she

eturn

D0581955

# The
# LICENCE
# OF WAR

Also by V. C. Letemendia

*The Best of Men*

# The LICENCE OF WAR

## V. C. LETEMENDIA

Jonathan Cape

London

Published by Jonathan Cape 2014

2 4 6 8 10 9 7 5 3 1

First published in Canada in 2014 by
McClelland & Stewart, a division of Random House of Canada Limited

First published in Great Britain in 2014 by
Jonathan Cape
Random House, 20 Vauxhall Bridge Road,
London SW1V 2SA

www.vintage-books.co.uk

Addresses for companies within The Random House Group Limited can be found at:
www.randomhouse.co.uk/offices.htm

The Random House Group Limited Reg. No. 954009

A CIP catalogue record for this book is available from the British Library

ISBN 9780224089395 (Hardback edition)
ISBN 9780224089401 (Trade paperback edition)

The Random House Group Limited supports the Forest Stewardship Council®
(FSC®), the leading international forest-certification organisation.
Our books carrying the FSC label are printed on FSC®-certified paper.
FSC is the only forest-certification scheme supported by the leading
environmental organisations, including Greenpeace.
Our paper procurement policy can be found at:
www.randomhouse.co.uk/environment

Printed and bound by CPI Group (UK) Ltd, Croydon, CR0 4YY

*To Emily and Oscar*

"... [T]hough there was a considerable part of the Kingdom within the King's Quarters, the Inhabitants were frequently robbed, and plunder'd by the incursions of the Enemy, and not very well secured against the Royal Troops, who begun to practice all the Licence of War."

– Edward Hyde, First Earl of Clarendon

"This is certain, that a man that studieth revenge keeps his own wounds green, which otherwise would heal and do well. Public revenges are for the most part fortunate ... But in private revenges it is not so. Nay rather, vindictive persons live the lives of witches; who, as they are mischievous, so end they infortunate."

– Francis Bacon, Baron Verulam, Viscount St. Alban

# PROLOGUE
## Seville, Spain. 4th October 1643

At the holiest moment in the Mass, as bread and wine became the body and blood of Jesus Christ, Don Antonio de Zamora was counting under his breath. *Uno, dos, tres, quatro* . . . He had spied his target on the previous Sunday, only to lose her among the faithful crowded into the vast nave of Santa María de la Sede, yet today God had placed her conveniently close: a row ahead of him, just across the aisle. *Cinco, seis, siete* . . . It would take no more than twenty, he estimated. *Diez, once, doze* . . . She began to fiddle with a hairpin in her expensive lace mantilla. *Diez y seis, diez y siete* . . . Her spine stiffened; he might have stroked his finger along it. *Diez y ocho, diez y* . . . On the count of nineteen she turned, as if he had tapped her on the shoulder, and the look upon her face confirmed what he already knew: that he was as handsome and desirable as in his youth. Regretfully, he lowered his eyes. While he needed a new mistress, he could not afford another spendthrift *sevillana*. He might ask Gaspar to find him a simple country girl and employ her at El Caballo Blanco, to save on her keep and enable him to visit her at his pleasure.

When Mass ended, Antonio ushered his family from the cool, dim cathedral into the blinding autumn sunlight, past the beggars gathered at the steps: the maimed on crutches or dragging their sad carcasses through the dirt, and a gaggle of gypsies and their children, whining and flattering. An ancient wretch with stumps for arms had the effrontery to pester him. "I fought in the northern wars as you did, sir – spare an old soldier a coin!"

"It *is* the Feast of St. Francis," Antonio's wife said, reaching into the pocket of her gown.

"A saint who chose poverty over riches," Antonio reminded her. "And each Sunday it is the same with you, Teresa. Cease your foolishness, or we'll soon be begging ourselves."

They walked in procession towards their coach: he and Teresa; their surviving son, twelve-year-old Felipe, and sole unmarried daughter, María de Mercedes; Teresa's elderly widowed aunts; and lastly the servants. Antonio felt both pride and a secret amusement that the crest of his parentage, de Zamora y Fuentes, was emblazoned on the door of the battered vehicle. He could maintain the semblance of rank. But what was rank without money? He was even in debt to Gaspar. The mistress might have to wait.

His cogitations were interrupted by a harsh breath from Teresa, who dropped her hand from his sleeve. "Look over there."

She pointed to a gypsy standing alone, vainly trying to soothe the fretful child she was carrying. The girl wore a ragged dress and shawl faded to dingy grey, and her black hair was matted with dust. The set of her features and her large dark eyes possessed striking beauty. Such a waste, thought Antonio: her charms would coarsen with breeding and hardship. And however boldly they sang and danced, full-blooded Roma women could not be had, except by force. Intimacy with an outsider meant exile from their kin.

"I agree she is an alluring creature," he observed.

"I am not speaking of her," said Teresa. "Look at her babe."

The brown-skinned boy was around six months of age and resembled his mother, except Antonio was shocked to see that his irises were a distinctive pale green. "How very strange," Antonio said. "Do you honestly believe . . . ?"

Teresa was already advancing on the pair. "What is your name, girl?"

The gypsy bowed her head obsequiously; she had not yet noticed Antonio. "Juana, my lady."

"Show me your son." Juana held him out; he was whimpering, clinging to her dress. "Who is his father?"

The girl opened her mouth to reply. But when Antonio approached her, she jumped back as though bitten by a snake. He shivered. Gypsies were supernaturally gifted; he had never encountered this one before, to his recollection, so what had she detected in him?

"She has told me all I need to know!" said Teresa, turning to sweep off to the coach.

Antonio restrained her. "My dear, you have woken in me the spirit of Christian charity. When did you last eat, Juana?"

"Three days ago," the girl said, staring at his face.

"And your boy?"

"He had a crust dipped in water this morning."

"Why are you by yourselves, and not with the rest of your tribe?" Juana said nothing. "Follow the coach to my house, and my servants will direct you to the kitchen, where you shall be fed."

"Don Antonio, you are shameless," Teresa scolded.

"On the contrary, *amor de mi vida*, I wish to correct your assumption. Are you going to let your son starve?" he inquired of Juana, who had not moved an inch.

"For his sake, sir, I accept."

"When you have eaten, you must promise to come and thank us."

"Yes, sir," she said, as if she were granting him the favour.

He and Teresa joined their family in the coach, and the gypsy trailed behind a smaller cart bearing their servants. Silence reigned on the brief journey to the de Zamoras' dilapidated ancestral home; and during the midday meal, Teresa darted peevish frowns at Antonio.

"Where is the girl?" he asked the servant clearing the table.

"She's gobbled her weight in bread and soup, sir, and is reading palms in the kitchen," the servant said.

"Fetch her."

"What madness, Don Antonio," complained Teresa. "She will seize the chance to steal a piece of our silverware."

"Unlikely, my dear," he said. "Practically every bit of it has been sold."

Juana padded in with the child draped sleeping upon her shoulder. The food had brought colour to her cheeks, and a confidence to her bearing. She scrutinised each member of the family, and next the room. Antonio wondered if she could judge the state of his affairs from the peeling walls, woodworm-riddled floorboards, and moth-eaten tapestries. Then she performed an odd obeisance, half bow, half curtsey. "May the saints bless you, for rescuing me and my sweet innocent boy when we were at death's door."

"Answer me, Juana," said Antonio, "who fathered your son?"

She hesitated, scuffing at the floor with a dirty toe. "He was . . . an Englishman, sir."

"An Englishman, in Spain?"

"No, sir: I met him in The Hague two winters past."

"What was his business?"

"He'd been a soldier."

"Where is he now?"

Her lip curled. "God knows. He left me as soon as *he* knew I was carrying his child. And my people wouldn't have me any more, because he was a *gajo*."

"A *gajo*?" echoed María de Mercedes.

"He was not a gypsy," Antonio explained; so Juana was indeed an exile, and vulnerable. Yet her reply had elicited in him a peculiar unease. "How could you be certain he was from England?" he demanded of her.

"I myself thought he was lying, he was such a dark man. And he talked a lovely Spanish – as lovely as yours. He spoke many tongues, besides. I wouldn't understand them, being as I am an ignorant gypsy," she added, with the false humility of her race.

"What was his name?"

"In The Hague they called him Monsieur Beaumont."

Antonio leant closer. "*Beaumont?*"

"So he was French," said Teresa.

"He told me his father was from England, my lady," Juana insisted. "And his mother was a noble lady from Seville."

Antonio's heart thundered within his ribcage. Grabbing his wine glass, he swallowed a large gulp.

"As I remember," put in Teresa's senior aunt, "one of the de Capdavila y Fuentes wedded an English lord."

Antonio forced a shrug; Juana was edging towards the door. "Ah yes," he said, "I forget his name."

"What is that stink?" exclaimed María de Mercedes.

"The baby has soiled itself," Teresa said, covering her nose. "Please, Don Antonio, get rid of them."

"Anything to oblige you, my dear." Antonio leapt from his seat, strode over to Juana, and snatched her by the wrist. She had to run to keep up with him as he marched her through the house and into the courtyard. Neither spoke a word until they arrived at the gates to his property; by some miracle, the child still slumbered, oblivious.

"Ay," cried Juana, "you are hurting!"

Antonio tightened his grip. "What did you see in me today?"

"I saw Monsieur. You would be his image if he was older."

"How old was he?"

"Five and twenty, or a little more – I couldn't say. You *gaje* are different from us. Why, who is he to you?"

Antonio's head was spinning as though he had drunk a whole cask of Malaga. "You're to go back into the city, Juana, to an inn, El Caballo Blanco, near the church of San Pedro. Tell Gaspar Jimenez that Don Antonio de Zamora wants you to stay there."

"When will you come to me?" she asked warily.

"When I choose," he said. "And if I don't find you, I swear by the devil, I'll hunt you down. You can watch your child die first, before you meet your Maker."

# *Part One*

England, October–December 1643

# CHAPTER ONE

**I.**

King Charles was hunting stag in the royal forest, with his party of lords and gentlemen, and a pack of eager hounds. They had disappeared from view into a thick mist that drifted through the trees. Like smoke on a battlefield, Laurence thought, as he reined in to wipe sweat from his eyes. He did not enjoy the chase.

"Your Highness, you must be more careful," he warned the young Prince, who had pulled up impatiently at his side; the boy was riding too fast, and his horse had already stumbled once on a tree root.

"If we don't hurry, Mr. Beaumont, we may lose them," Prince Charles shouted. "I want to watch the kill." Before Laurence could stop him, the boy put spurs to his mount and galloped ahead, vanishing among the trees.

Laurence became aware of an extraordinary silence. No birdsong or soughing of branches above, no rustle of animals in the bushes. He was alone. Then Sir Bernard Radcliff emerged out of the mist and walked towards him. Laurence felt astonished: he had last seen Radcliff in the grounds of the Earl of Pembroke's London house, dying from a multitude of wounds inflicted by the Earl's guards.

"I understand your surprise," remarked Radcliff, with a superior smile. "But don't forget, your precious tutor Dr. Seward instructed me in magic, as well as in the casting of horoscopes. The dead can be revived, sir, if one knows the proper rituals."

"You were wrong about the King's death," said Laurence, his voice sounding puny as a child's in the vastness of the forest. "It wasn't to happen when you predicted."

"It will happen soon, nonetheless."

Radcliff's smile faded as spectacularly as he did, dwindling to a wisp of fog; and now Laurence discovered himself in a small clearing where the King's body was laid out upon a makeshift bier of bracken and dry leaves. Pembroke stood over the bier, like an old vulture in his sombre cloak, leaning on a cane. Nearby were his guards with Prince Charles, who was kneeling, white-faced, wrists and ankles tied, a rope around his neck.

Pembroke turned a bleak stare on Laurence, and shook his head in reproof. "I had planned that he would reign under my authority, after his father's tragic accident. Alas, he watched the kill. That was your mistake, Mr. Beaumont. You ought to have kept him by your side."

Trembling, Laurence drew his pistol from the holster of his saddle. "You'll never get away with the murder of two kings." He fired. The shot ricocheted off Pembroke's cloak, as if he were wearing steel. Laurence gaped in terror as the speeding ball changed course, and plunged into the Prince's breast.

Laurence jolted awake and tasted blood in his mouth. Exploring with his tongue, he identified the source: he had bitten into the tender flesh inside his lower lip. Dawn was breaking, and he could hear the Oxford bells chime seven.

Isabella slept on next to him, one shapely arm flung over the counterpane, her peaceful expression a contrast to his unquiet mind. He longed to rouse her and tell her about the nightmare and what had inspired it: how through the initial year of this civil war he had helped thwart a conspiracy to kill the King. It frustrated him that the criminal designs of Pembroke and Radcliff had to remain a strictly guarded secret: in Radcliff's case, to protect his widow; and in Pembroke's, because the King had chosen not to expose his former friend as a traitor. Yet what troubled Laurence far more was that in the domain of politics and intrigue he could not be open with the woman he loved. Isabella was still close to the man who had once been her guardian, the new Secretary of State, Lord George Digby, whom Laurence trusted no further than he could spit.

He sank back and nestled against her, inhaling the scent on her naked skin: attar of roses, orris root, musk, and frankincense; and a more animal trace, from their passion of the night before. Yesterday he had asked her a second time to marry him, and she had refused. "Must we fight everyone?" she had said. "That is what our marriage would entail." He was prepared to fight. But was she?

## II.

"I opened Pandora's box, and evil flew out," Seward muttered, as he hurried along Merton Street. He could imagine what Beaumont would say: that he should not have upset himself by gazing again into the King's future.

Passing Oriel College, he turned north, and threaded his way up to Broad Street, into St. Giles. As if in defiance of the war, Oxford was stirring to its usual business: traders were setting up their stalls, servants emptied slop buckets into the gutters, drovers plodded behind sheep and cattle, and carts rolled in loaded with hay from the countryside. Near the Church of St. Mary Magdalen, Seward's path was blocked by a troop of laughing soldiers headed for their billets after night patrol on the city defences. He waited impatiently for them to go by, then carried on at a frantic pace up the Woodstock Road, dived into a side street, and arrived breathless at Mistress Savage's house.

The door stood wide, and a young maidservant was sweeping the threshold. She stopped when she saw him, her broom in mid-air. "I am Doctor William Seward, of Merton College," he panted. "I have urgent news for Mr. Beaumont."

"Please sit in the parlour, sir," she said, "and I'll wake him."

Seward fell into a chair, and mopped his brow with a corner of his cloak. A few minutes later, Beaumont ran down the stairs, his pale green eyes anxious and his inky hair tangled from sleep. He wore just his breeches, which hung dangerously low. Even agitated, Seward could not keep his own eyes from lingering on that smooth, olive-toned body, so youthful despite its many scars.

"What's wrong, my friend – are you ill?" Beaumont asked, crouching beside him and laying a hand on his thigh.

"No, Beaumont," Seward said. "I have been working through the night."

"It's too much for you, at your age. What's your urgent news?"

"I was working on . . . a horoscope."

"A royal horoscope? Oh Seward, I thought we were finished with all that."

"I could not rest until I had drawn His Majesty's chart again, now I had the true hour of his birth," Seward whispered. "I *had* to learn how far Radcliff had erred in calculating the date of his decease with the incorrect hour."

Beaumont rose and took the chair opposite, propping his elbows on his knees. He cupped his chin in his hands and squinted at Seward through his lashes, as he had been wont to do as a gangly boy of fifteen when concentrating on his lessons. At one and thirty, he was lean-muscled and broad-shouldered, and more graceful, yet his movements had not lost their impulsiveness; nor had his character. "What did you find out?"

"By my reckoning, His Majesty has about six more years to live. Not even six; to be exact, five years and a little over three months – and he will die on the thirtieth of January."

"Then you needn't have been in quite such haste to tell me," Beaumont said, with a slight smile.

"Radcliff did not err, as to the circumstances: the King *will* perish by violence."

"Is that so surprising? We *are* in the midst of a war, though I pray to God it doesn't last five more years."

"If I have read his stars correctly, it is a war he might lose, together with his life."

"Will you alert him?"

"You know very well it would be high treason to predict his death."

Beaumont hesitated. "Last night I dreamt of him dead, perhaps as you were at work on your calculations."

While he recounted the dream, Seward listened intently. "It is a clear warning to you, about the future," he said, at the end.

"No, Seward: though I admit I was disturbed by it, I see it as a mess of my past worries and complete nonsense." Beaumont began to laugh. "Still, Radcliff resurrected gave me a bit of a scare. And I had to envy Pembroke his armoured cloak."

"Don't be flippant. It is telling you that while you may not be pleased to serve Lord Digby, you must serve him as you served Lord Falkland, may God rest his soul, if you are to protect the lives of your King and Prince Charles."

Beaumont relaxed back, and crossed his long legs. "How are things at Merton these days, with the Queen in residence?"

Seward snorted. "Now you are being evasive."

"What would you prefer me to say? I am *not* pleased to be in Digby's service. I'd rather have stayed in Wilmot's Lifeguard."

"Your talents would be wasted in the ranks. Besides, Lord Wilmot is an arrogant, immoderate fellow."

"Minor flaws, compared to those of certain others in His Majesty's camp," Beaumont said, shrugging. "And he's also the King's Lieutenant General of Horse and one of our best commanders. Most important to me, he was a true friend when Falkland died."

"He kept you drunk."

"Yes, for which I'm eternally in his debt," retorted Beaumont, with a heartfelt emotion that made Seward a little sheepish.

"I understand how stricken you were by Falkland's demise. And I know you do not have a great respect for Lord Digby," Seward added, more quietly.

"You're wrong there," said Beaumont, not bothering to lower his voice. "I have the greatest respect – for his guile and utter lack of scruple. Without those qualities of character, he'd never have obliged me to work for him. In my view, his appointment will be disastrous for the royal cause, and I dread to think what sort of cunning schemes he'll suggest to the King, now he has more power in His Majesty's Council. I'll be his spy as I was Falkland's, out of duty to the King and the Prince, but I won't pretend I like it."

"As I did once observe to you, Doctor," remarked a husky drawl from the stairs, "if only Beaumont were not so useful."

Isabella Savage unnerved Seward on most occasions. This morning as she came towards him he could hardly look at her. Her satin robe clung to the curves of her body, her dark coppery hair flowed loose, and her feet were bare. "Madam," he said, getting up to bow, "excuse my early visit."

"It's a pleasure to receive you." She strolled over to Beaumont and caressed his cheek with her fingertips. "I trust you were not among the scholars evicted from your chambers upon Her Majesty's installation at the College?" she asked, as Beaumont slipped an arm around her waist.

Seward felt his cheeks redden. The heat between them was always palpable, yet today it seemed to him almost a physical presence, as though living in sin under her roof had intensified their sensual bliss. "No, madam: age has its privileges."

"Indeed it should. To quote the wise Cicero, it is a burden as heavy as Aetna."

Seward did not respond. Beautiful women were dangerous enough without an education; but that Mistress Savage should dip her nose into the classical authors and then flaunt her learning struck him as the height of immodesty, no less offensive to him than her déshabille.

"And to quote my father, Seward is a veritable jewel in Merton's crown," Beaumont told her, drawing her closer and leaning his head against her hip.

Seward rose, now thoroughly unsettled. "I should leave you in peace."

Beaumont gave one of his wicked smiles, flashing his white teeth. "Small chance of any peace: my mother is in town, determined to arrange another betrothal for me. You might encounter her at the College. She's lodged near to the Queen."

"She called on us yesterday, Doctor," Mistress Savage said. "How Beaumont takes after her – even in that flare to her nostrils."

"Much as his brother Thomas resembles his lordship their father as a young man," said Seward, wondering what had transpired at the meeting between these formidable females.

"I must visit her around midday," said Beaumont. "If you're not busy or sleeping, Seward, I could pass by your rooms."

"Please do."

Beaumont sprang to his feet; someone was rapping at the door. "Dear me, I hope that's not her," he exclaimed, with a comical frown at Mistress Savage.

He went and opened to a man in the Secretary of State's livery; Seward thought he had the air of a weasel. "Good morning, Mr. Beaumont," he said, studying Mistress Savage with salacious interest. "His lordship requests that you attend him immediately at his offices."

"Would you remind me of your name, sir?" asked Beaumont.

"Quayle, sir."

"Mr. Quayle, pray inform his lordship that I'll attend him as soon as I'm more decently dressed."

"I can wait for you, sir."

Seward took the opportunity to leave. "Until later, Beaumont. Good day, Mistress Savage."

On his way down the street, he heard a door slam shut. He glanced over his shoulder to see Quayle snooping through her front window.

## III.

Lord Digby sat at Falkland's old desk, his round visage freshly shaved and his blond hair impeccably curled. He was still in his dressing gown, a quilted garment of scarlet satin, and on his head was a lace cap. To Laurence, he resembled some sleek Flemish cardinal in his Vatican chambers.

"How are you, Mr. Beaumont, and how is our darling Isabella?"

"We're well, thank you, my lord."

He surveyed Laurence keenly with his protuberant blue eyes. "Have you broken your fast yet?"

"No, my lord," replied Laurence. "I was in too much of a rush to obey your summons."

"That is lucky for you: what I have to show you might otherwise upset your digestion, as it did mine."

Digby motioned to Quayle, who advanced with a small package of rolled-up linen held at arm's length. "Where should I deposit it, my lord?"

"On the floor. Have a look, Mr. Beaumont. It was in a bag of correspondence that arrived this morning from London."

An ominously ripe odour emanated from the package. Laurence squatted down and unfurled the linen. A pair of human ears fell out of the cloth onto the flagstones with a wet splat; they were blackened and oozing decay. "Oh Christ," he said, recoiling. "Whose are they?"

Digby clapped a hand to his mouth. "Had they been yours, sir, I might have recognised them from the gold ring in your left earlobe," he said, in a muffled voice. "On more careful examination, you will behold a pearl earring." Laurence now noticed it, beneath the gore. "The ears belong, or should I say *belonged*, to an agent of mine, Hector Albright, who ran certain errands for me in London – soliciting funds and pledges of more active support from our Royalist friends, and so on. I assume that he was seized and tortured under questioning by whoever committed this barbarity."

"Was there any message for you, apart from his ears?" Laurence asked, straightening, nauseated by the smell despite his empty stomach.

"None at all. I tend to doubt he survived the mutilation. In his last letter to me, he wrote that Parliament, under the auspices of John Pym and his ludicrously titled Committee of Public Safety, had imported a spymaster from the Low Countries to root out suspected Royalists in the City. He might be the butcher."

"Did Albright know his name?"

"Unfortunately not." Digby gestured for Laurence to cover up the ears. "It could, however, be on the list that I inherited from my Lord Falkland." Producing a sheet of paper from his desk, he flourished it at Laurence, who inspected it as if he had never seen it before. "Five names, of purported rebel spies. Are they familiar to you?"

Falkland had posed Laurence the same question; and he gave Digby the same answer. "No."

"I told you I want you to investigate it, as your first assignment in my service. Falkland notes here that he got the names from a Sir Bernard Radcliff, with whom I believe you were acquainted, yet he did not say who Radcliff was to *him*. What can you tell me about Radcliff, Mr. Beaumont?"

Again, Laurence would have to twist the truth to keep secret the plot against the King: although the list itself was not connected, Radcliff had given it to Falkland as part of a desperate bid to save his own neck after his guilt was revealed. "I was introduced to him by my friend Walter Ingram," Laurence said, starting with the truth. "He married Ingram's sister. I met him just a couple of times. He was killed back in August – I can't remember how he died," he added mendaciously. "But Prince Rupert might: Radcliff was an officer in his Horse. I was unaware of Radcliff's association with Lord Falkland."

"What rubbish," Digby said. "You were Falkland's chief agent. You knew all of his spies."

"No, my lord: as you had your Albright, Lord Falkland must have had his Radcliff – without my knowledge."

Digby cast him a sceptical glare. "At any rate, I am sending you into London, sir, to find out about this list, the rebel spymaster, and what happened to Albright. I have someone to accompany you. He has served as courier to Their Royal Majesties in many a delicate situation. He is a goldsmith by trade – ample justification to visit Oxford frequently, bringing wares from his shop. Quayle, get rid of that package and fetch in Mr. Violet," Digby ordered.

Quayle reluctantly scooped up the offensive bundle and carried it out.

Laurence, meanwhile, felt a mild foreboding: he had heard of Violet as a slippery character who managed to elude arrest by the authorities in London. Might Violet be playing on both sides of the game?

A man not much older than himself entered and bowed, doffing his hat. His plain fawn suit matched his complexion, and his sparse hair, and beard. "Your lordship – sir," he greeted them, in a reverent tone.

"Mr. Violet, this is Mr. Laurence Beaumont. We were discussing Albright's fate."

"Dreadful, my lord, very dreadful."

Digby made a humming noise in his throat. "Old Queen Bess used to call *her* spymaster Walsingham 'Moor,' and 'her Ethiopian,' because of his swarthy skin," he said. "The title would fit Mr. Beaumont admirably, don't you agree, Mr. Violet? His mother hails from Spain." Violet appraised Laurence, as if not sure how to answer. "His exotic charms prove an invaluable asset to him with the ladies," continued Digby, "yet they render him conspicuous, as does his height. He was nearly seized in London this spring, when we last attempted to encourage an uprising for His Majesty."

"Might he adopt the guise of a foreign merchant, my lord? I have truck with Venetians, now and then. Do you speak Italian, Mr. Beaumont?"

"I do," said Laurence.

Digby beamed. "An ingenious idea, Mr. Violet. Prepare to travel with him tomorrow. How long will the journey take, in your estimation?"

Violet scratched his nose pensively. "If we set out in the morning, we should be in Reading by dusk, my lord, and the next day ride on to the City outskirts, to the house of friends of mine. We'll bide there overnight, and then pass through the fortifications on the morrow. I can accommodate you at my establishment in Cheapside, Mr. Beaumont."

Laurence merely nodded; about sixty miles to London and his Arab stallion could ride forty a day without tiring. In less than the time estimated by Violet, he could be with his own trusted friends in the heart of Southwark.

"Thank you, Mr. Violet," said Digby. "Is he not the quintessential mole?" he inquired of Laurence, when Violet had gone.

"He appears so, my lord."

"He disappears, sir, unlike you," Digby said, with a feminine giggle.

"My lord, when you asked me to serve you, you suggested that you would give me *a free hand*."

"How I appreciate your gift of memory – but those were your words, not mine."

"Whatever the case, let me deal with this investigation as I think fit."

"I am sorry, sir," Digby responded unapologetically. "I cannot afford your capture by Parliament, and Violet is a native of London. He knows his way around far better than you."

"I'm sure he does, my lord. But wouldn't it be wiser for us to travel and operate separately, to avoid suspicion? I have my methods of coming and going, as he has his. If he's seen with me in Cheapside, we may both be in danger of arrest."

"No, you must stick with Violet. And in case of any difference of opinion as to your work, you are to follow his advice. You shall spend this morning together organising your plans. And don't forget to copy out that list of names. He should have a copy, also." Digby tossed the sheet at Laurence, who returned it.

"I have it memorised, my lord."

Digby was twirling a blond lovelock between his well-manicured fingertips. "You must invent some excuse to Isabella for your absence. We cannot have her fretting about you."

"With respect, she's not a child and I'd prefer to be honest with her."

"My dear Mr. Beaumont, honesty is not in your nature. And in your duties for me, I have every right to command your discretion. Is that understood?"

"Yes, my lord."

"*I* can still see the child in her," Digby said, more amiably. "And years of caring for her as my ward have endowed me with an acute understanding of *her* nature."

"Of course, my lord," said Laurence, imitating Violet's reverential tone.

## IV.

"Mr. Pym has been at the Commons all day, sir," the secretary said to Veech. "Do not be long with him. He is very tired."

"It was he who called me here to Derby House," said Veech, and strode into John Pym's chamber.

Pym was huddled in an armchair by a roaring fire, a blanket over his knees. On a table at his elbow lay an untouched plate of bread and meat, a vial, and a horn cup. Sweat shone on his forehead, and the pain in his bloodshot eyes told Veech that he was suffering from a bout of the sickness rumoured to afflict him more and more. It might soon kill him. And who then would take up the burden he had assumed: of solving the disputes in Parliament between moderates and radicals, and among the religious sects; of forging an alliance with the dour, canny Scots; and of levying funds for what so many viewed as a traitorous, ungodly rebellion against their anointed monarch?

"What tidings, Clement?" Pym asked hoarsely. "We have not talked in a while."

His insistence on Christian names irked Veech. These Puritans loved pretending to themselves that they were all the same before God, even as they looked down their noses at their servants. "I caught a spy, a week ago. He gave his name as Hector Albright, and under examination revealed that contraband may be about to enter London smuggled in empty wine barrels belonging to the Vintners' Company – arms, or powder, I'd suppose."

"Another foiled Royalist plot could be helpful to us. You were not with us then, Clement, but last May our discovery of the King's scheme for a revolt in London worked marvellously to our advantage. There is nothing like fear of an enemy within the City to unite the factions in Parliament," Pym said, shaking his big head.

"With your permission, I'll have an extra watch put on the docks and conduct a search of all imported barrels."

"Yes, yes, though you may need a warrant from Parliament for the search. The Vintners are a respected Company."

"Many of them are malignants," said Veech.

"What a term for our enemies: *malignants*!" Pym grabbed his vial, poured a few drops into the cup, and swallowed the mixture. "I have a malignant enemy lurking within *me*, Clement, though it is not binding the rest of me together. It is tearing me apart. I might not witness the end of this great struggle to restore our freedoms." He paused, wheezing. "You were in the Holy Land, and on the Barbary Coast." Veech tensed; how much did Pym know of his personal history? "Are we Christians any more righteous in our conduct towards each other than are the Jews and the Mahommedans?" Pym went on.

"The Jews live to count their money," Veech replied: it was a harmless question. "And they skulk about serving whoever will let them live. As for the Mahommedans, they're the finest and bravest of warriors, and the most brutal when they exact revenge."

"I pray that such brutality will not become *our* habit. Sometimes I wonder if I am wrong to oppose my fellows in Parliament who would compromise with the King, for the sake of peace. What is your opinion, Clement?"

Veech stifled a laugh. He had encountered no just rulers and very little justice in the lands that he had travelled, and in his view, Charles Stuart was a king who had declared war on his own people. As for brutality, once the beast of war was let out of the cage, it would not slink quietly back in. And Pym had brought Veech to England to be the beast, to do what Englishmen quailed from doing, though they wanted it done. "I have no opinion, Mr. Pym," he said. "I obey your orders."

Pym coughed, and licked spittle from his lips. "Where are you keeping the spy?"

"I'm not keeping him any more: he died in gaol."

"How?"

"How most men die there – of a fever."

"God rest his soul," Pym said quickly; he did not believe the explanation, Veech thought.

"Albright couldn't tell me who has charge of Lord Digby's operations in the City," Veech said. "But Digby had written to him about a Mr. Beaumont, who was Lord Falkland's intelligencer."

"Beaumont would be an obvious choice. It was he and the King's cousin by marriage, Lady d'Aubigny, who brought in a royal authorisation for the May revolt. Beaumont escaped, while the lady fared less happily. She was arrested at the French embassy and imprisoned briefly in the Tower."

"You set her *free?*"

"How else could we treat a young woman of noble blood whose husband fought bravely and died at Edgehill Field? We are not yet as vengeful as the Mahommedans."

"I trust we wouldn't have to set Mr. Beaumont free, if he were arrested."

"No, but he is also of noble stock, son to Lord Beaumont of Chipping Campden. If you arrest him, Clement, he must not die of gaol fever," Pym said, in a deliberate tone. "After his trial, a ransom would likely be offered to us, or an exchange negotiated for some prisoner of ours held by the King."

*Would you pay a ransom for me, in the same circumstances?* Veech could have asked. *Or would you let me hang, because I am not the son of a lord?* "Who can give me a description of Mr. Beaumont?" he inquired, instead.


**V.**

Lady Elena Beaumont delivered Mitte, the Queen's lapdog, a surreptitious kick to stop the spoilt animal snuffling round her skirts. The other ladies assembled in the Warden's chamber at Merton College, where Queen Henrietta Maria held her cramped little Court, did not notice: they were listening, rapt, to the tale of Her Majesty's perilous voyage to England from The Hague last February. Lady Beaumont could have recited it from memory. "*Imaginez-vous*," cried the Queen, and chattered on in her accented English about how her women had expected to drown in the stormy waters of La Manche, and had confessed their most secret sins to her, as they might to a priest; and how Parliamentary ships had tried to prevent her vessel from landing; and how, as they arrived at Bridlington Bay, they were bombarded with enemy fire; and worse yet, how they were forced to escape from the house where they had sought refuge and hide in a ditch, leaving poor Mitte behind.

"And Your Majesty had the courage to go to her rescue," effused one of the ladies.

The Queen set back her narrow shoulders. "Courage runs in my blood. I am the daughter of France's greatest king, and my husband has himself dubbed me his She Generalissima, on my request."

"Please tell, Your Majesty, about how your brave cavalcade was met in Stratford by your royal nephew," another lady said wistfully.

"Who would not lose her heart to Prince Rupert – he is so gallant and handsome," the Queen concurred, "but he can be so brusque in his manners. It is the German in him."

Lady Beaumont clenched her jaw to suppress a yawn. As she stared out of the window at the quadrangle below, she at last saw her son walking out from beneath the Fitzjames Arch. He was late, as usual, and in animated conversation with a College servant. His boots were worn and unpolished, he was without hat or sword, his hair was carelessly tied back with string, and he could not have shaved for a day or two. What would Her Majesty think?

When the Queen's page admitted him, Laurence bowed with his customary elegance to Her Majesty and the ladies. They got up to curtsey, Lady Beaumont included, though the Queen stayed seated.

"My Lady Beaumont," said the Queen, showing her prominent front teeth in a smile, "he is you, in masculine form! Since you are the only gentleman here, Mr. Beaumont, you must sit beside me, and I shall choose a young companion to sit on your other side." She surveyed her ladies, as if judging a competition. "Mistress Penelope Furnival!"

A blonde girl hurried to claim her prize. Lady Beaumont's pulse quickened: she and the Queen had thoroughly explored the requisite issues of heredity, land, finance, health, and temperament for this match; and all appeared promising to her. But Laurence had slipped the net of betrothal twice in the past, and now there was the additional complication of Isabella Savage. Lady Beaumont considered herself no mean judge of beauty, and she could not deny Isabella's attractions: a profile worthy of an Italian Madonna; skin the colour of rich cream; a figure slender yet ripe; a striking blend of intelligence and artfulness in her heavy-lidded, gold-flecked hazel eyes; and voluptuousness in the lines of her mouth. And who knew what courtesan's tricks she employed to keep a man of Laurence's experience beguiled in her bed.

Laurence smiled at Penelope as he might at his sisters, then focused his attention on the Queen. "I gave Penelope the part of the goddess Aphrodite in our masque last night, Mr. Beaumont," the Queen told him, "and I played her mother, Dione."

"Your Majesty was generous, to surrender a role for which you are so eminently suited."

The Queen's eyes sparkled. Everyone knew of her fierce devotion to the King, but Lady Beaumont had also noted her penchant for the company of good-looking young men, and for flirtatious banter. "I *had* to play Dione, sir, to His Majesty's Zeus. You should have witnessed his entrance: he was lowered to the stage in a golden carriage, to a bolt of lightning and a rattle of thunder!"

"It is wonderful that he can still find time for these entertainments," Laurence said.

Lady Beaumont caught the sarcasm, though fortunately it was lost on the Queen, who leant over and touched his sleeve. "It would be

a delight to see you in Greek dress. We are too constrained and . . .
*déguisés* in our modern clothes."

"I agree with Your Majesty: they are a terrible limitation to
physical activity. In fact, I think we men should abandon clothing
altogether and exercise naked, as did the Greek athletes."

The Queen burst into laughter and clapped her hands. Her ladies
joined in, though some of them were blushing to the roots of their
hair. "Might you accept a part in our next entertainment?" the Queen
asked him.

"Your Majesty, I have no talent for acting."

"Necessity must demand that you play many roles, in the service
of our Secretary of State."

"Not half as many as he likes to play himself," Laurence said to
her, as though in confidence.

"Oh how right you are! His lordship is addicted to mischief."

"Your Majesty," intervened Lady Beaumont, "would you have the
grace to excuse me and my son? We have a family matter to discuss."

"On condition that you sup with us this evening, Mr. Beaumont,"
the Queen said, as he rose.

"It would be an honour, Your Majesty, but tonight I must prepare
to quit Oxford on a mission for his lordship."

"Ah, well – then may God speed you on your journey, sir."

Lady Beaumont steeled her wits for combat and followed her son
out, down the stone staircase, and into the quadrangle. "Laurence," she
began, "what think you of Mistress Penelope?"

He turned upon her his annoying smile. "She's very pretty."

"Yes, she is. You might not remember: she is daughter to Sir
Harold and Lady Margaret Furnival, of Lower Quinton. They are
almost our neighbours, but six miles or so from us at Chipping
Campden, across the Warwickshire border."

"Are they!"

"I am hoping to arrange for you a more private interview with her."

"To what end?"

"So that you may learn if she will suit you as a bride," said Lady Beaumont, her patience evaporating.

"I believe the English Church only allows a man one bride at a time." She gasped, as the significance of his words sank in. "Other faiths are more accommodating to human nature, though not liberal enough," he went on infuriatingly. "If a man can have several wives, it seems to me that a wife should be allowed as many—"

"You have not . . . *married* that woman."

"Not yet, but I did ask her to marry me."

For a second, Lady Beaumont was dumbstruck. "Have you taken leave of your senses?"

"Far from it, madam – all of my senses tell me that I want her for my wife."

"From what *I* have heard about her at Court, without the kind intervention of Lord Digby she would be shunned by respectable society. She does not even know her own father, and she is notorious for her past affairs. It was sufficient insult that you dared present her to me yesterday! Oh Laurence, marriage to her is out of the question. Or . . ." A sudden thought flew into Lady Beaumont's mind. "Is she with child?" His smile did not waver, but she saw a flicker in his eyes. "Laurence, that *you* should be deceived by such an old ruse. You cannot be sure the child is yours."

"She is not with child."

"Then bid her goodbye, before it is too late. You cannot destroy the good name of your family, and ruin your father's health. Your duty is to him, as his heir."

"Yes, it is," Laurence said, his face softening.

"When might you come home to see him?"

"I'll ask Lord Digby for permission, when I return from his business."

"Will you promise until then not to engage in a lawful union with Mistress Savage?"

He sighed, and nodded. Reaching for her hands, he pressed them affectionately. "I must go."

"Where are you going now?"

"To call on Seward."

Lady Beaumont drew away. She could not bear his friendship with that old sodomite, but nor could she argue against it: Seward had been her husband's tutor before he was Laurence's, and Lord Beaumont thought the world of him. Yet whenever she heard his name, she shuddered inside, for a reason of her own.

## VI.

"Do you ever tidy your rooms, Seward?" asked Laurence, looking round at the shelves piled high with dusty tomes and crowded with rows of jars and vials, and alchemical equipment; and on the big oaken desk, more books and scrolls of tattered parchment, and Seward's silver scrying bowl engraved with arcane symbols. On the filthy floor were still more books and scraps of discarded paper, and plates that he must have put out for his cat to lick clean. In one corner stood the cupboard where he kept his packets of dried herbs and powders, odd-shaped stones and bones and crystals, and his bottles of awful home-made wine. Those from his friend Dr. Clarke's cellars, however, were always delicious; and it was just such a bottle that he and Laurence were now sharing. The rooms never changed, and neither did Seward's gaunt face and skeletal frame; and Laurence had not once seen him in anything but his black scholar's gown and skull cap.

"There is order in my apparent chaos," said Seward, fixing his rheumy blue eyes on Laurence as he polished his spectacles on the sleeve of his gown. "And who are you to criticise? As if you were the tidiest of people."

"I grant you, I am slovenly in some respects," said Laurence, "but I do make a point of soap and hot water, and clean linen – and occasionally I buy myself new clothes. You were wearing that same cap on the day we were introduced in my father's library."

"No, Beaumont, it is a facsimile thereof. The original met a sad end on the day I acquired Pusskins." Seward looked over with paternal pride at the striped cat sleeping curled by the fireplace. "He was a tiny kitten, but he ripped it to shreds with his needle-like claws and teeth."

"Perhaps he thought it was a rat."

Seward did not laugh. "You are in peculiarly high spirits, my boy, considering the day you have had. And you are obviously bridling at Lord Digby's command that you work with this fellow Violet, whose allegiances you doubt, to find a man who butchered one of His Majesty's spies." Laurence shrugged; Seward did not even know of Lady Beaumont's lecture. "*Could* this villain's name be among the five on Radcliff's list?"

"I'd bet the list isn't worth the paper it was written on."

"For what reason?"

Laurence took a sip from his cup. "You yourself called Radcliff a lying rogue, and he was bargaining for his life when he supplied those names. He probably invented them. And anyway, if Pym got his spymaster from the Low Countries, he might not be English, whereas all five of the names most definitely are. And he can't have been very long in England if Albright only mentioned him in that final letter to Digby. I didn't hear so much as a whisper about him while I was in Falkland's service."

Seward adjusted his spectacles with a bony hand, and read aloud what Laurence had scribbled on a sheet of paper. "'Victor Jeffrey, Anthony Burton, James Pritchard, Christopher Harris, Clement Veech.' Radcliff produced the list in August. It is possible that the butcher had arrived in England before then, and that Radcliff possessed the connections in London to learn about him."

"Yes, it is possible. Seward, I'm not going to London with Violet. I intend to leave tonight, alone."

"That would be the height of idiocy," Seward reproached him. "No matter your instinct about him, you cannot disobey his lordship."

"His lordship is most welcome to dismiss me afterwards, for insubordination."

"Are you talking in jest?"

"I'm absolutely serious. I passed the entire morning with Violet, and nothing in his behaviour or speech convinced me to rely on him. And if I *am* wrong about his loyalties, he must be under watch by Parliament as a known courier. As I said to Digby, we'd double our risk by moving about together. My friends in London have saved my life on several occasions, and I won't have them exposed to more danger than they face each time they help me. I can make contact with Violet when he gets to Cheapside."

"What if Lord Digby comes here asking after you?"

"You can tell him the truth."

"Does Mistress Savage know what you are about to do?"

"No. His lordship insisted that I be discreet, and that I concoct a pleasing fiction for her to explain my absence – as if she's unaware of my duties and what they might involve. It may be better for me to go without explanation, and let Digby tell her what he chooses. I'll set matters straight with her when I return."

"If she comes to me, what am I to say? I shall have to lie."

"Hardly a novel sin for either of us – we're still lying our heads off to cover up Pembroke's conspiracy," Laurence pointed out.

"Beaumont," said Seward, in a hushed tone, "what must I do about the King's horoscope? I have been pondering: should I alert him?"

"Do any of us wish to know when we're to die? *I* don't."

"You are young. It is natural that you should fear death."

"The King hasn't yet celebrated his forty-third birthday. Is there no room for error in your calculations?"

"There is always room, in any human interpretation of God's holy will," Seward admitted.

"In that case I'd suggest you keep silent."


As Laurence was leaving through the College gatehouse, a man in a suit of blue velvet and a cloak trimmed with gold braid came swaggering along Merton Street. "Lord Henry Wilmot, you dazzle me with your splendour," Laurence said. "I presume you've no army manoeuvres today."

Wilmot stopped and slapped him on the shoulder. "Good to see you, Beaumont. What are you doing here?"

"I was paying my respects to the Queen."

"I'm about to do the same myself. She has plans for me." Wilmot grinned and tugged at his luxuriant moustache. "Connubial plans. I've been far too long without a wife, *and* without a son and heir. Ten years of dutiful fucking, and my dear departed Frances proved dry as a stick."

"Has Her Majesty a prospective candidate?" asked Laurence, impressed by the Queen's industry as a matchmaker.

"A rich widow – too Puritan in her religion, but I'll soon change that."

"With more dutiful fucking?"

Wilmot whipped off a kidskin glove and smacked him on the ear. "I shall miss your insolence."

"As I shall yours."

"God damn it, I'm sorry for you, man," Wilmot said, sobering. "Digby's no Falkland."

"That he isn't."

"I haven't forgotten the eve of Newbury Field, and the Council of War – Digby and His Teutonic Highness Prince Rupert and I were scrapping like dogs over a bone. Not Falkland – he was . . . serene. Even then, he must have decided how his life would end. Later I tried to stop him from—"

"We both tried," Laurence cut in, thinking of his own words to Falkland. *Remember your wife and children. They may be worth dying for. His Majesty's cause is not.* Falkland had still ridden to his death.

"He was more concerned about you than himself that night. Mistress Savage had broken with you, at the time."

"So she had."

"All is sweetness and light between you and your lover now, is it?"

"I've no complaints."

"I don't doubt it, my old cock. If I wasn't in the market for a wife, I might give you some competition for her."

"She'll be flattered to hear that, my lord."

Wilmot punched him playfully on the chest and sauntered towards the gatehouse. "Wish me luck with the Queen!"

Before going home, Laurence bought Isabella a present. His only other had been a necklace purchased from his friend Mistress Edwards. Today he chose a book.

Isabella came to the door herself. "Lucy is out visiting," she said. "She promised to return by the hour of curfew. Though she persists in denying it, I think she has a lover somewhere. What do you think, Beaumont?"

Laurence recognised Isabella's brittle tone; and he could guess the cause of it. "I think you have something else to ask me," he said, trying to embrace her.

She ducked aside and went to sit in her chair, next to the window that gave onto the garden where they had spent many afternoons conversing and playing chess. "How was your first day in his lordship's service?"

"Shorter than I'd expected. He introduced me to a Mr. Violet. I'm to work with Violet, but I didn't much like him."

"I know Violet – he's an unctuous man. And . . . did you find her ladyship your mother at College?"

"Yes, and I told her of my proposal to you."

"You did not have to. What did she say?"

"*Exactly* what I expected." Laurence knelt at Isabella's slippered feet, pulled the book out of his doublet pocket, and placed it on her lap.

"Is this a gift?" He nodded. She opened it to the flyleaf, and her face melted into a smile. "Thank you, Beaumont."

"Would you read for me?"

"You may disapprove of my pronunciation. I didn't have the benefit of a tutor such as Dr. Seward when I was learning my Latin. Where should I begin?"

"At a random page."

"Let me see . . ." She leafed through the book, and her eyes danced at him. "I shall start here. '*If you listen to my advice, you will not be in too great a hurry to attain the limits of your pleasure.*'"

"Your pronunciation is perfect," he said. "Don't stop."

"'*Learn, by skilful dallying, to reach the goal by gentle, pleasant stages. When you have found the sanctuary of bliss, let no foolish modesty arrest your hand . . .*'" And as she read on, he slid his hands up, gradually, beneath her skirts, to that sanctuary.

## VII.

"I am selfishly glad Beaumont accepted Her Majesty's supper invitation," Digby said to Isabella, as Quayle brought them a water bowl and napkins to cleanse their fingers after the meal. She was particularly gorgeous tonight, in her bronze silk gown and her favourite necklace of enamelled rock crystal and amethysts; and he could imagine the source of her languid, dreamy air.

"I was not about to go with him, Digby," she said.

"Oh I'm sure the Queen wouldn't care that you and he are living together without the Church's blessing, but I daresay His Majesty would object. How different he is to his father, whose Court was as licentious as a Bankside brothel. So, my dear, how did you spend the afternoon?"

"I was reading Ovid's *Ars Amatoria*."

"Hmm – as I recall, a disquisition on love, two-thirds of it advice for men, and a third for women. What was said of Ovid . . . That he would have been a better poet had he controlled his genius instead of permitting it to control him. Could that apply to our Mr. Beaumont?"

"No more than to you."

"*Touché!*" giggled Digby, tossing aside his napkin. "Have you read the sequel, *Remedia Amoris*? It contains the most excellent advice for those who would be cured of their love."

"Why should I wish to be cured?"

Digby felt a pang of sorrow for her. "Isabella, have you told him about your youthful mishap and its attendant consequences?"

"He knows everything about it."

"Still, as heir to that fine Cotswold estate he will want children. You said to me that your face and your body have been *your* fortune, but that they could not last forever. As Ovid says, time is the devourer of all things. What will happen then?"

"If you are eager to learn, persuade his friend Dr. Seward to cast my horoscope."

"You must get bored, in that house," Digby said, after a silence. "Were you not supping with me, you would be twiddling your thumbs waiting for him to come home to you, like a good little wife. Except that you are not good, Isabella, and you are not married to him. Do you not crave the thrills of your former life, when you and I worked together? It was I who sent you to seduce Beaumont, if you remember."

"Do you regret it?" she asked, as though challenging him.

"Regret is a pointless emotion. It is more profitable to look forwards than to look back."

Isabella laughed and kissed him on the cheek. "Digby, you *are* a man of the future."

"Yes," said Digby, pleased by her observation, "I believe I am."

## VIII.

For three days, Antonio had stayed away from El Caballo Blanco. He knew from Gaspar that Juana and the boy were ensconced there, in a back room, and his mind was now busy conceiving of an excuse to his wife, not for a visit to Juana but for a voyage to England. Divine Providence had engineered the events of St. Francis's Feast Day; and the reawakening of a family tie could solve the problem of his depleted finances. Yet above all, it would appease a hunger for revenge that had gnawed at him for years.

Straight after dispatching the gypsy to Gaspar's, he had written to a retired fellow officer, Don Miguel de Perez, whose sons Sebastián and Santiago held positions at Court in Madrid. Antonio had asked for news of the war between King Charles of England and his Parliament.

Don Miguel's reply arrived the next day, verbose and crammed with important names; the old windbag was basking in the reflected glory of his progeny.

King Charles and Queen Henrietta Maria, daughter of the valiant Henry of France, are driven to solicit money, arms, and recruits from any royal house in Europe that will assist them! And the rebellion of their heretical subjects has worsened, spreading across his entire realm, with small likelihood of a settlement. These details were relayed to Sebastián in person by His Majesty King Philip, who had them from the former ambassador to Spain, John Digby, Earl of Bristol . . .

Antonio read no further. He would never forget John Digby's appointment to the Spanish Court, in 1611. That same year, James Beaumont had come to Seville.

"The bitch has a sailor's tongue and a violent temper," Gaspar grumbled, pocketing the money Antonio had given him. "She fought like a devil when we forced her to wash. I had to burn her rags – they were crawling with lice. Were I you, Don Antonio, I'd screw her cunt to my satisfaction, and boot her out."

"As long as I pay you, she stays," Antonio said.

He found Juana sitting on a pallet cradling the boy, who was suckling at her breast while she tore into a leg of roast chicken with her strong white teeth. Clean, in a decent gown, her hair combed to a shine, she excited Antonio even more; and her boy had an angel's countenance. *And my eyes*, Antonio said to himself.

"Don Antonio," she said, in her gypsy whine, "how can I thank you for your charity?"

"You can tell me about Monsieur."

"He's of your blood, isn't he," she asserted, in her normal voice.

Antonio lunged forward and grabbed a fistful of her hair. "No questions, *mi gitana* – I want answers. How did you two meet, so far from home?"

She winced, dropping her chicken leg. "My people had followed the Spanish troops north. Our camp was attacked, and they were all slaughtered except for me. The countryside wasn't safe, so I went to The Hague."

Antonio let go of her hair. "And then?"

"I was begging near a brothel – the custom was mostly rich folk who might have pity on a poor starving gypsy. But when I asked a man for a coin, he started to beat me. Monsieur heard my shrieks."

"He was in the brothel?"

"Yes. He and the Jew who owned the brothel fought with the man, and sent him packing. Monsieur had the Jew shelter me, afterwards – it was bitter cold, that winter."

"How very charitable of *him*," Antonio commented, his eyes on her smooth young breast. "So, he was one of the Jew's customers."

She unlatched the child, and pulled up the front of her gown. "No, he wasn't. The Jew ran gaming tables, and Monsieur was his card-sharp. They were good friends and had made a pile of money together. Monsieur had a special gift with cards."

"What sort of gift?"

"He could remember them in his head, however many rounds were played. And he was a clever cheat."

"What did he tell you of his father and mother?"

"That crone at your table – didn't she speak of an English lord? *His* father was a lord. Monsieur wouldn't talk much about him. When-ever he did, he'd look as if he might weep. He talked even less about his mother, just what I said: she was a noble lady from this city." Juana paused, eyeing Antonio. "I don't know how he was raised, there in England, but if he was my son I'd have taught him better. He was the whores' whore, at the brothel. That's what I called him, for pleasuring them in their off hours. He had no pride."

"I thought he was a soldier."

"He had been, but he'd deserted. He had taken a musket ball here." She stabbed a greasy finger at her right side, below her ribs. "He'd lost the guts to face fire." Antonio hid disgust: a cardsharp, friends with a Jew, and a coward! "That was why we fled The Hague," she rattled on, regaining her confidence. "The army would be looking to hang him when it turned to spring, and I had to get back to my people. And others were after him, like the man who'd beaten me. He'd wounded Monsieur when they fought, but that wasn't enough for him: he wanted Monsieur dead. If Monsieur's still alive, he'll have the scar – from a broken bottle." With the same finger, she traced a line from her left thumb up along her forearm. "And he'll have a mark here . . ." She tapped the outside of her lower lip. "From a stiletto. Monsieur deserved *that* one – he'd been cuckolding the fellow."

"And when did Monsieur have *you*, Juana?"

Histrionic outrage crossed her face. "Not 'til he'd chased me through France and into Spain. He was mad for me, and when at last he caught up with me, he raped me, over and over."

"Until he learnt about the child."

"Yes," she said, primly.

"You are full of shit, my girl," Antonio said. "If he was mad for you, he would have raped you before you fled The Hague. But you might be telling the truth about why he cast you off. Why would he care to be saddled with your spawn, or with you, if you became a nuisance to him."

Antonio was gratified to see the confidence drain out of her. She hugged the child to her breast. "What more do *you* want of me?"

"You are to stay here, and behave yourself. I am leaving town for a while."

"Why must we stay?"

"Because I say so."

"How long will you be gone?"

"You ask too many questions. And don't you dare dream of running, or you know what will happen." He examined her for a moment, tempted. Then he decided to wait, like Monsieur; often a pleasure delayed tasted sweeter.

Back home, Antonio dug out from a coffer in his bedchamber the leather coat he had worn through many of his campaigns; the bloodstains had faded to rust. He slipped it on and surveyed his lean, broad-shouldered figure in the glass. He had a head of thick, distinguished salt-and-pepper hair, most of his teeth, and few aches apart from a throb in his right calf from an old rapier wound. Not bad, for a man of fifty-three.

He was still admiring himself when Teresa walked in. "Don Antonio, why are you dressed in that coat?"

"My dear, I had meant to inform you at supper tonight: I must embark on a voyage, to England."

"*England?*" she repeated, as though it were an alien planet.

"Today I received a letter from the Earl of Bristol, a dear friend of my late maternal aunt, Elena de Capdavila y Fuentes. He was English ambassador to our Court, when I was in my twenties."

"Why should he write, after all these years?"

"I was as puzzled myself, yet my aunt had always recommended me to him," Antonio bluffed, "which brings me to the content of his letter. Our sovereign King Philip has graciously agreed upon a loan to Charles of England, to aid him in crushing a rebellion that has broken out in his kingdom. Bristol wishes to entrust me with the task of delivering the funds. It may involve some danger, but the reward is impossible to refuse." Antonio named a fabulous sum. "I am to ride for Madrid tomorrow to collect the loan. A royal guard will escort me overland, to set sail from the port of La Coruña."

Teresa did not speak; and he held his breath. Then she clasped her hands together, tears spilling from her eyes. "Oh, Don Antonio, we are saved! God has finally listened to my prayers."

"And mine," said Antonio, exhaling a long sigh of relief.

"And it is such an honour, that you should serve two Royal Majesties." She dashed away her tears, and with the staggering practicality of women carried on, "You will have to order a suit of warm clothes, and woollen undergarments and hose, the instant you arrive in Madrid. The English climate is reputed to be horrid: nothing but fog and rain and snow. And why not take Diego Sandoval with you? Agustín is too elderly and frail to travel as your valet, but Diego would do well in his place. According to Agustín, he already speaks English. And he would jump at the chance to leave Seville."

"So he would," agreed Antonio; Diego was his valet's nephew, a scholarly youth whose library of forbidden books had attracted the ire of King Philip's Inquisition. "You are not just beautiful, *mi querida* – you are a fount of knowledge and wisdom," he praised his wife, glad that her knowledge did not extend to politics: as if the King of Spain's coffers were not as empty as his own, and the country not ruined by its war with France. "I'll talk to Agustín. Diego and I will have a lengthy voyage before us. Plenty of time for him to teach me English."

## IX.

Laurence rode through the night, stopping now and again in the small hours of morning to rest his horse. He trotted it into the village of Chelsea around four o'clock the next day; rather better than Violet's estimation, though he attributed his swift, uneventful journey as much to the stallion's endurance as to the sway of Prince Rupert's and Wilmot's cavalry over the countryside. The commanders were conducting regular patrols in the vicinity, mainly to obtain supplies, but also to harass any Parliament troops unfortunate enough to cross their path.

Laurence stabled his horse with a trusted ostler at an inn near the Chelsea turnpike and went down to the meadows bordering the riverbank; he would have to while away the remaining daylight hours hidden. Rain began to bucket from the skies, so he sheltered in a barn, dozing fitfully on a bale of damp straw, his pistols at the ready.

By evening, the rain had tapered to a drizzle. He drew up the hood of his cloak, slung his saddlebag over his shoulder, and squelched through water-logged pasture towards the quay where the fleets of barges moored. Nearer the quay, he stopped short, dismayed by the sight of Parliamentary militia: a troop of them were apparently inspecting goods destined for the City. By their cloth caps and cheap, thin cloaks, they looked to be London Trained Bands; raw fellows, to judge by their unmilitary bearing. He started off once more at a casual pace, keeping to the shadows, and jumped onto the vessel furthest from them. Crouched behind a row of grain sacks, he waited for them to finish, and for the barge to head out on its journey downriver. After a few minutes, he swore at his ill luck: from the loud tramp of shoes on the wooden deck and snatches of conversation, he realised that his barge, out of all those he might have chosen, was to carry not only goods but the militiamen as well. Raw fellows they might be, but he could not afford the risk. He would have to sneak back onto the quay.

He was contemplating his move when a voice cried, "Who's there?"

The best defence is attack, Laurence reminded himself. He stuffed his pistols into his saddlebag and emerged, to stare into the barrel of another pistol, held by a nervous militiaman. "What the hell are you doing – put aside your weapon," he told the man, and gestured at the sacks. "Has duty been paid on this cargo?"

"Duty?" said the man, lowering the pistol.

"Excise duty," Laurence replied, with curt officiousness. "If it hasn't been paid to Parliament, I must have it from the owner of the barge. Where can I find him? Come on, come on, answer me."

"I don't know, sir, you must talk to Corporal Draycott. He's in charge."

"Where's Draycott, then?" said Laurence, wondering how long he could maintain his performance.

The man went over to a section of the barge where his companions stood bunched, their caps and cloaks dripping. Rain was falling heavily again, and Laurence seized the excuse to bury his face deep into his hood. "Where's the Corporal?" the man asked them. "Is he on board yet?"

The crew were loosening the ropes that secured the barge to the quay. Laurence calculated the gap in between, as well as his odds of fooling the Corporal, which he decided were slim to negligible. He clutched his saddlebag to his chest, sprinted for the edge, and leapt. Though he cleared the distance, the ground was slippery, and he landed on his knees. "Stop him!" yelled a chorus of voices. A shot whizzed past as he scrambled to his feet. He ran, boots slithering, lost his balance, and fell face down in the mud. When he lifted his head, he saw that he was hemmed in by militia. They dragged him up, crowding round in fascinated silence as he spat and wiped his mouth on his sleeve.

"Give me your saddlebag," said the man who had accosted him. Laurence obeyed. The man searched inside, and produced Laurence's pistols. "Excise, eh?" He whistled admiringly at them. "Not with a pair of flintlocks like these."

# CHAPTER TWO

Laurence sat shivering, knees drawn to his chest, head bowed against the wind, cursing himself under his breath. He had been hauled unceremoniously onto the barge, where the militia had confiscated, along with his pistols and saddlebag, his cloak and doublet, and the knife he always kept in his doublet's breast pocket. They had tied his wrists and ankles with a rope and fastened it to an iron ring embedded in the deck. As the barge nosed its way through murky fog, they had left him alone, in spite of his repeated demands to talk to their corporal. A brutal interrogation probably awaited him, and God only knew which of his severed parts Lord Digby might receive in a package. He should have ignored his instinct, and travelled with Violet.

At last a man approached carrying a lantern. He wore a buff coat, the orange sash of Parliament, high boots, and a good beaver hat. "I am Corporal Giles Draycott of the London Bands," he informed Laurence, in a courteous, educated voice. "Who are you and what were you doing on this barge?"

"Corporal Draycott, there's been a mistake," Laurence said, in a brusque though somewhat friendlier tone than he had used with the militia. "I applaud the vigilance of your troops, but they've arrested the wrong man."

Draycott set the lantern on the deck, and squatted down. In the flickering light, Laurence discerned intelligence and gentleness in his face, and a likeable straightforwardness in his eyes. They were perhaps the same age. "Pray explain, sir," he said.

"You must keep what I tell you between us. I'm an agent of Parliament returning from Oxford. I was in haste to report vital news to the Committee of Safety at Derby House. That's why I took passage on your barge. Don't bother to ask my name – I'll give you a false one, on the instruction of Mr. Pym himself."

"Heavens above," murmured Draycott. "But why did you claim to be an excise officer, and then try to flee?"

"Why would I admit who I am to a common trooper? I tried to flee because I knew I'd be delayed and questioned."

"If you won't give your name, are you carrying any credentials?"

"*Credentials?* Sir, there are enemy spies everywhere, including among our militias, who would not hesitate to cut my throat if they found me out. I've put my cover at risk by telling you even this much. I'm not well known yet in England, which has been an advantage to me thus far," Laurence went on, inspired by Digby's portrait of the butcher. "I was away, fighting in the wars abroad. Now, untie me, and you must let me off as soon as the barge docks."

"How can I, when for aught *I* know, *you* might be an enemy spy?"

Laurence sighed, thinking. "Corporal, did you hear of the King's plot for a revolt in London this spring?"

"The whole City heard."

"I helped to detect it, when I first came back from the Low Countries. If you want proof of who I am, ask me anything you want about it."

Draycott seemed to consider. "Tell me how Lady d'Aubigny and Lady Murray smuggled in the King's Commission of Array authorising the revolt. Their coach was thoroughly searched when it entered London."

Laurence could provide a bit of the truth for a change. "The document was hidden down the front of Lady d'Aubigny's dress, where she assumed no gentleman would search, and none did. I was warned she had it on her, and I followed her, the day she delivered it," he added, less truthfully.

"To Sir Edmund Waller's brother-in-law."

"No, to a man named Chaloner, who later passed it on to him."

"The ladies were fortunate to be spared a public trial," Draycott remarked.

No idle observation, Laurence suspected. "They were saved by their rank and their sex," he said, feigning scorn.

"Yes – for so-called rebels, we behaved ourselves scrupulously towards them. They were shielded from the common view through-out, to the disappointment of most Londoners. Lady d'Aubigny was rumoured to be exquisite in appearance – tall and flaxen-haired," Draycott said, his eyes watchful.

"Lady d'Aubigny *is* exquisite, though she's small in height, and her hair is dark brown," said Laurence, amused: he could have offered a more intimate description of her charms. "Rumour confused her with Lady Murray, who is tall and blonde, and less exquisite." Draycott's face relaxed, hinting to Laurence that he had survived a test and won a measure of trust. "I'd be pleased to satisfy your curiosity at length on another occasion," he went on, "but I swear, if you don't free me tonight, there may be grave consequences. Where is the barge to dock?"

"Lambeth," Draycott said. "I must convey the troops to Captain Harper, who's in charge of the fort at St. George's Fields. I'll ask his permission to accompany you back across the Thames, to confirm with Pym that you are his agent."

"And blow wide my cover? Pym won't thank you for it."

"Then supply me with some token of proof to take to Pym, in confidence. You'll be kept but a few hours at the fort. You have my word, sir."

It was more than Laurence could have hoped for: Lambeth was not far from Mistress Edwards' house; and during those hours at the fort he might exert his powers of persuasion on the Captain to release him before Draycott could reappear and unmask his lies. "Very well, Corporal. Until we dock, please ensure that none of my property goes astray – especially my pistols."

"They are a splendid brace – they must be worth a great deal."

"They were a gift from a friend who was killed in battle at Newbury. I value them as a memorial of him, not for their worth," Laurence said, with absolute honesty, thinking of Falkland.

"I'm sorry for your loss, sir. I heard it was a terrible fight, though I did not witness it." Draycott settled back on his heels and cast Laurence a rueful smile. "I haven't seen action, thus far. I was a lawyer before I enlisted this summer. I dealt mostly with crimes of fraud, cheating spouses, petty theft – and the odd murder."

"You moved fast through the ranks, to be made a corporal."

"My learning and profession got me where I am. For how long did you serve abroad?"

"S-six years," said Laurence, his teeth beginning to chatter.

"You must be cold, sir," said Draycott.

"Frozen would be closer to the truth."

"We thought you might have messages sewn into your cloak or your doublet. I'll have them returned to you." Draycott rose, picking up the lantern, and walked away; and a militiaman soon came with the garments. After Laurence put them on, his bonds were refastened, and again he was left alone.

As the barge neared Lambeth, he could distinguish the imposing silhouette of the Abbey and the outlines of Westminster Hall and the Palace of Whitehall across the river. The men were jostling for a view, talking more cheerfully among themselves, obviously keen to get home after their day's patrol in bad weather.

"Who's for a flagon at the Dog and Duck tomorrow?" one of them shouted out.

"Can't afford it on our pay," grumbled another.

"What pay? We're owed since August."

"Hush and ready yourselves, boys," Draycott told them.

Laurence braced himself, hanging onto the iron ring as the barge lurched to a standstill. A militiaman freed him and cut the rope from his ankles, leaving his wrists tied, and hustled him onto the pier where

Corporal Draycott was supervising the stragglers. Then they marched along empty streets, meeting a sole nightwatchman who saluted them with his torch. Ahead Laurence saw more lights, and the fort, a new, solid construct with bulwarks on all sides.

"Corporal," he said to Draycott, at the entrance, "I'd appreciate your discretion about me."

"Captain Harper will want to know why we took you prisoner."

"You're a lawyer, aren't you? Be economical with the facts."

Draycott chuckled. "I'll do my best." He guided Laurence down a chilly passage to a room where an officer was warming himself by the hearth. "A good evening to you, Captain Harper," Draycott said, in a different, rather hostile tone.

Harper had a bulbous nose, his gut overhung the orange sash about his waist, and his mouth was pinched tight as an arsehole. His piercing close-set eyes resembled a pair of currants stuck in a bowl of dough; and they fixed at once on the rope around Laurence's wrists. "Who's he?" he said, jerking a hand at Laurence.

"He was apprehended on our barge, as we were setting out from Chelsea," Draycott replied. "I told him we would have to keep him here while I go to Derby House and confirm his account."

"What account?"

Draycott glanced at Laurence, half apologetically. "He informs me that he is an agent in Mr. Pym's service, on vital business for the Committee of Safety, and can reveal no more about it. He can't even state his true name, on Mr. Pym's command."

"Scurvy, black sort of a rogue, isn't he," said Harper, studying Laurence up and down. "Mongrel blood, I'd wager."

"Untie my hands, and give me a pen and paper," Laurence said to Draycott. "I'll write you a message for Mr. Pym."

Draycott obliged, and Laurence scribbled out some meaningless lines of code; he was starting to fear that he would not convince Harper. Sure enough, as he was giving Draycott the message, Harper said, "Lock him up before you go, Corporal."

"You've no need to place me under restraint," Laurence objected. "I pledged to Corporal Draycott that I would wait for him."

"He answers to me, sir. And you shall wait in one of the cells."

Draycott led Laurence out, along a flight of stone stairs, to a cell bare except for a necessary bucket. "I'll be as quick as I can," he said.

Laurence's stomach constricted as the door closed and the outer bolt squealed shut, leaving him in total darkness. It brought back memories of his hellish weeks imprisoned in Oxford Castle where he had suffered torture almost to breaking point. He had only just managed to keep silent, then, to protect Lord Falkland from calumny. He felt no such allegiance to the present Secretary of State.

## II.

Diego Sandoval could pass for English, with his curly auburn hair and freckled complexion. He was short in stature, and though well proportioned, a trifle round-shouldered, as befitted a scholar. Neatly apparelled in his dark suit and hose, a small white ruff at his throat, he looked the picture of a keen young valet, yet the impish gleam in his eyes hinted at a wayward streak as dangerous as his collection of banned books.

"Don Antonio," he said, "I cannot express my gratitude to you for this opportunity to broaden my horizons."

"You are not travelling with me for your own pleasure but for mine." Antonio locked the door of his private office; he wanted no interruptions. "I hope your bags are packed, because we leave at dawn."

"It's been a while since I was last in Madrid," Diego commented, smiling.

"We are not bound for Madrid."

Diego's smile faltered. "But my uncle told me—"

"Shut up and listen. And if you breathe a word of what *I* am about to tell you, I'll have the Inquisition on you like a pack of hounds before you can say a Hail Mary. Is that clear?" Diego nodded. "We're to ride for Cádiz, instead, from whence we'll take ship for England."

"Has King Philip already dispatched to you the funds for King Charles?" Diego queried, seemingly unflustered by Antonio's threat.

"No. We'll collect them in Cádiz, together with diplomatic papers, to ensure my safe passage."

"I'd suggest that you carry two sets of papers, Don Antonio, one genuine and one false, that you can present according to the situation in which we find ourselves. Vessels departing from our ports may be boarded and searched these days, given our war with France. Also, the rebel English Parliament has seized control of King Charles's navy, and your mission to England is anathema to Parliament's interests. As soon as we cross into English waters, we may be in very *hot* water, and those funds could fall into rebel hands."

Antonio had an urge to smack Diego's impertinent face. But the advice was sound. "Aren't *you* a clever monkey. And how would I obtain my false papers?"

"I have some skill at forgery," replied Diego, with a modest lowering of his lashes.

"Could you provide me a sample of your work tonight?"

"If I might borrow paper and writing instruments from your office. Don Antonio, it would further assist me if you could be more . . . truthful about the purpose of our voyage," Diego went on, his eyes still lowered.

Antonio started to laugh. "I might, if you teach me a little English. For instance, how do you say, *un paso en falso, y acabo muerto?*"

"If I put a foot wrong, I shall end up dead," Diego responded, without hesitation.

## III.

As the cell door swung open, Laurence squinted into the flame of a torch. Harper's bulk loomed over him. "Come with me."

"Have you heard from Mr. Pym?" asked Laurence.

Harper did not reply.

Sweating and dry in the mouth, Laurence went ahead of him upstairs. Draycott was standing by the fire in a weary attitude. "There *has* been a mistake, sir," he said to Laurence. "I spoke with Mr. Pym's secretary. We must beg pardon for the delay we caused you." Draycott frowned at Harper, who flushed. "Mr. Pym is pleased to receive you, sir," Draycott added, to Laurence. "A guard from the fort will escort you to Derby House, lest any further mishap interfere with your duties."

"I won't require the guard, Corporal, only my belongings." Draycott handed Laurence his saddlebag, and he checked that the pistols and knife were inside. He smiled at Draycott, and grinned nastily at Harper. "Thank you and goodnight to you both, gentlemen."

His knees were shaking on the way out; it had been far too easy. In the street he stopped to get his bearings, and pulled his hood over his head. As he took a step forward, a tall, thickset man in a long, flapping coat and wide-brimmed hat burst from the shadows on the opposite side of the street and hurried towards the fort. Although the man's face was invisible, the sheer determination in his gait suggested danger to Laurence. The man slowed, raising his arm as if to aim a pistol. Hastily Laurence swerved into the closest alleyway, and began to run eastwards to Southwark.

## IV.

"I don't know what he is to the Committee of Safety, Corporal, but I wouldn't trust him to empty my pisspot," muttered Harper. "You should follow him with some of our boys – see which way he went."

"*Captain*," said Draycott, "I've been to Derby House and back, in godawful rain, to establish the fact that our prisoner was none other than Mr. Pym's agent, Clement Veech. I might have spared myself the journey. I knew he was telling the truth, on that barge. Even if I lack your years of soldiering, from time to time my legal skills have their uses."

"Oh yes? And how's that?"

"When I questioned him about the Royalist plot, he provided details with which few people are acquainted. For example, that Chaloner received the Commission of Array *before* Waller got possession of it."

Harper appeared suitably mystified. "And he gave me an exact description of Lady d'Aubigny and her friend, Lady Murray."

"Friends of *yours*, are they, Corporal Draycott?" Harper sneered.

"No, Captain, but I happened to be taking a deposition at the Tower when they were brought in as captives of Parliament. No one had been allowed to see their faces, but once inside the Tower precincts they had to remove their veils. Veech could not have described her so well, unless . . ." Draycott broke off as the door banged open.

A man stood in the entrance, his long, baggy, foreign-looking coat slick with rain, water trickling from the brim of his hat, a matchlock pistol in his right hand. "Who was it that went out of here just now?" he demanded, in a rich, sonorous voice.

"Who the devil are *you*?" exclaimed Harper.

The man surveyed Harper and Draycott as though they were piles of dung upon the pavement. "Clement Veech, servant to Pym."

Draycott and Harper exchanged stares. "What?" cried Draycott, to Veech. "But Pym's secretary was sure that *he* was Veech. My description fitted him perfectly."

"How did you describe him?"

"As tall and dark, with an authoritative manner," Draycott said, realising that Veech was neither as tall nor as dark, nor of the same build. And he was much older, his broad, full face creviced with lines, whereas the other man had a thin, high-cheekboned, foxlike visage.

"What else, Corporal?"

"I . . ." Draycott quailed beneath Veech's gaze. "I recounted what he had said to me: that he had served some years in the Low Countries before returning to England, and was presently coming from Oxford under cover with vital news to report to Pym."

"The last part should have given him away: I've never been in Oxford. What colour were his eyes?" asked Veech, pointing a finger at his own, which seemed to Draycott a fathomless black.

"They were extremely pale in shade – a . . . a greenish yellow, I believe."

"You fools – you let go Laurence Beaumont, Lord Digby's chief spy." Veech turned on his heel. "Call out the troops, Captain Harper. If we move fast, we may still catch him."

## V.

Laurence could barely see through the downpour. His breath came in uneven gasps as he tore through the desolate lanes, his nerves working like a quarried beast's, his heart thumping. He imagined he could hear the splash of boots behind him, over the ceaseless wash of rain.

It was not his imagination: the boots were gaining on him; and now he heard the rattle of steel, and shouts. Slithering into a doorway, he flattened himself into the shadows, and cocked one of his pistols. He must be only a short distance from the south end of Blackman Street, where there was another, even bigger fort than the one he had left. Mistress Edwards' house lay to the north of the street, in a narrower section crowded with tenements. Somehow, he must get past the fort and up the street.

He launched out of the doorway. "Stop or we'll fire," voices bellowed immediately; and fire they did. He bent low and raced on. Halfway up Blackman Street, a ball singed his cloak. Fear made him reckless. He whipped around and fired, with no idea who or what he might hit. An agonized howl rang out, and he recognised Draycott's voice crying, "Dear God, no!" and Harper bawling, "Damn you, men! After him!"

With the last of his energy, Laurence hurtled up the street, skidded to Mistress Edwards' door, and hammered on it with his fists. It opened almost at once, and he staggered inside. "Shut it, quick," he hissed, and unseen hands obeyed.

A candle flared, illuminating a lugubrious, stubbly face, and a white nightgown. "Troopers after you, Mr. Beaumont?" Barlow asked in his funereal tone, as if inquiring about the weather. "You get upstairs, sir, and let me deal with them."

**VI.**

Laurence blinked awake after a profound and dreamless sleep to see Cordelia, his favourite of Mistress Edwards' ménage, seated on the edge of his bed. She glowed with surprising health in her shabby, patched dressing gown. "Cordelia, you look very well," he said, smiling at her.

She wriggled a hand beneath the bedclothes, and pinched him on the thigh. "Not six months since you last hid with us, and here you are, in trouble again."

"In far less trouble than I might have been, thanks to Barlow."

She mimicked Barlow's rumbling voice. "'How dare you disturb me at this hour of the night? I'm a tax-paying citizen. I shall complain to the authorities, I shall.' Oh, he was a laugh with the troopers, sir."

"*I* wasn't laughing."

Her hand strayed higher. "Fancy some sport?"

"I would, but I'm promised to a certain lady."

"Did you get married?" she asked, continuing to explore.

"N . . . no, but I hope to marry her."

"Where is she?"

He shifted away; Cordelia had provoked in him the inevitable reaction. "At Oxford."

"Well, then! What she doesn't know won't hurt her. And the flesh does seem willing . . ."

"It is, but I can't." He reached down, and stilled Cordelia's hand. "Thank you, though," he said, giving it a friendly squeeze.

Cordelia pouted and lay back on the bed. "Didn't we have fun in better times, before you left to fight abroad, and before the rebels took over and made every day a Sunday," she reminisced. "The place was lovely: hangings and paintings, and feasts – gentlemen coming and going until the break of dawn – with more *coming* than going, I'd say. Not that you've changed, sir, which is why a little sport—"

"Hey, what's this?" he interrupted, noticing her rounded belly. "Mistress Edwards must have had a change of heart, in her old age."

"She has, sir." Cordelia stroked her stomach proudly. "I'm over four months' gone." Then she saddened. "The Mistress won't do as she used to for us girls, ever since she lost Jane in August."

"Lost?"

"She couldn't staunch the bleeding."

"Oh God, poor Jane," he murmured, understanding. "What a way to die."

"We buried her in the yard of St. Saviour's. Ned Price persuaded the clergyman that she was his sister, and pure as the driven snow. You haven't met Ned, have you, sir."

"Who's he?" said Laurence, distracted, thinking of Isabella. In her youth she had been lucky to escape Jane's fate.

"A player's son, a nobleman's castoff – it's a fresh story every day," said Cordelia. "Only Mistress Edwards knows the truth, but she won't tell us. You can be the judge of him yourself: he's in the kitchen with Barlow."

Conditions had deteriorated in the front room where Mistress Edwards received her gentlemen callers. From his last visit Laurence was accustomed to its disguise, a necessary precaution since Parliament deemed her business a serious crime: plain whitewashed walls, bare floor, and hard, high-backed chairs around a table on which a selection of religious books and tracts were laid out. But now damp bubbled behind the plaster, and a depressing odour of rot hung in the air.

"Barlow?" he shouted out.

His guardian angel sloped in, followed by a younger man. "Mr. Beaumont, Ned Price," Barlow introduced them.

"A pleasure, sir," declared Ned Price, his grey-blue eyes sparkling, and bowed with a flourish. Laurence extended a hand. "Oh," said Price, looking bemused as he clasped it, "I see you prefer the Puritans' manner of greeting."

"We *are* in a house of prayer," said Laurence, "and they do have some habits to recommend them."

Price was of average height, his hair a middling brown, and his features, otherwise as undistinguished, were infectiously animated. A sanguine temperament, Laurence thought; and whatever mystery shrouded his origins, Price cut a fine figure in his slashed doublet and breeches, lace collar, and calfskin boots. While Laurence had never bothered about his own dress, his upbringing had taught him the difference between quality and fake goods; and he had learnt during his rather less-privileged years as a spy and cardsharp to note every detail of what others wore. Price's collar was an imitation of Brussels spinning, and the suit tailored deceptively well from cheap, flashy fabric.

"My friend, you really must stop saving my life," Laurence said to Barlow, gripping his meaty paw.

"All right, then, sir – I shall."

"No, truly, man, I have to thank you."

"Barlow needs no thanks – he derived immense gratification from baffling those dunderheads," Price interjected exuberantly.

Barlow ignored him. "I was on my way to bed when the shots rang out, sir. Did you get one of them troopers? Your pistol smelt to me as if it had been fired."

"I fired once, and I must have wounded somebody," said Laurence, hoping that he had not hit Corporal Draycott. "I heard a cry of pain, at any rate."

"A shame *I* wasn't here with Barlow," said Price. "I'd have gone to the door posing as a man of the cloth who had visited to instruct Mistress Edwards' household in their Bible studies." He lifted his eyes to the ceiling, and talked through his nose like a divine. "'A malignant fugitive, on the loose in this neighbourhood? We shall not sleep safe until he is apprehended!' What do you say, Barlow?"

"I say you are in love with yourself, Ned Price."

"Don't talk of love to me, you heartless monster. Barlow still hasn't remunerated me for a job of work we did the other day," Price explained to Laurence, "so I couldn't buy supper last night for my sweetheart."

Laurence was tickled to catch Barlow's familiar euphemism: a job of work. Price must be a thief, like Barlow.

"Is she the serving wench you've been ogling at the Saracen's Head?" Barlow asked.

"Mistress Susan Sprye is not a wench, Barlow. She's of yeoman stock and hails from the West Country."

"What does she want with you, you penniless bastard?"

"I'm penniless because *you* haven't—"

"Quiet, now – the mistress is coming."

Laurence heard the tap of a cane. As Mistress Edwards entered, he fought to conceal his shock: she had never been a large woman, and arthritis had plagued her for as long as he had known her, but in less than half a year she had shrivelled to skin and bone, and her formerly sharp eyes had clouded over. She had even neglected to dye her hair; grey strands peeked out from her clean white cap.

"Mr. Beaumont, welcome." He kissed her gnarled hand, and she smiled as flirtatiously as ever, revealing her stained false teeth.

"Cordelia told me about Jane," he said, drawing out a chair for her. "I'm so sorry."

Her wrinkled lids lowered briefly, as if she found his words as inadequate as he did. "I cherished that girl as a daughter."

"She's in heaven now, madam," Barlow grunted.

"Can whores go to heaven?" she asked Laurence, in a cynical yet curious tone.

He knew she was anticipating her own death. "If there *is* a heaven, it would be a gloomy place without them," he replied.

"You may leave us, Ned Price," she said with regal hauteur, and invited Laurence and Barlow to sit. "I can tell what you're thinking, sir," she said to Laurence, when Price had disappeared. "Let's not discuss it."

Laurence nodded. "How is your business?"

"Cordelia, Perdie, and Rose are with me, and my maid Sarah, of course, but I couldn't keep the other girls on a fraction of our old custom. It's the taxes, sir: men can't afford the luxury of my house, with Parliament skinning their pockets. Barlow's had to go back into his trade, and I had to sell my jewels for a song – apart from that necklace you bought off me fair and square." Mistress Edwards winked at him with a touch of her old gaiety. "Did it please the lady?"

"Very much. She wears it often."

"Did I say it was a gift from a suitor of mine? I could have married him and settled down, but I was wild, then, and heedless of the future." Mistress Edwards paused for breath, her hollow chest heaving. "Oh, sir, I can't count the number of girls I got out of their difficulties. I didn't never falter, until Jane." She scowled at her hands. "They was trembling worse than leaves. I shall not touch another girl. But what future will Cordelia have, with her baby?"

"At least she's happy about it."

"She's over the moon, the silly creature. So what brings you to London, sir?"

"My work for the Secretary of State. I'll find somewhere else to hide by tonight. Things are hard enough for you without the danger of sheltering me."

"No, sir: them troopers have ferreted about here countless times, with nought to show for it. We could close the door to custom, if you'll recompense me for the lost earnings. It won't be a fortune, but I might charge a little more than we generally take in, for the risk."

"Tell me your fee," said Laurence.

"I'll think upon it." She smiled again, always pleased at a good bargain. "What's your errand, sir?"

"I have a list of names to investigate. They may be of Parliamentary spies. Sir Bernard Radcliff drew it up."

"Radcliff?" She pulled a handkerchief from her sleeve, coughed into it, and tucked it back, not swiftly enough for Laurence to miss the vivid blood in her spittle. "The Radcliff who used to visit us before the war?"

"The very same. And on his list may be the name of a new man John Pym has recruited from abroad as his spymaster, to search out the

King's allies here in London. From what I know of *that* fellow, he's a ruthless sort." Laurence described to them the grisly package of ears.

"Then he don't deserve to live." Mistress Edwards rapped her knuckles on the table. "And if we can do some damage to Pym by hunting him out and killing him, I shall die content. Pym and his dogs of rebels have ruined my livelihood and now they're sending me to my grave. I'd like to strangle them all, for the misery they've caused us."

Laurence was silent, abashed by the force of her hatred. She had suffered from the war in ways that he had not, despite venturing his life, both in battle and in his clandestine activities.

"Who's on the list, sir?" Barlow asked, as though already planning their demise.

"Victor Jeffrey, Anthony Burton, James Pritchard, Christopher Harris, and Clement Veech."

"They ring no bells for me," said Mistress Edwards.

"Nor for me," said Barlow.

"I also have to get a message to a goldsmith, Thomas Violet, who has his shop in Cheapside," Laurence said.

"That's easily done," Barlow told him. "My nephew Jem could pop round and deliver it for you."

Mistress Edwards patted Laurence on the wrist. "You must not stir from my house until the hue and cry dies down. Barlow, could Price inquire about them names? He has a wide acquaintance."

"That he has, madam – wide as the day is long," Barlow agreed, scratching his stubbly jaw.

Laurence felt instantly uncomfortable. "Can I trust him?"

"He won't betray you, sir," Mistress Edwards said. "In some matters, he can't even trust hisself, but he wouldn't betray any friend of mine. And my girls will want to help, too."

## VII.

"If this horrible racket persists, you will be accused of conjuring demons in your rooms," Clarke warned Seward, his fat jowls wobbling.

Pusskins was crouched motionless at the door to Seward's bed-chamber, ears flattened, and coat and tail puffed up, emitting unearthly yowls. Shut inside was a stray cat that had followed Seward home when he had been picking mushrooms earlier in the College meadow. He had not had the heart to turn it away.

"But, Clarke, if I open the door, there will be bloodshed! Might you take it to your house in Asthall?"

Isaac Clarke dumped his enormous weight into a chair, and brushed some of Pusskins' hairs fastidiously from the hem of his robe. "If I do, you will be unable to bring your demon when you come to stay with me there."

"In that case, I must put the poor thing out. Clarke, restrain Pusskins, whilst I secure the object of his wrath."

"And let him tear me to pieces!" said Clarke, not budging from the chair.

"How could he, you great elephant? You are a thousand times his size. Grab him by the scruff of his neck."

No sooner had Clarke heaved himself up than there was a knock at Seward's front door, and a low voice inquired, "Dr. Seward? Are you in?"

The men regarded each other apprehensively. "Is it *that woman?*" Clarke mouthed. Seward nodded. "Whatever can she want?"

"She has come to ask me about Beaumont," Seward mouthed back. With extreme reluctance, he went to answer the door.

"Oh," said Mistress Savage, evidently disappointed to find Seward had company. "How are you, Dr. Clarke? Forgive me, Doctor – you are busy."

"Madam, I was about to leave – a good day to you," Clarke said. "I shall see you in Hall, Seward." He skipped nimbly past her and off towards his rooms, with a speed that belied his girth.

"Enter, Mistress Savage," said Seward, "but beware of my cat."

Pusskins ceased yowling and studied her with marked interest, then trotted over to her. She stooped to stroke the animal, a privilege that was Seward's sole prerogative. "How may I assist you, madam?" he demanded.

She let the cat alone and glared at Seward. "The day before yesterday, the day you called at my house, Beaumont returned from a meeting with Lord Digby and announced to me that he had to sup with the Queen. I therefore accepted an offer to sup with Digby, expecting Beaumont home later. But he didn't come home and nor, as I learnt subsequently, did he attend Her Majesty at supper. The next day I went in some distress to his lordship, who told me Beaumont was supposed to leave for London on his business – but not until that morning, and with another agent, for greater safety. Lord Digby is as consternated as I am. I know Beaumont came to see you," she carried on, now more pleading than angry. "Did he tell you what he was about to do?"

"No," said Seward, feeling a grudging empathy for her. "His disobedience is reprehensible," he added, more honestly.

"And dangerous! And has he so little concern for my feelings that he should leave me without explanation, without so much as a good-bye?" Seward took this as a rhetorical question. "Doctor," she said, "what's that scratching noise? Have you mice in your bedchamber?"

"It is a stray feline. Pusskins is bent on destroying him."

"As is true of most males, your cat can't tolerate a rival."

"I was hoping to liberate the beast, but I fear for its life if I try."

She gathered up Pusskins into her arms. "I'll hold him." Seward unlatched the door. A thin black form slinked out, and a pair of emerald eyes peered up at them. Mistress Savage began to smile. "I happen to have an infestation of mice in my kitchen, and this creature is starved."

"Then it is yours."

"I should call him 'Beaumont,' but that would be one too many, under my roof."

Seward considered. "As a youth here in College, Beaumont earned the epithet of 'Niger,' because of his dusky skin."

Mistress Savage offered Pusskins to Seward, and plucked up the stray. "Niger he is. I thank you, Doctor – for the cat, and for the name."

Seward could not help smiling himself. "Listen to it purr. It knows you have rescued it from imminent death."

"Let's pray that Beaumont has nine lives," she said, as he ushered her out. "He's spent more than a few of them already."

## VIII.

Sarah had lit a fire in the hearth, and Laurence had provided money to buy Mistress Edwards' household what he suspected was their first decent meal for some time. After they had eaten their fill, Price asked, with a blithe enthusiasm that worried Laurence, "Where shall we begin tomorrow, Mr. Beaumont? We might catch some gossip in Westminster about that man Pym hired."

"You might," Laurence acknowledged nervously; he could picture Price in his gaudy clothes lurking at the doors to the House of Commons, and getting himself arrested.

"We've the list, sir." Cordelia prodded a finger at her temples. "We whores don't forget gentlemen's names. We can disguise ourselves as straitlaced Puritans, like we did for you before, and inquire around there."

"One of you girls can set up a stall in the precincts," Mistress Edwards said, "selling flowers."

"Or religious pamphlets," Perdita said. "We've heaps of *them*."

"There'll be talk of last night at St. George's Fields, sir," Barlow put in.

"And hereabouts – what with all the shots them militia fired, they woke the entire neighbourhood," said Mistress Edwards.

"I could go to the fort," volunteered Price.

"Hmm," said Laurence. "On the subject of last night . . . Harper and Draycott might purposely have let me go, in order to see where I'd lead him, but I'm not convinced of it. Harper was furious that he had to free me, and Corporal Draycott seemed genuinely embarrassed by the whole affair. And they waited too long to pursue me. I believe Pym's secretary *had* corroborated my lies to Draycott, and that for some reason, for a short while, I had them fooled."

"Someone must have tipped them off, after you'd gone," Barlow said.

"Yes, and I may almost have bumped into him." Laurence told them about the man in the flapping coat; his skin prickled at the memory of that determined stride. "I don't know why, but I feel certain he's Pym's new agent – the butcher."

"If he is, he'll be out hunting for you, Mr. Beaumont," concluded Mistress Edwards.

## IX.

"For God's sake, Tom, they could at least shoot to kill!" yelled Ingram, over the cheers and the crack of fire, as Tom's troopers galloped through the park after their prey. They had left some of the deer maimed and thrashing, while other wounded beasts blundered into the undergrowth trailing coils of guts.

Tom motioned for his servant Adam to stay behind, and cantered his horse up to Ingram. "You may be soon to marry my sister," he said, an aggrieved look on his sweaty face, "but you should address me by my rank when on patrol. How would you like it if I called you Walter, in front of my men?"

"Forgive me, Major Beaumont," said Ingram, aware that Tom was hurt by more than the neglect of his rank. His brother Laurence had always been "Beaumont" to Ingram, and Tom had always been "Tom"; he had been a child of ten when Beaumont and Ingram had first met at Merton College.

"Perhaps you're not happy serving under the Beaumont colours," Tom went on. "You should have told me so, and stuck with your brother-in-law Radcliff's troop after he died."

*Radcliff maintained better discipline*, Ingram wanted to say. "No, sir: I'm unhappy that those beasts are in torment."

Tom shrugged, and shouted to his men, "Finish them off, and we'll eat roast venison tonight." Then he said to Ingram, "Let's ride to the house."

"Yes, sir," said Ingram, dreading what was to come: the owner of this Northamptonshire estate, Mr. Sumner, was fighting for Parliament.

As they raced down a hill, an old-fashioned, timbered building came into view, surrounded by an assortment of barns and stables. A far cry from Lord Beaumont's Palladian mansion, Ingram observed, but his lordship's house would be no less vulnerable to pillage. These days the armies on both sides were seizing all they could, from friend and foe alike, caring little about what they destroyed in the process.

In the courtyard, Tom waited for some more of his men to arrive, then ordered them to dismount and follow him. He marched up the front steps of the house and banged on the door. A wizened manservant opened to them. Tom pushed past into the dark, wood-panelled hall.

"Madam Sumner," he said, "you have guests."

A woman in sombre mourning dress stood before them. Around her were a clutch of older women, similarly attired, their faces pale with fear. "Who are you, sir?" she asked, in a defiant voice.

Tom bowed. "Major Thomas Beaumont, of His Royal Highness Prince Rupert's Lifeguard. We have the Prince's authority to take from you whatever provisions we need."

"Major Beaumont, were you not taught the manners to bare your head when you introduce yourself?"

"I'd show you greater respect, madam, were your husband to show the same to his King. But you have my word as a gentleman that you will not be harmed if you and your servants keep out of our way."

"Then be done with your thieving as fast as you can."

Tom turned to his men. "Curtis and Smith, upstairs. You fellows, to the stables. Wheel out any wagons or carts you can find, and start loading them. You, to the barns. Round up the livestock." They scattered, knowing the drill. "And empty the cellars. We'll drink a health to His Majesty when our labour's done, if her wine's not too sour. Ingram, look after the women. My word is my word."

Ingram saluted: this was his penalty.

"How much time will they take to despoil my husband's estate?" Madam Sumner demanded of him, as the house began to tremble with the thunder of boots.

"I can't say," Ingram replied. "You and your ladies might seek somewhere quiet to sit, where you'll be safe from disturbance."

"*Quiet? Safe from disturbance?*" She clenched her fists. "A week ago I lost my eldest son in a skirmish, and today I am losing my home."

"We *all* have lost," Ingram told her, his temper fraying. "My sister's husband died before he could see the child she was to bear him. And Major Beaumont's sister lost her husband at Chalgrove Field. She was made a widow at not twenty years old."

"Is that how you excuse his conduct towards us?"

"No, madam. That's how I explain it."

"Let us go to the garden where there is little to steal, other than my herbs and rosebushes," she said to her womenfolk.

"I'll go with you," Ingram said.

"Are they such brutes, that we require a guard dog?"

Ingram let the question pass, and followed them.

Even from the garden, they could hear smashing glass, thumps, and crashes; and doors splintered by violent kicks; and harsh exclamations as the men swarmed about in search of booty. A few of the women were weeping, but not Madam Sumner. Her courage reminded Ingram of his doughty aunt, who had worked so hard to preserve her livestock from Prince Rupert's raids in Gloucestershire the previous spring. "Sweeping the commons, they call it. Robbery, is what I say," Aunt Musgrave had protested to him, though she was a staunch Royalist.

"You do not appear to share their appetite for destruction, sir," said Madam Sumner. "Or are you imagining your wife and estate in these circumstances?"

"I have no wife, madam," Ingram said. "But I'm to marry at Christmastide, if our whole world hasn't fallen apart. My betrothed is the Major's youngest sister." He saw her eyes widen. Trust a woman, he thought: in the absolute chaos of her own life, she had caught the ill feeling between him and Tom.

As the autumn sun dipped and the garden grew chill, Madam Sumner implored him to go in and ask when the soldiers would depart. Walking through the hall, he saw that it had been fouled with excrement; and not by a single man, but by the efforts of several. "Swine," he muttered.

He found Tom in the courtyard, where troopers were herding horses, cows, pigs, hens, and geese from the barns, and loading wagons with sacks of feed, barrels, and the carcass of a huge sow dripping blood at the neck. More men poured from the kitchens weighed down by silver and pewter jugs, goblets, and salvers, legs of mutton, baskets of eggs, and loaves of bread, as if in preparation for a feast, while smoke rose in plumes from the outbuildings.

Tom and a horde of others were congregated by an open cask, filling their mugs. "Ingram," he called over, "come and wet your whistle." When Ingram made no move, Tom grinned and strolled over to him. "What's wrong, man? Has one of the ladies swooned?"

"I beseech you, *Major Beaumont*, to call your troops to order, before they're too drunk to obey you."

Tom stopped grinning and leant forward, to hiss in Ingram's ear, "Talk to me once more like that and I shall raze this house to the ground."

"This house might be your father's."

Tom's eyes flashed. Then he threw back his head and laughed. "It was a joke, Ingram. Why in God's name can't you take a joke?"

# CHAPTER THREE

## I.

Two days after Laurence went into hiding at Mistress Edwards' house, troops from the nearby fort came by every dwelling and business in the neighbourhood with copies of a broadsheet, on which was an artist's depiction of the fugitive. Parliament was offering the princely reward of a hundred pounds for his capture.

"It's nothing like," said Barlow, as they examined the image. "And you don't have a moustache. Read me what's beneath it, sir."

"'Laurence Beaumont, Intelligencer to the Cruel and Devilish Catiline, the Lord George Digby. A bloodthirsty, evil-faced man, six foot tall, black and spare, five-and-twenty to thirty years of age.'"

"What's all this about cats?"

"Catiline was a Roman politician infamous for his conspiracies," Laurence explained. "His lordship would be flattered." But he felt aghast at his own fame, and a hundred pounds was a tempting sum.

That same day, he and Barlow made a trap door in the ceiling of Mistress Edwards' bedchamber, so that he could climb beneath the rafters in case of emergency, and Barlow started to spread word that there was illness in the house. "Most contagious – we've had to close our door to visitors," he told a gentleman who had knocked furtively hoping for a spiritual consultation with Perdita. Blackman Street became a gaol, from which only Sarah, Barlow, and Price could come and go, and the sale of religious pamphlets at Westminster was cancelled. Meanwhile, Barlow's nephew Jem, a pug-nosed, stunted boy of about sixteen, had found Violet's shop boarded up. The goldsmith had not been seen in Cheapside for some time; he had apparently omitted to pay his taxes. The shop remained shut as the week dragged to an end. This was another setback for Laurence: how would he make contact with Violet, when finally the man got to London? Nor was there any sign of relief from neighbourhood patrols, which agitated him more and more, for the sake of his friends. Again, he blamed himself: although reason and instinct had fuelled his decision to disobey Lord Digby, he knew that a measure of spite had also been involved, which was both unprofessional and petty of him; and he wished now that he had confided in Isabella.

On the evening of Laurence's eighth day at Blackman Street, Price walked in on him and Barlow sitting glumly across from each other at the table. "The Trained Bands won't be patrolling for much longer," Price announced. "The Earl of Essex has issued a call for reinforcements. They'll be off on campaign, and both of the forts near us will be short of troops."

"How d'you know that, Price?" Barlow asked.

"From a washerwoman at the fort in St. George's Fields," he said, straddling a chair. "She's sweet on me, the old trollop. Today she told me that Captain Harper and Corporal Draycott brought in a wounded man on the night our Mr. Beaumont escaped. His leg was bleeding, and they carried him away that very night, even though they have a surgeon at the fort. She never saw him herself, but he must have been an important fellow, because he was taken to Derby House."

"You may have injured Pym's spymaster with that shot of yours," Barlow said to Laurence.

"Oh Christ," said Laurence, horrified. "If he's the man who nearly accosted me outside the fort, I believe he won't stop searching until he catches me. I must flee London, as soon as the militia leave."

"You're right, sir," nodded Barlow, "though Mistress Edwards will be sorry. She so wants a taste of revenge on John Pym before she dies."

"She'll be sorrier yet if I'm found in her house – and so will you all. That was good work, Price, but not good news."

A petulance crossed Price's face, as though Laurence were spoiling his fun. "But what about that list of names? And what about the man Albright, whose ears were shorn off? You can't go now, sir – we've just started our investigations."

Laurence reflected: Price had indeed done good work. "If you discover anything more, you can report to me in Oxford – if I ever get back there alive. And if I don't, you can report to Lord Digby."

The petulance vanished, and Price's eyes gleamed. "Might I call myself your agent?"

"I suppose you might."

"You can count on me, sir – you won't regret it." Price bounced from his chair. "Gentlemen, it's time for *me* to leave. Early tomorrow I've an appointment with Mistress Sprye, of the Saracen's Head tavern. I think I'll take her for a walk by St. Saviour's, and lay a posy on Jane's grave."

## II.

For over a week, Draycott's egregious confusion of Veech and Beaumont had deprived him of sleep, appetite, and peace of mind. Captain Harper was treating him with utter scorn, and when he returned from duty to his house off Chancery Lane, Judith would keep asking the reason for his despond. He could not bring himself to tell her, until the morning that he came down to breakfast and she pointed at a broadsheet lying on the kitchen table. "What a dreadful face."

"Wife," he said, "send the children upstairs with their nurse. We must speak, in private."

Once he had poured out the whole story, she counselled him. "Giles, you should apologise to Mr. Pym's secretary, or he might shoulder the blame for this dangerous man's escape. I am only thankful you were not killed by him that night, or horribly injured, as was Mr. Veech."

Pym's secretary received Draycott with alarming news: the great man had been about to summon him to Derby House for an audience. What punishment would be in store for him? Yet after he gave his account of events, Pym merely said, "You made an honest error, Giles Draycott, as did my secretary. And remember who you were dealing with: Laurence Beaumont must excel in deceit." Pym took from his desk a copy of the same broadsheet. "Have you seen this?"

"Yes, sir – it frightened my wife. She could not understand why I was hoodwinked by such a sinister-looking man, but the artist did him an injustice. The image is not like him at all." *It is almost more like Veech*, Draycott nearly added. "He was . . . handsome and engaging in his person. His manner, as much as what he said, made me believe him."

"Hence my summons: we require a better description of him. I do not mean of his appearance – that information we have. Clement Veech wants to ask you about your encounter with him."

"How is Mr. Veech?" inquired Draycott, wishing he did not have to think again about the mad chase through rain-soaked streets, the explosion of fire, and Veech collapsed howling on the ground.

"He has begun to recover, in the care of my physician. Up to today, he was too feverish for conversation. My secretary will take you to him. Giles," said Pym, "though I am not acquainted with the details of his past, I sense that Clement Veech has endured terrible suffering. It must have hardened him. Suffering can have that effect, or the opposite."

Draycott studied Pym's grey face and sunken eyes; the man knew of what he spoke.

"You must prepare yourself for the smell," Pym's physician murmured to Draycott outside the door to Veech's chamber. "He is still wearing the clothes he was brought in with. I can tend the wound, but otherwise he forbids me even to touch him."

"And his fever?"

"It has abated, and his delirious visions have stopped, praise God. He seemed tormented by them, and was crying out in a foreign language."

Draycott entered the darkened room, and approached the bed; the stench was like that of a charnel house he had once been forced to visit, to inspect the body of a murdered woman. "Mr. Veech?"

"Come closer, Corporal Draycott," said Veech. His skin seemed preternaturally blanched, apart from the shadowed sockets of his eyes. His left leg, resting on a bloodstained pillow, was exposed to the thigh, leaving the wound open to view; it looked as if some carnivorous animal had gnawed a hole above his kneecap. "If you are about to shit through your teeth, sir," Veech said, "there's a pail under the bed."

Draycott swallowed. "Thank God you are recuperating."

"God?" Veech laughed quietly. "It was I who told the surgeon how to remove the ball, and rinse the wound with vinegar. I'll be lucky to walk again."

"Mr. Pym said you wanted to question me about Mr. Beaumont."

"I heard you're a lawyer, with experience of the courts. In the course of our duties, you and I are both trained to watch and listen for the small things that betray a man's character, and to record them to memory. Is that not so?"

"Yes," said Draycott.

"Then you'll be able to tell me what Mr. Beaumont wore, what was in his saddlebag, his exact words to you, how he spoke, his gestures – everything you can recall, down to the very scent of him. I must know him, sir, like the back of my own hand."

**III.**

Weeds were sprouting over the mound where Jane was buried, and soon, when the earth settled, her grave would be impossible to locate. Price knelt to place on it a bunch of flowers that he had gathered in the nearby fields; she would forgive him for not buying an expensive posy from the street-sellers. He was remembering his last night with her after he had a spectacular win at dice, and how she had screamed with laughter and flailed her legs in the midst of congress when he had tickled the soles of her feet.

"A penny for your thoughts, Ned?" asked Susan Sprye, her brown eyes melancholy; he had told her that Jane was his sister.

"Jane and I used to play together among these graves when we were children," he said, with a doleful sniff. "We loved our parish: St. Saviour's is one of the best churches in London." He rose and brushed the soil from his knees. "Come, I'll show it to you."

The huge oak door was unlocked. Inside, a verger was sweeping the floor of the chancel. Otherwise Price and Susan were alone. Price wanted to curse as he looked round. How St. Saviour's had changed since that bunch of zealots had seized power: the altar draped in a white cloth rather than splendid brocade, statues of saints gone or left headless, and the wall-paintings defaced. Rocks had been thrown at the stained-glass windows, and sunlight streamed through the holes.

He and Susan paused in the nave to admire the vaulted ceiling, and then he beckoned her to one of the canopied tombs, thankfully undisturbed. "It belongs to the poet, Gower. He's been dead over two hundred years. He was rich, and famous. The neighbourhood is celebrated for its poets and playwrights."

"And for its strumpets," she giggled.

"William Shakespeare worshipped here," boasted Price.

"Who's he?"

"He was among our greatest playwrights, and he was also a player, in the time of Queen Bess, and His Majesty's father, King James. He's been dead not thirty years."

"Well before my day," Susan said archly.

She was a fetching girl, in her dark red cloak; buxom, yet not fat, and fresh-skinned, with a bloom of pink in her cheeks. She was self-assured, and a bit saucy, too; traits Price appreciated in the female sex. They made conquest more of a challenge. "My father was a patron of Shakespeare's company," he went on. "He yearned to tread the boards himself, or so my dearest mother told me before she passed away, though such a thing would have been far beneath his rank."

"So you *are* a gentleman," she remarked, as if she had entertained her doubts.

"Yes, but . . . I was born out of wedlock. My noble father was generous enough to recognise me in his will."

"Is that how you get by, Ned Price? How you afford your costly clothes?"

He let the question pass, and drew her to an older tomb, with the effigy of a knight on a crumbling stone slab. "He may have fought in the Crusades."

"Crusades?"

"Long ago, armies from every corner of Christendom rode off to free the Holy Land from the infidel Turks – the Saracens."

"As in the Saracen's Head!"

Price nodded. "Thousands perished in the name of religion. There's war for you."

"Will you fight in *this* war?"

Her tone was probing; and she was from the Royalist West Country. "If I fight," he said, in a low voice, "it will be for the King."

She gulped and fluttered her lashes. "I'd hoped you weren't a rebel, Ned, but I didn't dare ask."

"I didn't dare admit I was loyal to him, Susan. Or . . . may I call you Sue?" Price bent to kiss her, and when she offered no resistance, parted her lips with his tongue. A cough from the chancel suspended his explorations; the verger was glaring at them. Price whisked her behind a pillar. "Sue, I've adored you since first I laid eyes on you. I am mad for love of you." He kissed her again, and delved a hand into her cloak.

She shoved him away. "You scapegrace, don't you mistake me for a loose woman. I was raised in Bristol, a city of sailors who've been about the world, and I know something of it. Now you behave your-self." She offered her arm to him, chin in the air like a queen. "Tell me more stories of these dead folk."

Price nattered on for a while, amused by her naive responses. But eventually his supply of stories wore thin, and his stomach began growling. "I'm hungry, Sue," he said. "Let's go out to a chophouse."

"Not yet." She led him towards a marble wall tablet crowned by winged eagles, and gestured at the names inscribed on it. "Who were they? More poets?"

Price scanned them impatiently. "No, they were St. Saviour's rectors. You won't want to hear about . . ." Then he looked a second time.

## IV.

"Victor Jeffrey, Anthony Burton, James Pritchard, and Christopher Harris," recited Price, in a triumphant, singsong voice.

Laurence jumped up from the table where he had been at cards with Cordelia and Perdita, and slapped Price on the back. "Mr. Price, you are priceless."

"But, Ned, you forgot Clement Veech," said Cordelia.

"I didn't – his was the only name missing. Still, isn't it the most extraordinary coincidence, sir?"

"Yes and no. The man who provided those names was a visitor to this house. He must have known Southwark. Perhaps he went to pray at St. Saviour's to atone for his sins," said Laurence, thinking to himself that fornication with whores would have been a mere peccadillo on Radcliff's part, as compared to attempted regicide.

"Why would he want you to believe the vicars were spies for Parliament?" asked Perdita. "And why add the name of Clement Veech if it wasn't on that tablet?"

Laurence shrugged. As Seward had said to him, Radcliff was a lying rogue, and the list may have sent him on a wild goose chase. "It could be somewhere else in the church. He could have borrowed it from anyone."

"I went to see my washerwoman, after I left Sue at the Saracen's Head," Price said next. "Harper's detachment is to quit London within the week. More militia are setting out from across the City."

"Thank God," exclaimed Laurence. "Then I've not long to wait."

"Let's have a proper feast before you go," suggested Cordelia. "We did that before, when you had to leave, and . . . who knows when you'll come back again."

Laurence emptied his pockets of coins. "Here's for the feast. And while Sarah's out, she could buy an ounce of poppy tincture for Mistress Edwards."

"Few of the apothecaries sell poppy nowadays," Price told him. "The Bands have commandeered their supplies."

Cordelia winked at Price. "You've got light fingers, Ned – steal it from the Bands."

Laurence hurried upstairs to inform Mistress Edwards of Price's news. She was lying fully dressed on her bed, though in a concession to comfort she had removed her teeth. Without them her cheeks were hollow and her mouth puckered as a dried fruit. In one hand she held a small pewter bowl, for expectorating, and in the other a bloodstained handkerchief. "Of course you must seize this opportunity to fly, sir," she mumbled, once he told her. "And I am glad if we've been of help."

"You have been invaluable, as always," he said.

She patted her counterpane with a gnarled claw, for him to sit. "So has your money, to us. I may put some of it aside for the girls, for when my time comes."

"I wish I could have got you your vengeance on Pym."

"You might yet, though I doubt I'll live to hear of it."

Laurence felt his eyes sting, and covered her hand with his; how frail were those old bones to the touch. "What will become of the house?"

"I've asked Barlow to sell it and split the proceeds with the girls. Perdie and Cordelia are good for nought else than whoring, and I don't know what Cordelia will do when her baby's born. Rosie has family in Chelmsford, out Essex way. As for Sarah, I believe that Barlow might make an honest woman of her, after I die."

"Barlow and Sarah? I'd never have guessed: what a pair of sly devils," he joked, to lighten the conversation.

"Now don't you go teasing Barlow, sir. He's bashful when it comes to love."

"Unlike Price," Laurence remarked, curious to find out more about his new recruit. "Price is sharp, isn't he."

"So sharp he'll cut hisself, if he doesn't take care."

"Cordelia said you knew the truth about his origins."

Mistress Edwards wagged her head. "He doesn't know it, sir, and nor do I want it known, but he's my grandson."

"Why must it be a secret?"

"It was his mother's wish. My only child, Cicely was. I'd sent her to be raised by decent folk, so she wouldn't follow in my footsteps. She married young, to a charming scoundrel. Daniel Rawson had three wives hidden away, besides her, and his business was robbing travellers on the roads. He gave a wonderful speech at Tyburn, the day he was hanged." Mistress Edwards laughed sourly. "Ned's inherited his charm and his silver tongue, but not his name. Cicely's father was a Mr. Price, from somewhere in Wales."

"What happened to your daughter?"

"She came back a widow to Southwark with Ned – they lived apart from me, not at my house. Ned was bright at his lessons, and at first she had hopes for him. But he fell into vicious company. She died broken-hearted – he was seventeen, then. And I thought to myself, if I couldn't stop him from being a thief and a trickster, I'd keep my eye on him so he wouldn't end like his dad. I had Barlow take Ned under his wing." She gave Laurence a piercing look. "Ned's not turned out all bad. He's half my daughter's, and she was a dear, honest lass, God rest her." Laurence said nothing, waiting. "Would you be a friend to him, sir, and get him out of Barlow's trade, while he's still young enough to learn another? He has such promise, and I'd die happy if I knew it wasn't wasted."

"I have in fact agreed to something of the kind," Laurence told her, and kissed her withered cheek; he would not have refused her, anyway.

"Bless you, sir, that is a true relief to me, more than revenge on Pym." She dabbed her eyes with the handkerchief. "Now on to present matters," she said, in a stronger voice. "The Bands may be marching out, but there'll be other troops after you – and every citizen loyal to Parliament or to their pockets. Remember my Maud, who married a sea captain and sailed to the Indies?"

"I wouldn't forget *her*: she was the tallest woman I've ever met, and she could pick me off my feet."

"Open my oak press, and look inside. She left me a patterned gown to cut down for my own use, but I won't require it where I'm going." Mistress Edwards watched as he drew out the pieces: bodice, skirt, and sleeves. "Hold them up to yourself."

Laurence did, and was surprised. "A fit . . . except Maud was somewhat better endowed in the bosom than I am."

Mistress Edwards cackled. "We'll stuff the bodice, and give you a modest collar to your chin. Rose is clever with paint, and you're a fine-boned, smooth-skinned lad, not a hairy ape like Barlow. You'll pass nicely, if the troopers keep their distance."

"If they try any mischief with me, they'll be sorry for it," said Laurence, in a high, prudish voice. "I don't tolerate unwanted advances."

Mistress Edwards burst into more cackles, triggering a cough that deprived her of speech for some minutes. She spat into her bowl and mopped her lips. "As we're talking of advances, sir, I hear my girls don't please you this time round. Cordelia told me you're to wed your lover. Did she make you swear to be faithful?"

"No, it's a question of trust, on both sides," he said. He would have liked to confide in her about his situation with Isabella, as he had in his friend Ingram's wise aunt, Madam Musgrave. While different in character, she and Mistress Edwards shared a maternal quality singularly lacking in Lady Beaumont.

"If I was you, I'd enjoy the moment," Mistress Edwards advised. "It's what everyone should do, what lives dangerously. And you mustn't offend a girl like Cordelia. She's got her pride, sir, as well I know: I've had her working at the house for me since she was thirteen."

On the night that the Trained Bands marched out for Essex's camp, Barlow called together the household. "You can't risk travelling through town, Mr. Beaumont," he said, "so you must go south and cross the Thames beyond the fortifications at Vauxhall. Tomorrow Jem is coming by with a donkey cart. We'll lay a bale of straw in it, and tuck you down into it as if you was an invalid lady on death's door. The militia will stop the cart as you pass the fort at the bottom of our street, on the Newington road. Jem will deal with them. Then he'll let you off at the river. Gain the other side, and you must press southwest, the quickest route out of Parliament territory."

"I'll paint your face a yellow shade, sir," said Rose, "and we can bind your head and most of your face as if you had the toothache, so there won't be much for the troopers to look at, and you won't have to speak."

"Let me ride up front with Jem," said Cordelia. "He doesn't have a woman's wiles."

"No, it wouldn't be right, not in your condition," Laurence objected.

"It's my belly that will do the trick, sir. I reckon most of the militia have wives of their own."

Sarah had procured a leg of mutton, oysters and winkles from the Southwark fishwives, a cheese, a quince tart, a cask of Canary, and two bottles of burnt wine. Although Mistress Edwards joined them, Laurence saw that food had become a painful nuisance to her. She sipped a small glass of Canary, and within the hour asked Barlow to carry her upstairs.

As the night progressed, Rose and Cordelia sang a duet, accompanied by Price on a cracked and broken-stringed lute, and Perdita recited a scurrilous verse she had composed itemising the vices of their

Parliamentary callers. "Booze enough for me," Barlow announced when the cask was dry, and wobbled off to bed. Sarah left discreetly, soon after him. Laurence brought out the burnt wine, a potent distillation that reminded him of the winter he had spent at Simeon's brothel in The Hague, where there was always a plentiful supply. It sped through his veins like opium, allowing him to forget, temporarily, the strain of the past ten days, and the perils of the morrow.

By the second bottle, Price and Rose had fallen asleep at the fireside. Perdita had reached the melancholy stage of inebriation, her arm draped about Laurence's shoulders, and Cordelia was nibbling the remains of the tart. Laurence excused himself to visit the privy. When he returned, Perdita and Cordelia had disappeared; to bed, he presumed, and he decided to follow their example.

Up in his chamber he undressed, tripping on his breeches. As he sank gratefully in between the sheets, he heard muffled laughter; and under the bedclothes his fingers met a firm, rounded stomach.

"Awake, my turtledoves," shouted Price, sauntering through the door without troubling to knock.

Laurence frowned at Cordelia, naked by his side. She squinted back at him, naughtily. "Er . . . what hour is it?" he asked Price.

"Past eleven o'clock, sir." Price brandished a little vial. "For Mistress Edwards, courtesy of the Trained Bands. My washerwoman sneaked it out of the surgeon's chest."

Laurence sat up, his head pounding, and motioned for Price to throw it over. He caught it and sampled the contents. "Thank you again, Price."

"Ned, did you say eleven o'clock?" Without heed for modesty, Cordelia leapt out of bed. "Go and wake Perdie and Rose, if they're still asleep. We must get busy."

"Busier than you were last night?" sniggered Price. And he shot Laurence a conspiratorial look, as if to say, *We're all the same beneath the belt.*

**V.**

However acutely she resented the humiliation of facing Mistress Savage a second time, Lady Beaumont could not retreat to Chipping Campden until she had done everything in her power to wrest Laurence from the woman's clutches. She knew from Lord Digby that her son was still out of Oxford, and so she chose early morning to knock at Mistress Savage's door, hoping to find her alone or, better yet, dallying with some other lover.

The young maidservant showed Lady Beaumont into the parlour, which appeared to her a more spacious room than on her last visit just over a fortnight before, and far preferable to her own stuffy lodgings at Merton. On a table between two chairs polished to a shine with beeswax was a pitcher full of late pink and white roses; a pile of books lay nearby, scholarly tomes, some of them in Latin and Greek. The windows gave onto a small garden, inviting in the late October sunshine: a tangle of the same pretty rosebushes crept over Cotswold stone walls, bordered by oak and beech trees that were shedding a few of their autumn leaves. Such tranquil domesticity hinted at a good housekeeper, not a talent she had expected in Mistress Savage, and at an ominously settled state of affairs.

Mistress Savage entered, immaculately dressed, and dropped a curtsey. "Your ladyship," she said, "how kind of you to call, but I am afraid that your son is not here."

"I came to speak with *you*, Mistress Savage," said Lady Beaumont. "I am to return to Chipping Campden on the morrow, but first I must have satisfaction on an issue of concern to the Beaumont family. Laurence informed me that he wishes to marry you. As a woman of the world, surely you understand – that cannot be."

"A woman of the world?" Mistress Savage repeated.

Lady Beaumont abandoned subtlety. "He may do as he likes with you as his mistress, but you shall not be his wife."

"You speak as if I had insisted on that privilege."

"Was it not your idea?"

"No, your ladyship, it was his, and his ideas are his own on almost everything, in my experience. Please, be seated." Mistress Savage took the other chair. "Though I am under no obligation to explain myself to you, I can tell you that I never once asked to be his wife."

"I see," said Lady Beaumont. "Do you know of his father's ill health this summer?"

"Yes. I trust his lordship is fully restored?"

"He is, but the apoplexy could recur, with any untoward shock or distress. Our eldest daughter is now a widow because of this war, and our sons' lives are at risk. His lordship is most anxious to ensure the continuance of his line, before he dies." She glimpsed a puzzling sadness in Mistress Savage's eyes, and went on, encouraged. "If you truly care for Laurence, you will break off this . . . attachment, and let him marry honourably, as he should."

Mistress Savage was silent for a while. "Your ladyship," she said, at length, "I have the utmost respect for your family. And if you think I am trying to inveigle my way into your son's heart for the sake of a title or riches, or both, you are wrong. I have my honour, too."

"A woman's honour is a different thing, and from what I have heard, yours was lost long ago."

"Since we are being so very plain," Mistress Savage rejoined, "I must argue with your definition: what *you* call a woman's honour is like a piece of property, which may be freely given, bought, or stolen from her depending upon circumstance. Her true honour is *indeed* a different thing."

"And this is pointless talk. Will you break with him?"

"Not on your bidding."

Lady Beaumont got up to leave. If Mistress Savage remained obdurate, she would have to appeal to a higher authority.

**VI.**

Seated in his reception chamber at Christ Church, his small figure dwarfed by his ornate armchair, the King was reading a letter. He looked up distractedly as Digby and his father were shown in. "M-my lords," the King acknowledged them, in his slight Scottish burr. "I have j-just received this d-dispatch from my nephew Rupert." His stammer was more marked than usual, Digby noticed; he must have had worrying news. "He is urgently requesting m-more ammunition for the g-garrison at Newport Pagnell," the King continued. "He says that if the t-town falls to the rebels, the lines of c-communication between London and the North will be swiftly reopened, much to our detriment."

"His Royal Highness is ever in a hurry," Bristol murmured.

"You mention London, Your Majesty," said Digby. "Our Mr. Violet was briefly there and has returned with heartening reports of the quarrels in Parliament over its alliance with the Scots. Those of its Members who would choose freedom of conscience over the dictates of the Presbyterian Church are restive, and some are so hotly against the ecclesiastical state ruling in Edinburgh that they might be prepared to split with the Scots-loving Presbyterians – *if* they could be assured their liberty of worship."

"My Lord Digby, what c-common ground have I with these independent sects, apart from an aversion to the Scottish K-kirk?" inquired the King, sitting forward. "As Head of the English Church, I cannot tolerate every stray sect in my kingdom, especially when their beliefs defy the principles upon which our Ch-church is founded."

"Perish the idea, Your Majesty! Yet if you were to demonstrate a certain flexibility of mind, you might woo some of these freethinkers to our side." Digby cast him a winning smile. "We have had stranger allies."

"But did they not recently sign their Solemn League and C-covenant with Edinburgh?"

"Your Majesty, that agreement is tenuous," said Bristol. "Edinburgh may consider it as a guarantee that the rebels will impose the Kirk's Presbyterian rites throughout England, but many in Parliament view it as a contract entered into simply to obtain military support for the war.

They have no real intention of carrying through on their religious promises."

"And Violet says that the main architect of the agreement may soon take his final bow upon the stage of politics – and of life," Digby added. "Though Pym has slaved day and night to achieve his goal, he often cannot attend sessions in the House due to his sickness. When he dies, these cracks in the façade that he pasted over will resurface, and possibly widen. They might be exploited to our advantage."

"And if the Highland Scots rally to your cause," said Bristol, "they will threaten the rule of the Kirk on home soil. That could put paid to a Scottish army for the rebels."

The King sat back in his armchair, stroking his beard.

"Ah well," said Digby, "we shall have to see how events turn out." He knew from the King's expression that the seed was planted; now he had only to water it at judicious intervals. "Violet also reports that the citizens of London are being bled to the bone, Your Majesty. They are taxed on everything, and life has become a dreary affair, with fines and punishments imposed for the slightest breach of order."

"The last measure I can understand," the King said. "I hear of so much intemperate behaviour in Oxford: duels, drunkenness, improprieties towards women, and blasphemous language. Has Violet been in communication with our f-friends in the capital?"

"Yes, he has, Your Majesty. Despite our unfortunate venture in the spring with the Commission of Array, and the gaoling of some known Catholics, your friends are chafing for an opportunity to assist your cause." Digby glanced at his father.

"A friend of ours there, named Major Ogle, reports the same, Your Majesty," Bristol said. "He, too, is convinced that these independent sects are hostile to the Scottish settlement, and that Londoners in general are tiring of war."

"Their womenfolk proved as much by marching upon Whitehall to call for peace," remarked Digby.

"The gentler sex is oft the wisest," the King observed. "'Wise as serpents, and harmless as doves.'" He stood, and picked up his silver-topped cane. "On that note, I am about to take the air with Her Majesty."

"The skies promise rain, Your Majesty," Bristol said.

"Then we shall walk in the covered passage by our two colleges."

Digby hid mirth. According to gossip, the royal couple used it for more than walking; it was the one place they could be alone, away from their courtiers.

"Oh, my Lord Digby," the King said, "my son Charles has asked me if Mr. Beaumont could instruct him in the art of writing ciphers – an apt study for a prince. Might you spare your agent, for a couple of hours here and there?"

"Why yes, Your Majesty. Mr. Beaumont is out of town for the nonce, but I shall apprise him of your wishes on his return."

"Charles is very attached to him – after Rupert, of course! Charles worships his cousin as a hero."

"His Royal Highness Prince Rupert is a hero to us all," said Digby, assuming his smoothest tone.

"Prince Charles may have to wait for those lessons," Digby confessed to his father, as they left Christ Church. "Violet was apprehended at once by the City militia and questioned about his outstanding taxes, so it is highly likely that Beaumont will be caught. I'm half tempted to let him pay the price for his disobedience."

"Should he be examined, a great many inconvenient secrets might spill out. And what a price he'd pay, after eluding arrest once already this past spring. At the very least he would hang, George, as others did who were connected to that *unfortunate venture*, as you called it. Don't forget he is *your* spy, and you have been painted as an arch fiend by Parliament."

Digby rolled his eyes. "I thank you for reminding me. It would be a shame to lose him. I'd solve a different problem, however," he went on, more lightly. "Lady Beaumont came to see me in some perturbation over his offer of marriage to Isabella."

"Marriage?" exclaimed Bristol. "Has he gone that far?"

"He did promise her ladyship that he would not take Isabella to the altar until he had spoken with Lord Beaumont. She wishes me to work upon Isabella, so that he can be betrothed to the daughter of some neighbouring family – a Mistress Furnival. She went to talk to Isabella herself, to no avail."

"Isabella is an ideal mistress, by any man's estimation, not a suitable wife. She must realise that the marriage will never take place. She has had enough disappointments in life, but if love is blinding her to the truth, you have a duty to enlighten her."

"You are in no position to speak of her disappointments, or of my duty to her. It is partly thanks to *you* that she was ruined as a girl and is now unsuitable for a wife."

"How was I to know she would be seduced at that house?"

"My honoured father," said Digby, stopping and turning on him, "you might as well have put a lamb in with a wolf. I was but twenty at the time, and even *I* could have predicted the outcome."

"Well *none* of us could have predicted that she would be fertile at so young an age," retorted Bristol.

"And who decided that she should be submitted to some filthy witch for an operation that almost killed her? She could have had the child in secret and been none the worse."

Bristol bowed his head. "What's done is done, and you have been a faithful guardian to her since then. Bring her to reason. She will understand it's in her best interests."

"And offer her what, in exchange for relinquishing the prospect of marriage to the man she loves?"

"You could rescue her good name by getting her a husband – one who would not object if she continues as Beaumont's mistress. It was your intention to find a match for her, and you should act soon, before the bloom is off the rose."

"You contradict yourself. You have described her as the ideal mistress, not a suitable wife."

"Don't be facetious with me, George. We both know of a widower with heirs who would happily overlook her past and allow her the . . . liberty she might desire: our friend in the Vintners' Company."

"I have considered Sir Montague," Digby admitted, peering up at the clouds; his father was correct about the rain. "And I have tried to suggest to her that her talents are wasted here in Oxford. Yet I cannot imagine she would agree to such an arrangement, unless Beaumont gives her more heartache."

"George, think of what we are planning in London. Sir Montague is resourceful, but like Pym he is often ill. We may need someone to continue his work for us, if his health fails."

"Dear me," sighed Digby. "It is a game of chess. Which piece to sacrifice?"

"Oh, Isabella would not be in any personal danger. Remember how leniently Parliament treated the Ladies d'Aubigny and Murray. She would be titled herself, as Sir Montague's wife." Contemplating the match, Digby experienced a shade of guilt most rare in him. "Why not strike while the iron is hot – in Beaumont's absence?" his father persisted. "Go and speak to her."

"Very well – I shall try."

"On a graver issue," Bristol said, "will His Majesty deign to court the independent sects in Parliament? We know how immovable he is on matters of religious doctrine."

"Were he not, he might have avoided a war. But this would hardly be the first time he made a promise he did not intend to keep."

"And the stranger the ally, the less compunction he will have in breaking it. I shall encourage Major Ogle to pursue negotiations with them."

"Yes," said Digby. "In a few months, our efforts may bear fruit."

"Niger is an enchanting little fellow," Digby declared, tickling the cat's silken ears with his fingertips. Isabella had greeted him at the door cradling it in her arms.

"Will you come into the parlour, Digby?"

"No thank you, my dear – I cannot stay long. What a pity the Doctor was not helpful as regards your inquiry, when he gifted you your companion."

"It seems Beaumont was as secretive with him as with us," she said tartly.

"Secretive is not the word for Beaumont's conduct! I'd have been pleased for him to tell you I was sending him to London – after all, I told you myself. He lied to us. But you may be sure he confided in Seward, and that Seward is lying, probably on his request. Sometimes I think the venerable Doctor is the only person Beaumont trusts. He does not trust me, and . . . I tend to wonder if he trusts you." Digby let fall a silence. "This business of his wanting to marry you – was he still asking, before he left?"

"Oh yes. And he had talked of his proposal to his mother. Her response was as he had expected. Can you believe – the day before yesterday, she came here herself and asked me to end our liaison. She is direct, I must admit," Isabella said, smiling, "though she kept notably quiet about her scheme for his betrothal. How Beaumont would laugh. He considers it such a joke."

"Does he? How odd . . . She came to see me, too, and I received a somewhat . . . contrary impression." Isabella's smile faded. "You must corroborate my account with Beaumont, but her ladyship told me that he has agreed not to pursue his suit to you until he discusses this other prospect with his father. And he acknowledged to her that his duty is first to Lord Beaumont." Digby watched Isabella; she controlled her emotions so bravely. "Isabella, Beaumont is full of passion for you, as are you for him, and such feelings can cloud judgement. Think how many of us, carried away by the moment, make promises we can never hope to keep," he continued, reminded of the King. "Beaumont wishes you to be secure in his love, and he means it. I once considered him incapable of love, but I was wrong. The trouble is that even if you defied his family and married him, you could not give him what he wants. And in the recesses of his mind, he knows."

She resumed her smile, though it was now forced. "Do you claim to know him better than I?"

*Tread delicately*, Digby warned himself. "I may care more for your future than he does. You suggested that I ask Dr. Seward to cast your horoscope. *I* would suggest, Isabella, that you consult the Doctor about Beaumont's inner nature."

"You have accused the Doctor of lying to me. Why would I get an honest opinion, this time?"

"Lies can be as revealing as the truth."

"Trust you to say such a thing," she remarked insouciantly, but he could read the hurt in her eyes.

## VII.

"O Lord, may thy heavenly angels guide me in my search," prayed Seward, his chest fluttering, like the beat of an angel's wing.

Tonight he had filled his scrying bowl not with plain water, but with a decoction of herbs and roots that he had gathered at the appointed dates and times, some in the dead of night, and others under the noonday sun. He had recorded the recipe years ago, and then misplaced it until recently among his books. It was from Robert Fludd, as was the bowl, bestowed on him shortly before Fludd died.

Fludd had passed it to him, saying, "William, remember: all truth lies in the harmony of microcosm and macrocosm."

"Might the truth one day free us from ignorance and superstition?" Seward had asked. "I do believe it, but do you?"

Although Fludd had not answered him, Seward maintained his faith. At his great age, he might never see the day when enlightenment dawned upon the world, and nor would he find a student to pass on his store of occult learning. He had made a dire mistake, once, in thinking that Bernard Radcliff might be worthy of the latter privilege, and had taught him too much. Radcliff had desired earthly power, not spiritual enlightenment, and his ambition had led to his death.

Seward shook off the memory, and slowed his breathing, gazing into the dark liquid. "What will be His Majesty's fate?" he whispered. "How will *he* die?"

For a long time, Seward saw only his own reflection. Then a mist floated across the surface, his nerves began to tingle, and a vision appeared. Two figures, their backs to him, were walking side by side, swaying as if drunk, their cloaks rippling and billowing in a powerful wind. The shorter man clutched his hat tight, while his companion gestured extravagantly with both hands. In the next second, a sudden gust blew away his own hat before he could catch it. He turned, and Seward had a clear view of his face. As rapidly, the vision evaporated, leaving Seward shocked and mystified: had he seen the present, or far into the future? At least he understood the men's strange gait: they were on the deck of a ship.

## VIII.

"What's that you're eating?" Antonio asked Diego, between gritted teeth. In the last few days their vessel had hit rough waters and he had been wretchedly seasick, unable to stir from their miserable berth below deck; and he was still furious about losing his prized cocked hat in a wind.

"Ginger, Don Antonio," Diego replied, chewing as contentedly as a cow on its cud. "A root very efficacious for nausea. I had the presence of mind to buy myself a small supply before we left port."

"Why in hell have you waited so long to give some to *me*?"

With his pocket knife, Diego sliced off a section of the dry, knobbly root and offered it to Antonio, who crunched at it, grimacing at the taste. "I've been thinking," Diego said, in the deliberate tone Antonio had come to recognise.

"Yes, Diego?"

"As you have at last confided in me that we're not on a mission to bring funds to King Charles, and as I realise that we have no diplomatic papers to protect us, other than the ones I forged, we'll want help upon our arrival in London."

Antonio glowered at this piece of wisdom, as unpalatable to him as the ginger root. He had been driven to show the forgeries when the ship's captain had asked for their travelling documents. To Diego he had explained that he had deceived everyone about the purpose of his journey so as not to be bothered by questions. "And all you need to know is that I am seeking to re-establish a family connection in England." To his annoyance, Diego had crowed with laughter. "*I* knew from the start that your pretext was false, Don Antonio! As if King Philip has money to spare for Charles of England."

"You might like to find yourself a friend," Diego now continued, "such as . . . the Spanish ambassador."

"I should also like to be twenty years younger and rich as Croesus," scoffed Antonio.

Diego stopped chewing. "His name is Don Alonso de Cárdenas."

"Who told you that, my clever monkey?"

"I've been following events in England ever since I began to learn the language. You said you have friends at King Philip's Court – well I have friends in Madrid. Don Alonso has been King Philip's envoy in England for about the past five years," Diego breezed on. "From what I managed to glean, he encountered many difficulties early in his appointment, the first being his greatest disadvantage: he spoke practically no English."

"Is that so," said Antonio, mastering his temper; the ginger was working magic on his queasy stomach. "What else can you tell me about him?"

"He may be no friend to King Charles. Queen Henrietta Maria is French, and we are at war with France. Or should I say, losing our war with France."

"As I am perfectly aware. Have you a better reason?"

"The English royals have been seeking aid from the Protestant House of Orange, in the Netherlands, to which Spain is equally hostile. And our King Philip has a strong interest in limiting the influence of his French and Dutch enemies abroad. In short, Don Alonso may be more kindly disposed to the English Parliament than to King Charles," Diego concluded, popping another slice of ginger into his mouth.

"Kindly disposed to a bunch of rebels?"

"Yes – on the instruction of *our* king."

Antonio pondered: this did not fit with the tone of Don Miguel's letter. How could Diego know more about English affairs than Don Miguel's sons? "Surely neither our king nor Don Alonso can afford to be openly hostile to King Charles."

"You're right, Don Antonio. It's my guess that they'll preserve a polite façade of diplomacy until they see how the civil war unfolds."

"*Civil war?*" Antonio shook his head in amazement. "Are you suggesting that King Charles might be defeated?"

"You're a soldier, Don Antonio – you have experienced the vagaries of warfare," said Diego. "I've only studied them. But history teaches us that rulers *can* be defeated by their subjects, and I'd venture to predict that whichever side in this conflict has the most money and is least plagued by internal strife will win."

"In that case, Diego," Antonio said, "you will write me an introduction from His Majesty King Philip to Don Alonso stating simply that I am in England to visit a dear friend of my maternal aunt: John Digby, Earl of Bristol."

# CHAPTER FOUR

L aurence ran a hand along the window frame, feeling in the darkness for the midpoint, where the inside latch was situated. Prying the blade of his knife between window and frame, he teased at the latch until it came free, and pushed open the window. Barlow would be amused, he thought, as he hoisted himself onto the sill and crawled though. Sliding his feet over, he dropped to the kitchen floor. Instantly his heart jolted in his chest: a ghostly figure was looming up at him wielding a brass candlestick, poised to strike. "Lucy, put that down," he whispered.

"Mr. Beaumont! Why'd you have to break in?" she said angrily, though she did as he asked.

"I lost my key. I tried throwing stones at your windows, and nobody heard." Laurence tossed aside his saddlebag, went to grab a tinderbox from the mantel, and bent to light the fire.

She was shivering in her nightgown. "Shall I call the mistress?"

"No." As the flames began to crackle in the hearth, he stripped off his wet cloak and sank onto a chair to remove his boots. Cold and unutterably tired, he wanted to go straight to bed; but he was also dirty, stinking of sweat, and ravenous. He dragged himself to his feet again, fetched the heavy copper, and poured water into it from a pail. "How is she?"

"She's been worried to death about you. More than a fortnight since you left."

He hung the copper over the flames. "Have we any food or drink in this house?" Lucy disappeared into the pantry and returned with a wine jug and a half-eaten pie, dumping them on the table. "Thank you, Lucy," he said. "You may go."

"Don't forget to douse the fire."

He paid no attention, cramming pie into his mouth and chasing it down with wine, and eventually she stalked away. After he had washed and followed her instruction, he wrapped a towel around his waist and hurried upstairs to Isabella's chamber. She lay on her side beneath the covers; he could just distinguish her dark hair spread out, against the whiteness of her pillow. Then her hair moved, eerily, as if of its own accord, and separated into an independent form: a cat! The animal scampered past him, brushing against his ankles, and darted from the room.

"My God, whatever next," he murmured, closing the door behind it.

Isabella rolled over to face him. "Beaumont! Do you know what agony you've put me through?"

He climbed into bed and pressed against her, luxuriating in the warmth of her body. "I'm sorry, Isabella – I wanted to tell you that I was leaving, and what for, but—"

"Then why didn't you?"

"Digby forbade me."

"Liar." With impressive speed, she reached back and slapped him hard on the cheek. "You deceived us both."

Swinging himself on top of her, he pinned her by the wrists. "And I promise to explain my reasons. But not now."

In the morning, Laurence woke before her. He examined her face, and was pained to see an unhealthy cast to her complexion, and circles under her eyes. And he remembered that for the first time ever in the ten months of their tempestuous yet all-consuming relationship as lovers, she had denied him the pleasure of satisfying her. It was altogether an inauspicious welcome.

Slowly her lashes flickered open. "What are these?" She touched a finger to his forehead. "Traces of a woman's paint?"

"I had to escape from the City in female disguise."

"Were you inspired by my example?"

He laughed; he had once scolded Isabella for dressing as a boy, to run from Parliament troops. "No. The owner of the house where I took refuge, Mistress Edwards, suggested it."

"So there *was* a woman."

"She's an old friend of mine, more than sixty, and very ill. She's sheltered me on several occasions, at considerable risk to herself."

"Oh," Isabella said, in a slightly mollified tone.

"Did Digby inform you that he had intended anyway to send me to London?"

"Yes, on the morning after your departure when I went in search of you to his offices. *He* had no issue with you telling me."

"Now he's the one who's lying," Laurence protested. "I lied to you in only one respect – about having supper with the Queen, who *had* invited me. I'd decided to disobey him by leaving early and by myself. Obviously I didn't want him to find out. But when he ordered me on this mission, he expressly commanded me not to talk of it with you. Had I disobeyed him in that regard we wouldn't be arguing." She frowned dubiously, which hurt Laurence far more than her slap. "Would you take Digby's word over mine?" he asked, staring into her eyes.

"Why would he lie to me about such a matter?"

"To cause trouble between us. It was you who warned me he'd try to break us apart."

"Yes, I know," she admitted. "So why *did* you not wait to go with Violet?"

Laurence repeated to her the reasons he had given Digby. "I'm not even sure if Violet was in London."

"He was. He brought his lordship a detailed report on the quarrels within Parliament, and . . . other useful intelligence."

"Good for him." Laurence took her in his arms; he felt no softening of her attitude. "What else is bothering you, my love?"

"Her ladyship your mother paid a second visit here, before her departure for Chipping Campden."

"Ah," he said, releasing her. "You must have had a delightful exchange."

"It was most delightful, and I am beginning to agree with her: I might prefer the role of mistress to that of wife," Isabella said, brightly. "We would be wise to recognise our limits, don't you think?"

"Is that her view or yours?"

"Be honest, Beaumont – can you picture me at home with her ladyship, grumbling about the servants over our embroidery?" Laurence was silent; he could not. "She hinted that our marriage would be the death of your father."

"Nonsense – he married for love."

"Whatever the case, you neglected to tell me that you're considering the betrothal she has arranged."

Laurence sat up in bed. "That is false."

"You promised her not to marry me until you had spoken to Lord Beaumont about it," Isabella rushed on. "And you pledged to do your duty to him, which, *clearly*, is to wed the girl they have picked out for you."

"Did my mother also pay a visit on Digby?" Isabella nodded. "I suppose this creative version of the facts came from him."

"Then what is your version of the facts?"

"I have promised to speak to my father," Laurence said, without shifting his eyes from hers. "I would be . . . undutiful to marry without his knowledge, although had you accepted when I proposed to you, I'd have overlooked my duty to him. But I haven't changed my mind. I want you for my wife, Isabella. In the past, he accepted that I should be free to choose, as he did. I believe the more he gets to know you, he'll understand," he concluded, uncomfortably aware that he knew little himself about Isabella's life prior to meeting her. She disliked talking of it, and had told him only that her mother had died when she was a girl, and that after she was seduced and endured an abortion, she had become Digby's ward.

"It is the opposite," she said. "The more your father knows, the less he will understand. Did you intend to reveal to him that I cannot bear you children – and why?"

"No, because I still believe you can."

She wilted, leaning her head on his chest. "Why do you persist in your delusion?"

Laurence felt again the peculiar awe that crept over him whenever he recollected his night at Yusuf's house. "Before I returned to England two summers ago, I was in Spain. I met a man on the road to Cádiz who took me to his home. The lady of his house, Khadija, was an African, a seer who spoke to me of my past, of things that she couldn't possibly have known unless she had a mysterious gift. She also said I would love a woman named after a great queen, and that this woman would give me a child. I am convinced, in my heart, that the woman is you."

Isabella's expression struck him as baffled, and pitying. "Oh Beaumont, countless women are named after great queens, your own sister Elizabeth included. I am amazed that you, who are suspicious of everything under the sun and do not even believe there is a God in heaven, should put such faith in a vague prophecy."

"It amazes me, too, and I can't explain it, although she made another prophecy, not vague at all, that *was* fulfilled. It concerned a . . . political affair, here in England." He saw a gleam of interest in Isabella's eyes. "I can't say more about it for reasons of state, but trust me, her prediction was uncannily accurate."

"If I'm to believe you about one prophecy, and if I'm to trust you, surely you can trust me with the other."

"It's a secret that's not mine to share."

"Is our friend Dr. Seward privy to it?" Laurence did not answer, irritated by her tone. "I assume he is. And is Digby?"

"Isabella, stop."

"How you intrigue me, Beaumont – you and the Doctor, and your secrets." She flung aside the bedclothes with an imperious gesture. "Make love to me, now."

His desire was so dampened by their conversation that he almost refused. But in the end, it was as easy for him as breaking into her house.

## II.

Laurence shaved meticulously for his audience with Digby, and dressed in fresh linen, and a black suit of clothes that he hoped would lend him appropriate gravitas. He had last worn the suit at the trial of the man responsible for his torture, who had been sentenced to hang mainly on his evidence. He was as determined this morning not to give Digby the advantage. Nor would he discuss his relations with Isabella.

"How wonderful that you are safely home to us, sir," Quayle said, at the door.

"Thank you, Mr. Quayle. Is his lordship in his office?"

"No, sir, he is at fencing practice, with the Prince of Wales and two gentlemen from Her Majesty's Court."

Quayle led Laurence out into the adjoining herb garden. The Prince was in combat with a man Laurence recognised as Henry Jermyn, Colonel of the Queen's Lifeguard. He had heard of Jermyn as an affable and gregarious fellow, liked by everyone; a rare thing these days. Jermyn had been in The Hague with Her Majesty while she was raising funds for the war, and had accompanied her back to England, earning a baronetcy for his devoted service.

"Good morning to you, Mr. Beaumont," the Prince hailed Laurence. He was tall for his thirteen years, and would grow head and shoulders above his father, judging by his large hands and feet. His swarthy, rather plump cheeks glistened with sweat, and his big dark eyes were full of mischief. "You *are* looking splendid, sir. Have you an important event to attend?"

"Extremely important," said Laurence, bowing to them all. "I am here to see the Secretary of State."

The Prince burst into giggles.

"Ah, Mr. Beaumont," Digby said, puffing a little, "may I introduce Mr. Jeffrey Hudson." Digby's partner was a young dwarf, blond like him, flourishing a miniature rapier.

"You've taken on a fearsome opponent, my lord," Laurence remarked.

"Indeed, his stature belies his skill: he's caught me off guard several times."

Hudson scowled up at Laurence. "Mr. Beaumont and I met once before, though he failed to allow me the honour of an introduction."

"I humbly beg pardon for that, sir," said Laurence.

"Lord Jermyn, Mr. Beaumont," said Digby.

"I know much about you, sir, from our mutual friend Lord Wilmot," Jermyn said, with a graceful smile.

"Well," said Digby, "since Mr. Beaumont has arrived, he and I must go to business. Pray excuse us."

The Prince lunged forward and rested the tip of his rapier on Laurence's chest. "You shall go nowhere, sir, until you promise to instruct me in the secret art of breaking codes!"

"With pleasure, Your Highness, if you'll promise not to run me through," said Laurence, which set the Prince giggling again.

"Business before pleasure, Your Highness," Digby told the youth, and guided Laurence inside, to his office.

As he undressed to the waist, Digby called for Quayle to bring him towels and a fresh shirt. His belly reminded Laurence of a child's, soft and dimpled; and he must have caught Laurence inspecting his embonpoint, for he said, "I was on trimmer form when riding with my regiment. Now I am closeted indoors at Council meetings, and every evening we feast at Court. You can have no sympathy for me, being such a scrawny fellow."

"It is you who should have sympathy for me, my lord," Laurence said. "I can never put fat on me, however much I eat."

Digby let Quayle towel him down, his flesh mottling with the friction, and then assist him to dress once more and comb his hair. Laurence waited, anticipating a stern rebuke; he had not yet been invited to sit. When Quayle left, Digby at last motioned Laurence to a chair, and sat down himself at his desk. "I shall not waste breath on chastising you for your impromptu departure. Was your journey profitable?"

"In part," said Laurence. "I learnt that four of the names on Radcliff's list are also on a memorial tablet in St. Saviour's Church, in Southwark. They're of dead vicars."

"Then the list is a fabrication?"

"Not necessarily – the names could have some other significance. Clement Veech was not on the tablet."

"He may have been buried elsewhere in the church. Did you look?"

"No, my lord. I couldn't even visit St. Saviour's myself." Laurence told of his arrest by the Trained Bands and the circumstances of his release, and how he had gone into hiding with a price on his head.

"'Intelligencer to the Cruel and Devilish Catiline, the Lord George Digby'!" chortled Digby. "I would have appreciated a copy of that broadsheet." Then he sobered. "Who carried out your investigations for you?"

"The same friends who hid me."

"What of Albright, and Pym's spymaster?"

"I learnt nothing about Albright, but by accident I may have shot and wounded Pym's spymaster." Laurence explained about the man taken to Derby House. "That was why I chose to leave so precipitately, before my mission was accomplished."

"You could have been as dead as those vicars," said Digby, with a hint of possessive anger. "You cannot return to London."

"No, but it's possible that my friends might unearth more intelligence and report it to me here. And Violet should beware if *he* goes back into the City: if he doesn't pay his taxes, the militia will have a good excuse to arrest him."

"He has since fulfilled that obligation."

"Was *his* journey profitable?"

"Oh yes, sir. He says the question on everyone's lips is who will succeed the ailing Pym as a unifying force in Parliament, which is more and more divided. The independent sects doubt that their freedom of worship will be respected once a Scottish army is on English soil.

Parliament will be beholden to Edinburgh, and there will be Scots Commissioners in Westminster to insist that the rebels keep to the terms of the Solemn League and Covenant." *Hardly news*, Laurence wanted to say. "Violet made contact with a gentleman, a Major Ogle, who has reported earlier to us on these murmurings of internal dissent," Digby continued. "Major Ogle is now conducting discreet negotiations with some independents and moderates in both Houses, all of them dismayed by the terms of Parliament's Scottish alliance. My father and I cherish hope that His Majesty might offer them certain religious concessions, to bring them into our fold."

"But, my lord, His Majesty has never seen fit to bend, on matters of religion."

"He has suggested to us that he would consider it."

Laurence was momentarily confounded. If the King was prepared to accommodate the freethinking sects and the moderates in Westminster, there might be a chance he would bend on other issues. Could a peace be reached, after more than a year of bloodshed, and many rounds of failed negotiations between the two sides? *You can't stop this war*, Laurence had told Falkland, on the eve of his death; yet might it be stopped? Then an image floated into Laurence's mind of the King's face, refined, dignified, and immeasurably obstinate. Some deception was about to be practised here, though by whom and upon whom Laurence was not sure. "A most encouraging development, my lord," he said to Digby. "Who is Major Ogle?"

"He is an ally of His Majesty, and completely trustworthy, my father assures me. Alas, he is for the present detained by Parliament in Winchester House."

"Ah," said Laurence; the Major's gaol, used mostly to incarcerate prisoners of rank, lay a short distance away from Blackman Street. "And how, exactly, is he able to conduct confidential negotiations while behind bars?"

"With the assistance of the gaol keeper, a Mr. Devenish, who is among the freethinkers disturbed by Parliament's Scottish bedfellows.

Ogle might soon be . . . liberated. We shall speak more of him anon. Isabella must have been immensely solaced by your return," Digby said, in a changed, apparently genuine tone. "She has had a multitude of worries, lately." Laurence said nothing, thinking of Lady Beaumont. "Did she mention to you that her friend Mr. Cotterell is unwell?"

"No, my lord," replied Laurence. "I remember him, as a gracious old gentleman who once lodged us at his house."

"He wrote to her that he may not have long to live, and asked her to visit."

"I could take her, with your permission."

"Thrilled as I am to hear you beg my permission for anything, sir, I shall arrange for her conveyance, and a party of guards to accompany her. You two have been so long apart," Digby added. "Let me not keep you from her today. You may attend me again tomorrow, sir."

## III.

Laurence came home to find Lucy in a panic. "The mistress is sick, sir. After she broke her fast, she brought up her food, and said she felt dizzy. I put her to bed, but she wouldn't let me fetch a physician."

A wild hope gripped him as to what these symptoms might portend, and he raced upstairs. Yet when he saw Isabella shivering beneath piles of covers, glassy-eyed and flushed, he realised that she must be suffering from a bout of her recurrent fever; he had witnessed it before, and it always left her completely drained.

He knelt down at her bedside and stroked her burning cheek. "Your enemy is back. How fast it takes hold."

"Just hours. I knew as soon as I put food in my mouth – it tastes like iron on the tongue."

"I might ask Seward for that remedy of his – it seemed to help you, last time." He smoothed the hair from her forehead. "What else can I do?"

"Tell Digby I'll have to delay my journey. My friend Mr. Cotterell—"

"Yes, yes, I will – Digby spoke to me about him. Are you warm enough?"

"I am either freezing or on fire, in turns. Beaumont, I was unkind to you."

"Don't give it another thought, my love," he said, kissing her, and tucked the bedclothes snug around her.

At Merton, courtiers were strolling in the quadrangles, and a band of musicians were playing viols for their entertainment. As Laurence sped beneath the Queen's rooms, he felt a distinct relief that his mother was no longer in town. When he got to Seward's door, he found it ajar. He pushed it wider, and a gust of acrid smoke filled his nostrils. Obscured by the fumes, Seward stood at the hearth, vainly flapping his arms to clear the atmosphere. He wore an apron on top of his academic gown, and his cap was askew. Laurence walked in, and immediately started to cough. "Seward?"

Seward turned with a cry of joy, and shuffled up to throw his arms about Laurence. "Beaumont! I was on tenterhooks wondering what had happened to you in London."

Laurence pointed at the alembic over the hearth. "What explosive potion are you brewing?"

"It's for my eyesight." Seward removed his spectacles to wipe off the steam on his apron. Then he set them back upon his nose and surveyed Laurence. "You appear in fine health. And it has been a while since you wore that black suit."

"I'm in fine health, Seward, but Isabella has her fever."

"I suppose you came not to recount your adventures, but to obtain more of my Jesuit's bark."

"I came to do both," said Laurence.

Seward went to his cupboard and searched among the shelves for the vial. "She visited me soon after you had left, to ask your whereabouts – as I had predicted. As predictably, I had to lie to her, which displeased me." Hence her remark about secrets, Laurence thought.

"I was sorry for her, Beaumont. I gave her a cat rather like you in appearance, and proposed that she call it Niger," Seward added, still searching.

"As my substitute?"

"No, to deal with the mice in her kitchen. Aha!" He picked out the vial and handed it to Laurence. "Do you recall the proper dose? And have her maid boil some barley in water for her with a little salt and sugar. She must drink as much fluid as she can, while sweating out the fever."

Laurence stuck the vial in his pocket. "Thank you."

"In thanks, I want to hear about your exploits."

"You will. I also have something astounding to tell you about His Majesty." Laurence sat down and began with the events in London and his flight to Oxford; then he described his audience with Lord Digby and the King's novel interest in religious compromise.

As he was talking, Seward heaped ash on the fire, removed the alembic, and decanted the steaming liquid into a pot. Then he settled into his chair, and they looked at each other without speaking. "My boy," Seward said eventually, "could it be a sign of God's mercy towards the King if these negotiations with the freethinking sects and the moderates bore fruit, and brought peace to his kingdom? Might he be saved from an early and violent death?"

"You've often accused me of jumping to conclusions, Seward, yet yours beats all." Laurence sighed, rubbing his eyes; they stung from the smoke and sheer fatigue. "I don't know much about God's mercy, but I do know a bit about His Majesty's character. If his armies were on the verge of defeat, I'd understand his change of heart. For the moment, they are not. And I mistrust any negotiations in which Digby is involved."

"His father Bristol is a man of good faith."

"Reputedly so, but I know nothing about the intermediary they've chosen, the curiously named Major Ogle, who is in Winchester House prison – on what charge I forgot to ask. He may be another of their shadowy London friends, like Violet. Digby told me that Ogle may soon be *liberated*. I'm not an astrologer, but I can foresee what that might mean." Seward frowned at Laurence. "He'll be sprung from gaol, perhaps by the gaol keeper, who Digby says is one of these independents. At any rate, don't get too hopeful, Seward, although I hope I'm wrong about the King." Laurence stood up. "I should go to Isabella."

"Wait – I have something astounding to tell *you*," said Seward, in such a way that Laurence sat back down. "A couple of nights ago, I applied myself to my scrying bowl, seeking an answer as to His Majesty's fate. I received a vision. As Fludd warned me, and as I have learnt in the past, the bowl does not lie, but it shows only what it wants, and sometimes so unclearly that I cannot understand what I see. This vision, though brief, was crystal clear."

"Was it of the King?"

"No. I saw two men on board a ship. One of them had your face, Beaumont – I swear, the likeness was striking. He appeared older by at least twenty years, and so I thought he might be you, at some future time. His expression, however, was unlike any I have seen in you: full of resentment, and vengeful."

"If my life continues on its present course, he and I may yet be twins."

"It's not a joke," Seward chided. "Upon further cogitation, I am sure, for no reason I can give, that he is alive in the present – that he is not *you*. He cannot be other than your kin. Your Spanish kin, I would deduce."

Laurence got up again. "It's an odd vision, and I'll leave you to brood on its significance. I have more tangible matters to worry about."

Seward rose also. "I feel as sure, and with as little reason, that he intends you harm."

"Then we must pray for a shipwreck," Laurence said.

**IV.**

Price considered it one of his attributes that he could never hold onto money for very long: he was as generous with his own as with that of other people. And he had a superstitious idea that the more easily it was spent, the faster even more would accrue to him. Flush with coin from Mr. Beaumont and after an unusually lucrative job of work with Barlow, he had moved out of his stinking room near Fish Street and into a pleasant chamber at the Saracen's Head. He had paid the land-lord, Robin Nunn, a week in advance for it. Sue was now convinced of his gentlemanly status, and acknowledged him publicly as her sweet-heart. He had not yet attained his goal with her, but he had every expectation of success.

On All Hallow's Eve, as he was lounging on his featherbed sip-ping from a bottle of wine and contemplating an invitation to cele-brate that unholy night with Barlow and Mistress Edwards' ladies, someone knocked at his door. He went to answer. "Well how are you, Jem?" he said, wondering if the boy had heard about his change in fortunes and had come to cadge a loan.

Jem looked very smug, in a new doublet far too big for him and a ridiculous old hat of Barlow's. "I've got something you want," he said, with his cocky grin. Price stepped aside for him to enter. "Aren't you comfortable these days," Jem said, peering round, doubtless calculat-ing what might be lifted and sold if Price ever had to depart in a rush.

"State your business," Price said.

Jem's eyes rested on the bottle of wine by Price's bed. "Mind if I take a drink, Ned Price?"

"Suit yourself."

Jem darted forward and grabbed it, and swigged a mouthful. "Fine wine," he declared, expertly smacking his lips.

Price snatched the bottle from him. "What have you got?"

"A name," said Jem. "Worth twenty pound."

"Why would I pay that much for a name?"

"I'll give you a clue. Mr. Beaumont would want to know it, and badly. I'd wager he'd pay yet more. I'd take him the information if I could, but I don't like to leave the City. Haven't in all my life," Jem added, with pride.

"Give me another clue."

"Remember them dead vicars?"

"Y . . . yes," said Price.

"Remember that missing name? Clement Veech?"

"Who is he?"

"Twenty pound and I'll tell you."

"If you're fooling me, Jem, I'll have the money back and give you a beating free of charge."

"On my soul, you won't regret a penny of it."

Price clambered onto his bed and stood up unsteadily, hanging on to one of the four posts. He reached into a hole in the canopy over his head and plucked out the stocking where he kept his money. He counted fifteen pounds into the palm of his hand, stuffed the stocking into its hole, and climbed down. "Here's three quarters, and you'll have the rest when I return from Oxford."

"Twenty pound, *now*. A bargain's a bargain."

"You little thief." Price hunted in his pockets for the other five, and dropped the whole sum into Jem's grimy palms. In a matter of seconds, Jem dispersed them cunningly about his person, some into his capacious doublet and down the front of his ragged breeches, and the rest into his hat. "Talk," said Price.

"Clement Veech is the rebels' spymaster."

Price emitted a low whistle. "How do you know?"

"'Cos I got brains, Ned Price, that's how. I went round Derby House and had a look about. A busy place it is. Next day I followed a man in, as if I was his footboy. I sneaked into the kitchens, still looking and listening, and while I was there, a fellow in black walked in and started scolding the cooks. He said Mr. Veech wouldn't touch their food unless they put more spice in it, and that if he didn't eat, his leg wouldn't heal, and Mr. Pym was depending on him to get better. My throat's dry." Price gave him the bottle. Jem continued, after a gulp. "It so happens that was Veech's surgeon. When he'd gone, the cooks was gossiping about him, and about this Mr. Veech and his odd habits, how he wouldn't let the servants clean his chamber, and such like. And they was laughing about Mr. Pym, too, and how he kept calling them by their Christian names, and how would he and Veech appreciate to be called 'John' and 'Clement' by *them*! They said when he's dead, which he will be soon, 'cos he's on his last legs, the man who'll fill his boots is a different kettle of fish, a man called . . ." Jem scratched his beardless chin, in the manner of his uncle. "Sinjin, I think it was. Then I reckoned I'd heard enough, so I made misself scarce."

"Who else knows, save me? Have you told Barlow?"

Jem chuckled dismissively. "I wouldn't get twenty pound off Barlow – he'd give me a box on the ear if I so much as thought to ask."

Price had to laugh. "I might do it for him."

"I did tell Mistress Edwards. She said, fair's fair – you talk to Ned, and he can go and tell Mr. Beaumont in Oxford."

"Bless her, so I shall." Price pondered sending the boy again to Derby House in the hope of more discoveries, but it would cost him; and he hated to postpone the enormous satisfaction of reporting to Mr. Beaumont.

"Will you be at the house tonight?" Jem inquired, as Price showed him out.

Sue was in the passage carrying a tray, her face wreathed in smiles. "I might, I might not," replied Price.

Jem strolled away, casting a manly, appraising glance over his shoulder as he passed by Sue.

She bustled into Price's chamber and set the tray on the floor. "A taste of supper for you, Ned. Who was that ragamuffin?"

"No one you'd care to know." Price shut the door and embraced her; he could smell the combined fragrance of young sweat, lavender, and baking on her skin. And it occurred to him exactly how to seduce her. "My love, can you keep a secret?" She nodded. "I've been yearning to tell you: I have a new friend, a Mr. Beaumont. He's an agent of the King. He was on a mission here, and asked for my help. He would have been arrested by Parliament, had I not smuggled him out in disguise. And today I found him vital information that I must relay to him in Oxford."

She bit her lip charmingly. "I thought you were going for a soldier."

"There are other ways to serve His Majesty," Price said, assuming a noble, self-sacrificing expression.

"Oh Ned, you *are* brave. When must you leave?"

"Tomorrow."

She let him ferry her to the bed, and they sat down. "Will it be . . . dangerous?"

"Yes. But it's my duty, Sue."

"Ned, you love me, don't you?"

"I do."

She gathered up her skirts, and pointed to the garter at the top of her plump left thigh. "Tonight I shall tie three knots in this, and tuck it under my pillow."

"What for?" he said, more fascinated by her thigh.

"To bind you to me. The country folk say that on All Hallow's Eve, it can give a girl power over the man she will marry."

He dared to caress her garter. "I *am* in your power, Sue. I'm on fire for you."

"And I for you. Shall we . . . shall we be married, Ned?"

"I swear, *if* I ever return . . ." He kissed her, and she allowed him to unlace her bodice, and lower the neck of her shift to cup her breasts in his hands. "I swear that you shall be my darling wife," he promised.

"Ned," she said, stroking his moustache with her fingertips, "you can write. Will you pen a letter to my father?" He merely smiled at her, intoxicated by his triumph. "You should beg his leave for my hand. That is the custom."

"Sue, I told you, I must go to Oxford. I can't think past that."

"You could write before you set out."

"Don't you trust me, when I have trusted you with my secret?"

"I've trusted you with my virtue, Ned." She sat up to tighten the strings on her bodice, and shake out her skirts. "Susan Price," she murmured, longingly.

He pinched her cheek. "Hurry or you'll catch a lambasting from Mr. Nunn."

After she had gone, he looked for bloodstains. There were none anywhere that he could detect. What if she was not so virtuous, after all, he thought, and had a practical reason to rush him to the altar? She was as cunning as Jem! He had believed her a virgin, when it was she who had played him along. But he could play the role of deceived lover, when he got back from Oxford. Or would he come back? He imagined Mr. Beaumont congratulating him, singing his praises to Lord Digby. He might win a knighthood, and marry an heiress. "Sir Edward Price," he said to himself loudly, in an aristocratic accent; and in his own voice, more quietly, he said, "Why ever not?"

## V.

Veech admired the two sections of smooth wood that he had pierced with holes at top and bottom, through which he had threaded leather cords. Shaped to the contours of either side of his knee, they would support it as he learnt to walk on crutches; he had borrowed the design from the infidel surgeons, whose skills far surpassed those of English medical men.

"What is it – a brace?" Draycott asked.

Veech slipped it over his foot and up his leg, to the bandaged wound. "Yes, I made it myself."

"Are you still in much pain, sir?"

"It's worse and worse, the more I move the joint. But I must move, or the blood in my leg will become stagnant and putrefy. Listen to those crowds," Veech remarked, of the noisy mob outside Derby

House. "Isn't it a peculiar turn of events, Corporal, that tonight they should be celebrating the discovery of a Catholic plot to blow up old King James and both Houses of Parliament?"

"Why do you say peculiar, Mr. Veech?"

"Parliament is now at war with James's son, who is married to a Catholic. How things have changed, in less than forty years."

"Parliament doesn't blame King Charles alone for this war. His chief counsellors pushed him to it, above all Lord Digby, many are convinced."

"If you remember," said Veech, adjusting his brace and tightening the leather cords, "one of the plotters hanged, drawn, and quartered in the churchyard of St. Paul's was Sir Everard Digby, a kinsman of his lordship."

"That *is* peculiar," Draycott admitted. "I had forgotten."

"My own father watched the executions as a young man, and *he* never forgot the spectacle. Sir Everard was the first of three to die on the scaffold, that January morning," Veech went on; he could still hear his father's deep voice telling the story. "In his address to the crowd, Sir Everard claimed he had done no wrong in the lights of his religion, but asked God, the King, and the entire kingdom to forgive him for breaking the law." Veech laughed. "Religion excuses everything, even the murder of a king. There's a tale that, as Sir Everard's heart was cut still beating out of his chest and the executioner showed it about, declaring, 'Here is the heart of a traitor,' Sir Everard piped up, 'Thou liest.' Now, Corporal Draycott, I've seen the heart cut out of a man and I can assure you, he was quite incapable of speech."

Draycott averted his eyes, as though repulsed. "The penalty for traitors is cruel, some might say barbarous. Yet I suppose it must be, in retribution for their crime, and to deter others from following their example."

"Oh I approve of it, Corporal: it reduces all men to the same level, whether they be the noblest or the lowest in rank. Yet even the most barbarous of deaths can't deter a man who believes his immortal soul will fly straight to heaven." Draycott said nothing. "Mr. Pym tells me you are to be blooded soon, as the expression goes."

"Yes, sir: I leave the day after tomorrow. I'd thought that we would join the Earl of Essex's army, but Captain Harper's troops are to assist Sir William Waller in the attack on Basing House."

"Basing House . . . What is its importance?"

"By all accounts, it's a nigh impregnable papist stronghold, the Marquis of Winchester's seat, and lies on the main road into London from the western counties."

"How can a house be impregnable?"

"The oldest part was built as a fortress, hundreds of years ago, and is linked by a bridge and gateways to the newer part – four storeys high. Basing has held out more than a year for the King."

"Well, well. Are you ready to fight?"

"I must be."

"Judith will pine for you," Veech said, knotting the cords on his brace. He saw Draycott blush. He had quizzed Draycott about his marriage, which sounded a dull affair arranged so that Draycott could inherit his father-in-law's practice and a house near Chancery Lane. "Now for me to stand, Corporal. Fetch me those crutches propped against the wall." Draycott passed them to him. He wedged one under his left armpit, and pushed up off his chair with his right hand. He gritted his teeth, and after a couple of tries, rose shakily.

"I could hold you, to support you better," Draycott suggested.

"You let me be," cried Veech. He thrust the other crutch beneath his right armpit, steadied himself, and took a few paces forwards. His head swam and his wounded leg was screaming at him. He felt himself about to fall. "Get the chair." Draycott slid it behind him just in time, and he slumped into it, his crutches clattering to the floor. "When I catch Beaumont again in London, he shall suffer for this. Mr. Pym wants me to treat him with kidskin gloves. But by then, I won't be answering to Pym."

"You can't be certain that Beaumont would venture back here."

"I'll find a way to bring him back – and to pay him back, too."

"You mustn't overtire yourself, Mr. Veech," said Draycott, as if to change the subject.

"Are you growing fond of me?"

"I am . . . concerned for your welfare, as is Mr. Pym."

"Corporal," Veech said, "you're not made to be a soldier. The reek of battle will offend your delicate nose. So I've a proposition for you. Since you were the one who let Beaumont escape, and are to an extent responsible for the fact that I am permanently lamed, you must help me get retribution. Pym has agreed that I can hire you as my assistant."

Draycott looked uneasy. "What would my duties entail?"

"*Entail!* Such a lawyer's term. You'd have but a single duty: to do my bidding, whether or not it abides by the rule of law."

"Then I can't accept."

Veech smiled, despite the throbbing in his leg. "You may reconsider, when you're out on campaign: no marches in the bitter cold, no sleeping on the ground with the damp numbing your bones, no flux from bad rations, and no risk of imminent death or injury. You'd go home to your wife's bed unless I called you out, and sleep peacefully in the knowledge that you're aiding in the capture of an enemy of Parliament. We are at war, sir," Veech added softly, "and war permits us licence."

"Even in war, there are rules of conduct," Draycott said, as softly.

"Not for the victor, in any war I've known." Veech started to unfasten the cords of the brace. "I wish you luck, sir, and I hope you return alive to me."

## VI.

Laurence was watching Isabella pack the last items into her travelling chest. "You're not well yet. Why not rest a few more days?"

She shook her head. "I've delayed my journey over a week. If you were in my place, and Dr. Seward were ailing, you would go to his bedside, would you not?"

"Yes, I would."

"Mr. Cotterell is *my* Seward, Beaumont – I owe it to him. I owe you for nursing me so devotedly, but leave I must. Please," she said, shutting the lid of her chest, "take this down for me."

On the stairs, Laurence heard voices from the kitchen: Lucy's and a man's, which he recognised with some disquiet. He left the chest by the front door and went into the kitchen. In mud-splashed clothes and boots, Ned Price was sitting on a stool by the fire toasting a slice of bread on the end of a knife with one hand and petting Isabella's cat with the other. When he saw Laurence, he jumped up, an excited expression on his face. "Mr. Beaumont, I come unannounced."

"So you do," Laurence said. "How are you, Price?"

"Saddle-sore," laughed Price, rubbing his bottom. "And that damnable horse of mine threw me twice. Nearly cracked my head open." He indicated a bruise on his forehead. "Then I had trouble finding you in Oxford. But by God's grace, here I am. Lucy said you were busy upstairs helping Mistress Savage pack, and as I was starved after my ride, I asked her for a bite to eat." She was not pleased, Laurence noticed, as she doled out a bowl of stew for Price and thrust it at him. "Thank you, Lucy," Price said, dipping his bread into the sauce, and ate greedily.

"Mr. Beaumont, I should attend to the mistress," said Lucy, and walked out.

"*You're* not leaving town, are you, sir?" Price queried, through a mouthful.

"No. Have you news for me?" Price nodded, chewing. "What is it?" Laurence asked, less patiently.

Price swallowed and licked his lips. "Clement Veech is your butcher."

"My God . . . How did you learn that?"

"I had the idea of sending Jem to Derby House, to spy for me, and he overheard talk that confirms it. He even got a glimpse of

Veech's doctor." Laurence listened without interrupting as Price described what the boy had told him. "Who's Sinjin, sir, the fellow who's to replace Pym?"

"Oliver St. John. He's one of the leaders in the Commons, and prominent in the Committee of Safety. He has close ties with the independent sects. His brother-in-law, Cromwell – another Oliver – is a rising star in Parliament's northern army. No news of Albright?"

"No, sir."

"That would be too much to hope for. Price, you truly did well. You and I should go to Lord Digby, once I've seen Mistress Savage off."

Price waved a hand at his travel-stained clothes. "I can't be introduced to his lordship as I am."

"You've just ridden in from London. He'll understand."

"He might, but I'd be ashamed."

Laurence was about to remonstrate further when Isabella came in, wearing her cloak. Price set down his bowl and bowed to her. She frowned at Laurence, who said, "Mr. Edward Price – Mistress Isabella Savage."

"Good day to you, Mistress Savage." Price glanced sidelong at him, as if in congratulation. "I am a friend of Mr. Beaumont's from London."

"Are you," she said; no curtsey, Laurence observed.

"I gather you are to embark on a journey, Mistress Savage."

"Yes, I am. Are you staying long in Oxford?"

"A couple of days, madam."

"Then our acquaintance will be brief. Goodbye, Mr. Price." She offered her arm to Laurence. "Beaumont, the coach awaits." They walked in silence to the front door and out into the street, where she said, "Although I don't know him from Adam, I don't like the looks of him."

"You're too quick to judge," Laurence said, perturbed nonetheless: he respected her opinion, particularly about men.

The driver was loading Isabella's chest onto the roof of the coach. Lucy sat within, her expression as frigid as the early November day. Laurence helped Isabella to ascend, shut the door, and leant through the window to kiss her.

"I'll write to tell you that I've arrived safe," she said in a gentler voice, as if to make up for her previous bluntness. "Beaumont, take care of yourself."

He kissed her again. "Remember me to Mr. Cotterell. I hope he has a speedy recovery – for his sake and mine. And don't forget that I love you."

"I won't, if you don't forget to feed my cat," were her final words, as the driver whipped up the horses.

"She's a goddess, Mr. Beaumont," Price announced. He was still in the kitchen, sitting on his stool, legs stretched out towards the fire. "Mistress Edwards' ladies can't hold a candle to her, not even Cordelia, who's one of the prettiest women I know."

"Will you stop calling me 'Mr. Beaumont.'"

"What *should* I call you, sir?"

"Not 'sir,' either." Price flushed. "I don't like titles," Laurence said, ashamed of his own bluntness. "If you're Price to me, I'm Beaumont to you." He went into the pantry for a bottle of wine, and filled two glasses. "Let's drink a health to Jem, shall we?"

"It was my idea, sir – I mean, Beaumont."

"So why not come with me to see Digby?"

"I'll be ready for the honour of an introduction once I buy myself some decent clothes."

"His lordship can pay for them," joked Laurence, but Price did not smile.

"May I consider myself an agent of the Secretary of State?"

Laurence thought of his promise to Mistress Edwards. "Price," he began, "I know you were Barlow's accomplice." Price reddened again and glared at his muddy boots. "I've been a thief and a spy, and there's much in common between stealing property and stealing information. Both require similar skills of us, and we often share the same end – ignominious and unlamented."

Price stared up at him. "When were *you* ever a thief?"

"Never mind about that. I just wanted to warn you. And to be frank, I've known more honour among thieves than among spies."

"It can be no worse to be a spy than to live as I have."

"All right, then. I'll require Lord Digby's approval."

Price broke into a childlike grin. "Thank you, Beaumont. But . . . you won't . . . you won't tell his lordship what I was?"

More lies, Laurence reflected; and as if Digby would care, as long as Price was useful. "I leave it to you to give him an account of yourself," he said. "Make it simple and not too far from the truth – and don't change your story."

"What a find, Mr. Beaumont!" Digby beamed across his desk at Laurence. "He can be our new man in London. Since we lost poor Albright and you have become *persona non grata* there, we are rather short of agents."

"He must be properly trained first. I need at least a fortnight with him, or else we may lose *him* to Clement Veech."

"You are relieved of your other duties until then. I shall have a mission for him, when you think he is ready. You'll both hear about it, in time. Isabella left today, as arranged?"

"Yes, my lord, as you arranged."

"Good. Our Mr. Price can stay with you while he receives the benefit of your training."

"I don't think Isabella would appreciate that."

"I pay the lease on her house, sir, and she may not return for *at least a fortnight*, unless Mr. Cotterell suffers a rapid decline. Why did Mr. Price not come with you to report his news? It is not what I would expect from an eager young man."

"He felt ashamed to be presented to you in his travelling garb."

Digby laughed at this. "Now I know more about him: he is vain of his appearance."

"As are many of us."

"Not you, sir," Digby said. "When you polish *your* appearance, there is always an ulterior motive at play. You wear a fine suit of clothes as other men wear armour – to do battle."

## VII.

Through wet mist, Draycott scanned the lofty walls around Basing House. "No wonder it hasn't been breached yet," he said to Captain Harper, who was guiding their party of newly arrived officers on a reconnaissance. "A whole town could fit within this estate."

Harper sneezed, using his fingers as a handkerchief, and wiped them on the skirt of his coat. "We launched the first assault with all of our artillery. Our musketeers seized the church and a few outbuildings that the malignants had already burnt down, but we made scant progress otherwise. The rain drove us back as much as the efforts of our enemy inside the walls."

"How many are they?" one officer asked.

"We estimate about five hundred, and there may be reinforcements on the way. That's why we must begin again at dawn. Waller has sixteen troops of Horse, about half as many of dragoons, and three score infantry divisions, including the three regiments from London. He plans to storm the defences from various sides. We'll receive our orders tonight."

Draycott felt sorry for his brigade. The men had not slept since marching out of the capital with their fellow reluctant auxiliaries from the Trained Bands; all were camped beside the artillery range on Cowdrey Down, a bleak area of field with no natural shelter.

"I hope your boys are prepared for a fight," Harper said to the officers, as they turned their horses about.

"As soon as they saw the size of the place, they were discouraged," said the same man, with a boldness that Draycott envied. "And how can we expect volunteers to serve indefinitely, miles from home and on such irregular pay? They came straight from eight days and nights of patrolling the City defences, and they're not accustomed to marching so far. Many of them haven't a pair of boots to their name, just thin-soled shoes – and in such freezing weather!"

"They won't notice the weather once they hear the cannon fire," said Harper. "They'll be too busy pissing in their breeches."

Twilight was fading when Draycott rejoined his Southwark brigade, whose principal concern was to keep themselves warm and dry over the coming hours; only the higher-ranking officers had billets in and around the small town of Basingstoke, and tents were scarce. Winds, icy for the second week of November, whipped across the fields, and a sprinkle of rain fell as the men ate their cold rations of meat and biscuit. Draycott walked about procuring bandages and stockings for blistered and chilblained feet, and a dram of spirits from the quartermaster for those who were sneezing and feverish. He distributed what spare blankets he had; the men were already beginning to doze off.

Later, squeezed in between some of his fellow officers, warming his chapped hands over a smouldering brushwood fire, Draycott thought of home. The eldest of his three sons, Gregory, had been ill again, his eyes bright and cheeks hot as Draycott had kissed him goodbye. "I'll have to purchase more physic, Giles, but we still owe the apothecary," Judith had said; she had looked on the verge of tears, though Draycott knew she would hold them back until the children were abed. Dear God, he mused, tonight could be his last on earth. How would his family get by? Not that life had been smooth, for the past year or so. With the uncertainties of war and the steep rise in taxes, Londoners balked at wasting unnecessary time and money on legal suits. Draycott's practice had dwindled, earning him about the same paltry income as he earned now, in the militia. He and Judith had quarrelled more and more; and her mother had interfered, criticising Draycott's professional acumen as compared to his late respected father-in-law's.

He found himself considering the opportunity Veech had dangled before him. As a small child, Gregory had been fascinated by firelight. He would sit entranced before the hearth; and he required no watching, for unlike other children he never once stuck his little fingers in to get burnt. Draycott felt as fascinated by Veech: the man seemed to possess extraordinary power, even incapacitated as he was. Yet Draycott feared getting burnt.

Draycott woke in darkness to the roll of drums. Damp had penetrated every layer of his clothing, and his feet, though stoutly shod, were numb. He assembled his men for prayers, and a quick breakfast of cheese and more hard biscuit. Then he went to saddle his mare, Betsey, pitying her for the danger she would face, and mounted, to lead the brigade through the fog to their positions by the northerly walls of Basing House. They had to wait for the fog to lift before starting the bombardment.

Around midday a thunderous roar from their artillery was answered by cannon fire from the top of the old section of the house. Draycott's men were stationed behind another regiment of Trained Bands. When the order came to advance, this regiment, equipped with ladders, ropes, and grenades, set about scaling the walls, a perilous objective, since they were under the constant fire from above. The occupants of the house were shooting off musket balls, and flinging what appeared to be roof tiles at the Parliament troops. Female voices screamed oaths at them, and Draycott saw blood pour from the eye of a man yards away as one of the projectiles hit its mark. Coughing and spitting from the clouds of black smoke that filled the air, dodging as balls whizzed past, he struggled to contain his panicked troops. They were firing too early, cutting down men from the regiment in front of them.

"Hold your fire or aim high," Draycott yelled, but they would listen neither to him nor to the commands of drum and trumpet. And as the siege wore on, they acted more and more like frightened cattle: some attempted to retreat, some stumbled into those ahead, and still others were wandering about blindly, having dropped their weapons. By the dimming afternoon, they would advance no further and a mournful cry went up: "Home, home!" Draycott and the other officers tried to rally them, in vain. They were of one mind, and surged away from the house, back towards Cowdrey Down.

Draycott was hopelessly watching them flee, when Harper came charging through the melée. "You lily-livered fools!" he shouted at the men, and to Draycott he barked, "We must turn them about."

Harper had no better luck. He disappeared into the clouds of smoke, while Draycott was swept along in the tide of retreating men. "Pick up your muskets, for God's sake," he urged them. Betsey, who had been quivering at the awful cacophony, reared up with a scream. Draycott lost his seat, thrown into the mud as she raced off after the crowd. He staggered to his feet, pain stabbing his spine, and ran, tripping and slipping over bodies, pushed from behind, until he gained more open ground. The gunpowder could not conceal a slaughterhouse stench, and when he looked down at his coat and breeches and boots, spattered with filth and gore, he was sick to his stomach.

At the camp, he witnessed defeat: soldiers clustered in forlorn groups, and piles of bodies, dead, dying, and wounded. A man tugged at his sleeve, the officer who had spoken to Captain Harper about the men's woes; Draycott nearly failed to recognise him, his face was so blackened with smoke.

"The Bands are refusing to fight on, Corporal," he said. "General Waller has said he'd hang any who desert, but I think they'll be too numerous for him to carry out his threat."

"Praise Heaven for that," said Draycott, stupidly glad.

He wept as foolishly when he discovered Betsey, skittish but whole, penned with a bunch of other runaway mounts. As he rubbed her down, he whispered calming noises in her ear, and blessed God for sparing her life and his.

The next morning, he counted seventy of his brigade killed. The regiment in front had suffered more casualties, some self-inflicted as he knew. Rumours circulated that Parliament had lost over three hundred altogether. In a downpour of sleet and snow, the shivering, bedraggled Bands assembled to march back to London; Waller was withdrawing his own regiments to the garrison at Farnham rather than engage the enemy again. On the ride home, Draycott decided: he would accept Veech's offer.

## VIII.

Laurence and Price had worked hard, to gratifying result. In roughly a fortnight, Price had memorised and churned out ciphers, and acquired the art of opening and resealing letters, smuggling messages in ingenious places, and concocting invisible inks. Laurence had drilled him as to when and how to hold his tongue or supply misinformation if captured and interrogated. Rather more slowly, Price had learnt the basics of horsemanship. Laurence had been dismayed by Price's ineptitude in the saddle, but in his past life he had not needed to ride very far, let alone gallop or jump a horse. Laurence had put him through his paces, impressed by his grit, given his many tumbles and bruises. They had also rehearsed manoeuvres of defence and attack. Laurence had shown him some deadlier tricks of the trade: how to be efficient with a ligature or a knife, or with his hands. Despite his thieving, Price was unaccustomed to the use of violence, and clearly alarmed by it.

"Scoop out a man's eyes with my bare thumbs?" he gasped, when Laurence tried to teach him the technique as they grappled together in mock combat on Isabella's parlour floor. "I could never do it, and I should hope you've never had to."

"Oh but I have, and if it's you or the other man, you may surprise yourself," said Laurence, feeling suddenly old.

"Have you . . . have you ever killed in cold blood?"

"More than a few times – as have some thieves."

"Not this one," said Price.

"Then be welcome to the brotherhood of spies, and occasional murderers," Laurence told him.

———

Price claimed some expertise with a rapier, but confessed to inexperience with a pistol; so that, too, became a part of his training. "Now I think about it, Beaumont, I might do with a few more fencing lessons," he admitted, at target practice one day in the fields bordering the River Cherwell.

"I'm as bad a swordsman as you are an equestrian, Price," Laurence said, truthfully. "You must ask his lordship to find you a different instructor."

Price seemed disappointed. He squinted at the target: a sack stuffed with straw and stuck on a pole, at about the height of a man. "When *can* I meet his lordship?"

"You wanted to wait for your new clothes."

"They were delivered yesterday morning, while you were sleeping."

"In that case I'll arrange an introduction for tomorrow."

"When do you expect Mistress Savage back?" Price asked, in a casual tone. Ignoring the question, Laurence loaded another pistol. It was obvious to both of them that Price could not stay in her house once she returned. "Had I a woman as beautiful as she is, I wouldn't let her out of my sight," Price carried on. "You know women, Beaumont. It's not their fault they can't be trusted. God made them that way, as He made us their superiors. Take my Sue, for example, the wench from the Saracen's Head."

"You told Barlow she was a lady, not a wench."

"I was wrong: she pretended to me she was virgin before she let me bed her. It's she who's wrong now if she expects me to marry her. I suppose it's much like you and Mistress Savage," Price said, in the same casual way. "I mean . . . She *is* a lady, but . . . you wouldn't marry her, would you?"

Laurence hesitated, as though debating his answer. Then he turned, raised the pistol, and blew Price's hat clean off his head.

Price gaped at him. "By Jesus, you could have killed me!"

"Yes," said Laurence. "I could have."

# CHAPTER FIVE

"Cold enough to freeze a man's balls!" Price shouted gaily to Laurence, over a vicious wind buffeting them from the north. The ground beneath their feet was crusted with slippery rime, and they were more skating than walking along the street to Digby's door.

Laurence grabbed him by the collar of his cloak, at which he skidded to a halt. "Wipe the grin off your face. And remember: don't speak unless questioned, and keep your answers brief and to the point. What comes out of your mouth is more important than those clothes on your back. And don't smile. His lordship may smile, and he will, but not you."

Laurence saw in Price's eyes a hint of the fear he had demonstrated when that ball had sent his hat flying. Earlier in the morning he had paraded before Isabella's glass in his new doublet and breeches, bowing and saluting effusively to his image. Too late to say anything about the ostentatious purple hue Price had selected for his garments, Laurence had felt obliged to correct his etiquette. Though a quick study in many respects, Price had a great deal to learn about his trade, and the circles into which he was so ambitious to move. In one respect, however, Laurence would let him learn by himself. He had fished repeatedly for Laurence's opinion of Digby, and Laurence had refused to comment.

Quayle announced to them that his lordship was in conference with the Earl of Bristol. "We can return at a more convenient hour," said Laurence.

"Oh no, sirs, their lordships will be pleased to receive you," said

Quayle, peering at Price as he took their cloaks and ushered them into Digby's chamber.

Digby and his father were seated at one side of his desk, and rose in unison to acknowledge their visitors. As a younger man, Bristol must have been blond and round-faced like his son. Now in his sixties, he was grey of hair and beard, and Laurence detected in his careworn visage a less optimistic temperament. Digby, in contrast, exuded satisfaction.

"Gentlemen," he said, "what an unseasonably cold day! May I present my honoured father, the Earl of Bristol."

"May I present to your lordships Mr. Edward Price," Laurence said, bowing. Price followed suit, as Laurence had taught him.

"Mr. Beaumont, I think we met at Chipping Campden when you were a boy," said Bristol. "How fares your noble father, Lord Beaumont? And how is your lovely mother?"

"They're both well, thank you, my lord, and they haven't forgotten their debt to you."

"Many years ago, when ambassador to Spain, I gave Lord Beaumont an introduction to his future wife," Bristol explained to Price.

Price neither smiled nor spoke.

"I gather you have done work for Mr. Beaumont in London, Mr. Price," Digby said, in a more efficient tone, "and that he has been training you in the skills of an agent. Tell us a little about yourself, sir. What was your former occupation?"

Laurence listened with interest, wondering how inventively Price would lie.

"I had none, my lord," said Price. "I was living off a small annuity bequeathed to me in my father's will. I had hoped to enlist in His Majesty's cavalry a year ago, but I was injured after a fall from my horse, and only mended from it recently."

"Would you not prefer army service to our more . . . covert duties?"

"With respect, my lord, I believe that I can best serve His Majesty by serving your lordship, if you will condescend to hire me."

"On Mr. Beaumont's recommendation, I shall."

"Thank you, my lord." Price looked about to continue, until he caught Laurence's eye.

"Allow us a moment alone with Mr. Beaumont, sir. Quayle, find Mr. Price some refreshment," Digby murmured, and Quayle showed Price out. Digby motioned for Laurence to sit. "A keen fellow, sir."

"He is, my lord," said Laurence, "but his training is incomplete."

"You have had over a fortnight with him. He should be ready to take to the stage."

Laurence deliberated whether to object and cast aspersions on Price's aptitude or to agree, and let him sink or swim on his own. "I could advise you better as to his readiness, my lord, if I knew what mission you had in mind for him."

Father and son were quiet. Digby toyed with a button on his doublet, while Bristol studied Laurence with a speculative air.

Digby broke the silence. "Mr. Beaumont, His Majesty said that you above anyone could be trusted with the secrets we are about to reveal to you. He told us that you helped him in the past with a matter of grave importance to himself and to His Royal Highness Prince Charles, in which he still depends on your complete discretion."

"A matter he would not discuss, even with us," Bristol put in.

Laurence kept his face impassive. In thanks for concealing the plot against His Majesty's life, he had been given the highest recommendation; and now he dreaded what secrets he was about to hear.

"I told you of His Majesty's coming negotiations with certain independents and moderates in Parliament for a reform of the English Church," Digby continued.

"Yes, my lord, and you said that your intermediary in the negotiations, Major Ogle, might soon be freed from Winchester House. Has Parliament acceded to his release, or is his sentence drawing to a close?"

"Neither, sir," said Bristol. "The keeper of the gaol, Mr. Devenish, will . . . *free* Ogle upon receipt of a warrant from His Majesty, so that Ogle can come to us here and expedite our settlement."

"Devenish will let Ogle escape?"

"I can rely upon Mr. Beaumont to be direct," Digby said to his father, laughing.

"But, my lords, can you rely upon Devenish?"

"I think we can, and we must press ahead with our negotiations," said Bristol. "Pym has not entirely cemented this Solemn League and Covenant with Edinburgh, and even should all go smoothly for him, the Scots will face a battle with the weather if they try to send an army south before the spring. If His Majesty can reach his own terms for a religious compromise with the moderates and independents over Christmastide, the prospect of Scottish troops marching into England would be hailed with far less enthusiasm in Parliament."

"Pym's faction may find itself out in the cold," elaborated Digby. "And Londoners are cooling in their enthusiasm for war. We hear that Parliament has caused much offence by searching house to house for deserters since Waller's disastrous attempt on Basing House. The City is so upset that it may petition for the return of all of its three regiments, which would leave Parliament's southern armies in sorry shape." He paused, evidently waiting for Laurence to speak, but Laurence said nothing. "I forgot to mention to you that, while in London, our Mr. Violet was in talks with some powerful dignitaries and merchants of London's Corporation, many of whom Parliament is burdening with extortionate taxes," Digby recommenced. "They might be persuaded to treat directly with the King if they are guaranteed a general pardon and the satisfaction of their debts, in the event of a Royalist victory. London may therefore be ripe for revolt, just when Parliament's fighting force is at its lowest ebb."

"If I've understood you, my lords," said Laurence, after another pause, "His Majesty is considering two separate alliances, one based upon religious concessions with the discontented Members of Parliament and the other with members of the City Corporation."

"You understand perfectly, sir," said Digby.

"Beg pardon, but I'm not yet clear: in the case of the first alliance, he's approaching the Members as a peacemaker. In the case of the second, he would seek assistance of these . . . prominent citizens in London to stir up an armed revolt, as he attempted last May."

"We have hope, in this instance, of a more successful outcome. And it is not so much an *armed* revolt, as a means of acquiring *new friends*."

"It appears to me that he would wear two hats at the same time."

"Oh dear, sir," Digby sighed, glancing at his father, "*there* you have misunderstood His Majesty! He wishes a conclusion to the war, and to the discontent of his entire kingdom! He would make welcome *all* of those who share in his desire."

*By promising them quite different things*, Laurence added. "Thank you for enlightening me, my lord."

"We must tell you of a related development," said Bristol, in a lower voice. "As you know, the rebel garrison at Aylesbury blocks our easiest route for a march upon London. That garrison is, however, in a parlous state – the soldiers unpaid and threatening to disband. Their senior officer, Lieutenant-Colonel Mosely, has privately expressed to me his deep regret that he took up arms against his King. He is acting as a conduit for my correspondence with Major Ogle, and has pledged his word, in exchange for a fair sum, to surrender the garrison to us at the start of our spring campaign. Once Aylesbury is in our hands, the way will be open for Prince Rupert to move swiftly on the capital."

"If it is not *clear* to you so far, Mr. Beaumont," said Digby, "we will reap the fruit of our labours before the Scots can rush to Parliament's aid. And when we have London, the war may be over as quickly. What say you to that?"

Laurence struggled to answer: it was precisely the sort of intrigue that would appeal to Digby's labyrinthine mind; and His Majesty, confident in his Divine Right to rule, would think any means fair to defeat his opponents. "My lords, I have to question whether your strategies will combine to positive effect. The moderates and independents in Parliament won't look favourably upon an officer who betrays his garrison, or on City dignitaries who are bribed to go over to the King."

Digby glared at Laurence as if he had suggested some indecency. "*Betrays? Bribed?* I would not choose such words."

"*They* will use such words, you may be sure of it."

"Sir, reflect on the timing," intervened Bristol. "With Ogle free, His Majesty's religious agreement should be reached by Christmastide. By spring, when Aylesbury is surrendered to us, it will be late in the day for those Members of Parliament to voice their scruples."

"My lords," said Laurence, "I desire a happy result for His Majesty as much as you do, but he only discredits himself by making overtures on every side and playing them off against each other."

"Have a care, sir," gasped Digby, "in choosing *your* words!"

"It is to His Majesty's credit that he seeks an end to bloodshed," Bristol reasoned. "Is not some slight subterfuge justified, to save Englishmen's lives?"

"Mr. Beaumont is usually a cynic," Digby said snidely. "But this morning I would almost think him possessed by the spirit of Lord Falkland, in his moral indignation."

"If we set aside morals, my lords," said Laurence, "either of these two Parliament men – Devenish or Mosely, or both – could betray *you*. Then you would face the same situation as in May: the Committee of Safety would broadcast the discovery of your subterfuge, Londoners would rally around Parliament, and His Majesty would lose the good will of many of his subjects." When the lords were silent, Laurence thought he might as well be hanged for a sheep as for a lamb. So he carried on, "I was asked for my opinion, and I'd say as much to His Majesty: I think it laudable that he should concede to greater freedom of worship, and openly pursue the chance of peace with all those in his kingdom who are sick of bloodshed. But your hopes for London and Aylesbury are not based on sound foundations, in my professional judgement. In truth, I wish you hadn't shared them with me."

"We had to, sir, on the King's request, and we thank you for your opinion," said Digby. "But you are my agent and you are to follow my orders, whatever your moral or professional qualms. Now, you inquired as to my mission for Mr. Price."

"Yes, my lord," said Laurence wearily.

"He and Violet will go together to London. Violet is familiar to the authorities, so I shall send Mr. Price into Winchester House, to complete the arrangements for Major Ogle's release. Price will be taking him money and the requisite papers. And when that is accomplished, Price will stay in London. He will infiltrate Mr. Pym's network of agents, and offer to spy for Clement Veech. We need a man inside who can report to us on what Veech might be hearing about our designs in the City."

Laurence felt as though he were engulfed in quicksand. "That's subtle work, even for an experienced man. Veech will sniff Price out before you know it, and Price will break under questioning."

"As might you."

"As might I, or anyone else. But why throw him in so deep, when he hasn't been tested?"

"Are you the tiniest bit jealous of your territory, sir, or of your protégé?"

Laurence did not bother to dignify this with a response. "Let him visit Winchester House, and take Ogle what's needed. Then he must return to us for further instruction. And we shouldn't send him back into London until Ogle is safely in Oxford."

Digby opened his mouth, but Bristol again intervened, placing a hand on his son's sleeve. "Needs must, Mr. Beaumont, when the devil drives, and we are desperately short of men in the capital. Besides, we have every faith in your selection of Mr. Price, and in the thoroughness of his training. In concession to you, however, we shall let him decide for himself whether he is ready to undertake these more subtle duties. Please, have him come in."

Laurence could not argue. He rose and went to the door. Price was chatting with Quayle in the hall outside; when he saw Laurence, he hurried over.

Laurence had a second to whisper in his ear. "They're sending you to London, and will ask you to enter into Veech's service and supply us with intelligence on him. *Refuse, if you value your life.*" The moment Laurence stopped speaking, he realised he had said the stupidest thing possible.

Price's face shone. He walked in, ahead of Laurence; and while Digby explained, in the briefest detail, about Winchester House, and then described the trickier part of his assignment, he listened avidly.

"A risk is always rewarded by His Majesty," Digby said, smiling at Laurence.

Price did not hesitate. "I am honoured to accept, my lords, and I pray that I shall prove worthy of your trust."

Still smiling at Laurence, Digby produced a purse from the drawer of his desk and gave it to Price. "An advance on your wages, Mr. Price. Mistress Savage's house may become somewhat crowded when she is home from the country, so Quayle has prepared a chamber for you here, in my quarters. You may go with him to inspect it, and then you are invited to dine with me and my father. Mr. Beaumont, I thank you for a most informative conversation."

"Might I beg a word with Mr. Beaumont before he leaves?" Price asked, his expression now that of a child about to be separated from its mother.

"We'll talk when you come to collect your belongings from the house," Laurence said to him. "Good day, your lordships."

Laurence strode out and snatched his cloak from Quayle. Tugging it around his shoulders, he tore off into the street and back towards the Woodstock Road. He was so angry that he did not feel the cold, though it was indeed foul weather, and he could not blame the Trained Bands for running home. He would be as glad to desert from Digby's service. And what more could he say to Price about the enormity of the task he had accepted? Price would not listen to *him*. Laurence next considered appealing straight to the King, to reconsider these rash schemes. But he knew that His Majesty would not listen, either. Both were already seduced, by their own aspirations and by the Digbys.

There was a carrier at Isabella's front door, shuffling his feet to keep himself warm. "Mr. Beaumont? A letter for you, sir," he said.

Laurence took it, hoping for her writing on the cover, but instead recognised Walter Ingram's. He paid the man and went inside. As he threw off his cloak, her cat appeared as if out of thin air and circled him mewing; he had forgotten to feed it since the day before. And how dismal the place looked: the table was strewn with evidence of his labours with Price, and dirty glasses, plates, and knives, and stumps of burnt-out candles; skeletons of roses poked from a vase on the window ledge surrounded by a drift of decaying petals; balls of paper lay scattered across the floor; and every surface was dusty with ash from the fireplace. He went into the kitchen, the cat trotting at his heels, and rooted out some leftovers of a ham joint and a bowl of soured milk for it. Then he found a bottle of wine and started to drink as he read Ingram's letter; he had not seen his old friend in months.

Ingram opened with kindly inquiries, and a short account of his actions in Prince Rupert's autumn campaign. "'Major Beaumont' likes his elevated rank," Ingram commented. Of his own sister, Sir Bernard Radcliff's widow, he wrote, "Kate was delivered of a healthy boy on the last day of September, but the fenland air in Cambridgeshire did not agree with her. She left the Radcliff estate in the care of her steward, and has gone with the baby to Aunt Musgrave's." Laurence smiled: proud Lady Radcliff was once more dependent on the hospitality of long-suffering Madam Musgrave. "Our troop stopped by Chipping Campden on All Saints Day," Ingram went on. "Tom wanted his lordship your father to supply some of his horses for the men, and funds for their equipment. His lordship admitted to me that he was not sleeping well, and had pain in his joints. I seized the chance to warn him about the damage that I have seen wrought to other great houses, knowing how he cherishes his beloved collection of art. We also talked more cheerfully of wedding plans. Anne and I are to marry on the seventeenth of December, with modest ceremony. Hard times do not warrant lavish celebrations, and his lordship has dug deep into his pockets to finance Tom's troop, or should I say, the Major's. We pray you can come to the wedding. Aunt Musgrave is especially keen to embrace you." Laurence smiled again, remembering her wise, affectionate face and bearlike hugs. "If you see Dr. Seward at the College, please greet him for me." Below his signature, Ingram had penned an afterthought. "His lordship and her ladyship are very distressed, Beaumont, that you will not sever your ties with Mistress Savage. They asked me, as your friend, to urge that you do so. I told them how she helped to save your life when you were imprisoned in Oxford Castle. Nonetheless, I understand their feelings. We shall have occasion to discuss yours, God willing, since his lordship has invited me to stay at the house over Christmastide."

How typical of Ingram to sympathise with both sides; yet the issue must be resolved. Laurence decided to ask Digby for a couple of days' leave to go home, as soon as Price set out for London.

## II.

"Mr. Beaumont was predictably difficult," Digby complained to his father, as they took a turn in the herb garden before dinner. "I do wonder why His Majesty insisted that we ask for his opinion. I also wonder about this secret business in which he helped the King. As Secretary of State, I should be privy to it. If only I could raise Falkland from the grave: *he* must have known about it, and, I am convinced, destroyed all record of it prior to his mad decision to ride into the fray at Newbury and get himself slaughtered."

"My dear son, calm," said Bristol, his breath fogging in the misty air. "It is a good habit to listen as much to advice one does not want to hear as to that which one does. Mr. Beaumont may be right that Mr. Price is still wet behind the ears, and that a more experienced agent should be in London to handle him."

"Don't speak to me of ears," Digby said, cringing at the memory of Albright's. "And who else *have* we in London?"

"Were Isabella there, she could supervise Price and the necessary imports for our plan. She possesses both experience and subtlety in such matters. George, you must persuade her to wed Sir Montague. You can assure her that it would not trouble him if she and Beaumont remained lovers."

"The old roué might derive pleasure from watching them together. Gossip always had it that he was something of a voyeur."

"Work upon her, then."

Digby began to smile. "I *am* working, through Mr. Cotterell. I wrote to him of her position and told him truthfully that Beaumont would hurt her, and that she would be foolish to spurn this opportunity for marriage and a comfortable future. Mr. Cotterell is particularly sensible to her feelings. And she will heed his advice, where she might believe mine prejudiced."

"She owes her very survival to him and his late wife. They nursed her so kindly back to health, after . . ." Bristol stopped, and sighed.

"It might be easier to have Mr. Beaumont out of town, around the time that she is to return. I can then judge what progress Mr. Cotterell has made in his efforts."

"Yes, it might. But where and on what pretext will you dispatch Beaumont?"

"I shall think of one," said Digby.

**III.**

Veech could see that John Pym was clinging to life by a thread. His skin had a chalky hue where it was not blotted with sores and broken blood vessels, his clothes sagged on his frame, and when he spoke, his voice was so faint that Veech and St. John had to lean in to catch his words. "Oliver," he said to St. John, "show Clement what evidence of the King's duplicity we have lately received."

St. John looked to Veech a pompous fellow, with his curled hair and fancy clothes; he had been the King's Solicitor-General, a position stripped from him before the war by His Majesty for political reasons. "This is a copy of a letter from a Major Ogle, prisoner at Winchester House, to the Earl of Bristol," St. John said, handing Veech the paper.

"The original letter was forwarded to the Earl through our commander in the Aylesbury garrison, Lieutenant-Colonel Mosley. Major Ogle is a sincere yet misguided gentleman who believes he can find common ground between the King and Members of our Parliament disaffected by our alliance with the Scots. He has outlined the terms upon which they might support the King, and, moreover, has stated that as proof of good faith, our garrison at Aylesbury might be surrendered to the Royalists in January."

"How can Major Ogle make such a claim from a gaol cell?" Veech asked incredulously, eyeing the letter. The chain of involvement fascinated him, however: if Bristol was a part of the King's scheme, so was Lord Digby, and so must be Laurence Beaumont.

"Because Lieutenant-Colonel Mosely has encouraged him in that expectation."

"In which he is deceived?"

"Entirely deceived, and he is equally deceived into thinking that the keeper of Winchester House, Mr. Devenish, is his friend and accomplice."

"It is a most scurrilous affair," said Pym, his sunken eyes half closed. "The King can have no true desire for a reform of the English Church, or he would have acceded to Parliament's demands on that count during last year's peace talks. Oliver, you must forewarn the Members of Parliament, but let us keep this business quiet. With God's blessing, our treaty with the Scots Commissioners will be concluded in the next few days. It is imperative that we show them a united front. Mr. Veech, have you any tidings for us?"

"I continue to search cargo," said Veech, "but no arms or powder have been discovered, as yet. I heard, however, that His Majesty's agent Mr. Violet was here not long ago, and visited with important folk in the City, some of them Catholics."

"You should have brought Violet in for questioning, Mr. Veech," said St. John.

"That would be to kill the goose that lays the golden eggs, Mr. St. John. I'll take him, when the time is right."

Pym frowned at Veech. "Clement, I had report of Hector Albright. Someone who saw his body told me it had been . . . mutilated, by *you*."

"He did not die from having his ears clipped," Veech responded obliquely.

"That was not all you did to him," murmured Pym, in a sickened tone.

To judge by the expression on St. John's face, he could not give a damn, so Veech let the comment pass.

## IV.

"Your Majesty's profile was admirably captured," Digby said to the King, of the new medals struck to award his soldiers for gallantry in the field. They were leaving the mint at New Inn Hall, where quantities of College plate were being melted down and turned into coin for the war effort. "In the next issue, however, might I suggest an equestrian portrait? It would convey a martial tone in keeping with the medals' purpose."

"I shall bear that in mind," said the King. "Has Violet set forth yet with . . . what is his name . . . ?"

"Mr. Price, Your Majesty. Yes, three days ago. They may be in London by now."

"I am sorry that Mr. Beaumont d-disapproved of our plans."

"Were he so very averse, he would have come and told you."

"Yes, I think he would."

"And it is, shall we say, a *deformity* of his profession to see flaws in every plan. Experience has taught him to trust nothing and no one."

The King hesitated at the door to his coach. "I hope you are not on bad terms with him, because of his opinions?"

"We parted on the best of terms, after I granted him a week's leave to call upon his father, who has been asking him to visit for some time."

Assisted by an equerry, the King lifted his fur-lined cloak to ascend the muddied stair. Then he beckoned Digby to the window.

"Prince Rupert comes tonight into town, to sup with us at Christ Church."

"He must be fresh from harassing the Earl of Essex's regiments," Digby observed, concealing irritation; inevitably Rupert would attend their meeting of His Majesty's Council later, and throw his weight around.

"Her Majesty wishes for you and Jermyn to leaven the atmosphere at table," the King said, with a twinkle in his eye. "My nephew can sometimes discourse too long on military manoeuvres for her taste."

"She may depend upon us for lighter fare," said Digby, and bade the King goodbye.

How to exploit this evening to his own advantage, Digby ruminated, on the way back to his quarters: he and the Queen both viewed Rupert as their main rival for influence over her husband, and they could not resist poking fun at the humourless young man, who missed even the most blatant of jokes. Jermyn was more cordial towards the Prince, yet Digby often managed to eke a smile out of him with some veiled witticism at Rupert's expense.

"My lord, you have visitors from London," Quayle said, as Digby bustled in out of the cold. "Two – er – *ladies*, who are in search of Mr. Beaumont. They are in your antechamber. I took the liberty of serving them wine."

Digby handed Quayle his cloak and hat, and smoothed down his hair, before entering the room. The women had drawn up chairs at the fireplace, and were sipping from their glasses and teasing Isabella's cat with a ribbon; Beaumont had consigned the animal to Digby's care on his departure. The prettiest, a blonde with dimples at either corner of her mouth, was pregnant, Digby noted. Although both wore high-cut frocks of sober colour, as they rose and curtseyed he had to agree with Quayle: there was something unladylike about them.

"My Lord Digby, we thank you for receiving us," the blonde said, in an accent of mixed gentility and common London twang. "May I introduce Mistress Perdita Hughes." Her companion was a redhead, with pillow lips. "And I am Madam Cordelia Weston. We are friends of Mr. Beaumont."

"Merely friends, my lord – we know that he is soon to be married," said Mistress Hughes, reassuringly. "We come with sad news for him, from the capital."

"Oh?" said Digby. Whores, he realised: expensive whores; and they were taking the measure of him, as expertly as he was them.

"A lady very close to his heart has passed on," said Madam Weston.

"That is tragic!"

"Mistress Edwards was sixty-two in April, my lord," Mistress Hughes said. "A fair age, but it was still a blow to us."

"Was she your . . . mother?"

"No, my lord," said Madam Weston. "She might have been, such was the attention she doted on us. We were lodgers at her house."

"Paying lodgers," Mistress Hughes added.

"Please be seated, ladies," he said, and availed himself of a chair.

"Where might we find Mr. Beaumont, my lord?" Madam Weston asked, without further ado.

"I am afraid that he went out of town yesterday, to his family in Gloucestershire."

"When might he return?"

"In a week, or perhaps more."

"You won't be sending him into London again, will you, my lord?"

"Not after his most recent, arduous sojourn," replied Digby; by her attitude, she had more than friendly feelings for Beaumont.

"To be honest, our Mistress Edwards aided in his escape. He was hiding in her house, during his stay."

"What a service to His Majesty, and to myself! Were you ladies also of assistance to him?"

"We did our share."

"Cordelia, you did more than that," asserted Mistress Hughes, and to Digby, "She drove him through the defences in a donkey cart.

He was lying in the back, got up as a sick old woman. If it wasn't for Cordelia being in her delicate state, the militia would have searched the cart and found him."

"Then Mr. Beaumont is in debt to you for his life, Madam Weston," said Digby, impressed.

"He has done us many a good turn over the years."

"Why, how long have you known him?"

"Since thirty-five or six, before he went to fight in the Low Countries," said Mistress Hughes. "We were just girls then, weren't we, Cordelia, and new to the house. He is a sweet-tempered gentleman, and so respectful of the fair sex!"

"Who is he to wed, my lord?" Madam Weston inquired.

"A young maiden, from a neighbouring county."

"Oh – I'd pictured a woman. And Mistress Edwards said they'd been lovers for months. As a matter of fact, he bought her a necklace off the Mistress."

A bawd's necklace for his darling Isabella, thought Digby. "*That* passion has ended."

"Well, well, and I thought he was so taken with her as to refuse all others!"

Mistress Hughes nudged her friend's elbow. "He didn't refuse *you*, on his final night in London."

"Ladies," Digby said, as though to steer the conversation away from Mr. Beaumont's romantic affairs, "might you be acquainted with another of his London friends – Mr. Edward Price?"

"Ned Price?" said Mistress Hughes. "It was at Mistress Edwards' house that Mr. Beaumont met him, only last month."

Madam Weston expressed similar astonishment. "How might *you* be acquainted with him, my lord?"

"He, too, came to Oxford in search of Mr. Beaumont. He seems a fine young gentleman."

The women looked at each other once more. "He does like to be seen as such, my lord," said Madam Weston.

"I had considered employing him in some way or other, but . . . as His Majesty's Secretary of State, I must be assured of his probity."

"What's probity, my lord?" queried Mistress Hughes, with endearing innocence.

Digby surveyed them beneficently. "Tell me first about Mr. Price."

## v.

Laurence stirred, between sheets scented with Lady Beaumont's select combination of bay and rosewater, and opened his eyes to the hangings of his bed. He wished he could remain there indefinitely, cocooned in this womblike space, familiar to him since childhood.

He had trudged home in the dark through Lord Beaumont's park, leading his Arab stallion; over the final mile from the gatehouse, a stone had nicked its front right fetlock, and he had not wanted to aggravate the injury. Jacob, his lordship's venerable Master of Horse, had greeted him in the courtyard, promising the Arab a thorough rubbing down, a salve for its wound, and a supper fit for a king. Lord Beaumont's valet, Geoffrey, stood on the front steps to usher Laurence in and take his sodden cloak; and in the luxury of the Hall, Laurence had enjoyed as warm a welcome from Lord and Lady Beaumont, his sisters Elizabeth and Anne, and Tom's wife Mary.

As soon as he saw his father, Laurence decided to keep to himself his own problems with Digby and the King; there was a new stiffness to his movements, anxiety in his blue eyes, and more white in his beard and moustache. In contrast, Lady Beaumont's uncharacteristically amiable demeanour suggested to Laurence that she viewed his visit as a step towards reconciliation, and the betrothal. Anne was full of news about Ingram, and of thanks to his Aunt Musgrave, whom she had yet to meet; it went unsaid, Laurence remarked, that had Madam Musgrave not made Ingram heir to her substantial property in Faringdon, the match might have encountered some parental opposition. Normally so vivacious, Elizabeth struck Laurence as understandably dejected. This time last year, she was anticipating her own wedding day and a long future with John Ormiston, who had died in June at Chalgrove Field in the arms of his brother-in-law and best friend, Tom. Mary, meanwhile, looked to Laurence happier and less intimidated by the Beaumont household, and rather self-absorbed.

Burrowing deep into the soft feather mattress, Laurence closed his eyes, wondering for how long he could postpone the questions he had avoided last night. But a polite knock sounded at the bedchamber door and Geoffrey's voice called, "Master Laurence, his lordship asks you to join him in a ride about the estate, once you have broken your fast."

Jacob had saddled one of Lord Beaumont's horses for Laurence. "Your Arab will be right as rain in a day or so," he said, as he put out his hands for Lord Beaumont to step up and mount.

Laurence thanked Jacob and set off at a canter with Lord Beaumont, whose stiffness did not appear to affect him in the saddle. Leaving the gravel drive, they rode across fields spangled with frost towards the river, where Laurence had taught himself to swim as a boy, and where he still liked to bathe in the summertime. Snow was drifting from the sky, and a crisp breeze from the Cotswold Hills ruffled their cloaks, and the manes and tails of their horses. Near the riverbank they pulled in, and Lord Beaumont gazed over to the far side, his eyes tearing; from the cold, Laurence hoped.

"These days I am feeling my age, Laurence," he said, "and I have no need to remind you that the station into which we were born comes with as many duties as privileges. If, God willing, Mary brings her babe to term—"

"Mary is pregnant again?" interrupted Laurence. "That *is* good news, for her and for Tom."

"Yes, but she is less than three months' gone, and could suffer another miscarriage. And even should she bear a male child, Thomas is not my eldest son. You are, and I want to see your children before I die."

"I've always thought Tom might be more suited, as your heir," Laurence ventured.

"He cannot be master of this estate while you live," declared Lord Beaumont, with surprising force. "I have studied your natures, and it is his that worries me most. He has his mother's swift temper, and he clings on to his resentments until they fester in his mind. You are more akin to me, though you were a sight more wayward as a youth, and you have still a wild streak in your character that I both love and fear, and which perhaps has led you to doubt yourself in my role. When my father died, I had my doubts, and less experience of life than you. But doubt can be a healthy thing, if it causes us to reflect and act cautiously. And I am certain that you will defend the Beaumont estate with a noble spirit, and attend justly and fairly to the welfare of those whose livelihood depends on us. I pray, also," he went on, studying Laurence, "that you and Thomas will put an end to your old quarrels. You will have to be the peacemaker, because he cannot be the first to forgive – he wrongly considers it a sign of weakness. I believe he loves you, as I know you love him, and if you are patient with him and do not provoke him as you are wont to do, you will be rewarded by strong affection. He is as shy with such feelings as his mother, but they are there."

Laurence blinked away tears of his own: this sounded like a farewell speech. "I promise, if it's in my power, that we won't quarrel again."

"Laurence," Lord Beaumont said more sternly, "twice your mother and I tried and failed to find a girl who would meet with your approval. On the second occasion, you told us that you wanted to choose your bride, and I acquiesced. But you are on the verge of an unfortunate alliance."

"I beg to differ," Laurence said. "I'd be very fortunate to have Mistress Savage as my wife, and I won't dishonour her by retracting my proposal."

"Ingram gave account of her merits, and how she snatched you from the brink of death in Oxford Castle. For that, I thank her with my heart, and if you cannot leave her as a mistress, it is your affair. In marrying her, however, you would grieve us terribly. Dear boy, surely you have loved other women as you do Mistress Savage, and imagined the earth would cease to spin if you could not be together?"

"There was one," admitted Laurence.

"Just *one*, among them all?" asked Lord Beaumont, with a combination of humour and mild bemusement. "When was that?"

"The summer before last." Laurence thought back to the hot night on the rugged Andaluz hills when Juana had rejected him; so different from the present frigid morning in a carefully tended park. Lord Beaumont might fall off his horse if he learnt that the object of Laurence's mad obsession had been a gypsy thief. Nevertheless, to a degree Juana and his father shared the same view: *We did not create this world, Monsieur, but we must abide by its rules.*

Lord Beaumont cast him an inquisitive frown. "Would you still wish to be with her?"

Laurence could not lie. "No."

"*Quod erat demonstrandum.* I intend no dishonour to Mistress Savage, but I ask that you wait upon your offer to her. Should she inquire the reason, you may tell her it is on my request."

"I'm a bit too old for that excuse."

"So you are," said Lord Beaumont. "Over Christmastide, if possible before Anne's wedding, call upon the Furnivals and become better acquainted with Penelope. Try to see *her* merits. Your mother said you found her pretty, which is a start. Have I your word, sir?"

Laurence hesitated; he was about to betray Isabella, as she had predicted. "You have it," he said.

"I thank you, my son." Lord Beaumont leant from his saddle to press Laurence's arm. "And I've yet another request. We are concerned about Elizabeth. You and she were always close. She will not confide in Anne, but Anne is convinced that more ails her than the sorrow of widowhood. She might confide in you."

Laurence discovered Elizabeth in the parlour. She was sitting on the bench before her virginals, not playing the instrument but staring fixedly at the keyboard. He shut the door behind him, and edged onto the bench beside her.

"Liz," he said, "I can only imagine how painful it must be for you, with all the talk about Anne and Ingram's wedding."

"Let me guess the next platitude on your lips," said Elizabeth. "I'm still mourning my husband, and Anne's joy must bring forth memories of my brief happiness. The truth is, Laurence, I spent more time with Ormiston during our courtship than after the wedding, and living as his wife in his mother's house with his carping old maid sisters was intolerable." Laurence held his peace. "Now I'm disgusted by myself. Without the miniature portrait that he had painted for me on our betrothal, I might already have forgotten his face. And I loved him so much. I suppose I love him still, but it's like loving a ghost. How could it happen to me, in less than half a year? I'm evil and rotten, and cold inside."

Laurence tucked an arm around her waist. "You're none of those things, but I'll say this for you: you're as prone to exaggeration as our mother."

"There's more that I am ashamed of," she said, squirming away. Again, he waited for her to speak. "Do you recall when we talked, before my wedding night?"

"Yes, I do."

"I could count upon my ten fingers the number of times I lay with Ormiston, but I showed him how to please me, as you had described, and . . . *that's* what I remember most about him, not his face. I can't rid myself of the images that creep into my head, and the urges I have – and at the most inopportune of moments." He smiled, seeing the blood rush to her cheeks. "I shouldn't have told you – you take it as a joke." She gave him a fierce shove.

"I'm very glad you did. And though it's beyond even my dubious morals to administer the cure, what I think you need is a good . . . A good man," he finished.

She peered at him from beneath her lashes. "Is that what you meant to say?" They both started to laugh, quietly at first, and then uproariously, until they were collapsed upon each other, shaking with mirth. It was not the release she might have desired, yet it was better than nothing; and Laurence felt the better for it, too. "So I'm not sick?"

"Oh yes you are, along with much of humankind and pretty much the entire animal kingdom."

"You won't tell anyone."

"No, but I could suggest to his lordship that you might be interested to receive suitors."

"Wouldn't it be disrespectful to Ormiston's memory?"

"I didn't know him well, Liz, but *he* was a good man, and he'd want you to be happy."

"What will Tom say?"

*He will be furious*, Laurence replied to himself. "You can cross that bridge when you come to it."

"Isn't it odd: last year I married Tom's dearest friend, and this year Anne is to marry yours." Elizabeth's blue eyes, upward-slanted like his, were alert and a little scheming. "Might there be any potential suitors for me among your other friends?"

Laurence shook his head at her. "*You* work fast."

"There's no harm in asking. While you may not be one of them yourself," she added teasingly, "you must know at least *some* good men."

## VI.

Price followed the turnkey of Winchester House into what must once have been a majestic hall, but was now parcelled into a warren of small chambers, narrow corridors, and rickety staircases. At length the turnkey halted before a door, rapped upon it, and said, "Mr. Devenish, sir, a Mr. Price is here to see Major Ogle."

The door opened onto a cosily appointed room with a four-poster bed, padded armchairs, and Turkey hangings on the walls. Before the fire an old brindled dog lay snoring, its grey muzzle resting on its paws. Above the fireplace was a wooden board from which dangled dozens of keys. Devenish was of middle age and prosperous in appearance; fat from bribes like all gaol keepers, Price thought. "Who are you, Mr. Price?" Devenish inquired, when the turnkey had disappeared. Price showed his credentials, a note in cipher from Lord Digby. "Ah yes," said Devenish, and his left eye began to twitch.

"How fares the Major?" asked Price, in the neutral way that Beaumont had taught him.

"You may judge for yourself, sir," Devenish whispered. "I wrote to the Earl of Bristol again through Lieutenant-Colonel Mosely. Ogle will be let out, as soon as I have His Majesty's warrant. In my letter I gave the Earl a list of what else was needed."

Price handed over a bag. "You will find here the warrant, a safe conduct for Major Ogle to travel to Oxford, and a bill of exchange for a hundred pounds to deal with his expenses."

He expected some sign of excitement on Devenish's face, or at least a thanks, but Devenish only said, his eye twitching away, "No more than a short visit with Ogle, sir, and you must be gone." He selected a key from the board. As he opened the door, his dog struggled up on its stiff legs. "Down, Hodge," he said to it, with an affection that touched Price. The dog flopped gratefully to the floor, and rested its head back on its paws.

Through another maze of passages, they reached the cell, spacious and comfortable, with a high casement window to provide fresh air. Several men were playing cards, and one, youngish and honest-faced, smiled at Devenish as he might his host at a social gathering.

"Major Ogle, Mr. Price has been sent by your *wife* to assure her that you are in health, sir," said Devenish.

"Cousin Price, how are you?" said Ogle, rising. "Have you news of her and the children?"

"They are well, praise God, and praying for the day you're reunited," Price answered smoothly.

"You can tell her that Keeper Devenish treats us very considerately – an hour of exercise each morning, wine, and meat for supper.

We may be better off than most Londoners. Come and inspect the view: it's a pleasing prospect." Ogle drew Price over to the window. It gave onto Clink Street, with the river in the distance; the drop was too steep to afford escape. "Confirm to Lord Bristol that the parties are agreed on Church reforms," Ogle murmured. "When I get to Oxford, I'll furnish him with a complete account. But he must not delay in securing my freedom."

"He hasn't." Price grinned over at the pinpoints of light that twinkled on the far bank of the Thames. "You ask Mr. Devenish."

They said no more, and afterwards Devenish escorted Price to the prison entrance. "You could get lost, otherwise," he said.

"I thank you, Mr. Devenish," said Price, adding under his breath, "Both the Earl and His Majesty are happy to have such a friend in you."

Devenish grunted noncommittally, and retreated into his warren.

The turnkey was unlocking the main gate to admit a man in smart, sombre clothes with a satchel under his arm. "Good day to you, Mr. Draycott," the turnkey said. At once the name set Price's heart thumping: a Corporal Draycott, formerly a lawyer, had been with Veech that night when Beaumont had been chased through the streets. It was a coincidence Price could not pass up. He heard Beaumont's voice in his head: *Move slowly, breathe deeply, and look a man straight in the face without wavering. Always say as little as you can, especially if you're told the unexpected, and especially if you have to lie. And always remember your lies, which is why you should keep them simple, and mix in a little of the truth.* Price walked slowly through the gate, and called out, "Corporal Draycott?"

Draycott halted, polite confusion on his face. "Do I know—?"

"My name is Edward Price, sir, and I wonder if I might speak with you for but a minute," Price interjected, in an eager, yet not too eager, tone.

"How do you know *my* name?" Draycott asked, as Price approached him.

"I've family near the fort at St. George's Fields. You were an officer there, I believe."

"Yes, but not any more. What is your business, sir?"

Price looked into Draycott's eyes. "I can get you information
about a fugitive who escaped from the fort last month." He discerned
a smidgeon of interest.

"What fugitive?"

Price pulled a creased broadsheet out of his doublet. "Is the
reward still offered on this man?"

"No, it has been withdrawn," said Draycott in a colder voice.
"Too many people came forward – with *false* information."

"For the same reward," said Price, "I'll even help you catch him."

## VII.

Laurence wanted to go straight to Isabella's house on the chance that
she might have come home while he was at Chipping Campden, but
he felt bound to call first on Digby, who would know anyway if she
were back in Oxford. "His lordship is out, Mr. Beaumont," Quayle
said, at the door. "But His Majesty wished you to attend him immediately upon your return."

Through boot-high drifts of snow, Laurence slogged over to Christ
Church, and announced his presence to the King's equerry. He felt an
ominous sinking in the pit of his stomach as he was shown into the royal
chamber, where His Majesty and the Queen were at a game of draughts
with Prince Charles before a companionable fire. They might have been
a family like any other, Laurence thought, except that they were not.

"Mr. Beaumont, how did you find your stay in Chipping
Campden?" the King asked solicitously.

"It was most enjoyable, thank you, Your Majesty. Everyone is
busy preparing for my sister's wedding later this month."

"Is it not about time for yours, sir?" inquired the Queen.

"Your Majesty is ahead of me there," Laurence said to her, at
which Prince Charles snorted with laughter.

"I trust his lordship your father has had no t-trouble from Colonel Massey's Gloucester garrison?" the King said next.

"No, Your Majesty, though it is a worry to him that he may soon receive a visit from the Colonel's men."

"Pray God his worries will soon be removed. Let us talk, sir." The King rose and picked up his cane. "We shall go to the Great Hall."

The Hall was so chilly that they could see their breath in the air. The King waved Laurence to a bench at one of the long tables, at a distance from the liveried guards posted at the doors, and took a seat opposite. "I heard of your objections to our strategy for the c-coming spring," he began, in a subdued voice, "and your concern about our friends Devenish and Mosely. Yet from my own correspondence with them, I have no question as to their allegiance, Mr. Beaumont. These various plans of ours will unfold towards a single purpose, as I shall explain. It is my d-desire that you put the same faith in Lords Bristol and Digby as you have in me."

"Yes, Your Majesty," said Laurence; he had about the same amount of faith in all three of them, and it was fast eroding. And why should the King devote to him such personal attention, if there were not some doubt gnawing at the royal mind?

The King raised his eyes to the rafters. "Here, in this very place, I intend to call an assembly, late in January. It will be my parliament, to which *all* discontented souls will be invited, on terms of a free and general pardon, to profess their fealty to me. They will swear an oath that the Parliament sitting in Westminster is illegitimate and has no legislative authority within my realm. I shall embrace the independent sects, the City Councillors of London, and whoever has the courage to depart from the Lords and Commons, and from the rebel armies." Not a trace of his stammer now, Laurence noticed: the King was confident of success. "The idea for my assembly came from Edward Hyde, Lord Falkland's old ally," the King went on. "I cherish the thought that Falkland, whom you and I both esteemed so highly, would have approved."

"He was tireless in his efforts to restore peace to your kingdom," said Laurence. "If that is the result, Your Majesty, he will rest easier in his grave."

The King inclined his head in agreement. "The assembly will re-establish to my people that I am the source of law and order, and a peacemaker more dedicated to their welfare than to triumph in bat- tle. But, since we *are* at war, I am not averse to combining peace with a triumph. To mark the opening of my assembly, I shall announce that Prince Rupert has occupied the Aylesbury garrison. Mosely will have opened the gates to him, on the eve of our first sitting."

"Then he will march on London." Laurence kept silent about the obvious: this triumph depended entirely upon Mosely's good faith.

"Quite so. Your brother Thomas will share in my nephew's glory, as an officer in his Lifeguard. And his lordship your father can take pride that both of his sons have distinguished themselves in my cause." The King stood, and rearranged the folds of his cloak. "Upon my soul, we must put more braziers in here come January, or the members of my parliament will have numb backsides."

As they were leaving, he touched his small, fine-boned hand to Laurence's shoulder. There was roughly a foot in height between them; and how fragile he seemed. Laurence could easily have picked him off his feet and tossed him through the doors. "I hope I can count on you, sir, as I have in the past."

"Yes, Your Majesty," said Laurence.

The King dropped his hand. "What day is your sister to marry?"

"The seventeenth, Your Majesty."

"Your family will want you home to assist in these preparations. I shall ask Lord Digby to free you from your duties in plenty of time."

"Why thank you, Your Majesty," said Laurence. He felt like a dog that had been tossed an unsavoury bone. Digby must have relayed to the King his seditious speech about playing off one overture against another, and the King had not appreciated it, convinced as he was that he could do no wrong. This overture to Laurence, laced with fond references to the Beaumonts, was a reminder that he should shut his mouth and obey.

"Be there, be there," Laurence muttered, as he rounded the corner into Isabella's street. Although the bells were chiming five of the afternoon, the short winter twilight had long since turned to darkness. It might as well be the dead of night: perishing cold had kept most of Oxford's citizens indoors.

To his joy, candles glimmered in her front window, and he smelt wood smoke from her chimney. He did not wait to knock, and let himself in. By the door, he saw her travelling chest; she must not have had occasion to unpack. He shed his cloak and saddlebag, and hastened into the parlour where Isabella sat reading, her cat curled on her lap.

She looked as startled as the cat, which jumped off her skirts and streaked out. "Beaumont, when did you get to Oxford?" she asked, setting aside her book.

"Today." Lifting her bodily from the chair, he buried his face in her neck and inhaled the scent of her. "How I've missed you, my love."

"I can't breathe," she said, in his ear.

He released her, and inspected her hungrily. Her pallor had gone, as had the shadows of sickness around her eyes; but her expression was ambiguous, neither hostile nor welcoming. "And you, when did you return?"

"The day before yesterday."

"Is Mr. Cotterell any better?"

She sat down again and folded her arms around her waist. "A little, though he knows it is only a temporary reprieve."

"I'm sad to hear that. *You* look in much better health."

"Yes, I am."

"Isabella," he said, "what have I done this time to earn such an indifferent reception? It's true, I left the house in less than pristine order, but at least your cat didn't starve." He knelt before her and ran his hands up along her thighs. "Speak to me, please."

Isabella took his hands in hers, not as a lover, but to stop his caresses. "There's a note for you on the mantel, from a Madam Weston. I think you should read it."

"Madam . . ." He frowned. "I don't know of her."

"I believe you know her intimately," said Isabella, in a strained voice.

The note was signed "Cordelia." In a childish, painstaking script, she wrote that she, Perdie, and Barlow had come to Oxford. The women had called at Lord Digby's quarters for Laurence, while Barlow waited in the street. They had brought news of Mistress Edwards' death on the fifteenth of November: she had been buried beside Jane in the yard of St. Saviour's Church.

He glanced over at Isabella. "The lady who hid me in London has . . . has . . ."

"I am aware."

Laurence read on. Cordelia and Perdie had debated staying in Oxford to ply their trade, but in the end decided against it: Cordelia did not want to have her baby in a strange town, far from friends, and Perdie would not be left there alone. Cordelia blessed Laurence for his past kindness, and prayed they would soon meet again, if Mistress Edwards had her wish and His Majesty drove the rebels out of London. "She was a courageous soul," Laurence said.

"Was she also a bawd?"

"A highly successful bawd, until Parliament ruined her business."

"I gather you were her patron since the mid-thirties, and more recently availed yourself of her merchandise, on your last excursion to the capital."

He sank into a chair, annoyed at himself and at Digby. "How did Digby manage to extract that piece of intelligence?"

"It was accidentally volunteered. Oh Beaumont, a tumble with a whore I could forgive," she said, less caustically. "I should be thankful to her, given that she went to such lengths to help you. But you weren't honest with me when you came back to my bed. And you slipped fast, you who claimed that you were prepared to fight all society and your own family to wed a woman some people would judge not far above a whore." He tried to interrupt, but she cut him off. "I don't want to hear your excuses, and it did not upset me as much as Digby might have hoped. Yet it is a symptom of what's wrong between us."

He knelt once more by Isabella's feet, though he did not attempt to touch her. He had known her ecstatic, tender, enraged, sorrowful, and sarcastic. Today her face frightened him: she was resigned. "What is that?" he asked.

"Let's see if you can guess. You must have spoken to his lordship your father and her ladyship about us, and about the girl to whom they would betroth you?"

"I didn't speak to her ladyship on either score. In a whole week, she let the subject pass – I was astounded by her self-restraint. My father did inquire. I told him that I'd be very fortunate to have you as my wife, and that I wouldn't retract my proposal to you."

"Did you make any concessions?"

"I . . . agreed to meet the girl when I'm home over Christmas to attend my sister's wedding."

"So we could not be married before then."

Flooded with happiness, he seized her hands. "Then you'll accept me?"

"What I meant is that you have agreed to wait, to choose your wife," she said, pulling away from him.

"I'll go through the motions, Isabella – for my father's sake. I haven't the least intention of marrying her."

Isabella regarded him pityingly, as when he had told her about Khadija's prediction. "No, my dear friend. You shall pay her court, and wed her, and do your duty as your father's heir." Laurence gaped at her, speechless. "Beaumont, our problem is that we can't be honest with each other, as a married couple should, and our lies and evasions would eventually kill the love between us. We could fight society, and even your family, though it would be a war of attrition. But we cannot fight our natures."

"I swear I'll be honest with you, Isabella, from this day on. I'll tell you anything you want to know."

"Remember what secret I asked you to reveal?"

"That's not about us," he said, infuriated by her logic. "It's a matter of state which has no bearing on *us*."

"You think I might tell Digby. You think I can't be trusted as far as he is concerned, and you have always thought so."

She was entirely correct, although Laurence could not bring himself to confess it to her. "I won't allow Digby to break us apart."

"Another evasion," she said; correct again. "He will not break us apart, Beaumont, because *I* am breaking with you, of my own accord."

"No, no," he exclaimed. "You can't."

"I did not reach my decision lightly." Isabella looked past him, as if to concentrate. "I was so muddled that I sought the advice of two wise, elderly men. I told you that Mr. Cotterell is my Seward. As a girl, I was conveyed to his house more dead than alive after my ordeal, and I'd have embraced death if not for the loving support of him and his wife. While he understands my feelings for you and took an instant liking to you on the night we visited his house, he counselled me to think of my future and of what women such as I must contemplate: that as my attractions fade and I remain childless, you will wonder why on earth you burdened yourself with me."

"Isabella, I promise you—"

"Let me finish. I was still undecided on my return. Yesterday, before I learnt from Digby about Madam Weston, I called on *your* Seward. We talked of you, and of me. I confided in him my barren state, and what your African prophetess had foreseen. He was as surprised as I that you should believe her, though he gave weight to her words. He thought as I did, however, that the great queen's name cannot be mine."

"How could you listen to his advice?" Laurence burst out. "He's ignorant about women. He fears and despises them, for the most part."

"In fact, he refused to counsel me on the issue of marriage. But from what he told me about you, I made up my mind. And what Digby told me afterwards confirmed my resolve." Isabella slid from her chair and knelt, hands clasped as though she were praying; their faces were separated by a scant inch. "I love you, Beaumont, as I have never loved any man, and I think I always shall. But I would not be content as your wife, and my discontent would soon become yours. We would quarrel, as we have in the past – as we have in only two months under this roof – and we would grow to hate each other. I could not bear ever to hate you, and I want you to be happy with the girl you marry. And I would like you to be faithful to her, in as far as you can, which means that we must also part as lovers."

A terrible silence descended.

"Have you . . . told Digby of your decision?" Laurence asked finally.

"You are the first to know. You need not leave the house," she went on, more briskly, "but I would prefer that you spend tonight elsewhere. Tomorrow I'm going away again, and may not return to Oxford for a long time. I am sick of it," she added, with a vehemence he shared.

"Where will you go?"

"I'd rather not say. I'll be well provided for."

"I won't let you," he insisted, grasping her by the shoulders. "I can't live without you, Isabella. I don't want to live without you. We'll . . . we'll start anew. I can change. I *will*, as soon as I'm free of this . . . this vile, deceitful occupation that has made me into something *I* hate. We'll go abroad together, and leave the past behind us."

"It would follow us, Beaumont."

"Why should it? Please, please, Isabella, let me change *your* mind. I did twice before, when you tried to part with me. Let me do so again."

He hugged her to him and kissed her, and felt her body relent; and as they fumbled aside their clothes, he willed her mind to relent also. He would prove to her that he could be as honest and open in his heart as in his physical desire for her, and they would stay as tightly bound, flesh to flesh.

Afterwards they lay panting, still locked. Then she ran her fingers through his hair, and over his face. "My beautiful love, speak another word and you will spoil our precious moment. Let this be our goodbye, for the present. And when next we meet, it will be as old friends."

Laurence blundered down the street, scarcely conscious of putting one foot in front of the other. Although his head reeled, the truth was increasingly plain to him. Not Digby or his loathsome occupation as a spy, or his family, or even the world was to blame. It was his fault: he had withheld his trust from Isabella, who deserved it as Juana had not. Nor had he told Isabella what else the African had prophesied: *A woman has poisoned you,* Khadija had warned him, of Juana; and of the woman with the name of a queen, *if you do not spit out the poison, you will lose her.*

Since his insouciant youth, Laurence had adopted the habit of evasion as naturally as he had memorised his lessons, or learnt to cheat at cards. And he had been able to swim through life without getting badly caught on any shoals, until his years of soldiering and spying in the Low Countries, an experience which had nourished his suspicion of others, and his cynicism. He had suspended these instincts with Juana, and had paid the cost. His love for Isabella was strong and pure, and greater than himself, but he had not spat out the poison in his character; and because of that, he had poisoned his future with her.

He stopped, crumpled against a wall for support, and vomited into the snow what resembled to him a pool of blood. He was shaking in every nerve, and his teeth were chattering. Where to go? He could predict what Seward would say: *It would never have been a happy marriage. Your father could not have borne the disappointment. Mistress Savage recognised her proper place, and decided what is best for both of you. And your wounded heart will heal, as with the gypsy.*

On a cliff top near Cádiz, Laurence had almost blown out his own brains in his despair over losing Juana. He felt no such impulse today. Somehow, somehow, he might win Isabella back. And if not, to commit suicide would be another evasion; the mistake Falkland had made, though for nobler reasons. Laurence remembered how Wilmot had comforted him after Falkland's death. With grim purpose, he marched to the stables to fetch his stallion, saddled up, and rode for Abingdon, headquarters of the King's Lieutenant General of Horse. Whatever the future might bring, tonight he would seek refuge in Wilmot's bluff company, and drown his sorrows in drink.

## VIII.

Digby called late at Isabella's house. She answered the door, her eyes swollen and wretched. "My darling," he said, "I am so dreadfully sorry."

"Please do not add hypocrisy to your list of defects." She swept into the parlour. "Lucy and I will be ready to leave at dawn. Have you the samples?"

"Yes," he replied, following her. "Our powder maker insists that they are of the highest quality. Once I get your message that Sir Montague is satisfied, I will ship him the barrels." He handed her the two little oilcloth bags. "Be sure and keep them dry."

"Did you receive any word from Violet or Mr. Price?"

"Not as yet. When you reach London, you should make contact with them as I told you."

"Beaumont must not hear of our plans until after my marriage, or he may embark on some impulsive quest to stop me – from both endeavours."

Digby hesitated. "Is it . . . truly finished between you? You have no second thoughts? No lingering doubts?"

Isabella's eyes now glittered dangerously. "As you like to say, the die is cast."

"Then I have something else for you." Digby felt into his doublet pocket and produced a slim, purple-bound volume: his own copy of Ovid's *Remedia Amoris*. "You might consider it an early wedding gift."

*Part Two*

England, December 1643–April 1644

# CHAPTER SIX

**A**ntonio was disappointed in Don Alonso de Cárdenas, who seemed to him an odd, ugly little man, not the imposing figure he had expected to represent King Philip of Spain's interests in England. "Near on two months, you say, from the port of Cádiz?" Don Alonso asked, as they sat in the dark-panelled reception chamber of his London house.

"Yes, Don Alonso, and we weathered many a storm."

"Hardships must suit you, then: you don't look a day over forty." Don Alonso crossed his small feet in their tasselled Cordovan leather shoes, and stabbed a pudgy finger at the letter Diego had taken such pains to forge. "I needed no introduction to the ancient de Zamora family – I am acquainted with it by reputation, and yours is a long and brilliant record of service. It is also stated here that, eight years ago, you lost your eldest son Isidro to the Imperial cause."

Antonio nodded, genuinely sorrowful. "My wife Teresa and I mourn him to this day. I have but one son left to me, our youngest child. Thank heaven Felipe is only twelve and not old enough to fight, though I joined the ranks when I was not much older."

"You named him after our King. Is this your first visit to England?"

"Yes, Don Alonso."

"Do you speak any English, sir?"

Antonio heard Diego clear his throat; the valet stood beside the Envoy's equerry, near the doors. "I flatter myself that I have a talent for foreign languages," said Antonio. "English was not among them until I boarded ship. During the voyage, however, I gained some fluency."

"When *I* arrived, I could barely put together a phrase," said Don Alonso. "How I fumed over the irregularities of its grammar. It is even worse than . . . *French*," he added, delicately.

"Unlike French, it's a language easy to grasp in its essentials, and hard to master at a higher level of discourse," Antonio observed, stealing Diego's words to him. "And the accent is more of a challenge than that of French. Yet if a man doesn't make an effort to replicate the sounds of a foreign tongue, he becomes an object of ridicule to native speakers," he went on, remembering James Beaumont's villainous mispronunciation of Spanish, which he had delighted in aping for his pretty de Capdavila y Fuentes cousins.

"Foreigners are often mistakenly judged to be fools," the Envoy agreed, his sharp eyes fixed on Antonio.

"Yes, but we are sometimes in want of information, when we travel abroad. I myself had no idea that matters between King Charles of England and his rebel Parliament had grown so violent. Can you go about safely, as a Catholic and a Spaniard, in this city governed by heretic zealots?"

"They are not all zealots, Don Antonio, and they are bound to respect the immunity of my office. I keep to my private chapel for worship, and I am careful not to engage in any unwise correspondence with the Royalist camp. His Majesty King Philip wishes for Spain to present a strictly neutral stance towards both sides. We cannot tell what will be the outcome of the war."

That clever monkey Diego was right again, Antonio noted. "Is it possible the rebels could defeat King Charles?"

Don Alonso did not respond at once; a servant had entered with Venetian glass goblets and a silver flagon of wine. "To His Majesty King Philip, long may he reign and prosper," he proposed, after the wine was poured, and Antonio seconded the health. Don Alonso merely wet his lips with the wine, studying Antonio over the rim of his glass. Antonio waited for his answer, gulping the delicious Alicante. "It is not *impossible*, Don Antonio," he said, at last. "But they have lost their greatest champion in Parliament, John Pym – hence the windows draped in black and the crowds in mourning that you may have seen in the streets. He will be difficult to replace: he was an astute negotiator among the factions in Parliament. As a sign of the esteem in which he was held, he was buried yesterday in Westminster Abbey, after lying there in state for two days. The Abbey is where English royals and people of rank or other distinction are laid to rest. King Charles cannot have been pleased that Pym should be so honoured. If the Royalists recapture London, I would not be surprised if they were to disinter his body, chop off his head, and stick it on the end of a pike for public display, in warning to all would-be traitors. As one passes over to the south end of London Bridge, one may behold at least thirty of these severed heads thus displayed in various states of decomposition, with sightless eyes." Don Alonso shivered and took a minute sip of wine. "The juiciest morsels are picked out early by carrion birds."

"Eyeballs can be the tastiest part of a fish," laughed Antonio. "So, is there no chance of a peace?"

"A faint chance," the Envoy allowed, "but the conflict is not just in England. The Scots are reportedly bringing Parliament an army this spring, and King Charles has already fetched some of his regiments back from Ireland, mostly Protestants who had been serving against the Catholic tribes in that godforsaken isle, and were more inclined to fight for Parliament. The new shipments will probably be Irish Catholics, who are detested as much by Protestant Royalists as by Parliament. Those Irish live in bogs and go about half-naked, and their version of our faith is steeped in heathen lore."

"*Dios mío!* Will the armies not break from campaign, now that winter has come?"

"They will have to, because of the cold, even if the regime in London disapproves of traditional festivities to mark the occasion of our Lord Jesus's birth."

"Then it might be less dangerous to travel out of London, at this time of the year?"

"That would depend upon the traveller." The Envoy set aside his glass. "Don Antonio, pray tell me, what is your connection to the Earl of Bristol?"

Antonio recollected Diego's question to him on their voyage: "How well do you know the Earl?" "About as well as I know the Emperor of Japan," he had admitted. "So tell the Envoy the truth, or he may suspect you of some political motive in coming to England," Diego had advised.

Still, Antonio could not resist embroidering a bit. "While ambassador to Madrid over thirty years ago, he became close friends with my late maternal aunt, Doña Cecilia de Capdavila y Fuentes. He arranged a match between her eldest daughter, Elena, and an English nobleman, James Beaumont." Don Alonso was silent, his ugly face bland. "Beaumont bore his bride home, and my aunt never heard from her again. She went to the grave disconsolate. For her sake, I wanted to learn of Elena's fate, and, if she yet lives, to bring her tidings of her brothers and sisters."

"Did they remain in Seville?"

"The girls, yes – they took the veil. As for the boys, James Beaumont had purchased them military commissions, for when they came of age."

"They followed your illustrious career?"

"And were all slain in battle like my Isidro, God rest their souls," finished Antonio.

The Envoy paused respectfully, before inquiring, "Are you aware that the Earl of Bristol is a man of influence with King Charles and that his son Lord George Digby, now Secretary of State, stands impeached by Parliament as a traitor for urging the King to wage war against his people?"

This was more recent news than Antonio had received in Don Miguel's long-winded letter. "Why no," he said.

Don Alonso spoke in a voice as sharp as his eyes. "Don Antonio, shall we drop the pretence? I believe you were sent by our enemies the

French to stir up discord between Spain and the English Parliament."

"I was *not*, I swear by the Holy Church," cried Antonio, leaping to his feet.

"Then what *are* you doing here? Beware of lying to me. I can have you arrested and handed over to Parliament."

Antonio sank back into his chair and uttered a groan, secretly thanking God for Diego's warning. "It humiliates me to confess, but I have come here as a beggar."

"A *beggar*?"

"The Earl of Bristol and Lady Elena Beaumont may be my last hope of saving the house of de Capdavila y Fuentes from penury and disgrace." Antonio threw up his hands in a poignant gesture of despair. "Her brothers had children who now rely upon me for their daily bread. I have nothing left to give to them. I am struggling, as it is, to support my own family on my meagre officer's pension. Sometimes I envy Isidro his glorious death in the field – better to die a hero than live in ignominious poverty." He found himself weeping; it was not wholly a performance, for he loathed being poor. He let the tears run down his face until they tickled his cheeks, and he had to dry them on his sleeve.

Don Alonso considerately refilled Antonio's glass. "I shall assist you to find your cousin, the Lady Elena Beaumont, in exchange for two promises. You must have no communication whatsoever with the Earl of Bristol or his son. For the reasons I gave you, it would be most prejudicial to our embassy and to Spain. And I must forbid you or your servant to quit my house, until I grant you permission. If you cannot give me your word, you may go whenever you like, but I will not come to your aid if you fall foul of Parliament – or of King Charles."

"As to the Digbys, you have my word of honour," said Antonio, pleased that he could skip a potentially troublesome step in his quest. "But I had hoped to roam a bit about London."

"Let me explain what happened this very day," said Don Alonso. "An English priest, Father Bell, was hanged, drawn, and quartered at

Tyburn, the main place of execution here. He was a Franciscan who had been in Spain and our territories in the Netherlands. He was apprehended with a torn fragment of a letter written by him in Spanish addressed to *me*, which was sufficient grounds for his arrest. I tried to intercede on his behalf while he was in prison. *He* preferred a glorious death – as a martyr to our faith. In consequence, though the authorities cannot trespass on my immunity, I am under their watch, along with every member of my staff. Do you understand why I cannot permit you to leave the confines of this embassy?"

"I do," Antonio assured him, "and again I pledge my word: neither I nor my valet will set a foot outside. But might I request one more favour? I should write to my wife and inform her of my safe arrival."

"I have a diplomatic packet leaving for Spain tomorrow morning," his host said. "Your letter can be included with my correspondence."

"The low son of a whore," Antonio expostulated to Diego in the privacy of their bedchamber. "How dare he accuse me of spying for the French? Were I not dependent on his hospitality, I would have drawn out my rapier and thrashed his ambassadorial arse."

"He's not as silly as he looks, and none of his remarks were idle, Don Antonio," said Diego, stooping to help him off with his boots. "You must abide by his rules. Why risk arrest, torture, and an agonizing death when you have come so far, and are so near to your goal? It's a stroke of luck that you needn't approach the Earl of Bristol. You can rest in the comfort of the embassy and let Don Alonso work for you. And I won't have to forge you an introduction to the Lady Elena. He'll provide a more convincing one. Besides, we don't even know the location of Lord Beaumont's estate. We could be stumbling about for months between two hostile armies in abominable weather, whereas Don Alonso might give us papers of safe conduct and a map."

"All right, all right," said Antonio, defeated by his barrage of arguments.

"I'm so glad you confided in him your financial troubles. Your eloquence had me on the verge of tears." Diego looked up at Antonio. "But what else do you want of the Lady Elena?"

"A loving reunion with my cousin." Antonio unlaced his breeches and dug a hand inside to scratch his balls. "Now go to sleep, while I write to Teresa." To Teresa, and also to Gaspar, he thought: if he and Diego were Don Alonso's prisoners, the gypsy and her son must remain his.

Later, as he sat down at a side table and inked his quill, he heard Diego's voice, from out of the shadows. "Might I suggest, Don Antonio, that you put nothing in your letter that our host might deem . . . compromising."

Antonio turned round to glare at the youth; Diego was invisible beneath the bedclothes, apart from the top of his curly head. "Why the devil should I not?"

"If you do, I would bet you a thousand escudos that your letter will not leave his house," Diego said sweetly.

"Fuck your goddamned impudence," Antonio muttered, but he followed Diego's counsel.

## II.

Ingram felt happier than he had in months. It was the beginning of his yuletide leave, he was with Beaumont again, and every mile of his journey brought him closer to Chipping Campden, where Anne awaited him. In four days, she would be his wife. He and Beaumont had fallen a few yards behind Tom and Adam, who was leading a packhorse laden with gifts that Tom had purchased for the family; and as they rode, Ingram took simple pleasure in the tranquil Cotswold fields blanketed with fresh snow that glittered in bright sunshine. Over the muffled tread of their horses' hooves and the jingle of their harnesses, he could hear the familiar cawing of rooks in the bare tree-tops, and the twitter of smaller birds in hedgerows thick with holly. He might forget that England was a country at war.

The sole blight to his happiness was the state of his friend. Beaumont's skin was sallow, and the naturally dark pigment under his now-bloodshot eyes had extended down to his prominent cheekbones; he looked as if he had not eaten in weeks, although he had obviously been drinking. The left side of his jaw was bruised purple, and he could not wear gloves, despite the cold, because of scuffed knuckles on both hands. Before setting out from Oxford, Ingram had noticed on his clothes an overpowering smell of liquor and ladies' perfume. "Don't ask," he had said to Ingram, and with unusual restraint he had let pass the jokes Tom had cracked at his expense.

"There's Moreton-in-Marsh in the distance and you've barely spoken," Ingram remarked. "You're not far from home. I hope by then you'll be able to hold a conversation." Beaumont said nothing, so Ingram went on, "I gather you were engaged in some sport."

"Last night was particularly excessive."

"Ending in a brawl, I presume?" Beaumont nodded. "Over cards or women?"

"Cards. And I wasn't even cheating," Beaumont said, with an air of mock outrage.

"And then what happened – were you thrown in gaol?"

"Wilmot's rank saved me from the indignity. As you once told me, it pays to have such friends."

"Well, please don't get into any fights at *my* wedding," Ingram said, only half joking; the Beaumont brothers had drawn blood at Elizabeth's, after Beaumont had been caught with Isabella Savage up in his chamber.

Beaumont smiled, in the open, affectionate way that had endeared Ingram to him since their youth at College. "It would be a bore to repeat myself."

"How *is* Mistress Savage?"

Beaumont's smile vanished. "I haven't seen her for the past twelve days. We bade goodbye to each other, and she left Oxford for an unknown destination – unknown to me, at any rate. It was she who broke with me. I was at fault, and I don't care to discuss the details. And now I'm supposed to contemplate a betrothal." He told Ingram about Mistress Furnival, his talk with Lord Beaumont, and Isabella's insistence that he marry the girl.

"I *am* sorry, Beaumont."

"Don't say it's for the best."

"I won't. How are you finding Lord Digby's service?"

Beaumont jerked aside his head to spit. "I feel like an indentured slave stuck with an unscrupulous master – more than one, to be perfectly honest."

Ingram glanced towards Tom, who not long ago had almost sent his brother to an excruciating death because of his mistaken suspicion about Beaumont's loyalties. "You wouldn't go over . . ."

"No need to worry, Ingram. After turning coat when I was abroad, I know what it is to live with the consequences. And here I'd cause great distress to those I love. I think my father would understand, but it would divide our family, and that I can't do, in all good conscience. Moreover, I can't fight for a side which would ruin his house and fortunes, given half a chance. His welfare is more important to me, in the end, than my jaded political convictions."

"And Seward would never understand."

"No, he wouldn't, and there's another reason for me to stay with the King. I also think Prince Charles could be a fine monarch one day, if he doesn't succumb to the plague that's raging within our camp."

"Is there plague in Oxford?" Ingram exclaimed; he had not heard.

"A virulent and contagious strain – of mistrust, duplicity, and cynicism. I am very sick with it, and of it. The Prince isn't yet infected, which makes his company a balm to my troubled soul. I've been giving him lessons in ciphering, on His Majesty's request," Beaumont added, less sarcastically. "As a student, he reminds me of myself: quick to learn when he's interested and lazy when he's not. And he shows a most precocious interest in the opposite sex."

"As did you," Ingram said, laughing.

"So," said Beaumont, as if to switch the topic, "are all your family coming to the wedding?"

"No, just my brother Richard and Aunt Musgrave. Kate's baby is a sickly child, and she was worried to travel with him, and Richard's wife is pregnant again."

"How are Kate and your aunt rubbing along?"

"They are not, as Aunt Musgrave will no doubt tell you. Kate's the same ice queen as always, spoilt and ungrateful."

"I do look forward to seeing your aunt," said Beaumont. "She had some sage advice for me, in the past. This time I'm tempted to have a cry on her shoulder."

"Or into her expansive bosom – she would relish that. My poor aunt! Her lands have been raided twice now by our troops, and she fears the next to descend on her may be from Parliament's garrison at Gloucester."

"You were right to warn my father about his house," Beaumont recommenced, after a short silence. "He should hide some of his money and valuables, to preserve at least a portion of the family wealth. Then in the last resort, they could flee to France."

Ingram reined in abruptly. "France? Do you truly mean that?"

Beaumont reined in also, and shot him a stare. "Oh yes. My father would be hard pressed to abandon the estate, but my mother is more practical. I believe she'd urge him to accept exile, if the war deteriorates into a bloodbath."

"As *you* once said to *me*, military life has a tendency to corrupt." Ingram glanced ahead again at Tom. "What a spirit of churlish revenge enters men's nature when they're *en masse*. They would deplore it, were it inflicted on their own families. In October, Tom's troop sacked an estate, and while they were pillaging, they'd found occasion to shit and piss all about inside the house."

"Did Tom attempt to stop them, or did he join in?"

"Who knows, but he threatened to raze the place. When I begged him not to, he said he'd spoken in jest. I wasn't so sure."

"You forget that he has a highly developed sense of humour."

Ingram grinned as they spurred on their horses; this was more like his old friend. "I shall be pleased to have *you* as my brother, Beaumont. Just think: had you not whisked me from the battlefield after Edgehill and brought me to Chipping Campden, I'd be dead, or crippled."

"I'm afraid I see it quite differently. If your horse hadn't fallen on you and broken your leg, my sister would never have been moved to pity you in your convalescence, and she wouldn't be where she is now: in the unenviable position of having to marry you."

"That may be so," Ingram said, struggling to keep a straight face. "But if not for Aunt Musgrave's largesse, I would have been too poor to propose to her."

"*Not* so, Ingram," said Beaumont, smiling again. "I'd have won you a fortune at cards – through fair means or foul – to have *you* as my brother."

## III.

Veech limped slowly into his first private audience with Oliver St. John; Pym's desk was still draped in black cloth, he noticed. St. John stood by the window looking out. "Well, Mr. Veech?" was all he asked, and curtly, at that.

"Sir Montague Hallam of the Vintners' Company has a new wife – a marriage of convenience, or so it would appear for an old invalid," replied Veech. "His bride, Isabella Savage, is said to be a woman of uncommon beauty, and hasn't long to wait to be a wealthy widow."

St. John turned to face him. "I did not call you here to indulge in trivial gossip."

"Mr. Pym can't have told you, Mr. St. John: I've been watching Sir Montague for some time," said Veech, as if he had not heard the reproof.

"You are wasting the resources of Parliament. Of all the Members in the City Corporation, Sir Montague is among the most loyal to us."

Again, Veech paid no notice. "I received information from a man I'd posted in the alehouse where Sir Montague's servants go to drink, near the Strand. Last week, his valet let slip that Lady Hallam gave up a lover to get married." Veech saw a gleam in St. John's eyes: how these Puritans relished a juicy scandal. "He eavesdropped on her talking with her maidservant. The lover's name was Beaumont."

"And what do you make of that, Mr. Veech?" said St. John, in a politer tone.

"Sir Montague conducts regular business with Oxford. I've searched his barrels randomly, unbeknownst to him, and found no evidence to incriminate him – thus far."

"You searched them without proper warrant?"

"I shall have the warrant soon enough. As to other matters," Veech went on, "Mr. Devenish informed my agent Draycott that Major Ogle is petitioning the House of Lords to be released from gaol with a keeper, to obtain materials to prosecute his case. He will then be allowed to escape. It's my guess that he will stop, on his way to Oxford, to visit his purported friend Lieutenant-Colonel Mosely in the Aylesbury garrison."

"A neat plan, sir," St. John acknowledged. "He cannot suspect that both Devenish and the Lieutenant-Colonel are loyal to us."

Veech bent to adjust his brace; Pym would have made some kind inquiry about his leg, but not St. John. "When the garrison is supposedly to fall to the Royalists, who might be commanded to occupy it?" he asked.

"Who can say, Mr. Veech – the honour might go to Prince Rupert himself. Pray God, Essex's troops will be waiting to do battle with whoever is sent."

"His Majesty's beloved nephew would be a prize hostage for Parliament. Mosely could insist that he will open the gates only to Rupert."

"Are you proposing that we lay a *trap* for the Prince?"

"Yes, Mr. St. John," said Veech, wanting to laugh at the man's outraged face; what a performance.

"Rupert may be wary of such a condition."

"I doubt it, with the King so sure of Mosely."

"Even if Rupert were drawn in, he and his Lifeguard would fight to the death."

"No, sir: he's a mercenary – a professional soldier, if you prefer – and they don't *waste their resources* in bootless heroism when they know themselves outnumbered."

St. John was clearly too deep in thought to catch Veech's contemptuous use of his own phrase. "The Committee might consider it an . . . un-English tactic."

"Rupert is half-German and un-English in his tactics. How else did he earn the title of Prince Robber, but by sacking English towns and demanding tribute from the citizens?"

"And his brother Prince Maurice is still worse. By spring, Mr. Veech, the Committee of Safety will have a change of title," St. John said next. "The Scots Commissioners have requested it to be called the Committee of Both Kingdoms."

"Another marriage of convenience," said Veech, under his breath.

**IV.**

Blowing on his numbed hands, his stomach growling, Draycott paced up and down the chilly hall of Westminster. He had missed his dinner with Judith; Veech was an hour late for their appointment; and at half past three in the afternoon the light was fading, and he would have to go home, across the river, in bleak darkness. "I've waited long enough," he muttered to himself.

Then he saw Veech hobbling through the main doors, leaning heavily on a cane. "Mr. Draycott – were you about to leave? Forgive me, sir: Mr. St. John kept me at Derby House. Let's hire a hackney coach to take us to Ludgate. I daren't walk the distance in this weather, or my leg will seize up." When they had found a vehicle and were settled in, rattling up the Strand, he asked, "How is Mr. Price?"

"How do you think – he's been agitating for this meeting each time I see him," Draycott replied irritably. "He will not talk to me. Why have you delayed, if you're so anxious to capture Beaumont?"

"Is it not your practice as a lawyer to investigate the character of a witness, before you place any trust in his testimony?"

"Of course it is."

Veech was wedging his left foot against the door, to protect his wounded leg from the bouncing of the coach. "Mr. Price has acquaintances everywhere," he said. "At the Saracen's Head, where we're going, and in Cheapside, and in Southwark. They're a mixed lot, as mixed as their accounts of him. Some report that he's a thief and a cozening rogue, always out of funds because of his extravagant tastes. Yet the landlord of the Saracen's Head, Robin Nunn, claims he's a gentleman, and pays his bills. Price's mistress, Susan Sprye, is employed by Nunn as a serving wench. Price has promised to marry her, Nunn says. The man I sent on my inquiries tried to talk to her, but she was tight-lipped and hostile."

"Your description of Price matches a multitude of citizens in London."

"You're annoyed with me, sir, but be patient and hear me out. Mr. Price's friend in Cheapside is Thomas Violet, a goldsmith, and a known agent for His Majesty who goes back and forth from Oxford. I should say, I'm letting him do so, for the present, until I decide to take him."

"That is a curious association," agreed Draycott.

"As curious as Price's friends in Southwark. There used to be a famous brothel in Blackman Street. The bawd and her whores had since seen the error of their ways, and turned it into a house of prayer. Troopers searched it over and over, but could discover no signs that she was in her former business. She died in November, and a servant of hers named Peter Barlow now keeps the house. He's served his spells in gaol. He was a practised miller of kens, if you're acquainted with the term."

"Are you testing me, Mr. Veech? He was a burglar."

"And you must have come face to face with him, the night Beaumont escaped, when you went knocking on all the doors of Blackman Street."

"It's possible, though I'd be hard put to remember any one face, we questioned so many people." Draycott chose not to add that he had been so horrified, confused, and subsequently embarrassed by the whole train of events that he had done his best to forget them.

"My man spoke with Mistress Edwards' neighbour, who knows Mr. Price as a merry young blade. He visits Barlow to this day."

"Price is an informer. We can't expect him to be a choir boy."

"He's far from that. But let's return to the night of Beaumont's escape. A very short time before you knocked at Mistress Edwards' house, the neighbour heard footsteps and pounding on her door. She was scared to tell the authorities – Barlow's a rough fellow. And the next week, she heard there was sickness in the house, though Mr. Price went in and out freely. The house was shut to visitors until after the twenty-second of October, around when Price took his lodgings at the Saracen's Head."

Draycott held up a hand. "You've lost me, sir."

"On the *twenty-first* of October, an old lady was taken out of the house swaddled in blankets, and packed into the back of the cart. One of Mistress Edwards' women drove off the cart."

"The old lady was Mistress Edwards, I presume."

"No, sir: Mistress Edwards was a little old lady. This one was tall."

"Then . . . Beaumont was hiding at Mistress Edwards', and got smuggled out."

"And where does that leave us with Mr. Price?"

"He's a true scoundrel. He's about to inform on his friends, who abetted in Beaumont's escape." The coach made a sharp lurch, round Temple Bar into Fleet Street, and Draycott was thrown sideways against Veech, who thrust him violently away. "Excuse me," he said, staggered by the fury on Veech's face.

"That would be the most obvious explanation," Veech said, calm again, as though nothing had happened. "But Mr. Price may be yet trickier. On the day you met him at Winchester House, he had come to visit a prisoner there, our Major Ogle, who is getting ready to fly the coop. And they had a very quiet chat together, Mr. Devenish said."

"So what mischief is Price up to?"

"We must find out."

"Will you arrest the occupants of Blackman Street?"

Veech rolled his eyes. "You and Mr. St. John both are so eager for arrests, when it's the small fish that are bait to hook the biggest." The coach had come to a halt. Draycott leant through the window; in the twilight he could discern a signpost, of a turbaned face in profile with a hawkish nose. "I'll do the talking," Veech said. "You listen, and learn."


**V.**

Laurence had much to say to his father, on the ride to Sir Harold Furnival's house, and so he began at once. "I think you should profit from the break in hostilities over Christmas by hiding as much of your wealth as you can, as secretly as you're able. You'll need enough to support you to live in modest style for some years: gold, silver, jewellery – items that are portable and easy to conceal. Most of your servants would lay down their lives to protect you, but in the circumstances of war, you can't rely on their discretion. As few of them as possible should know where your valuables are hidden. And in the last extremity, I'd recommend that you might go to France."

Lord Beaumont frowned at Laurence as if he had proposed running naked through the streets of Chipping Campden. "I would rather be slain on my doorstep."

"I hope Parliament would treat you more respectfully than that, and, in the event of His Majesty's defeat, would pardon Tom. But I might not be as fortunate, given who *I* serve."

"I never liked you in such work, even when you served Lord Falkland."

Laurence refrained from pointing out how it was his father's well-meaning suggestion that he seek employment with Falkland that had sucked him back into espionage, on his return from abroad. "Even sooner, you may need money to pay the fines that will be levied on you, should our part of Gloucestershire fall to the enemy. And you should be prepared for what may happen to the house."

"Oh that I could wave a magic wand to render my marbles invisible, and my canvasses, and the books in my library," Lord Beaumont lamented. "Your mother would say they are just things, yet they are beautiful things that represent to me what separates us from *the character of the beast*, as Aristotle so aptly named it. I shall talk with her after the wedding, about what might be stored away. Now do not press me any more, Laurence. You will find that Sir Harold and Lady Margaret keep a large household, in the old style – a contrast to ours, not that Penelope seems distressed by the prospect of life at Chipping Campden. She has paid us a few visits, and grown close to Elizabeth. She is a sociable girl." He paused; and Laurence knew what was coming next. "You must forgive me, but I inquired of Ingram as to your relations with Mistress Savage, and he told me she had ended them. Is that so?"

"It is," said Laurence shortly, and for the rest of their journey they discussed other matters: the estate, his lordship's tenants, and Elizabeth's interest in a second marriage.

Sir Harold's was indeed a traditional country seat, from the crumbling stone archway bearing the Furnival coat of arms to the house itself, a timbered structure with diamond-paned windows and an overhanging thatched roof. The front doors opened directly into a hall festooned with ancient weapons, and the air was thick with smoke from damp wood smouldering in an enormous blackened fireplace. A couple of wolfhounds trotted up, slavering enthusiastically when Laurence patted their grizzled heads. He was surprised to see some thirty people assembled, most of them women and young girls, busy carding wool and spinning; tasks that Lady Beaumont assigned to her servants. They all rose to curtsey, some of them clearly in awe of the new arrivals.

"Your lordship, Mr. Beaumont," Sir Harold greeted them in a loud voice, striding up from his place by the fire. He had the rubicund complexion of a man who spent little time indoors, and his legs were as bandy as old Jacob's from years in the saddle. His manner struck Laurence as simultaneously fawning and self-satisfied, and there was a glint of avarice in his eyes as he appraised his guests. When his remarks about Laurence's prestigious service with the Secretary of State elicited no comment from Laurence, he turned his attention to Lord Beaumont. Laurence understood him: it did not signify whether he especially liked his future son-in-law; his daughter would be wife to the heir of a wealthy peer, and that was sufficient. Lady Margaret greeted them more timidly. She must have been as pretty as Penelope in youth, but her brow was now creased into an expression of permanent anxiety, and the way she deferred to Sir Harold suggested that she lived in fear of him.

"Pen is everyone's favourite," Sir Harold said, as the girl came forward. "She was even celebrated at Her Majesty's Court, and cannot stop talking about her sojourn in Oxford. Her Majesty and Lord Jermyn showed her the greatest kindness . . ." Laurence's gaze drifted as Sir Harold babbled on. A girl who resembled Penelope, but more humbly dressed, had risen from her spinning wheel. A sister, he assumed. Then Sir Harold distracted him, moving closer and talking in an even louder voice; and when Laurence looked again, she had disappeared. "We should let the young folk get acquainted," Sir Harold told his wife and Lord Beaumont.

Penelope slipped her arm into Laurence's and drew him a little aside. "You must find us very homely, Mr. Beaumont, after the splendours of Chipping Campden."

He could think of nothing to say to this. He wanted to like her: Elizabeth's friendship was a recommendation, and he could identify no flaw in her physically. Yet he could not help remembering the tiny lines at the corners of Isabella's eyes and mouth, witness to experience of both suffering and pleasure; and how the light would catch the gold in her irises and the copper in her dark hair.

"Sir," said Penelope, in a consternated tone, "I believe your mind is elsewhere."

"Oh no," he assured her. "Tell me more about your time in Oxford."

## VI.

Unabashed by the presence of the Beaumont family, Madam Musgrave assaulted Laurence in the entrance hall at Chipping Campden and crushed him to her, momentarily depriving him of breath. He was delighted to see her unchanged, still wearing her stiff, outmoded gown and yellow ruff. "Mr. Beaumont, can it be that you are even more handsome than I recollect?" she said, in a voice as booming as Sir Harold's, but far dearer to his ears. "Let's have a proper kiss, you young devil." And she smacked him on the lips. "Where is Walter's sweetheart?" she demanded, and embraced Anne with the same gusto. "Mr. Beaumont and I plotted this match," she informed Lord and Lady Beaumont triumphantly.

"Mr. Ingram and I are very lucky that you did," Anne said, smiling.

"Madam Musgrave, you will be thirsty after your journey," Lord Beaumont said, offering her his arm.

"I am, my lord," she rejoined, seizing it, and swept him into the Hall. The other women followed, leaving Ingram, Richard, and Laurence behind.

Richard bowed to Laurence, for the first time in their unfriendly acquaintance. Laurence bowed also, but could not resist the urge to provoke. "Mr. Ingram," he said, "I owe you an apology. From the day I met your younger brother at College, I have exerted an evil and debauching influence over him, for which, in the past, you quite correctly reproved me. And now I see the tragic consequences: he is about to marry my sister. I don't know how I can make amends."

Richard blushed and stammered, "There is . . . really no need."

Laurence and Madam Musgrave sat at cards into the early hours of the morning, long after the rest of the household had retired. His lordship's butler had furnished them amply with Jerez, and a platter of almond tartlets on her special request, and they were both somewhat tipsy. Laurence was letting her win and she knew it, but she was enjoying herself too much to object.

As he dealt out a fresh round, she observed, "Human nature is a constant source of amazement to me, sir: that two children from the same issue as Walter should end up such prim, pious creatures! Richard is a conceited idiot with no head for business, and Kate behaves as though she has never broken wind in her entire life."

"Perhaps she hasn't," said Laurence. "That would explain a lot about her character."

"Ah well," laughed Madam Musgrave, "I suppose we must forgive them. They were orphaned young, and Richard had to grow up fast, trying to be both father and brother. Mr. Beaumont," she said, wiping her sticky fingers on the skirt of her gown, "I have the distinct impression that, unlike Walter and Anne, you are unhappy in love and in want of advice."

"You're absolutely right," Laurence agreed, and confessed all.

"So it was Mistress Savage that we talked of at my house, when you asked if a woman could conceive after having a child torn from her womb."

"And you said it might be possible."

"But it may be only a faint chance, if you have not yet got a babe on her. She was wise to decline you. As for Mistress Furnival, give her children and she may be content to let you do as you please, if you're discreet and don't bring home any *gifts* from your travels," Madam Musgrave went on, grabbing another tartlet. "I should not have to remind a man of your age and experience that few marriages begin with love. You're a horse left too long to its own druthers. It will do you a world of good to settle down. And fatherhood – *legitimate* father-hood," she stressed, "may bring you unexpected joy. Now, there's a fee for my counsel, sir."

"You may ask anything of me – within the bounds of morals and religion," he added decorously.

She leant over to pinch him on the cheek. "I wish to be god-mother to your firstborn."

"You have a bargain, madam," he said, and they drank a health to it.

**VII.**

Price dismounted, thighs trembling and buttocks aching. Not once in his life had he ridden so far in such a short time: London to Oxford, to report to Lord Digby, who had ready for him a new suit of clothes, expensive though of a rather dullish russet colour; and then about thirty-five miles onwards to Chipping Campden.

Now Price appreciated his lordship's sartorial choice. Lord Beaumont's mansion was a model of restrained taste in the style of the Banqueting House at Whitehall, and to Price's eye, just as grand. Some day all this would be Beaumont's. It confounded Price yet more that Beaumont should go about with holes in his clothes and ragged shirt cuffs. And he seemed to have but a single decent suit to his name, of Puritanical black; and not even a servant to attend him.

Price was still gazing at the magnificent façade fronted by col-umns when an ancient bow-legged man in livery stomped over to take his horse. "A good morning to you, sir. Have you come from the church?"

"No, from Oxford," said Price, in the aristocratic tone he had been practising, and shook the snow from the hem of his cloak.

"Then you will have missed the ceremony, sir – it must be fin-ished by this hour. Ah, I see some of the gentlemen now." The man pointed to a party of riders galloping up the gravel drive. They swung gracefully from their mounts, handing their reins to younger grooms who had rushed to their assistance. Beaumont was not among them.

Price whipped off his beaver hat and bowed. "May I introduce myself: Mr. Edward Price."

They also bowed, though none doffed their hats or gave their names; they appeared more interested in the old man. "Jacob, spry as ever," one of them said.

"Seventy if I'm a day, sir," Jacob said proudly.

"Three score and ten," remarked Price, to join in the conversation. "And for how many of those years have you been his lordship's groom?"

"Jacob is not a groom, sir: he is my father's Master of Horse," another corrected Price with a blue-eyed stare. "I am Thomas Beaumont. Are you a guest of Ingram's?" Dark blond, pink-complexioned, and bearded, he was a couple of inches shy of his brother's height, not lean and rangy but strongly built, and he held himself straight as a ramrod.

Price hesitated, surprised, and then had to shout his reply: a procession of coaches was rumbling into the courtyard accompanied by more men on horseback. "In fact, sir, I am an uninvited guest, here to see your brother on Lord Digby's behalf."

"How he loves to receive such guests at our family weddings," Thomas said, with a wry edge, "though he might have preferred if you were of the opposite sex."

Price tried to stay by Thomas's side, as they ascended the front steps. Through the doors, he saw a lofty ceiling festooned with plaster wreaths, and an expanse of floor paved in black-and-white marble, ending in a flight of polished oak stairs wide enough for half a dozen souls to walk up side by side. Two statues, both the height of a tall man, flanked the doors to a great hall: a semi-clad nymph and a youth wrestling with a serpent. Price had to admire the nymph's pert breasts.

Thomas's group left him behind and thundered up the staircase, so he meandered into the hall. Tables were set with spotless linen cloths, silver plate, knives, spoons, an array of glassware, and even forks! Room for at least a hundred guests, Price estimated. Musicians were assembled on a dais playing viols and wind instruments, and in the hearth of a carved fireplace blazed a fire aromatic with the scent of pine cones. High over the mantel hung the portrait of a gentleman who resembled Thomas Beaumont, though his face wore a sweet, far-away expression.

Price accepted wine from one of the servants standing like soldiers on parade along the length of the hall. He was sipping at his glass when Beaumont came in with a companion. This must be Beaumont's old friend, Walter Ingram, thought Price, jealously; never had Beaumont turned such an unguarded, boyish smile on him. Beaumont was dressed not in black but in a suit of olive green that brought out the paler shade of his eyes. Today he looked fit to be a lord's heir. Ingram had on navy velvet slashed with a sky-blue satin. His was an open, humorous coun-tenance, and his light brown hair was thinning at the crown.

Price addressed Ingram first. He could tell that Beaumont was not pleased to see him: the enchanting smile had gone, and the guard was raised again in those slanted eyes. "May I offer you my congratu-lations, sir? Edward Price is the name."

"Thank you, Mr. Price," said Ingram. "Do you know my brother-in-law?"

"Yes, we are both in Lord Digby's service. How are you, Beaumont?"

"Frozen to the marrow," Beaumont replied. "That church is like a bloody grave."

"Forgive me for intruding," Price said, "but I have news from his lordship."

"I hope you'll attend the banquet, Mr. Price?" Ingram said.

"Thank *you*, sir – with pleasure."

"Pardon us a moment, Ingram," Beaumont said. He guided Price out of the hall, into a parlour of more human dimensions, and shut the door.

"Everything's set for Major Ogle's release from Winchester House," Price began, unable to contain his excitement. "Mr. Devenish, who is a worthy gentleman, told me that Ogle will be let out under supervision of a keeper, towards the end of this month. He'll then slip away and get himself to Oxford."

"What else?"

"I've had more luck." Price described his chance encounter with Draycott at Winchester House, leaving out mention of the broadsheet. "And three days ago, I met Clement Veech. He's hired me as his agent – exactly as Lord Digby had hoped."

Price expected a *Price, you are priceless*, but Beaumont said only, "Go on."

"Veech asked me about you. I said I'd ride to Oxford and see what I could find out. He was willing to wait. And here's the best part. Lord Digby suggested that I feed him *misinformation*, to confuse him, in case he has some idea of our true plans for the City this spring."

Beaumont laughed mirthlessly. "His lordship is full of plans, each cleverer than the last."

"Well *I* had one, for him. You heard about Mistress Edwards' death, and how her house was to be sold? I suggested to Lord Digby that he pay Barlow to keep it as a safe house. Lord Digby thinks—"

"I don't give a shit what he thinks," cut in Beaumont, startling Price. "The house isn't safe any more, and you must steer clear of it. Describe Veech to me," Beaumont said, in a less scathing tone. "You have a good memory – tell me every detail you can remember."

Mollified, Price considered. "He's tall, broad in the chest and brown-haired, with a heavy brow and deep, dark eyes. Though his face is creased as worn leather, there's a peculiar, soft aspect to his features, and his hands are white and fleshy. He was wearing the same coat as when you glimpsed him: long and baggy, with sleeves that hang low over his wrists. He walks with a bad limp, and he wears a wooden contraption around his knee. When he seated himself, he had to shift his leg into place, as if it were a dead thing. And when he was served his food, he put more salt and pepper on it than I've ever seen a man use before, and wolfed it down without breaking a sweat. He's got a voice as deep as his eyes, and he speaks quietly, with a sort of menace. But I have him fooled, Beaumont. And I'll soon have him eating out of my hand."

"He's more likely to bite it off. Price, one of the worst mistakes to make in our work is to see in a man what we want to see – it's a kind of wishful thinking that can lead us to underestimate our enemy. How was Draycott with him? Did they seem amicable?"

"No, but then Draycott barely talked. Veech wouldn't let him . . ." Price trailed off.

Two girls had burst into the room, arm in arm. The loveliest of them, a dark blonde, had Beaumont's Oriental, almond-shaped eyes and fine features. The other was blonder, with a more English cast of face, her expression as pert as the statue's breasts. Her eyes were on Beaumont.

Beaumont switched to an easy manner. "May I present my sister Elizabeth Ormiston and Mistress Penelope Furnival."

How unfavourably Sue compared, mused Price, as he examined these gorgeous creatures' unblemished complexions, the yards of satin in their gowns, and their fashionable pearl necklaces and earrings. "Mr. Edward Price, at your service, ladies," he said, answering their curtsies with a bow.

"Mr. Price," said Elizabeth, "you must be my brother's uninvited guest. Tom told me," she said to Beaumont, with a little wink.

"I *am* invited now, by the bridegroom himself," said Price, giving her his most dazzling and adulatory grin. "He asked me to attend the banquet, though I know nearly no one and may be at a loss for conversation – unless some kind person rescues me."

She stroked her fingers to her hair, an inadvertent gesture that Price read instantly. "We were about to drink to Anne and Ingram. Will you join us, sir?"

**VIII.**

"Seward, what ails you?" asked Clarke, as they sat before the last glow of a log fire, with Pusskins sprawled before them on the hearth. "We are about to start a season of rejoicing in the peace and quiet of my country house, and you are the epitome of gloom."

Seward could not lie to his friend. "I woke this morning with the certain knowledge that I must look into my bowl, and yet I sense I shall foresee a bad vision."

"You should have left that thing behind in your rooms. The eve of Christ's birth is no time for occult dabbling."

A peal of bells rang out from the village church, as though to emphasise Clarke's point. "Midnight," Seward said, redundantly. "Please, Clarke, go to bed and let me do what I must."

"If I find you here tomorrow morning struck dead by some infernal entity you conjured, I shall deny you Christian rites."

Seward managed a chuckle. "My spirit would haunt you forever after."

"It could scare me no more than you do now, you repulsive old skeleton," said Clarke, heaving himself from his seat, and lumbered upstairs.

As soon as Seward heard Clarke's rhythmic snores, a sound much like the purr of his cat, he went and filled his bowl from the jar of Fludd's liquid. He recited a prayer to invoke the angels' blessing, and waited, anticipating either a vision of the King's death or of the Spaniard who so resembled Beaumont. He had begun to guess what harm that man might be bringing to England.

In his youth, Beaumont had got one of his mother's maidservants with child; and as his tutor, Seward had endured a lecture from Lady Beaumont for allowing her son to develop unchaste habits. Bemused by her disproportionate rage over such a common offence, he had urged her to pardon the boy, saying, "Many of us have fallen into similar errors, in our early years." His mundane words had sparked in her a sudden alarm. She had as fast regained her composure; yet since that day, he had his suspicions about Beaumont's paternity. Beaumont had never shown any, and as for Lord Beaumont, he would often remark, accurately in Seward's view, upon the likenesses in character between himself and his heir. But if a secret existed, it must be kept, for if revealed, it could destroy the family.

The surface of Seward's bowl was at first a blank. Gradually he perceived a swirl of white: a snowstorm, through which he saw the figure of a man on horseback racing away from flashes of fire. As the man glanced back at whoever was trying to shoot him, his face was impossible to identify amid the gusts of flakes, though his panic was unmistakable. He twisted about and raced on, bent low over the pommel to avoid the shots. Not low enough, for a blazing ball streaked towards him, and he was hit. He swayed in the saddle. Could these be the King's last moments on earth, Seward wondered, feeling faint with horror. The vision dimmed, only to clear again: the man was now slumped forward, his head lolling and jouncing against the animal's neck, his arms dangling by its sides. The horse had slowed to a walk, and beside the imprint of its hooves in the snow, there was a trail of blood. Then the vision became obscure, and disappeared altogether.

## IX.

"Hurry and take your turn, Liz, before we fall asleep," Anne said, yawning. "This is even more tedious than watching Laurence win."

In the congenial atmosphere of the parlour, Laurence studied Elizabeth from across the chess board as she fiddled with her ivory knight. He had seen that languorous expression in her ever since the wedding banquet, when she had dedicated most of her attention to Price, and he did not like it. "I was pondering my strategy," she said, and set her knight down on the board.

"Not there," cried Ingram, who was playing every alternate move with her against Anne; Laurence had opted to sit out of the game, after they had grumbled so much about his string of victories.

"Too late." Anne snatched up the knight with a black pawn. "That's what you get for being moonstruck."

Elizabeth blushed, but did not deny the charge.

"Moonstruck by whom?" Ingram asked Anne.

"Mr. Edward Price. She's been conspicuously silent about him for ten whole days – which is how I can tell. Who is he, Laurence?"

It was a fair question, Laurence thought. Had Elizabeth met Price in his Blackman Street garb, or even in his loud purple suit, and had she heard him speak and observed him without his lately acquired gentleman's manners, she might have been less impressed. The Price to whom she had been introduced was partly a creation of Digby's, but also the product of Laurence's own assiduous tutelage, although Price had required no tutor to detect in Elizabeth what her trouble was and how he could appeal to her, which he had, with every possible show of gallantry. "I don't know him very well," Laurence said. "He was . . . helpful to me in some work I had to do, so I gave him a recommendation to Lord Digby."

"If Liz is moonstruck, you are being purposefully vague," said Anne. "Where is he from?"

Ingram answered for Laurence. "London, by his speech, and he was trying to hide it."

"Why should he try to hide the fact that he's from London?" demanded Elizabeth.

"He might be ashamed of his origins."

She screwed up her eyes at Ingram. "And that means he is beneath us?"

"What acrobatic logic," Laurence said.

"*Is* it? Because clearly *you* didn't appreciate his presence at the banquet, and for that reason dragged him away, when we could have offered him a chamber for the night."

"I did nothing of the sort – he told me he had to return to Oxford," said Laurence, which was the opposite of the truth: when Price had begged to stay, hinting that he could not afford accommodation elsewhere, Laurence had supplied him with money, and a servant to deposit him at the town inn.

"Why didn't he tell me?"

"Perhaps he was no longer entertained by our company, but didn't wish to be rude."

"I don't believe you. And how did you enjoy entertaining Penelope? If not talking of someone is a measure of attraction, you must be head over heels in love."

"'Often a silent face has voice and words,'" he quoted, evasively.

"I haven't heard that line since our time at Merton, Beaumont," said Ingram. "From Ovid's *Ars Amatoria*, is it not?"

"Right you are," Laurence said, recalling the afternoon when Isabella had read to him in her parlour.

Elizabeth heaved a frustrated sigh. "So how soon will you propose to Pen, Laurence?"

"Who's talking now, you or our mother?"

Elizabeth grabbed her discarded knight and hurled it at him. He caught it in mid-air, and placed it deliberately back on the table.

"Lady Margaret told me Penelope has a twin named Catherine," intervened Ingram, with his habitual tact. "Did you meet her at Lower Quinton, Beaumont?"

Laurence remembered the young woman who had left the hall as Sir Harold was speaking to him. "No, but I might have seen her briefly."

"Why wasn't she at our wedding?" Ingram asked Anne. "Were her parents afraid she might eclipse her sister?"

"Catherine is fragile in health, and extremely shy," declared Elizabeth, with great authority. "Pen says she'd never want to marry."

Tom broke up their discussion, marching into the parlour with his cloak and boots blood-splattered from his morning's hunt. "You should have been with us," he told Laurence and Ingram, as he pulled off a glove and reached into his doublet. "We shot a buck, and the dogs had themselves a fox. I met the carrier at the gatehouse – this is for you." He tossed a letter to Laurence. "And there's one for her ladyship. Adam," he yelled as he walked out, "fetch me hot water."

Laurence stuffed the letter into his pocket; it was from Digby, and he had no immediate desire to read it. Then a faint hope arose in his mind that it might contain news of Isabella, so he excused himself and went up to his chamber. The message was in a code he had designed for Digby.

Digby wrote that the King was much encouraged by correspondence with his London friends, and that a stunning development had emerged for the spring: His Majesty had news of a richer prize than those he was already expecting, around the time of the Royal Assembly's first sitting in Oxford. Digby provided no further detail. He concluded by wishing the Beaumont household a happy and prosperous yuletide, and urged Laurence to prolong his visit at Chipping Campden for the full twelve days of Christmas. Not a word about Isabella; and the extension of leave meant to Laurence that Digby wanted him out of the way.

## X.

In her private office on the third storey of the house, Lady Beaumont was inspecting bills from the feast. She considered the event a success, even if smaller and less elegant than Elizabeth's; and there had been no instance of gross misbehaviour to provoke any quarrels, as had occurred between her sons last year. Admittedly, however, she found Sir Harold a boor, and Ingram's aunt an embarrassing relic of old King James' licentious days. The next wedding to celebrate would be between Laurence and Penelope. Mistress Savage had demonstrated more sense than Lady Beaumont had given the woman credit for, in terminating the affair; and while Laurence had looked woebegone upon his arrival home, he had cheered; and he had behaved courteously towards Penelope. If he was light and reticent in his comments about the girl, that was his nature. He had also pleased Lady Beaumont on a different score: when she had complained to him about the brash young man who was captivating Elizabeth at the banquet, he had shown the fellow out. She had agreed that Elizabeth might receive suitors again, but not until Laurence was married, and definitely not of that kind.

Hearing the clink of spurs on the stair, she called out, "Laurence, is that you?"

"No, madam." Thomas appeared at the door, and passed her a letter. "From the Spanish Envoy in London. He has a most fanciful seal."

"The Spanish Envoy?" She scarcely glanced at it, surveying him instead. "Thomas, remove your boots, or you will leave muddy tracks all over the house."

"I'm off to wash," he said, and withdrew.

Lady Beaumont slit the seal with her paper knife, a miniature Toledo sword that had belonged to her mother, and that she had treasured since girlhood. She did not know Don Alonso de Cárdenas, nor could she imagine why he would write to her.

As she read beyond the formal greeting, the lines of script danced malevolently before her eyes. "Your cousin, the renowned soldier Don Antonio de Zamora, is in London, staying at the embassy as my guest. He has expressed a wish to reacquaint himself with you and your noble family, and bring you news from your homeland. He said that you have been parted these past thirty-odd years . . ." Conquering dizziness, she read to the bottom of the letter, and then reread it, to make certain she was not dreaming. How could this be? She would have to write to the Envoy and somehow stop Antonio's invasion, but on what excuse? And why in God's name should he come to her now?

She rose and went to the lacquered cabinet that she had brought with her from Seville as a bride. With a key on the chain at her waist, she unlocked the door, and pressed a panel that released a secret drawer where she stored a little rosewood box. As she had countless times, she picked it out and took from inside the medallion of reddish gold: on one side was engraved a cross, and on the other a sickle moon. *Our bad blood seems destined to surface in each generation*, Antonio had warned her.

Quickly she replaced the medallion, and thrust the box into the drawer along with the Envoy's letter. She locked the cabinet again, and left her office. She could hear the gruff tones of Thomas and Adam in Thomas's chamber; and as she reached the head of the stair, she saw her husband smiling up at her from the floor below. "My dear, you are pale. You work too hard on your accounts. Come, and leave business to itself."

"I shall," she said. Yet as she put a foot forward, the stairs transformed into the narrowest flight of steps, and the descent grew vertiginous, as if she were on the peak of a mountain. Lord Beaumont's face had dwindled to a mere speck, though she caught the echo of his voice, crying out for help.

# CHAPTER SEVEN

Everyone in the household was perplexed that her ladyship should appear in robust health, and then in the space of hours faint and keep to her bed for three days, refusing to eat or speak. Neither Martha, mistress of the stillroom, nor Lord Beaumont's surgeon could identify her malady. "The wedding drained her," was Lord Beaumont's explanation, and he stayed at her side until she had the strength to rise. By the fifth day, she was herself again, ordering about the servants, snipping at her children, and scolding Lord Beaumont for neglecting his own health. "It was no more than a passing ague," she said, but her swift dismissal suggested otherwise to Laurence. He shared her impregnable constitution, which had borne him safely through his few childhood ailments, fluxes, chills, periods of starvation, a nearly mortal wound, and as close a brush with death from torture. She was hiding something, though he could not think what.

On purpose he rode back to Oxford a week earlier than the end of his holiday, hoping to catch Digby off guard, but his lordship's offices were shut. Seward was still in Asthall with Dr. Clarke, so Laurence left his horse in the College stables and walked over to Christ Church in search of news about the stunning development Digby had mentioned. An equerry told him that the King was at the house of Sir Arthur Aston, the city Governor, but that Prince Charles would be pleased to receive him in the royal chambers.

He heard barking as he knocked at the doors, and the Prince rushed out, accompanied by Prince Rupert's famous dog, Boy, wagging its tail. "Enter, sir," said the Prince. "Rupert is here, and Harry Jermyn."

Jermyn greeted Laurence as cordially, and Rupert's handsome, stern face lit up. "Mr. Beaumont, how good to see you again," he said, in his German-inflected English. "I have often asked your brother Thomas after you. And my cousin tells me you are teaching him how to design ciphers," he added, ruffling Prince Charles' hair.

"Yes, Your Highness," said Laurence. "It's been my pleasure."

He had not seen Rupert in a while, and had forgotten how imposing the young man was, and not only in his height of well over six foot tall. Trained almost from infancy to his military career, Rupert had witnessed his first action when he was thirteen, no older than Prince Charles. At just twenty-four, he had a spectacular record of victory in this war, and his sole superior in the Royalist army was the old veteran, Patrick Ruthven, Earl of Forth, His Majesty's Lord Marshal, whose gout and intemperance might soon prejudice his abilities in the field. No wonder Rupert was so envied by the men of Laurence's age, such as Wilmot and Digby. But Laurence felt sorry for him: like Prince Charles, he had not yet been affected by the plague of intrigue and mistrust, and perhaps had not realised the extent to which his blunt manner, as much as his many talents and his privileged position with the King, had created him enemies in the Council of War.

"My Lord Digby is to return tomorrow or the next day, Mr. Beaumont," Jermyn said. "He departed later than he'd wished for his family seat at Sherbourne, because his valet was taken ill."

Prince Charles struck a languid pose, and mimicked Digby's speech. "Poor Quayle was terribly afflicted with catarrh." Next he became solemn and dignified, and adopted the King's burr and stammer. "Our physician d-de Mayerne would advise a hot mustard p-plaster."

"Now, now, Your Highness," Jermyn reproved him, although all three men were trying not to laugh.

"It's one of de Mayerne's less revolting cures," said the Prince. "I can't remember what he once smeared on my chest, but it stank worse than a turd."

"Mr. Beaumont, will you drink a cup of hippocras, or do you prefer your wine without sugar and spice, as I do?" inquired Rupert, waving to a sideboard laden with flagons and cups and salvers of sweetmeats.

"As you do, thank you, Your Highness," said Laurence.

When Rupert had served him with charming informality, Charles led him to a table covered by a vast sheet of paper. "Look what Rupert made me for Christmas. Isn't it magnificent?"

The gift was a map of the kingdom drawn in beautiful detail, with a breadth of geographical knowledge far beyond Laurence's, and an artistry to which he could never aspire. There were forests, rivers, mountains, and hills; borders, county boundaries, cities, towns, fortifications, and roads; and around the islands, ships sailed, and fish and bare-breasted mermaids cavorted among the waves. Rupert had constructed little flags attached to wooden sticks no bigger than toothpicks, in orange for Parliament and gold, red, and blue for the Royalists, and had dispersed them about the map to indicate the current possessions of each side.

"It is amazing, Your Highness," Laurence said frankly, to Rupert.

"My father believes these won't be orange for long," Prince Charles said to Laurence, indicating the flags at Aylesbury and southeast at Windsor, where the King's Palace was depicted, and down the snaking Thames to London.

Rupert's eyes were on Aylesbury. "Might we talk, Mr. Beaumont?" he asked. They left Charles and Jermyn with the map, and went to sit by the fireplace. "Major Ogle is in Oxford," he said in a low voice. "I gather you assisted in his release."

"Not I, but a man I trained – Edward Price," Laurence said, relieved: this part of the mission had succeeded, although he still feared for Price's survival as a double agent.

"Not just Aylesbury has been promised to surrender to us, sir, but also Windsor."

Laurence drank off his wine, thinking of Digby's reference to a richer prize. "I didn't know about Windsor, Your Highness."

"Mr. Devenish has requested of Lord Bristol a royal warrant to raise two hundred men who will march into *that* garrison once I've occupied Aylesbury." Rupert frowned at him. "Lord Digby said you were concerned that we should so rely on Devenish and the commander at Aylesbury. He joked to me that your brother's name was more suited to you than yours, and called you a doubting Thomas."

Laurence chose to be as blunt as Rupert. "My doubts persist. And I don't understand how the keeper of a London gaol can promise you Windsor, too."

"Ah well, in my view, Aylesbury is prize enough. The rebels could be so shaken by its loss that other ill-provisioned garrisons might follow in declaring for the King. You must take heart, sir: from our reports, the rebels' power in London has shrunk over Christmastide, and their Parliament is poorly attended. The House of Commons is reduced to a third of its size, and the Lords to a mere score. My uncle is certain that both will be stripped of all legitimacy when his Assembly meets here in Oxford. By then, with God's grace, Aylesbury will be ours."

"When is it to be delivered?" asked Laurence, holding back more scepticism.

"If weather permits, my army will be at the gates on the twenty-first of January, the day before the Assembly opens." Rupert rose as did Laurence, who was the shorter by two or three inches; a change for him. "I'll bear your doubts in mind, however, Mr. Beaumont."

Prince Charles and Jermyn were still poring over the map. "I recognise some of the mermaids," the Prince exclaimed. "*She's* the Duchess of Richmond." Laurence noticed Rupert flush; according to Wilmot he had fallen in love with her, though the Duke was his close friend. "And I'd wager Mr. Beaumont can tell us who her companion is. Pray you examine her, sir."

"Might she be the Duchess's sister-in-law, my Lady d'Aubigny?"

The Prince winked at Jermyn. "To your expert eye, Mr. Beaumont, are her proportions accurately represented?"

"Her face is very like," Laurence said judiciously; her breasts were larger in life, as he recollected.

"Rupert should have included Mistress Savage among them – she'd be perfect for a mermaid," the Prince said. Then he too flushed.

"Down, Boy," snapped Rupert, all of a sudden. The dog had its front paws on the sideboard and its nose in the sweetmeats.

Prince Charles ran to tug at its collar. "Stop, Boy, or you'll be sick again. Rupert, he won't listen to me."

While the princes were busy chastising Boy, Jermyn turned to Laurence. "Mr. Beaumont, my Lord Digby asked me to tell you, in the event that you got to Oxford before him: Mistress Savage was married in London last month to Sir Montague Hallam, and is living at his house in the Strand. He's a respected member of the Vintners' Company whom the King knighted for his services to the City. He has already pledged his fealty to the royal cause, in secret, through Digby's agent, Violet."

Laurence could not speak for a moment. "Is he a . . . friend of Lord Digby's?" he managed, at length.

"No, of Bristol's. Digby knew it would be a blow to you, sir," Jermyn continued, his face sympathetic. "But at least Mistress Savage will be in an excellent position to aid His Majesty in the capital."

The wine surged up nauseously into Laurence's throat, and he swallowed with an effort. "Then . . . is she now also an agent of Digby's?"

Jermyn looked bewildered. "She always has been, sir, has she not?"

## II.

"Ned," hissed Sue, nudging Price beneath the bedclothes, "who were you dreaming of? Who's Elizabeth, Ned? You were saying the name over and over."

"For Christ's sake, Sue, I'm barely awake yet and all I hear from you is who, where, what, Ned this, Ned that. Elizabeth was my mother's name, if you must know."

He swung his legs out of bed, sat up, and reached for the chamber pot. His immediate thought was that money went faster than he could piss. He was deep in debt to Robin Nunn, driven back to his old lodgings near Fish Street, and Sue had followed with infuriating tenacity. Veech had offered no advance upon hiring him, and he had seen neither Veech nor Draycott since that mid-December day. But at last he had received a message to meet them again this morning in the Saracen's Head, and he was determined to squeeze some coin out of Veech, though he would need his wits to earn it.

"Will you call on the vicar, Ned?" she asked, as he began to dress. He did not reply, his mind on Veech. "Ned? Three weeks you're home from Oxford, and I'm tired of your delays."

"I told you," he said, finally, dragging on his boots, "Mr. Beaumont was in Gloucestershire for Christmastide, and I didn't get paid. We'll have to wait until I have money."

"Well *I* can't wait. Ned, I am with child."

He turned and stared at her. "Oh Sue, are you truly?" She nodded, her mouth wobbling. *You're not bound to have it*, he nearly said. Then he thought of Jane in her grave, and felt remorse. "I'll write to Mr. Beaumont and ask him to dispatch what he owes me. And after that, I'll talk to the vicar."

"Aren't you happy, Ned?"

"Of course I am." He bent to kiss her on the forehead. "Everything will be fine, don't you worry." As he was throwing on his cloak, it occurred to him that he did not care for her to witness his meeting with Veech and Draycott: she would want to know who they were. "You sleep a bit longer, my sweetheart. Let me call at the Saracen's Head and tell Nunn your supper upset your stomach and you'll come by in the afternoon when you feel better."

Outside in the freezing dawn, Price swore some of his most indecent oaths: a future with Sue and a mewling babe scared him worse than jumping off London Bridge. He had not strived so hard and climbed so high to have his chances wrecked. Elizabeth was his destiny, and he deserved no less.

He walked northwest towards Ludgate, still pondering what to tell Veech. A crowd of unusual size had gathered at the end of Canning Street where the pamphleteers hawked their wares. "Hear ye, hear ye," bellowed one of the sellers. "A devious papist plot has been discovered in our city, hatched by Jesuitical snakes. All is to be revealed in Parliament."

Price stopped to buy a pamphlet, and as he read, his heart began to somersault in his chest. "Violet," he whispered. "I must warn Violet." He ran to Cheapside and the narrow close near St. Mary le Bow where Violet kept shop; the goldsmith had dutifully paid his taxes and was living above the premises, thus far unbothered by the authorities. Today, militiamen swarmed at Violet's door. Another fascinated crowd filled the street, and people were craning from upstairs casements. "Open, on order of Parliament," an officer yelled. The men pounded on the door with wooden staves, and eventually it splintered on its hinges. They barged inside, and Price watched haplessly as Violet was hauled forth. A hush fell among the spectators as the officer read out the charge: "Thomas Violet, you are under arrest for seditious practices, and conspiring with known Jesuits and papists to sow division between Parliament and the worthy aldermen of the City of London. I am hereby authorized to convey you to the Tower, where you will await examination by both Houses."

"I am innocent of all these crimes," protested Violet.

Soldiers wrestled him away, and as the crowd's murmurs swelled to a hubbub, Price elbowed a path out, and hurried trembling and sweating towards the main thoroughfare of Cheapside. What if Violet broke under examination and gave his name? Calm, calm, he told himself, or Veech would be onto him quicker than a fox upon a rabbit.

Veech and Draycott had occupied a corner table in the taproom. Veech was lavishly seasoning his breakfast of fried collops and eggs; Draycott had only a mug of ale in front of him. Veech nodded at Price, while Draycott's nervous eyes shifted from one to the other.

"Good day to you, gentlemen," said Price, and slid onto the bench next to Draycott. He had been hungry earlier, but as Veech stabbed an egg yolk with the point of his knife and yellow liquid oozed out like blood from a wound, his appetite deserted him. "What's all the to-do in the streets?" he inquired, pretending mild concern.

"People are rioting to show their disgust, because the King has tried to stir up more trouble within the City," Draycott replied. "It wasn't to be an armed revolt, this time – instead, he attempted to woo the Lord Mayor and Members of the City Corporation. He invited them to his version of a parliament that he's to call in Oxford later this month, where they would swear an oath declaring illegitimate our Parliament at Westminster. His letter to the Lord Mayor is to be published, as will other evidence of the conspiracy. Those most involved are Catholics."

"Praise God it's been thwarted," said Price.

Veech licked a smear of yolk from his lips, his attitude reflective. "I forgot to ask you, Mr. Price: what brought you to Winchester House on the day you encountered Mr. Draycott there?"

"I'd been to visit a prisoner, a cousin of mine," answered Price, wary at the change of subject.

"Hmm . . . Do you know the keeper, Mr. Devenish?"

"We've a slight acquaintance, sir."

"I have strong reason to believe he's a closet Royalist."

Price let himself appear astonished, rather than appalled, as he was: how could Veech have found out about Devenish's true sympathies? "Had he a role in the plot?"

"Oh, I doubt *that*. Intelligence suggests he may be mixed up in a quite different intrigue of the King's. I'm laying a trap for him, but I won't spring it just yet. So if you go visiting your cousin there, you be careful to give nothing away to Devenish."

"I shall, Mr. Veech."

Veech sat back and folded his arms across his chest. "So, what information have you for us about Mr. Beaumont?"

Price resorted to Beaumont's advice: combine lies with the truth. "As promised, I went to Oxford – to Lord Digby's offices. I claimed to be a friend of Mr. Beaumont's from London."

"Very bold of you," said Veech, in a tone neither complimentary nor critical.

"I'd made sure beforehand that his lordship was out of town for the holiday, as was Mr. Beaumont. A servant of Lord Digby's by the name of Quayle fell to talking with me. He hinted that I might soon see Mr. Beaumont in London again," Price lied.

Veech glanced at Draycott, who was looking down fixedly at the remains of Veech's breakfast, and then said to Price, "I'd like you to return to Oxford. I must know when Beaumont might be travelling here."

"I'll need funds, sir."

Veech dipped a hand into his coat pocket. As he pulled it out, his sleeve rolled up a few inches. Price could not tear away his eyes: Veech's forearm was even whiter than his hand and almost naked of hair, like a woman's, in bizarre contrast to his weather-beaten face and thick brows. With a quick, instinctive gesture, Veech straightened his sleeve. "This should do you," he said, counting out a pile of crowns.

"Thank you, Mr. Veech," said Price, shovelling them into his own pocket. As always, the possession of money miraculously restored his self-confidence. He would tell Sue he was going to Oxford to collect his wages from Beaumont; and in Oxford, he would tell Beaumont of Violet's arrest and Veech's suspicions about Mr. Devenish. It was too late to help Violet, but Beaumont had taught him the art of concealing messages. He would send Sue round to Winchester House with a gift of a pie for Mr. Devenish.

## III.

"What else could you expect, Beaumont," Wilmot had said, of Isabella's marriage. "She's Digby's puppet and dances to his tune. But why should *you*? He's fucking you in the arse and he won't stop unless you challenge him."

"Not to a duel," Laurence had said. "My paltry skills are no match for his."

"True enough, they aren't. So use your brains. Think of a way to quit his service for mine."

As before, Wilmot tried to console Laurence by plying him with liquor and introductions to other women. He found himself strangely uninterested in the women, and in the case of liquor, he began to worry about the increasingly slanderous statements that flew from Wilmot's mouth while they drank together at his quarters. "You ought to be more discreet," he warned his friend, but Wilmot would not listen.

Every morning Laurence rode from Abingdon into Oxford, to call again at Digby's offices, and at Merton for Seward. At last, on the ninth of January, he saw lights in his lordship's windows, and Quayle answered to him, glum-faced. "His lordship has bad news, sir."

Digby greeted Laurence by thrusting a newssheet at him. He had not finished reading when his lordship burst out, "*You* are responsible for Violet's arrest. If you had followed my orders in October, instead of making yourself so conspicuous to Parliament, he would not have been left stranded, forced to work alone in his addresses to the City Councillors."

"My lord," said Laurence, annoyed by this revision of the facts, "I told you Violet was in danger of arrest. And your orders to us in October were to investigate that list of Radcliff's, and Albright's fate. You didn't tell me about His Majesty's *addresses* until some time after I returned to Oxford. And if I might remind you, I never approved of them."

"We can only pray Violet is not tortured by that cruel spymaster, and that Mr. Price has eluded capture," Digby ranted on, as though he would hold Laurence to blame for all this, also.

"Violet may be sharp enough to hold his tongue, but I'd have to concur about Price: if he's arrested, he'll talk about his visit to Winchester House, and the whole point of Major Ogle's felicitous escape to Oxford will come out in Parliament."

"Might *I* remind *you* that you agreed to send him to Mr. Devenish."

"Yes, and it was a mistake. But you would have sent him, anyway, over my objections."

They glared at each other across Digby's desk. Then Digby said, in a malevolent voice, "I believe you and Lord Wilmot are jealous of the prestige that will accrue to my father, to me, *and* to Prince Rupert, when Aylesbury and Windsor are handed to the King."

"I don't give a damn about prestige, nor do I see why you should accuse Lord Wilmot of such pettiness."

"Oh no? In your moments of drunken fellowship with him, has he not confided in you how much he loathes me, and resents my trusted status with the King? How he yearns to discredit that *unlicked cub*, Prince Rupert, his main rival in our Council of War?"

Laurence felt a tightening in his stomach. "I must have been too inebriated to recollect, my lord."

"He is a sot, an ambitious wretch who would sell his own mother to enhance his reputation," shouted Digby, and slammed his hands on the desk.

"He's an officer of great courage and talent who is loved by his men."

Digby's cheeks coloured an apoplectic red. "Why do *you* love him?"

"Love is not the term I would choose."

"Why do you *respect* him, if you prefer."

"My lord, I respect anyone who can drink me under the table."

Digby's expression altered with unnerving speed, and he started to laugh. "I do enjoy your sense of humour, sir. Oh, by the bye, I have decided to terminate my lease of that house off the Woodstock Road, as it seems you are not living in it."

"I didn't consider it mine but Isabella's. I haven't spent a night there since we parted."

"Do you still have your key?"

Laurence hunted in his pocket and placed the key on Digby's desk. "Will that be all, my lord?"

Digby picked it up and examined it thoughtfully. "Why have you not asked me about her? Do you not want to hear about the work she is undertaking for the King?"

"No, my lord, to be honest I don't."

"Nonetheless," said Digby, "I must insist on telling you."

———

"Thank Christ you were home, Seward, or I might have stormed back to his offices and punched him in the jaw. So, talk to me," Laurence begged, as he stretched out his legs to the hearth. "I want your opinion: has he gone completely mad?"

Seward filled his pipe and lit it with a spill from the fire. "He definitely put Mistress Savage at risk when he gave her those bags of sulphur and saltpetre to smuggle into London."

"A minimal risk compared to the quantities that he plans to ship in next, in her husband's wine barrels, to await a Royalist march on London. He's dreaming if he believes they'll be spared from search because of Sir Montague's friendly relations with Parliament."

"He did tell you that Sir Montague has continued to sell wines to whoever will buy them, and has not changed his practice of exporting full barrels to Oxford and receiving them again empty. It is possible they might avoid detection."

"After the exposure of this late plot, all cargo from Royalist territory will be inspected with a fine-toothed comb. And if it's not discovered by Parliament, the powder may well spoil long before the King can attempt to retake the capital. Digby told me everything on purpose. He knew I'd be alarmed. Wilmot's right about him: he *is* fucking me in the arse."

"Or rather, he would like to but he can't," said Seward, with his crusty chuckle. "He is envious of your friendship with Wilmot and your passion for her."

"I suppose you mean that if not for her dubious paternity and the horrible episode in her youth, he might have married her," Laurence said, although he could not picture Isabella and Digby as husband and wife.

Seward laughed so hard that he choked out a cloud of smoke. "My eyesight may be dim, but sometimes you are as blind as a bat. He does not love her in that way. He is in love with *you*."

Laurence blinked at Seward. "Are you suggesting that he shares your proclivities? He's a contented married man, with children."

"Pah, what does that signify. He loves you and he is testing you: as to whether you will remain obediently in Oxford, or venture upon a suicidal errand."

"To fetch her out before the barrels arrive?" Seward nodded, puffing on his pipe. "If he's so enamoured of me, why send me to my death?"

"Where *his* passion in concerned, he is like a selfish child: if he cannot have what he desires, he cannot bear for anyone else to have it. He would rather see it destroyed. It takes a man such as I am to recognise these feelings. Sorry to shock you, Beaumont," Seward added.

Laurence patted him on the knee. "I've never been shocked by you, Seward, even when I was a boy of fifteen and you gave me that first sultry appraisal in my father's library. I am a bit surprised at Digby, however."

Seward regarded him more gravely. "Then do not go to London. I can tell by the look on your face that you are considering it."

"I've already decided to go."

"My dear boy, you suspect Lord Digby of madness, but *that* would be sheer insanity."

"My insanity once saved your life."

"So it did," Seward acknowledged.

"Now," said Laurence, "I may be about to dice with *mine*, but not with my Arab stallion or my French flintlocks. I'm leaving them here. Should something happen to me, Ingram can have them, as a belated wedding gift."

## IV.

"They sound like hounds baying for blood," Antonio said to Don Alonso; they were peering down at the rioters in the street below the Envoy's window.

"They will judge every Catholic in London a traitor, and every foreigner a priest or a spy, if not both," Don Alonso murmured, as a clump of hardened dung smacked against the windowpane.

"The army should disperse them."

"Oh no, sir: they are enjoying one of the few entertainments not proscribed by the authorities. We should step back. They often aim more dangerous projectiles at my house, though they will tire by the hour of curfew." Antonio went and threw himself into an armchair; he was equally tired of the Envoy, and the Envoy's house. "It is a pity for you that the plot should be blown open now," Don Alonso said next.

"Please explain," said Antonio.

"A friend of mine in the House of Lords told me that a Lord James Beaumont sat in the House during the King's Parliaments, prior to the war. He and his wife, Lady Elena, have two sons and two daughters. Their estate lies in Gloucestershire, some thirty or forty miles from Oxford." The Envoy hesitated, eyeing Antonio. "Around the middle of December, I addressed a letter to her ladyship on your behalf. I have had no reply."

"You knew since the middle of . . ." Antonio battled rage. "Your letter may have been lost. This time, I shall write to her myself."

"I cannot permit you. If I worried earlier that correspondence dispatched from my house would be intercepted by Parliament's spies, it is now a certainty. And the name Beaumont will attract immediate suspicion. Lady Elena's eldest son is Lord Digby's chief agent, and a wanted man in London. So you are a captive here, Don Antonio, unless you wish to face the baying hounds," Don Alonso said, looking as gloomy at the prospect as Antonio felt.

The hounds did slink off at curfew, and he and Antonio ate their supper undisturbed. When a messenger came with a diplomatic packet, Don Alonso bade Antonio goodnight and disappeared to work in his chamber. Antonio retired to his, to digest the revelation: this eldest son, the gypsy's lover, the reprobate, the deserter, the coward, was also a spy.

Diego was as yet unaware of Juana's existence on God's earth, so Antonio simply repeated to him what the Envoy had said. "Don Alonso was miserly with the facts, Diego. We have been at his house for a month, and he probably knew from the day we arrived where Lord James has his estate. That dishonesty cancels my debt of gratitude – and my promises. I will not stay another night. We shall head to Oxford."

"*Qué locura*," exclaimed Diego. "We'll be captured by the militia before we ever get out of London. I implore you, Don Antonio, have some sense."

"Oh shut up, you craven fool, and pack our bags."

"How will we find Oxford? We have no map."

"We'll ask directions, in our marvellous English. You've spent enough time chattering with the servants. What's our best way to escape from the house?"

"You may escape and go to your death," said Diego stubbornly, "but I'm staying."

Antonio hauled him up with both hands around his neck, and started to squeeze. Diego flushed beet-red, gulping for breath. "Either you come, Diego," Antonio said, "or I leave behind your strangled corpse. I ask you once more: how do we escape?" He relaxed his grip a little.

"By . . . by two or three of the clock, all his servants will be abed," Diego stammered. "The easiest way is through the kitchens, but the servants' quarters are in the same wing. The slightest noise and we shall be undone."

"Have faith in God, and in my Toledo blade, which I will put through your guts if you betray me."

At the appointed hour they stole out, carrying their boots. Diego went in front, loaded down with their baggage, and with Antonio clinging to the hood of his cloak. They tiptoed past the Envoy's reception room into the servants' domain; there was no noise, save for the scuttling of mice, and the kitchen flagstones were icy beneath Antonio's stockinged feet. He felt exhilarated to be in charge again, and worthy of the name he had acquired in battle: *El Valoroso*.

Diego whispered, "We're at the door."

Quietly they put on their boots, then Diego shot back the bolt with a hideous grating squeal.

"Open and run," hissed Antonio, and they tumbled out into the back lane and sprinted away like a pair of thieves.

The streets seemed to belong to a city abandoned. Moon and stars were obscured by cloud, and a wet snow drifted down. Antonio could not tell north from south, or east from west; and Diego was staggering and panting from the weight of their bags.

"We'll stop a moment," said Antonio, and they sheltered in a doorway. "We can't be far from the river."

"Houses and more houses, Don Antonio, and not a soul abroad," Diego moaned. "I should have let you strangle me."

"Hush." A rider was approaching. As the clip clop of hooves grew louder, Antonio unsheathed his sword. "When I step out, seize the horse's bridle."

The man was alone, trotting his mount steadily in their direction. Antonio saw the dull glimmer of a breastplate on his chest. Leaping from the shadows, Antonio slashed deep into the flesh of his thigh, and next into his sword arm. The man screeched and put spurs to his horse, but Diego had a firm grip on the bridle. Unable to go forward, the horse reared, and when it plunged back onto all fours, the man lost his balance. Antonio grappled for his wounded arm and leg, and dragged him to the ground. He wore no helmet, and Antonio heard the crack of bone as his head hit the cobblestones, where he lay splayed and immobile.

"Hurry," urged Diego; he had soothed the agitated beast, and was slinging their bags over its saddle. Antonio was about to drive the point of his sword into the man's exposed neck. "Don Antonio, we must fly."

Antonio sheathed his weapon and sprang into the saddle. He pulled Diego up behind him, and they set off at a gallop, the wind tearing at their cloaks. The moon had begun to glide from amid a dense mass of cloud, and ahead, Antonio saw rippling water. The

Thames, he thought jubilantly. "God is with us," he shouted back to Diego.

**V.**

Laurence had bought a brace of pistols to replace his flintlocks, and a sturdy, thick-pelted nag that would carry him about fifteen miles a day. The armies were still regrouping after Christmastide, and as he had expected, few travellers had braved the appalling cold. On the fourth morning of his journey, he set the nag loose near the village of Acton; a gift horse for whoever might pass by. He continued east on foot. By the edge of Shepherd's Bush Green, a regular stop for agricultural traffic into the City, a carter had left his wagon full of hay unattended outside an alehouse. Laurence wriggled in among the tightly packed bales, grateful for the warmth and shelter. At the fortifications near Tyburn Road, the carter drew up his wagon to exchange pleasantries with the guards; he was on his way to Smithfield Market, and they let him through unsearched. As he paused again at St. Giles in the Fields to breathe the oxen, Laurence extricated himself from the hay and jumped off the cart. He drew the hood of his cloak over his face, slung his saddlebag over his shoulder, and walked south along St. Martin's Lane to the Strand, swerving left at Long Acre Street to avoid the busy Covent Garden Piazza, and then down Bow Street.

Everywhere was evidence of the anti-papist riots: a litter of debris on the ground, broken windows, burnt-out shops, and parties of militia, one of them blocking Laurence's route to the Strand. He sneaked into the small laneways, and emerged at Temple Bar, near the top of the Strand; soldiers and armed servants in livery were on guard in the street, to protect the mansions of the rich from looters. When he inquired of a lady and her maid where he might find Sir Montague Hallam's house, they pointed to a brick edifice and hurried away as if he had the plague. Since he could not stroll up the steps to the house and bang at the door, he moved on, lightheaded from hunger and fatigue, towards Fleet Street, and on to Ludgate Hill.

At one side of the street was a baker's shop, and opposite, a tavern. Recklessly he chose the tavern. But at the threshold, he halted: why was the name familiar to him? Then he remembered.

The taproom was full of custom. He pushed through until he found a serving girl, and grabbed her sleeve. "Is Mistress Sprye here today?"

She shook him off with an indignant air. "Who are you to ask?"

"I'm Ned Price's brother – tell Sue I've brought the money I owe her," he said, imitating Price's accent. "Go on, then. I haven't got all day."

While waiting, he picked up a crumpled pamphlet from the floor. The papist conspiracy was now called Brooke's plot, he read, after Sir Basil Brooke, one of the Catholics who had secretly approached the Lord Mayor and Members of the City Corporation. These officials had informed Parliament directly of His Majesty's overtures. And this past Thursday, the eleventh of January, the author of the pamphlet declared in bombastic style, City Councillors, both Houses of Parliament, Scottish Commissioners, Independent divines, army commanders, and even a few Dutch ambassadors had dined together at the Merchants' Hall in a public show of thanksgiving and unity, as citizens had built a bonfire in Cheapside to burn idolatrous trinkets and images, and rejoice at their delivery from evil. Out of the long list of dignitaries who had participated at the thanksgiving feast, two names caught Laurence's eye: that of his old enemy, the Earl of Pembroke, and that of Sir Montague Hallam of the Vintners' Company.

He felt a tap on his shoulder, and looked round.

"I am Mistress Sprye, and who are you, sir?" She confronted him, hands on her hips. "You ain't any kin of Ned's, that I'd swear."

"No, but I *am* bringing you money. Where is he?"

"He's gone out of town. Who *are* you? You're not . . . you can't be . . . *Mr. Beaumont?*" she mouthed. Laurence nodded shortly. "He went to Oxford, sir, to see *you*."

Laurence swore. "When?"

"Five days ago."

"Did he have news for me?"

"If he did, he didn't tell *me*. Sir," she said, glancing around, "we can't talk here. I'll get my cloak, and then you follow me out."

She returned in seconds, and left the taproom at a brisk pace. Laurence pursued her, as she wove her way from the main thoroughfare of Ludgate into smaller streets, and then into alley upon alley, parallel to the river. He smelt rotten fish in the air, and the buildings around grew more and more wretched and dilapidated. Finally she slowed and crossed a muddy yard where a pack of children armed with sticks were beating a ragged youth twice their size. "Kill the priest! Kill the priest!" they shrieked. He was struggling to fend them off, saliva trailing down his chin; and in his face, Laurence saw a pathetic innocence.

"You little bastards, leave him alone," yelled Laurence, brandishing a pistol, at which they dropped their sticks and fled. The youth watched them incuriously, and proceeded to wet himself, with no apparent sign of awareness.

"Mr. Beaumont!" Mistress Sprye signalled Laurence over to a passage in a decayed tenement, and pushed open a door. "Our lodgings, sir," she said, visibly ashamed; at once stuffy and cold, the room was about the size of the bed that occupied it.

Laurence sat down on the bed. Something clunked against his foot: a bottle of wine. "May I?" He unplugged it and drank. "So Price and I just missed each other."

"Yes, sir." She sat down also, leaving a careful space between herself and Laurence, and wrinkled her brow at him. "Ned described you as very black, sir, but I thought you would be older, and . . . and much grander."

"I'm sorry to disappoint you," Laurence said, laughing.

"Oh, sir, what will he do when he doesn't find you? I hope he hurries home. We're to be wed." She blushed. "We've a child coming."

"My congratulations. He must be pleased," Laurence remarked, disingenuously.

"He wasn't when I told him. To be honest, sir, I'm not as sure of his affections as I'd like to be. Oh forgive me, sir – here you are, an important nobleman, and I'm blabbing out my woes to you. I wouldn't, if you hadn't shown the kindness to chase those brats away from that poor simple boy. They'll be the death of him one day."

She started to cry. For both herself and her unborn child, Laurence suspected, annoyed with Price, though his own past in that regard was far from irreproachable. He took a purse out of his saddle-bag and pressed it into her hands. "You should find better lodgings, or this place will be the death of *you*."

"Thank you, sir." She sniffed, and tucked it into her skirt pocket. "There's something you should know. That day I told Ned about the babe, he left in the morning, and got home later excited, as if he had a fever. He'd money from a man who owed him, and he asked me to buy him a handsome meat pie. So I did, sir. But when I came back from the Saracen's Head round curfew, Ned hadn't touched a crumb. Turns out he'd bought it for a friend. And he asked me to take it over, sir, the next day."

"Where to?"

"Winchester House. It was for the keeper, a Mr. Devenish."

"Oh," said Laurence, as if this meant nothing to him. "Was Mr. Devenish grateful?"

"No, sir, he didn't say a thing to me. Ned hung about a whole day – he couldn't sit still. He said he was expecting a message of thanks. When none arrived, he set off for Oxford. Sir," she went on, after a brief silence, "you don't look much like most people, and the militia will be watching for strangers. You could stay here, sir, if you have to. Though it's not fit for a man such as yourself, at least you'd be safe."

A convenient refuge, Laurence thought; he had hidden in far worse. But it would be unfair on Sue. Although she did not know it, she had already dipped a toe into the shark-infested waters of espionage. "I can't. Thank you, all the same," he said. "I must leave you now."

"Where will you go, sir?"

How many times Laurence had been posed that question, and had no real answer. Yet the pamphlet was giving him an idea so outrageous that the more he considered it, the more attractive it became.

The equerry escorted Laurence through a hall hung with pictures as impressive as those in Lord Beaumont's collection, and into a carpeted reception room. In a robe trimmed with ermine, the Earl of Pembroke sat in an armchair, his walking cane beside him. As in Laurence's dream, he resembled an ancient bird of prey, with his wrinkled, desiccated face and prominent nose; the thin fringe on his forehead could not disguise incipient baldness. Was it guilt that had eaten away at him, Laurence wondered, or life in the constant dread of being unmasked as a would-be regicide?

Quivering at the sight of Laurence, he dismissed the equerry. "God's blood," he exploded, "what in hell are you doing here?"

Laurence bowed politely to him. "You've changed quarters, my lord. I had to ask for your whereabouts at your other house, which brought back such memories to me, of the night I called there on you and Radcliff – the night of his death, and nearly of mine."

Pembroke leant back in his chair, and recovered a trace of his hauteur. "These are more modest apartments than any of my houses, but at least now I am in the heart of Whitehall."

"The Cockpit," said Laurence. "I'm surprised it should retain its old name, when the sport is forbidden by Parliament."

Pembroke did not smile. "I have been faithful to my bargain with His Majesty, and have kept my nose clean of intrigue. What does he want of me next?"

"It is I who want something of you."

Pembroke studied him incredulously. "Why were you not arrested by the militia? The City is crawling with them after His Majesty's recent plot and the murder of that officer last night."

"Murder, my lord?"

"A captain of the Trained Bands was found mortally wounded in the street near Westminster Abbey. With his final breath, he described his attacker as a tall, dark man who muttered words in Spanish to his accomplice in crime. Whoever they are, the militia are searching for them. And the description fits you rather well."

A trickle of sweat coursed down Laurence's spine. "I hadn't even heard about it. And nor had I anything to do with the King's designs upon the City Corporation. That was all an error, in my view."

"An *error*? I should hand you over to Parliament."

"You could, but His Majesty still possesses those incriminating letters of yours. He's been faithful to his side of the bargain, in hiding your treachery from the world. I am asking you to hide *me* for a bit."

Pembroke scowled. "Thank heaven I can trust my servants or your neck would be in a rope, and I would be ruined."

"My lord, I believe you were at a banquet on Thursday, at the Merchant Tailors' Hall. Are you acquainted with Sir Montague Hallam of the Vintners' Company, who also attended?"

"He has supplied my cellar for these twenty years."

"I would like one of your servants to deliver a message to his wife."

"Would you, indeed. What does it concern?"

"A private matter between the two of us."

"It's said she is a woman of extraordinary allure," Pembroke observed, with a seamy interest that amused Laurence.

"She is. She and I were . . . close, before her marriage."

"So she was your mistress. Was it for her that you came to London?"

"Yes, my lord."

"I did tell you once that you had balls." At last Pembroke smiled. "I was about to sup. Would you join me?"

"Gladly, my lord," Laurence said. "I'm famished."

The next day, Pembroke announced that he must go to his sitting in the Lords. "It is best for me to observe my normal routine, though most of the benches are vacant these days, and I shall have to listen to some interminable debate about the tax on coal. Write your message, and I'll have it dispatched in the afternoon."

Laurence composed a note in crabbed handwriting to Lady Hallam from a Dr. Niger, saying that the powders she had brought with her to London were extremely bad for her general health, and whoever had prescribed them was ignorant of their longer term effects. She would be in danger of her life if she took them in a dose with any other substance, and on no account must she send for more. He added that she should not trust any other apothecaries in town, because most of them were charlatans. He begged for her word that she would do as he advised, and he would write again to prescribe an effective remedy for her complaint.

Pembroke demanded to read the note. Laurence feigned embarrassment and prevaricated, but eventually surrendered it. "What manner of complaint has she, Mr. Beaumont?"

"One that she contracted from me."

"I doubt Sir Montague will catch it off her," Pembroke said, with a braying laugh. "He told me himself that he has not had a prick stand in years."

Over the course of two more days Laurence waited in agonized suspense for Isabella's reply, as he imagined Price must have waited for that of Mr. Devenish. Then towards evening, a cask of wine arrived from Sir Montague. At the bottom of the cask was a corked vial, and inside it a slip of paper. "'*Iacta alea est*,'" Pembroke read aloud to Laurence. "The die is cast. What does she mean by that?"

"She has taken the powders."

"'And please desist from offering me your advice. Look to your own future health, instead.' Dear me, sir, she will not forgive you for infecting her! I presume that you will soon be on your way, though before you go," Pembroke said, in a solemn voice, "I want to propose a new bargain: a favour of you, in exchange for information I gleaned today at Westminster. I shall have to confirm it, but if it is true, it will be of vital import to His Majesty."

"Please, continue, my lord," said Laurence, almost too heartsick to listen.

"I want you to plead my case with the King. Tell him that I repent. I cannot ask him to destroy those letters, yet a measure of *his* forgiveness would be a huge relief to me. We were friends, he and I, and if he would think less ill of me, I would leave the world comforted."

Laurence felt moved, despite all he knew about Pembroke: there were tears in those grey vulture's eyes. "And what have you for him, in return?"

"Tidings of another conspiracy against him," said Pembroke, "or, to be precise, against his nephew, Prince Rupert."

"By God," breathed Laurence, after Pembroke had explained. "I only pray I can report to Oxford in time."

## VI.

Laurence sprinkled sand upon the wet ink, and showed Pembroke the safe conduct he had forged, with the Earl's assistance. "How does it appear to you?"

"Quite well done, though if it doesn't convince the militia, I won't lift a finger to save you. And should it come out that you were here, I'll say you forced me at gunpoint to hide you."

"I'll corroborate your story, my lord."

Pembroke regarded him mournfully as he stuffed the paper into his doublet. "I have to confess that I appreciated your company, sir. I am without friends or family. I lost my eldest son to fever before he could cement our fortunes through marriage, my daughter's husband was slain at Newbury fighting for the King, and I am estranged from my wife, and from my finest treasures, which she keeps squirrelled away at my old family seat. I have nothing much to live for, and I foresee no benefit from this war. I fear that it will prove my undoing, that of my line, and that of England, too." Pembroke cleared his throat. "Will you require a horse tonight?"

"Yes, thank you. My lord, I am pleased that we're no longer enemies."

"Then work your magic upon the King, as you have worked it upon me, and persuade him of my contrition." Pembroke gave Laurence a sudden, sly look. "Do you ever ask yourself what might have happened, had my scheme succeeded?"

"I do. In fact, I had a bad dream about it."

"One last thing," said Pembroke. "If you think you had me fooled that you risked your neck to come here and warn your mistress off some quack medicine, you are mistaken. But I don't want the truth. The less I know, the sounder *I* sleep."

"This safe conduct has not been properly authorised by Parliament," barked the lone sentry at Tothill Fields. "I must search you, and afterwards you may ride to Derby House and apply to the Committee of Safety."

"You've no right to a search if you're not about to let me pass," Laurence said, as rudely.

The man grabbed his horse's bridle. "We're on orders, sir. Dismount."

It was the dead of the night, and beyond the torches at the fortification gates, Laurence could see no more than a yard ahead through the relentless snow. Thanks to Pembroke's expert taste in horseflesh, he was mounted on an animal bred for the chase. If he could burst forward and gather up speed, he could jump the gates, and he calculated that even a skilled marksman would have no clean shot at him once he was over. He slipped his knife from his doublet, swung one leg out of the stirrup and across the saddle as if to obey the sentry's order, and with a silent apology to both Pembroke and the horse, jabbed the blade into its skin, below the withers. It screamed, and the sentry had to let go and dodge or be trampled as it charged off, with Laurence clinging on sideways.

He managed to regain his seat and prepare for the jump, flattened against its neck. As it landed, he dared a glance behind him:

nothing but a white wall of snow. He heard the crack of pistol fire, and a ball whizzed by, and another; more sentries on the walls above were shooting at him. He was nearly clear of their range. Then a flash blasted towards him from an odd, oblique angle, and he felt as though a scalding fist had smacked into the muscle at the back of his right shoulder. Numbness spread instantly along his arm and his hand went limp. He dug his knees in hard as the frightened beast careered on, panting and snorting. They vaulted hedges and crashed through bushes and orchards, and forded a shallow stream; but on the far bank, after a while, they plunged into open countryside.

Laurence reined in. He took off his cloak to swab the beast's wound, superficial compared to his own. Clumsily, with his knife, he cut a strip of fabric that he rolled up and packed beneath his doublet over the hole in his flesh. With a second strip of cloak, he made a sling for his right arm; the cold would stem the bleeding that had spread stickily down his sleeve. He knew he might have an hour or so before the shock wore off and his strength would ebb. He threw the remains of his cloak about his shoulders and spurred on the horse, hoping it could take him some distance before it tired.

He tired first and slumped in the saddle, his face buried in the animal's mane, gritting his teeth at every jog and bounce as its pace reduced to a trot, and then a walk. He seemed to see ghastly images: of Isabella in a dank prison cell, and of a man in a long coat towering over her; of Prince Rupert, defiant yet resigned, surrounded by enemy troops; and of Tom's despairing face shattered by a hail of fire.

When Laurence next squinted up, an orange trail glowed among the clouds to the east: dawn was breaking. The bleak, snowy fields around him provided no clue as to where he was, and though he felt utterly frozen, his shoulder and back throbbed acutely and blood had soaked through his makeshift sling. The desire to sleep overwhelmed him, and he dropped the reins. Then he heard Seward's voice in his ear. "If you do not keep going, you will die." Too stupefied to understand how this could be, he nudged the horse to a trot. "A little further, my boy, a little further," Seward was saying. As the horse ambled on, Laurence's lids drifted shut; and he saw no more images, only darkness.

# CHAPTER EIGHT

I.

Antonio had ambushed a second soldier in London, this time without shedding a drop of blood: he had throttled the man with his belt. He and Diego had then stripped the corpse of hat, breastplate, clothes, boots, and other belongings, including sword and pistol, and divided up these English items for a disguise. Blessed again by God, they had passed unquestioned through the defences, each wearing half of the dead soldier's orange sash. Yet the weather had now deteriorated beyond belief: massive dumps of snow, and cold bitterer than in the Low Countries. They could hardly go ten miles a day and the light waned unnaturally early. Overnight they burrowed into deserted barns or hedgerows, teeth chattering, their faces, fingers, and toes frozen, huddled together like sheep in a storm. Every soul that they encountered had treated them with overt hostility, and Antonio swore they had been misdirected whenever they asked for the Oxford road. By the eighth day of their journey, in view of Oxford's walls, their horse caved beneath them and they had to plod the last few miles into town.

With the influx of troops and Royalist camp followers into the city, food was expensive and shelter scarce at any price. So when Diego at last secured them a corner on the floor of a common flophouse, Antonio proposed that they celebrate their luck at the neighbouring tavern.

They pressed through a crowd of drinkers, men and women. Antonio had been chaste as a nun since quitting Spain, and the sight of these English females in their immodest garments tantalised him; many of them were inebriated, which would be considered scandalous for their sex in Spain. "I might find a little sport here among these whores," he said to Diego.

"You can't be certain they're whores, Don Antonio – look what passes for wine in this establishment, and it costs more than a barrel in our homeland," Diego said. "We should buy fresh horses before our money runs out, and ride straight to the Lady Elena's house."

"I will not call on her dressed like a beggar."

"Isn't that what you said you were?"

Antonio shrugged. "Go to our quarters and stake out our patch of floor. I'll join you later."

"Be careful," were Diego's parting words.

While Antonio was finishing his cup, the crowd began to thin. A woman bumped up against him and cast him a saucy glance as she staggered towards the entrance. He watched her leave, and decided to follow. She crossed the courtyard, and disappeared into the nearby stables. Approaching cautiously, he peered in; skirts hoisted, she was urinating on the straw. Why waste coin on a trollop such as her, he thought. The instant she dropped her skirts, he lunged in and pounced, seizing her by the shoulders, and spun her about, slamming her face first against the wall. Before she could utter a cry, he whipped her skirts over her head, stuffed a wad of the fabric into her mouth, and leant on her with his full weight, forcing her legs apart with his knees. Drawing his hungry sex from his breeches with one hand, he delved for her cunt with the other. He had a finger inside her when she spat out the cloth and yelled, "Get off me, you poxy bugger."

"Who's there?" shouted a male voice.

Antonio shoved her aside and adjusted his clothes; she was scrambling away, still cursing. Blinded by the glare of a lantern, he unsheathed his sword.

"Beaumont?" gasped the man. "Dear God you're not, but you're a damned close copy. Who *are* you?"

As he stepped back in surprise, Antonio tore past, and out down the street to the flophouse. Pausing only to sheathe his sword, he darted through the door and trod round the other sleepers to Diego's corner. "Wake up!"

"*Qué?*" mumbled Diego.

"You will not believe: a moment ago, someone mistook me for Beaumont."

"What do you mean, *Beaumont?*"

"*What it means*, Diego, is that the Lady Elena has a son who must be my very image." Antonio felt simultaneously stunned and thrilled: he could guess which of the two sons it must be.

He was less thrilled the next morning when he and Diego were dragged from their sleeping spot by a gang of bullies who beat them soundly and then hauled them up before the justice of the peace. The woman he had accosted was no whore, but the tavern keeper's wife. Diego pleaded Don Antonio's case eloquently in court, stating that they were French mercenaries by the names of Antoine Desorme and Jacques Sand, come to serve in His Majesty's army. Antonio spoke no English, Diego explained, and had made a genuine mistake, thinking the woman had invited his attentions. The justice was not won over. He sentenced Antonio to five weeks in Oxford Castle gaol, and ordered them both to enlist in the ranks once the sentence was served, or else be hanged as deserters.

"So I must stew in gaol with you, Don Antonio, though I've done nothing to deserve it, *and* I saved you from worse punishment," Diego said afterwards. "In exchange you owe me the truth, about you and the Lady Elena."

## II.

"When you bow, do not flourish your hat as if you are hailing a coach in the street," Digby reminded Price. "And as you leave the chamber, you must back away facing His Majesty. Modulate your voice and guard your enunciation. I still hear traces of Cheapside in your vowels. Quayle, you need not accompany us – this cold will bring on your catarrh," he said, as Quayle assisted him with his cloak.

"My lord," said Price, "what if His Majesty asks us about Beaumont?"

"Let me respond."

As they walked through the snow to Christ Church, Digby congratulated himself on the improvement he had wrought in Price: a week of intense training and those gauche mannerisms were beginning to fade. Price had also demonstrated courage and ingenuity in London by inveigling himself into the service of Clement Veech, and by reporting that man's suspicions about Mr. Devenish. Could Price eventually replace Beaumont? Price's memory and wits would never rival those of Beaumont, who possessed not only the skills and experience for his role, but an abundance of God-given talent. *It would be a shame to lose him,* Digby had admitted to his father, when Beaumont had slipped off to London in October. An understatement; and now there was even less chance of his return.

The King acknowledged Digby and Price with a faint nod. "I have received a perplexing c-communication from Lieutenant-Colonel Mosely," he said to Digby. "He wants Rupert to d-defer the strike on Aylesbury for a couple of days. Why might that be?"

"I cannot imagine, Your Majesty, unless he is concerned about the weather," said Digby. "There is talk of a thaw, which would certainly impede the progress of any troops along the roads. But we cannot postpone the advance, at this late juncture."

The King stroked his beard, frowning. "Should we alert M-mosely of our refusal to delay?"

"Why worry! Rupert has never failed you, thus far. He advised, however, that the Lieutenant-Colonel be dispatched some means of blowing up the garrison's powder magazine, in case the rebels learn that the town is about to be surrendered to us. Then, *in extremis,* the Prince would take it by storm. Knowing him, I am sure this has been done." The King looked a trifle reassured. "Your Majesty, might I introduce my intelligencer, Mr. Edward Price, who helped in our arrangements for Aylesbury and Windsor."

"Ah . . . How long have you been with my Lord Digby?" the King asked Price.

"Since the autumn, Your Majesty," Price replied, in an awed tone.

"It was he who facilitated Major Ogle's journey to Oxford and warned us that Mr. Devenish is suspected of being our ally. Devenish must fear for his life," Digby added.

"We should arrange *his* escape to us," said the King. "He will merit a knighthood for his service. Have you news of poor Violet?"

Digby had not, much to his anxiety, but he was saved from having to answer; the doors flew open and Quayle rushed in. "Your Majesty, my lord, forgive me – Mr. Beaumont is come to his lordship's quarters with an urgent report from London, but he's badly wounded in the shoulder and fast weakening."

"Oh no, dear God," groaned Price, heedless of the King's presence.

"You must hasten to him, my Lord Digby, and I shall send him my surgeon," the King said, with evident distress.

Beaumont lay beneath piles of bedcovers, eyes shut, his face blistered raw. When Digby spoke his name, his lashes fluttered, and he regarded Digby as through a mist. "Rupert is in . . . *danger*," he said hoarsely.

"Fetch him spirits," Digby told Quayle, and hovered until Quayle brought the cup, which he held himself for Beaumont to drink.

Beaumont choked down a small amount. "Aylesbury is a . . . a trap. When Rupert enters the garrison he'll be taken . . . hostage."

"Hostage?" cried Digby.

"Yes – Mosely is true to Parliament, and so is Devenish. You must . . ." Beaumont let out a ragged breath. "You must warn Rupert."

"This morning Mosely asked that Rupert delay the strike on Aylesbury. *Why?*"

Beaumont screwed up his eyes, obviously attempting to think, through pain and exhaustion. "Because of Essex . . . He must be waiting for . . . for Essex to get there. Essex will seize the Prince, and cut his army off from Oxford, if it . . . if it tries to . . . retreat."

"Who gave you this information?" Beaumont's head flopped back against the pillow. "Tell me, tell me," begged Digby, shaking him in vain.

The King's surgeon and his assistant were hurrying in with their bags of medical instruments. "My lord, is he . . . ?" queried the surgeon.

"He is alive," Digby said, "but in sorry shape."

The surgeon rolled down the bedclothes, and he and the assistant moved Beaumont onto his side. His doublet and shirt were so encrusted with blood that the surgeon called for a bowl of water and a pair of scissors, first softening the cloth and separating it from the skin, and then snipping it away. When the garments were off, Digby wanted to avert his eyes: the flesh around Beaumont's wound was swollen and dark purple, and from the upper arm to the wrist, an inflamed red. "Even if I extract the ball, my lord, infection has entered his blood, which is most often fatal," the surgeon said. Widening the hole in Beaumont's shoulder with a pronged tool, he delved inside with his fingers. Almost immediately he pulled out the bloodstained ball. "It cannot have been travelling at great speed, to be so near to the surface – a blessing it struck meat and not bone."

"A *blessing*, when he will die anyway of infection?" shrieked Digby. He could watch no more. Staggering to his office, he plumped down at his desk, his mind in a whirl: Beaumont's news contradicted a slew of correspondence and Major Ogle's stout assurances as to Devenish and Mosely's good faith, to say nothing of his own and his father's expert judgment. How could they both be mistaken? He thought of Beaumont, his doubting Thomas, and tears sprang to his eyes. When had Beaumont been wrong?

But then he remembered: Mosely was not due to surrender the town until midnight of the following day. A courier on a fast horse could reach Rupert's camp by tonight. He yelled for Price. "You must take a letter to Prince Rupert. He is quartering at Ethrop House, not two miles from Aylesbury. Your speed is of the essence, sir."

"Yes, my lord," said Price.

Digby hunted out the book of figures that Beaumont had designed for his and Rupert's correspondence. Without preamble he wrote of Beaumont's shocking news, though he urged the Prince to send scouts to verify it, since it might be the error of a confused and dying man. Next he prepared himself reluctantly to inform the King.

## III.

Ingram estimated that the sky had dropped on the Royalist troops every conceivable variant of frozen water, from pellets of hail to thick snow, to a wet downpour of flakes that melted on contact, chilling man and beast alike. From time to time he lost sensation in his fingers, and had to pull off his gloves and rub the blood back into his hands. The men's noses dripped icicles, beards and moustaches were white with frost, their faces red and chapped. They were travelling without their helmets and breastplates, on the Prince's orders: he said the steel would make them colder. At least twenty beasts had slipped and broken a leg, and been shot and abandoned in the fields; some men were riding two to a horse. Ingram most pitied the foot soldiers, wading waist-high in snow, burdened by heavy muskets and pikes. Behind them, oxen lowed in protest as they were whipped on to drag the heavy artillery carts.

Tireless as ever, and as solicitous of his men, Rupert had been galloping up and down the ranks, shouting encouragement. "That's Quainton Hill," he bellowed at last, pointing at a snowy rise in the distance. "We're not far now from a hot supper!"

In afternoon darkness they trailed through the gates to Ethrop House, family seat of the Countess of Carnarvon. Officers and other gentlemen would sleep in the house, and the troops would bivouac in outbuildings, stables and surrounding cottages. The prospect of a cooked meal cheered them, above all: they had marched on rations of biscuit and cold beef.

"The Countess is the Earl of Pembroke's daughter," Tom reminded Ingram, as they rode into her courtyard. "She lost her husband at Newbury field. I wonder how she stomachs her father siding with the rebels."

Ingram thought grimly of what Beaumont had said about his political convictions. "So many families have been split. We're lucky yours isn't one of them."

He and Tom followed the Prince into the hall where the Countess and her household had assembled. She was surveying with some apprehension the crowd of men in their snowy cloaks and slush-covered boots. Ingram thought her round face handsome, despite her unfeminine aquiline nose. At her side was a blond-haired boy whose eyes were riveted on the Prince. "Your Royal Highness," she said, with a curtsey, "it is my honour to accommodate you. My late husband would have wished you to consider his home as your own."

Rupert bowed, and touched his lips to her outstretched hand. "Madam, I thank you for your hospitality. And who is this young man?"

"My son, Charles, His Majesty's namesake."

"I'd ride with you, Your Royal Highness, if I were old enough!" the boy piped up.

"Your mother must thank God that you are not," the Prince said, smiling at her.

"I hope His Majesty wins this war before my Charles is of an age to fight," she said, dignified in her sorrow.

Rupert's officers chose the best part of the hall, nearest to the fire. Tom insisted that Ingram share his place there, and slowly and painfully they thawed out; Ingram felt as if his limbs were ablaze. When food arrived, everyone gorged themselves on mutton, pease pudding, hunks of oven-hot bread, and barrels of ale; and afterwards, Ingram sat smoking his pipe while Tom left dutifully to check on his troopers in the outbuildings. Although the Prince and her ladyship had not yet retired, many of the men began settling crushed in rows on the floor, wrapped in their cloaks like bundled lovers, moisture steaming from their damp clothes. Their collective warmth and snores lulled Ingram into a slumber. He was nodding off when Tom came back and jabbed a finger in his ribs.

"See over there, Ingram – Price, the fellow who was at your wedding."

"And he's in conference with His Royal Highness, no less."

Rupert and Price stood alone together; Rupert was reading a paper in his hand. He stared from it to Price, shaking his head, spoke again to Price, and strode from the hall.

"What can that be about?" Tom asked Ingram.

"Whatever it is, it's alarmed the Prince."

Price was scanning the recumbent men. When his eyes fell on Ingram and Tom, he walked over without a trace of the breezy cheer he had shown at the marriage feast, and knelt down beside them. "Mr. Beaumont, Mr. Ingram. Your brother was wounded carrying us a report from London, sir," he said to Tom. "His Majesty's surgeon is tending to him, but there was little hope when I set out to come here, and by now . . ."

"What sort of wound had he?" demanded Tom.

"He took a ball in the shoulder."

"In the shoulder? Oh, he's survived worse in the past. It's sure to heal."

"No, sir: the wound has poisoned his blood."

"Sweet Jesus," murmured Ingram.

Price rose, frowning at Tom. "Excuse me, now. I must take a reply from the Prince to His Majesty."

He left Ingram and Tom without much to say to each other. "We should try to sleep," said Tom in a strained voice.

Ingram reached out to clasp him in a hug, but Tom pulled away.

## IV.

Late into the night, Tom could hear Ingram's muffled sobs and feel him quivering as they lay back to back. Tom could neither sleep nor cry.

Many times he had contemplated the possibility that Laurence might not be alive, over the six long years his brother had vanished abroad without a word home. Laurence had again evaded death, after his imprisonment last year. Tom did not dare imagine him dead now. And yet in the corner of Tom's mind lurked old, guilty thoughts of a different future for himself, as heir to the Beaumont estate and title. His child would inherit, if Mary bore him a son. More important still, he had yearned throughout his life to have his father's unmitigated love and respect; and for what seemed most of his life, Laurence had stolen these effortlessly away from him. He recalled scrapping with Laurence as a boy, when the five years between them had given Laurence the advantage in strength and size. He used to wriggle from Tom's grip like a fish and pin Tom on the ground, pretending he was about to drool in Tom's face. He never did; he was always too overcome with laughter.

## v.

On the morning that the King opened his Oxford parliament, Seward received a desperate summons from Lord Digby and hurried to his lordship's quarters. He felt torn between worry and anger: Digby could have sent for him when Beaumont had first arrived injured. He was aghast to discover Beaumont delirious with a raging fever; in spite of repeated bleedings, the royal surgeon informed him. The wound leaked discharge through a plaster of red lead boiled in oil, and around the hole where the ball had been extracted, flesh was blackening and dying. Seward asked the surgeon to leave. Then he set about cleaning the wound, fretting away the dead flesh with a razor, and dabbed into it his own poultice of honey, sage, alum, turpentine, and rye flour mixed with water. For three days Beaumont alternately raved and fainted, and Seward watched and prayed. He had nursed his friend back to health after more extensive damage from torture, yet on this occasion he had to contend with the adverse effects of bloodletting and the surgeon's nostrum on a body weak and infected. Beaumont was in no less peril.

But on the evening of the fourth day, the fever lowered, and Beaumont sank into a profound, opium-induced sleep. He woke about twenty hours later and gave Seward the ghost of a smile. "Where am I?"

"At his lordship's quarters," Seward replied, touching his hot forehead. "Praise be to heaven that your delirium has passed."

"Digby called you here?"

"Yes, my boy, though for the past days I've kept him from your bedside. In fact, I've had to turn away a horde of anxious visitors, such as your brother and Ingram—"

"But . . . what happened to Rupert?" Beaumont tried to lift his head from the pillows. "Was he seized?"

"Will you be calm? He is safe and sound in Oxford, and most grateful to you. I'll provide a full account of events when you are stronger."

"No, Seward, I want to hear it now."

"If you must," said Seward, secretly overjoyed by this sign of his friend's recovery. "It may distract you while I put a fresh dressing on your wound." He told Beaumont how the Prince had been forewarned on the night before Aylesbury was to be surrendered, and had ridden with his Lifeguard the next morning to a hill overlooking the garrison. "Mosely had no clue that aught was amiss, and sent out his young servant to meet the Prince, rather than sending his own brother, as he had promised. This confirmed your warning, Beaumont, and Rupert instantly chose to retreat. The thaw cost him near on four hundred men and horses, but nature deals an even hand: the Earl of Essex was as hampered by flooded roads, and could not prevent him from reaching Oxford."

"My God," said Beaumont, weakly.

"The whole debacle was revealed at His Majesty's Assembly in Christ Church," Seward went on, as he tied up the clean bandage. "Prince Rupert wanted to hang Mosely's servant *and* Major Ogle, who claimed he had been hoodwinked by the very men who aided in his escape to Oxford. The lad's youth pleaded for him and he is being held prisoner. Lord Digby and his father Bristol intervened to spare the Major."

"As well they should – they were as deceived. Seward, I need more opium."

Seward searched among the forest of vials and bottles on the bedside table. "My boy," he said, "his lordship is keen to know how you learnt that the Prince was to be taken hostage."

"His lordship must *never* learn how, but I will tell the King. My intelligence came from the Earl of Pembroke."

Seward almost dropped the bottle of tincture as he poured out Beaumont's dose. "By all the saints! I cannot wait to hear more, though you are in no state to talk, for the moment."

"Hurry with that," Beaumont said, of the opium, and swallowed it in one gulp. Then he went on, in a wondering tone, "Delirium can play the strangest tricks on the brain. After I was shot, when I was lost in the countryside, I imagined you were talking to me, urging me on. Your voice sounded as clear to me as it does today."

Seward felt tempted to speak of his vision, but Beaumont's eyes were starting to glaze over. "You were fortunate in that horse of yours – it must have scented the promise of oats and a good rub-down in Oxford."

"It saved me twice. I hope I didn't ride it to death."

"It's at Merton stables, in a stall beside your Arab. The grooms said no inferior beast could have made the journey."

Beaumont smiled again, drowsily. "It belongs to Pembroke."

**VI.**

Draycott saw Veech at his same table in the Saracen's Head; he was studying a ledger. "Good day to you, Mr. Draycott," he said, glancing up. "You look haggard."

Draycott took a seat opposite. "My wife and I have been keeping vigil four nights in a row, over our eldest boy, Gregory. Had I a choice, I would not have left him, he is so ill." Veech's face remained impassive.

"Have you children, sir?" asked Draycott, upset by his indifference.

Veech laughed savagely and shook his head. "I cannot think of one sound reason to bring another human being into this world. Now, to business." He passed Draycott the ledger, which was filled with entries in neat script. "I've been keeping a record of transactions between the Vintners' Company and certain buyers in Oxford, from the end of December through to January." Draycott examined them, his eyes stinging from fatigue. "Malmsey, Canary, Jerez . . . The gentlemen in Oxford enjoy their tipple," Veech carried on, "and then the empty barrels get shipped back to London by barge. What I have suspected for quite a while is that they are *not* empty, and contain contraband."

Draycott wanted to grab the book, hurl it across the taproom, and tell Veech to go to the blazes. He forced himself to concentrate. "Have you any proof?"

"Here's where I need you, sir: according to its licence, the Company is exempt from our searches unless some clear malfeasance can be proved. Yet the licence was granted by the King and is to expire on the first of March, a month from today. I want you to draw up an amended contract on behalf of Parliament that would allow regular inspection of the barrels as they enter the City – a necessary measure due to the circumstances of war."

"Commercial law is not my province, Mr. Veech. You should find someone with greater expertise to act for you."

Once more Veech shook his head, this time as if disappointed in Draycott. "Have you told Judith who's paying you to stay at home with your sick boy instead of marching in the cold with the Trained Bands?"

"I haven't mentioned you specifically, sir, but she knows that I am in Parliament's employ."

"I'll pay you extra for this."

Draycott's heart sank. The apothecary's latest bill was thirty shillings, and there was the surgeon who came every night to bleed their son; Judith would consider the money a godsend. "I must consult a colleague on the precise wording of the licence, and review similar contracts to ensure there are no loopholes that might be argued by the Company."

"How long will you require?"

"Two weeks, at minimum."

"Then I'll visit you to collect the licence in exactly a fortnight."

"No, I'll bring it to you," said Draycott; he could not tolerate the thought of Veech inside his house.

"If you wish. As it's approved by Parliament, you will convey it in person to the Vintners' representative, Sir Montague Hallam, and use your lawyer's wiles to make sure he signs, no later than the third week of February. I hear he's an agreeable fellow. You might become friends with him."

"Is that an order?" said Draycott, bridling at Veech's purposeful tone.

Veech did not reply; he was beckoning to a serving girl. "Excuse me, madam, is Mistress Sprye at work today?"

Draycott's ears pricked up at the name, though he kept quiet.

"She is, sir," the girl said sullenly.

"Send her to us." When the girl had flounced off, Veech observed, "Mistress Sprye cannot have seen her lover in weeks."

"Of course not: Price showed his true colours as a Royalist agent when he relayed your falsehood to Devenish at Winchester House. He'd be mad to set foot in London, now the King's designs on Aylesbury have been exposed."

Veech leant in closer. "The odd thing about Price is that he did not lie to me about Beaumont. *Beaumont was here*, so early I had no chance to issue an alert to the militia. On the seventeenth of January, a man of his description was stopped at Tothill Fields trying to *leave* the City with a safe conduct that made the sentry there suspicious. When he wasn't allowed to pass, he jumped his horse over the gates and got away."

"Well, well," said Draycott, rather pleased that Beaumont had again frustrated Veech.

"I know how to lure him back in, and this time he won't escape me," Veech said, his eyes gleaming. "As for Price, I believe he's a whore to both sides. He's true only to the colour of money."

"He *was* reportedly a thief."

"He's a thief and a whore." Veech shut the ledger; a comely young woman was walking towards them. "Mistress Sprye," he said, in a civil tone, "I am Clement Veech, and this is Mr. Draycott. We're friends of Edward Price, who went to Oxford lately on work for me."

She gave an impatient shrug. "He hasn't spoken of you to *me*."

"Has he ever talked of a Mr. Beaumont?"

"No, sir."

Veech nodded as if accepting her answer. "When you see him, madam, please tell him to call on me. I've a hundred pounds waiting for him. We thank you, and good day."

"And to you, sirs," she said, and left them.

"She couldn't lie to save her neck," said Veech. "Our names didn't register, but Beaumont's did."

## VII.

"Such a charmed existence you lead, Beaumont," declared Wilmot, perching on the end of Laurence's bed. "I gather the ricochet of that ball saved you from a smashed shoulder blade."

Laurence had to laugh. "I can assure you, my existence would be yet more charmed if the ball had missed me. I'm in considerable pain, and fear I may never get back the use of my right hand."

"That's why God made you left-handed, you old devil."

"Thank you for your words of consolation. And how are you?"

"Thriving vicariously on the honours of my commander-in-chief. Bugger me if Prince Rupert hasn't been created Duke of Cumberland, Earl of Holderness, President of Wales, and Captain General of four counties. Who can doubt that our golden boy will raise a massive army to conquer the west *and* repel the Scottish invaders from the north, *and* spirit across the seas a few thousand troops from Ireland to swell His Majesty's ranks? And if he does, Beaumont, it's largely your fault. He might have been Essex's prisoner by now."

"Hush," said Laurence. "I hear royal footsteps."

Wilmot rose to bow to Prince Rupert, with Boy at his heels, and Lord Digby. "Mr. Beaumont, are you faring better today?" inquired Rupert.

"I am, thank you, Your Highness. I expect to leave my bed tomorrow, if Dr. Seward permits me."

"I had asked you how my uncle and I might reward you for your dedicated service. You must have some idea, since you asked for us to meet together here."

"Yes I do, Your Highness." Laurence let fall a pause. "As soon as I'm able in body, I should like to resign from my Lord Digby's service, and fight for His Majesty under Lord Wilmot's command."

Digby flushed scarlet, glaring at Wilmot, who ignored him. Digby turned to the Prince. "Your Royal Highness," he said waspishly, "in his invalid condition, Mr. Beaumont has succumbed to Lord Wilmot's pressure. I must object: I will not let him go. Your Highness recently had proof of his inestimable value to us in matters of intelligence, although to this day he refuses to admit who told him of the trap that Mosely had laid for you."

"My lord, I have to protect my informant," said Laurence.

"Precisely my point," Digby said, to the Prince. "How can Mr. Beaumont quit my employ and deprive us of a source as deep in the belly of Parliament territory as Jonah in the whale?" The Prince was silent, his lips twitching as if the metaphor amused him. "I would urge Your Highness and His Majesty to decline his request, for the benefit of His Majesty's cause."

"Mr. Beaumont," said Rupert, "during your convalescence I pray you reflect on your decision. If you are of the same mind, my uncle and I will consider your wish. My lords, the Council of War meets in an hour. I'll see you there." And he walked out with Boy.

"My Lord Digby," said Laurence, before Wilmot could interject some inflammatory remark, "I thank you for accommodating me over the past fortnight, but tomorrow I intend to leave your quarters and stay with Dr. Seward until I'm strong enough to ride to Chipping Campden, where I hope to recuperate."

"Very good, sir," said Digby, and sailed from the room.

"We must celebrate, Beaumont," murmured Wilmot.

"Indeed we must, when I've regained my capacity for drink."

Price was at the doorway. "Mr. Beaumont, may I beg a word?"

"Don't tire him," Wilmot growled, and waved Laurence goodbye.

Price appeared crestfallen. "I have to confess: I slipped up with Veech, last time I was in London. He said he thought Devenish was a closet Royalist, and like a complete fool, I reported that to Devenish himself. How they must have laughed at my stupidity."

Laurence heaved a sigh. His shoulder throbbed, and from the chills rippling up his spine he could tell that he was feverish again. "It doesn't matter now."

"I also wanted to thank you, Beaumont. Lord Digby was sure you'd gone to London because you were afraid for Mistress – I mean, for Lady Hallam, in her business for the King. But you went for another reason, didn't you: you'd smelt a rat in that promise of the two garrisons, and you knew I'd be in trouble if Veech got wind of my game. You came to my aid."

Laurence cared too little and was far too spent to dispute this interpretation of the facts. "Price, you don't owe me any thanks," he said. "Just go, and let me rest."


**VIII.**

Ingram knocked, expecting Dr. Seward to answer the door. "Who is it?" he heard Beaumont call out.

"It's me, Ingram."

"The latch is off – come straight in." Dressed except for his doublet, a blanket across his knees, Beaumont was sitting at Seward's desk scribbling on a sheet of paper. His right arm was in a sling, and his shoulder bandaged under his shirt. Though he was still thin and sallow, the improvement in him delighted Ingram.

Beaumont set aside the quill and grinned. "How are you, my friend?"

"Very pleased to see you up and about," Ingram said fondly.

"Not as pleased as I am."

"How's your shoulder?"

"Much less painful. Look – I can move again." Beaumont wiggled the fingers of his right hand and shifted his arm about, in demonstration. "And my fever's gone."

"Dr. Seward has magical powers. It's the second time he's raised you from the dead, bless him. Where is he tonight?"

"In Hall, eating supper with Dr. Clarke. He told me that Rupert's to march back to Shrewsbury tomorrow morning."

"He is, and he's got a daunting task ahead, to amass an army sufficient to occupy the entire northwest for the King. Thank God he can count on strong support in Wales and the border counties. He's even started to recruit here in Oxford. He commanded Governor Aston to round together all the petty criminals in gaol who are of fighting age, and any rebel prisoners who'll turn coat to follow him."

"Common practice in the Low Countries," said Beaumont, "though he'd better watch out – they may be more of a nuisance to him than an asset. And you should keep an eye on your belongings."

Ingram drew from his doublet his letter and Tom's, to their respective wives. "These are for you to take home."

"Why didn't Tom come with you?"

"He sent his regrets. He's been busy buying supplies for the troop."

"What nonsense. He shares my mother's unjustified dislike of Seward. Although I know you both tried to visit me at Digby's quarters," Beaumont added, as if he had been unfair to Tom. "I'd like to say goodbye to him before you ride out with the Prince. Seward would leave us to talk." When Ingram hesitated, Beaumont went on, "Ah, so it's *me* Tom doesn't want to see. And I thought we were getting along quite well together, over Christmas."

"It's not to do with you," Ingram said, untruthfully. "He's been in a strange state ever since that business of Aylesbury."

"What could be the cause?"

Ingram thought of what Tom had said after he heard that Beaumont's life was out of danger. *My brother is indestructible. Alas for the rest of us mere mortals.* "Perhaps he at last realised that Rupert is not superhuman, and could fall prey to the enemy just like any other man. But his spirits are sure to lift on the march. When will you set off for Chipping Campden?"

"In about a week, I hope."

"You could be there by St. Valentine's Day, to make your addresses to Mistress Furnival." Beaumont did not smile. "What are you writing?" Ingram asked, to change the subject.

"A letter to the King."

"I gather from your tone that you can say no more."

Beaumont pushed his chair away from the desk and stood up. "Give Tom my love, and take care of yourself. Remember," he muttered in Ingram's ear, as they embraced, "you're also my brother now, and I don't want to lose you in some Welsh bog."


IX.

Laurence had scarcely greeted his astonished family and explained the circumstances that had brought him home when Lady Beaumont ordered him to lie down in his bedchamber. He was so stiff and worn out from the ride that Geoffrey had to help him up the stairs. But a few hours later, the valet roused him from deep sleep. "His lordship and her ladyship would like to talk with you in the library, sir."

Lady Beaumont wasted no time in preliminaries. "Laurence, we have had a visit from rebel troops."

Laurence sank into an armchair beside his father's. "When was that?"

"Last week. Their discipline impressed us: they asked only for a meal of bread and cheese, and a farrier to shoe their horses."

"They were Gloucestershire boys," said Lord Beaumont. "By chance I knew their officer: he had appeared before me at the County Assizes many years ago. It was a poaching offence, and he a decent man with children to feed. As he reminded me, I had spared him from the rope, and let him go with a small fine that I later reimbursed to him. He said he had not forgotten, and promised out of gratitude to keep his men in check, and to request the same of Governor Massey. But we would be foolish to depend on his good will alone."

"As soon as his troops had left, we took your advice," said Lady Beaumont.

"You hid your plate?" Laurence asked.

"Not our pewter, but all of the gold and the silver along with our best jewels are buried under the dovecote floor. Sundry other items dear to his lordship are dispersed elsewhere, in the outbuildings."

"How many of the servants know?"

"We could not have accomplished the digging unassisted. Although the work was done at night and by our closest servants, the rest were bound to wonder how come our fine pieces had disappeared. We elected to be honest, rather than let them believe that we had any less faith in them."

"And they have pledged their loyalty to us," put in Lord Beaumont.

"You were right," Laurence told them, though he knew the threat of retribution might loosen the tongues of even the most devoted members of their household.

"If the rebels decide to pillage the estate, we stand to lose everything else," said Lady Beaumont, in her brusque manner. "We cannot hide our sheep and cattle, or the game in his lordship's park."

"You would have to hide *me*. I was selfish to come here and put you at risk," Laurence said. "Let's hope word doesn't get to the Gloucester garrison."

Lord Beaumont cheered a little. "We've our own means of collecting intelligence, on that score. Our neighbourly spies in Chipping Campden town are on the alert, and will report post haste to the gatekeeper any rumours of approaching troops."

"With sufficient notice, you could ride north across the Warwickshire border," Lady Beaumont suggested to Laurence. "You would do well to ride there whatever the case. We might conclude the details of your betrothal this month, so that the marriage can be solemnised when Lord Digby next grants you leave."

"I might have to beg leave of Lord Wilmot. I tendered my resignation to Lord Digby. I only need His Majesty's approval for it."

"Was there an argument between you and his lordship?" she inquired accusingly.

"No, I've had enough of serving him, that's all."

"Thank heavens, my boy – he is a pernicious fellow," exclaimed Lord Beaumont, surprising both Laurence and his wife.

"My lord, how can you speak so?" she said.

"He is what Parliament says of him, my dear: an evil influence on our King. He has encouraged His Majesty to neglect the duties of a monarch towards his people. I might well ask you: how can His Majesty portray himself as a peacemaker, after these disgraceful schemes in London?"

"We read a broadsheet composed by the rebels, my lord. I am disappointed that you should give credit to their lies. Now, pardon me. I have accounts to draw up in my office."

When she had gone, Lord Beaumont cast his eyes towards the ceiling. "I cannot discuss political affairs with your mother. She has a vein of extremism in her, much like the Queen's. Her Majesty has been as malign an influence upon the King as Digby. And it is hard for me to accept that their obduracy in the face of Parliament's grievances may rob me of my sons, and land cultivated for six centuries by my ancestors."

"Do you ever think you chose wrongly, in siding with the King?" queried Laurence.

"Yes, but in conscience I could not do otherwise. I would be more wrong yet to change sides now."

Laurence sensed that his father was about to ask him the same question and would be saddened by a truthful answer, so he remarked, "Ah well, there must be pernicious rascals on both sides."

"And noble souls, such as Lord Falkland. Were he still alive, and Secretary of State, he might have convinced His Majesty to chart a wiser course."

"Oh no," said Laurence, unable to conceal his bitterness. "He had given up all hope. That was why he died."

## X.

Lady Beaumont unlocked her cabinet and drew out the letters from Don Alonso de Cárdenas. The most recent she had received two weeks ago, mercifully unbeknownst to anyone but the local carrier; it described Antonio's flight from the Envoy's house, and his probable involvement in the slaying of an officer in London.

> The militia searched in vain for the culprits, and I have endeavoured to learn independently of Don Antonio's whereabouts, to no result. My Lady Beaumont, your cousin is a reckless and violent man, whose sanity I begin to doubt. Forgive me my error, in telling him where to find you. I believe he will come to you soon. When he does, you must write to me at once. His presence in England is a threat to you, and to my position here as His Majesty King Philip's representative. I shall not hesitate to assist you, if it is in my power.

She closed her eyes and leant against her cabinet for support. Should she confide in her husband and her son, or await further news of Antonio? If she spoke out, they would ask why she had kept silent about the first letter. She might invent an excuse her husband would believe, but Laurence would not be fooled. She remembered his sceptical look when she had dismissed her illness at Christmastide as a passing ague; he would connect it to the letter. And there were so many obstacles that might forestall Antonio's arrival: capture by Parliament, death in a fight or from the cold. He could already have succumbed to one of these; it was now over a month since he had fled the Spanish embassy. Why prejudice the peace within her household for nothing?

# CHAPTER NINE

Among the first in gaol to be selected by Prince Rupert's recruiting officers was a pair of French mercenaries, Antoine Desorme and Jacques Sand. On the eve of their march to Shrewsbury, Diego explained to the officers that Antonio had served most of his sentence and he himself had been convicted of no crime. Might he absent himself briefly from camp to purchase some supplies in town, for the road?

He came back exultant, and reported to Antonio, "I found Lord Digby's offices and inquired about Mr. Beaumont of his lordship's servant, pretending to be a friend from the Low Countries. Mr. Beaumont is at his father's house recuperating from a wound. The house is as the Envoy told us, some thirty-five odd miles northwest, near a town named Chipping Campden."

"How fortuitous," said Antonio. "We're heading that way tomorrow. We can escape from the ranks once we get closer to our destination."

Diego seemed not to hear him. "I also asked after Mr. Beaumont's brother. Major Thomas Beaumont serves in Prince Rupert's Lifeguard. He rode out of Oxford about a week ago with the Prince, and must now be at Shrewsbury."

"So what? Shrewsbury is over a hundred miles away."

"Don Antonio," said Diego, "while the prospect of travelling such a distance in this brutal climate with a bunch of thieves, drunks, turncoats, and deserters is anathema to me, and I'm tired of posing as a Frenchman, the fact is that if *we're* captured as deserters, we'll face a hanging. I didn't waste a month of my life locked up with you, sharing the blame for your stupid offence, only to lose it because you haven't the patience to wait until we get to Rupert's camp."

"Why must I wait, you impudent boy?"

"You know almost nothing about the Beaumonts. You would confront a united force on home ground, without intelligence as to its weaknesses. You may think it convenient that Mr. Beaumont is there at the house, yet it's the opposite. He's a spy, and his expertise lies in detecting mischief. I propose, instead, that you open your campaign with his brother."

Again, Antonio had to concede to Diego's wisdom. "Mr. Beaumont may be skilled in detecting mischief, Diego, but I happen to know that he has a mischievous past. I've been saving up a story for you, about him and a gypsy from Andaluz. I believe we could put it to good use."

## II.

Price timed his arrival at Chipping Campden to coincide with the supper hour, hoping that Beaumont would not dispatch him to the town inn as soon as he had delivered his news. He further hoped somehow to catch Elizabeth alone, although even if she received him warmly, Lady Beaumont's opposition was predictable, judging by her disdainful attitude at the wedding banquet. More alarming was the thought that Beaumont might have revealed to Elizabeth the details of Price's past. Yet nothing ventured, nothing gained, Price told himself, as the manservant took his cloak in the entrance hall.

"The family is at table in the parlour, sir," the servant said. "Shall I announce you?"

"No, I thank you," said Price, in his best imitation of Lord Digby's accent. "You may whisper in Mr. Beaumont's ear that I bring him news from Oxford."

He waited, one elbow propped against the stone nymph's shapely hip, listening to the genteel murmur of conversation and the clink of cutlery. When Beaumont emerged from the parlour, Price felt reassured by his amiable air; he wore a sling to support his right arm, but looked in much better health. He guided Price into the Hall, which appeared more spacious and austere on this occasion. "So, what news have you got?"

"We've heard from Lady Hallam, through Violet's wife." Beaumont's face became alert. "Violet's still in the Tower, confined indefinitely at Parliament's pleasure. Thanks to his City friends, he hasn't been ill-treated, but his estates in Essex have been sequestered."

"Goodbye Violet," Beaumont said, in a tone that disturbed Price.

"At any rate," Price went on, "about the barrels: she and Sir Montague predicted they would be searched by Parliament, and organized for them to be emptied beforehand. She wished to convey her thanks to you, nonetheless, for your warning."

"*Has* the powder been smuggled in?"

"Yes, inside coffins. They were brought by river for burial to a crypt near Vauxhall. The authorities were too respectful to interfere with dead bodies. The powder will stay underground until it's needed."

"Vauxhall is a bad choice: the land's marshy. The powder will spoil if the crypt floods. And that could well happen before a march on London. What else?"

"That's all I have to tell you," answered Price, now distinctly piqued. "I should be getting back to Oxford."

"No, sup with us, Price, and stay the night here," said Beaumont. "I'll ask for a chamber to be prepared."

Tonight's was an intimate gathering, with none of the extended family members or dependents that Price would have anticipated in a noble household. Despite hunger, he restrained his appetite and said little. Lady Beaumont struck him as paler and thinner, her expression stern and withdrawn, and Lord Beaumont as benevolently vague. Price tried to keep his eyes from straying too often towards Elizabeth, but whenever he did venture a glance, she responded with a gratifying flush to her cheeks.

After the meal Beaumont excused himself and his visitor, and escorted Price upstairs and along a corridor to the chamber where he would sleep. A fire blazed invitingly in the hearth, and a jug of steaming hot water, a washing bowl, towels, and a ball of fragrant soap were arranged on a side table. "I must write a message for you to deliver to Digby tomorrow," Beaumont said. "We can talk more, in a bit. I'll bring us up some wine."

Price closed the door and collapsed onto the luxurious featherbed. He imagined Elizabeth lying with him, her arms twined about his neck. And Beaumont had stuck him in a corner of this vast mansion, expecting him to stay there like an obedient child! "I'm not good enough for your sister, eh?" he was complaining into his pillow, when a noise arrested him: the click of a woman's heels in the corridor. Someone knocked gently. He leapt from the bed, and answered, to Elizabeth.

"Mr. Price, are you retiring already to sleep?"

"Why . . . no, my lady," he replied.

She took a step nearer, leaving the door ajar. "How pleased I am to see you," she said, in the same spontaneous manner as at the wedding banquet. "I've thought often of you, since we met."

"As . . . have I of you," he said, cautiously.

"My brother is particularly mysterious about you. He's told me only that you were of assistance to him, and that he recommended you to Lord Digby." Price nodded, further encouraged by Beaumont's discretion. "Are you married, sir?" she asked next, so directly and with such candid interest that he hesitated.

"I am a bachelor, my lady, free to pledge my affections where I choose."

"Have you a . . . sweetheart?"

This time, Price did not hesitate. "No, my lady, and though you may consider me very forward, there is none other to whom I would rather pledge myself, than to you."

She sighed and offered him her hand, which he pressed to his lips. "I have been lonely, after the death of my husband. I never hoped to love again, as I did him. And yet . . ." She gave his fingers a little squeeze. "My strongest instincts inform me that . . . I am in love with *you*."

"My lady, those last words were on the tip of my tongue."

"You needn't worry that my parents might forbid me to accept suitors so soon upon my widowhood," she said, with an assurance that dizzied him. "They have agreed that I can, once Laurence is married. He and Mistress Furnival are to be wed in a matter of months."

"There might be other obstacles," Price said, yearning for her to demolish them. "I am not of noble birth."

"Nor is Anne's husband, Walter Ingram."

"I have no property to my name."

A shade of uncertainty crossed her face. "Ingram's Aunt Musgrave made him heir to her estate – that was what sealed the betrothal. But Laurence told Ingram he would have spoken in favour of the marriage, even so. He'll do as much for us. He's your friend, too, is he not?"

Price grew anxious: Beaumont could come upon them at any minute. "Yes, but my lady—"

"Elizabeth," she corrected him.

"Elizabeth, we must keep our love private between us."

"Doesn't Laurence know?"

"I would have been presumptuous to speak out, when I was afraid you might not reciprocate my feelings."

"Now you can. Or *I'll* tell him. And I can confide in Anne, not that she hasn't guessed."

"No, I beg you – we've met just twice, and I have many things to settle before I can ask for your hand. I've . . . I've debts to repay."

"Ah well, afterwards we won't have to concern ourselves about money. My bridal portion was restored to my father by Ormiston's mother upon his death, since he and I were wed less than a year. It's over a thousand pounds."

High stakes, thought Price. "Elizabeth, let's not be rash. In due course, I'll address his lordship for permission to court you. Anything else would be unworthy of us both. We should say no more tonight, but you will hear from me. Promise you will abide by my instructions?"

"I promise." She danced out, and blew him a kiss. "And I wish you happy dreams, sir."

Price shut the door again, trembling from head to toe. Impossible to maintain a conversation with Beaumont: his excitement would betray him, and that divine creature and her thousand pounds might be lost to him forever. He tore off his boots, undressed to his shirt, extinguished the candle by his bedside, and dived under the covers. He was praying for God to smooth his path towards marital bliss, when the clink of spurs in the corridor signalled Beaumont's approach.

A firmer knock sounded. "Price? Are you awake?"

Price stumbled from bed, ran his fingers through his hair to dishevel it, and padded to the door. He opened it an inch. "I'm sorry, Beaumont – the journey must have tired me out."

Beaumont had two glasses in his left hand, a letter in his right, and a bottle tucked into his sling. "Never mind, we'll drink when I get to Oxford in a couple of weeks. This is for Digby." He passed Price the letter. "*I'm* sorry, about my rudeness earlier. It was a consequence of anxiety, but I shouldn't have directed it at you."

"Oh, I understand. We could drink one glass," said Price, feeling somewhat calmed, and buoyed by Beaumont's apology, as frank as Elizabeth's declaration of love.

"No, no – one always leads to another, and you've a long ride tomorrow. Price," Beaumont went on, more quietly, "I met Sue when I was in London. She told me about taking Devenish the pie – and about the child."

"Trust her to keep a secret."

"She asked if I wanted to hide in her room. Of course, I couldn't accept."

"What was she thinking – as though *you'd* ever stay in a wretched hole like that."

"I'd have been grateful for it, but I might have brought her a lot of trouble. She was brave to offer."

"So she was." For the second time that night, Price summoned up his own courage. "But I'm afraid my fancy for her is over, Beaumont. Though I wish I could go and explain to her honestly, as a man should, I can't risk it, now that my cover's blown with Veech. I'm not worried about her," he said, forcing a grin. "She has a bevy of admirers at the Saracen's Head. She'll find a husband faster than I could say the Lord's Prayer."

"Then you might write and suggest that she does."

"She can't read." Price saw reproach in Beaumont's eyes, and felt annoyed. "Have *you* never got a woman with child that you had no desire to marry?"

"Perhaps many times, without my knowledge," Beaumont admitted. "I do know of one, when I was sixteen, and marriage was out of the question. She was a servant here."

"What became of her?"

"My mother dismissed her with a payment, and I was sent abroad on a tour. On my return nearly a year later, I'm ashamed to say I'd forgotten her."

"You had your problem solved for you."

"And it's not to my credit."

Price thought of Elizabeth: he would need Beaumont's good opinion of him in his dealings with women if he was to court her. "I swear, I'll do what I can to make amends with Sue."

"Well, then . . . If I'm not up before you leave, God speed. And goodnight."

"Goodnight, Beaumont," said Price.

**III.**

Laurence and his father were sitting in the Hall, gazing up at Van Dyke's magnificent portrait of his lordship. "Now that we have stripped ourselves of smaller treasures," Lord Beaumont said, in a conspiratorial tone, "might more items be preserved from the rebels, such as my canvasses, and my bronze statuettes from Venice? Or am I becoming greedy?"

"The canvasses are easily stored without their frames. You can remove them and the tapestries, and lay them flat under the rafters of the house. If you hang some of your less prized works of art in their place, Colonel Massey's troopers won't look very far, unless they're as discerning in taste as you are yourself. As for the bronzes," Laurence suggested, "you might sink them in the river – weigh down the lighter ones and chain them together."

"And what could be done with my horses? It will break Jacob's heart, should the rebels take them away. He has bred and raised them for generations, and is fonder of them than his own children."

"I don't blame him – horses must be less of a nuisance."

"On the subject of children, my boy, you ought to call upon Mistress Fur—"

"Who's singing at the virginals?" interrupted Laurence quickly.

Lord Beaumont keened an ear to listen. "Elizabeth has not touched that instrument since Ormiston's death! She may be recovering her old spirit. Would you ask her to play me my favourite air by Dowland? '*Come again, sweet love doth now invite,*'" he sang, in his tuneful tenor.

"I'm sure she'll be delighted to oblige you," Laurence said.

When he walked into the parlour, Elizabeth was still playing. The beatific look on her face changed, as he shut the door behind him. "What is it, Laurence?"

"Liz, are you in love with Price?"

She dropped her hands into her lap, and took a deep breath. "Remember when we spoke here about my situation, and I asked if you had any potential suitors for me among your friends?"

"Yes."

"And later you denied whisking Mr. Price away from Anne and Ingram's banquet, to keep him from me." Laurence nodded, now regretting that he had not told her more of the truth about Price. "And last night you invited him to stay. I presume *he* is your friend."

"He is, of a sort."

"Not like Ingram?"

"I have few, if any, friends like Ingram. Liz, you hardly know Price."

"You hardly know Pen Furnival, and you are about to propose to her."

"I'm not marrying for love. And our mother has gone to inordinate lengths to ensure that she'll make me a suitable wife."

"Why would Mr. Price not be suitable for my husband? Is it because he has debts?"

Laurence blinked at her. "When did he tell you that?"

"When I happened to pass by his chamber, as he was about to go to bed."

Laurence recalled Price, subdued at table, sneaking glances at Elizabeth; then sulky, upstairs; and next assailed by fatigue in the space of half an hour. "You *happened to pass by*?"

"I wished to bid him goodnight."

"And this brought on a discussion of his debts?" She coloured. "Did he profess his love for you?"

"We talked of our feelings."

"Ah, then it was a mutual profession," said Laurence; no wonder Sue had faded so rapidly from Price's fancy.

"Laurence, your protective urge is natural in an older brother, but I am a grown woman and I have been a wife. I might add that as a sign of his respect, Mr. Price has refused to court me without our father's agreement."

"I should damned well hope he has."

"I see no reason for you to oppose our courtship, unless you're aware of some dread secret he is hiding."

Price's secrets were tawdry rather than dread, Laurence reflected. "Price was born poor. He's had to do some less than . . . honourable things to survive."

"What things?"

"It's not my place to discuss them – it's his. But *I* have done some of these same things and worse, with far less need given my advantages in life. I know from experience how they can affect a man's character, to his detriment. Price may love you, but he may also love what you could bring him. I'm not sure which is most important to him. He may not be sure himself."

"What difference does it make, if we're happy together?"

"It could make a great difference, believe me: as his wife, you'll be his property by law – and your property will be his. Don't be in such a rush. You'll have other offers."

"Not while you men are busy fighting in this accursed war. I'd prefer to be widowed again, than miss an opportunity for happiness."

Laurence decided not to argue. He could rely upon Lady Beaumont to put a crushing end to Price's ambitions; and yet he hated Elizabeth to suffer the inevitable pain. "You might consult Anne, before your feelings run riot," he said. "She showed excellent judgement in her husband, and she's not as much of a cynic as I am."

Elizabeth gave an exasperated snort, turned to the keyboard, and launched into a loud, aggressive gigue.

**IV.**

Normally Draycott wore his best suit of black clothes but once a week, to attend church. This week, he had dressed in it twice: to bury his son, and now to visit Sir Montague Hallam. If not for the mourning band Judith had stitched on his hat, he resembled any lawyer visiting a client. Within, however, he felt as though every nerve in his body were scraped raw. Immersed in his grief, he walked right by Sir Montague's house; and he longed to carry on walking blindly down the Strand, for as far as his legs would carry him. It required an effort of will to retrace his path, ascend the steps of the handsome red brick mansion, and reach for the brass door knocker.

An elderly manservant accepted his cloak in the entrance hall, led him up to the second floor and through double doors into a wood-panelled gallery that spanned the length of the house, and then left him. On the walls hung tapestries depicting events in the life of

Jesus. The Crucifixion scene had the air of a village festival; its gay colours assaulted Draycott's eyes. He moved to Christ healing the sick; one was a child of about Gregory's age. Why had Christ not listened to his prayers, and healed his son? Judith had told him to have faith in the Almighty's Divine purpose, but nothing could justify the torment of those final hours. He nearly agreed with Veech: *I cannot think of one sound reason to bring another human being into this world.*

"My favourite is the temptation of our Lord," said someone behind him. "Satan has such a smile upon his face, as of a cat that has stolen the cream."

Draycott turned; from the low, gritty timbre of the voice he expected a boy. Instead it belonged to a dark-haired woman in shimmering satin whose loveliness momentarily erased his thoughts. The pretty young maid at her side seemed plain in comparison.

He bowed. "May I present myself: Mr. Draycott, legal counsel to Parliament."

"I am Lady Isabella Hallam. My husband will soon join us. Has Greenhalgh offered you wine?"

"No, my lady," said Draycott, trying not to stare at her.

"You must sample a glass of Burgundy from our cellar," Lady Isabella said, with a bewitching smile. "Lucy," she murmured to the girl, who slipped out obediently. "Mr. Draycott, let us be seated." As she took a chair and arranged her skirts, Draycott glimpsed a vivid rainbow flash from the massive diamond on her ring finger. "Sir Montague told me that you are come about the licence. You must have distinguished yourself, to represent Parliament on such a lucrative contract. The Company formerly negotiated with one of His Majesty's lawyers – an astute fellow, according to my husband, and an expert on wine."

"I can lay claim to neither advantage."

"You are modest, sir."

"No, my lady. I am honest."

"An honest lawyer. You are of a rare species."

Greenhalgh entered carrying a tray with three glasses on it, followed by Lucy with a crystal flagon. They placed them on a table near Lady Isabella, then Lucy perched on the cushioned ledge by the window, and Greenhalgh disappeared through the gallery doors.

Lady Isabella poured, and as she handed Draycott his glass, he could smell her perfume, delicate yet intoxicating. He could not remember ever being as close to a woman so beautiful. "A rise in duties will be unavoidable because of the war," she was saying. "Are there further changes that Parliament wishes to negotiate?"

"There are, as I must discuss with Sir Montague." He lifted his glass. "This is a treat for me: I seldom indulge in wine or spirits."

She pointed to the black band on his hat. "You are in mourning."

"My . . . my wife and I lost our eldest son to the phthisic. He was nine years old. It was as if he were drowning in his own blood and spittle. Oh my lady, forgive me for mentioning these details," he added, embarrassed. "We should thank God he is delivered from suffering."

"How trivial everything else must appear, in comparison, and how grossly unfair his death," she said, with such sympathy that his throat choked.

"Have . . . have you and Sir Montague children?"

"No, nor shall we." Draycott frowned: she could not be much over twenty-five. "He has sons and daughters from his previous two marriages, and grandchildren," she elaborated. "He has no need of a third family, at his time of life."

"That must be a sacrifice for you."

"Not at all, sir: it simplifies my existence."

Draycott heard a rattling outside the doors, and Greenhalgh came in pushing a chair constructed on small wheels, with a footrest that extended downwards from the seat. Its occupant was a gentleman in his sixties who must once have been good-looking but had run to fat. His noble Roman nose was speckled with the veins of a drinker, and his blue eyes glinted shrewdly beneath thick white brows. His mouth, framed by a clipped beard and moustache, was full and sensual. He wore a cap over his curled grey hair, a suit of dark red velvet with a broad lace collar, silk hose, and on one of his feet a black kidskin shoe decorated with rosettes. The other foot was bandaged.

"Good day to you, Mr. Draycott," he said, in a mellifluous voice. "My apologies for presenting myself in this absurd contraption – I'm not always confined to it, but today I am bothered by my gout. Bella, I shall dare a drop, though, to drink our guest's health."

After Lady Isabella had poured for him, she beckoned to her maid and whispered in her ear, while Draycott produced the new licence from his document case. When he looked up, Lucy had gone, but Lady Isabella showed no inclination to follow her.

Sir Montague unfurled the paper. "Exorbitant duties, Bella, as we had thought. Mr. Draycott, why should Parliament care to inspect our empty barrels? Has Parliament not weightier matters to attend to, such as the defence of London?"

Veech had told Draycott how to answer. "Since His Majesty's designs on the City last month, we are bound to inspect *all* goods for contraband. We know you as an honoured member of the City Corporation, and a loyal ally of Parliament – it is merely procedure."

"I thank you for reassuring me, yet I might argue that barrels sent back to us void of their contents are no longer goods, *per se*, but receptacles."

"I shall have to consult a colleague on the definition, sir. Pardon my ignorance, but why *are* the barrels returned to you?"

"They are made of English oak by skilled coopers. Inferior wood and poor construction result in spoilage. And the more a barrel is used, the more it tends to flavour the wine it contains, improving even a thin vintage." Sir Montague shook his head at his wife. "Can you believe the pettifogging, when we are in the midst of war?"

"We must applaud Parliament for its strict adherence to procedure," said Lady Isabella, with slight irony. "When will the inspections begin, Mr. Draycott?"

"As of the first of March, when the old licence expires, my lady," Draycott replied, bemused that a woman should participate so confidently in their talk. "Any sooner would be illegal."

"Then Parliament has broken the law," said Sir Montague. "A cargo of empty barrels sent a week ago from Oxford was searched in the docks by a servant of Mr. Oliver St. John, Mr. Clement Veech. It is not the sole instance, my agents tell me, and some of the barrels were badly damaged."

Draycott felt a stab of indignation. "Upon my honour, sir, I had no knowledge of it. I shall investigate the matter."

"What is past is past, yet these *legal* inspections may delay our shipments. You must insert a clause into our contract that any financial losses incurred will be compensated to us by Parliament. My lawyers can supply the monetary amounts, which will depend on the extent of the delay. What think you of the Burgundy, sir?"

"It is delicious."

Lady Isabella replenished their glasses. "Let us drink to all the lawyers who will be gainfully employed in drawing up a second draught of your contract, gentlemen."

Sir Montague chuckled and winked at her. Unsettled by their complicity and by her teasing, Draycott put down his glass after a small sip, and rose to bid them good day.

Lady Isabella accompanied him downstairs. As Greenhalgh was helping him on with his cloak, she said softly, "It was wrong of me to joke, when you are in distress at home."

"Please, my lady, think nothing of it."

"Lucy," she called out, "Mr. Draycott is about to go."

Lucy hurried out from some other room on the ground floor; she was holding a basket which she proffered to Draycott. Packed neatly inside were a roasted chicken wrapped in parchment paper, a loaf of new-baked bread, a cake, nuts, and dried fruits, and even a fresh lemon. "My condolences to your wife, sir," said Lady Isabella.

Draycott thanked her and left, more miserable than when he had entered. He desired her, and he despised himself for it.

———

"You made me look a fool," he railed afterwards to Veech, at their table in the Saracen's Head. "You should have told me about those barrels."

Veech paid no attention. "Did you meet his new wife?"

"Yes. Lady Isabella was very . . . gracious."

"Gracious, eh?" Veech laughed. "In two days, you'll take him an amended version of the licence." He waved a finger at the black band on Draycott's hat. "What's that?"

"It's in memory of my son. He died."

"Be rid of it before you call on Sir Montague. The licence doesn't interest me any more: I want you to become friends with Lady Isabella – *good* friends, if it won't tax you. From what I gather, she's not hard on the eyes."

"I am a married man, Mr. Veech."

"And *that* is an order, sir."

"What is your interest in her?"

"You'll know, presently," said Veech, scanning the taproom as if he owned it.

"Did Parliament accept my terms?" inquired Sir Montague; this time he had hobbled into the gallery leaning on an ebony cane.

"The rate of duty will be reduced by a quarter of the previously stated amount, if the Vintners' Company will let us inspect all barrels sent back to you," Draycott said, handing him the contract. "You'll be recompensed as you stipulated for delays to your trade. Mr. St. John sends his apologies for the illegal search, but asks why Mr. Veech should have discovered traces of sulphur in your empty barrels."

Sir Montague raised his bushy eyebrows. "Neither gentleman can know much about my trade. Sulphur is often added to preserve wine from mildew on a voyage, especially if it is being shipped from warmer climes."

"You must understand their concern: sulphur is a component of gunpowder."

Sir Montague was studying the licence. "I wish Bella were here to look it over with me." He signed, and then beamed up at Draycott. "I know you are puzzled that I refer to her in my commercial dealings, yet her wits are sharper and her education broader than mine, in many respects." He laid a hand on Draycott's arm. "Sir, while she and I are dear companions, she has few young people to entertain her. Would you sup with us now and again, at your leisure – as a friend, and not as the representative of Parliament?"

Draycott experienced another wave of self-disgust. "I should be honoured," he said.


**V.**

Sir Harold welcomed Laurence into the hall with a veneer of heartiness, thinly disguising impatience. "Ah, Mr. Beaumont, we have been asking ourselves when you might next grace us with a visit. How is your shoulder?"

"Better than it was, thank you," replied Laurence. "Sir, we had news at home that Colonel Massey has increased his raids to supply the Gloucester garrison. I can't afford a brush with rebel troops, so I must ride for Oxford as soon as I've presented my respects to your wife and daughter. I came to tell you that a date for the marriage—"

"Yes, yes, we must fix upon a date," Sir Harold cut in. "Her ladyship your mother agreed for us to host your wedding banquet – we're safer here from Massey's incursions. We'll just have time to prepare. Today's the fifth of March, and she was planning for a ceremony in the month of April."

"Forgive me, sir, but if you would kindly listen: a date can't be set until I've resolved a certain business in Oxford."

"Do you hear that?" cried Sir Harold to Lady Margaret and Penelope, who looked as disgruntled as her father. "What business is delaying you?" he asked Laurence.

"A matter of my employment with the Secretary of State," Laurence said, which shut Sir Harold up.

"It is a shame, Mr. Beaumont," Lady Margaret said, "but God willing, you and our Pen won't be apart for long."

"I thank you for your understanding. And now if you'll excuse my rude departure, I must bid you all goodbye." Laurence bowed shortly and turned on his heel.

Pen ran after him. "You are lucky to be going back to Oxford, Mr. Beaumont," she chattered on. "It is so dull in the country – I can't bear it, myself. I had thought that after our marriage, we might seek lodgings in the city. I have wonderful friends in Her Majesty's retinue, and Lord Jermyn is—"

"These decisions must wait, Mistress Furnival – and I *must* leave."

"I can't but remark how you have altered towards me," she exclaimed. "When we were introduced by Her Majesty, you were sparkling with wit and merry conversation, and you were so amiable at your sister's wedding feast. Aren't you pleased to be marrying me?"

"The truth is that I have too much on my mind to think very far into the future," he replied, pitying her. "And I really can't stay to talk."

"Sir," she said in a sterner tone, as they reached the doors, "I know you had a mistress in Oxford. I trust you have ended your relations with her?"

"Our relations are at an end. Goodbye, Mistress Furnival," he said, and kissed her hand.

"Don't I merit a kiss on the lips?" He obliged, as politely as he could. "Goodbye, sir," she said.

Not bothering to call for a groom to fetch his horse, Laurence went into the stables. In the darkness he almost tripped upon a boy who was crouched on the ground. "What the . . . ?" he muttered.

"Sorry, sir, sorry," the boy whispered back.

"Quiet," said a girl's voice. "And don't come closer, sir, or you may scare it."

As Laurence's eyes adjusted, he saw her, in the same pose as the boy. They were concentrating on a creature that rustled and fluttered about in the straw. "Scare what?" he asked.

"A magpie. We must catch it before the cats do. Oh look!"

The magpie waddled out of the straw, one wing drooping. The girl straightened slowly; her face was a serious, leaner version of Penelope's. She was the sister he had glimpsed on his last visit. Today her hair fell loose over her shoulders, her gown was stained at the front, and there was a smudge of dirt on her forehead. She reminded Laurence of someone, but whom? "You must be Catherine, Penelope's twin," he said.

"Yes, I am, Mr. Beaumont. Would you help us save the bird, sir? A hawk dived to snatch it, and in its fright it flew into the stable door."

"Have you somewhere to put it?"

The boy hunted about and brought forth an empty grain sack. Laurence moved nearer to the magpie. As if it knew that he meant it no harm, it made no attempt to escape, and he picked it up and placed it in the folds of the sack, where it sat glaring at him beadily.

"Please, take it into the courtyard," said Catherine.

Laurence carried out the sack, and the three of them peered at the magpie. He extended the damaged wing and stroked his fingers along the fine bone. "Here's the break. You could bandage the wing, and hope it mends."

"Would you do that for me?"

He raced to the stables for his saddlebag, where he kept a spare roll of the same muslin he had used for his own wound, and searched in the hay for a thickish stalk. He came back, and as Catherine held the magpie, he splinted the broken bone with a piece of the stalk, and wrapped the muslin around the wing and gently around the bird's body, avoiding its feet. "Change the bandage when it's soiled, but don't fasten it too tightly – the bird has to breathe. Do you know what magpies eat?"

"Seeds and worms."

He nodded, impressed. "In three or four weeks, you should be able to tell if the bone has knitted." He had not the heart to say that even if it did, the bird might never fly.

"I'll keep it safe in my chamber."

"Then you should hide your jewels. Magpies are reputed to steal whatever shines."

She smiled; one of her front teeth was chipped at the corner. "I have no jewels," she said. Then it struck him: though she was blonde and light-skinned, her dark eyes were wild like Juana's; but in their depth, they were like those of the African seer, Khadija. When he passed her the sack, his hand touched hers. "Thank you, sir. Such mercy towards a dumb creature is uncommon among men." Hastily she drew away, as if there were something improper in that brief, accidental contact.

"I must go," he said, remembering his own haste.

"Will, bring his horse," she said to the boy. "Goodbye, Mr. Beaumont."

"Poor thing," said Will, as they watched her walk towards the house, head bent, cradling the sack in her arms.

"The bird has a fair chance," Laurence objected.

Will gave him a sorrowful look. "The bird has, yes, sir."

## VI.

Under the boughs of a great tree that would soon be their gibbet, thirteen prisoners were praying, heads bared, hair tousled in the wind, as Prince Rupert's troopers crowded round jeering and hurling stones at them. Some were already bleeding from these well-aimed missiles; with their hands tied behind, they could neither defend themselves nor wipe away the blood.

"So, what was their crime?" Antonio said to Diego, who had been asking about in the crowd.

"To be captured, Don Antonio. Parliament decreed it lawful to hang any prisoners who came from Ireland to fight for His Majesty. The Governor of some town that fell to the rebels strung up a bunch of Irish. Prince Rupert learnt this morning. This is his reprisal."

Antonio approved. He had longed to see Rupert in the flesh. Two days ago, their motley troop of recruits had finally marched out of

Shrewsbury to catch up with Rupert's main army some thirty miles away; and last night, over their rations of beans and bread, they had heard much from his troops about his skill as a tactician. At any hour he would lead a small group of Horse from village to village and town to town on lightning raids for provisions, and his reputation for speed, agility, and invincibility made him feared but also adored. In Cheshire, as he had in Shropshire, he was drawing men to swell his ranks; and here he was again demonstrating his strategic use of violence.

Diego was more intent upon the crowd than the rebel prisoners. "Major Beaumont must be with the rest of the Prince's Lifeguard. If we don't find him first, he'll spot *you*, and you will have squandered the advantage of surprise."

When the nooses were lowered, Rupert pressed through towards the tree on his white horse. "I hold no grudge against you," he told the prisoners, "other than that you have treacherously taken up arms against your rightful King. You have been chosen by lot to pay for what occurred at Nantwich, when the same number as you were suffered to die by the noose. I have spared a fourteenth, who is delivering a message to the Earl of Essex: that in future, for every man put to death by Parliament otherwise than in a fair fight, I shall hang two rebels. Make your peace with God, and may He have mercy upon your souls."

"The licence of war, Diego," remarked Antonio. "One side breaks the rules, and the other must follow suit. And soon there are no more rules."

To the accompaniment of a drum roll, the hangmen tossed the ropes up over the boughs of the tree. A lone prisoner wept; the others burst into a defiant hymn, singing in unison, though their voices were drowned out by catcalls and laughter.

"Show some respect for their courage," the Prince yelled at his troops.

The singing hushed slowly, as each man met his fate by the slip of the rope. When it came to his turn, the last shouted out, "I go to a happier place, to the bosom of Lord Jesus, the King of Kings!"

"Or to the lake of eternal fire, you unrepentant heretic," Antonio scoffed at him.

All attention was fixed on the tree and the dangling corpses: the spectacle of death had sobered the crowd. Diego pointed out the officers who wore the colours of Rupert's Lifeguard. A smart company, thought Antonio with nostalgic envy, as he sought out a face that resembled his.

"Let me ask their drummer for Major Beaumont," said Diego.

Antonio's heart started to pound when the boy indicated a man on a grey and white mare: he had been wrong to look for himself in Elena's younger son; he should have looked for James Beaumont.

As if sensing Antonio's gaze upon him, Major Beaumont swerved about in the saddle. His astonishment was far greater than Antonio had predicted: his blue eyes popped wide and his mouth fell open.

"Major Beaumont." Antonio walked towards him. "At last I have the pleasure of your acquaintance."

"Who in God's name are you?" he asked, like a man confronting a phantom.

"Don Antonio de Zamora, cousin to your mother, the Lady Elena," said Antonio, sweeping off his hat. Major Beaumont remained dumbstruck, so Antonio talked on, in his best English. "I voyaged from my hometown of Seville to perform an errand in London for His Majesty King Philip, and whilst there as a guest of the Spanish Envoy, Don Alonso de Cárdenas, I mentioned that I wished to renew ties with my dearest cousin. He wrote to the Lady Elena on my behalf this past December, but had no reply—"

"Ah yes," interrupted the Major, some recognition dawning on his face. "She *did* receive his letter, at Christmastide."

"She may have written back to him, or to me, yet . . . with the war . . ." Antonio shrugged. "When I heard nothing in months, I had to make my own inquiries."

Major Beaumont dismounted, and bowed; his perplexity was comical. "Forgive me, sir, but you are the only member of my mother's family that I have ever met."

"She has not spoken of me?"

"Never in my whole life."

"*Qué sorpresa* . . . Are she, his lordship, and all your family in health?"

"Yes, when I left them."

"How many children are you?" Antonio asked him, in a paternal tone.

"There's my older brother, Laurence." He spoke the name as though it had a sour taste. "And two sisters, Elizabeth, who was widowed last year, and Anne, who was lately married. My wife also lives at my father's house, and expects our first child this summer. Have you not yet visited Chipping Campden?"

"I have not seen the Lady Elena in more than thirty years, Major – or may I call you Thomas? In Spain it is most . . ." He turned to Diego. "*Cómo se dice: descortés?*"

"Ill-mannered," Diego supplied.

"Ill-mannered to descend unannounced, even upon family, without invitation. The Envoy had told me that her sons served with the King, and so I went from London to Oxford, hoping to find you there, Thomas. I did not, though I found out you were in Prince Rupert's Horse. I therefore followed the Prince's army, in search of you."

"From Oxford all the way into Cheshire?" said Thomas. "But why—"

"My valet and I had the most appalling journey," Antonio hurried on. "Praise God, our tribulations were worthwhile. It gives me such joy to meet you. And I look forward equally to meeting your brother."

"He doesn't serve in the Prince's army – he's in—" Thomas stopped, and shook his head. "He'll be more amazed than I, when *he* meets you."

"Oh? And why is that?"

"He bears a striking similarity to you, as you both do to my mother."

"Does he."

"Your command of English is excellent, sir," Thomas said, as though he disapproved.

"I thank you. Have you and Laurence your mother's tongue?"

"Not I, but Laurence speaks it like a native. Sir, while I can't ask leave to accompany you to Chipping Campden, I could write to her, so that your visit won't be unannounced."

"After our introduction, there is no need."

Thomas surveyed Antonio and Diego with a different curiosity. "I don't mean to insult you, but if I knew no better, by your dress I would take you for some of our foot soldiers."

"Prince Rupert would not be pleased to recruit *me*," said Antonio, amused. "I was for years an officer in the Hapsburg cavalry, serving the Emperor who stole his father's kingdom and sent his family into exile."

"He wouldn't hold that against you, sir," Thomas said humourlessly.

"I am not here to fight, Thomas, but to strengthen the loving relations between our families."

A roll of drums cut into their exchange. "We're to march on." Thomas swung back into his saddle. "Let's talk again tonight, when we make camp." And with that, he trotted off.

"He's transparent as glass," Diego marvelled. "Not a whit of Mediterranean guile. And he hates mysteries, as he hates his brother. Don Antonio, we should disappear into our humble ranks and keep out of sight for a while. He will assume that we have gone to the Lady Elena."

Antonio grinned up at the hanging tree, and the thirteen bodies swaying in the wind; he fancied he could smell their shit-stained breeches. "Have you a plan, Diego?"

"I'm inspired by two old tales," Diego said, "of Cain and Abel, and of the prodigal son. You will give Major Beaumont a *version* of the truth. And not yet: let him lie fallow, then your seeds will take better root."

## VII.

The day after his return to Oxford, Laurence went to Christ Church hoping to obtain the King's permission to quit Digby's service, but the equerry said that His Majesty was too preoccupied, with unhappy tidings. Hillesden House in Buckinghamshire, seat of a loyal Royalist friend, had been demolished by Parliament troops under the command of Oliver Cromwell, and its owner taken captive to the Tower. Laurence thought of his father: such a fate would be his death. And for Laurence, there was also bad news: the King had left a message ordering him to report to Lord Digby's offices.

"I thank you for the note you sent, through Mr. Price, from Chipping Campden," Digby said at once, in his efficient voice, "and I shall consider your advice about our strategies in London, sir, but let us pass on discussing them. I need one of your brilliant figures for my correspondence. It will be a light and pleasant task, to ease you back into your duties."

Laurence pretended to accept defeat as regarded his service with Wilmot, and set to work. Meanwhile, whenever he and Price found themselves alone together, Price would invent some patently false excuse to disappear. One evening, Laurence burst into his chamber without knocking. "You've been avoiding me, Price. Is it because of the little chat you had with Elizabeth at my father's house?"

Price turned scarlet. "I acted towards her as a gentleman should. I trust she didn't suggest anything else."

"No, she's not a liar. But she is apt to be impulsive, and I won't have *any* man taking advantage of her, no matter who he is."

"Are you forbidding me to court her?" Price asked, a mixture of apprehension and defiance in his eyes.

*Yes I am*, Laurence wanted to reply. "That's for my father to do, should he so choose, and if he does, you'll have to accept his decision. I'm merely warning you to continue acting as a gentleman."

"You have my word, Beaumont."

"Good," said Laurence, "because I intend to hold you to it."

## VIII.

Beaumont tossed a sealed roll of paper on Seward's desk, lifted Seward from his chair, and gave him a mighty hug that knocked his spectacles askew. "Heavens, Beaumont, to what may I ascribe this violent outburst of affection?" gasped Seward.

Beaumont hopped up on the edge of Seward's desk and began to swing his feet about, as he would as a youth when in an ebullient mood. "I was taking a walk today in Christ Church meadows, when I came upon His Majesty and Prince Charles airing their dogs."

"A chance meeting?" Seward asked dryly, as he adjusted his spectacles.

"How *could* it be otherwise," said Beaumont. "The Prince hailed me over, and as we were petting the dogs, His Majesty had the grace to confess that Digby had convinced him he couldn't spare me for active duty."

"Which was no surprise to you."

"But it was to Prince Charles, who became positively irate. He started to talk about Pembroke's plot and how I had saved his father's life – and Prince Rupert from capture by Essex. And he said he'd consider it the height of ingratitude not to grant me my desire."

"His Majesty doubtless scolded him for his impudence."

"Not so. The King looked at him as if seeing him anew – as if seeing in him a future king. It was a . . . breathless moment. Then His Majesty bade me to accompany them to Christ Church, where he wrote and signed my release. His sole condition was for me to remain Digby's faithful servant until I'm fighting fit."

"Lord Digby will be beside himself with rage."

Beaumont shrugged. "There's nothing he can do about it."

"Are you certain it's what you want?"

"At least in *this* aspect of my life, I'm getting what I want."

"I did notice how silent you have been on the issue of your marriage."

"There I am well and truly trapped." Beaumont jumped off the desk, to pace about the room. "I'm sorrier for her than for myself."

"Do you dislike her?"

"No, I just foresee a loveless union." He told Seward about his flying visit to the household, and Penelope's eagerness to establish herself in the city. "My mother would never allow it. Oxford is far too ridden with vice." He stopped pacing. "I met Penelope's twin sister at the house. She rather intrigued me."

As he described the incident of the magpie, Seward's nerves began to tingle; he might have been scrying in Fludd's bowl. "What is her name, Beaumont?"

"Catherine," Beaumont said.

## IX.

"My nephew is on his way to Ch-chester, where he is expecting a f-further detail of Irish troops," the King told his Council of War, "but I believe we are agreed that he should suspend his recruiting in the west and hasten to the aid of our g-garrison at Newark."

"Should Newark fall, Oxford will be cut off from the entire northern reaches of England," growled old Lord Forth.

Digby suppressed a sigh: Forth was stating the obvious, simply to show he had heard what was being said. He was almost as deaf as a post, and for that reason always stood close to the King.

"The rebels have at least two thousand Horse and more than twice as many infantry laying siege to our garrison," Wilmot said belligerently. "Even Rupert can't raise an army of that number in time to relieve it."

"If His Majesty has one commander he can depend on for such a feat, it is His Royal Highness the Prince," Digby said, to provoke Wilmot, though he agreed with him about the odds of Rupert succeeding.

"Should we hold onto N-newark, my Lord Wilmot," the King said, "your t-task will be to join with Hopton and our southern army and attempt to break Sir William Waller's forces, now that we have accurate intelligence of his strength."

"Your Majesty, I broke Waller last year at Roundway Down, without Hopton's assistance. I shall be delighted to trounce him again." Wilmot smirked straight at Digby, while the King set his seal upon Prince Rupert's order.

Digby approached the King, and said smoothly, "Might I offer that my agent, Edward Price, ensure its safe and speedy arrival? His Royal Highness may remember how Mr. Price brought that vital dispatch to him at Aylesbury."

"By all means, my lord," said the King, and handed him the order.

"Mr. Beaumont has an announcement for you, my lord," Quayle informed Digby, when he got back to his offices.

He was drumming his fingernails on his desk as Beaumont came in. "Well, sir?"

"My lord," said Beaumont, his face bland, "His Majesty has acceded to my request: in a few weeks, once I'm fit, I may serve in Lord Wilmot's Lifeguard. Until then I am at your disposal." Digby could not speak for a second; hence Wilmot's complacent visage. "My lord, I am sorry—"

"No, you are not, sir," retorted Digby. "But as you said to me when you came into my service upon Falkland's death, be careful what you wish for. You have made your bed with Lord Wilmot, and you must lie in it. You should beware of catching some unfortunate complaint from the Lieutenant General."

"Such as what, my lord?" asked Beaumont. "Ambition? If so, I have already been exposed to a far more contagious strain."

Digby hesitated, to modify his voice. "You have done a disservice to the King and to me in your childish dream to play at soldiers again. Over the *few weeks* that you are mine, I shall keep you busy. But for the nonce, you may summon Price to me, and go for the rest of the day."

"Yes, my lord," said Beaumont, and left Digby to ponder his revenge.

## X.

Ingram had noticed how quiet and brooding Tom had been in the fortnight since those prisoners were hanged; it was a scene Ingram had not cared to witness. Then on the march from Chester to Newark, Tom had blurted out what had happened on that same day. "How I regret that neither you nor Adam had been there to reassure me:

sometimes I think I dreamt it all. Ingram, de Zamora was so much like Laurence. And I haven't seen him since! It's as though he disappeared into thin air."

"He must have gone to Chipping Campden," Ingram said, staggered nevertheless. "If we'd received letters from the family, we would have heard by now."

"If you write to Laurence, don't mention de Zamora," Tom said. "I want to tell him myself."

He and Ingram did not talk again about Lady Beaumont's Spanish kin. The army was travelling at a ferocious pace, mainly at night to escape detection by rebel scouts. Rupert had commanded swaths of hedge to be felled, to allow the passage of Horse, Foot, and artillery across country; and along the way, he had cleverly arranged to gather additional troops from local Royalist garrisons, sending some of these on ahead. They were to rendezvous with him at established points on his route, to keep the rebels guessing as to his numbers and the direction of his march. The Parliamentary forces besieging Newark might try to flee northeast if they had intelligence that he was actually sweeping down on them with more than six thousand Horse and Foot, an army twice as large as they could have anticipated.

On the evening of the twentieth of March, the Royalists camped a mere ten miles from Newark; they were to attack at dawn. Tom roused Ingram around two in the morning. The Parliamentary commander, Sir John Meldrum, had at last got wind of Rupert's approach, and had withdrawn to a derelict building that he had fortified. The place, called the Spitall, had once been a sick-house, and was linked by a bridge of boats to a flat island in the Trent River that flanked the town. Tom's men had been chosen with others to form an advance guard of cavalry to prevent Meldrum from slipping away: they would distract the enemy with a skirmish until the main body of the Royalist army could arrive.

Stealthily the advance guard rode into position between Newark and Meldrum's line of retreat; and by dawn, from the crest of a hill, they could view the enemy Foot and guns near the riverbank, with some fifteen hundred Horse in front. Resolving on a surprise charge, Rupert ordered his cavalry to assemble in three lines; he would lead the first of these. By nine o'clock they were ready.

Tom was beaming: they were to ride in the first line. He whispered to Ingram the Royalist password for the day: "*King and Queen.*"

"God be with you," responded Ingram, trying to hide his own fear.

"For King and Queen!" yelled the Prince, waving aloft his sword, and they sped down the slope, cantering faster as they clashed with Meldrum's Horse, which scattered like sheep. Ingram could not believe how they cleared a path through the melee without wasting a single shot. But Parliament's Horse counterattacked, and soon they were hacking and parrying on all sides. In the midst of the confusion, Ingram heard someone cry, "The Prince is surrounded!" Tom was pushing against the scrum of horses and men, thrusting his sword into the animals' flanks to get nearer to the Prince. When the enemy trooper directly in front of Ingram slid from the saddle, hit in the head by a glancing blow from Tom, Ingram caught sight of the Prince, in tight combat with three men.

As though protected by magic, Rupert cut one of them down with his blade just as his attendant shot dead a second. The third tried to grab the Prince by the collar of his cloak and had his hand sheared clean off by another Royalist officer. "Charge again, and drive them up to the Spitall," the Prince shouted, with a pure exultation that heartened Ingram: here was the joy of battle, and eluding death by the skin of one's teeth.

Under renewed assault, Meldrum's cavalry were fleeing back over the floating bridge onto the island, abandoning the Foot and artillery. Royalist scouts galloped up with intelligence that the mass of Rupert's army had now arrived, and that his musketeers were assaulting the bridge of boats, facing heavy enemy fire. On raged the fighting, for so long that Ingram was scarcely aware of the slant of the sun, but they gained the island towards afternoon. He and Tom were both unscathed, and the scouts were reporting few losses. Shortly after, they learnt that the Royalist Governor of Newark had blocked Meldrum's retreat to the north; and as darkness descended, word spread through the weary but cheerful ranks that Meldrum was suing for terms.

**XI.**

"'Our victory cost His Royal Highness less than a hundred lives,'" Laurence read to Digby, once he had finished decoding the report from Prince Rupert's courier. "'On his withdrawal from Newark to Hull, Meldrum had but two thousand Foot, stripped of all their weapons save their swords and some pikes. He left behind eleven brass cannons, two mortars, four thousand muskets, as many pikes and pistols, and more than fifty barrels of powder. The prize gun is a Basilisk four yards long that shoots thirty-two-pound balls.'"

"An enviable weapon," chortled Digby.

"It puts the best of men to shame," said Laurence. "And what else . . . 'A large contingent of the enemy also deserted to the King's side. A few enemy colours were seized from the rebels, only to be handed back to their officers by Prince Rupert himself, who went among his troops with drawn sword to restore order.' What an achievement: to move about a hundred and forty miles in eight days, and amass such a huge army on the way. His troops must have been pushed to the limit of their endurance, and then they had a battle to win. It was pure genius."

"And a crushing humiliation for a professional soldier such as Meldrum," Digby added. "Now for us to destroy Waller in the south and the armies of Lord Manchester and the Scots in the north, and the war might be won for His Majesty."

"My lord, I've received my marching orders from Wilmot," said Laurence. "I must leave for his regiment tomorrow."

"I know: he could not resist rubbing in *his* victory when I saw him at Council. I shall feel your absence, sir," Digby said in a gentler tone; after his initial, furious reaction, he had been suspiciously forgiving. "Their Royal Majesties are to celebrate Rupert's success with a banquet at Merton tonight around seven of the clock. Please do attend, Mr. Beaumont, and we can raise a glass in memory of our partnership."

"I shall, my lord," Laurence told him, "with pleasure."

That evening, Laurence packed his saddlebags, and cleaned and oiled his pistols; he would leave his Arab at the College stables, and ride out on Pembroke's horse. Seward had produced cups and a bottle of wine. "From Clarke, so it should be worth drinking," he said. "I shall have to drink plenty of it, to sleep through these festivities."

As the bells chimed seven, Laurence made a cursory effort to spruce himself up, and went out. Fires and torches were disposed about the quadrangles, and the courtiers milled about to the strains of music from the Queen's lodgings; and every so often a display of fireworks illuminated the sky with flashes of brilliant colour. Laurence accepted a goblet of wine from a butler and wandered towards the Chapel doors, outside which the King and Queen sat on a cushioned bench, amid a sea of ladies and gentlemen; Lords Digby and Jermyn were among them. In spite of her vivacious expression, the Queen appeared ominously frail and wan for a woman in the later stage of pregnancy; according to rumour, the child had been conceived during one of their Majesties' trysts in the covered passage by their colleges, although Laurence found this an unlikely indiscretion on the part of fastidious King Charles.

"Mr. Beaumont," said Digby, "Their Majesties have proposed a health to His Royal Highness Prince Rupert. Come lift your cup."

"Certainly, my lord," said Laurence, thinking how enthusiastic the Queen and Digby were to sing Rupert's praises, when they would as eagerly conspire to besmear his reputation.

"And shall we offer our next health to Mistress Furnival, sir?" Jermyn said to Laurence; Digby had left them to talk to his diminutive friend Hudson.

"To Mistress Furnival," said Laurence, and they drank again. "Are you acquainted with her family?"

"I've known Sir Harold and Lady Margaret since I was a youth, and Penelope since her birth."

"And Catherine, I presume."

A look crossed Jermyn's face that reminded Laurence of Will, the stable lad. "Did you see *her* at the house?"

"Yes, and I liked her very much."

"You must have charmed her from her shell. She generally avoids society – that's why she did not wish to be presented at Court with Penelope. Pen is acknowledged as the beauty of the family, sir – you are fortunate in your bride."

"And she will be as fortunate in her husband," said a voice at Laurence's shoulder.

He turned to see Lady d'Aubigny beside him; she was no less exquisite than he remembered.

"Will you take a cup of sack with us, my lady?" Jermyn inquired.

"Thank you, my lord, but I would prefer to steal Mr. Beaumont from you."

"Of course," said Jermyn, with the slightest smile at Laurence, and meandered towards Digby and Hudson.

"Are you alone, tonight?" she asked Laurence.

"I am," he said, thinking of their chequered history together: a brief sexual liaison while she was still pregnant with her late husband's child; a trip to London with His Majesty's doomed Commission of Array during which she had infuriated Laurence with her blithe indifference to danger; and then her generous word in the King's ear, solicited by Isabella, that had helped to rescue him from death in Oxford Castle.

Perhaps they were thinking alike, for she said affectionately, "I have missed you, sir. I want to show you a book, in the College library."

"A book?" repeated Laurence, as she led him over. The door was unlocked, and the library empty and silent, though not dark; moonlight streamed through the dormer windows in the roof. He surveyed the stalls of heavy tomes. "Which one is it?"

"It's here, sir." From a pocket in her skirts, Lady d'Aubigny withdrew a small volume. "Her Majesty lent it to me. It's from France – a rare item, much in demand."

She passed it to him, and he flipped through the illustrated pages. "I can imagine why . . . And it wouldn't be found in most college libraries."

She moved closer, and tapped her finger on a page. "Have you ever tried this?"

"I might have, though I can't quite recall," he replied; her attractions and the erotic pictures were a powerful combination. "And you?"

"No, but there's a first time for everything." Her fingers slid up his thigh, to caress him. "I believe you are tempted, sir."

"Your hand is on the evidence."

She removed her hand, and slid her hips onto the nearest library table. Adroitly she bunched up her skirts to reveal the tops of her stockings. "I should like to see your . . . evidence."

"If I may borrow my old tutor's dictum, my lady, *festina lente*." He approached, picked her up, and reclined her on the table. Parting her thighs, he lowered his head.

"You have done *this* before, sir, I'd hazard a guess," she observed.

He paused, to answer, "Oh . . . maybe once or twice." He resumed, his mind straying again to the day that Isabella had read to him from a more subtle book about the art of love. As his tongue had reached exactly this warm place, she had lost concentration.

Her ladyship began to pant. "Dear God, dear God! Ah! What joy!" she shrieked suddenly, pounding her fists on the table.

"Hush," he said, starting to laugh. He had forgotten how noisy she was in the throes of passion; and so, as he unlaced his breeches, he took the precaution of covering her mouth with his.

When at last they emerged from the library, he had no idea of the hour, but the feasting must have commenced some time ago, for the crowds had dispersed and they could hear a roar of conversation from the Hall.

"As I recollect," Lady d'Aubigny said, tidying her hair, "a banquet was held on the first occasion that I had the pleasure of . . . meeting you. This may be our final such meeting, Mr. Beaumont. I must surrender you to Penelope."

Laurence thought of Madam Musgrave's worldly advice to him. "You never know, my lady – life always has its surprises."

"Are you coming in to supper?"

"You must excuse me, but I have to rise early tomorrow," he said, feeling lazy after their energetic coupling; and their entrance together might provoke gossip.

"You have risen superbly tonight." Lady d'Aubigny kissed him on the cheek. "Goodbye, sir, and pray you keep safe that evidence of yours."

"Goodbye, my lady, and thank you for showing me that instructive book."

Seward had gone to bed, but Pusskins was still abroad in the front room, and snuffled at Laurence's clothes with avid prurience as he stretched out by the dying fire. "You've a nose on you like a hound," he told it, yawning, and drifted off to sleep.

# CHAPTER TEN

"**M**y lady, I am Colonel William Purefoy of the Gloucester garrison," the officer said, doffing his hat. "You must excuse our early arrival."

From her position on the top step, Lady Beaumont looked down at him. Only thanks to the gatekeeper had her family been warned in time to hurry out of bed and dress, and she was not in a forgiving mood. She saw the same emotion in the faces of Jacob and the grooms, who stood ranged defensively by his lordship's stables while about sixty of Purefoy's men dismounted in the courtyard.

Purefoy climbed the steps, obliging her to retreat into the entrance hall. As he walked in, his eyes settled upon Lord Beaumont's statues. "May I speak with his lordship?"

"I shall take you to him," she said.

"Have the men wait in good order," Purefoy called out to his adjutant.

She led him upstairs to the library, where Lord Beaumont sat in his armchair. The Colonel bowed and introduced himself, while she closed the doors behind her, and adopted a protective position by her husband's side.

"My lord and lady," said Purefoy, "as you must be aware, my troops occupied the town of Chipping Campden ten days ago, on the orders of Governor Massey."

"It puzzled us that you were so long in calling here," said Lord Beaumont, in a reserved tone.

"Governor Massey has granted me authority to provision my

troops from your stores, and if need be to quarter my men on your land. Although your sympathies are not with Parliament, I shall try to limit the damage to your property, but that will depend upon your compliance."

"What manner of damage are you planning to inflict on us, Colonel?" asked Lady Beaumont. She had promised Lord Beaumont to keep a civil tongue, yet Purefoy's supercilious attitude was more than she could bear.

"You must pardon my wife her outspokenness, Colonel," interjected Lord Beaumont, "but lately women have assumed new roles in the defence of their households."

"How right you are, my lord," said Purefoy. "In August of '42, my wife Joan had to defend my seat of Caldecote Hall against attack by Princes Rupert and Maurice, whilst I was away. With but eight men and twelve muskets at their disposal, she, her maids, and my son-in-law struggled to hold the princes off. They failed, and in the end Rupert burnt my house to the ground. In his generosity, he left my family unharmed. He even invited my son-in-law to join his regiment – an offer that was refused."

"As I can well understand," said Lord Beaumont. From the tightening of his grip on the arms of his chair, Lady Beaumont could see that he had caught Purefoy's veiled threat. "You were a Member of Parliament, Colonel, were you not?"

"First for Coventry, and then for Warwick. I presume you sat in the Upper House, my lord."

"Yes, though I did not attend as often as I should have, over the years."

"None of us were allowed the privilege, since His Majesty ruled without a Parliament for the greater part of his reign."

"True, sir: had he paid more heed to the voice of his people, this conflict might never have broken out."

"I am glad you acknowledge his fault," Purefoy said, with a sarcasm that infuriated Lady Beaumont: it was bad enough that her husband should criticise the King to a rebel, but worse that Purefoy should mistake a genuine opinion for sycophancy. "My lord, you recognise His Majesty's injustice, yet you have contributed to his coffers, and thereby to the war he is waging against his people. And you have given your sons into his service. If not for the intervention of your friends in this county and a certain officer at our garrison, your property might have suffered the ruin that befell mine."

A flush rose in Lord Beaumont's cheeks. "Sir, let me correct you on one point: I did not give His Majesty my sons. They are grown men with consciences of their own who freely picked – one more easily than the other – the cause for which they risk their lives. Had they decided to fight for Parliament, I would not have prevented them, though it would have grieved me. But it grieves me that they must fight at all."

"My words were poorly chosen," said Purefoy, in a somewhat chastened voice. He paused, examining the shelves laden with books. "You are renowned for your learning and your interest in the arts, my lord. I was most struck by those statues in your entrance hall. Did you acquire them abroad?"

"Indirectly, sir: I purchased them through an agent and had them transported from Milan."

"At enormous expense, I would reckon. They must weigh several tons."

"It was a complicated business," admitted Lord Beaumont. "Have you an interest in the arts, Colonel?"

"Yes, but I cannot turn my mind to idle luxuries at such a time as this."

"There we differ: for me, they are not idle luxuries. They are evidence of man's capacity to create, rather than to destroy, which is a solace to me, especially at such a time as this."

Lady Beaumont was losing patience with both of them. "Colonel," she said, "we have fired no muskets at you, and nor shall we impede the provisioning of your troops. May I remind you, lest you do not know, that his lordship's health is fragile, and we have our two daughters here, and our daughter-in-law who is with child."

"I pledge my word to respect your family, your ladyship," said Purefoy. "However, if any of you or your servants attempt any violence against my men, or should we learn that you are hiding from us plate or jewellery or coin or other valuables that might be used to further His Majesty's tyrannical assault on the lives and liberties of his people, I shall not hesitate to treat your house as Rupert treated mine."

## II.

"Together again, my old cock, and you've joined me when I need you most," Wilmot said to Laurence, over breakfast at his Abingdon headquarters. He bit into a slice of thickly buttered bread, and carried on talking with his mouth full; a contrast to Lord Digby's scrupulous table manners. "The King had promised me in Council that if Rupert succeeded in relieving our garrison at Newark, I would be sent to combine forces with Hopton in the south and take on Waller's army. But then it appears he had a change of mind and gave command to Lord Forth, who is of course Hopton's *great friend*."

"And His Majesty's Lord Marshal, your senior in rank. Isn't Forth already at Winchester?"

"He is, and yesterday we got a dispatch from him: he's so ill with gout that he can barely walk, let alone supervise an army in the field."

"Then Hopton will assume command."

"Exactly my concern." Wilmot banged a fist on the table, making their plates jump. "I saved Hopton's arse at Roundway Down and beat Waller soundly. Now my enemies in Council wish to deny me another triumph. They seem not to understand that if Waller triumphs, we could lose our entire southern army and a clear path to march on London." He shot Laurence an ominous look. "We may have to engage any day, though Waller's been dodging us while building up his own strength. He's had reinforcements from the Earl of Essex: Balfour's crack regiment of Horse. He could decide to sit down outside our garrison and prolong the stalemate, or he could strike while we're unprepared and far inferior in numbers. We're in damnable straits, Beaumont."

Laurence had to agree: this was not just an instance of Wilmot's injured vanity. "There's not much you can do about it yourself."

"I can still go to the rescue. The garrison is about fifty miles due south of us – you should reach it by tonight or early dawn tomorrow, depending on the roads."

"*I* should . . . ? But—"

"Listen to me, man," said Wilmot, seizing Laurence's sleeve. "You must address Forth privately on my behalf, to urge Hopton to call for my aid. The moment you bring me word, I'll be on the move, with my Lifeguard and three hundred of my Oxford Horse."

"You can't approach Forth without permission from the Council of War. You'd be up before a court martial."

"Not if I save our army from defeat. I am relying on you to bend the old man's deaf ear."

"Oh Christ, Wilmot! Even if he accepts your offer, what will happen when the King learns that you've vanished from your headquarters?"

"A raiding party took me a little out of my way," Wilmot said, with his confident grin. "When he finds out the truth, it will be too late."

"And should Forth refuse you?"

"He won't, if you put it to him as the lesser of two evils." Wilmot tossed back his mug of ale and stood up, signalling an end to their breakfast and to any more protests from Laurence. "Why didn't I see you at Their Majesties' banquet?" he asked, steering Laurence out to the yard. "Jermyn said you'd be there."

"I was reading in the library, and forgot the hour."

"You must have been buried in some captivating tome."

"Yes I was – a . . . treatise on strategic manoeuvres by a French author."

"Hmm. Has he any new ideas?"

"In fact he had some penetrating insights – and I'd thought the subject thoroughly explored. But they might be hard to execute without considerable skill and endurance on the part of the troops involved."

"Typical French," said Wilmot. "All very fine on paper, but totally useless in practice. Well, good luck to you, Beaumont. I picked a comrade of ours from my Lifeguard to ride with you. Be discreet – all he knows is that you're delivering a message from me to the Lord Marshal."

The man waiting for Laurence was Dick Mawson, a veteran from the foreign war who enjoyed his wine and women, and his ribald anecdotes. This morning he was noticeably solemn. "Were you seeing double last night after a few too many rounds?" Laurence teased him, as they mounted their horses.

"No, Beaumont, though it's odd you should say that," he replied, "because on a night late in January I mistook another man for you, until I had a close look at him. He would be about twenty or so years older, with cropped hair and a beard." Laurence remembered the Spaniard in Seward's vision; and he felt the prickling in his scalp that always warned him of danger. "Otherwise, as God is my witness," Mawson said, "he *was* your double."

## III.

After some inquiries at Winchester camp, Laurence and Mawson were directed to a large tent crowded with officers. Laurence left Mawson outside, and walked in to find Sir Ralph Hopton poring over a map. Now in his late forties, Hopton had fought in the Low Countries alongside his friend Waller, the man who had been his opponent at Roundway Down, and might be again if it came to a battle. Such were the ironies of civil war, Laurence mused, as he presented himself to the General and requested to speak to Forth.

"Lord Forth is ill and resting in his coach," said Hopton. "He has delegated authority to me. What is it you have to say?"

"My Lord Wilmot heard of the Lord Marshal's indisposition, sir, and is offering to bring reinforcements—"

"Lord Wilmot's offer is tardy," cut in Hopton. "We are to raise camp in a matter of hours and march towards the enemy lines. By tonight we should be within three miles of them, and in the morning we're to invade the village where the London brigades are billeted. Are you an officer in Wilmot's Horse?"

"I'm in his Lifeguard."

"Have you any fighting experience, or are you just one of those roaring boys he keeps for his entertainment?"

"I served six years abroad before entering His Majesty's ranks."

"Then I'll second you to Sir Edward Stawell's cavalry. We need every good man we can get." Hopton beckoned to a younger officer, whose proud, upright bearing reminded Laurence of Tom. "This is Mr. Beaumont, Sir Edward. He'll ride with you today."

"I have no breastplate or helmet, sir, and Lord Wilmot is expecting me at his headquarters," objected Laurence, but Hopton had turned back to his map.

"We can equip you," said Stawell. "Come with me." Laurence swore, more loudly than he had intended. "Mr. Beaumont," Stawell snapped, "the rules against blasphemy are strictly enforced here: twelve pence for every curse word. We don't approve of the vicious behaviour that Lord Wilmot allows in his Horse."

"Pray excuse me. I'll dispatch my companion with a message for Lord Wilmot while you calculate my fine." Laurence simply told Mawson to inform Wilmot that it was too late, and they parted after a hasty goodbye. "What's Waller's strength?" he asked, as Stawell took him through the camp.

"Our scouts estimate that he has some three thousand of his own Horse, and five thousand Foot, plus dragoons. And he has two regiments from the London Bands, and Balfour's cavalry. That's near on five thousand additional Horse."

Laurence swallowed more blasphemies: Waller had about twice the Royalist numbers. "How much do I owe you for my improper language?"

"I shall let it pass, on this occasion," Stawell said, in a cool tone. "Be warned, Lord Wilmot is not favoured by my men, and you may bear the brunt of their dislike."

"Then I'll be glad of a helmet and breastplate," Laurence said, as coolly.

That night Laurence lay rolled up in his cloak among the thousands of other soldiers bivouacked across the hilly countryside. He might as easily have been alone. Stawell's troops had given him a wide berth, responding with surly indifference to his attempts at conversation. He did not much care, preoccupied by Mawson's flabbergasting encounter with his double. He had never quite believed what Seward had told him about the Spaniards on board ship; was this now concrete proof of Seward's occult powers, or coincidence? He thought also about the odds of victory on the morrow, against a far superior force. His borrowed bits of armour were thin and dented, his right arm was still weak, and his shoulder muscle tender to the touch. After his musket wound abroad, he had happily exchanged active duty for the role of a spy. Had he made a bad decision in returning so soon to the field?

The next day, he rode with a vanguard of Stawell's cavalry into the nearby village, expecting a skirmish with the London brigades. Yet Waller had foxed them again by withdrawing his army to higher ground. Hopton ordered his forces up onto the slopes opposite, and vainly tried to lure Waller onto the plain below. Then scouts reported that Waller's vanguard of Horse, commanded by Balfour, was heading for the town of Alresford, about seven or eight miles from Winchester and in a crucial position on the main road to London. Stawell's regiment galloped off to occupy the town first, with the enemy cavalry thundering beside them. It was like some absurd horse race. They beat Balfour to the target, and had next to barricade the town as rapidly as possible to keep him out while they awaited reinforcements. Laurence toiled with Stawell's men to drag out carts, sacks, and bales of hay that could be torched; and they chopped down trees and ripped doors from barns and stables to block the streets. Not until long past nightfall did the main body of the army tramp in. They made camp on open ground between Alresford and the village of Cheriton, on the border of a wood, separated from Waller's army less than two miles away by a small hill and a vale.

At sunrise, Laurence woke to a man pissing so close to him that he had to leap up to avoid being wetted by the stream. Risking a fine, he commented disparagingly on the size of the man's member, and they came to blows. Laurence ducked a couple of punches and hit the man squarely in the jaw, sending him to the ground. "Wilmot's fart catcher," he taunted Laurence, through bloodied lips. "You should watch your back today."

"Go and fuck yourself," Laurence told him, "though it may be a challenge with that little prick of yours."

In a rebellious frame of mind, Laurence went out on sortie with a party of Stawell's Horse; they were to harass the enemy in the intervening ground between the two armies. But Waller released as few troops as Hopton, and no battle would be had that day. Towards dusk, although the Royalists captured another hill with a direct view of Waller's quarters in a hedge-enclosed field, they would have to spend the night in nearly the identical position as before. Hopton had ordered every man to stay by his horse, every foot soldier to keep his weapon near, and every officer to hold his place; and he had issued them with white tokens to wear in their hats, so that they could identify friend from foe.

Cold and bored, Laurence slipped away, leading his horse up the slope to the front lines where Hopton's musketeers were stationed to keep watch. Trees hid the enemy ranks down in the valley, but he could hear the faint echo of voices, the lowing of oxen, and the rumble of wheels. He tethered his horse to a branch and crawled on hands and knees to the crest of the ridge, wondering if anyone else had noticed these signs of movement. Then he tensed, catching a rustle in the undergrowth. "God with us," hissed a brusque young voice; it was the Royalist password, and Laurence answered in kind. "What in hell are you doing here?" the boy snarled at him. "You're not one of us scouts."

"Waller may be quitting the field."

"That's for me to report. Get to camp."

Laurence turned to fetch his horse. Mist obscured the valley, perhaps muffling the sounds of an army on the retreat. He was half inclined to ride straight to Wilmot and relay the news that Waller had once more dodged a fight. But he thought it best to stay, and see Hopton and Forth in the morning to deal diplomatically with any repercussions from Wilmot's unsolicited offer. It was sheer luck for the Royalists that Waller had chosen to withdraw. As for himself, he felt a cowardly relief.

## IV.

"Waller had not withdrawn, as we learnt the next day." Beaumont fell silent, staring at the floor. He looked remarkably smart in his black clothes, his hair damp from a bath, and his face properly shaved. "You did not tidy yourself up to visit *me*," Seward had observed on greeting him, but he had made no response. He needed to talk about the battle, so Seward had held back his own distressing news and listened.

"The mist was thicker at dawn," continued Beaumont eventually, "and by the time it dispersed, we saw that Waller's musketeers had occupied the wood. Our armies were only separated by the ridge he had seized, and by a valley that we couldn't enter except by a narrow lane bordered with tall hedgerows. He'd lined up infantry and guns behind the hedges. He knew our Horse couldn't push through to attack the main part of his army without suffering heavy losses. On a second try, Hopton recaptured the wood, and then we waited for hours and hours. And the men grew impatient. One of his commanders of Foot dashed out and launched an unexpected sally on the Parliament Horse."

"Poor discipline," said Seward.

"Extremely poor," said Beaumont, "and in the disorder, Balfour's cavalry swooped down upon our infantry. His Majesty's cousin, Lord

John Stuart, was sent to their aid, without success. Then it was the turn of my regiment, to run the gauntlet of those infantry and guns hidden in the hedgerows."

Seward shuddered as Beaumont described the scene: enemy guns burning great gaps in the spring hedges; men trapped, struggling to free themselves as their mounts collapsed beneath them; the stew of mud and gore; and the chaos of smoke and whistling shot and screaming.

"Stawell pressed all the way through with his vanguard. The rest of us were stuck and had to reverse down that narrow lane. When those of us who weren't killed or wounded escaped, we were ordered to keep charging. But with each charge, the enemy Foot drove us back up to the top of the hill, again and again. There was no point in fighting on." Beaumont smiled bleakly at Seward. "Hopton and Forth deserve credit for extricating the cannon, the baggage train, and the remaining troops. I heard that Forth commanded the final rearguard of Horse, and was the last to abandon the hill, in the company of his page."

"Brave man," said Seward.

"Nonetheless, it was a serious defeat – some three or four hundred dead, including a great number of officers. During the night I saw cartfuls of wounded roll in to Basing House, where we'd sought refuge. Stawell was captured, as was the leader of that mad infantry offensive. Every man from *his* regiment who hadn't been cut down in the valley was taken prisoner. His Majesty's cousin died of his wounds – Lord d'Aubigny's brother, twenty-two years old. That was Cheriton Field," concluded Beaumont. "Now a great part of our southern army is pretty much destroyed."

"Might Wilmot have saved the day, had he been there?"

"He would have improved our numbers and he might have put the fear of God into Waller's troops. But in my view, Seward, we shouldn't have engaged Waller to begin with – we were at a huge disadvantage. And Wilmot has thrown me from the frying pan right into the fire. This afternoon I must testify to the Council of War in support of his charge that Hopton's incompetence lost us the battle."

"By Jesus, he is a vainglorious fellow. His accusation is unjustified, and you must say so."

"I can't, or he may be stripped of his command. Although he has powerful enemies in Digby, Rupert, and Hopton, and the King openly dislikes him, he's as skilled an officer as Rupert. And his men are fiercely loyal to him. If they were to mutiny, the King would be in a catastrophic position."

"What sort of a friend is he to you – asking you to lie to Council?"

"It's not entirely a lie, and God knows as do you, I've told many more egregious falsehoods. I'll visit you later, Seward, and apprise you of the outcome," Beaumont said, turning for the door. "Wilmot is to meet me at Christ Church, before the other members of Council arrive."

"Beaumont, wait. I had a letter from his lordship, your father." Seward drew it from the sleeve of his robe and held it out. "His house has been occupied for Parliament."

Beaumont took the letter and read, chewing on his lower lip. "Written over a week ago. By now, the house may be in ruins."

"He says Purefoy is a gentleman—"

"The war is no longer *an affair of gentlemen*."

"Then we shall have to pray that Gloucestershire will soon be liberated."

Beaumont threw up his hands. "My dear Seward, can't you grasp the significance of our late defeat? Parliament has no more opposition in the southeast, and London is absolutely secure. When the Earl of Essex rebuilds his forces, he'll march on Oxford. The King will be cornered into a defensive war, unless Prince Rupert can subdue the North and the midlands, and rush to his aid. Rupert has wrought miracles in the past, but he has the Scots to contend with, as well as Parliament's northern armies. I suspect the King will be on his own."

"His Majesty's Oxford forces could repulse an attack by Essex."

"*If* we hang onto our surrounding garrisons, but as it is we're short of troops to provision them. I'd bet you money the Queen will be sent away for her confinement, and possibly the princes for their own safety. You should get ready to flee yourself. You'd be better off at Clarke's house in the countryside, even if his part of Oxfordshire falls to Parliament. Would you do that for me, *please?*"

"His Majesty is not defeated yet, and Oxford was retaken once before from the enemy."

"After the battle at Edgehill, but it wasn't a rout like Cheriton. Oxford may endure a long and bitter siege. And in the worst event, His Majesty would have to flee, rather than risk death or capture."

"His death is not imminent, according to the horoscope."

"Yes, well," said Beaumont, dubiously, "your visions may be more reliable than your astrological projections."

Seward frowned at him. "How do you mean?"

"My double you saw is flesh and blood. Someone I know almost mistook him for me, in Oxford. And I may have heard about him beforehand, from Pembroke."

**V.**

Wilmot was storming up and down by the closed doors of Christ Church's Great Hall. "Council has been postponed, Beaumont. Forth is too gout-ridden to rise from his bed, so I've asked for us to address His Majesty in private. What's the matter?" he said next. "You look as if you've had the wind knocked out of you."

"I have," said Laurence; he had anticipated enemy troops at Chipping Campden, but he had not reckoned on feeling such a burning, visceral desire to protect his family. "My father wrote to say that his house has been occupied by Colonel Purefoy, of the Gloucester garrison."

They were interrupted by a cough; Digby was sailing along the staircase that led to His Majesty's reception chamber. "Were you hoping for a royal audience, gentlemen? I doubt that His Majesty will acquiesce: he is very tired, and in no mood to hear your rants about his chief generals, my Lord Wilmot."

"He must, or lose the war," shouted Wilmot. "Forth is a bloody invalid, and Hopton has himself to fault that he's got no army left to command. *I* shall be bound to absorb the sorry scraps of his men into my Oxford regiments."

"Mr. Beaumont," said Digby, "you should have counselled his lordship on the perils of slander."

Laurence took a pace towards Wilmot, whose hand was straying to the hilt of his sword. "Please, my lord, let's ride for your headquarters."

"Why not settle our differences now?" murmured Wilmot, his eyes on Digby. Then he hesitated; an equerry in royal livery was clattering down the steps.

"My lords, His Majesty requests a word alone with Mr. Beaumont," the equerry said.

"It appears that our case may be heard," Wilmot sneered to Digby. "I'll see you back at Abingdon, Beaumont."

"How very uncouth he is," said Digby, as Wilmot swaggered off. "But what else can one expect from the son of a soldier of fortune ennobled only in the last century for his Irish campaigns. You have made a grave mistake, Mr. Beaumont, in transferring your loyalties to him. Good day to you, sir."

Laurence bowed to him politely, and followed the equerry upstairs.

In the royal chamber, the Queen lay on a daybed, her arms draped over her rounded stomach. With her were Jermyn and a lady-in-waiting, though not her husband. "Sir," she said to Laurence, after they had exchanged courtesies, "forgive me my ruse. Neither His Majesty nor Lord Digby knows of it, and no one else shall know of it, if we do not reach a solution to our problem. I am certain, however, that we shall. My Lord Wilmot is a friend to all of us here, and yet he has offended his king by threatening to impugn the conduct in battle of Sir Ralph Hopton. You are an astute man, Mr. Beaumont – you must understand that it is not in Lord Wilmot's interest to levy his charge. Surely you can persuade him to refrain."

"I'm flattered by your faith in me, Your Majesty," Laurence said, "but would not Lord Wilmot be more powerfully swayed by a direct address from one he holds in far greater esteem, such as yourself?"

He noticed her glance sidelong at Jermyn; they had covered this issue. "There are some who perceive me as exerting too much influence upon my husband's business," she replied. "And I did not fight at Cheriton – and neither did Lord Wilmot. If you who did were considered responsible for assuaging his lordship's fears as to the professional abilities of General Hopton . . ."

"Mr. Beaumont," said Jermyn, "we are depending on you."

The Queen extended her hand for Laurence to kiss. "A note from my Lord Wilmot would suffice, as confirmation. Bring it to us as swiftly as you can. And pray tell him that I have intervened for his sake, and cannot do so again."

"Yes, Your Majesty," said Laurence; he did not like the Queen, but she had demonstrated singular diplomacy today.

On the ride to Abingdon, he tried to shut out an insidious despair that had begun to colour his thoughts about everything, from the King's fate in this war to his family's predicament, to that of Isabella, and to his own situation. It was a mild, sunny afternoon, and all around him the countryside burgeoned with signs of spring. Yet as he veered his horse away from a line of treacherous mole hills that resembled little fresh-dug graves, he found himself contemplating death; and he wondered if men slain in their prime tasted any different to a worm than those who died peacefully of old age.

"My lord," he said to Wilmot, when he had explained Her Majesty's request, "you must heed Machiavelli's wisdom, and pick your battles. You went too far in your accusation, and you're lucky she's granted you a second chance with the King."

"He's afraid of the consequences, should I press my charge. He knows my men would rally behind me."

"What's more important to you," asked Laurence, "winning a war, or humiliating an officer whose troops you'll have to govern in your regiment? And why create more enemies in Council? Why prejudice your friendship with the Queen, and the marriage that she's helped to arrange for you?"

Wilmot was silent, tugging on his moustache. At length he said, "Mark my words, Beaumont, it's the last time I'll compromise my honour and my integrity as a general, or as a man. And in future, I insist that you stand by me *as my friend*, even if you think I've picked the wrong battle." Laurence watched over Wilmot's shoulder as he scribbled a paragraph, signed his name, and set his seal on it. "Mawson can take it to Oxford. You and I have some drinking to do."

## VI.

Sentries waved the shabby, bearded peddler through the Hackney Road fortifications without troubling to search his basket of ribbons, threads, pins, and needles. Price passed as unremarked through the Cheapside crowds and westwards along Paternoster Row towards Ludgate. But when he got to the Saracen's Head, as a precaution he sneaked round to the kitchen door, which was propped open for the benefit of the cooks labouring over their bubbling pots and spitting roasts.

"Good morning to you, sirs," he addressed them, in a wheedling voice. "Is Mistress Sprye at work today?"

"She ain't been here in over a month," said one of the cooks. "Mr. Nunn threw her out."

Price felt a twinge of guilt: he could guess why. "Where did she go?"

"To the devil, as should you."

Price walked east again towards Fish Street, though he thought it more likely that Sue had gone to her family in Bristol, or as he sincerely hoped, had acquired a new admirer. The tenement building repulsed him more than on the winter day he had left it; the same mob of hideous, malnourished children were playing in the yard, screeching as they kicked about an inflated pig's bladder. One of them pointed at him and chanted jeeringly, "Scarecrow, scarecrow!"

He turned into the passageway, and knocked on the door. "Is anyone in?" he called, not very loudly.

"Who's there?"

His heart plummeted. "It's me, Ned."

Sue opened, and gawped at him. She was clad in the gown she had worn on their tour of St. Saviour's Church, and he could detect the swell of belly at the front of her skirts. She had lost her country complexion, though not the sparkle in her eyes. "Don't you look a sight, Ned – I'd never have known you in those rags, with that ugly fringe of beard on your chin."

"It's my disguise. It's dangerous for me to be here, Sue – Parliament's spies will be searching for me."

She shut the door, and touched her stomach. "Still, it's high time you were back." Before he could stop her, she embraced him, knocking off his hat.

"Easy there!" He dumped his basket on the floor, and took a seat on the bed. Dismal beyond belief, he thought, surveying the stained walls and ceiling, the cracked horn pane window, and her laundry hung on a line of rope. "How've you been, Sue?"

"Mr. Nunn wouldn't keep me because of the morning sickness," she said, sitting down heavily next to Price. "He paid me a week's wages, and said he was sorry."

"*Sorry?*" echoed Price. "The heartless wretch."

"Where've *you* been, Ned? In Oxford?"

"Mostly, yes."

"Did your Mr. Beaumont tell how he met me at the Saracen's Head?" Price nodded. "At first I didn't believe it could be him – he's as black as one of them heathen mariners that live by the docks. And the way he spoke wasn't as I'd expected from the son of a lord. He was kind to me, though: he gave me money and advised me to get better lodgings."

Beaumont had not mentioned this to him, Price noted. "Why didn't you, then?"

"To save the money for our wedding, of course. And after Mr. Nunn dismissed me, I was afraid to move in case you wouldn't be able find me. I hate it here, Ned," she confessed, her brave front crumbling. "And I'm sick of those noisy brats. They did for the simpleton boy – he jumped in the river when they were chasing him and drowned, God rest his soul." She reached for Price's hand. "Thank heaven you've come for me, or I might follow his example."

"The fact is, I shouldn't have come at all," Price said, in a sombre tone, sliding his hand from hers to pull off his coat. "Lord Digby would fly into a rage if he knew."

"Who's Lord Digby?"

"His Majesty's Secretary of State. Mr. Beaumont and I are his agents."

"Ooh Ned, you *have* risen in the world!"

Price ripped apart the coat lining and extracted forty pounds in coin, piling it into her lap. "This is for you and the child, Sue. You'll have more when I can send it from Oxford. But as I said, I daren't stay with you here."

Nervousness crept into Sue's eyes. "A couple of men were in the taproom just over two weeks after I met Mr. Beaumont: a Mr. Veech and a Mr. Draycott. Mr. Veech said they were friends of yours, and that you'd gone to Oxford on work for him. He asked if you'd ever talked to me of Mr. Beaumont."

"What did you say?" he demanded, gripping her arm.

"That you hadn't. Then he said he had a hundred pounds for you, and you should call on him to get it. Who are they, Ned?"

"No friends of mine." Price shivered and released his grip. "Veech is a spy for Parliament, and Draycott answers to him. That's why I mustn't enter the City again."

"You won't have to. We'll go to Oxford together and be married there. We can set ourselves up nicely before the child is born."

Price had prepared his speech. "Sue, what was between us was an error for which I accept entire responsibility. But the truth is that I can't marry you."

Her expression hardened. "Have you another wife?"

For a moment, Price considered lying. "No."

"Then you owe it to me to abide by your promise."

"Even the King can't abide by his promises these days! We're a country at war, and I'm in the thick of it."

"You were in the thick of it when you courted me."

"Not as I am now. You deserve a life happier and more secure than you'd have with me – you and the child."

"It's *our* child, Ned."

"With your fine qualities, you'll have a string of suitors vying for you," Price breezed on. "You need a man with a decent trade, not that of a spy, which is what I am. We're not so different from thieves, us spies," he added, borrowing Beaumont's words.

"You *are* a thief – you stole my virtue."

"And I can't wrong you more than I already have. I'm thinking of your welfare. You may not understand that today, but you'll be grateful to me in time."

"Grateful?" she repeated, after a deafening pause. "To be used for your pleasure and tossed aside?"

"Now that's unfair. I could have written to you, to say goodbye. I risked my life to tell you to your face, and help you out with money." She glared at him and next at the coins, then brushed them from her lap as though they were soiling her. "Oh Sue," he admonished; some had rolled under the bed. He knelt to hunt for them but was loath to fumble in the litter of mouse droppings, and the accumulated dust and grime. "Have you got a broom?" he asked, straightening up.

"No, I've something else for you." A wave of tepid fluid stung him in the eyes. Sue was brandishing an empty chamber pot. As he blinked and spluttered, she threw aside the pot, seized a pewter candlestick and crashed it into the bridge of his nose. Blood gushed instantly from his nostrils and he howled in pain.

"Will you stop," he yelled, as she raised the candlestick for a second blow.

"If it wouldn't kill me I'd tear your child from my womb," she shouted. "A pox on you, you low deceiving rascal. Get out."

Staggering to his feet, Price snatched his coat and hat and basket of wares, and rushed to the door. He whipped it open, but not fast enough: the candlestick struck him squarely between the shoulder blades. He moaned and raced out across the yard clutching his free hand over his nose. The children doubled up with laughter and chorused, "Scarecrow, scarecrow!"

At the corner of Fish and Thames Streets, he stumbled over to a water trough, nudged away the horse that was drinking from it, and plunged his head in, gasping as he surfaced, having to breathe through his mouth. Gingerly he fingered the damage: his nose was broken. When the ripples in the barrel subsided and he saw his reflection in the water, he started to weep. "Stupid, goddamned fool that I am, no better than a dog returning to its vomit," he blubbered, picking up his basket, and traipsed towards the Strand. He would lurk there until dusk, when the patrols thinned, and he could approach the Hallam residence.

**VII.**

"Why should Sir Montague Hallam wish you to sup with him, Giles?" inquired Judith, as she sponged a stain from his Sunday doublet. "I thought your business was finished more than a month ago when he signed the contract with Parliament."

"He has some other legal issue to discuss," replied Draycott, hating the falsehood. He had torn up Sir Montague's note, an apology for the delayed invitation: Lady Isabella had been called to a sick friend, and was only recently back in London.

"Is this connected with your duties for Mr. St. John?"

"I'll find out when I see him, Judith."

"I wonder sometimes about those duties, you are so reticent about them."

"I am reticent on St. John's order," said Draycott; thank God that, as yet, he had never had to speak to her again of Veech.

"It seems to me he pays you a great deal for very little work."

"Should I complain?"

"Not when we're still paying off bills," she said ruefully, setting aside the sponge.

"There may be more work ahead that will keep me busy of an evening. With the extra money, you could hire a lady companion to sit up with you, as the children's nurse goes early to bed."

"Why would I sit up, Giles, unless I worried that you might not come home?"

"No need, then."

He dressed, combed his hair, and sprinkled a few drops of rose-water onto the palms of his hands to dab on his freshly shaven jaw. How appalled she would be if she knew what Veech had ordered him to do; and did the righteous Mr. St. John know?

Draycott tried to kiss her at the door, but she averted her face. "I'll prepare the spare chamber for you – you may be late."

"I can snuggle into our bed."

"Please, Giles, I've slept so badly ever since Geoffrey died. I had intended to beg of you . . ."

"What, my dear? Tell me – whatever can I do for you," he said, taking her in his arms.

"Do not . . . come to me at night."

"I haven't, Judith, in as long as we've been mourning, though it might have solaced us. Are you afraid to get another child?" he asked, remembering how he had felt. Time had blunted the edges of his bitterness, and now he thought a new life would bring them closer together; he missed his wife's body, as much out of affection as habit.

"I don't wish to have *any* more children."

The finality in her voice shocked him. "You would contravene God's law and my rights as your husband."

"That's why I am begging. You can say no."

He clapped on his hat. "It's not the moment to talk. Be sure and fasten the bolts on the windows, and don't answer the door. I promise not to disturb you tonight."

"Thank you, Giles," she said, as if he had accepted her wish.

——

The gallery looked cosier to Draycott on this mild April evening, as he waited for Sir Montague and Lady Isabella. Candles glowed in sconces on the walls, and the vivid colours of the tapestries were muted by shadow. To distract himself from thinking about Judith, he began to peruse a stack of books on the window seat. They were in Latin; Sir Montague was schooled in more than wine, he supposed. The slenderest of them, bound in purple calfskin and embossed with gilt letters, was Ovid's *Remedia Amoris*. During his Cambridge days, he had read *The Metamorphoses*, though his tutor had deemed some of Ovid's works immoral and had forbidden them to the students. Intrigued by the title, Draycott opened the book. On the flyleaf was a handwritten dedication in flowery script: "In the hope that you may be inspired to forget the past and embrace the future. I remain, as ever, your faithful George, Lord Digby," and beneath it, "Christmastide, 1643."

Draycott snapped the book shut. Sir Montague's faithful George was one of Parliament's chief enemies, and Veech might call this evidence of Sir Montague's guilt in the affair of the barrels. Or was it? They knew Sir Montague did trade with Oxford Royalists. But *faithful George* hinted at more than a business relationship. And what past was Lord Digby urging him to forget?

Draycott heard footsteps and the swish of skirts. He restored the book to the pile and hurried to station himself in front of Lady Isabella's favourite tapestry, pretending to admire it.

She entered with Lucy. "Mr. Draycott, Sir Montague had an unexpected appointment in Whitehall, and had no chance to send you word. He was obliged to go out: the Earl of Pembroke is a valued customer, and most partial to my husband's claret."

"No matter, your ladyship," Draycott said. "I'll look forward to the pleasure of his company on some other occasion."

"Please stay, sir, if *my* company won't bore you. Over these past weeks I attended a beloved friend in his last illness, and I am in want of cheerful conversation."

He reconsidered, noticing the hollowness to her cheeks, and the shadows beneath her eyes. "Then I shall, my lady, and I am sorry for your loss."

"Our sorrows can't compare: you suffered the death of a child, while my dear Mr. Cotterell was an old man who had lived a fruitful and contented life. Now, let us eat."

They went into a parlour on the same floor where a round table was set for three. A bright candelabrum illuminated the gleaming plates, and cutlery, and crystal glasses. On the parlour walls he saw not tapestries but two portraits of a dour, elderly couple in high ruffs. "Sir Montague's late parents," she explained. "They held the wine trade in contempt, though they were not too proud to live off his profits. He derives a perverse satisfaction from tippling under their noses. I find them disconcerting, myself: their eyes appear to follow one about – an artist's trick, in the angle of the pupils. Lucy, remove Sir Montague's place, and then you may be at your leisure," she told her maid.

Draycott resolved to enjoy the meal, though he knew how Judith would detest him supping in such intimacy with her ladyship, even if Greenhalgh was present to serve them. The food tasted as delectable as the wine: speckled trout in a butter and caper sauce; a dish of widgeon stewed with prunes; and a syllabub.

Lady Isabella talked about Sir Montague's clients in Parliament, and his sympathy for the Earl of Pembroke, who led a solitary existence. Then she switched to politics. "I gather that Lord Essex feels himself slighted, these days, by the Committee of Both Kingdoms," she remarked, as Draycott ate his syllabub. "He and General Waller behave no better than quarrelling schoolboys! He has claimed that Waller's victory at Cheriton will not signify unless he is given men and materiel to augment his own army for an attack on His Majesty's garrisons around Oxford. But it's my guess that Parliament will give Waller his pick of the cavalry and of London's Trained Bands, and leave Essex yet more discontented. They should beware: their squabbles could cost us the war."

"Your ladyship is well versed in military affairs," Draycott said. "My Judith can't bear to read the broadsheets. She's sickened by the bloodthirsty atrocities reported there."

"They're often wild exaggerations of the truth or pure invention. Nevertheless, they are a powerful weapon. Infinite money may be the sinews of war, as Cicero wrote, but the nourishment of hatred is as vital, to keep the populace engaged. And broadsheets are cheap to print and easy to distribute."

A stunning thought came to Draycott: might the Latin books be hers and Lord Digby *her* faithful George? This would fit with Veech's interest in her. "Are you familiar with the works of Cicero, my lady?"

"I haven't read his whole opus – he can be dry, at times." She settled back in her chair, fiddling with the stem of her glass. "What inclined you to Parliament's side, Mr. Draycott?"

"His Majesty's arbitrary rule and the religious meddling of his queen. I wouldn't like to see our country papist again." Draycott hesitated. "Sir Montague must be of a similar view."

"My husband is and has always been a businessman. He sells to whoever will pay his price, as you are aware from his dealings in Oxford." Her face softened, and she rested her elbows on the table, cupping her chin in her hands. "I should have asked: how is your wife, sir, in her bereavement?"

"She was the strongest of us at first, yet recently she has been inconsolable."

"She is a woman – she had to be strong when you were not, and now she has to vent her feelings." Draycott smiled at Lady Isabella's perspicacity. "Have you been married long, sir?"

"Ten years. I was assigned as clerk to her father at eighteen, after I was up at Cambridge. He helped me gain admission to Middle Temple, and once called to the Bar, I joined his practice. He had planned for me to wed Judith, his sole child. Upon his death I would inherit both the practice and a house of his, which I did. Judith's mother preferred to maintain a separate household."

"Some marriages are happier in the absence of a mother-in-law," Lady Isabella said, laughing.

Draycott laughed also. "In my own case, I have to agree. How were you introduced to Sir Montague, my lady?"

"Through my former guardian. I was orphaned young: my father died before my birth and my mother when I was a little girl." Draycott listened on, but a peculiar sensation began nagging at him: as though there was a third presence in the room apart from those he could see. Then abruptly he caught his breath. "What is it, sir?" she asked.

He pointed at the portrait of Sir Montague's father on the wall behind her. "I could have sworn that . . . his eyes moved."

She twisted in her seat and glowered at the portrait. "I have implored Sir Montague to hang those canvases in his dressing closet, but he will not do it. He is entertained by my dislike of them. Come, sir, let's go to the gallery. We shall have a sip of Malmsey, to soothe our nerves."

"No, thank you, my lady," said Draycott. "*My* nerves are a sure symptom of weariness. I should go home." As before, she descended with him to the entrance hall. "Pardon my silly fright," he apologised, now thoroughly ashamed.

"It's that pair of baleful ghosts. But you must not let them scare you. Don't be a stranger to us." When he had put on his cloak, she gave him her hand; and as he brushed his lips against her knuckles, he could smell again that exotic perfume on her skin.

"Goodnight to you, my lady. Please convey my greetings to Sir Montague, and my regret that he could not join us."

"I shall, and goodnight, sir," she said.

Draycott walked out onto the Strand, which was quiet save for some militiamen steering away a bedraggled peddler, an incongruous figure in this rich neighbourhood. How tragic that Lady Isabella's guardian had not chosen her a younger husband, he thought. If the copy of *Remedia Amoris* were hers, might Lord Digby have been her lover? Was Digby urging her to forget their past, and embrace a future with Sir Montague? Or did the book belong to her husband, and was Digby counselling the widowed Sir Montague about his marriage to Lady Isabella? Whatever the truth, Draycott knew that he ought to tell Veech about the dedication. But the consequences for her petrified him.

## VIII.

Tom and Adam tethered their horses by an ancient humpbacked bridge that spanned the River Severn. They were some miles east of Shrewsbury, in desolate countryside. Tom strained to catch the thud of hooves, but could hear only ewes bleating to their lambs in the pasture, and the forlorn cawing of rooks. He pulled off his gloves to wipe his sweaty hands on the front of his coat. "Why the hell did he insist on this godforsaken spot when we could have met at the camp," he muttered to Adam.

"I don't know, sir."

After an hour or so of waiting, Adam gestured to the far side of the bridge: two riders were approaching at a gallop. "Look at him," Tom said, as the Spaniards slowed pace and crossed the bridge towards them. "Isn't the likeness incredible?"

"That it is," gasped Adam.

The Spaniards reined in and leapt from their horses. The valet bowed, but de Zamora only beckoned to Tom, and said, "Come."

They walked together onto the bridge, leaving their servants behind.

"Were you at Chipping Campden, sir?" Tom asked, now wondering if de Zamora had chosen a private meeting place because he had bad news from home.

"No."

"Then where have you been in all this time?"

De Zamora sat down on one of the bridge's drystone walls, and contemplated the eddying waters of the Severn. "Answer me first, did you write to her ladyship about me?"

"I've written neither to her, nor to my father. I thought you would have visited them by now."

"Who else have you told that I am here in England?"

"My brother-in-law, Ingram, who rides with my troop."

"But not your brother?"

"No, I wanted to tell him in person. I haven't yet had the chance."

"Ah, thank heaven," sighed de Zamora. "Because what little you told *me* has changed everything. I have been searching my soul long and hard ever since, and I arrived at the conclusion that God put you in my path before him, to stop me from ruining the happiness of your family, which is the furthest from my desire." A quiver of apprehension passed through Tom, though he did not interrupt. "Thomas, I was not sent to England by King Philip. I came to fulfil a promise to *my* older brother, Jorge. He revealed a secret to me on his deathbed that I kept for over thirty years, until I learnt that my days were numbered, and felt driven to embark upon my journey."

Tom frowned. "You seem to me in perfect health."

"The rot lies within – the worm inside the apple." De Zamora buried his face in his hands. "You must advise me. I cannot die with this heinous omission upon my conscience, and yet . . . I shrink from the duty."

"What is your brother's secret?"

De Zamora glanced up, evidently bracing himself. "I shall begin with some history. Unlike you and your brother, Jorge and I were as peas in a pod, though a year and a half separated our births and our characters were quite opposite. As a child, I endured many an undeserved whipping on his account. We both entered the army young, but while I served obediently and rose through the ranks, he flouted the rules, led a dissipated life, and was nearly hanged as a deserter. At twenty-three, his crimes caught up with him: he was mortally wounded, stabbed in the belly by the husband of his mistress."

"Christ Almighty," said Tom: Jorge's misdeeds sounded familiar.

"Let me turn back two years, Thomas. When his lordship your father was paying court to your mother, Jorge had inflicted on himself a mild injury to evade military service. He was in Seville spending his nights in debauchery and his days in flirting with his pretty cousins. I believe he cherished a special fancy for Elena, and it enraged him that your father's suit should have been accepted by his aunt Cecilia, Elena's mother." De Zamora paused. "In his final moments on earth, Jorge confessed to me and to a priest that the night before Elena left Seville with her betrothed, he crept into the chamber where she slept, and . . . robbed her of her maidenhood."

Tom's gorge rose; he was imagining his mother raped by a man with his brother's face. "It can't be true."

"I have on me his apology to her, Thomas, most of it dictated – he was too feeble to hold a quill towards the end. He begged me to take it to her, and I gave him my promise." De Zamora reached into his doublet and brought forth a dog-eared letter, the parchment faded to a yellowish brown. "I can translate if you wish."

"No," said Tom, grabbing it. The Spanish was inscrutable to him, but he saw that the letter started in spiky, uneven script that grew increasingly erratic. The rest was in a flowing hand. There were three signatures at the bottom: one scrawled, "Jorge de Zamora y Fuentes," followed by "Antonio de Zamora y Fuentes'" in firm writing, and "Luis Iglesia, Societas Iesu" in the flowing hand.

"Now you may understand what changed for me when we met," said de Zamora, in a sepulchral tone. "You told me of the Lady Elena's silence about her Spanish family. I thought she might at least have talked about those of us who had done her no wrong, but the whole subject must have been too painful for her. Then you told me how your older brother Laurence was like me. Has he my dark complexion and green eyes?" Tom nodded, trembling. "They are inherited from the Fuentes branch of the family, Thomas – your maternal grandmother and my mother were sisters, both dark and green-eyed. My mother married my namesake, Antonio de Zamora, and Lady Elena's was wed to Giraldo de Capdavila."

Tom thrust the letter at him. "I've had enough of your family history, sir."

"I must know one more detail of yours: your brother's date of birth."

"He was born on the sixth of June, sixteen twelve."

"*Madre de Dios* – then it is possible."

"*What* is?"

"Your brother could be Jorge's son."

De Zamora might have punched Tom in the guts. Yet how it all made sense: of his mother's silence, of her sudden illness upon receiving the Envoy's letter about Antonio, of Laurence's wanton nature, and of the long estrangement between himself and his brother.

"Thomas, this is so complicated – more than I ever predicted when I sailed for England. I had hoped the Lady Elena would be glad that Jorge had repented of his sin. But should she have borne his child, and should my suspicions come to the ears of his lordship your father or your poor brother . . ." De Zamora shook his head, his expression noble and determined. "I cannot do it. I shall write to the Lady Elena and say that I am dying, and must forgo our reacquaintance to settle my affairs in Spain." He balled up the letter in his fist, and raised his arm to toss it into the river.

"Stop," shouted Tom. "Laurence must see it."

"And put doubt in his mind as to his paternity? That would be cruel, Thomas."

Tom wanted to laugh, for in *his* mind it was as plain as day. "Oh no, Don Antonio, you would do him a favour."


IX.

Antonio said nothing while he and Diego galloped their horses well beyond earshot of the bridge; he was too confused. Diego spoke first. "So, Don Antonio, has he told his brother of you? Did he write to his lordship or her ladyship?"

"Thus far he has kept quiet."

"Phew! Did he suspect Jorge's story?"

"He gobbled it up. As for your beautiful forgery, had I thrown it into the water, he would have dived in after it."

"Then what went amiss? Will he go running to his parents for their version of events?"

"I doubt it, he was so aghast at the insult to his mother's virtue. But hear this, Diego: he proposed that he and I meet with Laurence. He said that once Laurence sees the deathbed confession, he will be relieved of an enormous burden that he has always wished to be rid of."

"What burden?"

"Lord Beaumont's title and estate. Apparently he will be over-joyed to cede them to Thomas, if the taint of illegitimacy can somehow be hidden from public knowledge. And Thomas thinks his brother will find a means, such is his distaste for the inheritance."

Diego looked sceptical. "Thomas is lying, the greedy fellow."

"I swear he's not. As you said, he is transparent."

"Yes, well – his brother's no saint, just as the gypsy told you. *You* should hear what gossip I winkled out of the valet, Adam: how Lord Beaumont dotes on his heir, his *prodigal* son, though Laurence has given his father nought but heartache, with his drinking and gaming and whoring, and has teased and mocked his brother mercilessly since their childhood. The Christmas before last, Thomas came to blows with him over some harlot he had fucked shamelessly under his father's roof."

Antonio burst into laughter. "Now I am beginning to like him. Are they still enemies?"

"They've been friendlier of late, but Adam intimated that the truce is paper-thin. So why would this rascal surrender a title and a fortune in land and wealth to a brother *he* doesn't like?"

"Not to earn a seat in heaven," Antonio responded, laughing again.

## X.

In the kitchen at Blackman Street, through mouthfuls of eel stew, Price poured out to Barlow and Sarah what had transpired since Beaumont had hired him as an agent, ending with his ignominious arrest in the Strand. "I was found guilty of loitering beyond the hour of curfew, and spent ten days in the Fleet because I couldn't pay the fine."

"And to think you were afraid of being taken by Veech," Barlow commented. "Why didn't you send for me at once?"

"I hadn't a brass farthing after the turnkey was finished robbing me. It took me that long to raise money to pay someone to fetch you."

"Picked some pockets, Ned?" Sarah asked.

"There were none worth picking."

"Did you bend over your sweet bum to pleasure the turnkey?" Price grimaced and flung down his spoon; she was close to the truth. "Was it he who mashed your nose in?"

"No, it was Susan Sprye, the thankless bitch." Price could not resist a boast. "I've better prospects in mind: I'm about to court Madam Elizabeth Ormiston for my wife. She's Mr. Beaumont's widowed sister."

Sarah howled uproariously, slapping her thigh. "You've lost your wits, Ned Price."

"We are in love, Sarah."

"You may be besotted with each other, for all I know, but blood is blood and yours ain't blue. You've more chance of mating with one of them lions caged up in the Tower."

"Mr. Beaumont said he has no objection, if his father gives me leave to address her."

Barlow stomped out of the kitchen and came back with a hand mirror that used to belong to Mistress Edwards. "Wake up, Ned, and open your eyes."

"You weren't never the prettiest of fellows – just middling, I'd say," Sarah added, "but now you are downright ugly."

Price flinched from his image and changed the subject. "Is it safe for me to stay, Barlow?"

"The Southwark militia are thin on the ground these days," Barlow said. "Most of the brigades are to march out on campaign with Lord Essex. And why would Veech trouble to keep watching the house? Mr. Beaumont ain't been near in months, the ladies have gone to Rose's family at Chelmsford, and I've sworn off my old trade."

"My next concern is to communicate with Lady Hallam, on Lord Digby's business. Her ladyship won't trust anyone save me," said Price haughtily, still smarting from their abuse.

"Then you'll need a new disguise," said Sarah, "to match your new nose."

## XI.

"Ah Beaumont, come in," cried Seward. "We are all hustle and bustle at Merton. The Queen is leaving us for Bath, Clarke informs me, and then she will travel onwards to Exeter for her confinement."

"And tomorrow the King is to prorogue his Assembly," Beaumont said, with artificial cheer. "His army will take to the field, to cut off an attack by Essex and the redoubtable London Trained Bands."

"Is Lord Wilmot's Horse to ride out with him?"

"Yes indeed." Beaumont looked down at Pusskins, who was sniffing at his boots. "That cat of yours would benefit from a little exercise. He's as round as Dr. Clarke."

"It is the season: each spring, he busies himself destroying a host of newborn mice and rats."

"I ate a few rats in the war abroad, when I was serving with the Spanish."

"How was the meat?"

"Quite tasty, but, as they say, hunger is the best sauce."

Seward eyed his friend. "You have more news for me, other than that you are off on campaign."

"I received a puzzling note from Tom," Beaumont confessed. "He wants us to discuss an urgent family matter, too delicate to broach until we're face to face. It's not in Tom's nature to be *delicate*."

"Might it concern your father's health, or the occupation of the house?"

"Perhaps both. At any rate, Wilmot's granted me leave to ride out and call on the Furnivals before we become embroiled in action. They may know more about what's happened at Chipping Campden. And I should set a day for my marriage – it's the only thing I can do, to give my parents some comfort in their beleaguered state."

"You should get a message to her ladyship about your Spanish double."

"And tell her what, Seward? That a relative of hers by blood was caught assaulting some woman in an Oxford pothouse famous for its drunks and thieves? Or that he might have murdered an officer of Parliament, while in London? If he *was* the murderer, which I can't confirm, she might well congratulate him."

"You could at least warn her that he is here in England," Seward said darkly.

## XII.

Veech trained his perspective glass on the window of Lady Hallam's bedchamber. He was familiar with her nightly routine: towards the hour of eleven, she would go up to be undressed by her maid. Strumpet that she was, she never drew the curtains. And what a time it took her to discard all her layers, and unpin her hair, and have it brushed. Then she would stand by the window in her flimsy nightgown and look out, as though she could see him watching from the thicket of trees across the street. He studied the curves of her body. Those full, high breasts struck him as awkward, vulnerable appendages. They reminded him of a church he had once visited in Italy dedicated to St. Agatha, and the old priest who had recounted her legend to him. Devoutly Christian, she was thrown into a brothel by a Roman envious of her love for God. When she still refused to renounce her faith, despite being forced to serve as a whore, the Roman had tortured her and cut off her breasts; and she had died a martyr. "Now there's an idea," Veech said to himself, laughing, and put away his glass.

# Part Three

England, April–July 1644

# CHAPTER ELEVEN

## I.

"My visit will again have to be short, with all the patrols on the roads," Laurence told Lady Margaret as she led him into the hall. There he found the same gathering of gentlewomen and girls at their domestic labours, Pen and Catherine included. Today Catherine looked less wild, her hair dressed, and her gown neat and clean; and now that he saw the twins in such close proximity, he observed a stronger resemblance between them, yet Catherine's face seemed to him older than Pen's by some years. "Have you any word from my family, your ladyship?" he inquired.

"I am afraid not, sir – their house must still be under occupation, though we did hear a rumour that Colonel Massey might summon his men back to Gloucester garrison. Sir Harold is in the far meadow with our shepherds. I'll bid him to come to us at once."

"I thank you, but there's no need," Laurence said, pleased to avoid the man. "If you would inform him that in a bit over a week I've another very brief leave to ride out for the wedding ceremony, and then I must return straight to Oxford."

"Sir, that is impossibly soon," said Pen. "My gown will not be ready."

"And the banns should be asked three Sundays in advance, in Chipping Campden parish and in ours, and we've a feast to prepare," said Lady Margaret, with mild reproach.

"These are not normal circumstances, ladies. My own family can't risk attending the ceremony, and if Parliament discovers I'm in the neighbourhood, you'll be visited by rebel troops. My capture would put a tidy conclusion to my prospects as Penelope's husband. There must be no feast, simply a quick exchange of vows."

"The war interferes with everything," complained Penelope.

Laurence turned deliberately to Catherine. "What happened to the magpie? Has his wing healed?"

"I'm not sure, sir," Catherine said, "but he's got a fine appetite. I keep him in a cage, in a barn near the stables."

"Sir Harold failed to comprehend why you took pains to rescue it, sir," said Lady Margaret. "I had to explain to him that you were merely humouring our daughter's tender heart."

"You're entirely wrong, my lady," said Laurence. "I was humouring myself. As a boy, I kept a sort of hospital for wounded creatures. If I couldn't save them, I would dissect them for my lessons in anatomy."

"Mr. Beaumont must excel in the study of anatomy," Penelope remarked. "I hope he will instruct me in it, next week."

Her mother and the ladies blushed and tittered, but not Catherine, Laurence noticed. Was it true what Elizabeth and Jermyn said: that she did not wish to marry? Or was she offended by her sister's joke? He assumed an air of masculine command. "I'd like to see that magpie, on my way out."

"Mr. Beaumont," said Lady Margaret, "you don't have to humour her further when you are in such a hurry."

Catherine shifted in her seat; and in her eyes he read a mute appeal. "Once more, I am humouring myself," he said, "and it will take me no time at all."

"Your sisters shall accompany you, Catherine. Pen, dear?"

"I would rather not," said Penelope.

In that moment he knew: they would come to detest each other, as a married couple. "Good day to you then, ladies, and until next week."

A pack of girls pursued him and Catherine into the courtyard, squealing as they entered the shadowy barn when a mouse scuttled for shelter in a bale of straw. In one corner was a wooden cage. Catherine knelt down by it, as did Laurence. Unfastening a door on top, she deftly withdrew the bird, and set it on the floor. Immediately it tried to hide behind the cage. "Don't," she said, to the children crowding round. "You're frightening him."

"We'll do as we like, Miss *Cat*," snapped the tallest girl, a miniature of Penelope.

"Get out and shut the door," said Laurence. The other children ran off, but she lingered. "And you," he told her, at which she flounced out, pouting. "Why does she talk to you so rudely?" he asked Catherine.

Catherine said nothing. She untied the magpie's bandage, stroked its feathers into place, and offered it to Laurence. He extended the wing and felt for the break, though his eyes were wandering: to the light pattern of freckles on the bridge of Catherine's nose, the thick fringe of her lashes, and a tiny scar on her forehead. Her ears were not pierced, unusual in a young woman. She had mentioned that she had no jewellery, yet even her little sisters wore earrings. Why not her?

"Is it better, sir?"

With an effort, Laurence focused on the magpie. "How long has he been here?"

"We rescued him on the fourth of March, and today is the sixteenth of April."

"How well you remember."

Just as he heard the clip clop of hooves from the courtyard, a veiled expression came over her face. "My father is home, sir. You must forgive Pen's boldness," she went on, as though someone were dictating her speech. "She's so eager to be married to you."

"But not until her gown is ready. And you – are you eager to be married?" Catherine inhaled sharply; Laurence might have pricked her with a pin. He let go of the bird, which began to flutter about, experimenting with hops off the ground. He waited, and still she did not answer. "Is there some . . . impropriety in my question?"

She ignored it altogether. "Should I make him a new bandage?"

"No. Look at him – he's testing the wing. He has to learn how to fly again."

She fixed on Laurence her dark, compelling gaze, and a thought crept into his head; to act on it would interfere with everything, like the war. "What if he can't, sir? What then?"

Sir Harold was shouting, "Mr. Beaumont? Mr. Beaumont! Where are you?"

*Go to hell*, Laurence told him.

"Sir," she persisted, in a low, desperate voice, "if he can't fly, would it be right to keep him in this cage for the rest of his life? Perhaps we shouldn't have rescued him. It's worse to be offered hope, only to be disappointed."

"Catherine," Laurence said, as urgently, "did you know that the male magpie is almost identical to the female? They could be twins by their appearance, but within they're different. You may be your sister's twin, but I think you're very different in character. And I think she and I are not suited for marriage. Would *you* ever—"

"I'm more different from her than you know," Catherine interrupted. "My father is calling you."

Laurence rose, cursing his own vanity: why should he have expected a reciprocal attraction? She was biting her lower lip, eyes screwed shut. "Which of you is the oldest, you or Penelope?" he asked.

"I am," she said, without looking up, "by an hour."

"Thank you," he said, and walked out to Sir Harold.

"I should have thrown that damned bird to my dogs," Sir Harold boomed jovially. "What a silly girl she is, to be so infatuated with it. Pen has more sense." He clapped a hand on Laurence's shoulder. "A storm is blowing our way, sir, and it will be no weather for riding. You must stop fretting about the rebels, and pass the night with us."

A veritable storm, thought Laurence, as Sir Harold marched him into the house.

Penelope was clearly delighted by his reappearance, and Lady Margaret announced to her husband, "Mr. Beaumont has said that he wishes to marry Pen in a little more than a week."

"On which day, sir?" said Sir Harold, apparently untroubled by religious preliminaries.

Laurence adopted Lady Beaumont's most glacial tone. "It *was* to have been the twenty-fourth of April—"

"Oh, but the twenty-fourth is not a Sunday," interjected Lady Margaret; then she caught his use of the past tense. "Will you postpone it, after all?"

"I am reconsidering it altogether, my lady, since I hear from Catherine that *she* is your eldest daughter."

Sir Harold snorted. "She had no business prattling on to you. I told you she's a silly creature."

"I dislike your attitude, sir," Laurence said. "Had I not met her by chance last time, in the . . . the stable, I would never know of her existence. You've done her a gross discourtesy: convention requires that I should have proposed to her first."

"But, Mr. Beaumont, Catherine does not want to be married," said Penelope, with a patient air.

"That's not the point. She was allowed no opportunity to refuse me. And as for you, Mistress Penelope, though I might have taken you as my bride, I confess, I had grave doubts about our happiness as man and wife."

She coloured. "Doubts, sir?"

"When, pray God, the war ends, and should I survive it, I intend to pass the rest of my days cultivating whatever is left of my father's estate. You find the countryside dull, compared to the society you enjoyed at Oxford. I think you would be miserable leading such a life with me." Laurence softened his voice. "You have youth, beauty, and charm to recommend you. You will have many other proposals of marriage. It would be unfair of me to continue my suit."

"You would insult me if you broke it off," cried Penelope.

"Mr. Beaumont, we cannot, at this late stage," expostulated Sir Harold. "It will be imagined you heard of some stain upon Penelope's honour, and that would sadly diminish her prospects. And we had considerable expense with our lawyer, sir."

"True – as has my family." Laurence pretended to reflect. "However, if I marry Catherine for the reason I've stated, there will be no aspersions cast. And I would satisfy myself and my family that there's been no discourtesy on your part."

"You *cannot* marry Catherine," gasped Lady Margaret, as though Laurence had amorous designs on her husband.

"Why not, your ladyship, if she will accept me?"

"She is a . . . a shy, retiring girl whose health is affected by the slightest change."

"Then the life to which I aspire could fit her very well."

"She is impractical, sir: she could not manage a household. She has no conversation, no wit, and no womanly talents."

"She can learn how to manage a household, my lady, and in our albeit limited acquaintance, she has lacked neither for wit nor conversation. And I'm not certain what you mean by womanly talents," Laurence went on, "but if my supposition is correct, those can also be learnt."

Sir Harold was scratching his beard, paying no attention to the horrified faces of his wife and daughter. "Should she accept you, she will bring with her the bridal portion that we offered you for Penelope. How will we provide for Pen, when it comes to her turn?"

"As I assume you will provide for the rest of your lovely daughters, sir."

"But Pen wishes to marry this year."

"I will accept Catherine with half her portion," said Laurence, astonishing himself. As he spoke, he thought of his father and mother, and of all the careful negotiating that must have preceded the betrothal, and of what they might have lost to the rebels.

"What of Catherine's . . . health?" quavered Lady Margaret.

"Mr. Beaumont is right," Sir Harold said. "A quiet life in the countryside is exactly what her health requires. You have a bargain, sir. Fetch Catherine," he told his wife.

Tears glistened in Penelope's eyes as she watched her mother obey. Then she sailed from the hall with a dignity Laurence had to admire. Her miniature scowled venomously at him, and followed.

Catherine came in wiping her hands on her skirts; she eyed Sir Harold warily. "Cat," he said, "Mr. Beaumont has accused us of disrespect in not permitting him to address you, our firstborn daughter, before Penelope."

"It is of no importance to me, sir. He is already betrothed to Pen."

"Convention is important to *him*, and though we have apprised him of your many defects, he insists on addressing you all the same. You have our blessing to accept. So, what do you say?"

"Will you marry me, Catherine?" Laurence asked.

She hesitated, evidently stunned. Then she said firmly, "Yes, I will."

Laurence raced across the courtyard towards the stables. Rain pelted from a bruised sky, and the roads would be a quagmire, but none of this dampened his mood. He would write to his parents after the wedding; by then he would have pleased them in one regard, and as to the bridal portion, he would find some way of making amends.

"Mr. Beaumont, wait! Please, please, wait!" He skidded round in the mud. Catherine was splashing to him through the puddles, her hair tumbling loose of its pins, her face distraught. "They kept the truth from you. You didn't know."

"Didn't know what?"

"About *me* – I have the falling sickness," she said, in an angry tone. "That's why my family hides me from visitors and treats me as though I were weak-minded. I can never marry. I thought my father would have told you. His greed got the better of him, and everyone else was too ashamed and too frightened of him to speak up. I'd have told you myself, but I'm forbidden to talk of it. You are free, sir, to marry Pen."

"Come here." Laurence snatched her to him and pushed the wet hair from her forehead. "Was that how you got the scar – when you had a fit?"

"Yes, and how I broke my tooth. My father had to pry my mouth open with a stick so I wouldn't choke on my tongue. Now you see: I cannot be your wife."

"My God," murmured Laurence, thinking of Will's expression and of Jermyn's when they had spoken of her; it was she who Will had called a poor thing. This would explain why her ears were bare of jewellery that might be ripped out during a convulsion.

"Please, sir, let me go." She tugged away more forcefully, and they slithered and nearly slipped in the mud. "I've learnt to live with my unhappiness. I will not bring it on you."

"But do you want me, Catherine? Do you?"

"From the day we met," she said vehemently. "I still can't marry you. Forget you ever asked, and marry Pen."

"I don't want her – I want *you*. Listen." He clung to her and talked into her ear. "When I was a student at College, there was a boy afflicted with your sickness. At first it shocked us, but our tutor taught us that it was nothing to fear, and that the Emperor Caesar was subject to fits, and they didn't stop him from ruling. And they won't stop me from marrying you." He kissed her hard on the lips. "Catherine, *is* there anything else to stop us?" She relaxed into his arms, and shook her head. And next, to his surprise, she kissed him back.

## II.

"What a brilliant disguise, Mr. Price," said Lady Hallam, as she and her maid examined him up and down.

"Why thank you, your ladyship," Price said. He was dressed in the soft cap, leather jerkin, and baggy breeches of a trooper with the Trained Bands. Gone was his peddler's beard, which was no sacrifice, but Sarah had shaved off his moustache, cropped the shoulder-length hair he had been so proud of, and plucked his eyebrows to lend him a naive, doltish expression. His flattened nose was still swollen, although the bruising had paled to a primrose yellow. When he had knocked at the servants' entrance and asked to see her ladyship, the old butler had summoned Lucy instead, who would show him no further than the kitchen.

"I couldn't tell who he was, until he spoke," she said to her mistress.

He saw a change, too, in the former Mistress Savage, if less dramatic than his own. The candles burning in sconces over the hearth illuminated not just the flash of a great diamond on her ring finger, but also harder angles in her cheeks and jaw; and the tense set of her mouth and smouldering frustration in her eyes reminded him of Sarah's words. *One of them lions caged in the Tower.* "How is my Lord Digby?" she inquired.

"His lordship was in health when I last saw him, as was Beaumont. Beaumont has left him to serve again in Wilmot's Lifeguard." Price had hoped for some sign of interest in her, but there was none. "He's to marry soon," he went on. "This past Christmastide he introduced me to his future wife. She's young, and very pretty."

"I am overjoyed for him. Lucy, keep an eye on the front hall, lest we have visitors." Once the girl had gone, Lady Hallam said crossly to Price, "I expected you a fortnight ago."

"An accident delayed me."

"Might Veech know you are in London?"

"I pray not, but I've tempted fate too long – I'll ride for Oxford tomorrow. You may send to his lordship through my recruit, Peter Barlow."

"Who is he?"

"A trusted friend of mine and Beaumont's. His nephew Jem will call on you within the week, in the guise of a baker's apprentice. He can collect your messages and Barlow will arrange for their delivery."

"Has Barlow memorised our cipher?"

"No: though he reads a little, he can't write."

"Then what use is he? We need more than errand boys – we need skilled agents. Do you realise, sir, that with no likelihood of His Majesty advancing on London, our allies here are isolated as never before?

They'll be afraid to offer him their support unless we can supply them with accurate intelligence about what is happening, both outside *and* within the City."

"As well I understand," said Price, stung. "You don't have to teach me my business."

"Mr. Price," she said, as though addressing a child, "Veech nearly caught my husband smuggling in that powder, Violet is lost to us, and I cannot work alone. Digby has let things slip, and badly, if he has no more capable agents here – and you had better make that plain to him."

"You may depend on Barlow. It was he who got Beaumont out of London last autumn."

Lady Hallam's eyes narrowed; and Price felt he had scored a point. "Was Barlow then living in Blackman Street?"

"He is to this day," replied Price, wondering what Beaumont had told her about the place.

"Is he a thief, like you?" Price could not answer, speechless with indignation: had Beaumont told her this, also? "Some *ladies* who resided at the house came to Oxford in November, to inform Beaumont of Mistress Edwards' decease," she went on. "Beaumont was away, but Lord Digby enjoyed a fascinating talk with them."

And kept it secret, Price thought. "Barlow isn't thieving any more," he said defensively, "and nor am I."

"Why would you, now that you are in his lordship's pay. It was a mistake to lie to him, Mr. Price: although he does not care that you were a thief, he will always remember that you lied."

"Beaumont suggested it," said Price, which was not exactly the truth.

"So it was Beaumont's mistake – unless he had a good reason to cultivate his lordship's mistrust of you. Beaumont is clever in that regard, as you should be aware. You may report to his lordship that I am making some progress with Mr. Veech's associate, the lawyer Draycott. Mr. Draycott is a man of hitherto spotless morals, but his eldest son recently died, his marriage is strained, and I doubt he is happy serving Mr. Veech. He has become a kind of . . . friend to me."

"It sounds as if you're plotting his seduction," Price said, to insult her.

She smiled at this. But her smile vanished as Lucy hurried into the kitchen. "My lady, Mr. Draycott is at the door with a militiaman! Should Greenhalgh turn them away?"

Price swore under his breath. "Draycott knows me – he might recognise me even in this disguise. Let me escape through the back."

"No – there could be more troops outside," said Lady Hallam. "Wait with Lucy." She murmured something in Lucy's ear and glided towards the front hall.

Lucy snuffed out the candles over the hearth and drew Price into the shadows. He heard Lady Hallam announce loudly, "Mr. Draycott, and . . . Corporal Stanton of the Strand detail, are you not, sir?"

"I beg pardon for disturbing you, my lady." Price recognised Draycott's genteel accents. "We spied a man skulking around to the rear of your house, and the Corporal thought we should investigate."

There was a pause; Price squinted at the back door, calculating.

"Gentlemen, I believe I can explain – please follow me. Lucy?" she called.

It was a signal: Lucy grabbed Price and jammed her mouth onto his, blocking the men's view of him with her head as they walked into the kitchen.

"Dear Lucy, when will you learn: you must not receive your paramour without my permission," Lady Hallam scolded her. "And it is almost curfew."

Lucy twisted about in Price's arms. "It may be our last kiss, my lady. He's off to march for Lord Essex's camp on the morrow."

"Nonetheless, what nuisance you caused Mr. Draycott and Corporal Stanton."

"Lovelorn creatures, we can't blame them." Stanton's voice had a Cheapside ring. "Which of the Bands do you serve with, young man?"

Price saluted, feigning bashfulness; he did not venture out of the shadows. "The Southwark brigade, sir," he said, in his old, London accent.

"May God keep you safe, my lad, and you give those malignant dogs a right drubbing."

Lady Hallam wagged a finger at the pair. "Half an hour, and not a moment more."

"I am sorry we alarmed you unnecessarily, your ladyship," Draycott said.

"Gentlemen, my husband and I are indebted to you for your vigilance. We were to take a glass of wine upstairs in the gallery. Might you join us?"

"I'd be honoured, my lady, if I wasn't on patrol tonight," said Stanton, with audible regret.

Price listened to their retreating steps, and waited for the front door to shut. Then he whistled between his teeth. "That was close. I thought she'd never get rid of them."

"Oh she hasn't, yet," said Lucy.

He next heard Lady Hallam saying, sweetly, "I must apologise to *you*, Mr. Draycott, for practising a feminine deception: Sir Montague is abed – he was in pain from his gout. I so appreciated your company the other night. Would you stay, for a little while?"

"I ought not to, my lady," said Draycott, "but . . ."

Their voices faded as they carried on up the stair. Price was aroused: by his narrow escape and Lucy's charms, and most of all by Lady Hallam's ruthlessness. How vividly he could imagine her seducing Draycott, the lucky bastard.

"You stop that," Lucy said; without noticing, he had pressed his hips up against hers.

"Give us one more cuddle," he teased, "before your brave lad goes to the wars."

In answer, she unbolted the door and pushed him out.

**III.**

Under an azure sky scattered with thistledown clouds, courtiers, soldiers, and townsfolk had assembled in Abingdon's Market Place to witness the King and Queen bid each other goodbye. Digby generally eschewed public displays of grief, but he was sniffing and dashing water from his eyes along with everyone else: today the royal couple were like any other man and woman in love, about to be separated in dangerous times. He would also miss his friend Jermyn, who was to accompany the Queen on her travels.

"To think that Their Majesties have had less than a year together since her return from The Hague," he lamented to his father.

"I pity those boys, as much," said Bristol. The two eldest Princes stood beside Her Majesty's carriage, Charles fighting bravely for composure, with ten-year-old James sobbing on his arm. "I heard that Her Majesty consulted her astrologers, and was told she would be reunited with her sons – but not in England."

"And what about her husband?"

"The stars were silent on that issue."

"The stars, or the astrologers?"

"Who would have the temerity to predict that she might never see him again?"

"A fool or an honest man, if they are not the same thing." Digby bustled through the crowd towards Jermyn. "Jermyn, shall we write?"

"Yes, but of innocent matters," Jermyn said. "And do beware of disputes in Council, especially with Rupert and with Wilmot, whose late fit of pique might have cost the King dear. Her Majesty will not be there to pour oil on troubled water – though Mr. Beaumont deserves much of the credit on that last occasion. I should like to have said goodbye to him."

"He and Wilmot must be in attendance." Digby peered about. "Wilmot is so very fond of the Queen."

"Wilmot is here, but not Beaumont. Prince Charles told me he has gone into Warwickshire to visit his betrothed."

"Ah," said Digby thoughtfully.

"And now," said Jermyn, embracing him, "*our* time has come for a parting of ways."

"I shall pray for you, and for Her Majesty in her confinement."

Digby watched Jermyn take up his position at the head of the Queen's Lifeguard, while footmen lifted Her Majesty into her carriage and shut the door. The King stayed beside the window, clinging to her hand. As the vehicle picked up speed, he had to step back with the utmost reluctance, tears streaming down his cheeks. A second carriage followed, occupied by her ladies-in-waiting, her lapdogs in their straw baskets, and the dwarf, Jeffrey Hudson; and the procession was tailed by more mounted troops dressed in Her Majesty's bright livery. Digby waited no longer. Blowing his nose into his handkerchief, he turned for his quarters; Jermyn had inspired him with a plan.

## IV.

Laurence and Prince Charles were alone among the trees, where the King lay dead on a bracken bier. The forest rang with the yelping of hounds, coming closer and closer; and somehow Laurence knew they were after human prey.

Charles fell to his knees by the corpse and struggled to drag it from the bier. "We must take him away or they will tear him apart!"

"No, we have to save ourselves," cried Laurence. He grabbed the boy and thrust him towards a giant oak. "Climb, for your very life." They clambered into its lower boughs, but the Prince could not find a foothold on the mossy bark higher up: the soles of his boots kept slipping, and he was panting for breath. The dogs were crashing through the undergrowth on all sides. Some slavered and pawed at the base of the tree, while others leapt growling upon the bier, jerking their heads to and fro to rip flesh from bone. "Don't look down, just climb," Laurence urged the Prince, pulling him by the arms. The boy's cloak had snagged on a branch, and as he wriggled to free it, he began to slide inexorably from Laurence's grip. He

hung by the wrists, then hands, then the tips of his fingers, screaming, "Help me, Mr. Beaumont! Help me!" until Laurence lost him
altogether.

"Beaumont!" Laurence started awake. "Out of bed, my man,"
yelled Wilmot, through the doorway. "The King wants to see you."

His Majesty and Prince Charles were at breakfast in the reception
chamber. Both appeared to Laurence as if their sleep had been as
haunted as his. The King sipped gingerly from a cup, a plate of oat-
cakes and cold meats before him. Charles, his eyes reddened and sore,
was tossing scraps beneath the table to his dogs, whose loud masticat-
ing sent a shiver along Laurence's spine.

"You m-must excuse our gloom, sir," said the King. "We are
missing our She Generalissima."

"Lord Wilmot told me she departed yesterday, Your Majesty.
I regret that I wasn't there to wish her God speed."

The King nodded, unsmiling. "Mr. Beaumont, you have proved
yourself devoted to my cause in the past, and you were instrumental
in resolving the differences between my Lord Wilmot and General
Hopton. I understand your d-desire to serve in his lordship's
Lifeguard, yet we are about to enter upon a n-new stage in our war
against the rebellion. And I am persuaded that your talents would be
best employed elsewhere."

"Yes, Your Majesty?" Laurence queried, deeply apprehensive.

"Since we may soon take to the field, my Lord D-digby has proposed that you be given charge, under his aegis, of training scouts to
reconnoitre for our armies. We have not yet s-spoken of this to Lord
Wilmot – I thought it only right to ask you first if you will accept such
an important responsibility."

"We know we can count on you, Mr. Beaumont," said the Prince.

Laurence could not argue. "I thank you for the honour."

"You should thank Lord Digby," said the King. "He considers
you indispensable."

"His lordship should at least spare Mr. Beaumont to attend his own wedding before we open our campaign," Prince Charles said to his father.

"On what d-day are you to marry, sir?"

"A week today," said Laurence, "or so I had hoped."

"I gather that, for a distressing reason, you will be unable to celebrate at your father's house. In consolation, I shall insist that Lord Digby grant you a brief honeymoon."

"Thank you again, Your Majesty, and Your Royal Highness."

Laurence was retreating to the doors when the King said, "On second thought, sir, *you* may inform Lord Wilmot of your change in assignment, and lay to rest any objections that he might raise. I have neither the time nor the patience to hear them, myself. Lord Digby expects you to report to his quarters by the hour of curfew."

"The snake," Wilmot raged, as Laurence packed his saddlebags. "Digby was just waiting for the Queen to leave, to pull off his trickery. She would have championed my part."

"No, my lord, not again. She overreached herself already to protect you."

Wilmot seized Laurence's arm and swung him round. "Don't you forget, Beaumont: you promised to stand by me as my friend. Whatever fresh tricks Digby has up his sleeve, whatever anyone is plotting against me, I must be the first to know. You're still my champion, as I am yours. I demand the same loyalty as you gave to Falkland. Swear to me that I shall have it, through thick and thin."

"I swear," said Laurence, with a sense of profound foreboding.

**v.**

Laurence stopped on the corner of Digby's street; a vaguely familiar figure in a leather jerkin and cloth cap was sauntering towards him. "Beaumont, don't you recognise me?"

"I almost didn't," said Laurence, with perfect honesty.

"Were you coming to see his lordship?"

"Yes. As of today, he's taken me back into the fold."

"I *am* pleased to hear. He went with Quayle to be fitted for a new pair of boots. I got back to Oxford this morning, and was about to grab a bite to eat at the tavern. Why don't you join me?"

Laurence accepted, wondering uncharitably whether Elizabeth's infatuation would survive the man's transformed appearance. When they had settled themselves at a table and Price had ordered a meal from the serving boy, he asked, "Who broke your nose?"

"Sue did, when I broke with *her*."

"She should fight for money."

"I gave her money, and this is how she thanked me for it. And next thing I was thrown into the Fleet. Barlow rescued me and whisked me to the good old house. Oh I know what you're thinking, Beaumont," Price gabbled on, "but he said it was quite safe. And Sarah did a fine job of work on me." He plucked off his cap to reveal his polled head. "Can you believe, I passed muster with Draycott and a Corporal from the militia when they caught me at Sir Montague's house." He guffawed, describing the incident.

The serving boy had brought him ale and a platter of bread and cheese. As he reached for the bread, Laurence stayed his hand. "You shouldn't have risked another visit to the neighbourhood, after one arrest."

Price shook off Laurence's grip. "I had to talk to Lady Hallam, on his lordship's order."

"What was Draycott doing there?"

"He's become a friend of Lady Hallam's. She's . . . entertaining him." Price reached again for a piece of bread, and crammed a wedge of cheese into it. "Once she has him by the short hairs, she'll find out from him if Veech is getting suspicious. And I've set her up with Barlow and Jem, to act as her couriers."

With a mixture of fear and distaste, Laurence listened on. His day had started badly; how much worse could it get? "Veech will have Jem tailed to Blackman Street," he said, when Price fell silent.

"Tail a baker's apprentice?" Price drained his cup. "I doubt it. What's the matter with you, Beaumont? You look as if you might be sick. Does it upset you that Lady Hallam's playing games with Draycott?"

Laurence controlled a mighty impulse to add to the damage Sue had wrought on Price's nose. "Veech must have told Draycott about Sir Montague and those barrels. Draycott is a novice spy, but as a lawyer he's trained to hunt for information."

"And so?"

"Veech may have sent Draycott to play the same game with Isabella as she's playing with him."

"Well I'd like to know what game you and Digby are playing with *me*," said Price, in a hurt tone.

"What do you mean?"

"Thanks to Perdie and Cordelia, he heard about my past. He's known since November. Why didn't you tell me?"

"Because I don't give a shit about your past. I'm more concerned about the future." Laurence rose, searched for some coins in his pocket, and threw them on the table. "You can help me send a message to Sir Montague's house – for Lucy, from her lover in the Trained Bands."

"Are you asking me to take it to London?"

"To Aylesbury, to the London carrier."

"Aylesbury is held by Parliament."

"You'll pass muster, in your disguise. You might even get yourself recruited."

Lord Digby was still out when they returned. Laurence sat at his lordship's desk and selected the bluntest of quills, the most clotted pot of ink, and a sheet of paper.

"I thought you were left-handed," Price said.

"I am," said Laurence, holding the quill in his right. "Deer harrte," he began, in clumsy script, "I pray thou arte in gude helthe, as am I, prayse Godd, though mie shoon are worne from marching so farre on the high waie. We gott to Aielsberrie towne on the eighttenth daye of Aprill and I tekk this oppertunity to paie a frend to rite. How

sadde I was forst to leve thee, my sweate. I have no caues of com-
playnt to goo for a soldier, butt ewer since I did quitt Londonn I have
missed thee lyke mie rite hand. Tell hr laidieshipp I spied a grate
bigge ratt when I was in hr kitchin. Tis the clement wether which
brings out his kinde. Ewen if he doe seeme harmlesse suche rattes
bite and scrat pepell. Shee shude bewear and have hm cott befoar he
bringes hr woars veerminn. And tell hr nott to buie anie moar bredd
from that lowe prentiss boie. I herde his shoppe gott veerminn as
welle and his bredd int fitt to eate." He closed with more endear-
ments, and signed, "Thy love, Hennery Illingsworth."

"What's in the name?" asked Price.

"I once borrowed it from a dead boy and it brought me luck. It
might again." Laurence blotted the ink with sand, then went over to
the fireplace, rubbed some ash on his hands, and decorated the paper
with smudged fingerprints. He folded it, and sealed it with a big
splodge of wax. He did not know Lucy's surname, so on the outside
he put: "For my Laidie Hallammes mayde, Lucy," and the direction in
the Strand.

When Price had left with it, Laurence sank his aching head onto
the desk and thought of Isabella. During their long, lazy talks at her
house in the Woodstock Road, she had shared his cynicism about the
royal cause, though she had often said she could not afford to bite the
hand that fed her; Digby's, presumably. Marriage had removed any
financial worries, so why was she continuing to risk herself as Digby's
agent, knowing that the entire London network had become a sham-
bles, and Veech was breathing down her neck? "Try just for one day
being a woman in a world ruled by men," she had told Laurence, before
they had become lovers. When he had proposed to her, she had refused,
saying that marriage to him would entail fighting everyone, and that
she would always be afraid with him because he was not the sort of
man to lead a quiet life. Yet *she* did not want a quiet life: she had ignored
the warning he had sent from Pembroke's house, and she might ignore
his latest, if ever it arrived. Perhaps she liked the distraction of intrigue.

Perhaps she felt immune to death, a sentiment Laurence understood intimately but which might be her nemesis. And he knew in his heart, with acute guilt, that were she to reply to him begging him to come and spirit her out of London or indeed out of England to a new life, he would do it, despite his commitment to Catherine, who needed and deserved so much love.

He sat up and tucked the quill into place, and used the cuff of his shirt to mop away a few specks of ink. As he was shuffling the sheets of blank parchment together and stacking them neatly where they belonged, a slip of paper fluttered to the floor. He retrieved it, and read the single line written there, in Digby's script: "Sir Harold Furnival of Lower Quinton, Warwickshire."

## VI.

"Why are you here?" demanded Draycott, ready to slam the door in Veech's face.

"For the pleasure of an introduction to your wife." Veech limped past him into the kitchen, where Judith was stirring a pot of caudle over the fire. She inspected Veech hostilely; Draycott's emotions must have been obvious.

"Judith," he said, "may I present Clement Veech, agent to Mr. Oliver St. John."

Veech appraised her with utter indifference. "Has your husband told you that we are working together?"

"No, sir," she said, "though he has spoken of Mr. St. John."

"Has he told you of our work?"

"It is legal work, sir, is it not?"

"Mostly legal. We're bringing to justice some citizens of London who would create mischief for Parliament." Veech sat down near the fire on the polished oak settle that had belonged to Judith's father, and extended his bad leg. "You mustn't worry if he keeps late hours from time to time. He's better off in my employ than he was in the army."

"In *your* employ?"

"Yes, madam. Where are your children?"

"They are upstairs with their nurse."

Veech yawned and now gazed pointedly at Draycott, who said, "Judith, leave us, please."

She shifted the pot from the fire, and went out.

"Small thanks from her, considering how well I've treated you," Veech said. "When were you last in the Strand?"

Draycott waited to reply until he heard the creak of the stairs, and then of the floorboards overhead. "Six days ago."

"Did Lady Hallam receive you alone again?"

"Yes, Sir Montague had gone to bed early. I stayed only an hour."

"What did you talk about?"

"I believe it was the Queen's flight from Oxford. Lady Hallam expressed pity for her, having to travel in her . . . condition . . ." Draycott broke off and stared: Veech had plucked a knife from his capacious pocket; it was more like an old-fashioned dagger, with a crown on the top of the hilt.

"And?" said Veech.

"She thought it a sign of the King's . . . Mr. Veech, what on earth are you doing?"

Veech was busy whittling at the arm of the settle with his blade as a delinquent youth might carve his initials on a church pew. "I am bored, Mr. Draycott. I'll stop when you say something of interest."

Draycott could only watch a moment more. "I . . . found a book in the gallery. I read an inscription on the . . . on the flyleaf: 'In the hope that you may be inspired to forget the past and embrace the future. I remain, as ever, your faithful George, Lord Digby, Christmastide, 1643.'"

Veech stilled his knife and dropped it into his pocket. "And what did you make of that, sir?"

"I presume the book was a gift to Sir Montague, and the inscription referred to his new life with Lady Isabella. He has Royalists among his customers. Lord Digby must be one of them."

"The book is hers. Lord Digby was her guardian, and he arranged her marriage to Sir Montague." Veech rose ponderously and joined Draycott by the hearth. "So to what past, you might inquire, was Digby referring?"

"You tell me, since you have all the answers."

"To the past she shared with her lover, Laurence Beaumont."

"By God." Draycott shook his head, dumbfounded. "How and when did you hear of this?"

"Sir Montague's old valet was overheard gossiping, in December. It seems the affair was no secret in Oxford."

Draycott remembered walking Beaumont to the fort; with his lanky stride and amiable calm, he had behaved like a man out for a breath of fresh air rather than a captured spy. Draycott also remembered his smile: not a trace of fear, and dazzling, on a face as seductive as Lady Isabella's. And a fresh image crept into Draycott's mind, of her and Beaumont intertwined.

"Judith must wonder at that look in your eyes," said Veech. "I don't blame her." He dipped his thick forefinger in the caudle, tasted it, and spat into the fire. "Your wife is too mean with her honey pot."

"Any more of your insolence and I'll strike you down," Draycott said, between his teeth.

"You wouldn't have the guts." Veech limped towards the door. Then he swerved about. "Lady Isabella is Lord Digby's agent, as is her cripple of a husband. Had I told you earlier, your honest face would have betrayed you to them. Now I must have a watertight case for their arrest or the charges of treason may not stick in court. In a week or so, you are to hide a packet of correspondence in Sir Montague's house."

"What if I refuse?"

Veech cast a slow glance around the kitchen. "You can't value them more than this little haven."

"Are you threatening my family?"

"I will do what's necessary to get the man who crippled *me*. If the

Hallams are condemned, Digby will send Beaumont to her aid. And I'll be waiting for him."

"Mr. St. John cannot approve of your tactics, sir."

"Complain to him, and see what happens." Veech unlatched the door. "My regards to Judith," he said, as he departed.

Draycott tossed the caudle into the flames. He was standing frozen, holding the empty pot, when Judith charged back in and dashed it from his grip. "Giles, you lied to me about your visits to the Strand."

"And you should not have eavesdropped. I was on confidential business."

"It is a foul business. This evil man Veech thinks you lust after Sir Montague's wife. Do you?"

"No," yelled Draycott, feeling his cheeks burn. "But you are right about Veech – he is a most evil man. I've decided, Judith: I shall speak to Mr. St. John today and tell him everything."

Judith met his eyes as though he were a stranger. "I'm taking the children to my mother's. You may come to me when you are free, of Veech – and of that woman's spell."

She ran from the kitchen, and he did not attempt to go after her. Grabbing his cloak off the peg at the door, he stumbled out of the house.

"Mr. Draycott!" Draycott heard Lady Isabella's voice and stopped to look round; he had been blundering down her street in a panic of indecision, torn as to whether he should confront St. John or confide in her. She and Lucy were a few yards behind him, the hoods of their cloaks pulled over their heads; and behind them was a footboy carrying several parcels. "I called you twice, sir," she said. He reached for his hat, then realised he had left it at home. "Thank heavens Lucy and I dressed for this awful weather – but you're wet to the skin. Were you coming to visit my husband?" Draycott had no reply. "He is not here, sir. Greenhalgh took him to spend the afternoon at his son's, in Chelsea Fields. Please, step inside out of the rain or you'll catch your death of a cold."

Draycott shivered in the entrance hall while Lucy fetched towels for him; he had declined the offer of one of Sir Montague's robes, and of a glass of spirits. "I apologise for the fuss," he said to both women, when she returned.

"May I write my letter now, your ladyship?" she asked.

"Yes, you may do so in my chamber," said Lady Isabella. "Lucy received a note yesterday from her sweetheart," she explained to Draycott, as the maid went ahead of them upstairs. "He had someone else pen his message, unschooled fellow that he is, and even then we were hard pressed to decipher the script." She led Draycott more slowly up to the gallery, and waved for him to sit beside her, by the fireplace. "You are perturbed, sir. Is there more illness in your family?"

Draycott opened his mouth, intending to talk about Veech. "I have . . . fallen in love with you," he murmured, instead.

"Oh, Mr. Draycott, is it love, or loneliness and confusion? Because *I* am as confused. I have been pretending that I've not a care in the world, when I am desperate for your advice. Will you listen to my trouble?"

"Yes," he said, dreading what might surface; would she speak of Beaumont?

"You know that my one-time guardian is Sir Montague's friend. He is a Royalist, and an esteemed counsellor of His Majesty. Towards the winter of last year, he asked my husband to help him with a certain scheme that the King had in mind for London." She hesitated, lowering her eyes. "Sir Montague was fortunate to avoid discovery of what was in his barrels."

"Ah, then . . . it was as St. John's agent Veech suspected."

"My husband will not risk himself again. The stress upon his health almost killed him."

"So he is out of danger, as are you," said Draycott, enormously reassured: he would report an expurgated version of this to St. John and put an end to Veech's investigations.

"No, Mr. Draycott," she said. "The truth is . . . *I* am still helping His Majesty."

Draycott stiffened; she might have closed her fingers over his heart. "Surely Sir Montague would advise you to cease whatever you are doing, for your safety and his."

"It is the opposite, sir: he wants me to continue, out of loyalty to the King and to my guardian. You see, my guardian had always inspired me with a fascination for politics, and when the war erupted, I undertook to assist him in purveying news from Oxford to London. Since I am now established here, he wishes me to act as a conduit for messages to various Royalists within the City. I owe to him my education and my marriage – all I have. I readily accepted to do this work for him. How can I stop?"

"Oh, my lady," sighed Draycott, "I am as compromised, by Clement Veech. I accepted to enter *his* service, to my infinite regret. He holds himself above the law, and has hinted that my family may suffer if I don't do his bidding. He ordered me to insinuate myself into your husband's good graces, and yours – to spy on you."

"But I thought . . . I thought you were my friend," she said, with a little catch in her voice.

"I am, I swear, which is why I am confiding in you. I could not have borne the deception, and I will not obey him, whatever the cost to me. I won't . . . I won't!"

"Then what is to become of us?" She leant forward and touched her hand to Draycott's knee. Instinctively, he rested his head against the smooth curve of her shoulder. When she did not move away, he started to kiss her neck, and cheek, and her lips. Not for years had he kissed Judith so passionately, and Lady Isabella seemed to be surrendering to his caresses.

A sneeze made them jump apart.

Draycott leapt to his feet. "Who was that? Lucy?"

"It can't be – it came from the parlour." She hurried from her chair, and he followed. They found the parlour vacant. The portraits stared down at him, taciturn and immobile. Then he detected the ripple of a shadow under the table, and a slender black cat peeped out.

"You naughty boy," she exclaimed. "Here's the culprit, sir: Niger – as in the Latin."

Draycott burst into laughter, from sheer nerves. "What a handsome devil, with his beautiful green . . ." But he left the word *eyes* unsaid, for hers were swimming with tears. Guilt overwhelmed him. "My lady, can you forgive my misconduct? I wronged both you and Judith, and I should go home."

"You did no wrong," she said, with such earnestness that he felt himself absolved. "Mr. Draycott, Sir Montague is soon to be absent for some days. Please might you call on me then, and we can decide on a course of action?"

He nodded, terrified: his fate and hers hung in the balance.


**VII.**

"Pinch me, or I'll imagine that I'm dreaming," said Seward, as Laurence filled their cups. "Here we are at last on the eve of your marriage. A health to you and to Catherine – may she have the patience of Job."

"To Catherine," said Laurence.

"Clarke would swoon if he tasted this wine. Where did you obtain it?"

"I stole it from Lord Digby's cellar."

"How appropriate, to drink to a bride you robbed from under her sister's nose. Has his lordship allowed you a honeymoon?"

"A week's leave."

"He is magnanimous in victory, as you were graceful in defeat. What will you do with Catherine, Beaumont?"

"I know you're a bachelor, Seward, but must I acquaint you with the facts of life?"

"I mean," said Seward testily, "where will she reside, after the ceremony? By your description of her family, she might be happier at Chipping Campden."

"She might, though *I* can't take her there. I may not be able to stay at her father's house if Massey's troops are in the neighbourhood. In that event, I'll use the rest of my leave to visit Tom. Rupert's camp is about seventy miles northwest – a couple of days' ride."

"Have you been speculating as to his delicate family matter?"

"Yes, and it's still a mystery to me."

Seward pottered over to his cupboard. "I have something mysterious for you that I have been saving for years." He rummaged about the dusty shelves. "Where is it, where is it. Aha! Catch, my boy." He threw over to Laurence a leather pouch.

Laurence opened the pouch and shook out a ring of coppery gold set with a dull red stone. "For Catherine? Thank you, Seward."

"Look closer, at the inside." Holding it to the flame of Seward's candle, Laurence saw minute symbols engraved in a continuous line all around its inner surface. "They are in no language that I read," Seward said, coming to lay a hand on Laurence's shoulder. "The ring must be of ancient origin, and could have magical properties. It may help Catherine with her falling sickness."

Laurence frowned up at him. "You always gave me to believe that was nothing to worry about."

"In a man, it is less worrying, but if Catherine suffered a severe fit while pregnant, she might slip the child."

"Why would the ring help her?"

"I inherited it from a friend of my mother's, a wise woman versed in herbal lore and spells. She had the gift of healing people and animals, and probably of cursing those who offended her. She was drowned as a witch in the reign of King James, when I was not much older than you are now. I recorded a number of her receipts before she died, and there is only one of her concoctions that I have *not* yet tested: a deadly poison. As for her poultices and sleeping draughts, they have never failed me – or you, Beaumont," Seward added gently. "Her sleeping draught weaned you off your beloved poppy tincture on two occasions: after your beatings in Oxford Castle, and after your recent wound."

"Well, well," said Laurence. "Then I have more cause to be grateful to her."

Seward pointed at the ring. "Try it." Laurence tried; it stuck at the second joint of his ring finger, but slid neatly onto his little finger. "Will it be Catherine's size?"

Laurence pictured her hands, grubby from touching the magpie. "It might be a bit large."

"If so, she can wear it on a chain about her neck. You must not alter it, or you will lose the inscription. Wear it yourself, for security's sake, until you have pronounced your vow."

"Should I tell her your story about the witch?"

"You don't want to scare her."

Laurence studied the ring again, and smiled. "From what I know of her thus far, I don't think I would."

# CHAPTER TWELVE

Clustered in the nave of St. Swithin's Church were Sir Harold and Lady Margaret, a vicar in a neat surplice whose expression reminded Laurence of a paid mourner at a funeral, and two other, burly men he did not recognise. "Mr. Beaumont, how you like to keep us in suspense," said Sir Harold. He was stuffed into an old-fashioned padded doublet and breeches, and his beard had been trimmed; Laurence could see the meat of his jowls over his high lace collar.

"Forgive me, sir," said Laurence coldly, "but the roads were in a terrible state, and I had to stop by your house for directions here."

Sir Harold presented the strangers. "May I introduce Dr. Offstead, who will join you and Catherine in holy matrimony. I thought also to bring my lawyer, Mr. Spriggs, and my bailiff, Mr. Morris."

*In case I tried to renege on our bargain?* Laurence nearly asked him. "And where is Catherine?"

"She felt faint, and went to walk in the churchyard," said Lady Margaret. Despite her browbeaten expression, she looked attractive, in a gown of more recent make than her husband's suit. "Do you wish to change out of your riding garments, sir?"

Laurence experienced a momentary shame for his travel-stained clothes and boots. "I'm afraid Catherine must have me as I am."

"She will not argue with that," Sir Harold said. "Go and fetch her, my lady."

"Mr. Beaumont," said Dr. Offstead, while the men waited, "I have taken it upon myself to compose an enlightening homily on the duties of conjugal life, since you have not been married before."

"I thank you, sir, but we had agreed on a quick exchange of vows."

"Have you the ring, or was she already given it on her betrothal?"

Laurence held up his hand; he had kept on the ring, out of respect for Seward.

"Your taste is as modest as our ceremony," Sir Harold said to Laurence, "and as your choice of bride."

Laurence bit back a retort; the women were coming towards him along the aisle between tall box pews. Catherine's bulky costume was of faded cloth and obscured her slight frame, and her hair had been scraped into an unflattering knot. She did not appear faint, however: her dark eyes met his without wavering.

"Dearly beloved friends," commenced Dr. Offstead, in a sing-song drone, "we are gathered together here in the sight of God, and in the face of His congregation . . ."

As Laurence listened on, he thought how much Catherine must have suffered that he did not know about from her contemptible father, her cowed mother, and her spoilt sisters. He had undertaken a great responsibility in asking for her hand, and she had been courageous to accept him. Now he was determined to try and put aside his love for Isabella, even if he could no more banish her from his heart and mind than he could erase the scars upon his skin, or forget his anxieties about her precarious situation in London. For better or for worse, he and Catherine were linked. She was uncharted territory, as was he to her, and he felt in himself the same combined thrill and trepidation as when he had set sail for the Low Countries in quest of new adventures.

Dr. Offstead's voice recalled him to the present. "Mr. Beaumont, wilt thou have this woman . . . ?"

After Laurence had spoken his vow, Catherine spoke hers clearly and calmly. He pulled the ring off his finger. As it came free, it leapt into the air and fell with a tinkling sound on the weathered flagstones. Might Seward consider this an ill omen, he wondered, bending to pick it up. Yet as he slid it onto Catherine's left hand, it was a fit; as though she had always worn it.

Dr. Offstead pronounced them married, Sir Harold congratulated them, and Lady Margaret burst into tears, whether out of joy or some less happy emotion Laurence did not especially care. He tucked Catherine's arm into his and guided her from the church, wishing he could run away with her.

"Mr. Beaumont," she said, "there was to be no feast at the house because of what you told my mother, but our neighbours learnt of the marriage, and my father insisted on inviting them. If it's not safe for you to come, please don't."

"I'll come," he said, wondering again about the omen.

Sir Harold had to shout over the babble of his hundred or so guests, and the strains of a band playing fiddles, horns, and pipes. "People must marry, sir, war or no war, and we had to share this day with our friends."

"And with the Gloucester garrison," said Laurence, infuriated.

"What would you have us do? Send them home?"

"It's a bit late for that, but you should post a lookout to watch for any intruders."

"You must fancy yourself a very special item, to warrant such attention from our enemies," Sir Harold joked, though Laurence caught a nasty edge to his tone.

Catherine disappeared with her mother, until they were all summoned to table. Sir Harold had plied Laurence with drink; and he was feeling rather less nervous, and dangerously uninhibited, as Catherine sat down at his left side. He would have liked to whisk her upstairs and rip off her ugly gown. Sir Harold sat on his right, and Lady Margaret had her place by her husband. Her other daughters were ranged at the end of the table. Penelope avoided Laurence's eyes, but her miniature cast him a baleful stare, which he returned in kind.

Dr. Offstead recited the grace, and Sir Harold followed with a health to the married couple. "Catherine Beaumont," he marvelled afterwards, and to Laurence, "Will you deliver a speech, sir, in your father's stead?"

"No, sir: it would be unfair on these hungry people," said Laurence. Gentry and commoners were cramming food into their mouths with oily fingers, slurping wine from their pewter cups, and hurling bones over their shoulders to the dogs. "How's our magpie?" he asked Catherine, who was neither eating nor drinking.

"He – or she – can fly around the barn."

"Then it's time to release the prisoner."

"We're both impatient to be released." Catherine touched a finger to her ring. "You chose this well."

"I didn't choose it – a friend gave it to me. He said it had belonged to a witch. And he thinks it may help you with your sickness," Laurence added; the wine had loosened his tongue.

"So I must never take it off. Have you told your father about me?"

Her meaning was unmistakable. "Not yet," he replied.

"I wish you had, before we married. I'm entering your family under false pretences."

"There's nothing false in you, Catherine."

She made no response. The din from the tables below had anyway swelled to such a level that conversation was becoming impossible.

At length, platters were cleared, and Sir Harold bade the musicians strike up a merry country jig. Catherine leant over to speak in Laurence's ear. "Would you come upstairs, sir? I want to show you our first wedding gift."

Heads swivelled as they left together, and Laurence heard some ribald comments about him serving himself early to the tastiest dish. And why not, he thought.

At the top of the stair, he caught her in his arms. The thick fabric of her gown was unyielding as chainmail; and he sensed her resisting. She pushed open the bedchamber door and pointed to a canvas hanging on the far wall. "I don't know who sent it here . . . though you may."

The canvas was painted with masterful skill. Seated semi-clad in ethereal robes, her perfect breasts all but exposed, a goddess smiled languorously at a plump cherub floating in the sky. He held a bow and arrow, in his face the tacit question: where should I aim? On her lap, suggestively placed, lay an oyster shell.

Laurence's arousal drained out of him as if he had been kicked in the groin.

"She's beautiful, isn't she," Catherine said, looking straight at him.

"Yes, she is."

"Who is she?"

"I believe she's . . . Aphrodite, the goddess of love."

"What is her story?"

"Let's see if I can remember," Laurence answered evasively. "Cronus, the god of time, wanted to become the most powerful of all the Titans, so he castrated his own father Uranus. She was born of the foam that rose up as his parts were thrown into the sea. Because the other deities were jealous of her beauty, Zeus, king of the gods, married her to a lame blacksmith, Hephaestus. But she took many lovers, among them Ares, the god of war. The cherub is her son, Cupid." He studied Isabella's visage on the canvas, aware that he owed Catherine a more direct explanation. "It must have been painted about five or six years ago. The model would have been about your age."

"Pen told me that you had a mistress in Oxford. Is she Aphrodite?"

"Yes. Her name is Isabella Savage. Was, I should say. She's married now."

"Did she send us the portrait?"

"Certainly not."

Catherine breathed a little sigh. "Then who did?"

"A troublemaker." He drew Catherine towards him, searched for the pins in her hair, and pulled them out one by one. "Where did you find this ancient costume?" he asked, as he investigated how to unhook it.

"It was my mother's wedding gown," she said, her breath quickening. "Pen thought I should wear it."

"Then she's also a troublemaker. And *I* think you'd look much better without it."

He had discovered the hooks and was working on them assiduously when rapid footsteps pounded up the stairs, and Lady Margaret burst in. "Mr. Beaumont, there are soldiers on the main road, heading towards the house!" she shrieked. "You must flee!"

"We have unfinished business," he told Catherine. "I'll be back for you, as soon as I can."

"It can't be too soon," she said, and let him go.


**II.**

"Rain, rain, and more rain," groaned Ingram, as he struggled to light his pipe with a smouldering flint beneath the shelter of a dripping hedgerow. Prince Rupert's camp was an ocean of mud, the air seasoned by a potent waft from the open latrine ditches. Nothing could be kept clean or dry. Ingram's chilblained toes squelched inside his leaking boots, and he was itching from lice in clothes that he had not removed for weeks and now seemed a part of his skin. Mould flourished everywhere: on any item of leather not properly cured and polished, in the bread and cheese that he had eaten at breakfast, and in the now threadbare fabric of his sleeping blanket. Weapons rusted and jammed, men and horses took ill, and tempers had grown short among those, such as he, who had no indoor billet.

Ingram's pipe started to glow and he sucked in deep of the smoke, as though it might provide some warmth. On the far side of the field, a troop of musketeers were at drill. One youth had dropped his weapon in the mud, to the fury of the supervising officer who was screeching: "Present upon your rest! Blow off your loose powder! Draw forth your firing stick! Hurry up, you laggards."

While Ingram was watching them, smoking contentedly, a rider on a black horse cantered past the ranks. Ingram would recognise that horse anywhere. "Beaumont," he shouted, and sloshed towards his friend.

Beaumont reined in. As he leapt from the saddle, water cascaded from his cloak. "What a Biblical flood," he said, slicking away his wet hair. "It's been some time, my friend." He gave Ingram a slippery hug. "How are you?"

"The only dry thing on me is my pipe. And you, Beaumont – did you come from Oxford?"

"Yes, though . . . I stopped in Warwickshire, to be married."

"To be . . . ?" Ingram punched him on the shoulder. "My congratulations. I'm sorry I couldn't witness the ceremony."

"Not many did. And alas, I had to leave my bride unsatisfied. A party of men from the Gloucester garrison interrupted our embraces. Had they arrived a bit later, they might have caught us *in flagrante delicto*."

"There's a silver lining to every cloud," said Ingram, laughing. "So, what brings you here?"

"Tom wrote to me saying he wanted to see me about a family matter. Has he had more bad news from home?"

"Not that he mentioned. But he's gone to Oxford. The Prince was summoned there for a Council of War and Tom volunteered to ride with him, precisely to see *you*."

"God damn . . . Have you any idea what this is about?" Beaumont's eyes narrowed. "Yes, you do."

"I'd be breaking my promise to him—"

"Please, Ingram – if it's important, I should know." Ingram thought back to that day, etched in his memory because of the hangings; and as he recounted Tom's startling tale, Beaumont frowned, as though fitting together a mental puzzle. "Antonio de Zamora," Beaumont said quietly, at the end. "Where is he now?"

"Tom hasn't seen him since, as far as I'm aware. Were he at your father's house, I'd have expected news of him in our last letters from the family. It is odd that he should simply vanish, unless he came by a mishap."

"I somehow doubt that." Beaumont was mounting his horse. "Sorry to rush off, Ingram, but I must find Tom before he quits Oxford. Don't say a word to anyone else about de Zamora."

**III.**

Tom walked out consternated from Lord Digby's offices. De Zamora was waiting in the street, picking at his teeth with a fingernail and smiling at the passersby. Tom led him away, wishing he were not so obtrusively like Laurence. "His lordship's servant says that my brother is in Warwickshire solemnising his marriage. He may not be back for another five days."

"I am desolated that we must postpone our meeting – but what joyful news," de Zamora said, throwing up his arms in an extravagant gesture. "Perhaps he may soon engender an heir to the Beaumont estate – though, with God's blessing, you and your wife will be the first to give Lord Beaumont a grandson." He cocked an eyebrow at Tom. "You are a trifle perplexed, Thomas. Has the marriage come as a surprise to you?"

"Of course not," snapped Tom. "Now, sir, I must rejoin the Prince for supper at his quarters. I hope your valet has secured you lodgings."

"I left him counting the fleas in our bed at the Green Dragon Inn. Do you know of it?" Tom nodded: it was in a rough neighbourhood habituated by criminals. "Five days in Oxford." De Zamora cast his eyes heavenwards. "*Dios mío*, to think of the expense."

Tom scowled and dipped into his pockets. He withdrew a gold unite, which was all he had. Rupert's officers had not been paid in a month. "It's the last time, sir."

"Thomas," de Zamora reproached him, "I am only here for your sake. I might have sailed for Spain, had you not urged me to show Jorge's confession to your brother."

"Oh yes? How would you afford the passage?"

De Zamora roared with laughter. "Such wit, just as I had begun to doubt whether you possessed a sense of humour. When shall *we* next meet?"

*Never again*, Tom wanted to say. De Zamora was a liability to him in Oxford. And what if Laurence arrived early, and by chance met de Zamora before Tom had spoken to Laurence himself? "Stay close by the Inn," he said. "You'll hear from me when my brother gets to town."

"I look forward to that, Thomas," de Zamora said, and he sallied on down the street, whistling.

Tom still could not believe what Lord Digby's servant had told him. Why would someone so averse to marriage charge off in the midst of the spring campaign to wed a girl in whom he had demonstrated not the slightest interest? And how could the Beaumont family leave rebel troops at the house to attend the ceremony? No, thought Tom: Digby must have sent Laurence on a clandestine mission. And there was one man who might be able to confirm this.

"Come in, Thomas." Seward stepped aside for Tom to enter, and shut the door. "Might I assume that you are looking for your brother?"

"I rode from Shrewsbury to find him. Lord Digby's servant said he's away – getting married."

"So he is. Pray you sit." Tom fell into a chair. "He may be as astonished as you are that he has taken a wife," Seward said, with a wheezy chuckle, "but when we spoke before he set out, he was very happy."

"I am as happy, for him and our family," said Tom, pondering uncomfortably if it could signify a change in Laurence's attitude towards the inheritance.

Seward settled into the other chair, and knotted his bony hands in the lap of his soiled robe. "You wrote to him of a family matter that you wished to discuss. Does it concern a visitor from Spain? From your mother's family?"

Tom quivered with rage. "Ah, so her ladyship confided in Laurence about the letter, and he gossiped about it to *you*."

Seward's eyes bulged, behind his spectacles. "What letter?"

"The one she had at Christmastide from the Spanish Envoy in London. Please, Doctor, don't pretend ignorance."

"I swear, neither Beaumont nor I knew about that letter."

"Then how did you know de Zamora was in England?"

"De Zamora – is that his name?" A guarded expression crossed Seward's face. "Back in January, a man was seen in Oxford who markedly resembled your brother. He found out about it himself only this month. Who else could the fellow have been, other than a relation of her ladyship's?" Tom kept silent; he had feared a similar encounter today. "And you, Thomas, what do you know of him?"

"I met him at Prince Rupert's camp," Tom said, resenting Seward's inquisitorial manner. "He is our mother's cousin from Seville. It was he who told me the Envoy had written to her on his behalf. I've brought him to town with me. He's eager to consult both of us brothers on this matter, which pertains to our family alone, and which has prevented him, up to now, from calling on her ladyship." Tom sprang to his feet and paced to the door. "That's all I have to tell you."

Seward's voice stopped him in his tracks. "Thomas, while I have scant evidence to rely upon except my instinct, I am absolutely sure that he intends harm to your family. Beware of trusting him, and do not let him create strife between you and your brother."

Every hair on Tom bristled. "I can trust my own instinct. And you are not a part of our family."

"Nonetheless," Seward said, in the same chilling voice, "I was tutor to your father, your brother, and to you for a brief time, and your brother is my dearest friend. I would give my life for him, as he almost gave his for me. Whoever would harm him is therefore my enemy, also. May I remind you, Thomas," he continued more softly, "how in the not so distant past, *you* could have done him great harm, though without intending it. You must cleave together, from now on."

"My thanks for your unsolicited advice, Doctor," said Tom. "Should you speak with Laurence before I have the opportunity, please direct him to Prince Rupert's quarters. Goodbye."

Tom left feeling like a drunken man hit by a blast of arctic air. The future he had described to de Zamora, in which Laurence gratefully conferred on him the privileges of heir, now appeared to him an outrageous dream, provoked by that deathbed confession. But would it appear to Laurence more like a betrayal?

## IV.

On the crest of a hill, screened by a copse of trees, Laurence dismounted and tied his horse to a branch. He had a clear view for a good three miles all around; no sign of rebel troops near the Furnival house. He should have called there instead of sending a message for Catherine to meet him in this secluded spot, as if they were illicit lovers rather than husband and wife. Selfishly he had wanted her alone. And yet afterwards, as he had warned her in his note, he would have to leave her again with her family and make haste for Oxford.

Finally he spied her in her plain gown, her head and shoulders wrapped in a shawl, toiling towards him, not alone but with Will. They were carrying the magpie's cage between them, possibly as a pretext for her excursion, he thought. He ran to grab her side of it, and she dropped behind.

Not until they had reached the copse of trees, and he and Will had set down the cage, did he notice the dark purple welts on both of her cheekbones. "Catherine, what happened? Did you have a bout of your sickness?"

"No, sir, it was my father's gift to me on our marriage day," she said dryly. "Once those troopers had hunted for you in vain, they ordered him to empty his coffers. He had to surrender Pen's dowry and more, to get rid of them. He struck me because I told him it was his fault he'd been robbed."

"Has he done this to you before?" Laurence demanded, ready to leap on his horse and dash over to give Sir Harold a taste of his own medicine.

Will spoke for her. "He doesn't often mark her as badly, sir, but he was in a tantrum. She wasn't to stir outside 'til the bruises had gone, so I had to swear to her ladyship that we were off to free the bird, and would come straight home."

Catherine bent on one knee to open the cage. She scooped up the magpie, released it onto the ground, and watched it tread tentatively through the grass. "Fly," she whispered. "I pray you, *fly*."

Laurence might have prayed had he any faith. He examined her, in her huntress pose; her dark eyes, clouded and inscrutable above the bruises, were riveted on the bird. Then it startled him with a piercing squawk, and spread its wings. A strong breeze began to blow, billowing out their clothes, and the magpie was wafted clean into the air. They tracked its progress as it soared majestically over the trees and became a gleaming mote on the horizon.

Catherine's shoulders slumped, and she covered her face with her hands.

"Catherine," said Laurence, "I'm taking you to my father's house. It's only five miles south of here."

She stared up at him. "I know where it is, but you can't put yourself in danger again for my sake."

"I've got a fast horse – we won't be caught. Remember," he added, with teasing severity, "as my wife you promised to obey me."

"So you ought, Mistress Catherine," said Will.

Laurence hoisted her to her feet. "Will, inform Sir Harold that his bird has flown. If he causes you any trouble, ask at Chipping Campden for Jacob, Lord Beaumont's Master of Horse. Tell Jacob from me that he has a new groom."

"Yes, sir, bless you, sir," exclaimed Will. "Goodbye, sir, goodbye, Mistress Catherine." He retrieved the cage, and sped away down the hill.

Laurence led Catherine into the copse where his Arab stallion stood swishing its tail. He had his hands on either side of her waist, to lift her into the saddle, when she held back. "There is one thing, before we go. I'm not yet your wife."

How Catherine reminded him physically of Juana, with her narrow hips and small, firm breasts, and a similar animal scent to her skin. Accustomed as he was to practised sexual partners, it had required some patience, self-restraint, and not a little art to bring her to climax. When at last she arrived, however, he felt that she had given herself not to him but to the pleasure of her own body, which had aroused him far more.

"My mother and her gentlewomen told me that you would hurt me, and that I would find no joy in it," she said, as they tidied their clothing. "I know they wanted me to be afraid."

"Hmm . . ." said Laurence. "Perhaps they were speaking from their experience."

"Then I'm sorry for them. And I'm sorry, in a different way, for Pen."

"As am I, the poor wronged creature. Should I exchange you for her?"

"I'm not *that* sorry," replied Catherine, and she began to laugh so spontaneously that he joined in; it was the first time he had heard her laughing.

Eventually they mounted, and Laurence spurred the Arab to a gallop. Avoiding the road, they cut across fields dotted with sheep suckling their new lambs and ploughmen driving oxen through the freshly tilled earth; still not a sign of rebel troops. At the northern border to Lord Beaumont's property, he slowed the horse to a trot; looming ahead were the high drystone walls that surrounded his lordship's park. "We must part company at the gatehouse," he told Catherine. "The gatekeeper will go with you up to the house."

"No, let me down here," she said, loosening her arms, which had been snug about his waist, but he urged the horse on, until they were almost at the gates.

He reined in; he could hear male voices and the rumble of wheels on gravel. "Wait." He swung a leg over his horse's neck, slid off, and ventured closer. Lady Beaumont was descending from his lordship's coach, aided by her driver and the gatekeeper. Since their conversation suggested no immediate peril, Laurence decided to show himself.

"Laurence," she gasped.

"Is everyone well at the house?" he asked, pained to see new threads of silver in her hair and deeper lines around her eyes and mouth.

"Yes, yes," she said, speaking rapidly, "though Purefoy's men stole so much from us, we shall have a hard year ahead. Our sole consolation is that none of his lordship's treasures were discovered. And the troops left us, the day before yesterday. Governor Massey ordered them back to the garrison."

"Ah . . . So is it safe for me to stay?"

"It is most *un*safe – Purefoy sent that raiding party to Lower Quinton on the day of your marriage, and has paid informers in Chipping Campden town to alert him if you are spotted in the neighbourhood. But, Laurence, Sir Harold wrote to us that you refused Penelope to marry her twin, Catherine. Why? And you gave away half the bridal portion. What folly – we were counting on the money."

"I'll compensate you for it. There is something I should tell you about Catherine. She has the—"

"Great heavens," interrupted Lady Beaumont. "Why did you not say that you had brought her with you?"

Catherine was coming towards them leading the Arab. "Good day to you, your ladyship," she said, curtseying. "I am Catherine Beaumont."

Lady Beaumont surveyed Catherine's grass-stained gown, her bruises, and her tousled hair. "You are welcome. Bid a swift farewell to your husband, and attend me in the coach."

Laurence kissed Catherine on the forehead and said, under his breath, "Her bark is worse than her bite." Catherine smiled, and went dutifully to the coach.

"Wonders will never cease," said Lady Beaumont, as the driver helped Catherine inside. "I am impressed by the latitude of your taste in the female sex."

"Thank you for the compliment."

Lady Beaumont walked him to his horse. "Now, you must go. Are you returning to Oxford?"

"Yes." He hesitated to mount, fingering the reins. "I can't leave without asking: have you seen or heard from your cousin, Antonio de Zamora?"

Her eyes flickered, in a way he could not read. Then she said, too easily, "I have not. How come you know of him?"

Laurence brushed aside the question. "*You* knew since December that he was in England. You had a letter from the Spanish Envoy, around the time you were sick. Was it the letter that brought about your illness?"

"I can assure you, Laurence, I would not fall sick because some member of my family chose to visit us. Yes, I heard from the Envoy, but not from Antonio. Answer me: how did you learn he was here?" She frowned when Laurence explained what Ingram had told him. "So that is why he has not yet appeared on our doorstep: he was sniffing out Thomas first."

"What do you mean by sniffing? And why Tom? Why not sniff *me* out, if he was reluctant to come straight to you?"

"Perhaps he could not find you."

"Why is he here?"

"I suspect for financial reasons. He never had a penny to his name. If he thinks he will profit from his lordship, he's sorely deceived, especially after what we have lost to the rebels, and your reckless behaviour over the marriage portion."

Laurence heaved an exasperated sigh. "Tom said he's just like me."

"And so? Our looks are common in my family: his mother and mine were sisters more alike than the Furnival twins. Be warned if you cross paths that he is an inveterate liar. Allow me to deal with him, should he appear, though by Thomas's account he has been invisible for almost two months. He may have perished from the English cold. It would be a rude shock, after Seville," she concluded, sardonically.

"Then . . . he's no threat to you?"

"Antonio a threat? How you exaggerate. He may well prove an annoyance, but I am far more worried about our fortunes, his lordship's fragile constitution, my sons who are fighting in a war . . . even the gatekeeper's wife whom I came today to visit, who is in agony with her ulcers. Now ride out at once, or you'll bring us even greater worry by getting yourself captured."

Laurence felt as though he were banging his head against one of the drystone walls. He considered telling her about the murdered Parliamentarian in London, and about the incident of the woman in Oxford. No point, he thought, looking at her face: she would dismiss them both. "Please give my love to the family," he said, swinging into his saddle. "And be gentle with Catherine. She hasn't had any love from hers."

## V.

Laurence left his horse at the Merton stables and walked over to Christ Church. A visit to Seward could wait; first he had to know if Prince Rupert was still in Oxford. Upon inquiring, he heard from a royal equerry that Rupert had gone with His Majesty on a tour of the Abingdon garrison, where Rupert had quartered his men along with Wilmot's cavalry. "Then His Royal Highness will be here a while longer?" Laurence asked.

"Oh yes, sir: he is to inspect *all* of our surrounding garrisons," the equerry said, as though it were a herculean task.

This pleased Laurence: he could drop by Seward's rooms, and find Tom later towards evening, at Abingdon. But he was thwarted near the College gatehouse: Digby and Quayle were coming down Merton Street, and Digby immediately hailed him. "Mr. Beaumont, you are back early from your honeymoon. Were you on your way to my offices? Splendid – we shall go together." He placed a gloved fingertip on Laurence's arm to guide him there. "I trust the wedding met with your expectations."

"Yes, my lord: it was a quiet ceremony."

"And how did you and your bride like my gift?"

"Like is not the word, my lord: we were humbled by your generosity in parting with such a magnificent work of art."

"It is you who made the greater sacrifice, sir, in parting with the original."

"My sacrifice was rewarded," Laurence replied equably, though the comment irked him.

"Well, to business, sir. We have been holding interminable sessions of Council, to profit from Prince Rupert's stay in Oxford. He may soon be bound to go to the aid of York, which is under siege by both the Scots and Parliament's northern forces."

"That *is* bad news," said Laurence; York would be a disastrous loss. "When is His Majesty taking to the field?"

"As it turns out, he may not," said Digby, with a hint of petulance. "Rupert has persuaded him to sit upon our garrisons in the Oxford area, rather than provoke an engagement with Waller or Essex. Rupert believes those generals lack the strength to attack our ring of fortresses, even if they were to combine their armies, which is unlikely, given the animosity between them. Nor – according to Rupert – can they push farther west, with His Majesty so entrenched."

A defensive war, thought Laurence. "The Prince may be right: His Majesty can't afford another Cheriton. Parliament would gain control of the south."

"Lord Wilmot has objected to Rupert's plan. He has told Council that we have neither sufficient troops nor materiel to furnish the garrisons properly, and Rupert will be taking powder and supplies north with him, depleting our reserves. Besides, the success of Rupert's strategy depends not only on his relief of York but on his brother conquering the West Country. Yet Prince Maurice is well over a hundred miles away, besieging the port of Lyme Regis to no ostensible result."

"Has Lord Wilmot a better strategy?"

"He prefers attack to defence," answered Digby, as Quayle scurried ahead of them to open the door to his lordship's offices. "He would reduce our garrisons around Oxford to build an army large enough to strike at Waller, while the Parliamentary generals are unprepared and squabbling over command of their southern forces."

With a dancer's grace, Digby stepped through the door, handed Quayle his cloak, and beckoned Laurence to his inner sanctum. "What think you of that, Mr. Beaumont?" he said, seating himself at his desk.

"If the strike were repulsed, Oxford would be under siege, and His Majesty and his sons might fall hostage to the enemy. In this instance, I have to disagree with Wilmot: his strategy is too much of a risk. I prefer Rupert's."

To Laurence's surprise, Digby seemed piqued. "You have not seen the growing influence that Rupert wields over the King, and the gargantuan contempt with which he addresses His Majesty's civilian and military advisors. Lord Forth is bridling at his high-handedness."

"Tact is not among the Prince's many attributes, my lord."

"Tact is not the issue, sir – we predict he will demand political power when the war is done, for himself and for his brother Maurice. They will not trundle home to live in impoverished exile."

"Wouldn't they be owed something for their efforts in His Majesty's cause?"

"What if, God forbid, the cause does not prosper? Rupert is a mercenary: he will urge his uncle to arrive at terms with Parliament."

"I'd see no wrong in that, my lord, but then I was a mercenary, too, as were Wilmot, Forth, Waller, Essex, and countless others on both sides. It would be unjust of either side to prolong the war – as His Majesty would surely agree, given his sincere pursuit of peace from the outset of this conflict."

Digby must have caught Laurence's sarcasm; a flush rose in his cheeks, and for a moment he did not speak. "In the event of our defeat," he recommended, "those terms might include a cosy place for Rupert in England. But for myself, I would foresee an *impoverished exile*, at the very best."

"Your lordship would be wise to go abroad beforehand, as perhaps would I."

In a typical lightning shift of mood, Digby cast him a glowing smile. "Let us not expend our energies on hypothetic argument. Now that your conjugal life is so felicitously arranged, you must devote your attention to the duty His Majesty assigned you. Whatever strategy is adopted by Council, we shall require new scouts."

"I'd propose to recruit more than scouts, my lord. We need better informers in Waller's and Essex's camps, and men to reconnoitre a path of escape for the King to Rupert's headquarters in Shrewsbury, and to secure safe houses along the way for his shelter. Governor Massey has summoned his troops back to Gloucester," Laurence added. "*His* spies in Oxford must have reported on the King's preparations for battle. That leaves the northern reaches of the Gloucestershire open to us, for the time being, and Massey's raids will have alienated the local populace. If we offer them encouragement, they will stick by the King, who may be in desperate need of friends there, should Oxford be threatened."

"You may write me out an estimate as to the cost. Sir," said Digby, in a less confident tone, "I am concerned about our London network."

"Why, what have you heard?" asked Laurence quickly.

"My concern is that I have not heard anything. Since Mr. Price's return to Oxford, Isabella has failed to communicate with me through the couriers he recruited."

Laurence remembered Price's airy optimism about Barlow and Jem; had Veech already seized them? "She may be lying low," he said to Digby. "I sent her a message over a week ago, through Price, warning her to stop her games with Draycott and Veech."

"You might have asked my permission, prior to sending it."

"You would have done the same, my lord, if you knew the danger to her. Price acted rashly when he hired those people."

"Are they not friends of yours who rendered you excellent service in the past?"

"Yes they are, and for that reason Veech will be watching them. I told Price they might be followed to and from her house. I could waste no time in alerting her."

Digby pursed his lips. "I would not have objected to your warning her on that score, but it is not for you to put a stop to her activities as my agent."

"My lord, this is not some trivial issue of authority. Neither of us wants her to be arrested by a brute like Veech. And clearly Veech has a tight hold over Draycott. She and her husband were lucky to escape when they played about with gunpowder. Now she's playing with fire."

"It was she who suggested that she win the affections of Mr. Draycott, in order to obtain intelligence on the notorious Clement Veech. And she had a more daring plan in mind, which she may have postponed as a result of your message: to effect the demise of Mr. Veech."

"I hope she's abandoned it altogether," said Laurence, when he could find his voice.

"You underestimate her skills as an agent," Digby said, but so weakly that Laurence let the rebuke pass.

"What will you do for her, my lord, if she's taken?"

"I shall rely on *you* to think of something," Digby answered, in the same hapless tone.

## VI.

By the hearth in his cottage billet, Tom was sipping at a mug of watery ale, trying to ignore the chorus of snores from the other officers rolled up in their blankets, and the stink of his wet boots and stockings that were laid out on the hearthstones by his equally smelly bare feet. What a day, though it had distracted him from the nagging problem of de Zamora. Here in Abingdon, the King and Prince Rupert had discovered empty casks, rotten food, and ordure scattered about the camp. Loose women had taken up residence among the cavalry, some claiming to be wives, though their rouged cheeks and bold manners hinted otherwise to Tom. And on the faces of Wilmot's men he had seen open disrespect towards Rupert. The lot of them deserved a court martial.

Tom tossed the dregs of his ale into the fire, and allowed his eyes to close, focusing his thoughts on Mary and their coming child. It would be born in midsummer; but a few months to wait.

"Sir," he heard Adam say quietly, "your brother is here." He jerked straight in his chair and opened his eyes; Laurence was stepping round prone bodies, his saddlebag slung across his shoulder.

He squatted down by Tom's side, and smiled. "I went all the way to Prince Rupert's camp to see you. Ingram told me we'd passed each other like ships in the night."

Tom could not return the smile; his jaw was locked. "So, you and Penelope Furnival are husband and wife."

"I didn't marry her – I married her sister, Catherine. I stopped by our house to leave Catherine there, though I couldn't stay. Everyone is in good health. Purefoy's troops have departed for Gloucester."

"Thank God for that," said Tom, a little relieved.

Laurence produced a flask from his saddlebag. "Have you a cup?" He steadied Tom's shaking hand, and poured him a measure. "Tom, you're not feverish, are you?"

"No. To you and your bride." Tom took a large swallow. "By Jesus, this isn't wine," he spluttered.

"It's aqua vitae. We need strong stuff, to match the subject of our conversation – Antonio de Zamora."

"Damn Ingram – he broke his word."

"On my prompting. Tell me everything, Tom."

Tom gulped more of the potent spirit, which marvellously clarified his thoughts: he would talk of the deathbed confession, but not of what he had said to de Zamora about Laurence and the title. If de Zamora raised this with Laurence, Tom would call him a liar and challenge him on the spot to a duel that Tom felt sure he could win. "I kept from Ingram that I met the Spaniard a second time," he began, holding out his cup again; his hand had ceased to shake.

**VII.**

"If our mother was seduced or . . . or raped by de Zamora's brother, it would explain many things, Seward: why she never speaks of her Spanish family, her illness around the time that she heard from the Envoy, and her wish to deal with de Zamora alone, to hide the truth." Laurence scrutinised Seward's face in the candlelight; they were sitting across his desk from each other, in the positions they had once occupied as tutor and pupil. "Why do I suspect . . ." He rephrased his words. "You're less appalled by this than I was. You didn't . . . *know*?"

"Of course not – and it is a dreadful story," murmured Seward, his eyes downcast.

"It is, and yet she demonstrated no equivalent emotion when I asked her about de Zamora. Not that she couldn't be masking her feelings – she's a woman of steely resolve. But the more I consider his story, the more I mistrust him."

Seward glanced up. "On what grounds?"

"To begin with, he kept his secret for over thirty years. He was a soldier – he could have been slain at any point, leaving his brother's request unfulfilled. Then, in his retirement, he did nothing to find my mother. Only when he discovered he hadn't long to live, did he come to England. Why would a dying man undertake such a risky and arduous voyage?"

"For the benefit of his soul?"

Laurence shrugged. "Once he arrived here, what did he do? If I were him, I'd have headed straight to Chipping Campden without wasting any of my few remaining hours on earth. Let's follow his movements: he was in London before Christmas, and near the third week of January he assaulted a woman in Oxford."

"Hardly the behaviour of a dying man," interjected Seward.

"Unless he feared it might be his last taste of quim. That night Mawson called him 'Beaumont,' and the name must have registered. He could have located me then in Oxford without difficulty: I was bedridden with my shoulder wound. Instead he journeyed miles in the

winter cold to catch up with Tom – and not until March did he introduce himself. When Tom told him he resembled me, he behaved as if
he were surprised. Yet he must already have guessed from his encounter with Mawson that one of us was his double."

"He might have," Seward agreed.

"Then he vanished, and wasted *another* month apparently worrying about the damage his brother's confession might cause to our
family. On his second meeting with Tom, he said God had put Tom
in his path before me. It wasn't Divine Providence. I think he elected
to tell Tom, and not me, about *his* double, the reprobate brother. As
he may have planned, Tom is now wondering if I am Jorge's son –
with all that *that* entails. And according to Tom, de Zamora still
seems in robust health."

"His entire story may be fabricated. He is here to cause harm, as
my bowl forewarned. I should have spoken of the vision to Thomas
when he came to me."

"A good thing you refrained. Tom was sufficiently upset, as was
I, though I tried to hide it from him. Poor Tom, I know what he's
thinking: that I have no real desire for what he's always wanted. And
he was right, until not so long ago." Laurence broke off to calm himself. "I even raised the issue with my father this past autumn. He said
to me that Tom could not inherit while I was alive. That was when I
understood my duty. And . . . and when I heard about the troops at our
house, it became yet clearer to me."

"My boy," said Seward, "in some respects you grew rather too
early into your manhood, but in others, you were somewhat retarded."

Laurence smiled. "Thank you, Seward."

"What is your next move with de Zamora?"

"Tom will arrange for the three of us to meet tomorrow night, at
the inn where he's lodged."

"I shall pray for you and Thomas," Seward told him. "It could be
the gravest peril that you will ever confront as brothers."

## VIII.

"If you were about to invite me, sir, I won't trouble to come in." Veech handed Draycott a thin, sealed packet at his door. "Plant this tonight. I've informed Corporal Stanton you'll be visiting her late. He knows no more than that. Bide until morning if you can, to allay her suspicions. Stanton says her husband went to Rochester in the coach, and won't return until next week. I'll stop here again tomorrow afternoon to find out where you hid the evidence, and then we'll go on a hunting party with the militia."

"Why not wait, to catch Sir Montague as well?" asked Draycott, as scornfully as he could.

"He'll be drawn in after she's arrested."

"But . . . you will require a search warrant to enter the house."

"Leave that to me. Once she's in my custody, perhaps Judith and your children will run home to you."

Draycott recoiled. "What do you know about them?"

"I know where they are. You've lost one child. You wouldn't want some accident to befall another." And Veech turned, to limp off down the street.

Draycott wished he had a loaded pistol to discharge at Veech's retreating figure. He slammed the door and broke the seal on the packet. The pages were covered in a cipher; had he weeks, he would be unable to make sense of it. Still in a quandary as to what he should do, he unbuttoned his doublet and used a knife to unpick some stitches in the lining. He stuffed the pages back into the packet and forced it far inside the thick layers of cloth, rebuttoned his doublet, grabbed his hat and cloak, and headed for the Strand.

## IX.

Antonio dropped a coin onto the floor by his bed, and started languidly to fasten his breeches. "Take your money and go."

The girl was on her knees between his thighs, spitting into her apron. "You promised me twice as much."

"That was to fuck you. You should not have tried to sell yourself to a gentleman at your time of the month."

Snatching up the coin, she scrambled to her feet. "Most gentlemen hereabouts don't care."

"Oh get out," said Antonio.

She nearly collided with Diego, who came rushing breathlessly into the chamber. He shut the door after her, and announced, "I have seen him. And, saints above, he *is* your very image."

A thrill coursed through Antonio, more pleasurable than the service for which he had just paid. "Continue, Diego."

"I followed him to Merton College, where Thomas went after you two last spoke. And he knocked at the same door, and was admitted by the old man."

"Who can *he* be? Did you inquire?"

"Yes, in the gatehouse. The porter said that his name is Doctor William Seward. He's a scholar learned in philosophy, medicine, and astrology. So I said that *I* was a student of medicine, and had heard of him by repute."

"You are a paragon of ingenuity."

"I'm not finished," Diego said. "I mentioned that I had seen a tall, dark man entering his room but a moment earlier. Was this person also a scholar at the university? Oh no, that would be Mr. Beaumont, the porter said. Dr. Seward had been his tutor, and now they're fast friends. And what sort of a fellow is Mr. Beaumont, I said?" Diego imitated the porter's speech, in English. "'Charmin' as can be, sir, and he treats us like we was as good as he, though he's of noble blood.'"

"Then he must be soft in the head," muttered Antonio.

"It supports Thomas's contention that he doesn't wish to be a lord."

"He may not want the responsibilities of a title, but I doubt he'd appreciate being told that he's a cuckoo in his father's nest."

"I think we should talk to the Doctor, Don Antonio."

"Why, my clever monkey?"

"He's known Beaumont for half of Beaumont's life. And old men are easily intimidated. I asked the porter if I might request a consultation, on a medical issue. He said that Dr. Seward had condescended to heal him of his warts, and would surely assist a scholar such as me."

"On this occasion, your ingenuity may prove redundant," Antonio said. "Thomas and his brother are coming here tomorrow night, to meet with me."

## X.

"Mr. Draycott, thank God," exclaimed Lady Isabella, opening the door to him herself.

"My lady, are you all alone in the house?" he asked.

"No, but my husband took Greenhalgh with him to Rochester. Lucy is abed with a chill."

When they were seated in the gallery, Draycott inhaled a deep breath. "Clement Veech informed me today that Lord Digby was your guardian, and that you and his agent, Laurence Beaumont, were once lovers," he said, altering the truth a little. He was too ashamed to admit that he had told Veech about the inscription in her book, even if it offered no material proof of treachery, as Veech obviously knew; hence the incriminating packet.

"Of what significance is my past to Veech?" She sounded more cross than frightened. "I did not choose my guardian, and as for my relations with Beaumont, they ended before my marriage."

"Last autumn when I was still an officer in the Trained Bands, I arrested Beaumont, although I was unaware of his identity at the time, and mistakenly released him. The same night, Veech apprised me of who he was, and while we were chasing him, he fired on us. He wounded Veech with a crippling shot to the knee. It was after my mistake that Veech hired me. He thirsts for private revenge on Beaumont, quite apart from the enormous prize to Parliament of capturing Lord Digby's most able man."

Lady Isabella's gold-flecked eyes darted to and fro. "Beaumont won't be caught here again," she said, as though stating a fact.

"My lady, tomorrow afternoon, Veech will bring me and a party of militia to raid your house, to find evidence to bring you to trial on a charge of treason. He knows you are Digby's courier. He will arrest you, and then Sir Montague, although you are his target: he is convinced that Beaumont will attempt to rescue you from gaol."

"He will find no evidence of treason in my house."

"He has ordered me to plant a packet of documents in cipher tonight, and then stay, and . . . and make love to you, so you would not suspect me."

Lady Isabella paled, and fluttered a hand to her breast. "And will you plant it?"

"No. I am your friend, as I promised you. Veech has wrecked my life, but he shan't have the satisfaction of wrecking yours, if I can prevent him."

"Bless you, sir, for your courage and your loyalty to me," she murmured. Then she asked in a harder tone, "Where is the packet?"

Draycott thought of Veech whittling away at the polished oak settle; and he thought of Judith and the children. "At my house."

"What will you do when Veech makes no discovery?"

"I'll have to act astonished, and swear that I did his bidding."

"You might say I gave you no chance to hide it."

"He would only send me back for another attempt."

She moved closer to Draycott; he could smell mint and cloves on her breath. "You said he has wrecked your life. What did you mean?"

"Judith has left me, and taken the children. She despises me for being in thrall to Veech. I could force her to come home, yet I can't make her love me again – if ever she did."

Lady Isabella kissed him. Her tongue slipped inside his mouth, and she raised him up and ran her hands down his chest, around his waist, and along his spine and buttocks. His heart was thudding; would she detect the packet? But she separated from him, and said in a low voice, "Can we comfort each other tonight?"

"Yes," he said, feeling as if his entire future had just changed irrevocably with that single word.

She ushered him from the gallery, through a passage, and into a dimly lit bedchamber. She sat him on the bed and like some handmaiden of yore removed his shoes and stockings, unbuttoned his doublet, took it off and cast it aside, drew his shirt over his head, and then stripped him slowly of his breeches and close trousers. No one had undressed him since his childhood, and not once in the entirety of his marriage had he been naked with modest Judith.

"Lie back," Lady Isabella told him, "and shut your eyes." He caught the smoke of an extinguished candle, and next a wonderful, unidentifiable fragrance. He felt her hands, smooth with oil, massaging his tight muscles, from his neck, to his shoulders, then his chest and belly, and on to his thighs and calves; everywhere but his rigid sex. Her touch, when at last she touched him there, was paradise, and his whole body sang.

# CHAPTER THIRTEEN

I.

Draycott woke in the featherbed to the lingering scent of Lady Isabella's perfumed oil. Embarrassment consumed him as he thought of their sinful night: although he had not lain with her in true adultery, after the massage he had allowed her to lavish on him more intimate caresses that had sent him into paroxysms of joy. Then he must have slept.

He dared to open his eyes. She was curled up next to him, fully dressed on top of the counterpane, her face so young and seemingly innocent in repose. Anxious not to rouse her, he eased himself from the bed, and gathered his strewn garments and shoes from the floor. He burrowed a shaking hand into the lining of his doublet. The packet was undisturbed. He ran to the window and peered through the curtains. The sun was still low in the east: about six of the clock, he estimated. In the street he saw the usual dawn traffic, and servants scouring the steps of the houses; and, to his alarm, a party of Stanton's militia on patrol.

He threw on his clothes, listening for any noises in the house. All was silent. Shoes tucked under one arm, he stole to the door; but as he reached a hand towards the latch, he heard her voice. "Mr. Draycott?"

He turned, his cheeks hot. "My lady, I don't know what to say . . ."

"Say that next time *you* will please *me*." She smiled serenely, and rose from the bed with a rustle of silk. "I'll accompany you to the front door, though we must be very quiet. And in the afternoon we shall meet again, in less happy circumstances."

"I . . . I have the packet on me," he stammered. "I wanted to show it to you last night, but I was afraid. I told you Veech had threatened my family. Yesterday he spoke of hurting one of my children if I didn't obey him. I never would have, my lady, as God is my witness. I was going to take the packet home with me, and burn it."

Lady Isabella stopped smiling and came towards him; she looked tormented, as though on the verge of some similar admission. Then a resigned sadness crossed her face, and she hugged him, as he might have hugged his sons. "You are a good man, sir, and he is a *monster*."

"No, I am weak. And I must convince Veech that I am weaker yet and in his power, or you and I will both be undone. He must find nothing here that could link you to Lord Digby or to Beaumont – no letters, or . . . lines in their writing." At once he knew from her eyes: she had guessed he had seen that inscription in her book. "Let me give you the evidence now, and you can destroy it."

"We'll destroy it together," she said. "He can search all he likes. He will find *nothing*."

Veech knocked around three of the afternoon. He sniffed at Draycott as he pushed past into the kitchen. "Sweet as a rose, sir. Stanton tells me you wandered out of her house early this morning. Did you fuck her?"

"By God, no. It was the strangest night of my life." Draycott had little trouble matching his face to the story he had rehearsed: it was enough to remember spending into Lady Isabella's agile hand while she delved the fingers of her other into a forbidden place. "She must have drugged me. She served me some wine that dizzied me, upon the second or third glass."

"Did you hide the packet?"

Draycott rubbed his temples as if his head throbbed. "Yes, in the gallery, while I was briefly alone – I . . . I must have put it somewhere among her books, but my senses were growing confused by then."

"Did she attempt to question you, in your befuddled state? Did she ask you about me?"

"Not that I recall, though I can't be sure. I wanted to leave, but she insisted that I lie down in her guest chamber. And I knew no more until dawn. I let myself out of the house – everyone else must have been still asleep."

"Could she have seen you hide the packet?"

"No – she had gone to prepare the chamber for me."

"What accounts for your scented skin?"

"The bed linen reeked with perfume. In the morning it nearly made me sick."

Veech examined him solemnly. "You understand what a poisonous, conniving bitch she is, Mr. Draycott. She had hoped to make you talk. That's why we have to entrap her. Now let's go a-hunting."

They took a hackney coach to the Strand, where Corporal Stanton and a half-dozen militia were gathered on the steps of Sir Montague's house. When Lucy answered the door, Veech shoved her aside and barged through to the entrance hall. "Summon your mistress to the gallery," he told her. "Mr. Draycott, lead the way for me and Corporal Stanton. You stay below," he ordered the troopers.

In the gallery Corporal Stanton fidgeted with his hat, inspecting the imprints of his muddy boots on the polished floor. "What a business for her ladyship," he said to Draycott.

Lady Isabella entered and addressed them calmly. "Corporal, Mr. Draycott, and . . . who are you, sir?"

"He is Mr. Clement Veech, my lady, servant to Mr. Oliver St. John," Stanton said.

"This warrant signed by Mr. St. John licenses me to search the premises," said Veech, thrusting it at her.

She read it, and thrust it back. "Your charge is pure slander, as I shall inform him. And I will not allow a search of this house in the absence of my husband."

"My lady, begging your pardon," said Stanton, "you cannot deny him access: he has the authority."

Veech was surveying her as he might a pox-ridden drab who had tried to proposition him. "How many apartments are there?"

"The gallery here, a dining parlour, and the bedchambers – mine, my husband's, and one more for our guests – and my husband's dressing closet and study. Downstairs are the servants' quarters, the kitchen, scullery, and pantry, and the privy offices. And beneath are Sir Montague's cellars, a storeroom, and the cesspit."

Veech limped out, and Draycott heard him telling the men, "Start with the guest bedchamber." He returned and meandered about the gallery, lifting the tapestries and brocade curtains to squint behind them. He halted by a table, on which a pile of books was tidily stacked, and opened one book after another. "Latin and Greek, my lady! I thought your husband was a man of commerce."

"Most of those are gifts from his patrons," she said. "He cannot decline them, even if he has no aptitude for languages."

Veech held each book by its bindings and smacked it against the edge of the table so that the leather cover ripped from the spine. He rifled through the pages, and dumped book upon book onto the floor by her feet; no *Remedia Amoris*, Draycott was relieved to notice.

"Mr. Veech, I must object!" cried Stanton, but he was interrupted by someone yelling from below.

"Corporal Stanton, sir, we've nabbed a thief."

Stanton beetled his brows at Veech and stalked out. "You come, too," Veech said firmly to Draycott.

On the front steps, two soldiers were restraining a thickset man whose wrists were tied together. He was crimson with indignation. "I know the rascal," Stanton said. "He's Peter Barlow of Southwark parish, and has served more than a few sentences in gaol as a housebreaker."

"You can have no honest reason to be in this neighbourhood," snarled Veech. Then he drew Draycott aside. "He must be the same Barlow that lived at the old bawd Mistress Edwards' house, and was Edward Price's friend."

"Is it against the law to walk the City freely?" Barlow protested; and the instant he spoke, Draycott identified him as the outraged citizen in Blackman Street, on the night of Beaumont's escape.

"Have you seen him before, Mr. Draycott?" asked Veech.

Barlow met Draycott's eyes without flinching. "No," said Draycott, appreciating the irony: Veech would have been with him when he knocked on Barlow's door, had Beaumont not fired that crippling shot.

"I admit, I did mill kens in the past," Barlow said, "but I've been clean and above board these six long years, and there's nowt to criminate me here. You must state your charge, or let me go."

"He's right, Corporal," Draycott said.

One of the soldiers passed Stanton a cloth sack. "He threw it into the bushes as we took him, sir."

Veech tore the sack from Stanton's grip and pulled out of it a loaf of bread with a tiny corner nibbled away, as if by a mouse. He dug his fingers into the nibbled corner and withdrew a tight roll of paper that he unfurled; and his mouth stretched into a grin. He gave the paper to Draycott.

"What does this mean?" said Draycott, privately horrified: the minute lines of script upon it resembled the cipher of the documents he and Lady Isabella had burnt.

Veech spoke into his ear. "Did you not have a look inside the packet I gave you?"

"No. Why would I?"

Veech pointed at the script. "The figure is Lord Digby's, copied by me from a cache of his letters Parliament had seized, at the outbreak of the war. And I invented as evidence against her ladyship a most treasonous conspiracy, inspired by her husband's barrels and poor Sir Everard, Digby's ancestor. She was watching you, sir, when you imagined yourself alone in the gallery. She got her hands on that packet and wrote out the contents while you slept." Veech was correct, Draycott realised, except in the details; but why had she not told him in the morning? So that was the cause of her tormented look! Did she mistrust him, or could *he* no longer trust *her*? He thought he might faint. His belly cramped, and he vomited onto the pavement. "You're not to blame she had the better of you," Veech said cheerfully. "Now we have her, and I'll soon learn where Barlow was to deliver his loaf of bread. Corporal," Veech said in a louder voice to Stanton, "convey the thief under guard to Derby House." Stanton was eyeing them both uneasily. "Not a word to her about Barlow and our discovery," Veech said to Draycott. "Let's go upstairs, and I'll show you how she spied on you."

They found Lady Isabella standing by the fireplace with her arm around Lucy, whose goggle-eyed fear reflected Draycott's own. "I must talk to Corporal Stanton," Lady Isabella said. "Where is he?"

Veech ignored her. "Mr. Draycott, lift up that tapestry of the Devil tempting Jesus, and see what's behind it."

Draycott obeyed. There were two holes in the wood-panelled wall, and in the fabric of the tapestry, two holes cut to correspond. Without Veech's prompting, as if in a hateful dream, he went from the gallery into the parlour and reached up to the canvas of Sir Montague's father. He ran his fingers over the eyes, and touched two grooves: the original eyes had been excised, and a slat painted to match inserted underneath. He left the parlour, to study the panelled wall between it and the gallery. When he pressed it with both hands, it shifted, and a door the span of his shoulders creaked wide. On the inner side of the door was a metal bolt. He squeezed into the space. Thin shafts of light from the gallery allowed him to locate, on the opposite wall, a hinged slat. He slid it away: a perfect view of the parlour; and through the holes facing the gallery, also a perfect view. And he remembered the eyes he had seen move, and the sneeze that had stopped his embraces.

He stumbled out and into the gallery, feeling nauseous again. "Who was hiding there last night?" he demanded of Lady Isabella, though he wanted to know as well about those other occasions.

"No one. It is my husband's secret," she confessed, with a mixture of shame and disgust. "He cannot have release like most men. He must view others, covertly, to achieve it. Before our marriage, he would hire pimps and whores to perform lewd acts for him while he looked on."

Veech was laughing. "How the idle rich amuse themselves, eh, Mr. Draycott? My lady," he said in a new, polite manner, "your distress gives me pause for thought. If you will write and sign a declaration that neither you nor Sir Montague is involved in any conspiracy against Parliament, I'll postpone my inquiries until he is home."

"I shall be pleased to deny the spurious charge, Mr. Veech, if you would order *all* of your men to quit this house at once. Including you, sir," she added, to Draycott.

"The troopers can go, my lady," said Veech, "and Mr. Draycott and I will stay only to supervise the phrasing of your declaration. It must be unequivocal." He went out to the head of the stair, and began shouting for the troops to leave.

With his back to the doors, Draycott bounded over to Lady Isabella and mouthed, "Veech has Barlow and your copy of the evidence. All he needs now to convict you is a sample of your writing."

"Does he suspect *you?*" she mouthed.

"No – he thinks you saw me hide the packet. *I lied to him that I had planted it.*"

Her expression changed, and she spoke in a cold, clear tone. "I wonder how you live with yourself, Mr. Draycott, after your pretence of affection towards me."

"I might wonder the same of you," Draycott retorted, imitating her humiliated distaste. He swung round; Veech was in the doorway, arms folded across his chest.

"Get your mistress pen and paper," Veech told Lucy. "Why the long face, sir?" he said amiably to Draycott. "Your work here is almost done."

## II.

"What a shit hole," Tom said; he and Laurence were gazing up at the dingy plastered front and broken windows of the Green Dragon Inn.

"Tom," said Laurence, "don't let him aggravate you, and don't be surprised by what I might say to him. And keep that sword of yours sheathed, unless we're attacked first."

He walked ahead of Tom into the close, smoke-filled taproom. War had not changed life for this underbelly of society: a dismal crew were tippling in an atmosphere pervaded by the stink of rancid fat, cheap ale, and sweat. A girl pranced on a table to the tune of a pipe and a tin drum, her breasts bared and her skirts hiked to the thighs; and in the near corner, a grizzled veteran puked onto the floor, to the satisfaction of a dog that lapped at the spreading pool.

Tom nudged Laurence's elbow. "That's his valet, Diego, over there."

Diego beckoned them through the taproom into a quieter, brighter chamber. In an alcove to one side was a small table lit by a branched candlestick where a dark gentleman sat by himself. "*Los hermanos Beaumont,*" Diego announced, and went back into the taproom.

Nothing could have prepared Laurence for the shock as Antonio de Zamora stood up and bowed. Dressed in a soldier's leather coat with a plain white collar at his neck, and high riding boots, de Zamora wore a sword of English design at his hip. His full head of hair, cropped like Diego's, was greying, as were his beard and moustache, and he was a little shorter than Laurence and a shade thicker through the waist. Yet they had the same high cheekbones and flare to their nostrils, and around de Zamora's mouth were etched the same smile lines that Laurence saw when he looked in a glass; and, most strikingly, they had the same green eyes.

He appeared as taken aback by the sight of Laurence. Then he beamed. "Laurence and Thomas, I am beyond words to express my joy," he said, in accented though fluent English. "Pray sit with me, sirs. I cannot recommend the food, but I have ordered wine to celebrate."

He motioned them to a bench, and distributed the wine. "Here's to your very good health on our special night."

"And to yours, Don Antonio," said Laurence.

"Your health," Tom said curtly.

De Zamora was studying Laurence, fascinated. "Did you get these in the war abroad?" He stroked his own cheekbone and lower lip where Laurence's were scarred.

"No, sir," Laurence replied, wondering what Tom told the man about him.

De Zamora next inspected the deeper scar on Laurence's left wrist, as if he had known where to locate it. "And how did you get *this* one?"

"From a game of cards." Laurence switched to Spanish. "Is it your first visit to England, Don Antonio?"

De Zamora switched also. "Yes, and I am sorry to say I find your country uncongenial. The sun has no warmth, the cooking is tasteless, and the wine worse than vinegar. The streets smell of ordure which even your incessant rains don't clear away. Englishmen are generally coarse-featured and ugly. There are a few pretty women, but there can be few chaste ones – the humblest orange seller in El Andaluz would blush at their immodest comportment."

"*I* have no objection to it," Laurence said, shrugging.

"Were you ever in Spain?"

"Two years ago, after I grew tired of fighting in the Low Countries."

"Whereabouts did you travel?"

"From the Pyrenees to Cádiz."

"A long way. Did you visit Seville?"

"Alas not, sir."

De Zamora winked at him. "The *sevillanas* are the comeliest in all of Spain. Some say it is because of their pure stock."

"Pure stock? One may talk of that in horses, but not in men and women."

"I beg to disagree. For example, the royal house of Hapsburg has interbred for generations to ensure the purity of their line."

"A dubious practice, to judge by the size of their chins."

De Zamora guffawed, and slammed his cup on the table. "Oh yes, they have jaws like lanterns! Thank God there were no such deformities in *our* family. Did my cousin, your mother, ever confide in you the rumour that somewhere in the past, infidel blood had sullied her father's noble strain?"

Laurence recalled what old Yusuf had said, on that uncanny night back in Cádiz: *I should call you a Moor like myself, if it would not offend you.* "I hope the rumour is true," he said. "I've inherited an immense respect for the Moors from my own father."

"From your *father*, eh? You'd be a dead man if you said that in Spain."

"Then there are some benefits to living in my uncongenial country."

"You don't wear a sword. Why is that?"

"It keeps me out of trouble."

"Ah yes, I gather duelling is a punishable offence in Oxford."

Laurence did not correct the misinterpretation; evidently de Zamora had not heard about his clumsiness with a rapier. "Don Antonio, my brother says that you journeyed here because of *your* brother, Jorge, and a request he made to you on his deathbed."

Sobering quickly, de Zamora produced from his doublet a creased paper and extended it to Laurence. "Did Thomas tell you the substance of this confession?"

"Yes, more or less." De Zamora frowned, as if disconcerted by Laurence's calm. "Is it in your brother's hand?" Laurence inquired.

"The initial part. The rest he dictated to Fray Luis Iglesia, who administered to him the last sacrament. He was barely able to sign, as you can see."

Laurence advanced the candlestick, and took his time to read. "He must have been grateful to have had his sins remitted," he said, as he gave the document back to de Zamora; he could sense Tom stirring on the bench, and jogged his thigh surreptitiously.

"The mercy of our Lord passes all understanding," said de Zamora. "But will my cousin forgive him?"

"I'm certain she will."

"Why are you so certain?" de Zamora asked, after a pause.

"Because of her religious faith: she'll be hugely relieved that his soul is not damned to perdition."

"I thought she had converted to your father's church, to be married."

"Repentance is repentance, even for Protestants."

De Zamora gulped from his cup; he was temporarily flummoxed, Laurence thought. "How would his lordship accept the news that she was not virgin when he married her?"

"As you observed, our women enjoy more freedom than in Spanish society. Virginity is prized, yet if I were to count how many noble ladies in England have a dalliance before marriage, I'd imagine that half are guilty to a degree. And in the reign of King James, when my parents made their vows, the number would have been higher yet. His Court was notorious for its libertine habits."

"Jorge confessed to worse than a dalliance. And what if his lordship discovered that she had been taken against her will?"

"That's the plight of some women even in marriage."

"A husband cannot rape his own wife!"

Laurence shrugged again, as if the point were not worth disputing. "Don Antonio," he said, in a patient tone, "I hate to make light of your brother's confession, since you have come so far, but . . ." He glanced at Tom, who now had the look of a man sitting on hot coals. "To be honest with you, our father's chief concern these days is to keep his estate from plunder and destruction. His house has been sacked once by enemy troops. On the next occasion, for all we know, they might reduce it to a pile of rubble."

"So his fortunes have been greatly depleted," de Zamora commented, with studious sympathy.

"Greatly," echoed Laurence.

"*Qué barbaridad.*" De Zamora replenished his and Laurence's cups; Tom's was hardly touched. "Thomas, you did not exaggerate when you said your brother spoke my tongue like a native," he said, in English. "And I thank you for advising me to consult him about this document. I had qualms about it disturbing your family, and he has laid them to rest. Now, let us get acquainted. I know a bit about your history, sir," de Zamora continued in English, to Laurence. "It reminds me of a picaroon romance: you deserted from the Spanish ranks, then from the Protestant forces, and you've been a cardsharp, and a spy! And you're something of a libertine yourself, as concerns the fair sex."

Laurence wanted to kick his brother beneath the table: who else could have been the source of these details? "I'm guilty as charged," he said airily, to de Zamora.

"Thomas was struck by the peculiar similitude between your character and Jorge's. It was he who encouraged me to speculate—"

"You're lying," burst in Tom, reaching for the hilt of his sword.

Laurence placed a restraining hand on his arm. "To speculate . . . ?"

"How such things must run in the family," de Zamora finished, with a significant smile.

"There are black sheep in every family – it's human nature. Don Antonio," Laurence went on, "our mother will be pleased to receive you, but do be careful. When in the neighbourhood of Chipping Campden five days ago, I had a near escape from Parliament troops. If you were captured, the fact that you're Spanish would probably hang you. Or you might be mistaken for Irish, which would most definitely result in a hanging. Or you might be mistaken for me, in which case you'd be questioned – rather painfully, I suspect – and then hanged. Tom may not have informed you: His Majesty's enemies have put a high price on my head."

"I am no coward. I have faced death in battle for more years than you have been alive."

"So you must know the difference between a reasonable and a foolhardy risk."

"Perhaps your Prince Rupert may drive the rebels out," de Zamora said to Tom.

"No, sir," said Tom. "We're soon to leave for his camp at Shrewsbury, and then we march for the north."

"But I do not wish to delay my visit."

"You must be afraid that your health might fail you, before you have the opportunity to be reunited with our mother," said Laurence, solicitously.

"Er . . . no: mine is a slow disease."

"Not one that runs in the family?"

"It's the result of a wound that I sustained in Flanders. I thank you for your warning, but Diego and I shall press on, nevertheless, to Chipping Campden."

"Ah well, the best of luck to you." Laurence rose, and Tom leapt to his feet.

De Zamora stood up, hesitating. "I could be persuaded to visit you again in Oxford, should all go according to plan with my cousin."

"According to plan?" Laurence repeated.

"Forgive my English. I meant to say, should the meeting be as pleasurable as ours," de Zamora said, with an elegant bow.

"You think I told him those things about your past, but I swear, it wasn't me," insisted Tom, on their way from the inn. "I have no idea how he found out."

Laurence turned to look at Tom and believed that much was true; his brother was a bad liar. "Come with me to Seward's rooms. We'll speak there."

Seward had a fire blazing in his hearth, and as they threw off their cloaks, he drew up to it his two chairs. Laurence chose to sit cross-legged on the hearthstones at a judicious distance from Seward's cat, which lay basking somnolently in the heat.

"How did it go?" Seward demanded of them.

"He and Laurence jabbered away in Spanish as if they were the dearest of friends," Tom said.

"We did, most unnecessarily," said Laurence. "I was as impressed by his command of English as by the forged deathbed confession."

Tom emitted a gasp. "Forged?"

"I'd bet my life that the priest's script and Jorge's are by one author."

"How could you possibly know?"

"Oh for Christ's sake, Tom, it's a part of my work to catch telltale strokes of the pen. Did you ever leave Adam alone with Diego?"

"Once, on the same day de Zamora showed me the confession. Why do you ask?"

"Adam can't abide me." Tom said nothing to this. "If it was the same day, however, it can't have been he who provided that colourful description of my years abroad. Nor was it you. But someone did. And de Zamora modelled Jorge's character on mine, though, as I hope you'd agree, he embellished on my sins. He wanted to convince you that I'm not our father's son."

"Gentlemen," interjected Seward, "pray recount your conversation tonight."

While Laurence repeated it verbatim, in English, Tom listened with an increasingly agonised expression. "How could you suggest to de Zamora that our father would not care if our mother had been raped before her marriage?" he exploded.

"Of course he would care. It was a ploy, to make de Zamora doubt the value of his forgery. But if there's one genuine aspect to de Zamora, it's his resemblance to *me*." Laurence took a breath. "Might he have seduced our mother? And could I be his son?"

Tom clutched his hands to his head, as he used to when miserable as a little boy. "Don't say that, Laurence! Don't even think of it."

*You must be thinking of it now*, was on the tip of Laurence's tongue, though he held back the words.

"You are talking illogical rubbish, Beaumont," said Seward. "Her ladyship explained to you how her mother and his were like twins."

Laurence nodded, without conviction. "What did he mean by his reference to the inbred house of Hapsburg: 'Thank God there were no such deformities in our family'?"

"He's the one who's deformed," shouted Tom. "He's the lowest of scoundrels, and I'm going to kill him."

Laurence felt a surge of fraternal love, and a desire to protect Tom from the menace they had just confronted, more insidious and potentially damaging than Colonel Purefoy's invasion of their home. In his present mood, Tom would reject a hug; and Laurence was himself emotionally shaken, and at risk of losing his composure. So he merely said, "All right, Tom, if you must, but as your brother, I ought to share responsibility for the gruesome deed – although in the interests of self-preservation, I refuse to engage in any swordplay. I'd rather test your witch's poison, Seward."

"Cold-blooded murder would pile crime upon crime," averred Seward.

"More to the point, it's unoriginal – too many tragedies end that way upon the stage." Neither Seward nor Tom cracked a smile. "We might find a less dramatic solution," Laurence suggested. "I never told you, Tom, but this past January a Parliamentary officer was slain in London by a pair of Spanish-speaking gentlemen. Why not hand de Zamora and his valet to the rebels? Or are you still thirsting for their blood?" In reply, Tom sprang from his chair, snatched his cloak and whipped out, slamming the door behind him. "And he accused Ingram of not being able to take a joke," Laurence murmured.

Seward leant over, and boxed Laurence on the ear with practised force. "How could *you* joke about so grave a threat to your family? And you mocked his devotion to you."

"I'm sorry, Seward. My humour wasn't intended to be at his expense. I don't underestimate the threat. In fact, it petrifies me. It's all so incredible. You should have seen de Zamora's face . . ."

"I *have* seen his face," Seward said quietly.

"Ah yes – stupid of me to forget." Laurence sighed, rubbing his ear. "I'll go after Tom and apologise."

"No, let him sleep on it, and may you both be wiser in the morning. And do not be infected by de Zamora's lies, or you will lose this battle against him. You are James Beaumont's son, and none other. Do you hear me?"

"I hear you." *Though I'm not sure,* Laurence added to himself.

### III.

When Laurence arrived at Digby's quarters in the morning, Quayle gave him a letter. "His Majesty and Prince Rupert are to resume their tour of the garrisons around Oxford," Tom wrote, "and I am to ride with them. As you are determined to handle our problem according to your own judgement, I wash my hands of it. We may not see each other again before I head for Shrewsbury. I sign, your loving brother Thomas."

Laurence dispatched an abject reply, but he knew Tom would not heed it. Then he sent one of his scouts to make inquiries at the Green Dragon. That day and on the days following, the Spaniards were still in residence. Could he have changed de Zamora's mind about a visit to Chipping Campden?

The atmosphere in Oxford was becoming more and more fraught, with the King undecided as to his next manoeuvre; and Laurence now had to concentrate on his work. Based on the concise illustrated manuals used to teach military drill, he started to assemble a similar handbook for the new scouts he was recruiting with Price's help. He wanted to ensure consistency and accuracy in gathering information, and to instruct the youths in building a chain of local people who could supply regular intelligence: commoners of both sexes and of varied age, preferably illiterates. In Laurence's experience, those who could neither read nor write often used their ears and memories to better effect than educated people; and they were more likely to pass unnoticed.

He had been engrossed in this project for less than a week when he was summoned early to an unexpected audience in Digby's inner sanctum; his lordship had been as preoccupied recently by Council meetings. "I am amazed at the speed of your progress with those young fellows," Digby declared. "I think Mr. Price is ready to take some of them into Gloucestershire, to test out their skills as you suggested, among the populace."

"But *they* aren't ready, my lord."

"You are too much of a perfectionist, sir! Besides, he has already gone with them, on my order and on his special request."

"You might have consulted me first."

"You borrow my words to you in our last, rather heated exchange. At any rate, he wished to address your father, for your sister Elizabeth's hand in marriage. Apparently you said you had no objection to his courting her, as long he obtained his lordship's blessing."

Laurence wished he could deny this. "When did he make his request?"

"A couple of days ago. He did not like to bother you by mentioning it. He confided in me how very short-tempered you are grown, of late."

"If only he *had* bothered me, my lord. I would have given him a letter to take to Chipping Campden."

"Would you have written him an unfavourable reference?" Digby asked, with a provoking edge. "His past is a mite shadowy. Have you apprised Elizabeth of it?"

"Please do not trouble yourself on her account," said Laurence, and went fuming back to his desk.

Although Price would face stiffer odds of winning Lady Beaumont's good opinion than Prince Rupert could expect in his campaign to boot Parliament out of Yorkshire, Price's duplicity upset Laurence. And how would Price swallow defeat when his suit was refused? Could he be trusted to behave as a gentleman?

IV.

"It is a rare, scabrous condition of the skin," Diego told the porter, who was trying to peek through the veil draped over Antonio's head. "Dr. Seward may be his last hope. He cannot speak or eat, his lips are so sore."

"The good Doctor can cure him, if God willing there is a cure," the porter said, and let them through the gatehouse.

Under a steady downpour, Antonio and Diego squelched across wet grass towards the newer quadrangle. "I am sick of this blasted country in which the sun never shines," he said to Diego. "Give me a quarter of an hour, and if I am still with the Doctor, return to the inn."

It was only mid-afternoon, but he saw candlelight in the window Diego had pointed out to him. As he raised his hand to the door, it swung open, as if by its own agency. "Enter," said a raspy voice.

Antonio strode in and lifted off his veil to behold a skeletal figure in a black cap and gown; the Doctor's bones would probably snap as easily as a bunch of dried twigs. Thick spectacles magnified blurry eyes in a ghostly complexioned face. Antonio bowed. "Dr. Seward, may I introduce myself: Don Antonio de Zamora y Fuentes, of Seville."

"An introduction is superfluous, sir," said Dr. Seward.

"You are a doughty old man, and how well you conceal your shock – far more skilfully than my cousin's sons, when *they* had their first glimpse of me."

"This is not my first glimpse of you."

"Ah, so you have seen me about Oxford?"

Dr. Seward did not answer. "Don Antonio, be seated."

Antonio sat down and inspected the room; it was a wizard's den! The walls were hidden by shelves stacked with dusty tomes, and mysterious apparatus. On the large desk in the centre of the room was a silver bowl full of inky liquid. The room smelt of tobacco smoke, a sickly whiff akin to holy incense, and another unpleasant, ammoniac odour.

"Why beat about the bush," Dr. Seward said next. "Your brother's deathbed confession is a forgery."

Antonio concealed shock of his own, and pretended outrage. "You insult me, and Jorge's memory, may God rest him."

"You showed it to the wrong man: Beaumont is expert in detecting such falsehoods."

"Then I commend his perspicacity," said Antonio, shifting tack. "But there is a grain of truth in that confession, as he may already have guessed. His mother was not virgin when James Beaumont married her. And he is indubitably my son."

"Is he?" asked Dr. Seward, with the same strange calm.

"You have only to look at us both. He even shares my peccadilloes, although he is missing some of my virtues, such as valour in the field. I suppose his shortcomings might be attributed to an inherent flaw in most bastards, as history demonstrates, or to the sin of consanguinity. In my country, the mere rumour of illegitimate birth is a serious stain on a noble household. Yet he led me to believe that Lord Beaumont would not turn a hair if the truth were revealed. I find that unlikely, but I'm baffled in general by English mores. What is your opinion, Doctor?"

"His lordship would be appalled and revolted that you took advantage of your cousin. But it would not alter his profound affection for her – or for his son. I am thoroughly acquainted with both of their natures."

"His son, his son," objected Antonio. "Why persist in calling him that, when the facts speak for themselves? Laurence was born on the sixth of June, of 1612, and I lay with Elena nine months earlier, on the night before Beaumont took her away. You must know the date of her marriage. In fairness, you should tell me."

"She was married in England late in November of 1611."

Antonio crowed with triumphant laughter. "Unless by some miracle the boy survived a most premature entry into the world, he *is* mine."

"It's your conclusion that is premature, Don Antonio. You did not listen to me: I said, *married in England.* When she arrived here, yes, she was with child. She was also married."

"But . . . how could that be?"

"She and her husband were wed in Bordeaux, from whence they sailed for England. He knew his parents would oppose his impulsive match with a foreigner and a former Catholic. He decided to present them with a *fait accompli*. A second ceremony was celebrated at Chipping Campden. She had a pregnancy of eight months, which is not unusual."

Antonio felt nonplussed. Then he thought rapidly. "Laurence may yet be of my seed. She would know – women have an instinct for such matters."

"She might, she might not. And you had just one night with her, while her husband would have had many. In the end, what does it signify, Don Antonio? You came here on a sordid enterprise. You will go to her and try your mischief, but mark my words: you shall suffer by it."

"That has the ring of a prediction, Dr. Seward."

The Doctor cast him a sinister frown. "As I told you, today was not my first glimpse of you. I saw you on your sea voyage, walking with Diego on the deck of your ship. You lost your hat to a strong gust of wind."

Antonio shivered and crossed himself. "How could you have seen that?"

Dr. Seward rested his eyes on the silver bowl. "It gives me visions, of past, present, *and* future."

Antonio launched up and stared into the opaque, reflective liquid. He saw himself, afraid. He wheeled round, unsheathed his sword, and brushed the old man's chin with the edge of his blade. "You practise devilry, sir, and I am about to send you to hell for it."

Dr. Seward examined the blade unperturbed, as if Antonio were holding out a flower. "*You* are the very devil, Don Antonio."

"Have you seen into *my* future, in your magic bowl?"

"You can slit my throat before I will answer that."

Antonio whisked aside his sword and struck the bowl to the floor. It fell with a clang, spilling its contents over the flagstones. He bent swiftly to grab it and tucked it under his free arm. The old man fought to claw it away, but Antonio shoved him sprawling into the dark puddle. "Now the devil has a looking glass. If you would have it back, ask my son to meet me tomorrow night – ten o'clock, at the Green Dragon – with, let us say, three hundred pounds, which I am sorely in need of. A good day to you, Doctor."

## V.

"I told you, I tripped on the hem of my gown," repeated Seward, grimacing from his bed at Clarke and the College surgeon, while Beaumont inspected the bruise on his buttock.

"You've not much padding left down here, Seward." Beaumont restored his clothing and tucked a blanket over him. "You were lucky not to break any bones."

"I offered to mix him a poultice, which he refused," the surgeon said reproachfully.

"I did warn you, my stubborn friend, that you needed a new pair of spectacles," Clarke said in his sententious way.

"I thank you both, gentlemen. Beaumont, you may show them out."

Beaumont obeyed, and shut the door. "Before we talk, can I get you something of your own to put on the bruise, or . . . or something for the pain?"

"No."

Beaumont sat down on the corner of the bed. "How *did* you fall?"

"I was pushed, by de Zamora." Beaumont opened his mouth to speak, but Seward cut him off. "That is as nought, compared to his crime: he has stolen my bowl! I knew he would come to me – I had even been watching out for him." In a fit of self-recrimination, Seward tore off his cap and flung it on the counterpane. "I should have been more prepared."

"How did you know? Did you see him in the bowl?" Beaumont asked, half sceptical, half wary.

"There was no magic involved. This morning the porter informed me that a young scholar from abroad might visit, to consult me as to a cure for his sick friend."

"And he fitted my description of Diego?" Seward nodded. "Why didn't you send for me right away?"

"You would have thought me a nuisance, interfering in your duties for his lordship."

"Never, Seward," said Beaumont gently. "*I'd* been keeping a watch on the Spaniards until yesterday, when it slipped my mind. So what happened?"

Seward hesitated; if he revealed the full truth, he would all but confirm Beaumont's suspicions about his parentage. "I accused de Zamora of forging the deathbed testament, and he admitted as much, without a shade of guilt. I said he had come to England on a sordid enterprise from which he would reap no gain. He observed that my words had the ring of a prediction. I suggested it was, and to scare him I revealed to him my vision – to gratifying result. Then I erred foolishly, in showing him the source. He seized the bowl, and when I tried to wrest it from him, he pushed me to the floor and bolted. I had to send Pusskins to fetch Clarke, who insisted on summoning the surgeon – quite needlessly, I might add. And then I sent Clarke to fetch *you*."

"Why didn't you send over your cat, instead?" Seward had to smile. "Now Seward," said Beaumont, "did de Zamora drop any hint as to his plans?"

"No, but he confessed to being extremely low on funds."

"Hmm. That may be why he hasn't left Oxford. He can't get any more money from Tom, nor would I give him any."

"My boy," sighed Seward, "how could I have forgotten the worst part." And he told Beaumont about the ransom.

"Do you have three hundred pounds?"

"Certainly not."

"Well neither do I."

"You must raise it."

"How, by tomorrow night? At a time like this, I can't play truant on his lordship to hunt out a rich game of cards. Could it be done through magic?"

"It's not a subject for jest. I can no more scry without my bowl than see without my spectacles."

"Even if we give de Zamora the money, I don't trust him to fulfil his side of the bargain and return your bowl. And he'll be able to travel, and we know where he'll go. It would be easier for me to arrest him and Diego on a charge of assault, and throw them in gaol."

"And risk that they might dispose of my bowl before you take them? Meet him with the money," Seward beseeched. "Once you have my bowl, you may resort to rougher tactics."

Beaumont assumed an air of wounded pride. "I hope you understand what you're asking of me: I'll have to crawl on hands and knees to beg a loan from Digby." He grabbed Seward's cap, and held it out in the style of a mendicant. "And what should I tell him, when he asks me what the loan is for?"

"Use your powers of invention," said Seward, reaching up to bat him on the ear.

Beaumont jerked away his head. "Strike me again, Doctor, and you can kiss your bowl goodbye," he threatened, mimicking the Spaniard's inflected English; and they both dissolved into salutary laughter. When they had recovered themselves, Beaumont announced, "I have a plan, if Digby obliges me with the three hundred pounds: to ransom the bowl, get the money straight back from de Zamora, teach him a lesson without his knowing who arranged it, *and* have him and Diego seized immediately afterwards. With his lordship's permission, I'll take some of our scouts out on a little training exercise."

"Beaumont, I called de Zamora the very devil," Seward said, suddenly panicked by what he had asked of his friend. "And the Devil is the Prince of Lies. He may tell you new lies, but you must on no account believe them."

## VI.

Lord Beaumont's servant had left Price waiting in the entrance, with the two statues; the house seemed to him ominously quiet and still, as though uninhabited. "God damn those rebels," he swore: the marble nymph's breasts had been hacked to stumps, and some churl had carved his initials and the year, 1644, on her left thigh. Price felt yet sorrier for the youth, whose genitals were missing.

He wandered into the Hall. The canvases, including his lordship's portrait, were gone, as was most of the lighter furniture: the padded footstools and little tables inlaid with ivory and precious woods. Gone also were the Turkey carpets, the tapestries and velvet curtains, the bronze statuettes, and the gold and silver salvers on the sideboard that Price had admired at Anne Beaumont's wedding feast. Colonel Purefoy might have ravished the room of its valuables, yet he had not deprived it of its grandeur: the magnificent proportions in their stark beauty awed Price more than before. It was like the vacant chamber of a dead king.

At the click of heels on the stair, he mustered up his courage and went back out. Elizabeth stood poised halfway in her descent, hopelessly desirable in her satin dress and ethereal lace collar. He doffed his hat and bowed. "Elizabeth?" She rushed down to him and searched his face with such sweet anxiety that he felt comforted. "I did worry that you would think me ugly now, though I didn't suffer as badly as that poor youth," he added, cocking his head towards the statue.

"My dear Mr. Price, what happened to you?"

"I was on a mission to London for Lord Digby, and tussled with the militia. I was thankful to get away with just a blow to my nose."

She stroked his shorn locks. "Why did you cut off your hair?"

"To pass for a rebel. I shaved my moustache, too. At least that's growing in faster. And I won't be sent to London again, at any time soon," he said, more confidently. "When we learnt that Colonel Purefoy's troops had retreated to the Gloucester garrison, his lordship dispatched me to establish a network of intelligencers in the Cotswolds – of local people faithful to the King."

"Will His Majesty avenge what those beasts did to us?"

"Have they robbed your family of everything?" asked Price, girding himself to accept the loss of her thousand pounds.

"Of a great deal, sir. My father has been so shaken by our losses."

"But might I address him, Elizabeth? I want his leave to court you."

Price had predicted elation, but she knitted her brows. "It is an awkward moment to speak to him of marriage, though I do so wish you could."

"Elizabeth?" called a peremptory voice. Price turned to see Lady Beaumont gliding out of the parlour; she must have been lurking there all along. She curtseyed minimally to his low bow, and examined his nose rather as had Lady Hallam.

"My lady," he said, "I came to request his lordship's leave to court your daughter."

"His lordship sleeps in the afternoon and cannot be disturbed. *We* may talk, however, so that your journey to us will not have been completely in vain. Elizabeth, you may join us later."

Elizabeth's lips parted as if she would object, but to Price's disappointment, she went obediently back up the stairs. He followed Lady Beaumont into the parlour; more stripped walls, though all of the furniture was intact. She did not invite him to sit, and remained standing herself.

"My Lady Beaumont," he recommenced, "I understand your surprise that I should seek to marry your daughter, on the strength of so short an acquaintance."

"Why should I be surprised, sir? You made your attraction to her manifestly evident on both of your previous visits, though she has not spoken much of you since the last occasion."

"I asked her not to, until I was sure I could provide for her as my wife. Now, I am happy to say, there is no impediment on that score.

And I believe that your son and my friend, Laurence, approves of the match," Price carried on, perhaps unwisely.

"Elizabeth shall select her second husband no differently than she did her first, may God rest him. And we know nothing of you or your family."

"I'll supply what information I can, my lady. I was orphaned at a tender age and have but the vaguest memory of my parents. They were of Welsh stock, and rose to prominence with the Tudors," Price continued, resorting to a favourite version of his origins. "Old King Henry granted their ancestors lands in Sussex, and used to hunt in their grounds, or so I was told as a boy. My father would have been heir to the estate, had he not married for love a woman whose family was in trade. He was cut from his inheritance, and driven to take up with his father-in-law's business."

"What business?"

"My grandfather was a vintner, a kindly man but extravagant," replied Price, borrowing from Sir Montague. "He raised me, after my parents died, at his house in the Strand. I was eighteen when *he* died and left behind him huge debts. I struggled to pay them, and in the end had to sell everything to his creditors, including his house. Then in the summer of '42, I determined to enlist in His Majesty's army." He paused; Lady Beaumont was studying him as if he were transparent, an expression he had seen often in Beaumont. "Fate played on me another cruel trick, my lady: on my way to join his standard at Nottingham, I tumbled from my horse and cracked my spine. I despaired ever of walking again. God took mercy on me, and by October of last year, my injuries were healed. That was when I met your son, who brought me into Lord Digby's service."

"Is that so," she remarked, still skewering him with her gaze.

"Your ladyship, my father's marriage cost me my position in the world, and I have had to win it back through my own efforts. I would not care to repeat his mistake."

"In marrying a tradesman's daughter?"

"No, my lady: I would not marry Elizabeth without her father's blessing."

"She shall not marry without it, sir. He will give you due consideration, after I have recounted to him your tale."

"My lady, please let me speak to his lordship whilst I am here. I do not know when I can next return, given the uncertainties of war."

"His lordship's health is as uncertain, sir, having had his house ransacked and his estate pillaged. I cannot allow it any upset." Lady Beaumont left the parlour, and once more Price had to follow, enraged by her rudeness.

Three women were at the head of the stairs: Elizabeth, with a defeated air; Anne, hers sympathetic yet resigned; and a blonde girl. Price thought of the Hall in its glory, and today, naked. Penelope and Catherine were clearly twins, but such was the contrast between them. Had Beaumont married this fey creature to exorcise Lady Hallam's curvaceous ghost? The women came down, and Anne introduced Price to Catherine, whose eyes were a deep brown, and peculiarly direct. On her ring finger, she wore a slender band set with a dull stone, a cheap-looking trinket compared to Lady Hallam's opulent jewel. Why had Beaumont not chosen something better?

Elizabeth gave Price her hand, and he touched it to his lips. "We must bid each other goodbye, madam," he said. "And goodbye to you, ladies, and to your ladyship."

Anne and Catherine gave their goodbyes, but Lady Beaumont did not answer. It was this final insult that resolved him: he would marry Elizabeth with or without her parents' consent.

## VII.

Around ten o'clock, Laurence gathered his boys outside the church of St. Martin's at the Carfax. He ordered one fellow to stay on guard there, while the rest accompanied him to the Green Dragon.

"He'll be fast with his rapier," Laurence reminded them, "and his valet may also be armed."

As the youths melted into the shadows, he entered the taproom alone carrying his saddlebag. Tonight the crowd was thinner and less raucous; even the grizzled veteran seemed sober, nursing a tankard of ale with his dog at his feet. Diego stood near the entrance to the eating chamber, and waved Laurence over.

"How's your master, Diego?" Laurence asked in English, to see if the valet would comprehend.

"*Triste, Señor Beaumont – muy triste,*" Diego replied obscurely, escorting him to de Zamora's candlelit alcove, and left them.

De Zamora addressed Laurence in Spanish, without a hint of his former bravado. "I congratulate you for detecting the forged confession. I had no brother. My mother died in giving birth to me, her sole offspring, and my father joined her in the grave a year later. Sir, let us start afresh. I wish for us to be friends, as well as kin."

"Don't you think it rather too late?" Laurence inquired. "You've done your best to pit my brother against me, you injured and robbed an old man who is *my* friend, and God knows what you're plotting to accomplish at Chipping Campden."

"Was the Doctor badly hurt?"

"He was, but he's improving. Where is his property?"

De Zamora untied a sack on the bench beside him, to give Laurence a view of the bowl, then shifted it out of Laurence's reach. "Since I am in desperate financial straits, I cannot retract my price for it. Yet I do regret my violence. I lost my temper because of his persistent denials," de Zamora went on, with a sigh. "As if it is not perfectly obvious that you are my son. As I explained to him, the evidence is plain as day."

Laurence fought to keep his expression bland; out of a desire to protect, Seward had erred again by not disclosing this to *him*. "He told me of your claim, Don Antonio," he said, carefully.

"It is no mere claim. Before we make our exchange, *mi hijo*, here is the full truth about why I came to England, and about my relations with your mother."

"Don Antonio, you're like the boy who cried wolf," said Laurence, though he was torn between dread and curiosity.

"Please hear me out," de Zamora said. "Grant me a chance – not to redeem myself, for I am past redemption for my sins – but to have myself understood. I never expected that my venture would conclude in so precious a discovery – *you*." Laurence could read agony in his eyes, and, to his own unease, an intense, passionate craving for affection. "I would not have travelled here except for a miraculous coincidence that occurred last October."

"Your stories are plagued with coincidences."

"Our whole lives are thus plagued, my son, as you will learn. It was on a Sunday, as my wife Teresa and I were leaving the great Cathedral of Santa María de la Sede after Mass." De Zamora leant forward. "A gypsy girl was begging outside. She had a babe with her, a boy with our green eyes." Laurence caught his breath, as though the tip of a knife had probed beneath his skin. "When questioned, she said that his father was an English mercenary who had formed an attachment to her in the Low Countries and had journeyed with her to Spain. There he had forced her to be his mistress, and abandoned her when she became with child. She named Laurence Beaumont as her son's father – and she called the boy Lorenzo. Imagine: Beaumont was a name I had not forgotten. Of course, she recognised you in my features. I could not let them go. I provided shelter for them at a friend's hostel, where they remain to this day. Lest you were wondering, it was she who told me of your exploits in the Low Countries."

"Ah," said Laurence, now too thunderstruck to frame a better response.

"I knew then that God had put her and Lorenzo in my path to answer my prayer. For over thirty years, I had sworn revenge on James Beaumont."

Laurence was exerting all of his expertise, as cardsharp and as spy, to hide his inner turmoil. "Please, continue," he said, focusing on the gap between de Zamora's slanted brows, to avoid his distracting stare.

"As for the truth about your mother," said de Zamora, "she and I were in love, but we could not marry. The house of de Capdavila was mired in debt, and I had no fortune to my name but a half-derelict castle – the de Zamora family seat. When James Beaumont came courting Elena, I was still working to establish my reputation as an officer." He broke off, and frowned. "You appear to find my story tedious, sir."

Laurence shrugged in a semblance of boredom. "It's a familiar tale, Don Antonio: the poor yet noble lover unjustly thwarted in his heart's desire."

De Zamora's eyes blazed at him. "You are cold, my son. It must be the effect of your rotten climate."

"Then it's my turn to apologise. You were saying . . . ?"

"The challenge of money, in itself, would not have prevented me from winning Elena," de Zamora resumed. "There was another obstacle. Her father, Don Giraldo de Capdavila, loathed me, as I did him. Before embarking on his final voyage to the Indies, where to my immense delight he subsequently perished of ague, he forbade me to visit his house. In his absence, I persuaded my aunt Cecilia to lift his interdiction, for the sake of her deceased sister, my mother. Yet she would sooner have sold her soul to the devil than let us cousins marry. When she knew of our mutual love, she decided to sacrifice Elena to the heretic Englishman, even though it tortured her that she would not see her child again. Thank God she could not take from Elena and me that ultimate night, on which you were conceived." De Zamora hesitated. "You must want to know if I forced myself on Elena."

"To me, what's past is past," said Laurence, though he yearned to know. "You've lost her, and you'll never have her back."

"That may be, but what of you and I?" De Zamora lunged across the table to grip Laurence's arm. "Can you honestly deny that you are of my seed?"

"My true father is the man who raised me."

"I hear doubt in your voice. You know you haven't a drop of

English blood in your veins. You belong in Spain, with me. Thomas shall have his estate, and all of us will be happy. We'll reunite blood with blood! Would you not enjoy watching your son Lorenzo grow up? He is a beautiful boy. We could watch him together, *my* Lorenzo."

The idea was so absurd that Laurence nearly laughed. Then he saw the extreme seriousness on de Zamora's face. Years of obsessive brooding had poisoned the man's brain, Laurence thought, almost pitying him; but that rendered him more of a danger. "No, Don Antonio, I belong here, in England." Laurence detached himself politely. "You should beware of the child. He may turn out a liar and a thief, like his mother."

"Did she lie when she said you raped her – repeatedly?"

"Is that what she said? Yes, she lied."

"Then it is my guess that you must have been in love, to travel so far and to stay such a time with her," de Zamora concluded, with an edge of victory.

"I had a lust for her, Don Antonio, but now I care nothing for her, or for the boy. He must be one of many bastards I've sired, here and there." Laurence stood up and slung his saddlebag over his shoulder. "We should get you your money. It's with the owner of a more respectable tavern near St. Martin's Church, less than a mile away."

"*What?* You don't have it on you?"

"I wouldn't carry ten pounds on me in this neighbourhood of cutpurses, let alone three hundred."

"You are luring me into a trap."

"If I'd wanted to entrap you, sir, you would not be at liberty tonight."

Laurence walked out to the taproom, with de Zamora in pursuit calling for Diego. "The lazy fellow must have gone to bed," he told Laurence agitatedly. "Let me wake him. I will not leave without him."

"We haven't the time," said Laurence. "We must finish our business before the other tavern closes."

"I'm a fool to trust you," growled de Zamora, but he went along. When they gained Cornmarket Street, Laurence drew him towards a modest house, its windows heavily shuttered. "If this is a tavern, why is there no sign outside?" he demanded.

"Its patrons are mostly town officials who can't be seen breaking the curfew laws," Laurence replied, which was the truth.

The crowd of well-heeled drinkers seemed to assuage de Zamora's fears. He sat down at an empty table while Laurence fetched the leather purse that he had left with the tavern keeper. Neither of them spoke as de Zamora unfastened it and poured out the coins into the skirt of his cloak, beneath the table. "Three hundred," he said with a grudging smile, when he had counted them back into the purse. "Diego thought the bowl must be worth much more to the Doctor, for his visions."

"Seward is an adept: he can see visions in any common looking glass."

"Then why did he fight me for the bowl?"

"It's a talisman bequeathed to him by his mentor – in the *black arts*," Laurence added; he had surmised from Seward's account that de Zamora might be superstitious.

"Thank God I am rid of it," said de Zamora, crossing himself. "Diego did not want to let it go. He has studied alchemy, and other subjects that our Church condemns as witchcraft. He was eager to test *his* powers of divination."

Laurence pressed a little further, in case Diego had any plans to retrieve the bowl. "He had a lucky escape, Don Antonio. Without knowledge of the appropriate rituals and incantations, he would have invoked evil demons and become possessed."

"Sometimes he is too clever for his own good. Sir, what now?" de Zamora asked, tucking the purse into the front of his doublet.

"We must say goodbye," Laurence said, picking up the sack.

"That makes me sad. I feel more affinity to you than to my other sons – not that I should be surprised: your blood is thicker with mine than you know."

This last comment disturbed Laurence. He had the impression that de Zamora had tossed it out as bait, so he ignored it. "When you decide to sail home, don't try the enemy ports," he said. "You might find a ship from Bristol, which is held for the King."

"How far is Bristol?"

"About seventy miles from Oxford, to the southwest."

"Should I greet Juana for you, on my return?"

"If it pleases you."

They quitted the tavern, each with his prize. Laurence's nerves jangled in anticipation of a setback, and he drew away instinctively when de Zamora opened his arms wide. "Does an English son not embrace his father, on parting?" de Zamora inquired, his cheeks glistening with tears.

"We clasp hands," said Laurence, and so they did.

"*Que Dios te bendiga, hijo mío*. I pray that I may see you again in this world."

"*Adiós*, Don Antonio."

As de Zamora's footsteps retreated, Laurence blew out an exhausted sigh and sagged against the tavern wall. The words still echoed: *your blood is thicker with mine than you know*. He had an urge to chase after the Spaniard and ask what it meant. And to think of Juana, and a child: no mystery there as to the true father.

Laurence whistled to the scout posted by St. Martin's Church. "All well, sir?" the youth said cheerily, bounding out from the darkness like an angel sent to dismiss the unclean spirits of night.

"Yes, though it took longer than I'd expected. Let's hope our boys haven't drowsed on their watch."

"Nay, sir, they'll be chafing for action. I'll join them, if I may."

"Good luck to you, and until soon," said Laurence. He headed for Merton, where the porter was snoring away on his chair in the gatehouse. "A quiet night?" Laurence shouted in his ear.

He stirred, and mumbled, "Very quiet, Mr. Beaumont."

"Some fellows will come by asking for me in a while." Laurence gave the scouts' names. "Direct them to Seward's rooms." He paid the porter a coin, and carried on across the Front Quadrangle, swinging the sack in one hand.

The buildings were shrouded in an inky pall, but he could have negotiated the familiar route blindfolded. All he could hear was the crunch of his boots on the gravel path and the clink of his spurs. Yet as he passed under the Fitzjames Arch he felt a minuscule breeze on his left side, and before he could dodge, a sharp blow stung him on the temple. A harder blow struck the same side of his skull. Pain translated to dizziness, and his legs folded beneath him. He hit the ground, and swift fingers wrested the sack from him. "*Duerme bien,*" whispered his assailant.

## VIII.

Antonio forged on through the desolate streets, shedding more sad tears: he was again *unjustly thwarted in his heart's desire*, as his Lorenzo had phrased it. He had hoped to begin a new chapter in the autumn of his life. "Lorenzo begged me to bring him home," he had imagined saying to Teresa. What priceless vengeance it would have been to steal the cuckoo from James Beaumont's nest! He had envisaged the pair of them, he and his Lorenzo, arm in arm together in the warm sunshine of his courtyard. They would be the talk of Seville, with their matching looks. He had even dreamt of them united on a crusade to restore the twin houses of de Zamora and Capdavila to their former glory. And then, humiliation! He had laid bare his soul, only to be rejected by a man made in his own image, yet with a heart of stone: upon parting, not an embrace but a frigid clasp of the hand; a palm dry and cool to the touch; and an impassive face.

Halting to wipe his eyes on his sleeve, Antonio saw the glow of lights from the Green Dragon's windows. A couple of men were engaged in conversation on the other side of the street, beneath the crooked overhanging fronts of the timbered houses. They strolled towards him, their manner leisurely; they might have been apprentices in their coarse clothes. One was holding an unlit pipe, and called out, "Have you tinder, sir, and a flint?" Antonio paid no attention. Then came a series of low whistles behind his back, and he knew he was surrounded.

"The brutes were skilled in their criminal trade," moaned Antonio, as Diego rinsed out a blood-soaked cloth. "They were so fast I had no time to draw my sword. One of them punched me *here*, on the site of an old break in my ribs, and after that I was easy prey. He may have punctured some vital organ, in which case I'll be dead by tomorrow. It took the last of my strength to get up the stairs to our chamber." Antonio inhaled a cautious, shallow breath. "And they stole my sword, along with the purse. It's your fault for not being with me, you idiot, and I would throttle you were I not in such agony."

Diego reapplied the cloth, dabbing at a cut in Antonio's forehead. "Don Antonio, they would still have beaten the hell out of us," he said, in a consoling tone. "And now we have the bowl, we can ransom it again. Beaumont will pay, for the old man's sake."

"That bowl has cast a spell on you, *maldito*! We could pay with our lives after what you did to him, and if so, I pray *you* go straight to hell." Antonio pushed Diego away, and struggled to sit up on the bed. "We must escape from Oxford tonight."

Finally the desperation of their plight appeared to sink into Diego's brain. He dropped the cloth and clasped his wet hands together. "How? We have no money, and you're weaker than a newborn lamb!"

"You're the genius – you think of a way."

Antonio was disgusted at himself: twenty or even ten years ago, he might have slain a couple of the brigands before they took him down. They had suffered not a scratch. Experience told him that his cracked ribs would not heal for weeks. And all he had left in funds was a bit of change from Thomas Beaumont's gold unite, and what he might get for that accursed wizard's bowl.

## IX.

The scouts came upon Laurence lying beneath the arch, in a daze. "His valet sneaked by the porter and attacked me," he said, as they helped him to his feet; they did not know about the bowl, nor would he mention it. "Hurry over to the Green Dragon and take them both."

"But sir, he'll go nowhere after our night's sport," one of the scouts assured him, flourishing the purse and de Zamora's sword.

"Just to be safe, throw them in the nearest gaol until tomorrow morning."

They assisted Laurence to Seward's door, gave him their trophies, and then went away, leaving him tottering on the threshold. He could not see out of his left eye, his ears rang, and he felt as though a giant mallet were hammering inside his head.

"Beaumont, who did this to you?" exclaimed Seward, as he stumbled in.

"Diego," he said, slumping into a chair. "He stole back the bowl from me, and I suspect he wasn't acting on de Zamora's order. He coveted it for himself."

"So we are where we began!"

"I have to trust my scouts will get it back, yet again. What a farce, worthy of the stage. And there's more to tell you, Seward, if you can dig me out some remedy for my headache. You'll never guess who's come back to haunt me: Juana."

While Seward went and searched in his cupboard, and began measuring and mixing, Laurence related his extraordinary conversation with de Zamora. "The man is utterly deluded," Seward cried, once Laurence had finished. "How could he believe that you would run off with him to Spain?"

"Because he *is* my father," answered Laurence, wincing as Seward applied a poultice to his swollen temple, "and you should have told me he said so, when you both spoke."

"I did not want to encourage you in a falsehood that is his chief delusion, and must not become yours. Talk to your mother, Beaumont, and she will confirm the truth to you."

"Why would she, after all this time, unless circumstances made it impossible for her to keep her secret?" Laurence squinted at Seward through his one good eye. "You may find it odd, but I don't honestly care who engendered me. Perhaps if I were younger I might, but at this stage of my life, I am who I am."

"That you are," Seward agreed.

"Yet I still have to know what truly happened between her and de Zamora. It wasn't her habit to lavish affection on any of us children, but she's always been coldest towards me, and when I was young, I'd catch her looking at me as if I disturbed her in some profound way. I want to understand why."

"I did not know you as a child, Beaumont, but you were a profoundly disturbing youth, and you are still no less vexatious to everybody, me included. How did you receive the Spaniard's news about the gypsy and *her* child? Your son, I mean. It must have awoken strong feelings in you."

"He described the coincidence as miraculous. To me, it was almost as great a surprise as Diego hitting me on the head. And he guessed, rightly, that I'd been in love with her. But if he'd hoped to reawaken *those* feelings, or stir in me some fatherly instinct, he was wrong."

"Are you being quite honest with yourself?" Seward inquired, softly.

"Oh yes. I only found out from Juana that she was pregnant on the night she rejected me, to return to her people. She confessed to me then that she had lied to them, saying I had taken her against her will – she was afraid *they* would otherwise reject her. Even so, I offered to do anything for her and our child. She wasn't moved. She said she'd never loved me, and that I was unclean, not being of her people. When I asked if the child was also unclean, she said it was *hers*. I don't blame her for lying, or thieving, or whatever else she might do to survive – her people are treated viciously everywhere, and she'd seen her whole family slaughtered. I admire her resilience and I wish no harm on either of them. I've no more feeling than that. If de Zamora is so besotted with the boy, he may continue to provide for them. Juana can be trusted to take full advantage, as she did of me," Laurence concluded. "Seward, my head is killing me."

Seward passed him a small cup. "Drink – it's the very last of my poppy."

"Thank you – much appreciated." He downed it and licked his lips. "The question is: what to do with de Zamora and his resourceful valet? In your words, cold-blooded murder would pile crime upon crime. I won't pay them to leave England, and I can't hold them indefinitely in gaol. So we must think of something else." A loud knock at the door startled them both. "Let's hope it's the scouts with that damned bowl." He tugged a pistol from his saddlebag, cocked it, and rose to open.

Outside was the youth who had waited for him at St. Martin's Church. "I'm sorry, sir," the youth said, "but the Spaniards have gone – vanished clean into the night."

## X.

Antonio stuffed the fabric of his cloak deeper into his mouth; he could hear Diego retching quietly beside him. This was hell, he thought: to be submerged in human shit, although the warmth of it calmed the stabbing pain in his ribs. Yet as the driver urged on the withered nag pulling the cart loaded with night soil, and it jolted and bumped along, he had to bite down hard on the cloth to stop from crying out. At last the cart halted. He was afraid to move or breathe. Then he felt Diego's hands scrabbling for his shoulders, and together they lifted their heads to peer out of the muck. They were both coated in it, and he could distinguish only the whites of Diego's eyes. Around them were open fields, and above them a clear starlit sky. The driver stomped off a short distance, humming a tune, and returned carrying a shovel.

"Stay," Diego whispered. He slithered to his knees, and hoisted himself nimbly from the cart. And when the man came in range, he dived for the shovel.

# CHAPTER FOURTEEN

I.

"We're too close," Laurence yelled to Wilmot, over the ear-splitting boom of mortars, as rubble landed like scatter-shot a mere pace away, alarming their horses. They wheeled about and galloped to safer ground, coughing and spitting from the clouds of powder. "What a massive waste, to build up walls and then blow them to pieces."

Wilmot looked as excited as a small boy watching his first fire-works. He and Lord Forth had argued against Prince Rupert's strat-egy to maintain the circle of garrisons around Oxford, and twelve days after Rupert rode back to Shrewsbury, Council had acted on this advice: the Royalists were moving out of Reading, their nearest stronghold to London. "We had to slight the garrison, Beaumont," he shouted. "We can't allow Essex to reap the benefits of our labour, once we withdraw."

"Now you explain it to me, my lord, it makes excellent sense, though *slight* is an odd word to use for all this destruction."

"You sarcastic bastard, I gather you disapprove."

"I do. We should have stuck to Rupert's plan."

"It wasn't practical, with our scant numbers and provisions. You haven't told me, what brings you here?"

"Digby and I have to make sure that no compromising docu-ments are left behind to entertain the enemy."

Wilmot pointed at Laurence's left temple; the skin around his eye was still bruised from Diego's attack nearly a fortnight ago. "I hope the other fellow came off worse than you did."

"I hope so, too," said Laurence, wondering again what had happened to the Spaniards: he had been unable to trace them, nor had he any news of them from home. A cacophony of bangs and blasts echoed through the air, followed by another hail of rubble. He and Wilmot retreated further, brushing fragments of masonry from their cloaks. "How about a wager?" he asked. "I'll bet you any sum you care to name that Abingdon will be the next to go."

"Why Abingdon?"

"It's the logical choice. Our three other garrisons have their own castle walls to protect them. Just Banbury, Wallingford, and Faringdon – that's a thin line of defence between Oxford and the combined armies of Essex and Waller."

"They're sworn rivals. They won't unite."

"If they do, His Majesty might be wise to cut his losses and negotiate."

"Would you say that to His Majesty's face?"

"Yes I would."

"You don't give a damn, do you – one of the many reasons I miss your company, and your counsel. And I'd have to agree: in those circumstances, a settlement would prevent more waste – of materiel *and* of life. But don't breathe a word to anyone that I said so." Wilmot pointed out a rider trotting towards them. "Here's Mr. Price."

"At last," said Laurence. "He's been away recruiting informers in Gloucestershire."

Price reined in, and removed his hat. "My Lord Wilmot, good day. Mr. Beaumont, his lordship wishes us to attend him."

"Your lord and master calls," said Wilmot. "Perhaps I'll catch you later, Beaumont, and we can *slight* a bottle or two."

Digby was quartered at a farmhouse about a mile beyond the fortifications. On the way, Laurence asked Price about affairs in Gloucestershire. "Colonel Massey's troops are staying very near Gloucester garrison these days," he said, his tone and demeanour distinctly restrained. "He must be on the defensive."

"How were you received at Chipping Campden?" Laurence inquired, suspecting that Lady Beaumont might be the cause of his mood.

"Her ladyship told me she would discuss my suit with his lordship."

"You didn't speak to my father?"

"He was resting and couldn't be disturbed."

"Ah . . . Did my family give you any letters for me?"

"None."

"Had they any visitors staying at the house?"

"Not as far as I know," Price replied shortly, and Laurence asked him no more.

A long table in the main room of the farmhouse had become his lordship's desk, but he was standing at a distance from it, when they walked in. A space had been cleared upon it, for a package. Digby greeted them with trepidation in his owlish eyes. "This arrived from London, and was to be sent to me in Oxford via our garrison here."

"Your latest gift from Mr. Veech," said Laurence.

"Open it, Mr. Beaumont."

As Laurence loosened the string, the smell hit him. He dumped the contents out onto the table: a slim roll of bloodstained paper, and a largish object wrapped in sodden linen. Already queasy, he unfolded the linen. Inside was a severed right hand, the thick hair upon it matted with dried blood. Every nail had been torn from the fingers. He recognised the criss-cross of scars on the big, lumpy knuckles: the insignia of a housebreaker. "Oh dear God," he murmured, turning away. He had grasped this hand in friendship, and in thanks for saving his life.

"Whose might it be?" asked Digby, sounding relieved.

"It's Barlow's," Laurence choked out.

"It can't be," cried Price, clutching at the edge of the table. "Barlow can't be dead."

"Mr. Beaumont," said Digby, "pray inspect what is written on that paper."

Laurence obeyed. "It's in cipher, in *her* writing."

Digby snatched it from him. "Yes, but . . . the cipher is old. Isabella was not acquainted with it." He dropped the paper, and looked up. "Parliament intercepted a trove of my correspondence in this cipher before war was declared. Pym's agents broke it, and I have not used it since. What can it all mean, sir?"

"For Christ's sake, we know what it means. Veech has arrested her."

"If so, Sir Montague's friends in Parliament will secure her release. We must remember that my Lady d'Aubigny was liberated from the Tower last year without penalty."

"That was last year, my lord, and she is His Majesty's cousin by marriage, not *your* spy."

"I hired Barlow as Lady Hallam's courier, and I must accept responsibility for his death," Price said woefully. "Let me go to London and fetch her out."

"No, Price," said Laurence. "Veech will send us your ears, or your hand, or . . . or whatever else he chops off your body. We know who he wants. Until he can entice me in, he'll hold her as his captive."

"You'd have no more chance of succeeding than Mr. Price," Digby objected.

"Even so, I'd attempt it. Though if I'm seized by Veech, you would pay a high cost. I know what it is to be tortured, and – how did you phrase it to me last year – *once tortured, twice shy.*"

"I should not have said that, sir. It was to provoke you."

"It's the truth, my lord. Think of what secrets might come out – yours and the King's. If you estimate it's worth the risk, send me to London. After today, Veech and I want mutual revenge."

"I must reflect on my decision." Digby indicated the hand. "Meanwhile, please dispose of this, sirs, and then transcribe what Isabella wrote. It might provide some clue."

Laurence wrapped the hand back in its linen shroud. "He was a fine man, wasn't he, Price."

Price nodded, sobbing. "He might . . . he might still be alive, Beaumont."

"He might. But if he's not, let's give at least this part of him a decent burial."

When they returned from their sad duty, Laurence deciphered the lines on the bloodied roll of paper: a message purportedly from Digby to Isabella detailing a plot to lay charges of gunpowder in the cellars of Derby House, to be exploded while the Committee of Both Kingdoms was in session.

"This was invented by the rebels to incriminate her, yet why would it be in her writing?" Digby asked.

"Perhaps Veech left some document for her to find. She must have copied it without understanding the contents. I trust it *is* pure invention, my lord?"

"Upon my soul it is, sir. It would not hold water in a court of law."

"I wish I could share your certitude," said Laurence. "There have been so many plots of late. Parliament might believe us capable of almost any base intrigue."

He waited for a reproof, yet Digby said nothing.


## II.

On a rare hot, sunny day, the young Beaumont women were out in Martha's herb garden picking broom buds to preserve in vinegar. Elizabeth, Anne, and Mary wore straw hats to protect their complexions, but Catherine had discarded hers and was working away diligently; as if by tacit agreement, she and Mary had chosen one half of the garden while the Beaumont sisters took the other.

Observing them through the open stillroom window, Lady Beaumont marvelled at the bond that had grown between Catherine and Mary in less than a month. Mary was noticeably happier, which boded well for her approaching confinement. The rest of the household, including his lordship, was still bemused by Laurence's enigmatic bride, and Lady Beaumont knew that Elizabeth would have preferred Penelope for a sister-in-law. She herself detected in Catherine a strong character and an alert mind, though she could not yet predict if they might clash with hers.

Martha glanced up from the mixture she was grinding, of cloves, cowslip petals, and fresh butter: her salve for cuts and wounds. "Master Laurence is a dark horse, is he not, my lady, to settle for such a creature. Country folk would believe she'd been touched by fairies – she's got that strangeness in her eyes. And now what can she be doing?"

Catherine had stopped to search into a thicket of broom. She called over Mary and held out her left hand; then they both started fumbling inside the bush. "She must have lost her wedding ring," said Lady Beaumont. "I would not care if she did – it is a drab little thing." Her attention wandered to Elizabeth and Anne; heads bowed, they were in tight conference.

"It's not fair, when *he* had his way," exclaimed Elizabeth, and flung aside her basket, sending up a shower of yellow buds.

Anne grabbed her by the arm. "Liz, you must be patient. You don't know the man."

At once, Lady Beaumont hurried out. "Elizabeth, Anne, tell me why you were arguing."

"We were not arguing," said Elizabeth. "We were discussing why I should not be allowed to consider a proposal of marriage, as agreed, since Laurence has taken a wife."

"Are you referring to Mr. Price?"

"Yes I am. I'd hoped you would have an answer for me by now, as to whether he can court me. And I *have* been patient. I've waited a whole fortnight, and not a word has been said – as if he had never visited here."

"Did Laurence recommend him to you as a future husband?"

"He has said nothing to Mr. Price's discredit."

"Nor has he given him a warm endorsement," Anne reminded her.

"Ah, you would compare my situation with yours," snapped Elizabeth. Then she caught her mother's eye and bit her lip.

"They are two very different situations," said Lady Beaumont. "We have known Walter Ingram for years. To judge from my short acquaintance with Mr. Price, which is as short as yours, Elizabeth, he is not the kind of man your father and I could ever approve of you marrying."

"But why? He's endured his share of hardships in the past, yet now he has an excellent position with Lord Digby, and the means to support me as his wife. And he is Laurence's friend."

"Think of your dead husband, and the man *he* was! He would turn in his grave if he knew you had fallen victim to that strutting peacock, with his false graces. I should write myself today and—"

"My lady!" Martha came rushing from the stillroom. "Mistress Catherine is ill!"

Lady Beaumont turned to behold Mary, both hands clapped to her mouth in a trite gesture of horror, and Catherine swaying to and fro, her eyes rolling in their sockets like those of a maddened horse. The girl collapsed to the ground and lay juddering, flailing her arms and legs. Martha got to her first and bent to restrain her thrashing limbs. Her skin was a bluish grey, and a dribble of foam issued from her lips.

"It's as if she's possessed by demons," Elizabeth whispered.

Catherine's jaw locked with a grinding of her teeth, and her body became rigid; she was uttering strangled sounds.

"She may have been bitten by a mad dog," said Martha. "I'll fetch my spirit of hartshorn."

Lady Beaumont knelt and gripped Catherine's shoulders; the girl had regained her breath, but the foam had thickened around her mouth. She jerked convulsively, her lids flickering as if she were in the depths of a waking nightmare.

Martha sped back just as Catherine relaxed and her eyes closed, her face blanched and peaceful. "It is the falling sickness," Martha asserted. "No need of hartshorn – the fit has passed. We must lay her in bed and she will sleep, and be quite herself again. I know from my uncle who had it."

"Is there a remedy?" asked Lady Beaumont.

"Some say a powder of mistletoe around full moon, though it didn't help my uncle."

"Did he die of the sickness?"

"No, my lady, and he lived three score years until his heart failed him."

Mary spoke, with a confidence Lady Beaumont had not heard in her before. "It was because of her ring. Her hands were sweating, she said, and it had slipped off into the bush. She was desperate to find it – she believed she should never remove it, or something terrible would happen. I picked it up, too late." She showed them the ring in the palm of her hand.

"Give it to me," Lady Beaumont said, and replaced it on Catherine's finger.

## III.

Eight days after the slighting of Reading, His Majesty's troops evacuated Abingdon covered by Lord Wilmot's Horse; and the following day, Essex occupied the town for Parliament. Malicious gossip circulated that Lord Wilmot had virtually gifted it to Essex, although it was not he but Lord Forth who had issued the somewhat premature command to withdraw. Laurence suspected Wilmot's enemies, mainly Digby, of spreading a slander that would further harden the King against a man he already so disliked.

Essex and Waller had more sense than to quarrel. Their armies now controlled the whole of Berkshire and were a mere four miles apart, converging inexorably on Oxford. And Price's fledgling intelligencers in Gloucestershire brought other bad tidings: Colonel

Massey had recalled his troops to their home garrison not because of any perceived threat from the royal army, but to launch an attack on Bristol. Though he could ill spare any of his Oxford troops, the King had to dispatch General Hopton to the west, to secure this vital port.

Back in Digby's Oxford quarters, Laurence received a letter from Lady Beaumont. She made no mention of de Zamora and assured him that everyone at the house was well, except for Catherine. "Yesterday she suffered an instance of the falling sickness. We understand why she did not speak of it: she was in fear of being sent home, where she had been cruelly treated by her father. I think you tried to tell me about her ailment on the day you brought her here. We are dismayed, however, that her family hid the truth from us, and that you, knowing of it, chose to wed her. Since it is too late to break the marriage, we can only pray to God she may bear you healthy children." And in a last sentence: "As you must have heard from Mr. Price, he visited us some weeks before Catherine's illness, in the hope of courting Elizabeth. Please instruct him to look elsewhere for a bride." Laurence composed a reply thanking his mother for the information, though he avoided the subject of Price. In a letter to Catherine, he urged her not to worry, and to take care of herself.

He had no time to dwell on these domestic concerns, and after night upon night without sleep spent perusing and relaying reports, all of which confirmed the steady advance of Parliament troops, he was anyway too fatigued. His own worries about Isabella and even the mystery of the Spaniards weighed less immediately upon his mind: Oxford was bracing for a siege.

**IV.**

"For this despicable act, and for refusing my summons to lay down their arms, the citizens shall have no quarter," Prince Rupert told his officers, as they slogged back into formation in the drenching rain. Their first attack on the small, virulently Puritan town of Bolton had been repulsed, but that was not the cause of his outrage: the defenders had hanged a Royalist captive, contrary to the rules of war.

"Why did the rebels do such a thing, sir?" Adam asked Tom.

"They mistook him for an Irish papist," said Tom. "There's an old history of hatred between Catholics and Puritans throughout Lancashire. Now we'll settle it, once and for all." He was so sure of victory that he and his lieutenants Curtis and Smith had placed bets as to the number they would slay. Bolton would add to Rupert's triumphs, on his path to rescue the garrison at York.

"They can depend on God's mercy but not on ours," the Prince concluded. "I command you as always to respect the lives and persons of their women and children."

Tom joined in the collective cheering. "Those Puritan swine call Bolton the Geneva of England," he laughed to Adam, while drums and trumpets sounded the order for a second attack. "When we're done with them, they'll call it their grave."

"Charge, in the name of God, and of your King," cried Rupert, flourishing his sword, and sprang forward on his white stallion.

The Royalists bore down upon soldiers and citizens, hacking to the right and left with their blades. Tom ran a trooper through the chest, and galloped on, nearly trampling an elderly civilian who had rushed out of his house wielding a musket. Tom stuck the fellow in the neck; a scarlet jet gushed forth, spattering him and his horse. His ears rang with screaming and bellowing and howling, and distressed neighs. And he breathed in the intoxicating reek of war: a meaty odour of blood, the sewer stench of human waste, powder, and thick smoke. He began to lose count of how many he had killed or wounded. When the action lulled, he took off his hat and used the rainwater from the brim to cleanse his grimy face. He looked back for Adam, and saw him unhurt and grinning.

Trumpets sounded again; the Prince was blasting past, with Boy loping at his horse's side. "A couple of hours have won us Bolton," he shouted. "You have licence to sack the town. The plunder is ours."

They stormed the citizens' shops and dwellings for the fruits of pillage, shooting or cutting down the remaining men, and hounding the women and children, stripping some of their clothes and pushing them naked from their homes into the foul pottage of mud and guts and excrement outside. Adam waited in the street holding the horses as Tom, Curtis, and Smith smashed through door after door. They were exhilarated, thirsty from their labours, and started to search for drink, but most of the Puritan households were dry.

"They weren't equipped to receive gentlemen like us," said Smith.

"Then they should pay for their want of hospitality," said Tom.

He chose a wealthier house where, in the sparklingly clean tiled kitchen, he found several casks of wine. Smith had gone to forage in the larder, and returned dragging a young girl by the arm. "See what a tasty morsel I have here! She was hiding in a corner behind a sack of grain." Curtis helped him wrestle her to the floor, and after a slap to the face, she stopped resisting. "A little maid servant, so fresh she can't have been docked yet," he said, as they pulled up her skirts.

"Do her the honour, sir," Curtis said to Tom; she was whimpering, her eyes darting from one man to the next.

Tom examined the unblemished skin above her stockings, and the sparse hair over her pudenda; she might be fourteen or fifteen at the most. "It's against our orders."

Smith was ogling the pink cleft between the girl's legs. He unbuttoned his coat and stroked the bulge at the front of his breeches. "We were to give no quarter, sir."

"We were to treat the women and children with respect."

"A tumble won't hurt her," said Curtis, leering at the girl. "Eh, puss, aren't you hungry for a Cavalier prick?"

"Take her, sir," said Smith, his voice urgent with lust. "You'll make our ride all the smoother."

Tom felt suddenly repulsed. But at the same time, he did not want to disappoint his men. "I need to piss beforehand," he said, and stepped aside, praying for divine intervention as he urinated on the expensive black-and-white tiles.

He was still holding his uncooperative sex when Adam yelled in, "Major Beaumont, sir!"

"We'll have our sport later, boys," Tom said, and laced back his breeches.

A man from Lord Derby's troop was waiting outside. "Major Beaumont, seven hundred rebels are trapped in a church about a mile west of us. We're to roast 'em alive."

They mounted and cantered off, leaping their horses over dead and dying, and the wreckage of household goods. As they reined in at the churchyard, Tom spied Rupert's white stallion, and the Prince himself. Kneeling round him in the mud was a bedraggled delegation of men from the church, pleading for their miserable hides. Tom swung down from the saddle, noticing barrels of powder lined up by the church walls. "Your Highness, should we roll in the kegs, and attach the fuses?"

"No, sir," said Rupert contemptuously. "I may be famed as the Robber Prince by His Majesty's enemies, but I will *not* be infamous as Prince Butcher. I shall spare these men, as an example of the King's mercy. March them from the church, and put them with our other prisoners."

"Yes, Your Highness," said Tom, livid: he would have shot every one of them himself. He beckoned to Smith and Curtis. "His Royal Highness has ordered me to stay and take charge here, but I'd hate to deprive you of your fun. Go and show that girl what expert swordsmen we are, so she won't forget us."

**v.**

"It was as if I were a bird gazing down from the skies upon a vast expanse of moor strewn with thousands of bodies, of dead and wounded men, and horses," recalled Seward, as he and Clarke sat together at their breakfast of bread and honey. "The turf was red, and the air black with smoke – the colours of hell. Then blasting winds carried me upwards, and my dream faded. What can it signify? Victory for His Majesty – or defeat?" he added, mourning again his lost bowl.

Clarke dabbed a smear of honey from his lips. "Before you went to bed, Seward, had you consumed any cheese? It is reputed to bring on nightmares."

Seward did not answer, distracted by the clink of spurs outside. "I have a visitor. Would you open for me, Clarke – my hands are sticky." While Clarke hoisted himself from his chair and trotted over to unlatch the door, Seward picked up his knife and concealed it in the sleeve of his robe.

"Enter, Mr. Beaumont," Clarke said, at which Seward put down the knife.

Beaumont wore the air of a somnambulist, although his glazed eyes suggested that he had had no sleep recently, troubled or otherwise. His chin was shadowed with stubble, his linen was dirty, and the fingers of his left hand were black with ink. "You must leave Oxford as fast as you can," he said dully. "Go to Dr. Clarke's house. Essex has crossed the Thames. He's been stopped for now, but he's holding his position right under our northern breastworks. Tomorrow he may breach them."

"Oxford cannot fall," said Clarke.

"Dr. Clarke, we have supplies for a fortnight's siege: not long enough for Prince Rupert to come to our aid. Not that he could, being occupied in Lancashire, as is Prince Maurice in the southwest. Our sole hope is to separate Essex and Waller and strike them in turn. It's a faint hope, at that, with our lesser numbers."

"Heavens above," gasped Seward. "What will the King do, should Essex penetrate the defences?"

"He's told Council that he may send the young princes out of harm's way, but that he won't abandon his army."

"He is courageous, to stand by his faithful servants unto the very last."

"No, Seward, he's damned pigheaded and heedless of their lives. Now will you both *get out*, tonight if you can."

"Oh dear, oh dear," muttered Clarke, and skipped to the door.

"You too, Seward." Beaumont looked about at the clutter of alchemical paraphernalia on Seward's shelves. "Take only what you need."

## VI.

"Have I heard you correctly, my lord?" said Beaumont, from his writing table littered with dog-eared maps, codebooks, stacks of papers, and ink pots. "The King is to go *hunting* today?"

"Yes, sir, in the grounds of his palace at Woodstock," said Digby, leaning upon Quayle's arm to step out of his shoes and into his riding boots. "The princes and his Council are to accompany him."

"Is it the moment for sport," Beaumont asked, in a tone of restrained disbelief, "while Essex is laying siege to our bridges across the River Cherwell, and Waller is pressing towards us from Abingdon?"

"His Majesty believes the exercise might help to shake off the despond that has descended upon us. After our hunt, he will hold a meeting of Council at Woodstock Manor."

"Why couldn't he hold it here in Oxford, instead of risking everyone's capture outside the city fortifications?"

"Capture by whom?" inquired Digby, as he donned his coat. "Essex is occupied battering away ineffectually at our eastern defences. And Waller cannot cross his army over the Thames and swing it northwest as far as Woodstock in the space of a day."

"Yes, Essex is occupied, my lord, and up to this point we have managed to prevent him from entering the city," said Beaumont, with exaggerated patience. "And I agree that Waller could not bring up his *entire* army. But we have only a hundred musketeers posted at Newbridge to stop him from gaining the west bank of the river, and their ammunition won't last long if he makes a determined assault on them. Once he crosses over, an advance party of his Horse can quickly cover the less than ten miles to Woodstock."

"How could he possibly know that His Majesty will be in Woodstock?"

"From his scouts, of course."

"Even should your dire predictions be fulfilled, we shall have the royal Troop to protect us," Digby said soothingly. He worried for Beaumont, who had been neglecting himself ever since they had received Veech's unwholesome package. The stubble around his mouth had grown into a ragged beard, and between visits from the scouts and his own frantic sallies to confirm their intelligence, he forgot to eat, leaving untouched plates on the floor as he scribbled away at his reports. "I know what has inspired your feverish toil, and your pessimism," Digby added, as he lifted his arms for Quayle to fasten the sash around his waist. "You are still grieving the fate of your friend Barlow, and you are as anxious as I am to find a solution to our . . . *difficulties* in London."

"How can we think of London, when Oxford is in such imminent danger?"

"I am amazed that you can think at all, sir, you are so deprived of sleep."

Beaumont cast Digby a glassy stare and turned back to his work. "Enjoy the chase, my lord."

The hunt was an undeniable success: the King proved in excellent spirits after shooting two magnificent buck, and his companions took down a host of lesser quarry. "This must be an omen, Your Majesty," Digby had observed of the buck. "We should name them Essex and Waller."

By early afternoon, stripped and gutted carcasses were roasting on outdoor spits, as His Majesty and the hunting party wandered about sipping wine from their goblets. The King's Troop ate their dinner outdoors in rustic style, while the King, the princes, and members of Council were called to table in the manor house; the enormous, rambling palace opposite was too dilapidated for comfort. After the platters were cleared from the board, the meeting of Council opened.

"Here is our choice, when we return to Oxford," said the King, his face now grave. "We c-can engage the rebels upon any advantage that we may perceive, or else m-march suddenly away, and let them decide either to besiege the city or to pursue us."

"In a fight, we would hazard all, Your Majesty," said Forth. "If the rebels triumphed, you and your children and your ministers would be taken, and God knows how Parliament would treat with you. I propose that we quit Oxford under cover of night with our more nimble troops, leaving a part of our infantry and our heavier artillery behind us to defend it."

"My lord Secretary, have you an objection to his plan?" the King asked Digby, who had been shaking his head.

"I would borrow a phrase from my predecessor, the late Lord Falkland, Your Majesty," answered Digby. "When it is not necessary to make a decision, it is necessary *not* to make a decision. In four days, Essex has got no closer to crossing any of our bridges over the Cherwell, and he has sustained serious losses: some five hundred of his men have been slain or wounded, or have deserted. In the past, his ranks, especially the London Bands, have suffered from a lack of fighting acumen. I would suggest we let him carry on at his fruitless labours for another week, which will further reduce and dishearten his men. He and Waller will probably quarrel yet again, and cease to coordinate their movements. We can strike Essex first, and remove the threat from the east. Then, should Waller bridge the Thames and come upon us from the southwest, we will not be encircled."

"Your Majesty," said Lord Wilmot, eyeing Digby disparagingly, "although it may *appear* that we can sit another week in Oxford, each day we delay, we deplete our supplies. I second the view of our Lord Marshal: those who would prove the most valuable hostages to the enemy should march out while our path to the west remains open. In territory friendly to us, we can levy men and replenish our stores. And in the meantime, we may have better news of Prince Rupert, in the north."

"I th-thank you for your counsel, my lords." The King surveyed the other members, some of whom were looking anywhere but at him or those who had spoken. "H-has no one else an opinion?" A tense silence fell. "*In nocte consilium*," the King said. "We shall quarter here for the night. Let us break Council to gather our thoughts, lords and gentlemen, and resume our debate before bedtime, in the hope of a resolution to our circumstances."

Wilmot and Forth stalked out to the grounds, to drink with the Troop, Digby supposed. Indigested from the rich meal, he retired to the chamber that he would share with his fellow Secretary of State, Sir Edward Nicholas. Quayle helped him off with his boots and coat; and he lay down on his bed, closed his eyes, and drowsed.

He and Isabella were hunting with the King, among the venerable oaks and ashes of Woodstock Park. She wore a costume of garish scarlet, a colour that surprised Digby; and as her horse raced ahead, Digby noticed to his further surprise that she was astride Beaumont's Arab stallion, and that her legs were immodestly bared.

"What a seat she keeps," said His Majesty. "Most women would envy her prowess – though not to the extent that most men would envy her horse!" Digby gaped: never had he heard bawdy talk issue from the royal lips. "Although you are an exception, my Lord Digby," the King went on. "I think it is the owner of that horse *you* would like to ride. I should know: I grew up watching my father at sport with his favourite boys. Sometimes they even shared his bed with my mother, so he could fondle them, the better to do his duty by her. But does *your* wife know of your secret desire?"

"My wife and I are inseparable," protested Digby.

The King motioned for Digby to look down at himself. To his horror, he saw that he was stark naked. The King leant towards him, and pinched the roll of flesh at his waist. "A little less venison next time, my lord."

Digby woke to Quayle shaking him. "My lord, Mr. Beaumont has arrived with urgent news for Council."

Digby struggled up, thrust on his boots, and rushed out to the room where they had eaten. The King and his Council members were assembled at the table, their faces turned towards Beaumont, who stood with his shoulders slouched, evidently past bothering to carry himself in an appropriate fashion before the King.

"P-please repeat what you have t-told us, for his lordship's benefit," the King said to him.

"Waller crossed the Thames this afternoon on a causeway of boats, and landed five thousand Horse and Foot on the other side," Beaumont said. "Some of his troops have advanced three miles north-west of Newbridge. If he's not checked, he'll shut off our lines of communication to the west."

"Are you certain, sir?" asked Digby.

"Yes, my lord. When I got a report of his movements, I went in person to confirm it, and ever since I've been shadowing his forces with the scouts."

"What now?" the King inquired, of Council.

"Mr. Beaumont, have we yet superior numbers in this immediate area, as compared to rebels?" Forth wanted to know.

"For the time being, yes, my lord," Beaumont replied, "but should Waller learn that His Majesty and the princes are here, he'll dispatch his cavalry for a lightning raid to capture them."

Forth addressed the King. "We must hasten back to Oxford, Your Majesty, though with our large party we cannot expect to get there much before dawn. Our infantry must be drawn off from the defences to rendezvous with us on the road, in the very early morning. They can keep Waller at bay until we are inside the city."

"If our plight is so desperate, would it not be the best course to surrender to Essex, Your Majesty, on conditions?" Secretary Nicholas said timidly.

"I may be f-found in the hands of the Earl of Essex," the King responded, tilting up his chin, "but I shall be dead first."

"In that case, Your Majesty," said Forth, "our chief business upon our return will be to effect your escape."

Digby stared from Forth to the King; and lastly at Beaumont, in whose eyes he read no emotion save an immense weariness.

## VII.

The gatekeeper's wife died of her ulcers late in the night, and her putrid corpse required swift burial. In the morning, her husband and family laid her to rest in the churchyard at Chipping Campden while Lady Beaumont took the coach to the gatehouse with Martha and a bevy of servants. She supervised a meticulous cleansing of the sick room, burnt the spoilt linen, and arranged a repast for the funeral party, which by afternoon was in a state of happy oblivion thanks to Martha's elderflower wine. "Our work is done," Lady Beaumont said. "Let us go home."

Geoffrey ran out to the coach as it drew up in the courtyard. "Your ladyship, we have guests, from Spain. Your cousin, Don Antonio de Zamora, rode in at midday accompanied by his valet. They are in the Hall with his lordship and the young mistresses."

"Goodness me, your ladyship," Martha exclaimed, as if Geoffrey had announced a visitor from the skies. "Why did we not see them pass by the gatehouse?"

"We were otherwise occupied," said Lady Beaumont crisply. "I must refresh myself, before I attend them."

She went straight up to her chamber, where she applied rosewater to her temples, neatened her gown and hair, and pinched her cheeks to bring the blood to them, wishing that her finest jewels were not under the dovecote floor: she was riding into battle without her best weapons. She thought of Antonio's keepsake, the two-faced medallion locked inside her cabinet. He could have it back, and that was all he would wring out of her, she decided, on her way downstairs.

Near the open doors to the Hall, her courage faltered. How unchanged was Antonio's voice: as she listened to the cadence of his rapid speech, it seemed as yesterday that she had last heard it. But she had not bargained on his fluency in English; she would have preferred him stammering and clumsy in the language she had prided herself on mastering. She could see her husband on the edge of his armchair, rapt, while Antonio talked and made expansive gestures with his still supple hands. Anne and Mary were as entranced as his lordship, although Catherine was studying Antonio as might a card player waiting for a cheat at the tables. A fresh-faced youth stationed behind Antonio's chair was watching everyone with avid interest.

Lord Beaumont rose when Lady Beaumont entered. "My wife, can you believe it? Did you ever imagine that you might be reunited with your cousin here in England?"

Antonio sprang up, one hand pressed to his heart, his face suffused with affection, and bowed to her. "*Mi querida Elena, está usted tan bella como la última vez que la vi.*"

"I thank you, Don Antonio," she said in English. She would not pamper his vanity by returning his compliment, though he was annoyingly well-preserved, with his plentiful head of hair and slender figure; and his eyes glittered with the same old arrogance. His complexion, however, looked to her unhealthy beneath his weathered tan. He was dressed in a stained leather coat and breeches, a less distinguished costume than the olive green suit of velvet that she always remembered on him, and his boots were worn at the heel. As she had suspected, he needed money; and she knew precisely how he would attempt to swindle it out of her.

"Why was I the last to learn of his visit to our country?" Lord Beaumont demanded, surveying the two of them with mixed joy and confusion. "He said that the Spanish Envoy wrote at Christmastide to tell you, my dear. And he has met both Thomas and Laurence, who said nothing of it in their letters home. He could not explain the omission, so I must ask you."

"It was for our security, my lord," she said, as the two men resumed their seats. "Had Colonel Purefoy somehow discovered that we were to receive a foreigner – a Catholic and a Spaniard – we might all have been endangered."

"How right you were," said Lord Beaumont. "What would we do, my lady, without your forethought? Don Antonio has kept for you his family news, but he has had many tales to relate to us of his adventures in England. He is recovering from a violent attack, and a wasting sickness that was nearly the death of him."

"I was set upon by Oxford thieves who stole my purse and sword," Antonio said. "For close on a month, I could not move without excruciating agony from my broken ribs, and then on top of it, I was delirious with fever and riven with pains from the flux. I commended my soul to heaven more times than I can count. But God in His infinite mercy spared me," he finished, "and here I am."

"We are as infinitely grateful to God, Don Antonio," she said, wondering how much of his tale was true, though it did excuse his pallor. "Might I inquire as to the length of your visit?"

"That will depend upon your hospitality, my sweet cousin, and that of his lordship."

"Our hospitality will depend upon the rebels, sir. Should we have the smallest fear that they may encroach again on our part of the county, you will have to go from this house."

"I would never dream of endangering you," Antonio said. "My Lady Elena, you do not appear to share my bliss at our meeting."

"Don Antonio, please forgive her," said Lord Beaumont, and to her, "You took so much upon yourself, nursing that poor woman, and then arranging her funeral."

"Yes, my lord," she said, "it was a tiring and dispiriting business."

"I pray Elizabeth is not so tired by it, and will come down to us soon? Don Antonio is anxious to meet all of our children."

"Elizabeth? She was not with me."

"But she asked my leave to walk over to the gatehouse, after the coach had departed. I saw her set out, carrying a basket on her arm. She must have had a change of mind, and turned for home." Lord Beaumont shook his head indulgently at Antonio. "You have daughters of your own, Don Antonio – you must sympathise: how difficult it is, for a father to understand their moods."

"Years ago, I surrendered that impossible task to my wife, Teresa, bless her heart," laughed Antonio.

Lady Beaumont turned to the young women. Mary and Catherine appeared no more than puzzled. Anne looked aghast. "Anne," she said, "Elizabeth may be in her chamber. Let us go and see." They left the Hall at a dignified pace. On the stair she grabbed Anne's arm and they raced up to Elizabeth's bedchamber. It was empty, and a note lay on the pillow. "Read it," she told Anne.

"'To my dearest family: it grieves me to distress you, but I could wait no longer to be with Mr. Price, to whom I consider myself betrothed. You must not fear for my honour or for my safety. His trusted servants are to escort me from Chipping Campden to Oxford, where he and I shall be joined in wedlock. I pray you will look well upon us as a married couple, wanting my happiness as I desire yours. He has pledged to provide for me and cherish me more than his life, and he is a man of his word. I remain your loving daughter, Elizabeth,'" Anne concluded weakly.

Lady Beaumont's mother used to comfort her that God in His omniscience had measured every burden placed upon His children on earth, even if they could not comprehend why they must suffer; and that He would give them just due in heaven for their trials. Yet today Lady Beaumont felt that God had pushed her too far. She sank onto Elizabeth's bed. "Did you know of this?"

"I swear not. She was angry on the day of Catherine's fit, but then she talked no more to me of Mr. Price. I thought she was reconciled to the impossibility of the match. She had become more cheerful recently. She must have had a message from him, though how it was delivered I've no idea. I ought to have asked her." Anne began to cry. "I blame myself."

"It is *he* I blame, the dissembling knave." Lady Beaumont spoke with new determination. "Geoffrey may yet catch her and these *trusted servants* on the Oxford road. Failing that, he must find Laurence in Oxford, and they must deal with the rogue together. I want to keep the truth from his lordship and from my cousin for as long as possible," she added, picturing Antonio's glee if he learnt about Elizabeth's disobedience in the name of love; he would call it more evidence of bad blood. "Go down to the Hall and say that she left word of her intention to visit friends in town. And say that I was all of a sudden overwhelmed by the surprise of seeing my cousin again, and wish to rest undisturbed until supper. Then have Geoffrey come to me in my upstairs office."

## VIII.

Laurence had galloped back from Woodstock with Lord Forth's command that the Oxford Foot were to meet His Majesty's Troop some miles north of the city defences. Afterwards, in a state beyond fatigue, he had collapsed upon his bed at Digby's quarters and slept like the dead. Shortly after dawn, a travel-worn Quayle had woken him to say that the royal party had marched through the night and was now safely inside the defences. Laurence feted this event by washing and shaving, and changing his linen.

"Lord Forth has been created Earl of Brentford by the King in reward for his service," Digby announced, when Laurence emerged from his chamber, "and in view of yours yesterday, the Earl wishes you to play a crucial role in His Majesty's escape. Once dusk falls, His Majesty, Prince Charles, and the Council of War – myself included – will slip out through our northern fortifications where our Horse is stationed. We must delude Essex as to our movements, so you are to spread word through your informers in his camp that we intend a strike on Waller in Abingdon. A troop of our Foot and some of our artillery shall then march south with full colours, in the hope of forcing Waller back from Newbridge to defend his garrison."

"You'll need sound intelligence from *his* camp," said Laurence, deciding quickly who should be assigned to which place.

By afternoon, Laurence's scouts reported that Essex knew of these Royalist troops marching on Waller, and was continuing his assault on the eastern side of Oxford; and Waller had indeed retreated from Newbridge to protect Abingdon. So far, so good, Laurence thought. The same Royalist troops could now withdraw again to Oxford, and launch a second feint on Waller tomorrow morning, to keep him distracted while the King's party rode further from the city.

Digby was packing at his quarters. "You will come with us tonight," he said to Laurence. "Mr. Price has volunteered to stay behind and supervise the destruction of my correspondence, should the rebels invade."

"Brave fellow," Laurence observed. "He'll face a hanging if he's caught."

Towards afternoon he sought out Price, who was across the street at their usual tavern, eating. Immediately Price set down his spoon, as if he had lost his appetite. "I hear you won't come north with us," said Laurence, "and I wanted to tell you: I admire your courage."

"Thank you," said Price, lowering his eyes.

"You've done yourself proud in his lordship's service, and you've been very patient with me. Forgive me my short temper, on numerous occasions. Well, Price, if . . . if we don't see each other again before I leave, I wish you the best of luck."

"And good luck to you, Beaumont," muttered Price.

Around nine o'clock in the evening, the King and Prince Charles hugged young Prince James goodbye; the boy would remain in the city, under the protection of Governor Aston. Laurence knew that it must have been a heartbreaking decision to divide the royal family once more, when the Queen was far away at Exeter awaiting the birth of her child, yet His Majesty had accepted it as necessary, lest he and Prince Charles be taken hostage. With his Council, his servants, his personal Troop, and various others who felt their lives in imminent danger, he set off quietly through Oxford's northern defences, where five thousand

Royalist cavalry were readying to follow him. Laurence rode beside Digby and the civilian members of Council, behind the royals; Wilmot's Horse provided the vanguard; and Forth joined His Majesty's advance with two and a half thousand musketeers purposely bereft of their regimental colours, and no heavy artillery or baggage trains to slow them down.

At dawn they reached the village of Yarnton, where the King had met up with his Foot twenty-four hours earlier. Although this stage of the escape had been accomplished in good order, Laurence was holding his breath for reports on enemy movements. Scouts galloped in to warn that Essex had at last crossed the Cherwell, and some of his men were as near as Woodstock. Part of Waller's army had spread up from Newbridge and were not five miles from Yarnton. His Majesty would soon be hemmed in, unless the two Parliamentary generals were still deceived into thinking he had not left Oxford. Laurence sent the scouts back to investigate, and His Majesty regrouped his forces to carry on marching northwest. By nine in the morning, as they assembled on Hanborough Heath, near the market town of Witney, news came that Essex and Waller were in pursuit, infuriated that the King had eluded them. To maintain his advantage, he could not rest.

## IX.

Price stood paralysed in Digby's main office, cringing at the memory of Beaumont's words: *I admire your courage.* After Lady Beaumont's insulting behaviour, Price had felt amply justified in arranging for Elizabeth's flight, yet he had not known then how perilous her journey could be, with the fighting so close, nor in what straits he would find himself. He might be dead when she arrived, if the rebels breached the defences. If Oxford held for the King, he would face the Beaumonts' collective wrath. And he had not just wrecked his friendship with Beaumont: as a consequence of breaking his word to the man, he had prejudiced his entire future with Lord Digby. Now he cursed his hot temper. He should have swallowed his pride and waited.

He began to sort through the stacks of confidential papers he must destroy, his hands sweating and smudging the ink. But gradually it came to him: in the very last resort, they might buy him his neck. He could claim to be a double agent working for Parliament, a mole within the offices of the Secretary of State. While he hated the idea of betrayal, he feared death still more; and what had he to lose?

A rap on the door gave him a nasty start, as though he had spoken his thoughts out loud. He did not at once recognise the man on the threshold: Geoffrey, Lord Beaumont's valet. They surveyed each other for a moment. Then Geoffrey said coldly, "I must see Mr. Beaumont."

"He's gone. He rode out of Oxford last night."

"Where is Madam Ormiston?"

"Is she not at his lordship's house?"

"Not since yesterday morning. She left a note saying she intended to join you here."

"That is a complete shock to me," said Price.

"How can it be, when she wrote that *your* servants would escort her from Chipping Campden?"

Price hesitated, dismayed; why had she included this most unnecessary detail? "I might have remarked to her that if she wished to visit Oxford, Mr. Beaumont and I had scouts in his lordship's neighbourhood who could provide a guard for his coach on the road. I was not encouraging her to quit his house."

Geoffrey stepped towards him. "Where are you hiding her?"

"I am not hiding her anywhere."

"By God I'd strike you down, were you not a gentleman," hissed Geoffrey, with a dubious emphasis on the last word.

Unwittingly, by invoking rank, he gave Price the advantage. "I cannot help what Madam Ormiston has chosen to do," Price said, in a haughty voice. "I would have advised her in the strongest terms against it. You may tell his lordship that if I have any news of her, he will hear from me. Now I must return to my work for the Secretary of State."

Geoffrey was in a fix, Price knew; he had experienced the same impotence faced with Lady Beaumont. When Geoffrey retreated, Price shut the door, and ran to the window. He watched Geoffrey mount his horse and trot off a way down the street, passing another man riding in the opposite direction: one of the scouts that Price had paid to assist Elizabeth.

Price bolted out to him. "Where is she?"

"With the ladies, sir, though we had a rough time of it getting her through," the scout said. "She begs for you to visit."

The apartment, on the upper storey of a draper's shop, seemed smaller to Price than when he had first come to rent it, before the guardians of Elizabeth's honour had moved in. The floor was now covered in mattresses, and the air ripe with sweat, stale milk, and unemptied chamber pots. Mrs. Giddens and Mrs. Connell, both officers' wives, rose to greet him. Mrs. Giddens had been nursing her infant and shielded her breast modestly with a shawl, and Mrs. Connell gathered up her little boy to make room for their visitor.

Elizabeth sat in a corner, with a miserable expression that lifted when she saw Price. The skirts of her gown were wet and muddy, and her hair windblown. He felt abashed: how could he have imagined turning coat and sacrificing such a brave, lovely girl? "Mr. Price, thank God," she said, holding out her arms.

"She had a dreadful journey, poor lamb," put in Mrs. Connell.

Price edged round the mattresses to Elizabeth, and knelt before her. "Dearest, how frightened you must have been."

"I was," she said, stealing both of her hands into his. "We could hear the roar of guns from far off, and then right by us as we were riding through the defences. And the smoke, and the stink, and those ugly trenches . . . But I shan't be afraid any more, with you. Please," she murmured in his ear, "tell me I won't have to stay for long in this squalid place, with these strangers."

"I am sorry, but you must, for now," he whispered. "Although not of your station, they are kind, decent women. Elizabeth, the King has fled north out of Oxford. Lord Digby and your brother went with him. The city may fall to Parliament, by tomorrow or the next day." Her face drained of colour. "You mustn't fret, my darling. Even if the rebels invade, you should be well-treated – these ladies have little children, after all." He reverted to more personal matters. "Did you confide in anyone at home that you were to join me?"

"No, but Anne might have suspected it."

"Your father's valet was in town looking for you."

"Geoffrey? So soon? Then we *must* be wed."

"There's no chance of that, at present."

"Yes: if Oxford falls, our whole world will crumble," she sighed. "We should have joy of each other, for however short a time. Let me be with you, married or not."

"I refuse to dishonour you," said Price. He would not surrender her if he could help it, yet nor would he throw away his hard-won position with Digby and his friendship with Beaumont if this could possibly be avoided. And there might still be a chance of her thousand pounds. "Elizabeth, you must tell everyone that you eloped of your own volition. Your family will forgive you that, but they won't let me near you again if they believed I had encouraged you."

"But you did! And I thought we would be married by the time they came after me."

"I thought the same," Price said honestly. "How could I have foreseen that Oxford would be so suddenly threatened? You must write to his lordship that you are safely accommodated with two virtuous married ladies who can bear witness to my faultless conduct. I'll write to express my consternation at your arrival, and pledge to bring you home the instant that circumstances permit, without mark upon your honour. My scout will deliver our letters post haste to his lordship."

"You would have me go home without making me your wife?"

"I must! Please, my sweet, do you want your father's health to suffer, for worrying about you?"

"You had no thought for his health when you wrote entreating me to come to you. Perhaps you would like me to ride back *post haste*, along with your scout."

"I would, but tonight it's far too dangerous for you to make the journey," Price said, clinging to her hands. "Do as I bid you and all will be well."

"I'm not a child, to be pacified by facile assurances," said Elizabeth with a hint of her ladyship's reproof. "But I shall defer to you, since I am in your power."

## X.

Soaked by a blinding rainstorm, the royal army had pushed westwards into the Cotswolds through thick mud. They could comfort themselves that the enemy would be even more hampered, as both Essex and Waller were travelling with bigger guns and with baggage trains. After a halt in Burford, they headed on through the spring dusk across the River Windrush to Bourton-on-the-Water, and camped in the fields and meadows surrounding the village. Mindful of Parliamentary patrols from the Gloucester garrison, Laurence then led his scouts on a reconnoitre northwest, fanning them out across the Cotswold Hills. They returned dirty and half asleep in their saddles as the eastern horizon began to glow. One fellow had barely escaped arrest on the outskirts of Tewkesbury, where the King had hoped to quarter by the following night: Parliament had occupied the town. The Royalist army would have to change course and make speed for Evesham, about as long a ride away, through more barren countryside. By the next day, they had covered the nearly twenty miles to Evesham, relieved at least that Oxford was temporarily spared a full siege while Essex and Waller were busy chasing the King. He himself would not be secure until he reached his stronghold at Worcester, another fifteen or so miles to the northwest.

On the sixth of June, Laurence's thirty-second birthday, the royal army arrived there, to a fervent welcome. Although the Royalists' spectacular pace had left Waller and Essex trailing behind them, they were incapable of further action; and he was far too tired himself to celebrate either the anniversary of his birth or the relative safety of the King's new haven.

Two days after, Digby called Laurence to his billet and asked him to encode a letter to Prince Rupert. It was uncharacteristically bleak: "Essex comes upon us one way," Digby wrote, "Waller likely to go about us on the Welsh side by Gloucester, Massey and the Lord Denbigh towards Kidderminster, both with considerable forces; and when to all this I shall add the uncertainty of your brother's succeeding before Lyme, and that Oxford is scarce victualled for a month, and for aught we know blocked up in a manner by the enemy's horse, Your Highness will easily frame for yourself an image of our condition . . . all the hopes of relief depend upon Your Highness's happy and timely success."

Once the courier had ridden out with his dismal communication, Digby told Quayle to fetch wine. He and Laurence sat brooding and drinking, until he broke the silence. "Why is it I have never seen you pray, Mr. Beaumont? Are you not a religious man?"

"Not particularly, my lord."

"I didn't think so. Isabella hinted to me that you were an atheist – not something you would want publicly known." When Laurence merely shrugged, Digby went on, "I wonder whether, in times of adversity, God might listen with greater interest to the prayers of His less observant children than those who pester Him daily with their trivial requests."

"Are you asking me to pray?"

"It could not hurt, though I'd hazard a guess that there as many men praying in the enemy camp."

"Rather more, *I* would hazard a guess. Do you believe that God is a Royalist?"

"His Majesty believes himself anointed by God to rule, so it would appear logical that God should be on his side. What is your view of that doctrine, sir?"

"Why do you care to know, my lord?"

Digby had no chance to reply. One of the scouts had burst in, red-faced and breathless. "My lord, Mr. Beaumont, I've come from reporting to His Majesty: Essex is on the move! He's preparing to march south, to the relief of Lyme Regis."

Digby and Laurence leapt up from their chairs. "How could this be? When did you find out?" babbled Digby, his voice shrill with eagerness.

"This morning we were spying in his camp, my lord, and saw him loading his heavy cannons onto carts. We learnt that he and Waller had held a conference at Burford with their chief officers, the day before yesterday. It was then that they decided the armies should split up."

"There's no shadow of a doubt?" asked Laurence. "You confirmed the reports from several sources, as you were taught?"

"Oh yes, sir," the scout said, flushing with professional pride.

"Essex must underestimate our strength, to leave the chase to Waller alone, but nevertheless . . ." Digby beamed incredulously at Laurence, who was as stunned: how could these experienced generals commit an error of such magnitude, when their prey, the greatest prize in the kingdom, was virtually trapped and ready for the taking? "Now we have only Waller to contend with," Digby chortled, clapping his hands together. "Damn me, Mr. Beaumont, God *is* a Royalist, after all."

# CHAPTER FIFTEEN

**I.**

Reclined upon her bed immersed in a book, Lady Hallam looked to Veech as if she were spending a quiet afternoon at her house in the Strand, except that she had not been able to change the high-necked gown in which she had arrived at the Tower, and wore no jewellery save her wedding ring; and her hair was simply dressed. She neither moved nor raised her eyes when he entered.

"What are you reading today, my lady?" he inquired.

"A work of Suetonius about the emperors of Rome. Do you enjoy the study of history, Mr. Veech?"

"To me, all history is the same: the victory of force." He crossed to the window. "What a clear view you have from here of Traitors Gate."

"How very subtle you are. Have you come again with your proposition?"

"I'm giving you a last chance to consider it. A few lines in your hand to Lord Digby, and you and your maid can go free. Or you'll go to trial, and Barlow's confession will condemn you both."

"Why have you not shown me this fulsome confession, as I asked you?"

Veech heaved a sigh. In truth, he had not got a single useful thing out of Barlow, and he had admired the man's fortitude. "You can hear it in court, my lady, if you wish."

"You must be pleased he's not alive to bear witness to the false-hoods you extracted from him."

"On the contrary, his death was tragic – gaol fever is an awful way to perish. And I worry about that sick maid of yours." Veech glanced around the cell. "*She* has no featherbed, no fireplace, no bowl and jug for washing, no close stool for her privy needs. And her cell is below ground and damp, and often floods."

"I have petitioned the governor of the Tower, who promised to bring her to my cell."

"He won't. He can't afford to spread the contagion among his wealthier inmates."

At last Lady Hallam looked up. Veech caught a shade of fear in her eyes, although none in her voice. "I demand to see my husband's counsel."

"He has declined your case, just as your husband has withdrawn his support from you. I told you: we found no proof against *him* in that house, other than of past immorality. And Barlow named you and you alone as Lord Digby's agent."

"Then I must be allowed some other counsel to advise me."

"Perhaps Mr. Draycott could offer his services."

"I've more respect for my close stool than for that spineless lackey of yours."

Veech wanted to laugh: it was an accurate description. "As I won't neglect to inform him. My lady, you may protect Beaumont at the cost of your own life, but is it fair that you should sacrifice your maid's? In better circumstances and with a physician to tend her, she might still have a hope."

"I will not succumb to bribery. And you are not king in this place. The governor has promised to—"

"I told you already, the governor won't abide by his promise," cut in Veech. "Why else has he kept you apart from the girl these three weeks, when you've begged every day for her to join you? The longer you hesitate, the worse for her, and her death will be on your conscience."

"If the governor will not bring her to me," said Lady Hallam, "I want to be moved to her cell."

"Do you, now," said Veech. "Well he might agree to *that*."

## II.

After a prodigious midday meal with the Beaumonts, Antonio retired to his chamber for a siesta to find Diego sitting on the bed, the wizard's bowl balanced on his lap. He had filled it with water and was intent upon the surface. "I warned you that thing is cursed," yelled Antonio, and smacked it to the floor. "Get rid of it, or I shall get rid of *you*."

"I understand your rage, Don Antonio," said Diego sympathetically. "You are a disappointed man. Shall I explain why?" He lowered his voice and began to count on his fingers. "One, you know as little about the true state of Lord Beaumont's finances as when we first got here. Two, you've failed to penetrate the Lady Elena's chilly indifference. No tears shed when you spoke of her mother's lingering death, and her brothers slain in the wars. As you said, it's as though she sliced out her own heart on quitting her native land. She and her eldest son are as similar in temperament as in looks – the opposite from his lordship, who wears his generous, honest heart on his sleeve. He's more Spanish, in that way, than either of them. Which brings me to *three*," went on Diego, still counting. "Like his son Thomas, he is blinded by his emotions – in the case of Thomas, pride, resentment, and greed, and in the case of his lordship, absolute devotion to his wife and to his eldest son. You can shout what you wish into his lordship's ear about the Lady Elena's past or Laurence's paternity and he will take no notice. If he came in upon you in the act of adultery with her, he would retreat blushing from the scene, and excuse it to himself as a moment of cousinly affection. And as to *four*: rather than being rabidly jealous of you, he relishes your company, which must be the ultimate insult."

Antonio flung himself down on the bed. "I refuse to admit defeat."

"Nor should you. As a matter of fact, I've made some unexpected progress on the issue of his lordship's finances." Diego bent and grabbed the bowl: an obvious challenge. Antonio ignored it and waited for him to continue. "In my conversations with the servants and the grooms, I have occasionally remarked that if I were his lordship I'd keep a portion of my wealth concealed from the enemy, and that there must be plenty of good hiding places about the estate."

"And what have the servants and grooms told you, monkey?"

"Not a word. Yesterday evening I was drinking beer in the stables with the grooms. All they would talk about was horse colic, and founder, and other such favourite subjects of theirs, so I got bored, and wandered out. As I neared the path that leads to the dovecote, I felt the effect of what I'd drunk, and stepped into the bushes. And as I was happily watering them, Lady Elena hurried along the path with a lantern, stealthy as a thief. The light disappeared – she was inside the dovecote. What could she want there, at past eleven o'clock, I had to wonder?"

"I trust you shook the last drops from your prick and followed her."

"Yes, I did, and when I looked in, she was on her knees digging at the earthen floor with a trowel. She lifted up a section, reached in her hand, and pulled out a small bag that she tucked into her skirt pocket. I had to hide in the bushes again as she prepared to leave, but as she had gone, I went back to inspect where she had been digging. She had foiled me: the door to the dovecote was stoutly padlocked."

Antonio whistled between his teeth. "*Madre de Dios*, they must be precious doves."

"There are others as precious to her ladyship under *this* roof." Diego stroked the rim of his bowl, meditatively. "The hardest to catch will be the tastiest, if you want vengeance."

"What a sin that would be," said Antonio, chuckling to himself. "How I wish we had with us our devout Jesuit, Fray Luis Iglesia, to hear my confession afterwards. But in any case, I am tempted. She's a fresh little bird, the wife of my Lorenzo."

## III.

The Royalists had spent a week recuperating in Worcester from their forced march, and then pushed towards Shrewsbury, in an attempt to lure Waller deeper into hostile territory and separate him further from

Essex's army. The King cherished hopes of support from Rupert, who was now in the north, and had written imploring his nephew to speed to the relief of York from Parliament's northern regiments and the Scots, but also to tidy matters up as fast as possible and come to his own aid. "His Royal Highness Prince Rupert must be like unto God: everywhere simultaneously," Digby commented to Laurence. Meanwhile, the Royalists were again low on supplies. Since Waller had not barred their line of retreat, they tailed back to Worcester, and the next day retraced their route through the Cotswolds, in the direction of Oxford.

By dusk on the sixteenth of June, they made camp around the village of Broadway, a short ride from Chipping Campden. Laurence requested leave for an overnight visit. Though he longed to see his father and Catherine, it was Lady Beaumont he needed most urgently to address.

He saw flame flickering by the old stone walls of the dovecote, as he dismounted and tethered his horse in a thicket of trees. He had sent the gatekeeper to forewarn her ladyship, and she was waiting for him, beckoning him into the dovecote like some sentinel guiding him into the netherworld, her shadow alarmingly magnified by the lantern that she held aloft. "Laurence, did you ride from Worcester? We heard His Majesty had escaped there."

"No, his army lies at Broadway." Laurence wrinkled his nose at the familiar, acrid smell of pigeon dung. "He's marching for Oxford to reunite his forces. I haven't much time: I'm due back in camp before dawn. Thank God I stopped at the gatehouse, or I wouldn't have known about your Spanish guests! Why didn't you write to tell me about them?"

"I *did* write, and sent Geoffrey to Oxford with my letter, but you had already left. In that letter I informed you we had yet worse to distress us." Lady Beaumont set her lantern down on the clay floor; illuminated from below, her features seemed to him as gaunt as Seward's. "On the very day our guests arrived, Elizabeth absconded. *She* is in Oxford, with that man Price."

Laurence now recalled Price's distant manner, and his courageous choice to stay in the city. "Damn him. And damn her for being
such a fool."

"Subsequently we received these." Lady Beaumont delved into
the pocket of her skirts and produced two letters, then held up the
lantern for him to read.

"Christ! At least he says they won't marry without your
permission."

"You must bring Elizabeth home, or she will be ruined. We had
to lie to Antonio that she had gone to be with friends in Chipping
Campden town. His lordship is heartsick."

"As I can well imagine – I'll do what I can." Laurence searched
for a way to broach the issue of her and de Zamora. "How is . . . your
cousin?" he said, at length.

"Antonio has not changed a whit. He fawns over his lordship and
the girls, and as I suspected, he is penniless. But he has had nothing
out of us, thus far, save his bed and board. Antonio is effusive in his
praise for you and Thomas. He talked of meeting you last month. He
claimed that immediately afterwards he was assaulted by thieves, and
then became gravely ill – hence his strange delay in visiting us. Can it
be true?"

"Who knows – he's forever vanishing and surfacing, and vanishing again. But I can guess why he delayed coming to Tom, and to me:
he must have been asking round about us, to find some way to play us
off against each other."

"Play you off? But . . . why?"

Silence descended, apart from the cooing of pigeons high above.
"Did you ever love him?" Laurence burst out. "Were you and he lovers?
Or did he . . . did he seduce you, before you were married?"

He felt as if he were shrinking beneath his mother's glare. "What
in heaven's name has he suggested to you, Laurence?"

"That . . . I am his son," answered Laurence, in a feeble voice.
"Am I?"

"Was he drunk?"

"No, far from it." Laurence spilt forth everything, like an evil vomit. Yet even as he spoke, trembling, of that night when a mutual desire had been illicitly slaked, he detected not a trace of shock, pain, or guilt in her expression. Instead, he saw only contempt.

"He is a sad character beneath pity," she said, at the end.

"He is *convinced* that I am his."

"He has probably lost his wits after too many blows to the head in battle. Or else his fabrications may be a form of inherited madness. Amazing that none of the Fuentes and de Capdavilas was born an idiot, given how they married into each other's families over the generations. The custom is yet more common among Spanish noble houses than it is here in England."

*Thank God there were no such deformities in our family*, de Zamora had said. Or were there? Laurence had himself questioned de Zamora's sanity. "Could you have married him, if your families had agreed?"

"They would *never* have agreed. My father abhorred him – that much of his story is true. And we were nearly as impoverished, on our side, after my father's death. I am ashamed to confess that my mother would not have accepted a Protestant foreigner for a son-in-law had she not been desperate for money. Naturally Antonio was envious of your father's wealth, and he was of the majority in Seville who deplored the match, though he pretended the opposite to your father."

"Might he have been intimate with you, without your knowing? Could he have come into your chamber and drugged you, or . . . accosted you while you slept?"

She began to laugh. "You *have* been misled, I presume by your adventures with my less reputable countrywomen. Virtue was so treasured a commodity in young ladies of my rank that I could not receive any male above the age of fifteen unless my mother's gentlewomen were inches from me. They guarded me and my sisters, day and night. Your father likened our courtship to besieging a fortress."

Laurence laughed also, picturing the young Englishman, hat in hand, scaling the ramparts of some formidable Andalusian castle to win his Spanish princess. But then, unexpectedly, his eyes stung with tears. "I thought that if the story was true, it would explain why you . . . why you and I have always been at odds."

Her face softened. "Your theory is more exciting than the truth, Laurence. Your wet nurse used to say that the first child is the most difficult, and you *were* difficult in character, impossible to discipline. Your father held the reins too loosely, and I could not tolerate his indulgence. Perhaps when you have children of your own, you will understand: it is only human to make mistakes. And we have both made mistakes, you and I."

"Yes," he admitted, "I know *I* have."

"Now," she recommenced, "I had wanted to deal with Antonio myself. But I am afraid that he is mad, and more dangerous than I had initially perceived. The Spanish Envoy said that he is being sought for in London, on a charge of murder – a hanging offence – and it appears that the Envoy is as anxious to be rid of him as we are. But I would prefer him banished to Spain. He has a wife and family, and he *is* my kin."

"He might leave voluntarily, for a sufficiently attractive reward. Not just money – something to flatter his pride. What is he most proud of?"

"He brags constantly about his glorious military record."

Laurence remembered how de Zamora had scorned his own less than glorious service in the Low Countries. "A commission from King Philip would do the trick. The Envoy might forge us a document and have it delivered to Chipping Campden, by a messenger with the proper credentials. Why not write to him tonight, and I'll take the letter with me to Oxford? All being well, he'll receive it within a week – there are regular diplomatic couriers travelling back and forth from Oxford to London."

"I shall write at once."

"I can wait here for you, to avoid another meeting with your guests."

Lady Beaumont picked up her lantern, and slipped her arm into his. The gesture astounded him. "They are abed in the south wing, Antonio with his nightly jug of wine," she said. "They are too far away to hear you come in through the stillroom door. And it would do your father such good to see you."

"I'd also like to see Catherine."

"She sleeps in Mary's chamber. I'll wake her, and send her to yours."

She held the lantern while Laurence fastened the padlock and tested it with a sharp tug. Then she led the way along the path through the kitchen garden. It was she who deserved a military commission, he thought; and how ironic that de Zamora's troublemaking should at last have brought them closer. He felt a giddy joy. With their old, bitter disputes behind them, it was as if every obstacle might be conquered and every wound healed in the family.

Catherine sat poised on the edge of the bed hugging her knees to her chest, her dark eyes following Laurence's movements as he undressed in the candlelight. "You were a long time with your father. What did you talk about?"

Laurence tossed his doublet on the floor and pulled his shirt over his head. "Oh, many things: the war, the house, Elizabeth, Mary, our Spanish guests – and you."

"I so wanted to tell them of my illness, but I knew I'd be safe from it if I wore my ring. I only fell sick because the ring had dropped from my finger."

"You mustn't worry, even if you fall sick again," he said, less persuaded of its protective powers.

She jumped down and whipped off her nightgown, as Juana had stripped before him in Pamplona when she had first seduced him; he shivered, watching her. But rather than take his hands to explore her skin, as Juana had done, Catherine investigated him with hers, running them along his neck to the muscles of his shoulders, pausing to stroke the depression from the musket ball; and next the older scar in his side. Impatiently he seized her hands. "Now it's my turn."

Lying next to her on the rumpled sheets, he inquired, "So what's your opinion of Don Antonio?"

She rolled onto her stomach and pushed away the tendrils of hair stuck to her damp forehead. "He builds a wall of noise to shield his true self, as the octopus blows ink in the water to confuse its enemies. And Diego spies on everyone. The servants are leery of him."

"They're right to be," said Laurence, as impressed by her aquatic metaphor as by her insight.

"The other day he caught *me* spying on him when he was by himself in Don Antonio's chamber. He was angry, but he didn't dare scold me."

"What was he doing?"

"Looking into a bowl."

Laurence frowned. "A silver bowl with an engraved rim?"

"Yes! How do you know?"

"It belongs to my friend Seward, who gave me your ring."

"Why does Diego have it?"

"He stole it."

"Did it also belong to the witch?"

"No – it was a gift to Seward from a man named Robert Fludd, who was his teacher in astrology, and . . . other arts. He believes it has magical properties."

Her eyes gleamed, and she nodded as if she understood. "Then I must steal it back for him."

"Are *you* a witch?" Laurence asked, half teasing. When she did not speak, he thought of Khadija, and the words nearly flew out of him: *or are you the fulfilment of a prophecy?* For Catherine had the name of a great queen, the daughter of Lorenzo de' Medici, who had ruled France as regent after the death of her unfaithful husband.

## IV.

From Broadway, the Royalists had proceeded to the market town of Witney, where His Majesty's Oxford forces marched out of the city to swell his ranks. "He must choose among three alternatives, Mr. Beaumont," Digby reported, after Council. "To stick by the Oxford defences, or venture into the neighbouring counties to play cat and mouse with Waller and Essex as he has been doing of late, or attempt to meet up with Prince Rupert."

"Which would leave the south to Waller and Essex," Laurence said.

No strategy offered the King a clear advantage, but in the end he chose cat and mouse, pressing over twenty miles northeast to occupy Buckingham on the twenty-second of June. It was a step into enemy territory, yet scouts established that Waller was lagging behind in Worcestershire and that Essex had continued westwards after his success in repulsing Prince Maurice's siege at Lyme, so the royal army was in no immediate threat of an attack. The King was restored to optimism, cheered by news that Her Majesty had been brought safely to bed in Exeter of a little girl, who would be christened Princess Henrietta in honour of her brave mother.

Long into the evening, Council debated further strategy, and when that session closed, Digby announced to Laurence, "Our impetuous Lord Wilmot has argued for a sudden strike on London, to cut short the war. What think you of that, sir?"

Laurence considered his response. He and Wilmot had agreed that the King would be wise to settle with Parliament rather than drag out the conflict; in itself, a potentially seditious proposition. Wilmot's strike would expose His Majesty again to capture, if the royal army were unsuccessful in breaching the capital's defences. Could Wilmot be contemplating a secret bargain with Parliament: peace terms, with the King delivered as hostage? Not only would it amount to treason, but given Wilmot's indiscreet mouth, it would be found out well before it could be executed. "Lord Wilmot is *too* impetuous, though I appreciate his desire to spare His Majesty's realm more bloodshed," Laurence said guardedly to Digby. "What's the King's view?"

"He would prefer to head north and join Prince Rupert, as soon as we have some tidings of the Prince's success in relieving our garrison at York. At any rate, sir, His Majesty wants advice from our Lords Commissioners and the Committee of our parliament in Oxford as to Lord Wilmot's scheme. I am to ride for Oxford tonight with Culpeper, and I should like you come with us."

"I'd be happy to, my lord." Laurence could dispatch his mother's letter to the Spanish Envoy, confront Price, and have a talk with Elizabeth, as a prelude to getting her home.

Digby hummed in his throat, studying Laurence. "If Lord Wilmot were to confide in you any ambitions that might run contrary to His Majesty's best interests in this war, I hope you would alert me, sir. I should take it as a betrayal – private *and* political – if you did not. And the King would think the same."

"The King can rest assured that Lord Wilmot always has his best interests at heart," Laurence replied.

Digby merely smiled.

## V.

Price dropped the bag of correspondence he had brought with him onto Digby's desk, and lit a taper. From his pocket, he rooted out a key and went to his lordship's strongbox. Digby had left funds there and Price needed money, not for himself, he reasoned, but for Elizabeth: less than three weeks of keeping her in Oxford had exhausted his slender reserves. And she was beginning to exhaust him. It had wounded her self-esteem to write that letter to her parents, and she stubbornly refused to return home, even though Price thought she might travel securely with an escort now that Waller and Essex had drawn off their armies. She alternated daily between sullen moodiness and clingy tearfulness, and her guardians were losing patience. "She thinks she's *Queen* Elizabeth," he had overheard Mrs. Connell complaining to Mrs. Giddens.

Price slid the key into the lock of the strongbox, then hastily withdrew it. Hooves were clattering along the street, now slowing as they neared his lordship's offices. Price went to look through the window. Dismounting were Digby and Culpeper, His Majesty's Master of the Rolls; and Beaumont, Quayle, more servants, and a party of guards. Beaumont came up first to the door, which Price ran forward to open, with a bright smile. "Beaumont, how unexpected."

Beaumont lunged across the threshold. "Where's my sister? Tell me, quick." Cowed by the menace in Beaumont's eyes, Price stammered the address. "Does Digby know she's here?" Price shook his head. "You'd better keep it that way," said Beaumont frigidly, and walked out.

Price saw him confer with Digby, mount, and ride off. Sweat broke over Price: one such glare from her brother and Elizabeth might weaken and confess who had planned the elopement.

"Mr. Price, at work so late of an evening?" Digby said, strolling in with Culpeper. "What dedication. Are my papers still intact?"

"Yes, my lord: I destroyed nothing. My lord, the courier gave me this a half hour ago, as I was at supper." Price showed him the bag. "I would have sent it on to you tomorrow morning. Such luck that you should arrive beforehand."

"Pardon me, Culpeper." Digby unfastened the bag with nervous hands and emptied it onto his desk. Price shared his relief: no sodden packages. Eagerly Digby selected one of the letters and ripped apart the seal. "This is from Violet's wife." As he read on, he began to breathe heavily as if climbing a steep hill. "The wretch," he cried. "The wretch has sold her to Parliament."

Price and Culpeper exchanged looks. "My lord," said Price, "who has Violet—"

"Not Violet, *Hallam!*" screeched Digby, crumpling the letter in his fist. "He has saved himself, at Isabella's expense."

## VI.

"Who's the black man?" whimpered the little boy, burying his face in his mother's skirts.

The two ladies regarded Laurence fearfully as he stood in the doorway, until Elizabeth clambered over the mattresses and clothes and pots and baggage, and threw herself into his arms. "This is my eldest brother, Mr. Laurence Beaumont," she said to her companions. "May I present the Mrs. Connell and Giddens."

He bowed, reluctant to enter. "Would you excuse us, ladies: my sister and I haven't seen each other in some time."

Elizabeth had lost weight, he noticed, and her pallor suggested not just a poor diet and lack of sleep but severe strain. "When did you arrive?" she asked, in a maidenly tone most unlike her normal voice, after he had walked her out and into the street.

"Tonight, with Lord Digby. What's the truth about you and Price?"

"Laurence," she began, "you may be under the misapprehension that it was Mr. Price's idea for me to—"

"I don't want to hear again what I read in your letters to our parents."

"You were at Chipping Campden?"

"For a short while, last week."

"Are they . . . are they so very angry?"

"They're more distressed than angry. It's quite obvious Price organised your journey here, so please don't lie to me about that. The scouts who accompanied you are not his servants but those of the Secretary of State, and to assist you was a dereliction of their duty. Price will be in trouble if Digby learns of it. How has he treated you?"

"With the most scrupulous respect," Elizabeth said. "On all of his visits, the ladies have been in the room, to ensure utter propriety. My honour and reputation are perfectly intact."

Laurence smiled at her use of superlatives. "I'm *enormously* comforted to hear that. But have you asked yourself why?"

"He hopes to marry me, with his lordship's consent."

"If so, he has rather blotted *his* honour and reputation, wouldn't you say?" Elizabeth said nothing. "Have you told him how much you're worth as a bride?"

"Yes, and he has declared that he would wed me without my portion. He praised you for setting the example, when you married Catherine."

"He has a lot of gall. I can't condemn him for his lies, since I resorted to a lie to have Catherine as my bride. But I wish *you* wouldn't lie, to protect him. I think he invited you to Oxford and then realised what he might lose as a result – a thousand pounds and his brilliant career with Lord Digby. I'm not sure which would cause him the most anguish."

"How dare you accuse him of such base motives," she cried. "I will not listen to another word against him." Before she could turn on her heel, Laurence snatched her by the wrists. She squirmed in his grip. "Let go of me," she shouted, at which a pair of beribboned gallants passing by halted in their tracks.

"Please behave," Laurence said, under his breath, "or one of these gay cavaliers might mistake our little quarrel for something else, and issue me a challenge. Liz, I know why you ran away. I did the same when I was a few years older than you. But there's a difference between us."

"You were escaping a marriage, while *I* was doing the very opposite."

"That's not what I mean. You're a woman. You'll pay far more in the eyes of the world for your recklessness in love."

"You taught me to damn the world."

"I never held myself up as an example anyone should follow." He released her wrists. "And while it may appear to you the height of hypocrisy, it's my duty as your brother to get you home. A shame you can't travel with us the day after tomorrow, when Lord Digby's mission ends. Chipping Campden is on our way back to rejoin the King. We might have taken you there."

Elizabeth's defiance ebbed. "Is Mr. Price to quit Oxford with you?"

"He is."

"Then I see no sense in staying. Why can't I come with you?"

"Digby will ask inconvenient questions. If you choose to damn the world, you should be ready for the consequences, and this whole affair doesn't look well on you. The less gossip about your honour and reputation the better, and Digby adores gossip."

She hung her head; it was too dark for Laurence to tell whether she was sulking, penitent, or simply unhappy. "Then how *can* I get home?"

"I'll have to beg Governor Aston for the loan of his coach and a guard, although it goes against my nature to ask such personal favours," he said. "You'll hear from me tomorrow. Oh – and there's a surprise waiting for you at our house: our mother's cousin is visiting, from Seville. I'd advise you to beware of him. He knows only that you were with friends in Chipping Campden town, and that's *all* he must know."

"A Spanish cousin?" exclaimed Elizabeth. "How remarkable, Laurence."

"Yes it is," he agreed, leading her towards her door. "And be prepared: he looks just like me, and he's an even bigger scoundrel than Price."


**VII.**

Upstairs in his chamber with the curtains drawn close around his bed, Digby surrendered to tears; he had not wept so copiously since he was a child. "Isabella, my darling," he blubbered, banging his fists against the pillow until goose feathers drifted out like an unseasonable snow, "why did I marry you to that cowardly cripple? I will not let you die, my dearest girl! I swear to you, I shall have you rescued!"

At length, he felt purged. He washed his face, picked the feathers out of his hair, and straightened his clothing. "A plan," he said, aloud.

"We shall think of a plan." He went down and called for Quayle, who beetled in through the front door. "Has Mr. Beaumont returned yet from his mysterious errand?"

"Yes, my lord," said Quayle, the corners of his mouth twitching. "He and Mr. Price are out in the street."

"Summon them at once."

"I can try, but they might not listen."

"Why is that?"

"They are fighting, my lord."

Digby stalked to the door and unlatched it. His guards were ranged in a circle, together with a couple of nightwatchmen wielding their lanterns; they wore broad grins, though they sobered on seeing him and fell back. Beaumont stood in the middle, his arms hanging loose by his sides, looking down disdainfully at Price, who lay sprawled on the cobblestones, clutching his hands to his face. "Gentlemen," Digby said, "what is this about?"

"I apologise, my lord." Beaumont bent and dragged up Price by the shoulders of his coat; his mouth and nose drooled blood, and his head lolled upon his chest. Beaumont half carried him inside and dumped him into a chair by the door, where he sat moaning lightly, while Beaumont wiped his hands on his doublet and inspected his knuckles. "We had a score to settle."

"And has it been settled?"

"For the moment."

"Then if you are not too weary after your exertions, you might peruse a communication from Violet's wife." Beaumont accepted the crumpled letter and read it as though the contents were no news to him. "What think you of Isabella's chances, sir?" Digby asked.

"She stands accused of a high crime, my lord: a miniature Gunpowder Plot."

"Tell me they would not send her to the block."

"I doubt that – the block is reserved for royalty and peers. Her husband was in trade and his knighthood only recently bestowed.

She'd probably get a woman's sentence for treason: to be burnt at the stake with a chain around her neck – though as often is the case, the executioner might do her the mercy of strangling her with it, before setting her on fire." Beaumont smiled acidly. "But, remember, my lord: she's no use to Veech dead."

## VIII.

Draycott swatted away flies; the stench of human waste was overpowering in the dark, airless little cell. From a high window, a sliver of sunshine penetrated. Lady Isabella was sitting on the floor, her hair tangled over her face, hands resting in her lap. Beside her, under a filthy sheet, lay a body. There was no furniture in the cell, not even a bucket for a privy, just a pile of dirty straw in one corner. More flies had landed in a black cloud over the body, and swarmed indiscriminately upon Lady Isabella.

"My lady," he said, *"why* did you ask to be moved here?"

"To be with Lucy." Her voice sounded gritty and thick, as if she had swallowed a mixture of sand and glue.

"When did she . . . ?"

"The night before last. Veech said she could stay here and rot. I told him I was grateful for her company. At least he had not employed violence on her, as he must have on Barlow."

Draycott sank down next to her. "Mr. St. John has appointed me to represent you. I could not visit you until now. I had to keep Veech ignorant of my loyalty to you, as he still is. But if I'm to help you, you must be honest with me."

"It was *your* small lie that shook my trust, and brought on disaster. After you said the packet was at your house, I felt something inside your doublet as we embraced."

He sighed, thinking of what had happened next. "Why didn't you destroy the evidence while I slept?"

"I had to test you. I felt sure you would tell me, in the morning. And I was right."

"You might have told me then what *you* had done."

"You were safer not knowing, good man that you are, and I was already waiting for someone to collect my copy. Although Beaumont had warned me not to use that particular courier, I had no alternative. I did not expect Barlow, and he came far later than I'd hoped." She studied Draycott through her tangled veil. "Now it is too late for *me*, sir."

Gently he pushed aside her hair, and saw the blotchiness in her skin, and the reddened sores around her nose and mouth. He remembered her sleek and elegant, admiring the Devil in the tapestry: *Satan has such a smile upon his face, like a cat that has stolen the cream.* All that remained of her elegance was the diamond on her finger. "I've seen the depositions against you," he said. "Barlow never betrayed you, and that copy you made has gone missing. The only sound testimony is from your husband."

"Who in exchange for *his* betrayal will be allowed retirement in The Hague," she added, as if amused.

"St. John and Veech are sending me to Lord Digby with a final offer: your sentence will be stayed and you will go free if Laurence Beaumont returns at once with me to London and submits to investigation by Parliament. And they want me to take Digby a letter from you pleading him to comply with these terms."

"Had I wished to save myself by sacrificing Beaumont, I could have done so on the day of my arrest."

"My lady, there is another way out." Draycott spoke yet more quietly. "As Veech believes I'm in his power, you must now let Veech think he has defeated you. Do as you're asked. Before I leave, I'll have him move you to your former cell and bring in a physician. It's in his interest that you regain your health. Then I'll need some token from you to persuade Digby and Beaumont to trust me, so that we can work together upon your rescue."

"None of you can perform miracles, Mr. Draycott."

"We might. Please, we must try."

She was silent for a while; and he feared she had lost all hope. "Bring me the book," she said, finally. "You know which one I mean."

He found Veech leaning against a wall at the entrance to the Tower Keep, squinting up at the ravens as they circled the battlements. "She has agreed to write," he said.

"Well done, sir. Are you hoping she'll be your mistress, once Beaumont is dead?" Veech now regarded him, pityingly. "Don't be a slave to your cock."

"I suppose, unlike most men, you are incapable of such natural feeling," Draycott spat back.

A strange mania flared in Veech's eyes. "What have you been told about me?" Draycott frowned, bewildered. "Answer me!" Veech slammed him to the wall, pinning his throat with an iron hand. He dug the other hand beneath Draycott's coat, in between his legs, and fastened around his genitals. "Answer me, sir: what have you been told?"

"Nothing," gasped Draycott. "I swear to God."

Veech let go of him, and the mania faded into a placid smile. "You're right. I'm not like most men. I don't share their weakness."

## IX.

Wilmot's bold proposal won no support in Oxford, and when Laurence returned to Buckingham with Lord Digby's party, the royal camp was in a febrile state: Waller had passed through Chipping Norton, about twenty-five miles away, and battle was imminent. Over the next few days, both armies manoeuvred closer to each other on the banks of the River Cherwell, seeking the most advantageous terrain from which to attack. Around ten o'clock on a rainy, foggy late June morning, His Majesty's forces assembled to the east of Banbury; and as sun peeped through the dispersing clouds, they saw the enemy a mile from them, on the opposite riverbank. Both armies then lumbered off in a race to secure a hill on the west side of Banbury. Waller seized it first, and in the afternoon sent out troops to skirmish tentatively with some Royalist Foot.

During the futile action, one of Laurence's scouts caught a musket ball in the stomach; he was the youth who had kept patient watch at St. Martin's Church on the night of the meeting with de Zamora. He died before the surgeon could touch him; Laurence was holding his hand.

The next day at dawn, His Majesty's forces mustered to venture north towards Daventry, to try to tempt Waller from his advantageous high ground. Trumpets and drums sounded as the army drew up in three divisions, and by eight o'clock it marched out through the open countryside. Forth commanded the vanguard with most of the baggage trains and some artillery, while the King, Prince Charles, and His Majesty's civilian advisors were sheltered in the front centre of the main body, with a second detachment of artillery for their protection. Behind them rode the Royal Lifeguard under the King's cousin, Sir Bernard Stuart, and Wilmot, who was strategically located to receive orders from His Majesty and pass them back to the rearguard, where his Horse was positioned with the cavalry of the Earls of Cleveland and Northampton, and about a thousand more troops and guns.

Frustrated to be stuck by Digby's side, Laurence had asked to go ahead of the vanguard with Price and most of the scouts. "You would expose yourself unnecessarily to fire," said Digby. "I do not wish you to meet the same end as that boy yesterday."

"But, my lord, I can't direct the scouts from here," Laurence argued; the vanguard would be the first part of the army to strike across the Cherwell at a place named Hay's Bridge. Only a few scouts had stayed with the rearguard, to maintain communication between the tail end of the beast and its brain, at the centre, and to survey the two other bridges that Waller might cross, one at the village of Cropredy to the northwest, and another to the south.

Some hours into the march under increasingly hot sun, the troops became restive: on the far bank not more than a couple of miles distant, the enemy was moving parallel to them in full view. In his years of military experience, Laurence had never seen the like: a slim channel of water separated the two behemoths, and each side bristled weapons, yet not a shot had been fired. Forth rode up to confer with His Majesty, and soon after a party of dragoons split from the main column and headed northeast. Laurence could predict their aim: to safeguard the bridge at Cropredy, in case Waller used it to mount an attack on the Royalist flank.

As the dragoons disappeared from view, Price came galloping towards the King's section and reined in on his chestnut mare; he was hatless, his face streaked with sweat. "Your Majesty, the scouts have intelligence that three hundred rebel Horse are on their way south to swell the Parliamentary ranks. They'll cross the river up at Hay's Bridge if we don't get there first."

Immediately the King issued orders for the Royalist vanguard and midsection to push forward and intercept the oncoming force. Laurence could envisage the loss of more scouts; Price had dashed back to the front line, anticipating his concern. Now all eyes were ahead, and the Foot and artillery wagons were straining to keep pace with the cavalry.

By midday they had passed the dragoons at Cropredy Bridge. There was no sign of the reinforcements that Price had reported, and Laurence thought that the vanguard must be safely over Hay's Bridge. When his section approached, he saw the bridge was no wider than a coach, but the river ran shallow beneath; Horse and Foot could easily ford it, while the artillery rolled across the narrow structure.

Around one o'clock, the front ranks of His Majesty's division had crossed and were reforming on the other side of the bank when cannon shot roared out from the direction of Cropredy Bridge. Waller had launched a surprise assault, and the dragoons would be no match for his artillery.

A hand seized Laurence's shoulder, and Wilmot yelled in his ear, "Beaumont, you've a speedy horse – go back and find Cleveland, and tell him to draw up for battle."

"Mr. Beaumont, you are to stay here," Digby countered, glaring at Wilmot.

"My lord, this is no time for a dispute – we're about to fight," Laurence told Digby. "I must obey Lord Wilmot's command."

"You shall obey *me*, sir," shouted Digby. "How dare you defy my authority?"

Laurence dared. Steering his horse out of rank, he splashed it again through the water, giving it free rein. Almost at once he saw black smoke billowing from Cropredy Bridge. When he got nearer, rebel Foot were pouring over it, while a mass of cavalry forded the river, rapidly outstripping the straggling hind section of the King's troops and chasing them north. The Royalist rearguard was nowhere in sight, and Waller's forces would be neatly positioned to cut it off from the body of the army, although Laurence judged that the rebels' artillery would take a while to set up before the guns could fire. He heard the thunder of cavalry ahead, and loud voices bellowing out the Royalist field word, "Hand and sword!" Too late to deliver any orders: Cleveland's Horse was about to charge the enemy Foot. But his right flank would be vulnerable.

Crouched low in the saddle, wary of stray shot, Laurence wove a cautious path back towards Hay's Bridge. Rebel troops were still on the offensive around it, though they could not pass over the narrow bridge: some quick-witted Royalist musketeers had barricaded it with an upturned carriage and were sniping at them from behind this cover. Dodging the melee, Laurence swam his horse through deeper water a little higher up, and scrambled up the bank. Soaked and breathless, he trotted through the ranks towards Wilmot and the King, who were viewing the scene anxiously, His Majesty with the benefit of a perspective glass.

"Those are not W-waller's colours," he exclaimed.

"No, Your Majesty: they're Lieutenant General Middleton's – he's a Scots veteran," Wilmot said, shading his eyes with one hand. "Waller himself may be engaged to the south of us. What news, Beaumont?"

"Cleveland needs reinforcements. He must have bypassed most of the rearguard – I couldn't see Northampton's men."

"We'll send in Sir Bernard with a detachment from the Lifeguard. He'll take the right flank, and my cavalry will take the left."

"You'll have to find your cavalry first," Laurence warned him. "I think they've dropped over a mile behind."

"We'll find them together. What the devil does he want now," Wilmot muttered; Digby was pressing his horse up to bar their path.

"Mr. Beaumont," Digby said, "I have had enough of your disobedience. You are to remain here with me."

Wilmot addressed the King. "Have I Your Majesty's permission to enlist Mr. Beaumont for the day?"

"He is needed more urgently to direct his scouts, Your Majesty – it is a waste to send him into battle," Digby objected shrilly.

The King glanced from Digby to Wilmot, and then to Laurence, who said, "It would be my privilege to ride with the Lieutenant General, Your Majesty."

"Then you may," said the King, "and God speed."

Laurence cantered off with Wilmot, followed by his Lifeguard. At the riverbank, Sir Bernard Stuart was assembling about a hundred of his Horse, leaving a reserve for another sortie if it were necessary. Wilmot bawled encouragement at him as they put spurs to their mounts and blasted past. Once across the river, they skirted Cleveland's Horse, which was now in stiff fighting with Middleton's; the rebel guns still had not organized to fire, Laurence noticed, and many of the Foot were scattered hither and thither, wasting shot ineffectively.

"Where's that goddamned regiment," growled Wilmot, a mile further on.

At last Laurence spotted a scout racing towards them. "Waller drove into us from the southern bridge," the boy said, reining in. "Northampton has the edge on him, my lord, but your Horse is in the thick of the action."

An attack on two sides, like a pincer, Laurence thought admiringly: Waller was an experienced strategist.

"Nothing for it, then," Wilmot said to his men. "We must do what we can by ourselves."

When they raced back to the field, Sir Bernard's Lifeguard had already achieved its goal: some of the rebels had retreated in broken formation to Cropredy Bridge. Cleveland had withdrawn his Horse and was making a stand in preparation for a second charge. Facing him were more of Middleton's Horse and knots of Foot loading their muskets behind tall hedgerows.

"Hand and sword!" roared Wilmot, urging his men on, as Cleveland's began to advance.

At a swift canter, they locked in combat with the enemy. Laurence struck at the thigh of the nearest rebel horseman; his blade sliced through, and the man lost his seat, to be trampled by his own mount. Another pointed his pistol at Laurence's face, but before he could fire, Laurence hacked at his forearm, and he dropped his weapon to clutch his bloodied sleeve. Deafened by a close shot, Laurence beheld Wilmot swaying in the saddle, also gripping his arm, encircled by Middleton's troops who knew they had a valuable prisoner. A young officer wearing the Royal Lifeguard's colours dived in to snatch Wilmot's bridle, and Laurence grabbed his pistol from its holster to fire on a trooper behind Wilmot. Red spouted from the man's forehead, and he crashed to the ground. Wilmot was free, though injured.

"Beaumont, to your left!" he cried.

Laurence saw a flash of steel: an infantryman's tuck, not an inch from him. He brushed aside the weapon with his own. Rather than pierce him, the sword arced and sank partway into the glossy breast of his Arab stallion, which screamed in pain, rearing and plunging; Laurence nearly slipped from his saddle as he reached down to withdraw the blade. The infantryman was staggering back to avoid the horse's flailing hooves. Laurence had a clear target. He righted himself, tore out his other pistol, calculated his aim, and blew a shot between the man's eyes.

**X.**

Still smarting from his humiliation, Digby had watched Wilmot's near capture and regretted that he was not taken hostage. The King had brightened, viewing the subsequent rout: Cleveland's second charge, bolstered by Stuart and Wilmot, was wreaking havoc on the enemy Horse and Foot. More than ten pieces of cannon had been left on the field as they bolted for Cropredy Bridge; they had even deserted their Master of Ordnance, who was instantly surrounded, and lifted his arms in a gesture of surrender. The Royalists attempted to recapture the bridge, but the Parliamentary guns stalled their advance, allowing most of Middleton's forces to escape. Opposite the bridge, at a distance from the gunfire, Sir Bernard Stuart had reassembled his cavalry. Cleveland's men were starting to round up prisoners, and wounded from both armies; most of the dead were enemy cannoniers.

"Your Majesty, did you hear the rebels' field word today: 'Victory without quarter'?" asked Digby.

"*They* shall have quarter," said the King, "once we have command of the bridge, and Waller sues for terms."

Later in the afternoon, Digby bade Quayle hand him his timepiece: three of the clock, and already the King's army had reunited in the field with few losses. His commanding officers now gathered about him to debate a renewed assault. Digby saw Wilmot gallop up, the picture of martial triumph, his coat torn and bloodstained, a sling about one arm, and the other hand bandaged.

"My lord, what a lucky day for you," Digby remarked.

"I was rescued twice in the second charge, thanks to some brave fellows," Wilmot said. "That boy Howard from the Royal Lifeguard deserves a knighthood: eighteen years old, and he fought like a gladiator when I was surrounded the last time. And I have our friend Beaumont to thank, also – and His Majesty, for permitting Beaumont to ride with me. It must have vexed you, my lord, to miss all of the action."

"And you must be in *excruciating* pain, my lord, from your injuries."

"They're scratches, as compared to some of my old battle wounds."

"I am immensely gladdened to hear that. Where *is* Mr. Beaumont?"

"He's tending to that stallion of his – it was gashed in the breast. He had a close shave himself in the final charge."

"Tell him to come to me," Digby told Quayle.

"Leave him be," Wilmot said, in such a threatening tone that he provoked gasps from the nearest officers.

Digby plucked off a glove, then hesitated. The occasion was not right; they would duel another day. "My lord," he said, "at the banquet held in Oxford to celebrate our victory at Marlborough, in December of '42, you accused me of trying to steal Mr. Beaumont away from you. He said he had no owner that he knew of. He was wrong. He answered to Lord Falkland then. And now he answers to me. By the bye," Digby murmured, "you have been heard to declare that His Majesty cannot win this war, and that a settlement should be negotiated with my Lord Essex to end it."

"Many of us feared defeat before the King slipped out of Oxford."

"I'd no more submit to Essex than would His Majesty."

Wilmot laughed in his face. "If you wish to talk so valiantly, my lord, you shouldn't have resigned your military commission last year. You didn't stake your life in the field today, as I did. And your pygmy barbs can't hurt me. I can take Beaumont from you at the drop of a hat. Just ask him where *his* loyalties lie."

## XI.

"I hope to God this works," Laurence said to Price. He had rinsed the stallion's wound with a solution of vinegar and water, and was now smearing on a remedy of Jacob's: a poultice of mashed-up stinging nettles and ground willow bark. "Price, were the scouts sure of their information about the enemy reinforcements? You should have dispatched them again to confirm it: three hundred rebel cavalry can't vanish into thin air."

"I know," said Price, in a sheepish voice. "I was so confused that I forgot. I might have cost us the battle."

Laurence eyed him coolly. "Don't exaggerate your own importance. Send the boys north tonight, to see what they can find out."

"Mr. Beaumont! Mr. Price!" Quayle was riding towards them from the main camp. "His lordship wishes to speak with you."

Laurence gave his stallion's nose a last affectionate caress, wondering what punishment Digby had devised for him. He and Price went with Quayle, past a smaller, roped-off section of the field crowded with enemy prisoners. Some were pleading for their wounds to be dressed, yet the field surgeons would only come to them after the Royalist injured had received care, by which time more dead would be heaped upon the pile of naked corpses.

"Sorry buggers," jeered Price.

Quayle led them to a tent where Digby was sitting on a travelling coffer, reading a thick volume: a Bible. He looked up and smiled. "Gentlemen, we may have another fight on our hands tomorrow. Waller remains camped on the other side of the river, and he has declined His Majesty's offer of grace and pardon if he and his officers and soldiers would lay down their arms. He claims that he cannot negotiate without Parliament's blessing."

"I was unaware of the offer, my lord," Laurence said.

"You were distracted from events while nursing your horse. I trust it will recover. Those Arabians are hardy beasts. And I must congratulate you both, sirs, on your conduct today. His Majesty made special note of your gallant rescue of Lord Wilmot, Mr. Beaumont. I acknowledge my error, in trying to prevent you from taking to the field. If we engage once more in the morning, I shall be pleased to put you again at Lord Wilmot's disposal."

"I thank you, my lord."

"Oh, you shall soon repay me, sir," Digby told him.

———

There was no action, and throughout the next day, both armies held their ground. At an open-air ceremony of thanksgiving, the King knighted several officers, among them young Robert Howard, for his part in Wilmot's rescue. Then around six o'clock, Price rushed in with intelligence confirmed by several sources: about four and a half thousand Parliamentary troops from London had occupied Buckingham and were aiming to join up with Waller. At this, the King drew off his army, crossed over the Cherwell, and marched for the Cotswolds, where he could await news from the north of Prince Rupert's progress.

On the second of July, the Royalists established their camp on the rolling hills by Moreton-in-Marsh, a bare six miles from Chipping Campden. Laurence was pondering whether to ask Digby's leave for a quick visit, until Digby announced to him, "Essex and Waller claimed that they could not respond to His Majesty's overtures without the agreement of Westminster. His Majesty is therefore sending a message of peace and good faith, and terms of pardon, to the rebel Parliament. Monsieur Sabron, the French agent, is to deliver it, and you shall travel with him. You will be protected from arrest on the way by his diplomatic credentials, and in London you will be as immune, lodged with him at the French embassy. I believe you know what you must accomplish for me, while you are in the capital. Save her, sir."

"My lord, I'll do everything I can, but please may I first say goodbye to my family?" Laurence begged, knowing how little protection the French ambassador would afford him. "It may be our farewell."

"No, sir. Monsieur Sabron sets out today for Oxford, where he will rest overnight at Governor Aston's house before carrying on to London. Your order is to accompany him. And you are not to discuss our business with him or with any officials at the embassy – or with *anyone*," Digby added, his face solemn and unyielding, rather like the King's. "I cannot have His Majesty hearing of it. He would accuse me of wasting my best agent on a hopeless mission of rescue. If he does hear, after the fact, I shall insist that you engaged alone on it and that I was unaware of your intentions. You are on your own, although I'll provide you with funds, from my pocket. Now go, sir, and make your-self ready."

Laurence considered writing to Lord Beaumont, yet what would he say about a venture that even Digby knew was all but hope-less? He thought of Catherine; he could not tell her, either, that he was about to risk his life for the woman he still loved, above her. Nor could he tell her that the faint prospect of seeing Isabella again filled him with longing.

## XII.

Stretched out on his back amid tall, thick grass, Tom could hear the echo of fire from the battlefield. If he turned his head in that direction, he glimpsed sporadic, dazzling little explosions; the other direction, in contrast, seemed an impenetrable darkness. He was vaguely aware of whispering around him, and furtive rustling noises. He nearly called out: he could not be the only man hiding here, of the thousands who had fled, Royalists, and men from the Scots and Parliament forces alike. But he was unarmed and defenceless. Who might come, if he raised his voice?

Tom closed his eyes, and tried to remember how he had been shot. It had all been such a chaos. When Rupert had sounded the order to withdraw, Tom had ignored it. Never had they caved to the enemy. One charge would win the day; his idol could not be van-quished. Yet everywhere around him had been a swarm of men, cavalry wheeling their horses about and infantry stumbling through the muck, over dead and wounded; and he had no choice but to follow. He had jerked so violently at his reins that his mount bucked and threw him, and joined the stampede. Struggling to his feet, he had seen Smith gallop to his aid and reach out a hand to pull him up behind. Tom had grasped it just as a musket ball skimmed past, effortlessly splattering apart Smith's face. Tom had stared at the gobbets of flesh and bone, and the singed hair on Smith's skull. Then out of instinct he had thrust Smith forwards and leapt into the saddle, determined to carry his friend from the field. The body was impossibly awkward, sliding and bumping against the horse's neck and breast; in the end, Tom had heaved it to the ground. Had he waited a fraction longer, the next ball, from a pistol, would have ploughed into Smith's right thigh and not his. The searing pain had torn through his muscle and spread, as if along a fuse, into his groin and lower spine. All he could do was cling to the animal's mane as it chased after the panicked hordes. He must have tumbled a second time to the ground, because he could not recollect anything else, until a few moments ago.

Tom pressed his fingertips gingerly to his head and felt no contusions; it was the bleeding and the shock that had knocked him out. He rolled onto his left hip and peered down at the ragged, oozing hole in his thigh. The pain had dulled, and his leg was tremendously heavy and stiff. Wrestling off the sash that Adam had tied proudly across his breastplate as they had prepared to ride into action, he bound the fabric over his wound, knotted it, and lay back once more, his sweating brow cooled by the breeze rippling through the grasses. He wanted to sleep. Footsteps, muttered talk, and the slow thud of hooves jolted him awake again. In the moonlight he distinguished clumps of figures, some leading horses. Two separated and walked towards him: they were bare-headed, and their faces must have been black with smoke; as they approached he could see only the whites of the eyes. "Tom?"

"Ingram?" Tom still could not recognise his brother-in-law's features beneath the grime, but he knew the voice. "How did you find me?"

The other man was Adam, who started to cry, in great choking gulps. 'Thank God you're alive, sir."

"We've been searching at least an hour for you in the moors." Ingram squatted beside Tom. "Where are you hurt?"

"I took a ball in the thigh, from a pistol," Tom said, wishing Adam would be quiet. "Did the Prince charge again? Did we rout the enemy?"

"They routed us. It was a defeat," added Ingram, unnecessarily.

"The Prince wasn't captured?"

"No, he's gathering what remains of his cavalry to press on to York, where we're to seek refuge. There are lots of us hereabouts. But we have to move – those of us who are able."

"Who's left on the field?"

"Newcastle's Whitecoats. They've refused to surrender, though they're out of ammunition. They'll be slain to the last man, unless Parliament shows them mercy."

"Oh Christ. Smith is dead."

"And Curtis. I'm sorry, Tom."

"Why say you're sorry? You always hated them both."

"It's no time to argue," Ingram said impatiently. "Adam, help me." He and Adam gripped Tom under either arm, and hoisted him into a sitting position. "You must stand on your good leg, and we'll put you on the horse. When we get to York, I'll fetch you a surgeon."

The pain flared in Tom's thigh and rage swept over him, as in childhood when he and Laurence would play games together, and he would be about to lose. The odds were unfair and he did not care to play on. "Leave me to die, Ingram. I'll die all the same, if they have to cut off my leg."

"Don't be a fool: you have Mary to live for, and your child."

They attempted to lift him onto his sound leg, but he howled and wrested himself free. "Go, both of you."

"Please, sir, please," sobbed Adam, "don't give up hope. I'll take you to Chipping Campden, same as Master Laurence did for Mr. Ingram after the fight at Edgehill, when he broke his leg."

Tom almost laughed. "Edgehill was a stone's throw from home. We're hundreds of miles away."

Ingram snatched Tom roughly by the front of his collar. "I never thought you were a coward. Now put your arms round my neck, and stand up, God damn you."

"Everything's finished, everything," Tom mumbled; but he gritted his teeth, and obeyed.

# Part Four

England and Spain, July–September 1644

# CHAPTER SIXTEEN

## I.

**M**onsieur Sabron resembled to Laurence an intelligent ferret, with his pointed nose and shrewd, humorous eyes. Rather than talk of war and politics on the road, they discussed French and English mores, Sabron's estate in Gascony, and horseflesh. Sabron commented admiringly on the two mounts Laurence had brought with him: Pembroke's, and the Arab stallion. "What a waste to ride that beautiful creature into battle," Sabron remarked of the Arab, and Laurence agreed; he had already decided to entrust it to Seward's care.

When they arrived in Oxford, he left Sabron at Governor Aston's house, declining to stay there overnight, saying that he would rejoin the diplomatic party in the morning. The more he knew Aston the more he disliked the man, who reminded him of Catherine's father; and it annoyed him to be in Aston's debt for conveying Elizabeth home. He rode the thirteen miles to Clarke's house, where he discovered Seward and Clarke in far better spirits than on those last days of May when Oxford had verged upon disaster. Unlike the discreet Sabron, they both peppered him with questions as they sat together after an evening meal in Clarke's hospitable front room.

"The King's fortunes have improved," Clarke observed, of the battle at Cropredy Bridge, and His Majesty's peace overtures to Westminster. "What will he do now?"

"That will depend on Prince Rupert's fortunes," Laurence said. "A victory over the Scots and Generals Fairfax and Manchester could swing the balance of the war, and will certainly determine the King's strategy in the south. If he retreats his forces to Oxford, he could still be trapped into a siege. Waller's army is depleted but not broken, and he's been granted reinforcements by Parliament. And Essex is a threat to the Queen in the southwest: she and her child could become his hostages."

Seward was peering at Laurence keenly through his thick spectacles. "Why should Lord Digby ask *you* to go with Monsieur Sabron to London?"

"He has a private business he wants me to settle with the French ambassador," Laurence replied, which satisfied Clarke; but not Seward, he could tell.

Once Clarke had lumbered up to bed, Seward invited Laurence out to the kitchen garden, where rows of vegetables and herbs were sprouting their summery green leaves. "Let's have the truth, Beaumont," he said as he filled his pipe.

Laurence explained about Veech's most recent package of the hand, and Isabella's arrest; and how he had fought by Wilmot's side in battle, angering Digby; and his order from Digby.

"I am amazed at his lordship sending you on such a fool's mission. The moment you quit the French embassy, you will be seized by Veech. And what is the chance that Lady Hallam would be condemned, even on her husband's evidence?"

"Digby can't take that chance, and nor can I."

"Have you any idea how to accomplish this impossible task?"

"Not as yet. If only I could rely on Barlow for help. Seward, you didn't happen to bring with you any of your sleeping draught?"

"Yes, as it happens."

"And . . . the witch's poison?"

Seward lit his pipe and exhaled a violent puff of smoke. "I've never used that particular receipt. It would require some time to find the ingredients and to distil."

"It was just a thought," Laurence said gloomily.

"Any news from home?" asked Seward, in a gentler voice.

Laurence told him about Catherine's illness and her belief in the powers of her ring; and about the Spaniards, and his revelatory conversation with Lady Beaumont. "We may have opened a fresh chapter between us. To borrow one of Ingram's favourite sayings, there's a silver lining to every cloud."

"So there is. And you must have no more doubts as to your paternity."

Laurence smiled; a hint of doubt remained. "We have to wait upon the Spanish Envoy, her *deus ex machina*. I dispatched her letter to him when I was last in Oxford. Ah, but there's more – your bowl is at Chipping Campden."

"I pray she comes to no harm by de Zamora's valet," said Seward, when he heard of Catherine's desire to steal it back. For a while they both contemplated the night sky, festooned with stars; a barn owl ghosted past them, like an enormous moth. "The symbol of wisdom," he murmured. "When will *you* grow wise? Catherine is your wife and deserves your full affection, yet it's plain to me that you are still in love with Lady Hallam."

"You're right, Seward: though I've tried hard to banish those feelings. And the truth is that I volunteered to go to London before Digby sent me. Isabella may not be condemned in court, but I'm afraid of what Veech might do to her. If I see an opportunity, I intend to kill him or have him killed. I owe it to Barlow, among others." He gave Seward's bony shoulder a squeeze. "You were worried about me riding into the fray. This is no more dangerous."

"You are well aware that it is."

Laurence looked across the garden to the field where Pembroke's mount was grazing alongside his Arab. "I really should return that horse to its master."

"Would you enlist his help again?"

"I'm low on friends in the City, and he was my trump card last time. By the way, I wrote to inform the King how Pembroke's intelligence saved Rupert from capture at the gates of Aylesbury, and received not a word in answer."

"Do you expect His Majesty to thank the man who plotted his death?"

"You're right again. I did warm to old Pembroke, however."

"He might not be thrilled to see you a second time. Beaumont," Seward recommended, "on the morning you advised me to flee Oxford, I had been telling Clarke about a dream that had visited me in the night, of a vast expanse of moorland strewn with hundreds upon hundreds of wounded and dying men. Clearly a huge battle had been waged, and as clearly lost, though by which side I could not tell. Might it have been Cropredy, where you were?"

"Not by your description. There was no expanse of moor, and the losses weren't huge, even if the rebels fared worse than we did. Have you dreamt of it since?"

"If I have, I can't recollect. My dearest boy," Seward said suddenly, "I fear that next I shall have nightmares of some . . . some part of *you*, sent in a package to Lord Digby."

"I hope it would be a piece of my mind," said Laurence. "I've never yet told him exactly what I think of him. Now, Seward, I want to know all about your sleeping draught."

## II.

A wagon harnessed to a pair of cart horses stood outside Sir Montague's house, from which Greenhalgh was directing a procession of servants laden with rolled-up carpets and tapestries, boxes, chests, piles of linen, and various canvases, among them those of Sir Montague's disapproving parents. "Good morning to you, Mr. Draycott," he said, bowing imperturbably.

"Is your master at last well enough to receive me?" asked Draycott.

"Yes, sir: he is in the gallery. May I announce you?"

"You are busy – I shall announce myself."

Draycott felt glad that the wall where the tapestries had hung was now blank; the spyholes had been plastered over. Sir Montague looked sicklier than before, in his wheeled contraption, his gouty foot swathed in bandages, shoulders sagging, hands clasped across his rounded belly, his face powdered white like a mask. His mouth appeared sunken, as if teeth had been drawn from both sides. "Have you come to reproach me, sir?" he greeted Draycott, with a cheerful smile.

"I came for a book of Lady Isabella's: *Remedia Amoris*, if you did not surrender it to Veech as evidence of her guilt."

"Oh no, it is in the guest chamber with the rest of her belongings. Go and select whatever you wish, and then we shall talk."

Draycott did not trouble to pretend ignorance of the room.

Her property lay mounded on the bed: shimmering satin gowns in pieces, her fur-trimmed cloak and muff, and flimsy undergarments. He picked up a lace shift and held it to his nose, inhaling her exotic scent. How crude and treacherous the body was, he thought next, upset with himself, and tossed aside the shift to rifle through a stack of books. Most were damaged by Veech's rough handling, but two were intact: the slim, purple volume and another by Ovid. There was no inscription inside *Ars Amatoria*, only a date in her writing: the seventh of October, 1643. On impulse, Draycott stuck both books in his doublet pocket. He heard a faint mew from beneath the bed and her black cat slinked out, horribly thin, its ribs protruding, coat dull, eyes crusted with dried mucus. He remembered the day they had found it under the parlour table, and how he had declared his love for her.

"Judith, forgive me," he said. He had spoken those words to his wife earlier in the day, at her mother's; after Veech's threat, he had arranged for her and the children to quit London by nightfall and go to the house of a legal colleague in St. Albans. "I will soon be free of Veech," he had assured her, and she had told him, most surprisingly, "I pray you kill the man."

"Bella's four-footed friend," remarked Sir Montague, when Draycott came back into the gallery cradling the cat to his breast. "I have seen neither hide nor hair of the beast since she and Lucy were arrested." Draycott was silent, repulsed by his apparent indifference to the women's plight. "Do please sit down, sir. I hear from Oliver St. John that you are going to Lord Digby with a bargain to exchange her for the elusive Mr. Beaumont. I am shocked that St. John should engage in such dishonourable dealings."

"Veech persuaded him."

"Even the loftiest souls can be corrupted in time of war," joked Sir Montague. "I must say, Veech is one of the strangest men I have ever met. I feel sure that some tragedy in his past has affected his brain."

"His hunger for vengeance is certainly out of proportion to the hurt Beaumont inflicted on him."

"I would tend to agree. After he questioned me, I asked him why he should so hate a man who shot him quite by accident. He told me of an old Arab proverb: that it is the last straw which breaks the laden camel's back." Taking a handkerchief from his sleeve, Sir Montague dabbed at his forehead and cheeks, smearing the powder; underneath were blood vessels the colour of dark wine, and skin the texture of parchment. "Who will Digby choose to sacrifice: his darling Bella or his chief agent?" he resumed. "It is an awkward business, choosing between love and expediency."

"It did not seem so very awkward for *you*," Draycott said.

"She would have done the same in my place," Sir Montague said, impenitently. "As for *you*, sir, she and I planned your seduction to glean what intelligence we could about Parliament's spies. You might have noticed how rarely I was at home whenever you visited. I never did witness you two together, if it's any consolation. She feared that I might be swept away by my enjoyment of the scene, and that you might discover me frigging myself in my hiding place. Lucy was her accomplice. And Lucy's paramour from the Trained Bands was a spy in Lord Digby's employ, a man named Price, also an associate of the late thief, Barlow. You knew him, I believe."

"Yes," said Draycott, staggered.

"Ah well, it is history. You are an honest fellow, unlike me, so let me warn you: should Bella go free, she will have no further use for you.

And you will have given that devil Veech the greatest satisfaction, by facilitating his revenge."

"When do you depart for The Hague?" Draycott inquired, eager to terminate their exchange.

"Next week, sir. Niger is *your* friend, now," said Sir Montague, as Draycott stood up to leave; the cat had fastened onto the front of his doublet with its claws, and was burrowing its head in his underarm. "Please accept him as a gift, and for your convenience ask Greenhalgh for his travelling basket. And farewell to you, sir – I doubt we shall see each other again."

## III.

"We could expect no less of the Prince," Digby gloated to Culpeper, as they walked through Evesham marketplace, skirting the piles of dung left from the day's brisk trade in livestock. That afternoon, Council had erupted into spontaneous applause: the King had received an express message that Rupert had crushed the combined forces of Parliament and the Scots three days ago outside York. "The north is all but lost to the rebels," Digby went on, batting away a fly with his kidskin gloves, "and here in the south Waller's men are deserting in droves."

"Let us await further report of His Royal Highness's victory before we crow too loudly," said Culpeper, with his customary prudence. "Still, it would give His Majesty's terms for peace a more favourable reception in London."

"I think he will soon be able to dictate whatever terms he pleases. That is why there is no better time to remove Lord Wilmot from his commission."

"You must have more evidence of Wilmot's treasonous talk than hearsay. His reputation in the field is golden, after Cropredy Bridge."

"As though he won the battle single-handed," Digby scoffed.

"My lord, the King cannot afford a mutiny in his Horse."

"If only I had a penny for each time I've heard that said, my dear Culpeper, I would be a far richer man. The King dislikes Wilmot as much as we do, and he is Rupert's main rival." Digby considered, humming in his throat. "I shall hint in my correspondence to the Prince that Wilmot is conspiring to supplant Forth as Lord Marshal. Rupert might now be able to spare us one of his cavalry commanders to replace Wilmot. George Goring is also a popular veteran of the foreign wars, and a fine leader of men."

"When he is not drunk," said Culpeper. "He is cut from the same cloth as Lord Wilmot: arrogant and ambitious. And you would be stretching rumour, as concerns Wilmot's ambitions."

"I beg to dispute that. Wilmot tried to interfere in the fight at Cheriton without consulting Council, don't forget, and afterwards threatened to levy a charge of incompetence against Hopton."

"Yet he held back. Why are *you* in such haste to move on him, my lord?" Culpeper asked suspiciously. "Is it to engineer your coup before his friend Mr. Beaumont can return from London?"

"*My* coup? You and many others in Council are as eager to see Wilmot ousted. And what has Beaumont to do with it? He is not a member of Council."

"No, but you may be sure he would forewarn Wilmot. Was that why you sent him away with Sabron?"

"I swear it was not," said Digby, concealing his alarm: the true reason must never come out.

IV.

"*Qué ruido,*" grumbled Antonio, as he and Diego trod cautiously up the stairs. "She sounds more like a cow in labour than a human female. And *we* are bidden to creep about the house, lest we disturb her."

Mary Beaumont's pains had begun at dawn, and all day she had been attended by her ladyship, Martha, a midwife from town, his lordship's surgeon, and the Beaumont daughters. To Antonio's irritation, Lord Beaumont had asked to pass the anxious hours in the society of Diego, whom he had overheard quoting from a poem of

Lope de Vega. Diego had promised to recite an entire play of de Vega's for his lordship in the library.

"I might select *Las Flores de Don Juan*," he mused to Antonio. "His lordship would appreciate the tale of a profligate elder son who games away the family fortunes, while his worthy younger brother struggles in poverty."

"On the subject of family fortunes," Antonio said, lowering his voice, "you are missing your opportunity to get inside that dovecote while the household is distracted."

"You might try yourself, Don Antonio. Perhaps with your sharp teeth you can chew through the lock on it," Diego said, and skipped off towards the library before Antonio could fetch him a smack on the ear.

Antonio prowled crossly back to his chamber in the other wing of the house. But as he turned into the passage that led there, his spirits lifted. Catherine was standing outside his door. She hesitated at the sight of him, like an animal undecided between fight and flight, and wrapped her arms protectively around her stomach. She had seemed sleeker and handsomer recently, and so fascinated by Diego that Antonio wondered if she was nurturing a girlish infatuation for the youth in her husband's absence; or was he imagining things, as a consequence of his own sexual frustration? He would find out.

"Mistress Caterina, what are you doing here?" he inquired.

"I was searching for Diego."

"Were you," said Antonio, bemused as ever by the candour of Englishwomen. "And what for?"

"His lordship wants him, in the library."

"He is already with his lordship," Antonio told her, mildly disappointed. "Why are you not at Mary's childbed?"

"Her ladyship said I would be a nuisance."

"And her ladyship is to be obeyed! Does your husband worship her as slavishly as everyone else in this house?"

"I don't know, sir – I've only seen them together once, when he brought me to Chipping Campden – the last time *I* saw him," Catherine finished, looking straight into Antonio's eyes.

"You must know very little, then, about his life before you married him." Antonio moved closer. The defect in her complexion, a scattering of freckles on her cheekbones and on the bridge of her nose, oddly enhanced her allure, though in his view by far the most attractive of the young women was Elizabeth. "Did he ever say to you that he had visited my country?" Catherine shook her head. "I'm not surprised. He left behind his Spanish mistress, a gypsy named Juana. I met her in my hometown of Seville, this past October. He had deserted her because she was pregnant, and she had afterwards borne his son. She had not eaten in days, and her milk had dried up." Catherine was listening with the air of someone tolerating an elderly relation's prattle. "When I learnt of her history, I felt bound to assist her."

"You are generous, sir," Catherine said.

"Does it not lower your opinion of him to hear how ruthlessly he abandoned her?"

"I can't judge him until I hear *his* version of the facts."

Antonio adopted a new line of attack. "You have a twin sister, no?"

"Yes: Penelope."

"An identical twin?"

"Not quite. She's much prettier than I am."

"Hmm . . . Your husband and I might be twins."

Catherine smiled, revealing her chipped tooth. "How could you be? You are of an age to be his father."

*What if I was his father, you saucy minx?* Antonio nearly challenged her; but he was in a mood to play. "He and I are alike in character, nonetheless. And, I fancy, in our tastes." He laid a hand on the small of her spine and drifted it south to her buttocks, high and firm as a boy's.

She twisted to peer over her shoulder at it, as she might a burr that had become attached to her skirts. "Are you lonely for your wife, Don Antonio?"

He cupped her flesh more insistently. "Are you, for your husband? Although . . . you have had such a brief acquaintance with him, and younger men can be too swift to take their own enjoyment."

"He is thirty-two – not so young."

"Still, a man of my experience could make you swoon with delight. Would you like me to unveil to you the mysteries of your body? I can teach you how to please yourself, *and* him."

"Thank you, but I prefer him for my teacher. He is neither too young – nor too old."

Antonio pretended to laugh, and dropped his hand. "Now you will go telling tales to her ladyship about my unseemly behaviour."

"Why would I bother – it's of no import to *me*."

Catherine tried to walk on, but he grabbed her by the sleeve. "Why are you holding your stomach like that?"

"Because I feel a need to void, sir," she replied, flatly.

"Go, then," he said, and released her.

She disappeared down the passage, and he to his chamber, where he lay down on the bed and glowered at the embroidered canopy above him. Everything was quiet. But then he caught a hubbub of voices, and next the shrill, penetrating wail of an infant. To think of Elena as a grandmother! He was moved, thinking not just of her, but of her mother Cecilia and his own mother, also an Elena, whom he had never known: three women with their distinctive Fuentes looks. He pictured Teresa's plump visage, now and when she was young; and a wave of homesickness overcame him, bringing tears to his eyes. His son Felipe must have celebrated a thirteenth birthday. How loving and respectful they were, as compared to most of the Beaumonts; and how he yearned for the sun-drenched earth of Andalucía, and the beauty of his city, with its quaint narrow streets; and the solemn architecture of the Cathedral; and the modestly clad *sevillanas* he used to flirt with during Mass. "I am tired of England," he said, out loud.

Rapid footsteps were pattering towards his door. He brushed away his tears and sat up to witness Diego executing a caper in the doorway, a silly grin on his face. "Don Antonio, Mary has had a son! He is to be christened James, after his lordship, and everyone in the house is invited to . . ." Diego tailed off, staring into the room, then rushed in to pounce on his saddlebag, which had been lying on the floor beside the bed. He hunted inside, and raised his eyes to Antonio. "It has gone," he announced, collapsing to his knees, and began trembling like a drunk deprived of his wineskin. "Who could have taken it? Who could have taken *my bowl*?"

Antonio understood instantly who had rid him of the evil thing. "All I can imagine, Diego," he said, "is that the old wizard stole it back through magic."

## V.

Pembroke had been slumbering in his armchair over a digestive glass of cordial when his equerry came to whisper in his ear. He sat up, spilling on the front of his doublet as Beaumont walked through to him. "By Christ," he swore. "I hope you were not seen entering my lodgings?"

Beaumont cast Pembroke his incandescent smile. "No, my lord. Thank you again for the loan of your horse. I returned it to your stables."

"How the devil did you sneak into the City without being apprehended?"

"I entered openly, with the French agent, Monsieur Sabron, under his diplomatic safe conduct. He and I were to stay at the French embassy, but to our dismay the ambassador refused me shelter – for the second time, I'm afraid. I ought to have known better than to depend on his hospitality."

"So you are dependent again on mine."

Beaumont was looking thirstily at Pembroke's glass. "How have you been keeping, my lord?"

Pembroke heaved a resigned sigh and waved him to a chair. "May we dispense with courtesies, Mr. Beaumont? What is Sabron doing here?"

"He brought an offer of terms from His Majesty to the Lords

and Commons. 'We being deeply sensible of the miseries and calamities of this our kingdom, and the grievous suffering of our poor subjects,'" Beaumont quoted, "'do most earnestly desire that some expedient may be found out, which by the blessing of God may prevent the further effusion of blood, and restore the nation to peace.'"

"You and your confounded memory. What are the terms?"

"Maintenance of the true reformed Protestant religion, with due regard to the ease of tender consciences, the just privileges of Parliament, and the liberty and property of any subject, according to the laws of the land. A general pardon, and a total disbanding of the armies and, as His Majesty phrased it, that 'we be restored to our rights.'"

"Parliament will not grace him with an answer, after Rupert's defeat at Marston Moor."

Beaumont's pale eyes were now full of sorrow. "They say bad news travels fast, yet the King had had no report of it when Sabron and I set out. We were devastated to hear from the French ambassador that as many as four thousand died on the field – it must be the highest number of any battle since war broke out. My brother and my brother-in-law may well be among them."

Pembroke let a silence pass. "And why have *you* come to London, Mr. Beaumont?" When Beaumont did not reply, he asked, "Has Lord Digby sent you to fetch Lady Hallam from the Tower?" He was rather pleased to see Beaumont astonished by his guess. "I found out that Lady Hallam, your former lover, was Isabella Savage before she wedded Sir Montague. He always called her Bella and never told me her maiden name. And as I had thought, those messages of yours and hers back in January did not concern a privy complaint, but some matter of espionage." Beaumont said nothing. Pembroke ventured a further guess. "On both visits to London, you came not just out of obedience to Lord Digby. You are still smitten, aren't you, sir – and *that* I can comprehend, if she is as captivating as she was in her youth."

"Then you were . . . acquainted with her."

"I remember her when she was first presented at Court, in the late thirties – a ravishing, witty girl, and a skilled horsewoman. Van Dyke painted her as Aphrodite. He had no need to improve upon the truth with his brush, as he did with most of his other sitters. Not that I could judge the whole of it, for it was almost the naked truth, if I recall," Pembroke added, watching Beaumont's face.

"Yes, I've seen the portrait – and it is the truth."

"How can you help her escape when you are so sought after by the authorities?"

"I might begin by sending out a few messages. They won't be dangerous to you, I promise."

"As if sheltering you is not sufficiently dangerous! You may not have heard the latest development in her case: her legal counsel left the City on an unknown business, so a new lawyer replaced him, to expedite her trial. She was condemned yesterday, to burn at the stake. Her association with Lord Digby proved her ruin."

Beaumont's mouth contorted with such acute grief that Pembroke felt a wave of compassion. Some youthful, untamed quality in the man reminded him of his son Charles, who had died before his seventeenth birthday of the smallpox in Florence. That bad news had travelled slowly indeed: Pembroke had not received it for three months, and for over a week afterwards he had isolated himself in these very rooms, too stricken to face the world.

"As the King was ignorant when he sent forth his peace terms, Digby had no clue as to the hopelessness of your errand," he said. "Sir, you will throw your life away, and in vain. I am sorry for Lady Hallam, and for you. It's a pity you did not meet earlier, before she lost her reputation. You might have taken her as your wife."

"I would have taken her without her reputation," Beaumont said quietly.

"I advised Digby to find her a husband then – she had a host of suitors, despite her natural birth. But he let her run wild. I presume you know that her mother was a friend of Bristol's, of good descent, though impoverished."

"Have you any idea who her father was, my lord? She doesn't know to this day, as far as *I* know."

"I assume it was someone in the Digby family. Gossip suggested that she was George Digby's half-sister, yet I'd swear Bristol did not father her: he was too proper for adultery. Mr. Beaumont, what tidings do you bring for me, from the King?"

"He was most thankful that you saved his nephew from capture by Essex," replied Beaumont, after another, significant pause. "As to his forgiveness, you may have to wait."

"Until hell freezes over," said Pembroke.

## VI.

Veech caught Oliver St. John on his way into Westminster Hall; St. John did not slacken his pace, forcing Veech to hurry, dragging his bad leg. "I know what you are about to tell me," St. John said brusquely. "Mr. Beaumont is at the French embassy. He may be a criminal and a malignant, sir, but we have no power to root him out of there."

"He left the embassy last night, almost as soon as he arrived," Veech said, relishing St. John's consternation as he spoke. "One of the ambassador's equerries is in my pay, and reported to me this morning how Monsieur Sabron pleaded with the ambassador to keep Beaumont's disappearance from public knowledge."

St. John pursed together his old crone's lips. "I trust your men are searching for him."

"Yes, sir, but our best chance is to catch him red-handed at the Tower. I shall place an extra detail of guards outside Lady Hallam's cell."

St. John stopped and turned on Veech. "If you apprehend him, he must be questioned not by you alone but by a delegation from the Committee of Both Kingdoms, and he must be tried and sentenced according to the *due process of law*. I should not have heeded your advice about him. He came to London of his own accord, and now we have dirtied our hands in trying to bargain with Lord Digby. Your judgement was clouded by vindictiveness. Good day to you, sir."

Veech grinned after St. John's upright back, and pushed through the usual crowds of Members, lawyers, clerks, petitioners, and hawkers towards Westminster Stairs. He took a skiff, the route so familiar to him that he could estimate how long his journey would take by the colour and flow of the water. Today he felt exhilarated, sitting in the bow, watching the boatman toil away as he had once toiled over his oar in the crystal seas of the Mediterranean, and beyond. He was inspired to send a third package to Lord Digby: a reminder of Lady Hallam. And then, finally, he and Beaumont would meet face to face.

## VII.

Laurence's message, delivered to Sarah by Pembroke's potboy, was answered the next morning after Pembroke had left for the Upper House. A young costermonger appeared at the kitchen door with a basket of cherries, and on a discreet sign from Laurence, the cook invited him to step in. He and Laurence were both tearful, speaking of Barlow. Jem explained that on the day of his uncle's arrest Lady Hallam had sent for him in the small hours to collect something from her. He was delayed by a bellyache, and in the end Barlow had gone in his stead, but not until afternoon. "He'd still be alive if not for me, sir. Sarah fetched his corpse at the gaol. She could hardly rekkernise him, he was so banged about! She had him laid near Mistress Edwards and Jane in St. Saviour's yard." Jem sniffed, and mopped his eyes on his dirty sleeve. "She says the old mistress would have been proud of him, though. He didn't just die a thief – he struck a blow for His Majesty's cause."

"So he did," said Laurence, thinking how much the King owed to his humblest subjects, and how little he would mourn a dead thief.

"We want vengeance, sir. Sarah won't stop 'til she gets it. Have you come to do away with the fiend what killed him?"

"I swear to you I will, Jem. First I need your help. I have to free Lady Hallam from the Tower."

"God's bodkin! If she was a common sort, that'd be easy. A noble-woman like her won't pass unnoticed."

"Veech will know I'm in London, to make things harder for you. But she can be disguised as a boy. She's had some practice at it." Laurence described his flimsy scheme, and gave Jem the bottle containing Seward's narcotic potion, and a large advance from Digby's funds. "I wish I could take on the risk myself."

"You can't," said Jem. "You was an ugly old woman once, but for this job of work we need pretty women, and a young fellow of about my size."

Around midday, Jem returned. "We'll have her out tomorrow tonight, sir. Sarah went round the Tower with Barlow's cousin's wife, Ruth, selling cherry pies, and they found out where Lady Hallam's being kept. Veech put a special watch on the cell – boys from the Trained Bands. The guards don't like these newcomers. And Sarah and Ruth have won over the guards. Sarah promised them a feast tonight, meat pies and ale, and plenty of ladies for their entertainment. Sarah's cousin Tim will have a boat at the dock, to get us to his house in Bermondsey."

"What about Veech?" asked Laurence.

"He'll be drawn out on a hunt, sir, looking for you – in *Cripple*gate," Jem added, with a malicious smile at his own witticism.

## VIII.

Lord Digby must have been angelic in youth, Draycott thought, but his cheeks had become pouched like a squirrel's; and his blond hair, neatly curled, was thinning at the crown. The robin's-egg shade of his eyes matched the gloves in his left hand. In his right, he held the letters that he had been reading at his desk, one from Oliver St. John and the other from Lady Isabella. He addressed Draycott in an icy tone. "Before we speak of these, how is she?"

"When I last saw her five days ago, she was regaining her health. She had contracted a fever from her maid, who died of it."

"Poor Lucy," said Digby, gazing at him as though he were responsible.

"My lord, we can still save *her* life."

"At the cost of Mr. Beaumont's? The very notion is odious."

"It is," said Draycott. "And I am not here to obey Mr. St. John, or Clement Veech, the man who encouraged him to make you this proposition. I detest Veech more than words can express. I wish he were dead." Draycott pulled two books from his pocket and gave them to Digby. "Please go to the note in the margin, on the twentieth page of *Remedia Amoris*. She has written a note for Mr. Beaumont, in the other book."

Digby flicked through to that page, read, then closed the book, and placed both volumes on his desk. "How can you prove to me Lady Hallam was not coerced into penning those lines insisting on your honesty, and that Veech has not overlaid one proposal with another, more cunningly framed, to lure Beaumont to *his* death? Why should he or I believe you, Mr. Draycott, when you and Veech serve the same master?"

"I am not asking Mr. Beaumont to come to London. What I require is his expertise, and if he has people there who could assist me—"

"Who you would then surrender to Veech."

"No, my lord. Allow me to speak with Mr. Beaumont or at least show him what she wrote. We've bought some time to plan the rescue. Even if she is condemned, St. John will not allow her sentence to be carried out until he has your answer."

Digby hesitated, twirling a lock of his blond hair round and round his fingertips. "What is inside that basket you brought with you, sir?" Draycott set it upon the desk, unhooked a latch on top, and lifted the lid. "Bless me – Niger!"

"She asked me to bring it to you, my lord. Sir Montague would have let it starve, and she feared to keep it at the Tower, lest Veech torture it in front of her."

"I thank you, sir." Digby called for his servant and murmured something to him. The man nodded, picked up the basket, and left them.

A moment later, a young man swaggered in; Draycott recognised him at once, despite his broken nose. He bowed to Digby, and sneered at Draycott, "How's Mr. Veech? Are you still tied to his apron strings?"

"Apparently not," said Digby. "Mr. Draycott tells me that he is prepared to betray Veech *and* his masters in Parliament by procuring Lady Hallam's escape."

"The liar," said Price. "He's Veech's man. He was sent to her house to winkle information out of her and Sir Montague."

"I was, against my will, as she knows," countered Draycott.

Digby held up his hand, like a schoolmaster before two unruly pupils. "Mr. Draycott, your brave offer is too late: Mr. Beaumont has already gone to London, to Lady Hallam's aid."

"Then he and I can work together! I have access to her cell, and the trust of her gaolers. And Veech shares the same mistaken opinion of me as Mr. Price. No matter how resourceful Beaumont is, he can't succeed alone."

"Don't listen to him, my lord," said Price.

"I have listened, and . . . no, Mr. Draycott," Digby said. "You shall be taken under guard to Oxford, and detained there as my prisoner until further notice."

## IX.

Lady Beaumont felt glad of Antonio's slothful habits: he had not yet descended from his bedchamber by half past nine of the morning, when she went out to greet a party of three riders who came galloping into the courtyard leading a couple of spare mounts. One of the party, dark and thickset, wore a ruby red velvet suit and matching cloak; the others wore livery.

The gentleman dismounted and bowed. "My Lady Beaumont, Capitán Enrique Iturbe, at your service. Don Alonso de Cárdenas dispatched me from London, in answer to your letter."

"Heaven be praised," she said, and dropped him a weak-kneed curtsey.

"It is your genius that deserves praise, my Lady Beaumont." Iturbe switched to Spanish as Jacob came to take the horses. "Following your suggestion, I have with me a document for Don Antonio de Zamora that purports to be from the Royal Court of His Majesty King Philip: an offer of employment that Don Antonio should find irresistible. He will not discover that it is fictitious until he lands on Spanish soil."

"May God bless the Envoy!"

"My lady, he is more than pleased to remove any potential threat to the harmonious relations between Spain and Westminster. And he told me that he will derive a certain *private* pleasure from sending Don Antonio home."

"Sir, you shall soon meet my husband, who is out walking with our daughters. For various reasons I have kept from him and from our household the truth about Don Antonio's misbehaviour in London, and the favour that I solicited from the Envoy. I must ask your discretion on those matters."

"You have it, my lady." They went together into the Hall, and when they were seated, Iturbe produced a scrolled document from the satchel he was carrying. "The offer, suitably travel-worn. The copy of the royal seal is an exquisite piece of work."

Lady Beaumont hesitated to take it; she could hear the clatter of boots on the stair. "It is him. He must have spied on us from his chamber window."

Antonio strode in, shadowed inevitably by Diego. "My Lady Elena, who have we here: a fellow Spaniard, if I am not wrong!"

Iturbe rose to introduce himself and performed a low obeisance. "I am speechless at the honour of your acquaintance, Don Antonio – hero of a hundred battles, famed throughout Spain for your courage in the Imperial cause. How well you merit the title by which you were known: *El Valoroso*."

Perhaps Antonio had not been vainly boasting, Lady Beaumont thought; or was Iturbe flattering him? "The Captain is come with unexpected tidings for you, Don Antonio," she said.

"No less well merited, sir, than your military reputation." Iturbe gave Antonio the scroll. "It is with supreme joy that I deliver this to you. I feared it would never reach you. I was months travelling over land, and by sea, and when I got to England I could not be sure that King Charles's enemies would respect my safe conduct. I also feared that I might be robbed of the advance payment I have for you, in the event that you accept our king's offer."

Antonio was reading with an ostensible mixture of bewilderment, pride, and greed. "From the Escorial Palace! On behalf of His Majesty King Philip . . . A commission to train his regiment of cavalry for a campaign in . . ." He frowned up at Iturbe. "Who suggested that His Majesty should call me out of my retirement, to so honour me?"

"A comrade in arms of yours in Madrid, Don Antonio. I cannot recollect his name, but he insisted to His Majesty that only you were capable of leading this onerous mission. Our ambassador in London was as hearty in his recommendation of you."

"Don Alonso? But we did not part on the best note."

"So he told me. You know these diplomats – caution runs in their blood. He has since forgiven you your improvident flight from his house. Now, our ship departs for Cádiz in about a week, and there will be no direct passage to Spain for another month. You will have to bid a hasty goodbye to the Lady Elena and her noble family, and ride with me for Oxford this afternoon. We shall then proceed straight to London, from whence we are to embark. But . . . I should first ascertain: will you accept His Majesty's commission?"

"Of course I accept," replied Antonio.

"It is all so sudden, Capitán," Lady Beaumont said to Iturbe, feigning regret. "His lordship will be as sorry as I am that Don Antonio must leave us."

"It causes me equal grief," said Antonio, straightening his shoulders, "but if His Majesty calls, I must obey. Diego, we shall prepare our baggage."

Diego's canny eyes sought her out, and she detected a marked suspicion in his face. Then he smiled politely. "At your command, Don Antonio."

As they were alone, Iturbe winked at Lady Beaumont. "When a man gives you a free horse, you do not look into its mouth to count its teeth."

"I pray he will not, though I am more worried about his sly valet. Is it true what you said about his reputation?"

"Oh yes – he was singularly brave, though on occasion too reckless of his life, and those of his soldiers. On the issue of prayer," Iturbe continued more quietly, "did you renounce our Holy Mother Church, when you married his lordship?"

"Why yes, or else his parents would have rejected me as his bride."

"Might I implore your discretion, for a secret of my own?" She nodded. "I am an ordained priest, unbeknownst to Don Alonso. I came to London, not from Spain, but from Brussels, to supply financial aid to my Franciscan brethren in England. If you desire, I could receive you back into the Church, and hear your confession."

Lady Beaumont thought of her mother at prayer, fingering each bead of the rosary, and that soft murmuring, like a lullaby: *Ave Maria, gratia plena, Dominus tecum. Benedicta tu in mulieribus, et benedictus fructis ventri tui, Iesus* . . . "No, sir," she said, with an effort, "though I thank you, and may God bless you in your work here."

## X.

"I swear that wizard's bowl was bringing us ill luck," Antonio declared, rereading his magnificent offer while Diego dusted off their saddlebags. "I hope you will stop sulking over it."

"I'm amazed, Don Antonio, that *you* should be in such high spirits," said Diego. "Had you stayed in Seville, you would have had His

Majesty's commission months ago. We've achieved precisely nothing in England. You came to destroy the peace of James Beaumont's kingdom, but you'll leave him happy in it as a pig in its sty. She and your Lorenzo, and even that doltish Thomas have proved immune to our ruses. And you've got hardly an English farthing out of the family."

"That's not true: I had a good bit of money from Thomas, and for the past month we've eaten and drunk like lords in this house. Besides, Iturbe has my advance payment, and I'll have yet more when I arrive in Spain."

"We may have a difficult journey home, beforehand, and who knows what awaits us there."

Antonio paused to reflect. Teresa might believe him dead, in the half year since he had written to her from London. And was Juana still at Gaspar's, dreaming of revenge on her Monsieur Beaumont? How deliciously perverse it would be to fuck her soundly, turn her out, and then raise her Lorenzo in the de Zamora household. Yet as he watched Diego stuff their meagre possessions into their bags, he thought the youth had a point: why quit the field of battle without a victory?

He marched to the door.

"Where are you off to?" Diego asked.

Antonio swung about. "You should address me more respectfully, Diego, if you wish to grow any older."

Diego's face darkened. "You got rid of the bowl, didn't you. You couldn't bear that it might give me power over you. You, *El Valoroso*, were scared of it, and of me."

"Don't be so conceited," said Antonio. "It *was* stolen from you, though not through magic: a little elf took it, probably on her husband's instruction. I nearly caught her in the act."

"Catherine," whispered Diego. "I should have guessed."

"Thank God she put an end to your dangerous games." Antonio unlatched the door. "Take our bags downstairs. Then exert your wiles on the Captain's servants and find out what gossip you can about him."

"Yes, *master*," Diego said, rudely.

Antonio sauntered out and along the passage. From another chamber, he could hear Iturbe singing, over the splash of water; the Captain was at his ablutions. On the stair, he listened for a moment to young James Beaumont's infant babble from Mary's chamber. She had not emerged in the four days since she had been brought to bed; a wise custom given how dreary most women looked after childbirth. He descended to the entrance hall and asked a footman where he might find her ladyship; and he grinned to himself when the man said she had just gone to the herb garden.

The door to the dovecote was open. Elena sat on a rung of a ladder that extended up to the roof, where the birds had their nesting holes. Her hands were pressed together like a supplicant's, and he recognised her words, in Latin. "Are you reciting a novena to speed me on my journey?" he inquired, startling her as he came in. "Or are you praying that the seeds of revenge I have sown within your family will not take root?"

She raised her eyebrows. "What *do* you mean?"

"I gave your sons the answer to a mystery that has puzzled them since childhood: they are but half-brothers. Although they may deny it to themselves, the truth is planted. They'll fall out over the estate, I promise you, and carry the sin of at least two de Capdavila y Fuentes generations into a third. As for you, Elena, you've made the best of a sorry bargain: you exchanged wealth for the man you loved." Antonio approached, holding out his arms. "Remember what we felt for each other. Your cold façade hides a soul in torment, full of lost hopes and dreams, and memories that I have awakened."

"Antonio," she said, in a bored tone, "you dwell in the past, trapped by your own lost hopes and dreams. They have addled your brains. God has blessed you with a chance to redeem yourself, in honourable service to your King. I am praying that you will become a better man for it."

Antonio had a mind to slap her, or crush her to his chest and revive her ardour with a passionate kiss. Instead, he pointed at the clay floor. "I happen to know his lordship's treasures are buried here.

What will you pay me not to inform the rebels when I get to London?"

For a second, the colour washed from her face. Then she shook her head slowly. "That Diego, your little spy." She withdrew from her skirt pocket a small box and held it out to him. "Here's *your* treasure. I never wore it. You can present it to one of your daughters, and scandalise her with the story behind it."

Antonio picked out the medallion. "Our bad blood, Elena – of Moors and Christians. I think I'll wear it myself." He slipped the chain over his head, tucked the medallion inside the neck of his shirt, and tossed aside the box.

She rose and smoothed down her skirts. "Excuse me, now. I must attend to my visitors. There is a spade in the corner, and you have a few hours before we say goodbye. If you are so sure about his lordship's treasures, I suggest you start to dig."

"Woman, you are tough as a pair of old boots!" He offered her his arm, which she accepted with a flicker of a smile. "I shall accompany you. You have not won, *querida*," he said, as they left the dovecote. "Bad blood will always surface. And what a sinful concentration of our blood flows in the veins of our son! I joked to him about the Hapsburgs and their interbreeding, but they have nothing on *him*."

He saw her expression alter abruptly, and not because of his little quip; Elizabeth was racing up the path towards them as though chased by a pack of wolves. "What is it, Elizabeth?" she cried.

"Catherine," Elizabeth panted.

Elena ran after her, round to the front of the house and up the steps; and Antonio followed, with the faintest misgiving.

Lord Beaumont and Capitán Iturbe stood side by side in the entrance hall while Anne and Elizabeth restrained Catherine, who was struggling like a tigress, her hair flying, her dress ripped at the front. The object of her fury, Diego, was pinioned by Iturbe's servants, his cheeks dripping blood.

"Don Antonio," said Lord Beaumont sternly, "your valet is a knave who has grossly abused our trust."

"I beg pardon, my lord – what crime has he committed?" asked Antonio.

"He crept up on Catherine in her chamber and accused her of stealing from him. Then he accosted her. Thank heaven she had the strength to fend him off and call for help. The Captain and his men were able to rescue her in the nick of time."

"Permit me to deal with him outside, my lord." Antonio wrenched the youth from Iturbe's men and kicked him in the rear so hard that Diego stumbled through the doors, tripped on the steps, and landed spread-eagled in the courtyard. Grabbing him up by the collar, Antonio dragged him a short distance away, and spat in his face, "*Hijo de puta*, what devil possessed you?"

"She nearly scratched out my eyes," Diego whined.

"*Cierra el hocico o te corto los cojones.*" Antonio kneed him in that tender spot and he crumpled to the ground, howling and clutching himself. "*Levanta el culo, desgraciado*," ordered Antonio, and turned for the house.

Lord and Lady Beaumont were on the steps with Iturbe, who said, in a horrified voice, "What a conclusion to your visit, Don Antonio."

"He shall be punished severely, my Lord Beaumont," said Antonio, "and I must apologise for the dreadful shock to Mistress Catherine. Look at us – we are all in a state of nerves! My lord, let's share a glass of your fine Malaga to restore us, and bid each other a proper farewell before our party sets out."

He expected Lord Beaumont to acquiesce, with his gentle bonhomie, but his lordship's face rivalled Elena's in its cold reproof. "No, sir: the Captain is determined to ride out at once. You could not be our guest forever, Don Antonio, much as we appreciated your invigorating company."

## XI.

Veech had ordered out a troop of militia to comb the streets of Cripplegate, on report that a tall, dark, foreign-looking man had been spotted in the area. He himself had gone to Southwark, and spent fruit-less hours searching there, even breaking into the house at Blackman Street. It was empty, and the neighbours could tell him little he did not already know about its inhabitants. He left a couple of men to watch it, and around ten o'clock, decided to check on the Tower.

Long before his skiff moored by Traitors Gate, he heard drunken singing. Only one sleepy guard was on duty to salute him as he clam-bered out. "I had a taste of ale, sir, courtesy of the chief gaoler," the guard confessed. "But you should see most of them – they'll have thick heads to pay, tomorrow."

Veech stiffened, sensing trouble. "Bring me the keys to Lady Hallam's cell."

The guard came back with a heavy bunch. "Those boys from the Bands are soused to the gills! I tried to wake 'em, sir, but they're sleeping as the dead."

Veech hurried up to the cell. The men assigned to her door were slumped snoring on the flagstones. The door itself was locked, however, and through the spyhole, he glimpsed the outline of her body beneath her blanket, and her dark hair on the pillow. "Lady Hallam," he yelled, fitting the key into the lock, "I bid you, get up." She did not move, even at the grinding of the bolt. He flung open the door, rushed in, and tore aside the blanket. Lady Hallam, as he might have predicted, was a con-struct of straw, bundled clothes, and a moth-eaten wig.

## XII.

At two in the morning, Laurence heard a series of rhythmic taps on Pembroke's kitchen window, and let Jem in. "She's safe in Bermondsey, sir," Jem whispered.

"Well done, Jem, well done. None of you was caught or injured?" Jem shook his head. "Thank God. No sign of Veech?"

"No, sir, but militia are searching high and low for you and her ladyship, and for us Barlows. There's a guard posted in Blackman Street. We have to make tracks."

"Will you leave London?"

"Leave London?" echoed Jem, as if the very idea were preposterous. "London is the centre of things. Barlows could not be anywhere else! We've a wealth of places to hide 'til the hue and cry dies off. What about her ladyship? She wants to join you here."

"She *can't*," insisted Laurence, terrified of the danger to her, and to Pembroke. "She must find her way to Oxford in her disguise. You tell her, Jem: she and I must stay apart, or your courage and hard work will have been wasted."

"How will *you* get out? We might help you, sir."

"No, you've risked far too much as it is." Laurence gave him more money, some for Isabella's journey and most of it for the Barlows. As he and Jem hugged goodbye, tears pricked again in his eyes. "Thank you all, my dear friends. This may be the last time we see each other, Jem."

"Don't you count on it, sir," said Jem, with the stolid assurance of his late uncle. "Fortune favours the bold. She's a lady, so she'll look after you. And remember, *your* work ain't done: you owe us the death of Veech."

# CHAPTER SEVENTEEN

## I.

"There's bound to be talk at Westminster," Pembroke commented over breakfast, when Laurence told him of Lady Hallam's rescue. "Will your anonymous friends spirit you as cleverly out of the City?"

"No, my lord," said Laurence; he had passed the remains of the night wishing he could have accepted Jem's offer.

"Would you borrow my horse once more?"

"Thank you, but I prefer to take my chances on foot. I'll leave when it gets dark."

Pembroke shoved aside his plate. "You won't have a chance in hell, sir. There will be militia everywhere. *Now* what's the matter?" he demanded of his equerry, who had entered with a peculiar look on his face.

He came over to Pembroke, and said in a hushed voice, "My lord, a sack of coal just arrived at your door."

"Why should I care to know – and why are you whispering?" inquired Pembroke.

"It is no *ordinary* coal."

Laurence scrambled upstairs to his chamber for his pistols. He cocked them and listened, his heart somersaulting in his chest, for the tramp of militiamen's boots in the hall below. Instead he heard Pembroke call out, in a sardonic tone, "Mr. Beaumont, you will never guess what I found in that sack."

Laurence went to the top of the stair and saw Pembroke walk forward with his equerry, who was supporting a bedraggled, dirty boy in a cloth cap and soot-stained jerkin and breeches.

———

Laurence carried Isabella into the chamber next to his and placed her on the bed. He could feel the jut of her bones through the coarse woollen garments. He took off the cap. Her hair had been cropped to her shoulders; it used to graze the base of her spine.

"I could not resist coming to you," she said. "Can you forgive me?"

"Oh yes, my love, I'd forgive you anything," Laurence replied sincerely.

"How foolish I was to ignore your warnings about Veech and that baker's apprentice, although Mr. Draycott is not a rat, but a fine, honest man." She told him her story, beginning with the evidence Veech had given Draycott to plant at her house and the terrible day of Barlow's arrest, for which she blamed herself; her imprisonment and Lucy's death; Sir Montague's betrayal; and her trial and sentencing, unbeknownst to Draycott, who had gone on his noble mission to Digby. "He loathes Veech, who cost him his marriage and threatened to hurt his children," she concluded.

"How many of us must want Veech dead. I do, and I've not even met him or seen him at close range."

"He is a ghastly creature, Beaumont. Sir Montague had an idea that some harm was done to him, twisting him and filling him with hate."

"Does he still wear a brace on his knee?"

"Yes, an ingenious contraption. He might not walk without it. But there's something else wrong with him. He's tall and broadly built, and yet . . . I can't describe it."

"Price said there was a soft aspect to his features."

She nodded vigorously. "A softness that ill matches his deep voice and otherwise masculine appearance. *I* last saw him three days ago, when the extra guard was put at my door. He didn't threaten me, for once. He simply asked for my wedding ring, a showy jewel from Sir Montague. And as he reached for it, his sleeve pulled back a little, and I noticed that his hand and the skin above his wrist were nearly devoid of hair."

Laurence pulled back his own sleeves and held up his hands. "So are mine."

"You're not like him." Isabella looked away, as if trying to remember. Then she quoted, "'And Jacob said to Rebekah, his mother, *Behold, Esau my brother is a hairy man, and I am a smooth man.*' He should be a hairy man, with his thick brows almost knitted into one."

"Well," said Laurence, "I can't explain it."

"Explain to me this: why is the Earl hiding you? Is he a friend of yours, from before the war?"

"No, and you must keep secret how he's helping us – Digby, above all, must never know."

"I promise. But what are we to do? We can't stay here together, can we? Where will we go?"

"Let me think about that." He smiled at her. "You're very tired."

She hid her face in the pillow. "And I am so aged, and ugly."

"You are as beautiful as always, though you do need a scrubbing," he said, comforted by her vanity, and kissed her on the cheek. "Now sleep. You can bathe when you wake."

On his return from the evening session at the Lords, Pembroke showed Laurence a broadsheet. "Lady Hallam's disappearance is a source of public wonder."

"'She is undoubtedly a witch, who cast a spell over her vigilant gaolers last night, and magicked herself into a boy . . .'" Laurence frowned at an intriguing detail: the gravediggers who had buried her maid claimed that a finger was missing from the girl's hand, obviously stolen by Lady Hallam for a magic charm. "It *is* true that she owned a black cat. What about Sir Montague, and his debauches in the Strand? Is there any truth to *them*?"

Pembroke emitted his braying laugh. "He could not have been an active participant. He must have lusted as vainly for his wife, the impotent old reprobate. He sold *her* to the very devil, to eke out a few more years of life for his rotten carcass. As the poets and moralists say, we are only granted what we most desire when we can no longer enjoy it. Ah well, at least we can enjoy his wine." He called for his equerry to bring glasses and a bottle of Sir Montague's claret. "A health to our witch upstairs," he proposed.

"And to Sir Montague's few more years," said Laurence.

When they had emptied their glasses, Pembroke sank into his armchair. "I used to be so certain of what I most desired: power, temporal and spiritual. It was a dream I have relinquished. My present dream is far less ambitious: to end my days at Wilton surrounded by my surviving children and my grandchildren, and by my collection of art."

"You and my father share a similar dream."

"And you, sir, what's yours?"

"My immediate dream is to vanish with Lady Hallam into thin air, and leave you in peace," Laurence said. "But of late, I've had more nightmares than dreams."

"*I* have long been plagued by a recurring nightmare. I am in the Banqueting Hall, with His Majesty and Prince Charles, who commands that I be taken away, and hanged, drawn, and quartered, and that my head be stuck on Traitors Gate." As well it might have been, Laurence thought, though he did not interrupt. "And next, Mr. Beaumont, the *King's* head lolls about on his neck, falls, and drops into my lap. I cannot shake it off, as though it is glued there. You may say the dream was a product of my guilty conscience, yet at the time I had designs upon His Majesty's life, I honestly felt no guilt."

*Do you now?* Laurence was tempted to ask. Although the image of the royal head disturbed him, he was not altogether surprised that he and Pembroke had both dreamt of the King's death. He considered telling Pembroke how the conspiracy to regicide had been based on an erroneous horoscope; but in the end he merely observed, "Perhaps our dreams unbury what we daren't admit to ourselves in our waking hours."

"Yes, perhaps. Before we retire, sir," Pembroke announced, in a different tone, "I shall order my coach for seven of the clock tomorrow morning, to go on a visit to my friend the Earl of Bedford at his Woburn estate. Like me, he was of the peace party at Westminster. He shifted allegiances too often between King and Parliament to deserve either side's trust, for which he has my sympathy, and he was pleased to quit politics. He is Lord Digby's brother-in-law, in fact – Digby married his sister, Anne."

"What a small world it is, among noble families."

"Your father did well to bring in fresh blood by marrying your mother."

"I believe her world in Spain was even smaller, in that regard."

Pembroke stood, and picked up his cane. "You and Lady Hallam shall travel with me out of London."

Laurence gaped at him. "But, my lord—"

"I have never yet been impeded by the militia," Pembroke continued, with his former, masterful authority. "If she's as convincing a boy as she was today and if you don't object to huddling beneath my seat in the coach, I think we can outwit them." When Laurence tried again to protest, Pembroke talked over him. "Wait and listen to what I want in exchange: those letters of mine and Radcliff's that you gave to the King. Then our debts will be cancelled, Mr. Beaumont. I shall sleep easier – and I might even be rid of my nightmare."

From the window of his bedchamber, Laurence looked out at a forest of stars above the roof of Whitehall Palace. Whatever they might portend was no less of an enigma to him than the transformation in Pembroke. A man who had attempted last year to kill him was risking everything to save him and Isabella. Was it for the letters, or did Pembroke seek the forgiveness of a higher power than the King's for his past treachery? Or had loneliness and boredom drawn him again into flirting with danger?

Laurence heard his door creak open. He turned to see a phantom drift through, shut the door, and glide into his bed. Without a word, he threw off his clothes and lay down beside her. Neither of them spoke, until the stars faded and the sky had lightened to a pale silvery grey.

How fragile she was, he thought, without her lush curves; and how bereft of worldliness, without her luxuriant hair and her exotic perfume. Yet her spell was as strong over him. "It's dawn," he murmured, "and we've been awake all night."

"I slept all day." She caressed the scar on his shoulder. "This is new. Where did you come by it?"

"I was wounded escaping from London, in January. Isabella," he went on, after a short silence, "Pembroke has offered to smuggle us out in his coach. You must wear your boy's disguise and sit next to his driver. I'll be hidden inside the coach, under his lordship's seat."

"Oh thank God. I am so eager to leave. But what will happen to us, Beaumont, if we succeed?"

"We'll go to Oxford. Then I must return to His Majesty's camp."

She exhaled a quick, impatient breath. "What will happen between *us*? No other man has lain with me, since we bade each other goodbye. I want none other than you. Oh Beaumont, why did I let Digby persuade me into that counterfeit of a marriage? Could we somehow undo my mistake?"

Laurence groaned and rolled over, covering his face with his hands. "You have a husband, and I have a wife."

"As Digby wrote to me – the girl your mother had chosen."

"No, I married her sister, Catherine."

"Catherine Beaumont." Isabella spoke as if tasting the name. "For these last hours you were able to forget her." Laurence said nothing: Isabella was right. "Are you in love with her?"

"No. But I am extremely fond of her, and I owe it to her to make her happy. I chose her because . . . she's the opposite of her sister. She's had a hard life. She has the falling sickness, and she was mistreated by her family."

"And you pitied her."

"I don't pity her in the least. I admire her. She has a free spirit and a brave heart, like you."

Isabella shifted in bed and took away his hands. "Then you still love me."

"With all *my* heart and I always will."

"Have you been faithful to her until now?"

"Yes, though to be frank, I haven't yet spent an entire night with her. The war has intervened. But my marriage is *not* a counterfeit. I can't leave her, Isabella."

"Will you tell her about *us*?"

"She knows of you. About this, I won't, unless she asks."

Isabella studied him, as though tracing every inch of his body and recording it to memory; and beneath the heat of her gaze, he felt the blood rush into his groin. "Beaumont," she said, "we're not done with each other." She knelt over his hips and took him inside her. As they moved together, he seemed transported to that fateful moment, on a cliff near Cádiz at the very end of Spain; he was aiming a pistol at his own temple, staring down at jagged rock and swirling tide where the gulls soared and swooped. He depressed the trigger and the ball blasted past, deafening him. And he saw Isabella's eyes widen at exactly the same time, as if she too had heard the explosion of fire.

## II.

After the initial, tantalising news of Prince Rupert's northern victory, the King's camp at Evesham had received uncertain, often conflicting messages, some optimistic and some alarming. Digby had read that cartfuls of dead and dying Royalist soldiers had been seen trundling through the gates of York, but he refused to believe this possible. Meanwhile, the King fretted about his wife, lying weak and helpless with her little daughter at Exeter: scouts brought word that Essex was within two days' march of there. His Majesty had written urging Rupert to go to her aid, yet in the absence of any communication from the Prince, he could wait no longer to address the threat.

The royal army pressed into the southwest, travelling in one day a full seventeen miles to Coberly, a village not far from Cheltenham. Digby was settling to bed when a royal page summoned him to an impromptu midnight meeting of Council. He dragged himself over, yawning, to find the King ashen-faced. "An express has c-come from my n-nephew, and others who f-fought in the n-north," His Majesty stammered, and asked Culpeper to read the reports aloud.

A major defeat had been inflicted on the Prince by the allied armies of Parliament and the Scots on the moors outside York. He had lost much of his Foot and heavy artillery, his cavalry had been scattered far and wide, and he himself had narrowly avoided capture. They could not precisely estimate the number of dead, but it might be close to four thousand. After the battle he had withdrawn to York, but that garrison would soon have to surrender. Short of powder and weapons, he was nonetheless gathering his regiments of Horse, and would retreat through Lancashire, with the aim of seeking safe haven at his headquarters in Shrewsbury. In a poignant aside to the King, Rupert mentioned that his faithful companion, Boy, had perished on Marston field.

None of the King's Council dared state the obvious: that it had taken almost ten days for the King to learn that the north was all but lost to him; a stunning failure of intelligence. For the rest of the night, Digby lay awake bemoaning the disaster, and not solely for the Royalist cause: his own assiduously planned scheme to pit Rupert against Wilmot and drive Wilmot from power was unravelling.

**III.**

"As soon as I have seen my family, Capitán, I'll ride for Madrid to take up my commission," Antonio said to Iturbe. "How pleased my Teresa will be to welcome her Odysseus home from his travels. She must have wondered at my fate."

From the deck of the ship, they were staring out towards the mouth of the Thames, while Diego investigated the berths below.

Diego had moped peevishly for a while after his outrageous conduct at Chipping Campden, but Iturbe's genial company on the road had forced him to behave; and the Envoy had shown them all unstinting hospitality once they had arrived in London.

"Don Antonio," said Iturbe, "I regret to announce that an unanticipated business will prevent me from sailing with you. I must stay in England until it is arranged to my satisfaction. I heard of it only yesterday, and I did not wish to spoil our last evening together. Now, keep that purse I gave you safe, on the voyage. There are often thieves among the crew."

"I've experience of English thieves to last me a lifetime," Antonio said. "And the Envoy gifted me a fine rapier that I won't hesitate to use, should any brigand cross me."

"Then I need not worry for you, *El Valoroso*," laughed Iturbe. After more courtesies, they parted. He strode off along the gangplank, and became lost from view in the crowds upon the dock.

Today the sun shone down out of a cloudless sky, as though to augur Antonio's swift passage to Spanish shores; and the scent of fish and seawater in the air, and the mewing cries of gulls, reminded him of the port at Seville. He began to dream of the happy surprise with which Teresa would receive news of the honour King Philip was bestowing on him.

"Did you say goodbye to the Captain?" Diego had returned very quietly to the upper deck, his bag slung over his shoulder. "If so, it's time for us to do the same."

"What rubbish are you talking?" asked Antonio.

"I'm not going with you. I confided in the Envoy about my situation, and he offered me a place at the embassy as his clerk."

"Your *situation*?"

"Don Antonio, the immortal Petronius tells us, *Qualis dominus, talis et servus* – like master, like servant. You've been my master, but I am not like you. In fact," Diego continued, "I'm your superior, and you've become a millstone around my neck. The Envoy has promised to further my career. I shouldn't be amazed if one day I hold high office as a diplomat. And if by chance we meet again, which I sincerely hope may never be the case, please don't expect me to acknowledge our acquaintance."

Antonio unsheathed his rapier. In a trice, a bunch of ragged sailors encircled him, and a stout, smartly clad gentleman of weather-beaten countenance hurried up to stand in front of Diego. "Sir, as captain of this vessel, I command you to put away your weapon and let this young man leave unharmed."

"Certainly, sir," Antonio said, and slid his rapier into its sheath. "Goodbye, Diego, and I wish you the future you deserve, in this god-forsaken country," he added, in Spanish.

"*Más vale maña que fuerza*," taunted Diego. He bowed mock-ingly, and sallied away.

Antonio looked round agreeably at the men. "I shall translate, for those of you unfamiliar with my language. How do the English say it – *brains are worth more than brawn*."

**IV.**

Although a hole had been cut into the floor of Pembroke's coach for Laurence to breathe, he was fainting and soaked in perspiration when the coach stopped towards midday, less than ten miles from Westminster. But they had passed through the defences. After he had shaken off his cramp, he and Isabella bade a grateful goodbye to Pembroke.

"My lady," said Pembroke, "were every boy like you, I should turn sodomite."

"Your lordship flatters me," said Isabella, with her old arch smile.

"I swear it is the truth. And remember, sir," he said, in a private aside to Laurence, "my assistance is not free of charge. How should we communicate?"

"Through the code you used in those letters you want back," Laurence suggested. "If all goes well, I intend to leave Lady Hallam at Governor Aston's house. I'll get a message to her, once I have news for you."

He and Isabella walked on until nightfall, when they searched out a dry spot in a hedgerow to sleep. Isabella's feet had bled into her ill-fitting boy's shoes, and she had been limping towards the end, yet nothing could depress her mood. He felt as blissfully complete. The sight of her face, the sound of her voice, the warmth of her body next to his, gave him delight both agonising and exquisite, because it could not last. In the morning, he managed to buy a horse at extortionate cost. Driving the animal harder than he thought fair with its double burden, he cut across country to Oxford, which they reached in darkness. Governor Aston invited him to rest a while, but he stayed just to scribble a note for Aston to send on to Chipping Campden, and kissed Isabella on the hand; the Governor was watching. Then, with a fresh horse from Aston's stables, he travelled southwest nearly eighty miles, tracking the King's army into Somerset.

He rode into His Majesty's camp muddy, reeking of sweat, saddle-sore, and so worn that he could barely think. At the cottage where Lord Digby was billeted, he received a frigid welcome. His lordship looked unwell, his eyes puffy, his mouth trembling. "I should felicitate you upon returning alive, Mr. Beaumont," he said, "though I surmise that you did not succeed in your endeavour." From his pocket he produced a diamond ring. "I received this with Isabella's finger inside. I presume it was cut off before she burnt to death."

Laurence started to laugh, to Digby's manifest horror. "My lord, as you may have guessed, Veech cut the finger – from *Lucy's* hand when she was already dead. And he took the ring from Isabella *before* her escape from the Tower. She's now at Governor Aston's house, alive and well, with all ten of her fingers."

Digby gave a little cry, and dissolved into tears.

When he had dried them, Laurence recounted to him the events at the Tower, omitting the names of those involved in her rescue. "And as to who assisted in our flight from London, my lord, I must remain as silent. These people ventured far more for Isabella than I, and their lives are still in danger, as a consequence. Did her legal counsel, Mr. Draycott, come to you?"

"Yes, at our camp in Evesham over a week ago, with some unlikely tale about wishing to go to her aid. He begged me for your help – to deliver you to Veech, if I am not mistaken. Mr. Price recognised him as Veech's accomplice. He is being held in Oxford Castle."

"God damn," swore Laurence. "If I'd known when I was there . . . He was telling you the truth, as Isabella will confirm. He's an honest man who was forced against his will to spy for Veech. He must be freed at once."

"You say he is honest, and yet you cannot be honest with *me*, sir, as to how you effected Isabella's escape *and* yours. I financed the operation – I deserve to know."

"Is it not enough for you that she was rescued?" Laurence asked, thinking his lordship more deserved a punch in the face.

"I believe you are shielding the same *friend* in Parliament who gave you intelligence last January of the plot to seize Prince Rupert hostage, and I would like to have his name. It's an issue of trust between us," Digby added, in a threatening tone. "Comply with my request and I will send Aston an order to free Draycott. Until you do, I see no reason to let him out."

"Then if you will pardon me," said Laurence, "I must seek an audience with the King, before I succumb to my fatigue."

"I hope you remember, sir: we agreed you would accept full responsibility for your venture to London. Should you discuss it with His Majesty, do please make clear to him that it was your idea. After all, the credit should be entirely yours, for your gallant and intrepid deed."

"Thank you, but I am unworthy of such lavish praise."

"My dear Mr. Beaumont, has no one ever told you that sarcasm is the lowest form of wit?"

"I can imagine no one better than you to remind me, my lord."

"*Touché*," exclaimed Digby. "If only you were as skilled with a rapier – it would give me great pleasure to spar with you. And now, sir, you would do well to avail yourself of soap and water, lest you offend His Majesty's nose. He is quartered in town at the house of a Mr. Dawes."

Without consideration for His Majesty's nose, Laurence went straight to the royal quarters. The King was exercising his dogs in Mr. Dawes' garden, and graciously agreed to see Laurence. He listened while Laurence described a somewhat different version of the events in London, telling him of Pembroke's exceptional courage. "Your Majesty, Lady Hallam and I are in debt to him for our lives, and I know he's filled with remorse for his past treachery."

"I am heartened by that, Mr. Beaumont," the King said, as he threw a ball to his frolicking dogs. "Were he to renounce his aff-fection to Parliament and join me here, I would be more heart-ened still."

"Yes I'm sure of it, Your Majesty, but he's of the opinion that he can better serve you by representing the interests of the peace party at Westminster," Laurence said, creatively.

"They must be a s-sorry bunch, these days," murmured the King.

"He did request a favour, in exchange for the immense risk he undertook for us, your agents."

One of the dogs had raced back with the ball, and deposited it at the King's feet. He bent to pick it up, examining it with a meditative air as the dog wagged its tail, panting, eager for the game to recom-mence. "What f-favour, sir?"

"If it please Your Majesty, he desires the return of those letters between him and Sir Bernard Radcliff, that weigh so heavily on his conscience."

The King fixed on Laurence his liquid brown eyes. "Mr. B-beaumont, you were the man who found him out. And as I remember, you were of the view that he should have been b-brought to trial, and that I showed him undue mercy."

"I did, Your Majesty. But, like the Earl, I have had a change of heart."

"I cannot accede to his desire. When, by God's grace, peace is restored to my kingdom, and I to my city of London, I shall consider a p-pardon to those who have unlawfully rebelled against me, my Lord Pembroke included. That is my answer, unless, as I told you, he will come unto my camp, in open proof of his fealty to me."

"I thank Your Majesty," said Laurence. "And if I could suggest to Your Majesty, he may be able to offer you further assistance in London, so long as he's not discovered by the Committee of Both Kingdoms, or by anyone in Your Majesty's camp who might inadvertently expose him to Parliament as your friend."

"Are you asking me to k-keep his name from my Secretary of State?"

Laurence met the King's eyes. "I am pleading with Your Majesty to keep his name a secret between *us*."

"Very well, sir, you have my promise." Laurence reiterated his thanks, and bowed; the King had turned back to his dogs. "Good boy, good girl," he crooned, as they gambolled about his ankles.

How to trust the promise of this king, Laurence wondered, as he walked away. Then he saw Digby coming towards him, evidently bound for the garden. Digby stopped to inquire, "Was your audience satisfactory, sir?" Laurence did not answer, brushing by so close that his lordship had to step hastily out of his path.

**V.**

Pembroke watched the troop of guards file in ceremony through the doors of the House of Commons; they were carrying the Royalist standards seized at Marston Moor. Once proud, the banners were now stained and tattered; pieces must have been torn from the cloth by greedy soldiers as trophies of war. "Alas for Rupert," he muttered, recognising the Prince's standard: black and gold for the Palatinate, and blue and silver for Bavaria.

He was about to leave when Oliver St. John came stalking purposefully in his direction. "My lord," St. John said, "we must praise God for this proof of our victory: forty-eight colours in all."

"I shall take your word for it – I have not yet had occasion to count them," said Pembroke, unwilling to show him any politesse.

"I gather you were absent from the Upper House this week."

"Yes: I made a journey to Woburn, to call upon the Earl of Bedford."

"On a political matter?"

"No, sir, it was to discuss some alterations that he is planning for his house."

"My lord, when you passed through the redoubt at Constitution Hill on your way out of the City, the patrol on duty saw a young boy sitting up beside your coachman. When you returned yesterday, via that route, he was not with you. Who was he?"

Pembroke feigned bemusement. "You show an uncommon interest in my comings and goings, sir."

"Not I, my lord – my agent Mr. Veech brought this to my notice. Mr. Veech is attempting to recapture Lady Hallam, who escaped from the Tower in the guise of a boy, two days before you departed for my Lord Bedford's house. He fears she may have slipped by our defences."

"Would he imply she did so in *my vehicle*?" asked Pembroke, so scathingly that St. John blushed. "The boy is kin to my steward, who had been training him in the duties of a page. I've no room for more servants in my small quarters at the Cockpit. Bedford offered to accept him into his household, and I conveyed him thence. Your agent can go himself to Woburn, if he is still curious."

"My lord, were you not acquainted with Sir Montague Hallam?"

"He was my wine merchant."

"And were you ever introduced to Lady Hallam?"

Pembroke laughed, shaking his head. "It is not my habit, sir, to keep company with tradesmen or with their good lady wives."

Ignoring St. John's embarrassment, he carried on towards the street doors. A dark bulky-figured man in a long coat blocked his exit. "My Lord Pembroke," the man said, in a sonorous voice, "I am Clement Veech. I apologise to your lordship if Mr. St. John and I caused you inconvenience with our questions."

Pembroke's fingers twitched on his cane. "Mr. St. John is a lawyer, sir. Before you cause me more inconvenience, you should inquire of him the penalty for defaming a peer of the realm."

"I only seek the truth, my lord, to bring criminals to justice, whosoever they may be. It's a virtue of this country that no man, not even the King, can be above the law." Veech retreated, and Pembroke went out swearing to himself.

## VI.

Buffeted by wind, the Royalist army stood massed on Dartmoor as the King and Prince Charles rode forward to acknowledge the knots of local onlookers. "Not many recruits to be had among these Somerset yokels, though they can boast to their grandchildren that they once saw His Majesty in the flesh," Digby observed to Laurence, whom he was keeping close to his side during the march southwest, and out of Wilmot's purview. His lordship had been all warmth and cordiality since their discussion of Isabella, as though repenting of his own ingratitude, which did not deceive Laurence.

Today Prince Charles presented himself with a new, adult dignity. Nothing like war to turn a youth into a man, Laurence thought, although his nightmares reminded him how vulnerable the Prince was still, as a boy of fourteen. The King, meanwhile, appeared in a sanguine mood: his beloved wife had eluded capture by Parliament and sailed from Falmouth over a week ago, leaving the baby princess in care of the Governor at Exeter, where the army was now headed.

"The King talks of demolishing Essex's forces, as he threw Waller's into chaos," Digby said. "Even our northern defeat has not cast him low – it has only endeared Rupert the more to him."

"'I shall conclude with this promise to you,'" the King's messenger was declaring, reading from His Majesty's script, "'that I shall look upon your cheerfulness in this service as the greatest expression of your loyalty and affections that you can make or I receive, which I shall requite, if it be in my power. If I live not to do it, I hope this young man, my son, your fellow soldier in this expedition, will, to whom I shall particularly give it charge.'"

His audience hurrahed and clapped, drums rolled, and trumpets blared. As the parade broke up, Wilmot cantered his horse towards Laurence and Digby. "My Lord Digby," he said, in his peremptory manner, "might I speak with Mr. Beaumont? I want to borrow his scouts tonight, to go on a foray."

"Do not be long, sir," Digby told Laurence, unctuously.

Laurence felt a quiver of anxiety as he rode after Wilmot, who reined in when they were some distance from the ranks and exclaimed, "Digby seems to think he's your goddamned wet nurse."

"He wants me by him because he doesn't trust me any more," said Laurence.

"Well he's stirring up trouble for *me*, spewing slander to the King. Beaumont, are you privy to his correspondence with Prince Rupert?"

"Not recently, though he uses a figure I devised for him."

"I know he's conspiring against me, reinventing himself as Rupert's ally. He may even be encouraging the King to demote me."

"That can't be true, not when we may soon engage with Essex," objected Laurence, appalled by Wilmot's grandiose fantasies. "The King will be relying upon you, as his best general of Horse."

"That's precisely it, Beaumont." Wilmot urged his mount up to Laurence's. "Digby has convinced the King that the war can yet be won in the field. He's a panderer of dreams to His Majesty. We've lost the north, most of England's ports, much of the midlands, and a large part of the southeast. The royal cause is doomed. If it weren't for Digby and that turd Culpeper, we could end hostilities in a matter of months – or before. Many of us in the army believe that if made the right offer, Essex will come to an accommodation. He's no friend to the radical Independents, either in Westminster or in the Parliament's northern armies. He'd settle for a peace, rather than protract a war that will ruin our country. And if he does, we shall save lives, to say nothing of our estates."

"Whatever happens to Digby or Culpeper, you know the King will never accept peace on any terms but his own. And Essex will refuse to negotiate without consent of Parliament, as he has in the past."

Wilmot tapped the side of his nose with a gloved finger. "His Majesty can't go on fighting without his southern army. And that army is with *me*, Beaumont. Who else has its respect? Not Forth. He must be tossing and turning every night, wondering how quickly the King will have Rupert replace him as Lord Marshal. No surprise Digby has been cuddling up to Rupert: the Prince will have vast power with the King."

"What evidence do you have of this?"

"Not as much as I would like, which is where *you* can help me. You must be able to get to his lordship's correspondence."

Swallowing a stream of invective, Laurence took a moment to compose himself. "You don't quite grasp my position with our Secretary of State. He was so infuriated after I rode with you at Cropredy Bridge that he sent me on an errand to London from which he must have hoped I wouldn't come back. And since then, he won't let me near his private communications."

"Find a means of reading them, Beaumont."

"As your friend, Wilmot, I beg you not to ask."

"I *am* asking. Don't forget your pledge to me."

"I can't promise you any result."

"There's my man," said Wilmot, slapping him on the shoulder.

**VII.**

On the twenty-sixth of July, Digby went with the King, Prince Charles, and the royal Troop to a joyful meeting outside Exeter, where they were greeted by Prince Maurice, Digby's father Bristol, the city

Governor, and most of the principal gentlemen and Commissioners of Somerset and Devon. An enthusiastic crowd waited cheering at the gates, but the King did not pause for an address; with his eldest son, Digby, and Bristol, he rode to the Governor's house to see his infant daughter for the first time.

In the afternoon Council assembled, joined by Maurice, whom Digby found even cruder in manner and more tiresomely overbearing than his brother Rupert. It was at length decided that while His Majesty's army replenished its store of provisions with the assistance of the local gentry and officials, Prince Maurice's army would serve as an advance guard to chase Essex into Cornwall, which was, in the King's words, a county most affectionate to the royal cause.

Before supper, Digby and Bristol adjourned to their chamber in the Governor's house; they had not talked in an age. "His Majesty did not exaggerate: Henrietta is the prettiest babe," said Digby, averting his eyes as his less fastidious father unlaced and sat down upon the close stool.

Bristol was quiet, concentrating, and then exhaled a contented sigh. "Pray God her mother reaches France safely," he said, beckoning Quayle to pass him a napkin.

Digby let him finish and restore his clothing, then dismissed Quayle and shut the door. "So, Rupert is heading south again, to his headquarters at Shrewsbury. How admirable he is, to have pulled back together a fighting force even while crushed by the death of his darling Boy at Marston Moor. And at last he has moved on *our* behalf."

"Ah yes?" said Bristol, as he gave his fingertips a cursory rinse in the water basin.

"He has dispatched General Goring – to the city of Bristol, by coincidence – in search of powder supplies."

"That is marvellous, George!"

"Marvellous but late." Digby unlocked the coffer where he stored his correspondence, and produced his copy of the King's letter. "Written on my advice," he said, handing it to his father.

"'Nephew,'" Bristol read aloud, "'this is most earnestly to desire you, as you love your own preservation and mine, to send me General Goring with all speed . . . I hope you will not delay the doing of it, for I assure you the importance of it is no less than as I have said, and for which I am sure you will thank me as soon as ye shall know the particular reasons of it . . . and so I rest, Your loving uncle and most faithful friend, Charles R.' This is dated over a month ago. Did the Prince not respond?"

"He did not. Then the battle at Cropredy redeemed Wilmot in the public eye, and the timorous Culpeper, among others, refused to act until we had accurate reports of the Prince's victory in Yorkshire. When the catastrophic news reached us, I gave up hope that Goring could be spared. And after I had taken inordinate pains to smooth over the differences between Rupert and myself! I have copies of those letters, too, in case *he* ever accuses me of conspiring against him."

"Keep him kindly disposed to you, George: write tonight, and thank him." Bristol regarded his son more soberly. "Now tell me about Isabella." He exclaimed under his breath, when Digby described Sir Montague's ignominious behaviour. "What a louse, and a traitor both to her and to the royal cause."

"Somehow Mr. Beaumont extricated her from the Tower, and she is now in Oxford. He said the rescue was not to be credited to him, but to his friends in the City – presumably the same bunch of thieves and whores whom he relied upon in the past. Yet at least one *friend* must be a man of some stature – in Parliament."

"Why do you say that?"

"Remember how Beaumont forewarned us that Prince Rupert might be taken hostage last winter? He said he got his intelligence from a friend of the King whose name he had to protect. I asked him plainly, on this occasion, whether the same person had helped him, and demanded to know the man's name. He flew into a temper and refused to supply it." Digby giggled. "How splendidly handsome he looked, like some Eastern sheikh snubbed by a slave! Then he stormed off to an audience with the King. I encountered him as he was leaving the royal presence, and he virtually thrust me aside. And when I inquired of His Majesty whether Beaumont had identified our allies in London who had done us such devoted duty, he said it was a matter between him and Mr. Beaumont. I *am* intrigued. I'll have to ask Isabella, when I next see her. She will tell me."

"She may not. And George, you must prepare to be hurt. Beaumont will stand by Wilmot."

"If he does, he shall be sorry for it. But why do you use that word, sir, *hurt?*"

"*Know thyself* was the ancient dictum. You are so busy speculating upon the motivation of those around you, that you neglect to study yours."

"I confess, honoured father, that I am still at a loss to comprehend you."

"You fancy yourself a playwright, in your idle hours." Bristol hesitated. "You might recall a line from a comedy – what is it that poisons *more deadly than a mad dog's tooth?*"

"*The venom clamours of a jealous woman,*" Digby replied easily, though he felt his cheeks grow hot.


"May it please Your Highness," he began that night, as he always did his letters to Rupert, "since my last unto you at Bath wherein I stated unto Your Highness the condition of our affairs here . . ." And he provided a succinct, cheery account of His Majesty's prospects with Essex. "Our great care at this time is for Your Highness," he went on, and referred to the supplies of powder Rupert had been requesting from his uncle. Digby continued, with a distinct frisson, "We are very glad to understand that Goring is come so near as Bristol; the business he came for shall be gone through with, the superseding of Wilmot; but till we have spoken with him, I cannot certainly tell Your Highness in what particular manner. As soon as it is done Your Highness shall receive an express; in the meantime, and ever, I beseech Your Highness to believe that I am Your Highness's most faithful humble servant, George Digby."

As he transcribed these lines into cipher, Digby mused over his father's remarks about Wilmot and Beaumont. He pictured Wilmot insolent, as when he had last demanded to speak alone with Beaumont, and then humiliated, as he would be in short order. What had those two talked about that day? Beaumont had ridden back looking as if Wilmot had asked to borrow his soul, rather than his scouts.

Hurriedly Digby sealed his missive, and woke Quayle, who was dozing on his pallet near the canopied four-poster where Bristol lay asleep. "Find Mr. Price. Tell him to come to me, *without* alerting Mr. Beaumont."

## VIII.

On the second of August, while the royal army was marching deeper into Cornwall with Prince Maurice's forces, a courier brought a bag of correspondence for Lord Digby, forwarded by Governor Aston from Oxford. Three of the letters were addressed to Laurence, who felt bound to open his mother's before those of Isabella and Seward.

Lady Beaumont had good and bad news: thanks to the Spanish Envoy, her cousin and Diego must now be on their way to Spain; and Ingram had survived Marston Moor, and was with Prince Rupert's army. Tom had fared less well. "Adam brought him home to us grievously wounded from a ball that had struck his thigh. He was spared the leg being cut off, but his wound had festered. I agreed with my lord to summon Dr. Seward, who is still here with us, and Thomas mends slowly." Laurence thought of her ladyship's antipathy to Seward; Tom must have been in truly dangerous straits. "We fear he may not be fit again for army service," she wrote on, "and he has taken this hard, despite the joy he has in his son, James, who thrives . . ."

Laurence turned to Isabella's letter. She said that her health was much improved, and that she had visited Draycott in Oxford Castle. "It is a strange reversal of his circumstances with mine. How

I dreaded setting foot in that place again, and the Governor of Oxford keeps his prisoners in the most degrading conditions. I told him Mr. Draycott must be moved to a better cell, which has since been done. Draycott has one aim, to be rid of our enemy, but the fulfilment of this depends upon your advice and his freedom." Below, she had copied a line in Pembroke's code. Obviously she had heard from Pembroke, which to Laurence boded ill. Would Veech have the gall to arrest a lord? And how could they plot Veech's death when Laurence was far away from Oxford, and further yet from London? "I have such memories of us," she ended.

Seward's script was brief. "This in haste; her ladyship will write of Thomas. Suffice to say he is recovering. As for recovery, your wife gave back to me what I had imagined lost forever."

That evening the combined Royalist armies, some sixteen thousand strong, made camp around the market town of Liskeard, near Bodmin Moor. Once Laurence had sent his scouts out to reconnoitre, he transcribed Pembroke's code: "The limping man knows all, but has no proof. He may get it, should he find your friends."

By dusk, the scouts began to trickle back with intelligence. Essex's forces lay about six miles to the west, in the direction of Lostwithiel: he had an estimated ten thousand men, and was hoping for reinforcements by sea from the Parliamentary fleet, and by land, possibly from Waller. "His boys must be hungry, sir," one of the scouts joked to Laurence. "The local people have refused them provisions."

"My lord," said Laurence to Digby, when he had relayed this news, "we could spread a rumour to Essex that His Majesty has twice his actual strength. As long as Essex is so poorly supplied, he'll try at all costs to avoid an engagement. And the longer we can pin him down and starve him out, the better."

"Why not come with me and propose this to Council tonight?" Digby asked.

"Thank you, but I must stay and wait for more news from the scouts," Laurence replied; he did not feel like listening to hours of debate among the King's advisors, nor did he want to be collared afterwards by Wilmot. Yet he could see Digby was offended that he should decline.

Over the following days, scouts reported that Essex was stretched thin to control the area around Lostwithiel and defend himself against a force that he now assumed was more than three times the size of his own. The King was also awaiting reinforcements: he had called for the only other Royalist troops in Cornwall to move in and block any chance of a Parliamentarian retreat. To make matters worse for Essex, a party of Royalist cavalry surprised some distinguished rebel officers who were carousing at the house of a nobleman, a few miles from Essex's headquarters, and most were taken prisoner; a source of great hilarity to the Royalists.

"Now that Essex is cornered and demoralised, His Majesty plans to offer him a pardon," Digby told Laurence, "if he will reconsider his allegiance to Parliament and join with the royal army to preserve the kingdom from further bloodshed."

"I doubt Essex will concede," said Laurence, with genuine regret: this would have put paid to Wilmot's scheming. Although he and Wilmot had steered clear of each other since their talk, he knew Wilmot expected information from him; and to preserve both of them from disaster, he would not so much as look for it.

Late on the night of the sixth of August, Wilmot's pageboy came creeping into the barn near Digby's billet where Laurence slept, and asked him to meet Wilmot at a stretch of down some miles west of camp. With a sinking heart, he threw on his cloak, saddled his mount, and rode over, checking behind himself every so often to ensure no one was tailing him.

Laurence found Wilmot on the windswept hill, gazing at the distant enemy fires. "Have you news for me, Beaumont?" he asked, without ado.

"I'm afraid not."

"Are you aware of the terms His Majesty is sending to Essex?"

"Yes I am, and Essex will reject them."

"Essex won't trust the King, with reason, but he might listen to an appeal from our army. We're to issue a second proposal, openly and with His Majesty's blessing. It will be dispatched tomorrow night, once his chief officers are at leisure to sign it."

Rain had begun to fall in torrents from the dark skies. Covering their heads with their cloaks, they sought the only available shelter: a copse of stunted trees surrounded by tall bracken.

"If the second proposal has His Majesty's blessing, why did you call me out to discuss it at such an ungodly hour, and in the middle of nowhere?" Laurence demanded.

"You must invent an excuse to accompany the army delegates, and when you get to Essex's headquarters, slip him a message from me. If he'll accept a cessation of arms, I shall guarantee, as Lieutenant General, that Digby and Culpeper will be removed from power."

Laurence shivered. *Madness, madness*, he wanted to say. "How on earth can you guarantee that?"

"I told you, I'll have the support of the army. You know how the King's civilian advisors are loathed by those they send out so gaily to die in battle."

"And would you subvert *the King's* authority?"

"As I'll explain to Essex, if need be and as a last resort, our combined forces will take His Majesty under our protection to London."

*Plain treason*, Laurence nearly shouted. "No, Wilmot, don't even hint at such an idea, or you'll prejudice your case with Essex," he said, in a low voice.

"It's past the time to mince words."

"You could pay with your life."

"As I might have at Edgehill, Roundway Down, Cropredy Bridge, and in countless skirmishes fought in His Majesty's cause," retorted Wilmot. "He's being poisoned by Digby and such like. And in the very slight event that he defeats Parliament in battle, he'd have to sell his crown to Rupert."

"I don't believe Rupert gives a fuck for the crown – he's a soldier, for God's sake." Laurence seized Wilmot's arm. "Is that truly what *you* believe, or is your lesser nature talking? Wilmot, please, I beg of you, think again."

"I *have* thought. You're as sick to the teeth as I am of Digby, and of this war." Wilmot closed his hand on Laurence's, in a tight grip. "Beaumont, will you do it for me?"

Laurence tried to answer, but his throat was parched. He tipped up his chin and opened his mouth, to catch a few drops of rain. Then he licked his lips, and gave Wilmot an almost imperceptible, reluctant, nod.

On the seventh of August, His Majesty's offer was conveyed to Essex, who greeted it with a blunt response. "'That he, the Lord General, would discharge his duty,'" Digby quoted to Laurence, "'and would advise the King to return to his Parliament.'"

"The same answer as always, my lord," said Laurence.

"We shall see if the army's proposal has better fortune. It will be dispatched tonight, signed by Prince Maurice, Prince Rupert *in absentia*, Forth, and His Majesty's chief officers."

"My lord, why don't I follow the delegates with some of our scouts," Laurence said casually. "While Essex is receiving the proposal, we might have a look round his camp."

"Yes, sir, why not," said Digby, far too readily.

Instinct told Laurence that Digby had either guessed or been explicitly forewarned about a secret communication from Wilmot to Essex. Whoever had reported this must have shadowed Wilmot or Laurence to their nocturnal rendezvous. The message to Essex had been burning a hole in Laurence's pocket ever since Wilmot's boy had brought it earlier in the day, concealed within a letter addressed to Mr. Beaumont. And even now, Laurence sensed that he was being watched leaving Digby's billet. A few troopers wandered after him, as at a leisurely pace he retired to the latrine ditches on the edge of the Royalist camp. They fell back when he chose a private spot, lowered his breeches, and squatted down. Surreptitiously he opened the message; it contained what he had heard from Wilmot, including the proposal to take His Majesty under protection to London. He ripped it up, tossed the shreds in the ditch, and with a stick poked every last one of them deep into the ordure. He would decide whether to approach Essex, and what to say if he did, once he got to the Earl's headquarters.

That night he and the scouts rode westwards, on the heels of the army delegation. They had not gone a mile when he saw another party of riders pursuing them, splashing through the puddles. Price was at the lead, with a dozen troopers bearing torches. Laurence reined in, and signalled for the scouts to halt.

"Beaumont," called Price, "Lord Digby wishes you to turn back, and let the others press on."

"Why's that, Price?" asked Laurence.

"He didn't say." Price trotted his horse nearer. In the fierce torchlight, Laurence stared into his eyes: here was the shadow. Price glanced away, at the scouts, and at his troopers. "I'm to escort you, Beaumont," he muttered, in an awkward voice. "We have orders to search you first, however."

"Search him, sir – what for?" a scout objected to Price; the loyal youths were bringing their horses around Laurence in a defensive knot.

"Please dismount, Beaumont, and raise your arms," said Price.

Laurence shrugged. "Go on without me," he told the scouts.

They galloped off, casting resentful backward glares at Price. The troopers set to work on Laurence, stripping him of his cloak and doublet, and hunting in his shirt and in the pockets of his breeches. He had to remove his boots and stockings and stand barefoot in the mud while they searched these items; they also unbuckled his saddle, lest he had tucked anything beneath it, and plodded about inspecting the waterlogged tracks left by the horses. "Price," he said, with an imitation of bored annoyance, "what in God's name is this about?"

Price guided him out of the troopers' earshot. "Wherever you've hidden it, you must give me Wilmot's letter. I promise you won't come to grief."

"What letter?"

"There's no point in denying it," Price babbled on. "Digby knows that Wilmot and some of his officers are seeking an accommodation with Essex. He knows you met with Wilmot last night, and that Wilmot intended to offer Essex secret terms. He knows you were to carry the letter."

"Yes I met with Wilmot," said Laurence, narrowing his eyes at Price. "But I have no letter. Where the hell did Digby get his information?" Price's mouth started to quiver. "Did he ask you to spy on me?"

"No, I was to . . . to keep Wilmot under surveillance, so that I could protect you."

"You lying piece of shit. Did you follow me from the camp that night?"

"I followed Wilmot. I was there before you arrived."

"Where were you hiding – in the copse of trees?" Price winced an affirmative. "What did you hear?"

"I heard enough."

"Did you hear me agree to take a letter to Essex?" yelled Laurence; Price could not have caught the minuscule nod of his head which had terminated the exchange.

"Not in . . . so many words."

"Didn't I teach you, in such circumstances, not to assume you have the facts?"

"I wish I was wrong, Beaumont. Listen to me: I'll say to Digby that you surrendered the letter freely – even that you'd never meant to deliver it. Give it to me and save yourself, for your sake and for the sake of your family!"

"If you dare speak to me about my family, I'll kick your goddamned arse again," Laurence spat at him, and sloshed over to snatch his cloak, doublet, and boots from the troopers. Ankle-deep in mud, he did not bother putting on his boots. "Arrest me, and I'll gladly face a court martial," he said, swinging into his saddle.

"You'll go to your ruin. Wilmot is already ruined, Beaumont. General Goring rode into our camp just as you set out for Essex's headquarters. Prince Rupert sent him."

"Ah," said Laurence. George Goring would unseat Wilmot. Digby had been ingratiating himself with Rupert so that the new appointment would appear to be on the Prince's recommendation and not his own, hated as he was by Wilmot's men. With the royal army on the cusp of battle, unless Essex conceded to its terms, few in the ranks would be so ignoble as to mutiny against an order from Rupert. Wilmot's vaunting ambition had flown him too close to the sun. He was falling, and Laurence would be unable to warn him. And the King must have been party to that whole scheme, his ear bent by Digby's seductive tongue.

## IX.

Laurence spent the night under guard. For some hours he was restless, contemplating Wilmot's fate and his own, and his feelings towards Price. Had the man genuinely wished to save him from a charge of treason, or had he betrayed him to gain favour with Digby? Laurence fell asleep without reaching a conclusion.

In the morning, he was released; the entire army had been called to assemble for a march. When the ranks were lined up in formation, he saw Wilmot, who appeared calm and confident, though from the redness of his face and his bloodshot eyes, Laurence knew he had been drinking.

The King rode forth to view the troops, and next, to a blast of trumpets, ceremonially produced a warrant for Lord Wilmot's arrest on grounds of high treason, and announced that Goring would assume his duties as Lieutenant General. Wilmot was at first angrily speechless, then asked to go back to his station with the cavalry; but he was taken away, to a huge commotion from the men, who booed loudly and demanded the reason for his disgrace. Accompanied by his chief officers, and with great aplomb, the King cantered over to each division of Horse and personally explained to them that Prince Rupert had requested the change of command, and that it was temporary, upon investigation of the charges against Lord Wilmot.

After the King had retired to his quarters, troopers ferried Laurence off to a short audience with the Secretary of State in the corner of the field. "I am disappointed in you, sir," Digby said.

"My lord, I had no letter on me to Essex," said Laurence. "And Lord Wilmot is not a traitor. You can't believe everything that comes out of his mouth under the influence of drink."

"And you forget the old saw: *in vino veritas.* You shall remain in custody until you provide me with a more honest answer."

Laurence surrendered his pistols and his sword. A small party of troopers kept guard over him throughout the day, while the King hesitated to commit to battle. By nightfall, the Royalist army made camp on a heath. Laurence rolled himself up in his cloak, and slept more soundly than he had in a long time.

At dawn, Price woke him with breakfast, and developments. The army had written a petition to the King signed by some forty-odd officers humbly asking why Wilmot should be dismissed. Later came His Majesty's reply, which Price relayed scrupulously to Laurence: "that no king ever did owe more to gentlemen and officers," but that Lord Wilmot had for the past three months tried "to bring His Majesty's person into contempt"; and that he was overheard stating that the King intended to place all power in Prince Rupert's hands; and that he, Lord Wilmot, would rather join with Parliament than submit to Rupert's dominance; and that he had proposed to set up Prince Charles as King, and had held traitorous communication with Essex.

Wilmot's message to the Earl had made no such suggestion about Prince Charles, and never had Wilmot to Laurence, even in his most inebriated rants. It struck Laurence as yet another ironic coincidence that he should have frustrated Pembroke's more deadly scheme to do the same thing.

"Not only is Wilmot charged with treason – so are others, you among them," Price said tearfully, "though I did what I could to plead your case with Lord Digby."

"I can't express the extent of my gratitude," said Laurence. "Now stop snivelling, and find me a pen and paper."

In his letter to the King, Laurence defended Wilmot, adding that although neither he nor Wilmot had committed any treasonous act, he would accept without complaint the punishment that might accrue to him. Beforehand, however, he asked permission to complete a final business for Lord Digby.

"Price," he said, as he melted wax for a seal, "your work is to watch people, so watch your own back with Digby. The more he praises you, the more you should worry. It's the last advice I'll ever give you."

"Do you despise me, Beaumont?"

"I've not got the energy for that."

"And what of . . . what of my suit with Elizabeth?" Price asked. "Do you think I still have a chance?"

Laurence had to laugh at his tenacity of purpose. "I can't advise you *there*, but if I were you, I wouldn't hold out too much hope."

## X.

"Mr. Beaumont is not alone in speaking out for Wilmot," the King said, as he and Digby perused Beaumont's letter in the royal tent. "Falkland's friend Edward Hyde came to see me, in some distress, and insisted that there was no sedition in Wilmot's heart, and that his mad ventures were born more of vanity and jealousy of Prince Rupert than a desire to supplant me."

"But Mr. Beaumont is lying about Wilmot's communication to Essex. I do not understand why he continues to shield him."

"He was as unswervingly loyal to Falkland."

"Who was a thousand times nobler than Wilmot!"

"N-nobler even than you?"

"I cannot pretend to be the best of men, Your Majesty," replied Digby smoothly.

"My lord, we have no substantive evidence of Lord Wilmot's treason in the form of a written message. And given the warm regard in which he is held by my army and our p-present situation with the enemy, we cannot risk f-further strife within our camp. I shall therefore send him into exile, to France. Mr. Beaumont shall have exile, also. My wife and, for that matter, my eldest son, would not forgive me if I inflicted a court martial upon his lordship or Mr. Beaumont. Prince Charles is unaccountably fond of those men. And they could render me service by attending to the welfare of Her Majesty."

"Your Majesty is lenient."

The King indicated Beaumont's letter. "What think you of this?"

Digby hummed in his throat before answering. "It would be an inestimable help to your cause in the City, and my Lady Hallam would doubtless be pleased to have revenge upon the man who nearly sent her to a torturous death. Yet the odds are stacked high against Beaumont succeeding. Nonetheless, it is typical of him to ask: he finds danger irresistible."

"Is that the draw, I wonder," murmured the King, with a thoughtful expression.

## XI.

His Majesty had given Wilmot and Laurence a little respite to settle their affairs and bid farewell to their families. They had not been allowed to speak in private. Before awaiting ship at Exeter, Wilmot rode for the Oxfordshire estate of his wife, Anne; he predicted that her responsibilities as a landowner would delay her from journeying to France. Laurence saw his own future as yet more uncertain, depending on whether His Majesty and Lord Digby acceded to his request: to let him find and kill Clement Veech. He owed Veech's death to the dead, such as Barlow and Lucy, but also to the living, most of all to Isabella and Pembroke, and to Barlow's family.

He was packing his belongings at Digby's quarters when Prince Charles came in unannounced. "Mr. Beaumont, are you . . . are you off to your father's house?"

"I am, Your Highness," Laurence replied.

"I think it terribly wrong that you should be exiled with Lord Wilmot, sir, when your guilt appeared far less sure even than his," the Prince exclaimed. "And I've not forgotten your courage in saving my father last year from that conspiracy against him."

A lump rose in Laurence's throat as he thought about his dreams of the King dead in the wood, and his panicked escapes with the Prince. "I was happy to be of service."

"Do you remember the day we first met, when Lord Falkland was Secretary of State?" the boy carried on more cheerfully. "How we sat in the garden outside his offices, and I asked you about your scars, and you started to tell me about that lover in Paris and her jealous husband?"

"Yes I do, Your Highness," Laurence said warmly.

"You never finished your tale. I should enjoy hearing the end of it, sir."

Laurence touched a finger to the old scar on his lower lip. "What was her name . . . Angelique. Very pretty but no angel. And far too talkative."

"As is the habit of most French ladies," interjected the Prince.

"At any rate," Laurence went on, reluctant to fault the Queen and her fellow countrywomen, "I was sitting in my chamber early of a morning, when three unknown gentlemen burst through the door."

"Angelique's husband . . . ?"

"And her brother and father. They grappled me to the floor, uttering some unrepeatable language, and then her husband whipped out a stiletto and sliced open my lip."

"That must have hurt like the devil."

"Your Highness, they had worse in mind. They were about to tear off my breeches and . . ." Laurence paused decorously. "Deprive me of my manhood, when I was rescued by another young woman."

"Another lover?"

"Not at that time."

"Afterwards were you lovers?"

"Yes, we were," said Laurence. An image flashed before him of Juana striding in, brandishing the Toledo sword that she had stolen; part of the theft that had led him to Pembroke's murderous correspondence. "That's a different story, Your Highness, and a much longer one."

"It must keep for when we next meet. You should beware in Paris, lest you encounter Angelique's husband again."

"Thank you for the warning, Your Highness," Laurence told him, in such a way that they both began to laugh.

"Sir," said the Prince, becoming serious once more, "you've always been frank with me. I wish to know the truth: was Lord Wilmot trying to collude with the rebels, to raise me above my father?"

"No he was not, and those who repeat such a falsehood are either mistaken or malicious, or both. He's devoted to you, and you can trust him with your life."

"I knew it," sighed the Prince. "When you and Lord Wilmot get to France, *I* trust you will look after my poor mother."

"We shall to the best of our ability, Your Highness."

The Prince advanced to clasp Laurence's hand. "I pray it will not be for many years, but when I am king, would you be among my ministers?"

"I would be honoured."

"My father has agreed to *your* wish, sir," the Prince said unexpectedly. "He has explained to me what you are setting out to do. For the love of me, take care."

# CHAPTER EIGHTEEN

## I.

"So the King has gone deep into the wilds of Cornwall," said Lord Beaumont, looking round from his armchair at his family and Seward, who were gathered together in the Hall. "We thought him in Exeter with Princess Henrietta. When did he march out, Laurence?"

"About a fortnight ago," said Laurence uneasily; the news of Wilmot's disgrace could not yet have reached them, and he shrank from breaking it. "How is Tom?" he asked. His brother was the only Beaumont missing.

"He has started to walk, on crutches," Seward answered, "though he keeps mostly to his chamber. Thank God the ball entered above the joint of his knee, and that his thigh bone was not damaged."

"We owe thanks both to God *and* to you, Doctor," said Lord Beaumont. "You saved Thomas from an amputation."

They were speaking over the lusty babble of Tom's son, wriggling on Mary's lap. Laurence had obligingly admired young James Beaumont: blond, plump, and vigorous, he was the picture of Tom as an infant, and Mary was every inch the proud mother, boasting about his insatiable appetite. Laurence turned to Catherine, who appeared remarkably at home in the household. When she had raced out to greet him in the courtyard, he had been assailed by a pang of guilt. "How long has our friend Will been here?"

"Since mid-July," she replied. "He's learnt more in a month from Jacob than he ever did at my father's stables."

"Your mettlesome stallion is getting his exercise, Laurence," added Lord Beaumont. "Dr. Seward brought him to us, and Catherine has taken a fancy to him. It's become her habit to ride him in the park each morning."

Laurence frowned at her. "I hope he hasn't thrown you?"

"Not once," she said, as if surprised that he should inquire.

"And . . . we are overjoyed to have Elizabeth with us again," Lord Beaumont said softly.

Elizabeth seemed to Laurence no less uncomfortable than he felt himself. She gave a slight shake of her head: a signal, he assumed, that they would talk, but in private.

"I just received a letter from Ingram, Laurence," said Anne. "He's at Prince Rupert's camp in Shrewsbury, and sends you his warmest regards."

"I must send him mine," said Laurence.

"And now we ladies should allow the gentlemen a while to themselves before we eat," said Lady Beaumont. "Since my cousin's departure, we have resumed supping early, at the English hour," she told Laurence, who read in her expression a distinct triumph as she ushered out the young women.

Lord Beaumont leant forward and squeezed Laurence's arm. "Though I am not fond of Lord Digby, it was kind of him to grant you leave to visit."

"Or did you render him some exceptional service?" queried Seward.

"In fact," said Laurence, "it's . . . not a leave."

"Then were you on a mission for him to Oxford?"

"No. *His Majesty* permitted me leave to visit, to . . . to say goodbye. I've been sent into exile with Lord Wilmot and certain others who stand accused of . . . treason," Laurence finished, contriving of no more diplomatic way to make his announcement.

Seward and Lord Beaumont stared at him slack-jawed. "How could that be?" demanded Lord Beaumont.

Laurence gave an abridged version of the truth. He could discern scepticism on Seward's face; and when he fell silent, his father was flushed scarlet in the cheeks, his eyes brimming with tears.

"In the whole history of our family, Laurence, never have we been tainted by the dishonour of treason. I accept your word that the accusation is as baseless as it is base. Yet I must ask you," he went on, in a pained voice, "since we did share our doubts in the past about the justice of His Majesty's cause: would you have supported Lord Wilmot in a secret negotiation to end the war?"

Laurence hesitated, afraid of the consequences to his father's health if he spoke his mind. "I might have," he confessed at length, "were I absolutely sure that it was not born of Wilmot's ambition, and that there was a chance Essex would accede to it – and if the terms were respectful to His Majesty. I would not support a proposal to set Prince Charles on the throne instead of the King. *That* was a lie framed by Wilmot's enemies. But Essex would never negotiate without the blessing of Parliament."

"Nor could such underhanded negotiations ever be respectful of His Majesty," Seward said, in his most tutorial voice. "You disappoint me, Beaumont."

"Digby told me the same: that I had disappointed him. Well," said Laurence, beginning to lose his temper, "*he* hasn't disappointed *me*. He's the snake I always thought he was, and every bit as ambitious as Wilmot. But unlike Wilmot, he has the ear of the King, whom he has persuaded into more *underhanded negotiations* than I care to enumerate. While I deeply regret bringing dishonour upon my family, I am pleased to be free of him, *and* the war. As long as he's Secretary of State, he'll only sink the King further into moral turpitude."

"A king is still a king, and is owed your fealty. To argue with that is to make common cause with the rebels."

"If I didn't so detest the oppressive nature of the London regime and its religious intolerance, and if our family wouldn't suffer so much from a royal defeat, I might consider it, Seward. As things have turned out, I can avoid that unpleasant decision and skulk away to France."

"What will you do there?" Lord Beaumont asked.

"Oh, play at cards with the Queen. According to Wilmot, she's very free with her wagers. If His Majesty's fortunes decline, you could all join me," Laurence suggested, less cynically.

"My dear boy, I would prefer to be buried beneath the rubble of my house. Let us not ill-wish His Majesty, however: from what you tell us, he has Essex cornered, and Ingram says that Prince Rupert is massing a great army in the west. We must pray for a swift conclusion to the bloodshed. So, will Catherine travel with you, or bide at the house until you are more prepared to receive her?"

"I'd like her to choose for herself."

Lord Beaumont nodded, as though to close the subject. "Go to your brother, Laurence. He must be waiting to see you."

When Laurence poked his head round Tom's door, Tom was sitting fully dressed on his bed, his crutches propped nearby. The right leg of his breeches was rolled to the thigh, which was bandaged. His entire body had wasted, and he struck Laurence as far older than his twenty-seven years, his features settling prematurely into harsh lines. "Laurence," he said, his tone neither amiable nor hostile.

"Tom, I'm sorry about your leg."

"I have Adam to thank that it wasn't sawn off."

"And Seward," Laurence reminded him, quelling a familiar irritation. "You were lucky. What a slaughter, at Marston Moor. It took well over a week for His Majesty to get an accurate report of the battle—"

"Let's not talk of it," interrupted Tom, as though personally humiliated by Rupert's defeat.

Laurence moved to a cheerier topic. "Your son's the image of you at his age. And Mary is . . . blooming."

To his relief, Tom did not mistake his comments for sarcasm. "I know – she's discovered her tongue and can't stop wagging it. She must have been saving up her prattle ever since we got married. Were you aware that she and Catherine have formed a strange bond?"

"Not so very strange, given our family," said Laurence, with a laugh.

"What's far stranger to *me*," burst out Tom, "is how a lying, sponging bastard such as de Zamora would be so rewarded for his past service to the Spanish king, though I suppose he might have been a valiant soldier, even if he is a complete blackguard."

"They're not mutually exclusive categories, in my experience."

"Speaking of blackguards, your so-called friend Price is another one."

"His conduct was reprehensible, as I made quite clear to him, so let's not talk of that, either," Laurence said shortly.

"How's my Lord Digby treating you?" Tom recommenced, after a slight pause.

"I've been dismissed from his service." Laurence described the charges against Wilmot and his associates, and the penalty they must pay.

"By Christ," said Tom. "Why didn't you inform the King immediately of what he was plotting?"

"Because most of the charges are false, and unlike Price, he is a *true* friend to me. Tom, you understand what this means," Laurence hurried on. "You'll take my place, if . . . if I can't return to England."

"You'll be leading a life of luxury in Paris while I sit uselessly at home," Tom said, scratching at the bandage on his knee.

"Not uselessly – you're needed here. And Seward says you're starting to walk. Why don't you hobble down to supper tonight? There must be something we could argue about, to amuse the family."

Tom squinted at Laurence, as if undecided as to whether he should be provoked. Then he grinned. "Perhaps I shall."

"Until later," said Laurence, ducking out; he had seen Elizabeth loitering in the passage.

She beckoned him into the library and shut the doors. "How is Mr. Price?" she inquired, tentatively.

"Rising in his career with the Secretary of State. He still has hopes of marrying you."

She hoisted her shoulders in a world-weary fashion. "I don't know what I want, Laurence. My time in Oxford was such a nightmare. And now I think that in my loneliness I may have viewed Mr. Price as I wished him to be, not as he is – though I believe he's a good man at heart, or he wants to be good, at any rate."

Laurence thought of Mistress Edwards' verdict on her grandson's character. "I doubt *he* knows who he is. And it strains him to the limit to be perfectly honest with anyone, including himself. I can't fault him, on that score. I'd be the pot calling the kettle black."

"You've certainly kept a great deal about him from *me*," said Elizabeth, in Lady Beaumont's chastening tone. "But what answer should I give, if he asks again for my hand?"

"You won't have to answer," Laurence said. "It will be done for you."

Over supper, he broke his news to the women. His sisters and Mary wept openly. Lady Beaumont, in characteristic fashion, directed her anger at Lord Wilmot. Catherine was subdued. Laurence explained that he had a last, private business to conclude on behalf of the Secretary of State, and that he would return in a week or so to bid them all a proper farewell. Catherine could decide, in the meantime, whether to travel with him to France.

At the end of the meal, Seward went out to Lady Beaumont's rose garden for his customary pipe of tobacco, and Laurence followed. "Seward," he said, "forgive me if I upset you by my lack of faith in the King. I would hate it to come between us."

Seward breathed a weighty sigh. "As would I, Beaumont, and you've made no secret of your views, to me or to his lordship, who confided in me his own low opinion of Lord Digby. The circumstances of your disgrace hurt us the most. Now, did you succeed in London?"

"Yes, though I had to depend on my friends and your sleeping draught." As they meandered through the flowerbeds, Laurence told him all about it, and the bargain with Pembroke.

"Why would the King hand over his treacherous letters?" snapped Seward. "You were forced into a fool's bargain, with a rogue."

"He helped us at huge risk to himself, and he's since fallen under the suspicion of Veech."

"Then he may receive his just deserts at the hands of Parliament rather than those of the King."

"Not if I'm in time to prevent it by eliminating Veech, although Pembroke may already be suspect to others in Parliament." Laurence stopped and faced Seward squarely. "Veech's murder is the business I pledged to conclude for the Secretary of State."

Grabbing a blossom off a rosebush, Seward rubbed it between the tips of his fingers and thumb, until the crushed petals scattered on the ground. "That's what will happen to you, should you re-enter London."

"As I'm well aware. I must lure Veech out, as he lured me in."

Seward studied Laurence in the twilight. "You are afraid of him, as a man," he said finally. "I have not seen you so afraid before."

"All that I know of him scares me," Laurence admitted. "And I've never wanted a man dead, as I do him. *And*, to complicate matters, I want his death to look like an accident that inculpates nobody."

"Why, Beaumont? In case Pembroke is accused of killing him?"

"I hadn't thought of that," said Laurence, laughing. "But no – my main reason is to clear the lawyer, Draycott, whose family Veech threatened." He described Draycott's mission to Digby, and how Draycott had been tossed into Oxford Castle. "I have the King's permission to liberate him on the grounds that he could assist me – as I think he will, though he deserves his freedom anyway. Yet his politics are with Parliament, and his entire life is in London. Were St. John to find evidence implicating him in Veech's murder, he would lose everything."

Seward was silent again, lighting his pipe. Through a cloud of smoke, he remarked abruptly, "Our chat about the witch's poison inspired me to hunt for a vital ingredient in the woods near Clarke's house."

"Eye of newt?" joked Laurence, though he was fascinated.

"Monkshood, best harvested in the autumn, but the root I dug up was unusually plump, for this time of the year. I dried it and ground it into a powder. Some of her other recommendations I determined were more superstitious than lethal, except fresh snake venom, which would be hard to obtain in Clarke's neighbourhood."

"I wish I'd known. I could have got you some – from Lord Digby."

Seward cast Laurence a devilish smile. "The venom was superfluous. I tried the powder on a sow that was diseased and unfit for eating. The beast was paralysed within an hour, and dropped down cold in three."

"Did the witch provide any antidote?"

"Belladonna." Laurence grimaced; he had once ingested a dose of that drug to bizarre and stupefying effect, until he had become unconscious from it. "And foxglove," Seward added, "though I did not try them on the sow."

"The antidotes must be as lethal as the poison."

"If taken alone in sufficient amount, yes. Together, they act in counterbalance: her poison slows the system, while her antidotes do precisely the opposite. I sampled a speck of the poison diluted in water. The taste is simultaneously sweet, pungent and acrid, and produces a tingling on the tongue and then numbness. It would be difficult to disguise in a cup of wine or ale."

Laurence remembered what Price had told him about Veech's abundant use of salt and pepper. "Would strong spices mask it, in a dish of some sort?"

Seward ruminated, puffing on his pipe. "They might. Veech would have an awful death: the mind is lucid throughout, as the body loses function and ultimately fails."

"Good," said Laurence. "Did you bring the poison with you?"

"Heavens, no – it is at Clarke's house."

"We might ride there tomorrow. I'll continue on to Oxford, to free Draycott."

"You haven't asked if Thomas is well enough for me to leave his bedside."

"We both know he is."

"Hmm," said Seward. "You remind me of another thing: when

he was delirious, he spoke of the battle at Marston Moor, and later I asked him to describe the terrain. I am now convinced: it was what I foresaw in my dream."

"Then . . . your dreams are as prescient as your visions. We could have let de Zamora keep that bowl, and saved ourselves a lot of trouble."

"Whatever the case, Marston Moor did not signal the defeat for the King, so as his lordship said, there remains hope for the royal cause."

Laurence shrugged ambivalently. "Since you *do* have your bowl again, why not try peering into the future of Mr. Veech?"

"I've no need of it to know that you require my expertise in your murderous operation. I'll accompany you, on to Oxford."

"Thank you, Seward. I wasn't sure how to ask that favour of you."

"One favour merits another – I am in Catherine's debt. You must ask *her* how she outwitted Diego," Seward chuckled. "She was as clever a thief as he."


When Laurence and Catherine retired to bed, he forgot to inquire, still preoccupied by the business of Veech; and then while making love to her, he could not help thinking of his last time, with Isabella in Pembroke's house. Their terrifying climax seemed to portend the death of a relationship. Yet little by little, Catherine softened and distanced the memory, and he became absorbed in the moment.

"I want to come with you to France," she told him, eventually.

"Things may be hard, at the beginning," he said; how to confess that he might not live to enjoy his exile?

"No harder than what you must do here in England," she said, with peculiar certitude.

"What is that?" he asked, unnerved.

Hopping naked from the bed, she crouched to drag out from underneath a large, flat object. "Will brought it for us from my father's house. Should we take it on our voyage?"

Laurence glanced down at the portrait of Isabella as Aphrodite. Then he looked up at Catherine. Her certitude had vanished and he witnessed in her face a struggle as naked as her body, between yearning and despair, as when they had examined the magpie's injured wing, on the day he had proposed to her. Could she have guessed from his reticence in the courtyard that he had been unfaithful to her with Isabella, and that in quitting England he must bid goodbye to the woman he loved? "No, Catherine," he said. "We'll leave it behind."

## II.

Lady Beaumont extinguished her candle, and rested her head back on her pillow. Three generations of Beaumonts were gathered beneath this one roof; and soon, God willing, there would be more children to assure the future of a line unbroken through the centuries since William the Conqueror bestowed lands in Gloucestershire upon his loyal henchman, Laurent de Beaumont. Despite Laurence's news, she felt an inner peace that had not graced her for longer than she could recall.

"God moves in mysterious ways, dearest wife," her husband said, surprising her; she had thought him asleep. "Although we could have wished for it to happen otherwise, both Laurence and Thomas may be spared from death in this dreadful war." His hand searched out hers, under the bedclothes. "And, my Elena, I have been meaning to tell you: I know you believe me rather obtuse, with my nose in my books and my head in the clouds. Yet my ears were not deaf to the hints dropped by Don Antonio."

"What manner of hints?" she asked sharply.

"You are and always shall be the love of my life, and you command my unconditional trust. But I would not love you and Laurence any the less, or be any less proud of you, were Don Antonio his true father." Lord Beaumont yawned, and snuggled up to her. "There! I have said my piece, and can sleep contented."

"I shall not sleep a wink," she rejoined, "while you persist in your absurd misapprehension. Antonio is one of the blackest liars in

Christendom, and it offends me that you should be deceived by his wicked insinuations."

"Please, take no offence. As a young man, when I courted you in Seville, I did not understand him. Now I do. He was in love with you, and, if I am not mistaken, you with him. I was the interloper. Perhaps he journeyed to England at his ripe age to find out whether I had made you happy."

"You have. And Laurence is without a doubt your son."

"I know he is," said Lord Beaumont, "in all that most matters to me. But I do confess," he went on, less gravely, "I liked Antonio. There is something to be said for a bit of wickedness. And we are not so old," he added, easing his body closer to hers, "that we cannot be a bit wicked ourselves."

Regular as a clock, he slumbered afterwards. Lady Beaumont smiled, listening to his snores. He had always been an attentive partner, though in their early years of marriage, she could have no joy of him. She had been spoilt by a far more experienced lover.

Elena's two brothers were still in skirts and she, the eldest, had been a month shy of sixteen when the family learnt that her father had died of ague in the Spanish Indies. His estates there had been mortgaged against his borrowings. Her mother could spare a small dowry for Elena, but the three other girls would have to choose between the convent and marriage to suitors of inferior blood.

Doña Cecilia had reluctantly admitted Antonio again to the house, in the absence of his hostile uncle, and while convalescing from a wound to his leg incurred in a cavalry charge, he became a frequent visitor. She blamed his unruliness on the fact that he had been orphaned as a babe, and had grown up unsupervised in the crumbling castle of his forebears; and he had enlisted in the Imperial army at the age of fifteen, which was no education in morals. Antonio's cousins adored him, as did Doña Cecilia's youngest and prettiest gentlewoman, Beatriz, who was Elena's special confidante. Antonio would dazzle them with conjuring tricks, spin tales of his campaigns, and sing to them in his seductive tenor. And when Doña Cecilia's more censorious ladies were temporarily distracted, he would remind Elena that she was his favourite. "To look at you," he would declare, "is like gazing into a mirror." She took this as a compliment, for she thought him the handsomest man she had ever seen. And she was not alone in wanting his attentions: Beatriz tormented her with gossip about how many hearts he had captured in Seville. But in a stolen moment, he said to Elena, "I love you above all others. Will you be mine?" And she answered immediately: "Yes."

She was waiting for Antonio to open the subject of marriage with her mother when an Englishman arrived in town on the final stage of his continental tour. Heir to a rich estate and a title, James Beaumont had a letter of introduction to the de Capdavilas from John Digby, the English ambassador in Madrid, who evidently knew of the distinguished family, though not of their penurious circumstances. Doña Cecilia was thrilled to receive him. Blond and blue-eyed, Beaumont had a gentle smile, impeccable manners, and a solid grasp of Spanish, but no sense of pride: when the girls poked fun at his appalling accent and his English clothes, he laughed along with them. Antonio would not have borne such an insult.

One night Elena's mother hurried into the girls' bedchamber. "My darlings, Don James has asked for Elena's hand! After I confessed to him our terrible straits, he made me an offer that will save us from ruin. Although he is not of the true faith, Fray Luis says that God will absolve me if I accept it, since I am acting for the good of our house."

"Don James is too late," announced Elena. "I have already promised myself to Antonio."

Her mother stared at her as though she had proposed marrying the boy who scrubbed out their chamber pots. "He has no fortune, and he is your . . . your cousin!"

"I don't care if he is poor, and there have been marriages between cousins in our family for centuries."

"I ought never to have let him back into our house," moaned Doña Cecilia. "But that settles it: you shall leave for England with Don James as quickly as possible."

The next morning, James Beaumont began his courtship. Elena was furious, and would not say a word. "She is shy," Doña Cecilia apologised, though she more often complained that Elena was incorrigibly headstrong and outspoken. Beaumont returned to his inn, and not a half hour later, Antonio marched over demanding to know the truth about this rumoured betrothal. Doña Cecilia addressed him privately, and Beatriz reported to Elena that he had walked out looking thunderstruck. The following day, Beaumont informed Doña Cecilia that Antonio had stopped at the inn to congratulate him and invite him as a guest to the house of de Zamora. "What a splendid fellow your cousin is," he told Elena, "and unusually broad in his understanding, to welcome a foreigner and a Protestant to his home." Elena was mute, this time from shock: she could not believe how easily her passionate lover had capitulated. "How silly could you be, to take Antonio's flirtations seriously," chided Doña Cecilia. "He will marry into wealth, Elena: I've heard he has his eye on young Teresa de Salves."

Elena sank into despond, unreconciled to Don James; and Antonio stayed conspicuously away from the house. Then on the eve of her departure from Seville, Beatriz drew her aside. "All is not lost: once your sisters are asleep, tiptoe to my bedchamber, where I've arranged for Don Antonio to meet you."

"He's come to rescue me," gasped Elena. "God bless you for this, Beatriz!"

Like a hero from Elena's romances, Antonio clambered in through the window and swept her to bed. His increasingly intimate embraces drove her into a voluptuous frenzy, and without a struggle she surrendered to him the prize that should have been James Beaumont's. "For a convent-bred virgin, you learn fast – although you do have the best of teachers," Antonio observed, reclining on the bloodstained sheets. "It's a pity we have only one night with each other."

"One night without the Holy Church's blessing," she corrected him. "We'll find a priest, Antonio, and be wed before sunrise. Then my mother will be powerless to undo the bond between us."

"The tragic fact is that we cannot marry," sighed Antonio, "because of your father Don Giraldo's improvident lust."

"What are you talking about?" asked Elena, bolting upright in bed.

"Let me explain. He courted *my* mother before yours, and became mad with envy when Doña Elena was married off to the ancient fellow whose name I bear. Don Antonio de Zamora couldn't raise his prick to save his life! And since Don Giraldo couldn't have the woman he desired, he took her sister for his wife and her for his willing lover. I am the fruit of their adultery. As she was dying, just after she brought me into the world, my mother confessed this to Fray Luis and to her beloved sister, whom she asked always to be kind to her poor ill-gotten child." He smiled at Elena. "You and I are both cousins *and* brother and sister."

Elena was at first speechless. Then she cried out, "Who told you such a despicable lie?"

"It's no lie. Doña Cecilia told me, the day I learnt of your betrothal. She would have kept everything secret, had I not professed my affections for you and commanded her to dismiss that milksop Beaumont. I can see why your father abhorred me – the hypocrite, condemning *me* for my dissolute ways. I also see why, when she begrudgingly let me back in, Doña Cecilia made me swear that I wouldn't touch so much as a hair on her daughters' heads. And I thought it was because of my famous reputation with women." Antonio's fingers wandered to the moist cleft between Elena's thighs. "If she knew what hair I am stroking now! I hope Don Giraldo is turning in his grave, don't you? Our sin is sweet revenge, on him and on the Englishman who is robbing me so unfairly of you."

Elena at last comprehended Doña Cecilia's haste in packing her off to England. Yet as she gazed upon Antonio in his naked glory, she wanted him, even at the price of eternal damnation. "Antonio, we are twin souls who belong together. What our father and your mother did is not our fault, so why should we suffer for it? And if we're married, *my* mother will *have* to keep the secret, for the reputation of our house. No one else need know."

Antonio removed his hand. "There is a tiny problem, my dear Elena: our marriage would be unholy, and forever cursed by God. You and I *are* like beautiful twins, but our common blood would produce monsters of nature – and everyone would know." He started to pull on his clothes. "We inherited our sinfulness, from our father's line. The blood of Moors ran in Don Giraldo's veins, from a coupling as illegitimate as his with my mother, and as ours." Out of his doublet he plucked a rosewood box and laid it beside her. "Open this when I'm gone, and wear what's inside, in memory of tonight. As a small boy, I found it hidden among my mother's belongings, and stole it as a keepsake. I never understood its full significance until my talk with Doña Cecilia: it must have been Don Giraldo's secret gift to his lover. How ironic, and how appropriate, that I should pass it on to you! Our bad blood seems destined to surface in each generation. Still, you shouldn't be too sorry for yourself, *mi hermosa*," he laughed. "Count yourself lucky that I was your first taste of a man. On your wedding night, you can close your eyes and dream of my hands and my lips on your body, and the thrust of my virile sex within you. I really must be off or Beatriz will scold me," he added, sauntering to the window. "She's in the courtyard, watching out for us."

Elena had been listening in stunned silence, but when he threw a leg over the sill, she rushed to stop him. There was her faithful Beatriz below, beckoning urgently to Antonio; and on his face she saw a cool complacency that mortified her. He kissed her on the cheek, swung down from the ledge, jumped and landed agile as a cat, and vanished with Beatriz into the shadows.

In the morning he did not come to say farewell, and James Beaumont interpreted Elena's anguish as normal for a girl parting from her family and homeland. While their cavalcade travelled the hundreds of miles to Bordeaux, where they would board ship for England, he tried to console her, with the help of her two Spanish maids. It was Beatriz she missed most, especially when, less than a month after her incestuous night, she knew enough to recognise the consequences. She steeled herself, behaved lovingly to Beaumont, and raised a thorny issue. What if his parents opposed the betrothal, and threatened to disinherit him if he did not break it? "You are of an age to choose your wife, so why should we wait? Let me convert to your church in Bordeaux, and we can marry there – then the match cannot be undone," she urged, almost as she had implored Antonio. Beaumont agreed, ecstatic, and when they arrived at Chipping Campden, Lord and Lady Beaumont were scandalised, but had to accept. James was their heir and sole son, and his now-Protestant bride was big with child.

Over the next months, Elena dreaded what was ripening within her, to burst from her loins ghastly and deformed, like a demon in her illustrated prayer-book. By some miracle, however, she produced a healthy boy; and while disappointed that he did not resemble his father, the elder Beaumonts overlooked this flaw in their delight at a grandson. Still she longed for Antonio and thought guiltily of his keepsake in her lacquered cabinet. Yet Antonio had been wrong about her husband. James Beaumont was no milksop, but her brave champion in an otherwise inhospitable world. She bore him two sons who died in their infancy: God's judgement. Laurence, in contrast, had barely a day's illness, as though his thick de Capdavila y Fuentes blood rendered him immune; and he was sunny-tempered, precocious, and naughty. Her husband doted on him, as did her Spanish maids, who taught him fluent Castilian.

On his fourth birthday, Elena caught one of them whispering, "The older he gets, the more I see his father in him. God knows how the rascal found an opportunity to seduce her!"

"*Donde hay ganas, hay maña*," chimed in the other. "Or as the English put it, where there's a will there's a way. After all, Don Antonio was screwing Beatriz under Doña Cecilia's very nose. I wouldn't be surprised if that minx acted as his bawd. And *he* was no better than a spiteful valet pissing in his master's soup. What he couldn't have for himself, he had to spoil for Don James."

The discovery of this double betrayal and of her own naïveté horrified Elena as much as fear of the truth spreading, and it killed her love for Antonio. She promptly told her husband and his parents that her gentlewomen were instructing Laurence in the Catholic faith and must be sent back to Spain. Lord and Lady Beaumont rejoiced that the papists were going home, warmed a little towards their daughter-in-law, and then died in quick succession while she was pregnant with her fourth son, Thomas. Although Thomas survived his dangerous early years, her guilty fear remained; and just once she had let a hint of her secret slip out, to Dr. Seward. For as Laurence grew from boy to youth, he was to her a monster of nature, transforming before her eyes into a second Antonio: beguiling, provoking, lazy, irresponsible, and sensually disposed; though like James Beaumont, he was not proud, and he lacked Antonio's vanity. In defence, she had blinded herself to everything else about him that was not Antonio. She had done her best not to love him. Praise heaven she had failed, as signally as Antonio had failed to tear her family apart.

Now she remembered Laurence's words to her, in the dovecote: *I thought that if the story was true, it would explain why you and I have always been at odds.* How her heart had melted, and how much it had cost her to hide her remorse. She had lied to him, and again tonight to her husband, not because she was afraid that they would stop loving her if she told the truth, but to ensure peace between Laurence and Thomas, so the bad blood in their generation would end. Too quietly to rouse her sleeping husband, she murmured, "*Mea culpa, mea maxima culpa.*" As for the sin of Don Giraldo and her aunt Elena, which Antonio had apparently kept to himself while in England, she would take it with her to the grave.

**III.**

Governor Aston greeted Laurence with cold contempt. "His Majesty has written to me of your and Lord Wilmot's late disgrace, Mr. Beaumont. He further informs me you are on a hunt for a man obnoxious to his cause, and has instructed me to assist you however I can."

This last part surprised Laurence, until he divined Prince Charles' influence at work. "I thank His Majesty and you, sir, in advance. I brought with me some articles that Lord Digby gave me to return to Lady Hallam, if I may."

Aston guided him into the reception room where Isabella sat, her hair elegantly dressed and her boy's clothes switched for a satin gown. His love for her flooded back with painful vengeance, and it worried him that a month in Oxford had not restored her vitality. While her face and shoulders were not as thin, her skin was still unhealthily pale.

"Mr. Beaumont, how are you?" she asked. By her concerned expression, she had also heard of his disgrace. "But . . . what have you there?" Laurence handed her two books that made her frown and bite her lip, a diamond ring that she accepted with a faint smile, and a woven basket that she opened with an exclamation of joy. "Niger!"

"He's a well-travelled cat, and far better behaved than Seward's, though he did puke once or twice on the way."

She picked Niger out and kissed his sleek head. "Thank you. He is the most precious to me of all."

"Surely not more than the ring, my lady," commented Aston, as if to a child.

"Oh yes, Sir Arthur," she said; and Laurence knew at once from her tone that she disliked the Governor as much as he did. "The ring I shall sell, to buy myself something new. I had to leave the rest of my jewellery in London, including a necklace of which I was particularly fond. I can't replace it, but I might find a poor substitute. I shan't sell the books, however," she concluded, regarding Laurence wistfully. "They both contain very sage advice."

Aston cleared his throat. "Sir, how do you intend to go about your hunt?"

"I'll start today," said Laurence, "by releasing Mr. Draycott from Oxford Castle."

"The same for whom you went to such great lengths, my Lady Hallam," Aston said. "Had I known earlier that he was of value to Lord Digby, I'd have provided him straight away with more comfortable conditions."

"I must insist on accompanying you, Mr. Beaumont," said Isabella, "even if I was once told *that* gaol was no place for a woman. I'll be fascinated to witness your second meeting with Mr. Draycott. On their first," she explained to Aston, "I believe it was he who took Mr. Beaumont prisoner, in the name of Parliament."

"This is no place for *anyone*, except perhaps Veech and your delightful host," Laurence muttered to Isabella, as the turnkey ushered them through. The common pound was even worse than he recollected; obviously the Governor had not a shred of compassion for his prisoners.

Isabella was shielding her mouth with a fold of her cloak. "How I remember coming here to rescue your tortured body."

"I haven't forgotten, either, what you did for me," he said.

Draycott occupied a solitary cell; while bare, it was at least clean. He had altered since that October night on the barge: there were streaks of grey in his hair, and deeper lines in his face. His skin bore the chalky tinge of incarceration, and he was unshaven. When they entered, he rose from his pallet bed and stared at them like a man in a dream.

"Good day to you, sir," Isabella said.

Laurence extended a hand. "Mr. Draycott, Governor Aston has invited you to be his guest in Oxford, from henceforth, unless you prefer these rather monastic quarters."

"Aston?" repeated Draycott, in an incredulous voice. As he took Laurence's hand, his eyes strayed to Isabella. Laurence felt sympathy: they were both in love with her, and neither of them could have her.

"I'm sorry, sir," Draycott said next, "but I cannot accept hospitality from a man I so detest."

"I quite understand – I share your opinion of him: he's an insufferable bastard." Draycott's mouth dropped open, and Isabella started to laugh. "We'll find you lodgings elsewhere," Laurence went on, "but before that I want to introduce you to an ally. He was my tutor when I was up at Oxford, and is now my close friend: Dr. Seward, of Merton College."

"Ah. I attended Cambridge."

"Cambridge, eh? You'd better keep that to yourself, or he may hold it against you."

"Then I shall, sir," said Draycott earnestly.

Isabella laughed again, and winked at Laurence. "You are unaccustomed to Beaumont's sense of humour, Mr. Draycott. It's been his weapon of choice, even in the direst of circumstances."

"Seward has prepared a yet more powerful weapon for us," Laurence told Draycott. "A special remedy for Mr. Veech."

Draycott looked round in astonishment at Seward's front room, though to Laurence it appeared tidy; Seward must have left much of his paraphernalia at Clarke's house. "Mr. Draycott," said Seward, once they had been introduced, "I know from Beaumont and Lady Hallam how Veech mistreated you, and how, unbeknownst to him, you tried to collaborate with Beaumont in her escape. Are you ready to collaborate with *us* in his murder?"

"I am, wholeheartedly," replied Draycott. "How will he die?"

"By poison," answered Seward, with a relish that tickled Laurence.

"That fits, Doctor: he is a weird and poisonous man."

"I have even speculated that he may have some rare disease, after hearing about the oddities in his face and figure, and the striking absence of hair on his arm."

"I've noticed those things, too," Draycott said. "It could be why he always wears his long, thick coat, whatever the weather. He also shrinks from contact. When he was brought wounded to Derby House after you shot him, Mr. Beaumont, he would not allow the surgeon to undress him. More recently, after I had visited you in the Tower, Lady Hallam, I accused him of being incapable of natural human feeling – I meant, towards women," Draycott elaborated, blushing. "He burst into a fury, and demanded what I had been told about him, and then he grabbed me by the throat and by my . . . private parts. When I swore I'd been told nothing, he released me and became as suddenly calm. And he said, 'I'm not like most men. I don't share their weakness.'"

"He might have other weaknesses," Laurence suggested, avoiding Seward's eye.

"Or be misshapen from birth," Isabella put in.

"*There's* an interesting possibility, my lady," Seward said. "Now, Beaumont, apprise Mr. Draycott of the plan."

Laurence addressed Draycott, without a trace of humour. "I'm afraid you play an essential role in it. Right up to the very end, my life and yours will hang upon your ability to convince Veech that you remain in his thrall, and that you wouldn't care a toss if I die. Should things go smoothly, it will appear as if his heart unexpectedly failed him. But if he has the least suspicion of you, we're finished."

## IV.

Veech was relieved that the humid weather had not penetrated St. John's offices: he already sweated inside his coat, and the brace pressed more tightly against the joint of his knee. At once he found himself staring: a dirty, wasted, sullen version of Draycott sat across the table from St. John.

"Mr. Draycott has suffered abominably in gaol, at the hands of the Secretary of State and the Governor of Oxford," said St. John, gesturing for Veech to take a chair.

"About five weeks away, and you've aged five years," said Veech.

"His lordship's agent, Edward Price, recognised me from our dealings here in London, and I was consigned without trial to rot in the pound at Oxford Castle," Draycott said, his voice low and resentful. "Neither he nor his lordship enlightened me as to the fact that Beaumont had by then gone to procure Lady Hallam's escape, which I learnt of only today, from Mr. St. John."

"There was no news of it in Oxford?"

"If there was, it did not reach me, in the depths of hell." Draycott sank his head into his hands. "The keeper of the Castle took every chance to abase us prisoners, with encouragement from that vicious papist Aston. We were mocked and taunted and beaten. And at their whim, the guards deprived us of food and water. Those less able to bear their thirst had to drink their own urine. I nearly prayed to die."

*There are worse things than death*, Veech wanted to say. "How did you get out?"

Draycott raised his head again wearily. "Last week I was moved to a separate cell. The turnkey would not say why. The next day, he gave me a sealed letter directed to Mr. St. John, a purse containing eighty pounds in coin, and a message for me that as soon as the town bells struck midnight, I would discover the door to my cell unbolted, and the guards would not stop me from quitting the gaol. When I tested the door, it opened to my touch, and out I went. The guards were all asleep at their posts."

"In a drugged sleep," said Veech, his heart skipping in his breast.

"Yes, as I since realise. I had to ignore the pleas of my fellow prisoners, and hurry on. At the gates, the sentries paid me no notice. In town I bought a horse, and then I rode for London. Until Mr. St. John showed me what was in the letter, I had no clue as to who had rescued me."

Veech frowned. "Mr. Beaumont. But why?"

"You will know Beaumont's motive, Mr. Veech, when you read this," said St. John, passing the letter to him. "He has made the Committee a proposal to which there is a certain logic, given his present situation and his character."

The sloppy scrawl puzzled Veech: it was not what he would

expect from an educated man. "'Sir,'" he read aloud, "'I write to you by Mr. Draycott, whose liberty I organised as a mark of my good faith in what I am about to offer you, before I leave England for an indefinite exile. It is true that I aided Lord Wilmot in his design to remove from power the Secretary of State, as part of terms for a peace with my Lord Essex. I wished to satisfy my private quarrel with Lord Digby over his callous neglect of Lady Hallam: in spite of her brave service to him and to the King, he would have let her go to her death. Without his knowledge, and together with my accomplices who are all of them skilled lawbreakers drawn from the rabble of society, I fetched her out of London.'" Veech frowned again: he still nourished his theory about Pembroke as a culprit, though his investigations had hit a cold trail. "'I must depart for France by the end of the month, and have no time to waste, so here is my offer to you. I have intelligence of the schemes fomented in the City by Lord Digby over the last year, as I was his instrument in effecting most of them. Some you are aware of, others were stillborn, and more are being concocted as I write. I can supply the Committee detail of these plans, and keys to the figures employed by Digby in his correspondence, which were my invention. Once abroad, I would also report from Paris any intelligence that may help to expose him as the villain he is.'" Veech paused. "How tempting."

"Yes, but there is a catch," said St. John.

Veech read on, to himself. Beaumont would meet with St. John, and no one else. He asked for Mr. Draycott to escort St. John to an inn, the White Hart, outside the village of Stokenchurch, near High Wycombe. A clever choice, thought Veech: he knew the village was a popular stopping place for travellers to change horses on the Oxford to London road. Although now in Parliament territory, it lay closer to Oxford: a twenty-mile ride. "I pledge to come alone and unarmed, on the afternoon of the twenty-fifth of this month of August," Beaumont continued. "If by dusk I have no word from you, I shall wait no longer. In the case you attend, should you seek to detain me or harm me, or should you later unmask me publicly as your informant, you will be doing Lord Digby a favour and yourself none, for you would lose your *pair of ears* in Her Majesty's Court."

Veech smirked about the pair of ears. "Arrogant fellow," he said, returning the letter to St. John.

"The Committee is inclined to accept," said St. John. "Apart from the worth of his revelations about Lord Digby, an informant of his rank in Paris would be a boon to us. Yet the meeting itself is but four days away, and the Committee hesitates for me to undertake the risk."

"You should not. I'll go in your stead with Mr. Draycott and a party of militia. We'll arrive in good time and scout out the meeting place, lest he's plotting an ambush. Any hint of trouble and I'll bring him to London."

St. John glanced at Draycott. "What say you, sir?"

"I think it beneath our dignity to parley with a traitor," Draycott said, sounding disgusted.

"We are equal traitors in the eyes of the King, Mr. Draycott. And we are not parleying with Mr. Beaumont," said St. John. "We are merely benefiting from his treachery."


V.

"Are you bound for Chancery Lane, Mr. Draycott?" Draycott nodded; he wished Veech had stayed behind with St. John, rather than following him out. "Then let's take a skiff together, to Temple Stairs."

As they sat side by side on the narrow board, Draycott noticed Veech's whole face glowing, like that of a starved man anticipating a banquet. "You talked of adversity in your Oxford gaol," he said, in a newly expansive, companionable manner. "For three years, after I had been submitted to unspeakable injuries, I was chained to a bench of this width, crammed into a pirate ship with other galley slaves. We were whipped to toil at the oars, and had to consume our rations and sleep and piss and shit without moving from our places, and without prospect of freedom, except through death, to which many succumbed.

Many tried suicide, and were kept alive and tortured for their crime."

Draycott concealed interest: both Pym and Sir Montague had been right about Veech's past. "How were you not driven insane?"

"I fixed my mind upon my brute survival, and put myself in a state of war with any who opposed me, which gave me licence to do whatever was necessary for my preservation."

"The rule of beasts, not men."

Veech laughed and shook his head. "Beasts are gentler to each other than men, Mr. Draycott. They haven't the instinct for deliberate cruelty."

"What was your life before that?"

Veech settled his elbow on the bow of the skiff, and studied the river traffic benignly, as though it were ferrying to and fro at his command. "I was born and bred in Wapping, and apprenticed young to a spice merchant. He had a lucrative business. I bargained for him in the foreign ports and supervised the quality of his purchases. I spied out the cheaters who would disguise their stale produce for fresh, or fake their bills of sale, or elude their debts. And I punished them, so they wouldn't repeat a swindle. I was eight and twenty, sailing for Naples harbour, when my ship was boarded by Barbary pirates. For a decade I vanished: into their galleys, and then into their fortresses on the African coast. But through a happy chance, I was granted my freedom. I entered a militia in Italy, and then the Dutch army, where I gained the more artful skills for which I was recruited back to England, to serve John Pym."

"What happy chance bought you your freedom?"

"I told my overseer of a revolt that some of us slaves had been planning among ourselves. I was ordered to extract the confessions of my co-conspirators and to execute them, slowly, to deter future rebels. It was a small price to pay, to be shot of my chains. I can guess what you're thinking, sir," said Veech, as the skiff pulled into dock, "but don't flatter yourself. All men are Judases, given enough incentive. Look at Beaumont, spilling his lordship's secrets to the enemy."

"He *is* a Judas, and a sly one, at that. He's outfoxed you again: you won't have your revenge."

"Oh yes I will. And the Committee will hear I killed him in self-defence. If you say otherwise, let me warn you: I know where you sent your family."

"This time you've no need to threaten me, Mr. Veech," Draycott said scornfully, though inside he was sick with fear: now he and Beaumont could not fail. "I couldn't give a damn for his life. Just swear to me that *when* he's dead, you'll leave me and my family alone."

"I swear I shall – it's the last I'll ever ask of you," said Veech, in such a tone that Draycott believed him. "Afterwards, should you so choose, I can arrange for you to resign honourably from Mr. St. John's service with a fine pension."

"Then for once," Draycott told him, "I'll *willingly* assist you."

# CHAPTER NINETEEN

## I.

Laurence squinted through his spyglass at the valley below. A party of ten riders was galloping down the track towards the White Hart Inn. He handed the glass to one of Aston's men, next to him; they were both flat on their bellies amid ferns still damp with morning dew. "Veech is on the brown mare. That long coat marks him out. Draycott's on the piebald. Remember *him* well – you must let him escape unharmed."

"Yes, sir," said the man, and passed back the glass.

Laurence trained it again on Veech, who had brought a smaller escort than he had expected. He himself was equipped with thirty troopers from Aston's guard concealed at strategic posts overlooking the inn, a lonely establishment situated about a mile from the village of Stokenchurch. Through the day and night they had spent encamped in the Chiltern Hills, they had seen no Parliamentary troops reconnoitring; perhaps a sign of too much confidence on Veech's part. So what plan had Veech for today, Laurence wondered nervously, and had he any whisper of suspicion about Draycott?

The riders dismounted in the yard, Veech hampered by his damaged leg. The rest of them, armed with carbines, spread out to inspect the property. When they had reported to Veech, he, Draycott, and a hulk of a fellow went in through the front entrance. Those remaining stabled the horses and dispersed, some to the rear of the White Hart and some to the grounds. The landlord's servants and early customers were now filing out from the kitchen entrance, in the direction of the main road.

"Where are they going?" asked Laurence's companion.

"Veech may think I have accomplices among them. It seems as if only the landlord and his daughter have stayed behind."

"Is it a problem for us, sir?"

"It's an advantage," said Laurence. "Too many cooks spoil the broth."

By three o'clock in the afternoon, he had spied no more riders, and no new activity at the inn. He adopted an old army precaution: to empty bladder and bowels prior to battle. Then he wrapped in cloth the vial of belladonna and foxglove that Seward had mixed with aqua vitae, tucked it into a pocket in his close-trousers, and fastened his breeches. If in the worst case he or Draycott had to consume any of the food Draycott was to poison, the correct dose to reverse the monks-hood's toxic effects would be a gamble to estimate: he and Seward had tested the antidote successfully on rats, but not on a larger animal. Nonetheless, he derived comfort from it, as a sort of talisman from his friend. Inside his doublet lining was the slim knife he always carried; otherwise he was unarmed. He repeated to Aston's man that the guard should stay alert and in position, mounted his horse, and set out for the main road, and on to the White Hart.

## II.

Draycott saw Veech tense and shift in his chair at the thud of horse's hooves in the yard; he had been sitting impassively at a table in the taproom on which he had laid out writing instruments, a sheaf of blank paper, and his matchlock pistol. "Is it him?"

Draycott rushed to the window. "Yes, and he is alone."

Veech nodded at the big militiaman. "Otis, go with Mr. Draycott."

They went out, Otis brandishing his carbine and Draycott his pistol.

Beaumont swung from the saddle and regarded them with aris-tocratic disdain. "Damn you, put away your weapons. As I promised Mr. St. John, I'm not armed."

Draycott envisioned himself in his lawyer's role addressing an unrepentant criminal; nothing must betray their complicity. "Raise your hands, Mr. Beaumont, and walk ahead of us into the taproom."

Beaumont scowled, though he followed the order.

Veech did not stand when they came in. He motioned Draycott to come over beside him, and then examined Beaumont as he might a hoard of treasure, his eyes glittering. "Mr. Beaumont, I am Clement Veech."

Beaumont surveyed him with apparent indifference. "Where's Mr. St. John?"

"He was kept in London, on Committee affairs. He requested me to conduct our interview."

Beaumont's nostrils widened like those of a startled thoroughbred. "His absence demonstrates bad faith," he said, and turned on his heel.

"Another pace towards the door, and I'll shoot," said Veech, picking up his matchlock. "Not to kill, to wound."

Beaumont swerved about. "When I shot you, I fired at random. I apologise, Mr. Veech. But I won't talk to you. The Committee has disrespected my terms."

"A traitor merits no respect, and you'll do as you're bidden." Veech lowered his pistol. "I must search you. Remove your doublet and give it to me." When Beaumont tossed it onto the table, Veech hunted through it. "You *were* armed," he remarked, of the thin blade he found there.

"With a knife for eating," Beaumont said derisively.

"The landlord is cooking us rabbit stew. You can eat with fingers and a spoon."

"I don't intend to eat with you."

Veech placed the knife on the table by his pistol. "Your boots." Beaumont dragged out a chair and sat down to pull off his boots. He kicked them under the table to Veech. "And your breeches, boot hose and stockings."

"What in God's name . . . ?"

"Do as I say," muttered Veech, continuing his hunt. Beaumont peeled off his stockings, unlaced, stood to drop his breeches, stepped out of them, and threw them violently onto Veech's side of the table. "And your shirt," said Veech, delving into the breeches' pockets.

"By Jesus," swore Beaumont, as he whipped it over his head. Balling it up, he hurled it at Veech; he was now naked except for his close-trousers. Draycott waited, agonised, for Veech to produce the antidote Beaumont was to bring. Yet Veech had lost interest in the clothing.

He got up and limped in a ponderous circle around Beaumont, studying him as though entranced. Draycott was surprised by the number and severity of scars on Beaumont's lean body; the darkness of his skin rendered them all the more noticeable. "You *have* been in the wars," said Veech, resuming his seat. "We share an acquaintance with pain."

"May I dress?"

"Not until you finish undressing. I want everything off."

Beaumont loosened the tie on his under-linen. He hesitated, as if out of modesty, a hand covering his groin. Then he shifted his hand away, and the light garment fell to the floor. Veech beckoned him nearer. His hands were curled into fists, and he was shaking, from rage at the humiliation, Draycott assumed; he could see no fear in Beaumont.

"Raise your arms, and come and stand in front of me," Veech ordered.

"Have you a perverted desire that you wish me to satisfy, Mr. Veech?" Beaumont inquired.

"I might think of one, since you suggest it," Veech said, laughing. As Beaumont approached within a few inches of him, he seized the knife and used the blade of it to lift Beaumont's privy member and then his scrotum. Draycott could hardly breathe.

"No more than you'd expect to find between a man's legs," said Beaumont. "*Now* may I dress?"

Draycott caught in Veech that same unwarranted rage. As swiftly, it dissipated. "You know what you remind me of, Mr. Beaumont – a

Lascar, or an Arab. Save for one thing." Veech stroked the blade to his foreskin. "I travelled to the East when I was about your age, and spent some years there," Veech carried on conversationally, as when he had told Draycott of his time as a slave. "I saw many a convert to Mahommet circumcised and it requires an expert hand – not a skill I possess – and even so, there can be accidents." Otis made a little choking noise in his throat that elicited another laugh from Veech.

Beaumont's eyes were fixed on Veech, not on the knife, but his mouth had started to tremble. "Were *you* ever a convert?"

Veech sobered instantly, and snapped, "No, I was not. On the subject of hands, open yours and hold them out to me, palms up." Beaumont hesitated again. As he obeyed, Draycott's heart sank: in his left palm was a cloth bundle. Veech grabbed it and unwrapped the cloth. "Your infamous sleeping draught?" he asked, of the vial.

"It would induce sleep, yes," said Beaumont, in a faint voice, "but that's not why I have it with me. It's opium tincture. My gut has been unsettled recently."

Veech unstopped the cork, sniffed at the contents, and licked the wet end of the cork. He spat on the flagstones and wiped his mouth on his sleeve. "You liar, it isn't poppy." He offered it to Beaumont. "Drink of it, to settle your gut. Not too much – we've work to accomplish." Beaumont accepted it and drank a tiny sip. "Give it here." Veech corked the vial and placed it on the table by his pistol. "You may put on your shirt. You won't need any more than that." Beaumont cast him a look of unmistakable dread, and proceeded to tug the garment on. "Sit opposite me and Mr. Draycott." Veech pushed the writing instruments and paper towards Beaumont, leant back in his chair, and folded his arms across the broad mound of his chest. "Start on the ciphers you designed for Lord Digby."

## III.

Laurence constructed charts of symbols and letters, and filled in the squares, pausing only to dry his sweating hand on the front of his shirt, or to dip the quill and commence on a fresh page. He had reams of codes and ciphers memorised, not that it mattered now. How foolish he had been. He thought of Lady d'Aubigny smuggling the Commission of Array into London tucked into her dress, where no gentleman would search; and none had searched her there, as he had said to Draycott on the barge. But Veech was no gentleman, and his own lack of forethought could be his death. The belladonna and fox-glove were gradually taking effect: his mouth was parched, his head throbbed, and his stomach ached. These changes heralded further debilitating symptoms: muscular spasms, dizziness and blurred vision, incoherence, and unconsciousness from which, on the last occasion, he had been fortunate to wake. Today he had swallowed less, but the concentration could be stronger. Yet he might welcome unconscious-ness; it was not hard to predict what Veech had in store for him.

His muscles began to twitch, and he struggled to write on. From the corner of his eye, he checked the angle of the sun's rays through the taproom windows. Was it four or five o'clock? He twisted his head to and fro as if to relieve a crick in his neck, and saw Veech's guard on a bench by the door, carbine on his meaty knees, toying with a length of rope; he had the protruding brow and jaw, and the ungainly build, of a giant, although his expression was more dim-witted than brutal. Draycott appeared petrified, in the literal sense of one turned to stone. Meanwhile Veech was casually scanning the completed pages. Laurence detected in his face and physique and fleshy hands the soft, sinister qual-ity that Price and Draycott had spoken of; and there was a power to his voice, and to those hooded eyes beneath his black brows. Laurence admired Draycott anew: he had known what a man they had to kill. How hopeless seemed their plan, though it was late in the day to abort.

"Otis, ask the landlord when his stew will be ready, and remind him not to skimp on the seasoning," Veech said to the guard, who rose on his massive feet and stomped into the kitchen.

Laurence was now twitching more uncontrollably. He darted a frown at Draycott: a missed chance for him to slip in the monkshood.

Veech sat forward; had he guessed who had been chosen as his murderer? But then he said, with mild concern, "Mr. Beaumont, your pupils are unnaturally swollen. I believe you've poisoned yourself, instead of me! We must work faster. I don't want to lose a single scrap of intelligence before you die."

Otis shambled in, and announced, "Half an hour, sir."

"Otis, Mr. Beaumont is having trouble sitting still. Take that rope and tie his ankles to the legs of his chair." Otis tied the rope tight, but it was no help to Laurence: the chair rattled along with his twitches. More concern crossed Veech's face, and he moved to snatch the quill from Laurence, and a sheet of paper. "How did you and Lady Hallam flee London after your friends rescued her from the Tower?"

Laurence moistened his lips with his tongue. "We . . . left in the Earl of Pembroke's carriage."

"Then he *is* a Royalist."

"He's as staunch for Parliament as your Oliver St. John, and he was as pleased to shelter us and get us out of London as I am to be here with you," Laurence said, his words tripping over each other. "But I told him if he didn't, I would air in public a compromising secret of his."

"What might that be? A vice akin to Sir Montague's?"

"No: a past act of disloyalty to the King, which would . . . would prejudice his reputation."

"How did you come to learn of it?"

"Through a . . . a coincidence."

"That's no answer. Why didn't he have you killed?"

"If he did, his secret would be leaked by my friends."

Veech bored into Laurence with his impenetrable gaze. "What is his secret?"

"I came to betray Lord Digby, not to inform on Parliament's friends. You're wasting your time, and mine."

"Yes, and yours may be running out." Veech scratched some lines on the page. "Where is Lady Hallam?"

"In Exeter, preparing to sail for France, where I'm . . . to join her."

Veech snorted, as though this were unlikely. "And Sir Montague?"

"In The Hague."

"Operating for Digby?"

"Of course not. He can't be trusted, after the bargain he struck with your Committee."

"Who has replaced him in London?"

"Why, have you more packages in mind, Mr. Veech?"

"Yes, I do." Veech smiled reflectively. "Your friend Barlow scarcely budged when my knife cut through his wrist. I thought his punishment fitting, for a thief. There's a fitting punishment for every man and woman. Lady Hallam escaped hers, I'm sorry to say, but you shall not escape. I might send her those parts of you she cherished most, as a *memento mori*." Laurence bit down on his lip; the spasms were worsening, as was his panic. "Dear God," Veech exclaimed, over the rattling and banging of Laurence's chair. "I am tired of the noise, and his jumping about." He picked up Laurence's knife, and then, as if on a second thought, set it down again. Reaching into his coat pocket, he produced a different knife, a good two or three inches longer and much thicker in the blade. "How well this has served me, in the past. Mr. Draycott," he said, holding it out, "take it and pin his right hand to the table. Let's see if it quietens him." Draycott blanched. "You cowardly hypocrite – you've dispatched men to the gallows for their crimes, and yet you can't shed a traitor's blood. Go on and do it, or I'll do it myself."

Through a floating haze, Laurence saw Draycott take the knife. He shut his eyes, and felt Draycott's reluctant hand grip his, to flatten it upon the surface of the table. "You *are* a coward – you haven't the strength to defy him," he hissed at Draycott.

"Why would I bother, for a traitor such as you," Draycott retorted.

Laurence screamed as the blade stabbed into his flesh. He opened his eyes; and there was his hand, pinned below the knuckle of his second finger. Blood bubbled around the puncture and less than an inch of steel showed above his skin. Miraculously it cured him of the twitching, and of his headache. He was conscious solely of the pain travelling up his arm, and the desperate need to stay lucid and talk to keep Veech's interest until they ate, before that knife could be put to other use.

Draycott had his own right hand clapped to his mouth.

"Mr. Draycott," said Veech, "go to the kitchen and tell the landlord to bring us food." Draycott stumbled out. "I want the names of Digby's London agents, Mr. Beaumont."

An hour, Laurence thought: the monkshood would strike in an hour. "Victor Jeffrey, Antony Burton, James Pritchard, and . . . Christopher Harris," he confessed abjectly.

"Thank you," said Veech, and copied down the names of the dead clergymen in St. Saviour's Church.

## IV.

The landlord's daughter was stirring a cauldron of stew at the range, supervised by two of Veech's men who had been ordered to stay there. "Someone cried out, sir," she said to Draycott, in a frightened voice.

The landlord was tapping a cask, his hands shaking as he held a jug to the spigot, spilling the ale. "What business are you conducting here?" he demanded. "I'm not a man of violence, sir, and I don't appreciate my custom being driven away."

Draycott's nausea disappeared. If he could stick a knife through the hand of a friend, he could murder his enemy. "We're examining a malignant, and you are not to interfere," he said. The landlord quailed; he might not favour Parliament, Draycott realised, hence the two men on guard. "Mr. Veech has had to employ some rough measures," Draycott told them, in a lower voice. "To spare this girl the sight of blood, I'll bring Mr. Veech and Otis their meal, and you can attend to yourselves and the boys outside."

"Aye, sir," they said.

Draycott took from his pocket the marked bags: one of salt mixed with ground pepper and various other spices, and one of powdered monkshood. He would have to act openly, contrary to the original plan. "Mr. Veech likes his dishes well seasoned," he told the girl. "He gave me these to add." He offered her the bags, in full view of Veech's men, praying she would not accept them.

"You do it for me, sir – I wouldn't know how." She pointed to a stack of wooden trenchers near the range. While the militiamen were busy refilling their mugs, Draycott spooned out a generous amount of stew for Veech, sprinkled it liberally with the contents of both bags, blended them in, and stuck the contaminated spoon in the same serving. A separate portion, for Otis, he sprinkled with salt and spices.

### V.

Laurence kept his eyes averted as Draycott gave Veech and Otis their trenchers.

"Not eating, Mr. Draycott?" asked Veech.

"You deprived me of my appetite, sir," Draycott said. "Should I feed Mr. Beaumont?"

Veech made no reply. When Laurence looked up at him, he was studying Draycott intently.

The landlord came with a tray bearing ale, tankards, and a platter of bread. He boggled at Laurence's skewered hand as he set the tray on the table, and he left hastily. *Eat, eat,* Laurence urged Veech; the pain of his wound was lessening and he sensed himself nearing oblivion. Purposely he jerked at his right hand to reawaken the pain. "May . . . I . . . have some ale?" he begged, his tongue thick in his mouth.

"Why not," said Veech. "In fact, you should try a bit of my stew." He shoved his trencher across the table to Laurence, his eyes still on Draycott. "Taste it for me."

Laurence might preserve his life, if one poison cancelled the other, only to die a yet nastier death, but to deceive Veech he had to eat. He scooped a heaped spoonful of the stew, gulped it down, and burst into a fit of coughing. "Hot," he gasped.

"That it is," spluttered Otis, grabbing for his ale.

Laurence jammed in more, and forced himself to swallow. "Enough, enough," said Veech with an edge of annoyance. "I know your game – to line your stomach in the vain hope it will save you from the poison." He gestured for Laurence to return his trencher, and tasted the sauce. "As hot as an Oriental dish – the landlord is profligate with his spices."

"It was as you wanted," Draycott said, in a servile tone.

"Don't mistake me: I find it most palatable." Veech dug out a piece of rabbit, devoured it, and soaked up his sauce with bread, evidently enjoying his meal. When he pushed away his spotless trencher, his cheeks and forehead were beaded with sweat. He pressed his thumb to his lips, and nibbled tentatively at them with his teeth. The numbness; Laurence could feel it on his own lips. Veech loosened his collar and fumbled open the upper buttons on his coat. "I'll step out for air. Stay," he said to Otis and Draycott.

Otis was mopping his streaming face on his cuff. "Mr. Draycott, sir, is there any more in that jug?" he asked, when Veech had gone.

"No," said Draycott, his pistol aimed at Laurence. "Have it refilled."

"Mr. Veech's orders were to stay," Otis said, unhappily.

They sat listening to Veech's uneven tread outside. Laurence peeked at Draycott, who signalled encouragement with a flicker of his lids; and Laurence responded with an infinitesimal flicker of his, to signal his despair.

Veech walked in paler and sweatier, limped more laboriously to his chair, and dropped into it. "So, Mr. Beaumont, what is my Lord Digby concocting next, for London?" His speech was slurred.

"He's to send in muskets, concealed in . . . in coffins, for a revolt this autumn," Laurence invented feebly.

"When and how will they arrive?"

Laurence heard himself drone on, as if his voice belonged to some other being over whom he had no agency; he had no idea of what he was saying. And Veech was pausing to frame his questions, and as he recorded Laurence's answers, the ink blotted on the page.

Laurence battled a great desire to sleep, and jerked his hand once more, but felt nothing.

"Mr. Veech," interjected Otis, "may I go out to piss?"

"Go, and tell the others that we're almost done here – Mr. Beaumont is fading fast." Veech drank from his tankard, setting it down with a bang. "Sour as vinegar." He winced, and rubbed his belly. "And all that spice was a disguise for rotten meat." He plucked up his quill clumsily. "Carry on Mr. Beaumont. You were saying that . . . that Digby has . . . bribed . . . a . . ." Veech yawned, the quill dangling over the page. "Why is it so . . . *warm?*" He gripped the edge of the table in an attempt to stand, his heels scraping on the flagstones. He sighed as if worried, and shivered; he was fighting to inhale. Ripping at the buttons on his coat, he tore it open. Laurence blinked awake and stared; was he hallucinating, or did the rounded shapes beneath Veech's shirt resemble breasts? Draycott was also staring. Veech slumped deeper in his seat. "What have I eaten?" he moaned. His skin had acquired a pasty greenish hue, though his eyes were bright and intelligent. "I am . . . p-poisoned! How did you . . . ?" he mouthed, at Laurence. The truth registered, and he glared round at Draycott. "Ah, it was *you*, you miserable worm – you turned on me! Then I'm taking you with me, to hell." He scrabbled for his pistol and cocked it, but as he tried to raise it, both of his arms slackened to his sides, and the pistol fell from his grip. He slid from the chair and thumped to the floor, striking his head.

"Thank God," Laurence murmured. "Is his heart beating?"

Draycott knelt and inserted a hand into Veech's shirt. "Yes, and his eyes are wide. He can see me. But . . . what is he? Part woman?"

"Quick, show me the pages he wrote." Draycott fetched them. Laurence wanted to read what Veech had recorded about Pembroke, yet his vision was so distorted that he could decipher not a word. "The quill," he said to Draycott. Blood was oozing out in a puddle from beneath his wound, soiling the paper. He signed his name, and dropped the quill. "If you can, tell . . . Sarah, Barlow's wife that . . . his death is avenged."

"I shall." Draycott shuffled the pages together and stuffed them into his doublet. "We did it! Now let me free you."

"No. Fire his pistol, for Aston's men."

"First let me help you!"

"No, no, just do as we agreed," Laurence implored, with the dregs of his strength. "You must get clean away."

"Beaumont," said Draycott, pleading, "*you're* not about to die?"

Laurence saw Draycott's face shrink, to the size of a walnut. And then it vanished.

## VI.

Slouched over the table, Beaumont might have been sleeping or dead, so pacific was his expression. He was breathing regularly, however, and that gave Draycott hope. The sooner Aston's men arrived, the better. Resisting an urge to pull out that ugly knife, Draycott ran back to Veech. He squatted to button Veech's coat, trying to avoid the staring eyes, retrieved the pistol, pressed it into Veech's clammy hand, aimed at the ceiling, and fired. He had to leap aside to dodge a hail of plaster; Beaumont did not move. Draycott flew into the kitchen shouting, "Hurry, hurry! Something is the matter with Mr. Veech!"

He, the landlord, and the two militiamen raced back to the taproom. They surrounded Veech, and the landlord bent and held his cupped hand to Veech's nose and lips. "His breath is very faint. What happened, sir?"

"I can't explain it," said Draycott. "He . . . he clutched at his heart, grabbed his pistol, and then fired, though I don't know why – and next he collapsed! He needs a physician."

"There's none in the village, sir! You'll have to ride to High Wycombe."

"Christ Almighty," said one of the men, looking over at Beaumont. "Is he dead?"

"Let him be, and get help for Mr. Veech," said Draycott.

The landlord sprang to open the door, and as if he had pulled the trigger on twenty pistols, a volley of shots rang out from the hills around the inn. "Who's that?" he cried.

Draycott pretended terrified ignorance. He had perhaps five minutes to escape with his cache of papers before Aston's men arrived. Loud yells broke out from the yard, and the girl hurtled shrieking from the kitchen and threw herself into her father's arms.

Otis burst in, waving his carbine. "A raiding party, sir! They're coming out of the hills. Must be hundreds of 'em!"

Draycott lunged for his pistol. "Get our horses – we'll have to ride through their fire! Tend to Veech as best you can," he barked at the landlord.

"And the other? The malignant?"

"Damn him," said Draycott, and sped out.

Aston's troops were pouring into the valley, their fire closer and closer. A few balls whizzed by, one clipping Draycott's shoulder as he and Veech's men mounted and galloped along the track towards the main road. Behind him he heard more explosions of shot, and the shatter of glass. Then abruptly, the shots ceased. He and the others slowed their pace to look back at the yard, where Aston's men were reining in their horses.

"Why aren't they giving us chase?" Otis panted.

"They can't be after us," said Draycott. "They must have come to arrest Beaumont, and with good reason: he was here to betray Lord Digby, the King's Secretary of State."

## VII.

"'Revenge is a kind of wild justice.'" Seward smiled down at Laurence, polishing his spectacles with the sleeve of his robe. "Thus wrote the late Baron Verulam, and thus Veech's revenge backfired upon himself. How do you feel, Beaumont?"

Laurence was trying to recollect how he came to be lying on Seward's bed. He had surfaced from unconsciousness, retching and confused, shortly after Aston's men had carried him there; on Isabella's instruction, as Seward had told him, while feeding him a soothing mixture for his stomach. Once assured that Draycott had got safely away, he had given Seward a probably muddled account of their ordeal. Then he had slept. His head now throbbed no worse than after a night's drinking with Wilmot; and though his right hand, encased in bandages, was extremely sore, the pain was a sign of life. "I feel wonderful, Seward – like Lazarus," he said. "And I owe to the Governor's men a most efficient rescue."

"They might have had no one to rescue, had you not partaken of that stew."

"I've got Veech to thank there: his suspicion of it saved me. I wonder how long he took to die."

"His heart stopped at dawn this morning, according to Aston's physician." Laurence sat up, amazed. "Since he was breathing when the men arrived, they decided to bring him with you to Oxford, in case he recovered," Seward explained. "Who knows how big a dose Draycott administered to him, but all the same, he must have had an iron constitution. I asked the physician to leave his corpse undisturbed, at the Governor's house, so that I may view it before burial."

"You *are* morbid. Why?"

"Because of what you said to me, as you were drifting off to sleep."

"About his . . . breasts?"

Seward nodded excitedly. "I have never set eyes on a hermaphrodite, and at my age I may not have another chance – and nor may you. Will you be fit to venture out with me, towards afternoon, in my scientific quest?"

"I must admit, I am curious."

"And as morbid as I am. What sort of voice had he, Beaumont?"

"Deep." Laurence could still hear it in his ears. "Far deeper than yours or mine, and resonant. It would have been a lovely singing voice."

———

Veech was laid out on a table in an empty room, his body covered by a blanket. Laurence shivered as Aston's surgeon unveiled his face: his eyes glared up at them with no less intensity than in life.

"A striking countenance," remarked Seward. He pried wide Veech's mouth with his fingertips. "No ostensible discolouration of the gums or tongue. It is a cunning poison – he could well have suffered a natural failure of the heart." He lowered the blanket to Veech's thighs and unbuttoned his coat. "Have you a knife, sir?" he said to the surgeon, who supplied one; he seemed as intrigued as Seward and Laurence. Seward slit the shirt to Veech's navel and exposed his chest. "They are paps, though not like a woman's. They resemble those of a young girl, or a much fatter man."

"And how light the hair grows on his chest and belly – as on his arms," the surgeon noted, drawing up Veech's sleeve to look at the skin beneath.

"Let us investigate further." Seward unlaced the breeches, and he and the surgeon hefted up Veech's hips to roll the garment down; Veech's body was as stiff as the table. Then with the air of a magician, Seward raised the hem of his shirt. Laurence and the surgeon cringed. Where his testicles should have been was a neatly scarred gap, and his penis had been cut to a stub. Laurence recalled that sudden rage. *No more than you'd expect to find between a man's legs.*

"Not a hermaphrodite – a eunuch," Seward declared. "I am familiar with the snipping of boys' cods to preserve their sweetness of voice. They remain smooth-skinned, and are reputed to acquire small breasts. But this must have been done to him when he was a full grown male, or he would have been more feminine in appearance, and had a higher voice."

"He said he was in the East, at about my age," murmured Laurence, "and had seen converts to the Muslim faith circumcised. I asked him if he was ever converted, and he said no."

"The truth was far more horrific. It is news to me that castration at that age would in time effect similar physical changes as on a boy."

"How did he not bleed to death or die of shock?" asked the surgeon.

"In the East they are renowned for the making and keeping of eunuchs," Seward replied. "Observe what is inserted into the opening of his member: something like a plug. Without it, the opening would narrow, and he would be unable to pass water. He would definitely be incapable of amorous intercourse."

"What astounding powers of deduction, Seward," Laurence said. "It's no surprise he wanted revenge on me: when I shot him, I piled insult upon injury."

Seward unstrapped the brace on Veech's knee to expose a lumpy, hairless joint. "The bone is deformed. He would have worn that brace for the rest of his days. Let us turn him onto his front."

The surgeon helped Seward wrestle the body over, and Seward tore off the coat and shirt. Veech's back was ridged to the waist with scars from a lash, and on the upper muscle of each shoulder he had been branded with a squiggle of Arabic letters. "His owner's mark, I would suppose," Seward said. "He may first have been a slave to others, and then was enslaved by his lust for vengeance. Now we know why he chose to mutilate his victims. And think of what he was planning for you, Beaumont: to make you like him. You should rejoice that you rid the earth of such a tortured soul."

"I feel no joy," said Laurence, thinking what strength of will must have been required to carry on living in that emasculated body. Veech had been in the business of secrets, while hiding a secret for which Laurence could imagine no fitting revenge. "Dress him and cover him again, Seward, and let the Governor bury him at once."

Aston had invited Laurence and Seward to sup with him that evening, an offer Seward told Laurence they could not decline. Before going to table, they requested of the Governor a private talk with Isabella, to apprise her of what had happened at the White Hart, and of the discoveries about Veech.

"You were not so wrong, my lady – he *was* malformed, though not from birth," Seward said. "I believe Beaumont pities him."

"Remember his cruelty," she said to Laurence. "He deserves no pity. In the final moment, he could have killed Mr. Draycott with that shot. We must find a way to tell Draycott you survived."

"We should have *some* agents left in London who might communicate with him, though I don't want to know who they are."

Isabella nodded. "And now, gentlemen, let us join Sir Arthur. He has news, from the King."

Yet Aston kept silent throughout the meal. Only when it ended, did he announce, "His Majesty wrote a week ago from Cornwall. He is still engaged in trapping Essex's forces and cutting them off from provisions, by land and by sea. He has some sixteen thousand Horse and Foot, and the Earl under ten thousand, so with God's grace we may foresee a happy outcome in that part of his kingdom. Mr. Beaumont, he asked me to inform you, on confirmation of your success in destroying Clement Veech: he will limit your term of exile to September of next year – a twelvemonth."

"How gracious of him," Seward exclaimed.

"Yes, indeed," said Laurence, with rather less enthusiasm; was this on Prince Charles' urging, or was some other, less benign influence responsible?

"There is, however, a condition to his mercy," Aston said. "You must sail with Lord Wilmot, who is in custody at Exeter. Tomorrow morning I shall have a troop ready to escort you thence – they are the men who recently did you service."

Laurence thought of Catherine, whom he had altogether forgotten while plotting and executing Veech's death. "I had promised to pass by Chipping Campden to bid my family goodbye, and my wife wished to travel with me."

"I cannot allow the delay, sir. You are a prisoner in *my* custody."

"She can follow you, Beaumont," said Seward, a mite reproving. "And your family will comprehend. Besides, a twelvemonth will fly by in no time."

"Let's drink to that," proposed Isabella, in a voice so artificial that Laurence could not look at her.

When they had drunk, Aston said, "Why not spend your last night in Oxford at my house, Mr. Beaumont, since you will be departing from here."

Like Draycott, Laurence decided to refuse the Governor's hospitality, but for a less noble motive: he might have been tempted to invade Isabella's bedchamber. "No, thank you, Sir Arthur: I'll stay at Merton with Dr. Seward."

"You must report to me, then, by nine of the clock."

Seward stifled a yawn. "It grows late, Beaumont."

Laurence turned to Isabella. "Lady Hallam, may I have a quick word before we go?"

"Why yes," she said, with a bright smile.

As he walked her out to the entrance hall, he felt his head swim as if he had swallowed another dose of belladonna. "What will you do now?" he asked. "How and . . . and where will you live?"

"I'll seek temporary lodgings in Oxford. Sir Montague and I are in correspondence to settle upon a modest stipend for me as his estranged wife. As for you, what a marvellous concession from the King."

"Is it?"

She examined his face more dubiously. "Your exile may be a mere holiday from work. What was it Digby said of you last autumn: His Majesty thought it most ill-advised that he should lack such a good man to assist him."

"I have precisely the same idea."

"Still, who can predict where we may be in a twelvemonth. His Majesty's campaign in the southwest is progressing well and the Governor mentioned to me that Prince Rupert is moving to establish his headquarters in Bristol, to be nearer to the King. He might outweigh Digby's counsel: the King is devoted to his nephew."

"The King prefers sanguine advice. What he doesn't hear from Rupert he'll get from Digby. Oh, Isabella, this war doesn't matter to me – what matters is you," Laurence confessed, wrapping his arms around her. "At Pembroke's house, you asked me how we could undo our mistake. We're not done with each other, are we?"

"No. We are friends for life. But as you said, your marriage is not a counterfeit. I want you to be a true husband to Catherine."

"How can I be, when I love *you*?"

"Trust me, you will come to love her." Isabella reached up and wiped away a tear from his cheek; her gold-flecked eyes were dry, yet full of tenderness. "Beaumont, if I don't rise early to see you off, would you understand?"

"Of course I would. I couldn't bear it, either: to say goodbye in front of everyone. Especially that bastard Aston," he added, forcing a smile.

"Then I'll say it now." She kissed him gently on the lips. "Farewell, my beloved friend."

"Not farewell," he said, and kissed her deeply; a lover's kiss. "It is *just* goodbye."

## VIII.

For hours, Laurence lay awake. His thoughts wandered, from that parting scene with Isabella to the whole drama of Veech's death. He was almost afraid to sleep, lest he be visited by some nightmare of Veech castrating him. But when finally he slept, he dreamt again of the King lying dead in the woods. He and Pembroke were standing by the makeshift bier, and Pembroke was slapping him on the shoulder. "You did it, Mr. Beaumont! Thanks to you, we can crown a new monarch."

Then young Prince Charles came towards them through the trees. He paused at the bier, and as he studied his father's body, Laurence saw a startling transformation sweep over him. He grew in height and girth, his complexion sallowed, his hair thickened and darkened into a luxuriant peruke, his youthful cheeks sagged, and his large, molten Stuart eyes acquired a wary, cynical wisdom. Lines of hard experience furrowed around his mouth, above which sprouted a thin moustache. He looked up at Laurence and Pembroke, and his full lips curved into a smile at the same time humorous, lazy, and sensual; and without speaking, he turned and strolled away, back among the trees.

In the dim light of dawn, Laurence washed and shaved, packed his saddlebag, and sat at Seward's desk to compose three letters. To Lord Beaumont he described the new terms of his exile, and regretted that he could not go home before sailing for France, where he hoped Catherine would soon join him. He sent his love to the household, and promised to write from Paris. His next letter was for Ingram, and contained much the same information. The third, to Catherine, was the briefest, though it cost him the most effort. He was not pleased, as he reread it. He should have told her that he loved her. Instead, it ended: "I shall be waiting for you."

Seward had chosen to say goodbye at the door. "I loathe the fuss of partings," he said.

"As do I," Laurence agreed. "To be honest, I'm rather glad I can't go home. And, as you said, a year is but a little while."

"At my age, a little while is all that I have left."

"Then you must take good care of yourself – no more working through the night on royal horoscopes." Laurence nodded at the silver bowl on Seward's desk. "But you might watch out for me in Paris."

"I'll try, Beaumont, though my instinct tells me that I shall see no more visions. Perhaps the bowl's magic was erased by Diego's theft. Perhaps I am losing my powers."

"As *I* told *you*: you don't need your bowl. You'll see the future in your dreams." Laurence considered mentioning his dream of the ageing Prince Charles, but time was short.

"Were Catherine of our sex, and I her tutor, I would teach her how to use the bowl," Seward said. "She'd be an able student."

"She's enough of a witch, as she is. She's already stolen the affections of my horse."

"She might bring it, when she comes to you."

"I asked her to do that, in my letter. Seward, joking aside," Laurence went on, "*I* have a strange instinct about Isabella – that something is ailing her, and it's not her old sickness. I know your feelings about her, but will you promise for my sake to look after her?"

"I promise, if you will try to put her out of your thoughts," Seward advised. "She's a strong woman, and a survivor of life's woes. Now, my boy, you must go. May God speed you to France, and don't forget to write to me."

"I won't, my friend – and goodbye." Laurence slung his saddlebag over his shoulder and gave Seward a last, tremulous hug. As he crossed the quadrangle, he waved, but he did not dare look back.

### IX.

"I still wish I knew how Governor Aston learnt of your meeting with Beaumont, and sent those troops to arrest him," St. John said to Draycott. They were examining the pile of papers on his desk, some stained with dried blood.

"From one of Digby's spies?" offered Draycott.

"It must have been." St. John indicated the stains. "The Committee asked me to confirm with you that none of Beaumont's intelligence was extracted under duress, which might impugn its accuracy. In the past, Mr. Veech's methods had come . . . into question. I should have asked you earlier: was force employed on Beaumont, and is this his blood?"

"There was no force used, sir – the pages were soiled by my own hands after I was injured, as I transferred them from my saddlebag into my doublet for safekeeping," said Draycott. He had sworn Veech's men to secrecy on this score, on the excuse that it would cast a slur upon the dead man's reputation, and he doubted St. John would trouble to investigate any further.

"Thank the Lord you received no worse than a graze to your shoulder. Alas for Veech – I would never have guessed he had a weak heart." St. John selected a different page, in crooked script, scattered with ink blots and smudges. "He must have been in the utmost distress when he wrote these lines."

"Had I known, I might have sent earlier for help. And if only I could have brought back his body for a Christian burial."

"You had to leave him behind or be captured by Aston's militia, in which case we would not have the papers. It is a shame Beaumont was captured, and will be tried and executed for his treachery to the Secretary of State. We would have benefited from such a mole in the French Court."

"Then his statements are of value, in the Committee's opinion?" said Draycott.

"At first we could not make head or tail of his writing – it was yet more unintelligible than his letter to me. But once the pages in his hand were copied out by a man skilled in cryptology, the extent of our wealth became clear to us. Lord Digby's schemes for London beggar belief in their audacity, and we can now break all of his figures. And we were able to confirm that another peer, who sits in Parliament, is not a secret Royalist, as Veech suspected." Draycott nodded, though he mused to himself: had Beaumont told the truth about Pembroke's allegiances? "We have decided to publish an abbreviated version of our treasure trove, to stimulate enthusiasm for the war among the London populace," St. John said gloatingly. "It will appear in the newssheets under the title, *Lord Digby's Closet Opened*."

From Westminster Stairs, Draycott took a skiff to Southwark. He disembarked and strode south into Blackman Street, past shops and houses, and a host of unsavoury alleys, until he came to his destination. He knocked at the door and a fat, unkempt girl answered, nursing a baby at the front of her milk-stained gown. "Good day, madam," he said. "I am in search of Sarah Barlow."

"I don't know of any Sarah Barlow," she said, with tired impatience.

Draycott extracted a coin from his pocket. "She dwelt in your house not long ago with her husband, Peter."

"You ask the neighbours, sir. We've only been lodged here these past three weeks."

He gave her the coin, and she closed the door. As he was debating which of her neighbours to try, an insolent voice called out, "What's your business with Sarah Barlow?" The speaker, a pug-nosed youth with crafty, mistrustful eyes, sidled up to Draycott.

"I've a message for her."

"What's that, then?"

"Tell her Veech is dead." Draycott felt a hot rush of pride, though in the depths of his conscience he did not like himself for it. "You tell her that Giles Draycott killed Clement Veech, and that Beaumont and Lady Hallam are both safe."

The boy's eyes lit up, and his mouth twisted into a grin. "I don't know of any Sarah Barlow," he cackled, and swaggered off into the maze of alleyways.

## X.

Under sunny skies, and with the aid of opportune breezes, Antonio's vessel had sailed swiftly along. He and the Captain, Tomás Echeverría, a jolly and sharp-witted Basque, had become fast friends, supping together each evening and exchanging tales of their various exploits. In retrospect, Antonio was pleased to have left Diego in London, and wondered why he had tolerated that impudent rascal for so long. And as the weather improved and he shook the chill of England out of his bones, he started to forget the torrent of emotions Elena and his Lorenzo had roused in him. He felt again master of his destiny: *El Valoroso*, returning home to begin a new and illustrious adventure. He would tell Teresa he had been entrusted with the military commission because of his success in conveying funds to the beleaguered King Charles.

His ship docked at Cádiz six weeks after setting out from London. Echeverría accompanied him to a fishermen's eating place on the wharf, and they shared a meal in the open air, paid for by the Basque. When they had finished, Echeverría produced a letter. "I was asked by Capitán Iturbe to wait until we were on dry land to give this to you. It has been a privilege to meet you, Don Antonio, and may your commission with King Philip bring you everything you desire."

Though tantalised, Antonio delayed opening the letter until they had said goodbye; it was from Elena. What might it contain? A secret declaration of love? He began to read.

My cousin, by the time you peruse these lines, you will have arrived in Spain anticipating fame and fortune in King Philip's army, in reward for the disappointments of your sojourn abroad. Yet you who fancy yourself so skilled in guile have fallen prey to a snare which, were you less a victim of your own greed and vanity, you might have averted. King Philip's offer was forged with pleasure by Don Alonso de Cárdenas on the inspiration of my son, Laurence, who is a source of great pride to me and to my dearest husband. Learn from your mistake and behave as a proper Christian should, for what years remain to you before you face Divine Judgement. And may your wife and children console you for the loss of that which you imagined yours.

Antonio reread the letter several times. Then he drew from his coat the scrolled document with the ornate diplomatic seal, tore both it and the letter into fragments, and tossed them off the edge of the wharf, into the sea. He was remembering Diego's taunt: that brains were worth more than brawn. The clever monkey must somehow have found out about the deception being practised on Antonio, and for once in his life had kept his mouth shut.

Four days later, Antonio galloped up to his house, sweating profusely; on this first of September, the air around him was like an oven, the soil baked and cracked beneath his horse's hooves, the scant grasses withered, and the leaves on the trees dusty from lack of rain. He dismounted in the courtyard, horrified by the signs of neglect and decay: weeds and crumbling stones, part of the roof concaved, a bare inch of stagnant water in the horse trough, and flies buzzing everywhere.

Agustín, Diego's uncle, hurried out with a mixture of joy and apprehension. "Don Antonio, thank the saints! We have been praying for you to come home. Such tragedy has been visited upon us."

"What tragedy?" cried Antonio.

"There was sickness here, and it took from us your son Felipe," quavered the old man.

Antonio found Teresa and María de Mercedes in the cool of the dark, shuttered main room. He wept inconsolably, embracing them. They, meanwhile, were as parched as the countryside: they had no more tears to shed. "At the height of the summer, this past July, the gypsy Juana came to our door with her child in her arms," Teresa told him, in a numbed voice. "She asked to see me, though I would not condescend to her request. She claimed to Agustín that you had promised to keep her at El Caballo Blanco for as long as you were away, but that Gaspar had refused to feed or shelter her, and now she and the boy were starving. She demanded to know when we expected you. Agustín did not believe a word of her story. He had to throw stones at her, to get rid of her. Before she went, she uttered something in her language, and spat upon the step. The same day, a wasting fever broke out and spread through the household. Felipe was the only one who died of it." Teresa paused, to cross herself. "I sent Agustín to talk to Gaspar, and to our surprise, Juana's story was true. Your money had run out. Gaspar had let her work in his kitchen, but she was rude and lazy and thieved from him, so he had driven her onto the street. We could not understand why she would have been so evil and ungrateful as to curse us, after you had showed her such Christian charity."

Antonio's blood boiled in his veins: the gypsy was to blame for all of his misfortunes, from the morning he had encountered her on the

Feast of St. Francis. "I intend to ask her myself, *mi querida*, as soon as I can get my hands on her," he said.

"We often see her begging outside the Cathedral, her and her child, though we do not go near them. And Gaspar knows where she camps at night," Teresa added, "in a cave by the riverbank."

After dusk, Antonio loaded his pistol and rode out to meet Gaspar, as previously arranged, with a bunch of his henchmen and their hunting dogs. They left the horses and took a narrow, winding path down to the river, through a stretch of gorse and wild rosemary; it was reputed as a hiding place for criminals and fugitives. Juana had chosen a secluded spot, not in a true cave but a hollow den in the bank. As they crept closer, Antonio spied her squatting by the flames of a meagre fire. He signalled for the men to crouch low and restrain their dogs.

For a while he watched and listened. She was singing as she turned a fish spitted on a stick, smiling every so often at the child who toddled about nearby. She looked as ragged as before, and as attractive to Antonio. Yet this was a new Juana: neither wheedling nor defiant, but calm and gentle, even maternal. And despite her circumstances, she appeared to him happy. How well his grandson had grown, Antonio thought, in almost a year. He was now a strong-limbed little boy, with a head of curly black hair.

One of the dogs let out a yelp. Juana peered around, sweeping earth over the fire to extinguish it; and clutching the stick of fish in one hand, she grabbed the child with her other, and scurried into her lair. Antonio motioned for Gaspar and some of the men to advance, leaving the others to fan out with the dogs and block her escape. He crept yet closer to the entrance of the den and whistled low. Gaspar and his companions sprang forward into the hollow and hauled her forth. The dogs were released and bounded up with a volley of barks, though on Gaspar's command they stopped short of attack. Juana was writhing and biting and kicking, but she became still when she saw Antonio.

"How are you, Juana, and how is your boy?" he inquired.

"I am barely alive, and he's with the angels, bless his poor soul. He starved because you refused us succour," she snarled, at Gaspar.

Antonio cocked his pistol and aimed it at her forehead. "A single false move, *mi gitana*, and I'll blow you to kingdom come. Leave us to speak alone," he ordered the men.

"Did you find Monsieur?" she asked, when they had retreated.

"Yes, in England. He is my son, Juana."

"I could have told you on the day we met. And his mother was your cousin, the fine lady from Seville who married the English lord. I overheard Gaspar talking of your Elena."

Antonio seized a handful of Juana's hair and pressed the nose of his pistol into the base of her throat. "You are always such a liar. Your son is not dead, but my Felipe is. Why did you put a curse on him?"

"I didn't, sir," she whimpered. "I swear, by the blessed Virgin, I shouted a few words in anger. They meant nothing."

He dragged her inside the dark, feral-smelling hollow, and threw her on the ground. The child was doubtless inches away; he made no noise. Keeping the pistol at her throat, Antonio knelt and pulled up her skirts with his free hand. He unbuttoned his coat, and unlaced. "You said Monsieur raped you. Was it like this?" Thrusting apart her thighs, he fell upon her and drove inside. He was steel, hero of more battles than he could count. And as he ploughed on where his Lorenzo had been before him, he saw Elena's face, young again, as on their fateful night. Sighing victoriously, he spent himself.

Juana lay motionless, eyes shut; she must have fainted. He withdrew. But as he set down his pistol to restore his clothes, her eyes flashed wide. She snatched the weapon in both hands, and levelled it at him. "No, it was not like this. Monsieur was *better* than you."

Antonio dashed the pistol easily from her grasp. With a soldier's blind instinct, as though in the midst of the fray, he lifted her up by her head; and with a quick, expert jerk he snapped her neck. She fell back limp.

Antonio sensed those green Fuentes eyes upon him, and cowered.

"It was her fault," he whispered, to the invisible boy. "She did not have to die."

"Don Antonio," called Gaspar, "*qué pasa?*"

The boy set up a keening wail. Antonio reached for him in the darkness, and hugged him to his chest. "I have lost three sons. I will not lose my grandson."

Gaspar had lit a torch. In the flame, he and the other men surveyed Antonio with vague distaste as he emerged, his coat open and his breeches half fastened. "She gave me her child, for the one she stole from me," he said to them, in a voice he did not recognise. And as he staggered off, he began to howl, louder than the boy sobbing in his arms.

## XI.

"This august occasion demands a verse," said Wilmot, gesticulating so blithely with the bottle he had been drinking from, that he nearly dropped it into the waters of Exeter harbour.

"A verse?" said Laurence. "In all our years of friendship, I didn't know you were a poet."

They were leaning over the stout oak rail of the ship, observing the scene: sailors running nimbly up and down rope ladders attached to its tarred sides, and merchants supervising the loading of their cargoes, and peddlers in small craft plying a last-minute trade with those already aboard. Laurence was most entertained by the troop of cavalry assembled on the crowded dock, to prevent him and Wilmot from jumping ship.

"Oh it's not *my* poem, Beaumont. It's a favourite of my wife's, bless her." Wilmot cleared his throat ceremoniously, and began:

> "*Fair stood the wind for France*
> *When we our sails advance,*
> *Nor now to prove our chance*
> *Longer will tarry—*"

"Excuse me," interrupted Laurence, "but the rest is hardly appropriate: we're sailing to France in peace, not to fight the battle of Agincourt."

"We'll fight our battles in Paris. I hear the Queen's Court seethes with more rivalries than a viper's nest – though you'll soon be out of it." Wilmot tipped the bottle to his lips and grunted. "Empty. Shall we replenish our supply?"

They wove a path among boxes and barrels, and crated livestock; and as they swerved to avoid a stray hen that had escaped from its cage, they came face to face with two familiar gentlemen.

"If it isn't Price and Quayle." Laurence wanted to laugh at the incongruous pair: Price in an elegant suit and plumed hat, looking agitated; and Quayle in his livery, wearing his typical complacent expression.

"Did your lord and master send you to bid us goodbye?" sneered Wilmot.

"My lord, Mr. Beaumont," said Price, "I have a message for Mr. Beaumont from my Lord Digby that requires his immediate answer."

Laurence accepted it from Price and broke the seal. "My answer is no," he said, when he had read it.

Price glanced at Quayle, whose eyes betrayed mirth, and then at Laurence. "Is that your . . . final decision?"

"Yes it is. How are the scouts?"

"They . . . they are well, and asked to be remembered to you."

"My best wishes to them, and convey my regret to his lordship that I can't oblige him." Laurence held out his left hand to Price; the other was still bandaged. "Goodbye, man, and I wish *you* well – in love and in war."

"I hope you have a safe voyage," Price said, in a mournful voice.

Quayle bowed obsequiously. "Goodbye, sir, and goodbye, my lord."

Wilmot frowned after them. "Oblige Digby in what, Beaumont?"

"He offered to absolve me of guilt in your overtures to Essex if I would return to his service."

"No exile?"

"You would have sailed alone."

Wilmot sniffed and tugged at his moustache. "I know Digby is worse than a whole nest of vipers, yet exile is a bitter pill to swallow, even for a year. You might think again. I'd miss you, my old cock," he added, with touching sincerity, "but are you sure you want to refuse?"

"I've never been as sure of anything in my life." Laurence draped an arm round Wilmot's shoulders. "*I* have a few lines, on this august occasion, but not from a poem. It's a favourite dictum of my father's, though he said he hadn't the courage to live up to it himself. '*Delicatus ille est adhuc cui patria dulcis est; fortis autem iam, cui omne solum patria est; perfectus vero, cui mundus totus exsilium est.*'"

"In English, please – my Latin's rusty."

"'He remains weak for whom his homeland is sweet; while he is strong for whom the whole earth is his homeland, and truly perfect is he for whom the entire world is an exile.'"

"Very noble," Wilmot said, "but might I remind you, Beaumont: you are far from perfect."

"You should thank Christ I am, or I'd make you dull company."

"So you would," agreed Wilmot. "Then since neither of us is perfect, let's go in search of more wine."

"An excellent suggestion," said Laurence, and guided him onwards.

# EPILOGUE
## Oxford, early December 1644

Seward woke bleary-eyed and cold from a nap in his chair. The fire had dwindled to a pile of ash and glowing embers, and afternoon shadows were slanting across his front room. His cat was pawing at the door, with distinct purpose. "You behave as if I were your servant," he complained, hoisting himself to his feet, and shuffled over to unlatch it. But when he did, he had to admire the beast's sagacity. "Good day to you, my Lady Hallam," he greeted his visitor, as Pusskins scampered off into the quadrangle.

"I am no longer her ladyship, Doctor," she said. "You see before you plain Mistress Isabella Savage."

"Pray you come in." He shut the door and waved her to his other chair, which she accepted without removing her cloak. "Governor Aston told me of Sir Montague's illness, and how you were with him in The Hague."

"I arrived to find him on his deathbed. He begged me for wine, to ease his passage, so I supplied it. Afterwards his children called me unworthy of his name and title, both of which I happily renounced in exchange for my widow's stipend." Mistress Savage placed a hand upon her throat. "I was also immensely pleased to get back from one of his daughters the necklace Beaumont gave me." She looked towards the fireplace and shivered. "Have you news of him?"

"Not since the end of October." Taking her hint, Seward went to the hearth and threw some bits of wood into the grate. "He is a poor correspondent."

"As he admitted to me, he has no talent for expressing himself on paper. How was he?"

"Delighted by the broadsheet I'd sent him relating his fantastical revelations to Parliament, and his mysterious escape from royal justice."

"I wonder if he's heard yet that most of those revelations were exposed as lies and the rest as stale intelligence. Such a laughingstock he made of St. John and the Committee of Both Kingdoms, not to mention the late Mr. Veech. What else did he say?"

"He'd grown fed to the teeth of Lord Wilmot's vituperations about Lord Digby and Prince Rupert, and preferred to avoid Her Majesty's Court," said Seward, resuming his seat. "He was spending his days reading the modern French authors, and occupying his nights at the playhouse."

She smiled sardonically. "I've always thought the French commendable, in letting women on the stage. Had his wife not joined him?"

"No, nor will she. Lord and Lady Beaumont considered it safer that she bide at Chipping Campden, as the period of his exile is so short."

"What a mistake," declared Mistress Savage. "It is far from *safe* to leave a man of his nature alone in a city full of temptations." Privately Seward agreed, though he kept quiet. "Were they worried about her falling sickness?"

"Ah, Beaumont told you," said Seward, surprised. "She has had no recurrence of it, to my knowledge."

"Then is she perchance with child?"

"If she is, I have not been informed."

"Doctor," said Mistress Savage, "you are the first to hear *my* news: *I* am carrying his child."

"Great heavens!" muttered Seward.

"You cannot be more astonished than I was. It's the issue of a night we spent together in London, after my flight from the Tower. We were weak in resolve, and I was weak in body – truly, it's a miracle

I conceived. Destiny is cruel: had I become pregnant a year ago when he and I were living here in Oxford, I'd have married him, over the objections of the whole world. 'Are you afraid to fight?' he asked me, at the time, and I *was*, foolishly afraid." She lowered her eyes. "He was certain I could have his child."

"Were you aware of your state before he sailed for France?"

"Oh yes – even as you were plotting the murder of Veech." Beaumont had thought her unwell, Seward remembered. "I had to keep it from him," she added. "Why spoil his future with Catherine?"

"He should know. It will be his duty to provide for you, and for the child."

She looked up sharply. "*You* know what happened to me as a young girl. I was badly damaged, as a consequence. In the unlikely event that I do not miscarry, the child and I may be in danger of our lives when I am brought to bed."

"God willing, you and the babe shall prosper."

"Lest I don't, I'd rather Beaumont think I had died of some other cause. I intend soon to leave Oxford, anyway, for a place where my belly won't be the subject of gossip."

"When is the child due?"

"In April. Can I count on your discretion?"

"You can, Mistress Savage. But . . . why did you confide in me?"

"Because I have the highest esteem for you, Doctor, and I trust you as his dear friend. And should the child survive, I want my son or daughter to have what I did not: a loving family. If I can't arrange this before the birth, I was hoping that for his sake you might help."

"Gladly, madam, for his sake and yours, yet I am an old bache-lor, in the wane of my days." Seward pondered a moment. "You should consult someone else whose confidence you can depend on: Walter Ingram. He has an aunt in Faringdon, Madam Musgrave, who is devoted to him and to Beaumont. From their report of her, she is a wise and resourceful lady. I suspect Beaumont might have consulted her about matters of the heart. He talked to me of her . . .

motherly qualities. She may be exactly the person to address, in your situation."

"Thank you very much, Doctor – I'll write to Mr. Ingram." Mistress Savage rose and approached Seward as if she might embrace him. Out of instinct, he shrank away. "You *are* an old bachelor," she teased, with a knowing glint in her eyes, as if she could have used a different term to describe him.

They were saying goodbye on the threshold when Pusskins slinked up, to sniff at her skirts. "He scents his rival," she observed.

Seward bowed to her respectfully; he had once thought her his. "Whatever I am, you must not be a stranger to my door."

"I won't," she said. "And do please advise Lord and Lady Beaumont that Catherine should be reunited with her husband."

After Mistress Savage had gone, he felt a profound sadness. "While I recognised her spirit and intellect early on," he told Pusskins, "her glamour and my stubborn prejudice blinded me to her other virtues. That Beaumont should be loved by two such exceptional women! What will become of her?"

Pusskins peered at the shelf where Seward had stored his scrying bowl, and uttered a silent miaow. His cat never did anything without a reason, so he brought his chair to his desk, fetched the bowl, filled it with dark liquid, and settled down to concentrate. He had scant expectation of success, as he invoked the angels' guidance.

Then his nerves began to tingle. On the surface of the liquid, he beheld with unusual clarity a magnificent Palladian house, against a bleak, grey winter sky. A scaffold had been erected in front of the sole upper window not blocked by boards or masonry; it was draped in black and crowded with people, many weeping, some praying, and soldiers in livery; and two in leather masks. They were gathered around a small, bearded gentleman who seemed to be delivering a speech. Below the scaffold, mounted troops were lined up to contain a larger crowd: more soldiers, commoners, and the wealthy in their carriages or on horseback, all in awe, craning for a glimpse of him. When he had finished his speech, he spoke a few words to the masked men. Assisted by an older figure in bishop's robes, he put on a white cap and tucked his hair carefully into it. He removed a jewelled badge that had been hanging from a blue ribbon about his neck and gave it to the bishop; and next his cloak and doublet. He must have felt cold, however, for he motioned to have back the cloak. He lifted hands and eyes to the heavens, and after a while slipped the cloak again from his shoulders and knelt low. There came a flash of steel, and Seward saw no more.

"Impossible," he whispered. Death in the field or by the stab of a conspirator's blade he might understand. Yet how could the King go meekly to execution by the stroke of an axe, in public view? And could this signify an end to the House of Stuart? An end, even, to the rule of kings and queens in England? For Seward knew that the bowl did not lie, though it showed only what it chose; and the royal horoscope had foretold that His Majesty would die by violence, in the month of January.

## The End

# HISTORICAL NOTE

As in *The Best of Men*, I tried to remain true to written accounts from and about the period. I owe a huge debt to Sir Edward Walker's *His Majesty's Happy Progress and Success from the 30th of March to the 23rd of November, 1644*. Walker does not feature in *The Licence of War*, but he was appointed Secretary to the Council of War in 1642, and Clerk Extraordinary of the Privy Council in 1644. He accompanied the King throughout this stage of the conflict, and while admittedly biased as a Royalist, he witnessed many of the events in this book.

The affair of Major Ogle (sometimes referred to as Captain Ogle) and the King's false friends, Keeper Devenish and Lieutenant-Colonel Mosely, is on record, as is the so-called Brooke's Plot in which Thomas Violet was a player. In the first case, I slightly changed the chronology of their communications with the Earl of Bristol and the King. When Prince Rupert arrived at Aylesbury expecting it to be delivered to him, contemporary reports state that he grew suspicious and withdrew solely because the Lieutenant-Colonel's brother did not come out to escort him into the garrison, as Mosely had promised; a young servant was sent instead.

I chose Oliver St. John for the role of espionage master in the Committee of Safety (later the Committee of Both Kingdoms) because, from the end of 1643, he was a major force within the war party in the House of Commons. He discovered and revealed Brooke's plot, publicised as *A Cunning Plot to divide and destroy the Parliament and the City of London*. Edward Hyde, Earl of Clarendon, in his *History of the Rebellion*, described St. John as "a man reserved, and of a dark and clouded countenance, very proud, and conversing with very few, and those men of his own humour and inclinations." He was "very seldom known to smile."

One major historian of the period, C.V. Wedgwood, places Wilmot at the battle of Cheriton; but as her reference, she cites Walker, who does not name him as part of the army sent from Oxford to join Hopton's forces. I therefore invented Wilmot's ambitious desire to rout Waller in the field without permission of His Majesty's Council, and his charge of incompetence against the defeated Royalist generals. The King's and Digby's letters are quoted verbatim from the originals, so clearly there was a conspiracy to remove Wilmot from command well before his overtures to Essex came to light. The reasons provided by the King for the accusation of treachery that led to Wilmot's dismissal are true to record, but no letter from him to Essex was found, to my knowledge. Goring was apparently reluctant to replace Wilmot as Lieutenant General, and would have preferred to stay with Rupert. The army's petition for peace was sent to Essex a bit later than I suggest, after Essex had rebuffed the King's terms.

King Charles really did go hunting in Woodstock while Oxford was in extreme peril; either an instance of astonishing sangfroid on his part, or outrageous carelessness. Accounts vary as to where exactly Essex and Waller met before they made their fateful decision to split up their armies, leaving Waller to pursue the King. Again I followed Walker, who named the location as Burford. This strategic error was the most amazing luck for the Royalists. I would argue that it had a greater impact on the future course and aftermath of the Civil War than Rupert's defeat at Marston Moor. If the two Parliamentary generals had stayed together and captured the King and Prince Charles, as was imminently possible, hostilities might have ended sooner, saving much bloodshed. And since the radical elements in Westminster and in the Parliamentary armies were then far less powerful than they afterwards became, Charles might have avoided the scaffold. It is interesting to note that Colonel William Purefoy was a signatory on the King's death warrant.

In *The Best of Men*, I took considerable liberties with the Earl of Pembroke, who I hope is redeemed in *The Licence of War*. In this book, I gave myself free rein with George Digby's sexuality. I cribbed my title, *Lord Digby's Closet Opened* – an anachronistic *double entendre* – from two sources: his cousin's recipe book, *The Closet of Sir Kenelm Digby, Knight, Opened*, written during the days of Queen Henrietta's penurious Court in France and published in 1668, and a highly compromising cache of the King's letters seized by Parliament and published as *The King's Cabinet Opened* in 1645. The virulent animosity between Digby and Wilmot continued abroad, and in 1647 they fought their duel, in Paris. Digby won, wounding his adversary in the hand.

King Charles apparently regarded Don Alonso de Cárdenas as "a silly, ignorant, odd fellow"; and he spoke little English, but he was cleverer than the King realised. As the war unfolded, he shifted towards an alliance with Parliament, despite the unfortunate incident of Father Bell, and recognised its authority in spring 1644. When the magnificent royal art collection came up for sale in 1649, he acquired many fine pieces, for and on the secret instruction of King Philip. Readers curious about these dealings can consult Jerry Brotton's wonderful *The Sale of the Late King's Goods*.

Finally, Sir Arthur Aston deserves a note here because of the unique manner of his death. He had fought as a mercenary abroad and in the opening stages of the Civil War, and was appointed Governor of Oxford in 1643 on the Queen's request. She felt herself safer with a Catholic in charge of the city, but he was disliked by both soldiers and citizens. The near contemporary historian Antony Wood described him as "very cruel and imperious," and Clarendon called him "a man of rough nature, and so given up to an immoderate love of money that he cared not by what unrighteous ways he exacted it." His term as Governor ended in September 1644, when he broke his leg in a riding accident.

He survived an amputation, and by 1649 was serving in Ireland. At the infamous siege of Drogheda by Cromwell's troops, he repelled a number of enemy assaults. Cromwell prevailed, and the town was brutally stormed without quarter. Aston himself was bludgeoned to death with his own wooden leg, which, it is said, Parliamentary soldiers believed to be full of gold coins.

# MAIN HISTORICAL CHARACTERS

**Charles Stuart**, King of England, 1600–49

**Henrietta Maria**, his wife, 1609–69

**Charles Stuart**, Prince of Wales, 1630–85: heir to the throne; restored as Charles II in 1660.

**Lord George Digby**, 1612–77: married Anne Russell in 1640; created Baron Digby in 1641; succeeded Lord Falkland as Secretary of State, after Falkland's death in 1643.

**John Digby**, first Earl of Bristol, 1580–January 1653/4: married Beatrice Walcott in 1609; father of George Digby; ambassador to the Spanish Court 1611–24; created Earl in 1622; died in Paris.

**Prince Rupert**, 1619–82: son of King Charles' sister, Elizabeth of Bohemia; older brother of Prince Maurice (1620–52); Commander in Chief of His Majesty's Horse in the first years of the Civil War; appointed General of the Royalist forces in November 1644; banished with Maurice from England by Parliament in 1646.

**Lord Henry Wilmot**, 1612–58: married Frances Morton in 1633, and upon her death, Anne Lee in 1644; appointed Lieutenant General of the King's Horse and created Baron Adderbury in 1643; created first Earl of Rochester by Charles II in 1652; father of the poet and libertine John Wilmot, second Earl of Rochester.

**Lord Henry Jermyn**, 1605?–January 1684/5: appointed Colonel of the Queen's Lifeguard in 1639; created peer in 1643; accompanied the Queen to France in 1644; rumoured to have enjoyed an affair with her, and even a secret marriage after the execution of Charles I; created Earl of St. Albans in 1660; Lord Chamberlain to Charles II.

**Philip Herbert**, fourth Earl of Pembroke, 1584–1650: married Susan de Vere in 1604, and upon her death, Anne Clifford in 1630; succeeded to the title in 1630, on the death of his brother, William; owner of Wilton House, Baynard's Castle, and lodgings in the Cockpit, Whitehall, where he died.

**Lady Catherine d'Aubigny**, née Howard, 1620?–50: married Lord George d'Aubigny, cousin of King Charles, in 1638; widowed in 1642; involved in a failed London plot in May 1643; remarried to James Livingstone, First Earl of Newburgh; died in The Hague.

**Alonso de Cárdenas**, 1592–1664: Spanish Envoy to London c. 1638–55.

**John Pym**, 1584–1643: married Anne Hooke in 1614; head of the Committee of Safety from July 1642; architect of Parliament's Solemn League and Covenant with Scotland; died probably of bowel cancer and buried in Westminster Abbey; in 1660, with the Restoration of Charles II, his body was exhumed, despoiled, and reburied in a common pit.

**Oliver St. John**, 1598?–1673: married as his second wife Elizabeth Cromwell, cousin of Oliver Cromwell; in 1660 published an apology for his past politics; lived abroad after 1662.

# ACKNOWLEDGEMENTS

I want to thank everyone who has inspired and supported me while writing this story, in particular Jennifer Roblin, for casting her superb critical eye on my early drafts; Liz Jensen, for excellent advice on a later one; and Dave Morris, for encouragement and helpful comments throughout. A warm thanks also to Luba Frastacky, since retired from the Thomas Fisher Rare Books Library at the University of Toronto, who kindly provided me with original source materials for my research. As always, I am immensely grateful to my agent, Sam Hiyate, for his unwavering optimism, enthusiasm, and professional dedication; to my patient and considerate editor, Lara Hinchberger, for her expertise; to the team at McClelland and Stewart, including Lynn Schellenberg, for her meticulous copy editing; and last but by no means least, to Dan Franklin at Jonathan Cape, for bringing Beaumont home on a second adventure. And I cannot forget to thank all of my family; my familiars Lupin and Daisy; the brave and loyal souls of Pinton and Tonpin; and, of course, my very best of men, Oscar Thiaw.